Mike Ashley is an author and editor of over eighty books, including many Mammoth titles. He worked for over thirty years in local government but is now a full-time writer and researcher specializing in ancient history, historical fiction and fantasy, crime and science fiction. He lives in Kent with his wife and over 20,000 books.

Also available

The Mammoth Book of Awesome Comic Fantasy
The Mammoth Book of Best New Erotica 3
The Mammoth Book of Best New Horror 14
The Mammoth Book of Climbing Adventures
The Mammoth Book of Comic Crime
The Mammoth Book of Egyptian Whodunnits
The Mammoth Book of Elite Forces
The Mammoth Book of Endurance and Adventure
The Mammoth Book of Explorers
The Mammoth Book of Eyewitness America
The Mammoth Book of Eyewitness Battles
The Mammoth Book of Eyewitness Everest
The Mammoth Book of Fantasy
The Mammoth Book of Fighter Pilots
The Mammoth Book of Future Cops
The Mammoth Book of Great Detective Stories
The Mammoth Book of Haunted House Stories
The Mammoth Book of Heroes
The Mammoth Book of Heroic and Outrageous Women
The Mammoth Book of Historical Whodunnits
The Mammoth Book of Humor
The Mammoth Book of Illustrated Crime
The Mammoth Book of Journalism
The Mammoth Book of Legal Thrillers
The Mammoth Book of Literary Anecdotes
The Mammoth Book of Locked-Room Mysteries and Impossible Crimes
The Mammoth Book of Maneaters
The Mammoth Book of Men O'War
The Mammoth Book of Mountain Disasters
The Mammoth Book of Murder and Science
The Mammoth Book of Native Americans
The Mammoth Book of Private Eye Stories
The Mammoth Book of Prophecies
The Mammoth Book of Pulp Action
The Mammoth Book of Roaring Twenties Whodunnits
The Mammoth Book of Roman Whodunnits
The Mammoth Book of Science Fiction
The Mammoth Book of Sea Battles
The Mammoth Book of Sex, Drugs and Rock 'n' Roll
The Mammoth Book of Short Erotic Novels
The Mammoth Book of Tales from the Road
The Mammoth Book of the Titanic
The Mammoth Book of UFOs
The Mammoth Book of Vampires
The Mammoth Book of Vampire Stories by Women
The Mammoth Book of War Correspondents
The Mammoth Book of Women Who Kill

THE MAMMOTH BOOK OF JACOBEAN WHODUNNITS

EDITED BY MIKE ASHLEY

CARROLL & GRAF PUBLISHERS
New York

Carroll & Graf Publishers
An imprint of Avalon Publishing Group, Inc.
245 W. 17th Street
11th Floor
New York
NY 10011–5300
www.carrollandgraf.com

First published in the UK by Robinson,
an imprint of Constable & Robinson Ltd, 2006

First Carroll & Graf edition 2006

ISBN 13: 978–0–78671–730–9
ISBN 10: 0–7867–1730–0

Printed and bound in the EU

CONTENTS

COPYRIGHT AND ACKNOWLEDGMENTS

"The King's First Achievement" printed by permission of Valerie Anand and the author's agents, the David Grossman Literary Agency.

"A Dead Man's Wish" by permission of John T. Aquino.

"Perfect Alibi" by Philip Boast, "A Disobedient Daughter" by Jean Davidson, "The Philadelphia Slaughterman" by Ian Morson and "Murder Unauthorized" by Amy Myers, all printed by permission of the authors and the Dorian Literary Agency.

"A House Divided" by permission of Judith Cutler.

"The Palatable Truth" by permission of Carol Anne Davis.

"The Restless Dead" by permission of Martin Edwards.

"To Walk on Thorny Paths" by permission of Paul Finch.

"The Duke of York" by permission of Patricia Finney.

"The Dumb Bell" by Kate Ellis, The Curious Contents of a Coffin" by Susanna Gregory and "Satan in the Star Chamber" by Peter Tremayne by permission of the authors and A. M. Heath & Co.

"The Tower's Man" by permission of Michael Jecks.

"Green Tarts" by permission of Deryn Lake.

"Ice Sailor" by permission of Laird Long.

"'O, Poisonous Weed!'" by permission of F. Gwynplaine MacIntyre.

"Tom of Ten Thousand" by permission of Edward Marston.

"The Dutchman and the Masagascar Pirates" by permission of Annette and Martin Meyers.

"Two Sides" by permission of Mike Stotter.

"A Taste for Ducking" by permission of Marilyn Todd.

"Death Knows no Compromise" by permission of Derek Wilson.

"The Comedy That Became a Tragedy" was first published in *Pearson's Magazine*, November 1899. Copyright expired on 31 December 2001.

INTRODUCTION: GUNPOWDER, TREASON AND PLOT

MIKE ASHLEY

The Jacobean Age might at first seem a rather obscure period for a volume of murder and mystery stories, until you think about it in more detail. The phrase is usually applied to the reign of James I, the first Stuart king of England. He was the son of Mary, Queen of Scots, and had been James VI of Scotland before he succeeded Elizabeth as James I of England in 1603. His reign lasted until his death in 1625 at the age of 58. It was a period that saw considerable changes in Britain, particularly the growth in Puritanism, but it also set in chain a whole series of events that would change the face of Britain forever – not just the eventual union of England, Scotland and Wales into the United Kingdom, but more immediately the Civil War that would see the execution of James's successor, Charles I.

James was not that popular a king. If there is one event we remember in history (aside, I suppose, from the Battle of Hastings and the Battle of Trafalgar) it is the Gunpowder Plot and the attempt by Guy Fawkes and his co-conspirators to blow up Parliament, including the king, in November 1605. James was intelligent and well-read – he did, after all, initiate the new translation of the *Bible* which has remained the "authorized" edition to this day – but he was also bigoted, rash and oblivious to the views of others. He believed strongly in the God-given "divine" right of kings. He had a passionate hatred of anything "supernatural" and his writings against witchcraft and demonology are renowned. He had a strong Scottish accent that few English could understand. He was openly homosexual, fondling his favourites in public. He had a rather disgusting habit of dribbling, he drank too much and had such a fondness for fruit that he suffered from frequent bouts of diarrhoea. But at least he was against smoking, so he wasn't all bad.

There is scope a-plenty for murder, mystery and mayhem in James's reign. One of the most notorious of all murder trials, about the mysterious death of Sir Thomas Overbury, occurred during his reign and features in this collection.

But why stop with James I? The phrase "Jacobean" also applies to his grandson, James II, albeit briefly, as this James, even more pig-headed and intransigent than his grandfather, lasted only three years on the thrones of England and Scotland before fleeing Britain to live in exile in France. Between James I and James II we have the reigns of Charles I and II, the English Civil War and the Commonwealth under Oliver Cromwell. Why leave those out just to split hairs over when "Jacobean" begins and ends?

So this anthology covers crimes and punishments throughout most of the seventeenth century, from 1604 to 1688 to be precise. It was a period which includes many well known characters, many of whom appear in this book, including Francis Bacon, Sir Walter Ralegh, Sir Robert Cecil, Pocahontas, Nell Gwynn, the artist Rubens and, of course, William Shakespeare. All but one of the stories are new, written specially for this anthology, and the one reprinted story is so rare I'll guarantee you won't have come across it before. I'm delighted to say that Fiona Buckley has written a new Ursula Stannard story, and P. F. Chisholm has written a new story about Robert Carey. Stories are set not just in Britain but in the American colonies, including the lost colony of Roanoke and the early days of New York and Philadelphia.

The stories feature many of the key events from this period, but often viewed from a new or different angle, and I was fascinated to see how the authors have brought new twists to interpreting events. This book contains quite a few surprises.

As always the stories are presented in chronological order so let us part the curtains of crime and head back four hundred years to the dawn of Great Britain.

Mike Ashley

THE KING'S FIRST ACHIEVEMENT

FIONA BUCKLEY

Although James, as James VI of Scotland, had long waited for the day when he would also rule England, the result was not quite what he had anticipated. Though intelligent, James was easily blinded by the glory of his position and failed to notice the realities beyond. England held a far more complicated and, at times, vulnerable position in European affairs than Scotland. One of the first problems he had to face was the state of war between England and Spain, which had dragged on for seventeen years. Both countries were tired and James was able to score an early coup by negotiating a peace treaty. Known as the Treaty of London it is the events leading up to that which form the background for the following story, which also allows us to meet such noted characters as William Shakespeare and Sir Robert Cecil.

The story features Ursula Stannard, the married name of Ursula Blanchard, the heroine of a series of books starting with The Robsart Mystery *(1997). Ursula is treated as one of Henry VIII's illegitimate offspring and thus the half-sister of Elizabeth I. Elizabeth finds she can trust Ursula, welcomes her into her court, and uses her as one of her spies. This story is set forty years after the events in that first book, but Ursula's abilities have not dimmed.*

Fiona Buckley is the alias of Valerie Anand (b. 1937), author of many historical novels starting with Gildenford *(1978), unusually set in the last days of Saxon England. Other books include* The Disputed Crown *(1982),* King of the Wood *(1988) and the* Bridges Over Time *series, starting with* The Proud Villeins *(1990), which traces the generations of a family from pre-Conquest England to the present day.*

1

"How on earth," said Mr William Shakespeare theatrically, "are we to rehearse any of our forthcoming productions when the King's Players are on duty every day, all through August, sweltering in scarlet wool breeches and cloaks, standing round a conference chamber and fetching mid-morning wine for the august delegates as if we were a gaggle of waiters?"

He was unassuming to look at and no longer young but he used both his voice and the English language like a good musician handling a dulcimer. "Why must we waste our time as a guard of honour," he demanded rhetorically, "while the Royal Council and the Spanish embassy argue over their peace treaty? Can anyone tell me? Thank you, Furness, a cup of good wine won't come amiss when we're the ones drinking it. I love your Venetian glass goblets."

"So do I. He may look like something that ought to be kept in a menagerie," said Richard Burbage in his beautiful and carrying actor's voice, "but he has the tastes of a civilized man."

"I *am* a civilized man," said Thomas Furness, accepting this backhanded compliment as though it were pure flattery. "I gave my daughter a set of similar glasses when she married," he added, holding up the exquisitely patterned example in his hand. "She has good taste, too."

He was as competent an actor as any, but he was too tall and massive for leading parts. His hands and feet were enormous, his face apparently the work of a sculptor who had given up at the rough-hewn stage and his voice resembled coal rumbling down a chute. He specialized in supporting roles in what had once been Queen Elizabeth's own theatre company and was now the King's Players for her successor King James. When such exalted Players as Richard Burbage and Edward Alleyn, or Will Shakespeare, who not only took major parts but wrote them too, accepted his invitations to dine, he was always flustered as well as delighted and doubly determined to provide good wine.

"Will is right," complained Burbage. They had abandoned the table and the debris of a prolonged dinner. All elegant grooming and graceful postures, he had draped himself over a window seat overlooking the street. "I know that room in Somerset House. It gets the sun. If this heat wave goes on, we'll all melt."

"Quite. A row of dear little puddles on the floor with our pretty scarlet liveries soaking in them, that's how we'll be." Shakespeare elaborated with enthusiasm. "Pools of what the Spaniards are now calling cochinilla dye will look very gruesome."

"I can't see why a peace treaty needs so much cogitation," grumbled Alleyn. He was less obviously handsome than Burbage but possessed of a presence that made other people shrink when he entered a room. "The old queen had a personal feud with Spain but King James hasn't and I daresay the Spanish want a new start as much as anyone. We want them to promise never to send another Armada and I don't suppose they want to send one anyway. One day should be enough to agree on that!"

"It's because it's important," said Shakespeare, "If they don't take at least three weeks over it, it won't *feel* important. You know, I have a notion that maybe we're going to be more than a guard of honour."

"What do you mean?" Furness looked startled.

"I mean," said Will Shakespeare, "that wherever old enemies try to make peace, there is someone who wants to maintain hostilities. I think there may be people who want the conference to fail. Passionate Puritans. Passionate Catholics. Odd, is it not? They are opposites and yet on this they agree. Like the two ends of a cord meeting if you bend it into a circle."

"I must say I hope life will be easier for Catholics henceforth," Furness said, strolling to the window and peering past Burbage at the scene below. In one direction the street led past Somerset House to the fine houses of the Strand, and in the other it stretched downhill towards the Fleet river. It was as usual crowded with coaches, carts, riders and pedestrians, but one coach was noticeable as it had just drawn up in front of the house next door.

"My father was a Catholic," Furness said, "and he was fined over and over for not attending Anglican services. Me, I'd rather keep the law and stay out of trouble. I never criticised Queen Bess. And I don't think I will now, either," he added.

"Why not?" asked Alleyn.

"Because, according to the widow next door, her departed majesty's half-sister Ursula Stannard is moving in as her tenant for a few weeks, with some of her family. Her steward came to London in advance to find a house for them and I think the main party has just arrived. That must be her, in grey, getting out of the coach down there."

"Ursula Stannard?" said Shakespeare. "*Really?*"

He and Alleyn joined the others at the window. Down below, there was a bustle of welcome for the coach and the riders who had accompanied it. A middle-aged man was handing a woman, probably his wife, down from his pillion and a pretty girl in a stylish riding dress was descending unaided from a good-looking roan horse. Two maidservants had run from the house to unload the luggage and a butler was helping an ageing lady in a dove-coloured dress, out of the coach. Rings flashed on her hands as she shook out her skirts. Another lady, in black, emerged from the coach after her and although she was the older of the two, she went at once to straighten the other's hat and smooth a straying tendril of snowy hair back into place.

"Is that Ursula Stannard? But she's old! Her hair's white." Burbage was amazed. "I can hardly believe it, knowing who she is."

Ursula Stannard's unusual past was one of those secrets which had been public knowledge for years. Her mother had been a maid of honour to Queen Anne Boleyn, and had been seduced by Henry the Eighth, with Ursula as a result. As a young woman at the court of her half-sister Queen Elizabeth, she had been employed not just as a Lady of the Bedchamber but also as an agent, helping to seek out plots and traitors.

She was wealthy, partly because she had inherited money and a fine house from her late husband, but also in her own right, for she had been well rewarded for her services. On one occasion, so rumour said, she had saved the queen's good name and possibly her throne. She had been given an estate of her own for that. To see her old and silver-haired took all of them aback.

"I wonder, though," said Shakespeare, "whether it's just a coincidence that she's here at the time of the peace conference."

"Surely not. She's been retired for years," said Furness. "I understand that the young girl is her granddaughter – the couple must be the girl's parents – and is to be presented to King James at Whitehall, and then taken to Greenwich to join the queen's household."

"Very peculiar," remarked Burbage. "The king and queen don't live together. A sorry example to set to the populace."

"I don't live with *my* wife, most of the time," said Shakespeare. "People work out their own ways of conducting their marriages. I have a wife, a son and two daughters and although I'm usually here and they're in Warwickshire, I'd die for any of them." His voice took on a tender note. "My daughters, especially. My dear daughters. Furness, can we all have another drink?"

2

From the moment my coach entered London on that summer afternoon, I sensed the change. This was not the London I remembered from sixteen years ago, the last time I had been there, when I came to congratulate Queen Elizabeth after the Armada was driven off. Now, it was 1604 and Elizabeth was dead. Her cousin King James of Scotland, ironically enough the son of Mary Stuart who had been one of Elizabeth's most dangerous rivals, had England's crown on his head and the change of ruler had, it seemed, infected the world though I, Ursula Stannard, living quietly in my houses in Surrey and Sussex, had not realized it before.

I saw it now, however. The people in the London streets looked different. Hats were taller, there were fewer ruffs. I saw many folk in the austere dress of the Puritan sect which I had heard was becoming so influential. There were more coaches about, too, modern ones, less clumsy than mine. The very air smelt different. To me, it was unwelcoming.

The journey had been no pleasure, either. At seventy, I could no longer sit a horse for further than a mile or two, while my friend and personal gentlewoman Sybil Jester was approaching eighty and couldn't ride at all. I envied my daughter Meg, who at fifty could still manage the journey on the pillion behind her husband, George Hillman. But the unwieldy coach in which Sybil and I had travelled wasn't much better than a horse. The two-day journey through scorching August weather from Withysham, my Sussex home, had been a purgatory of heat, dust and jolts. Why oh why had I ever listened to my daughter's persuasions?

"You know court protocol so well," Meg had said, flatteringly, when she and George and their youngest girl, Philippa, came to stay with me before taking Philippa to London. "You were so helpful when we presented our elder daughters. Will you come with us again and advise us now that it's Philippa's turn?"

So here I was, itching with prickly heat inside my long skirts and stiffened bodice and starched ruff, feeling my age, and wishing I'd said no.

I felt better once I was indoors and sipping wine in the little parlour of the house that my steward John Malton had rented for us. The glitter of the Thames beyond the windows was enough to make one's eyes ache, but the parlour was blessedly dim and cool, and comfortable too, with its cushioned settles and the spinet in one corner.

"I never expected to see London again," I said to Sybil. "It's strange, knowing the queen isn't here. We weren't always in accord, but – I loved her, you know."

"At least, you're not here this time to become involved in plots and politics and run into danger, the way you often were in the old days!" Sybil looked round the parlour. "These are good lodgings. They have their own steps down to the river, by the way; have you seen them? John Malton is efficient, I must say. Well, I suppose it's in his family. Didn't you tell me that his grandfather was a steward at Withysham, once?"

"Yes. John joined the army and disappeared to Ireland for a while, but when he applied to me on his return, I was happy to have him."

"He's done well by us," Sybil said. "And we have the whole house to ourselves except for our landlady and the maids."

"Our landlady isn't likely to be a trouble to us." I was amused. Mistress Catherine Bennett was a nervous creature in her forties, all stammers and curtseys and we had realized, the moment we arrived, that John Malton had got her thoroughly intimidated.

Judging from her unadorned black dress, she was of the Puritan persuasion but she had provided us with a whole list of little luxuries at her own expense, from bowls of Spanish oranges to perfumed hot washing water to the excellent white wine, cooled in her cellar, which we were now enjoying.

My amusement was brief, though. Talking of Malton had reminded me of other servants, of Roger Brockley and Fran Dale, my companions through so many years and so many dangers. They were long gone now, like the old adventurous days. Like Elizabeth. I missed Elizabeth above all. What sort of court would this be, presided over by the Scottish stranger James? What sort of England would he create? Not one I would recognize, of that I felt sure.

The parlour door opened, to admit Meg and George and their daughter. It also, surprisingly, admitted a wave of noisy music and masculine laughter from somewhere near at hand.

"What in the world . . .?" I demanded, starting up.

"I'm afraid there's a party next door," said George Hillman ruefully. He was a most amiable and tolerant man but even he blenched slightly, as the din crescendoed. "He's a King's Player called Thomas Furness and today he has guests. The landlady says they're probably getting drunk. But she also says he doesn't have gatherings like that very often. She says that normally, we'll hardly be aware of our neighbours."

"I hope not, indeed!" said Sybil indignantly.

The business of presenting Philippa to King James went well, however. He was more agreeable than I expected. His charming and dangerous mother had plotted to get Elizabeth assassinated and to seize her throne, if necessary with the help of a Spanish army; his dissolute father Henry Darnley had been murdered, very likely with Mary Stuart's connivance. But King James, though he had a slight physical resemblance to his father, was quiet and courteous. He greeted Philippa kindly and thanked me for my former services to the Crown. He said he hoped for a peaceful reign and a prosperous England. Almost, he made me feel in tune with the unfamiliar new world of his court.

Now, we had delivered my granddaughter safely to the queen's residence at Greenwich and were returning by river to our lodgings. "Well, that's done," I said, as our hired boat made its way upstream. "I hope Philippa won't be homesick. Queen Anna seems kindhearted."

"Yes, indeed," Meg said. "She's still struggling with the English language, isn't she? I suppose it's very different from Danish. At least she isn't pretentious. When we sent our eldest girl to court, she came back to us with nothing in her head but fashion and scandal."

"She also got a good husband," said George. "Nothing like showing a girl off in the right circles. Philippa will be all right. She has all your common sense, my love."

"Well, you two have no more daughters to launch and frankly, I'm relieved," I told them. I looked up at the sky. The weather had changed from a heatwave to overcast skies and out on the water, the wind was sharp. I pulled my cloak more firmly round me and added: "I've rented the house for two more weeks so that Meg and I can do some London shopping but I shall be glad enough when I set off for home, I must say."

"You need to rest. We're nearly back to the lodgings," said George. "Boatman, those are our river steps, over there. Pull in."

"I'll sleep after dinner," I said as we climbed the steep steps up to the river entrance of the house, with George lending Sybil a hand. "This evening, Meg, we might try out the spinet in the parlour. We could . . ."

"Welcome back, Mistress Stannard," said John Malton, stepping out of the door to meet us. Mistress Bennett was hovering just behind him. "I apologize for troubling you the moment you arrive but there's a young lady to see you."

"She's just come," said Mistress Bennett. "And she was that insistent about speaking to you. You were already getting out of your boat and I said to Mr Malton, she looks a decent body, nothing of the hussy about her, so why not let her wait in the parlour; they'll be here in a moment . . ."

"Personally, I would have turned her away and told her to come back at a more suitable time," said Malton. "But, as Mistress Bennett says, she was insistent. I therefore allowed her to wait. She wishes to see you, she says, concerning the Spanish conference, and it's urgent."

"What Spanish conference?" I asked blankly.

"Did she ask for my mother by name?" Meg enquired.

"Yes, madam. She also said the matter was of national importance."

"Really?" George had raised his eyebrows.

Sotto voce, Sybil murmured: "Oh, no!"

"All I want is a good dinner and then a nap in a quiet room with the shutters closed and a coverlet over me," I said sourly. "But . . ."

"Mother, you shouldn't be disturbed like this. George will deal with her. Won't you, George?"

"Certainly, if Mistress Stannard wishes."

"No." I shook my head. "If she asked for me, then I must see her. Did she give her own name?"

"Yes, madam. Eleanor Powell."

"I've never heard of her *or* this Spanish conference but I'll find out what she wants." I handed my cloak to Malton and nodded to the others. "I'll call you if I need you."

Mistress Eleanor Powell was in the parlour, seated on a cushioned stool. She was a sturdy girl with pleasant blue eyes and crimped brown hair and she looked both respectable and sensible in her black hat and cloak. Malton, annoyed by her intrusion, had evidently not offered to take them. Her dark green gown was a practical affair of thin wool, and her hands were clasped in her lap. There was a wedding ring on her left hand. She stood up as I came in, but I saw to my surprise that she was trembling.

"Please sit down again," I said. "You are Eleanor Powell? I am Mistress Ursula Stannard and I believe you wish to see me."

"You are *the* Ursula Stannard?" She sat down as bidden, but kept imploring eyes on me.

"I suppose so," I said, slightly startled. "Yes."

"Then it's you I want. It's vital." Her accent was that of an educated Londoner but her voice seemed oddly weak. She shook her head as though this somehow surprised her, or as if she wanted to clear her sight. "The Spanish conference," she said. "The peace conference. There are those who don't like it. I know nothing of court folk so I didn't know who to tell. I've heard of you, though. You'll know who to go to. You must tell someone – someone at court. You must warn them."

"Warn them about what?"

"About someone who wants to ruin the conference. It's difficult. I . . . I'm sorry," said my guest. She had gone very pale, "I don't feel quite myself. I . . ."

"Mistress Powell, if you could tell me a little more . . . *Mistress Powell!*"

Something was horribly wrong. All of a sudden, her eyes had widened and become huge and fixed. I stepped towards her in alarm and as I did so, she fell forward off the stool. Ignoring the creakiness of my ageing knees, I crouched down beside her. "Mistress Powell? What is it?" She had turned her head to one side as she fell and I saw that her eyes were open and fixed. I put a hand on her shoulder and then realized that what had looked like an accidental bunching of the cloak was due to something hard jutting out beneath it. At the same time I felt a dampness under my fingers and when I lifted my hand, I saw the scarlet stain.

I dragged the cloak aside. From her back, poking through the material of her dress, was the hilt of a little knife, or dagger. It was silver, chased with a delicate pattern. Blood stained the green fabric around it and some had soaked into the cloak which was too dark in colour to show it. There wasn't much, anyway. The blade of the weapon must be very fine, I thought. And the whole length of it had been driven into her body. Now, Eleanor Powell was dead.

I had seen violent death before, more often than I liked. I did not scream. Quietly, I stood up and called for the rest of the household. I thought I did so calmly, but something in my tone must have spoken of emergency, for they took only seconds to come crowding into the parlour.

"Malton," I said, "she was alive when she arrived. Has anyone else been in here since, between her arrival and ours?"

"No, Madam. It was only minutes. Mistress Bennett was with me and the maids were in the kitchen. I could hear them chattering and stirring things, all the time. Madam, when I was soldiering in Ireland, we were ambushed at one point and I saw a man, stabbed in the back like this, fight on for quite a while before he collapsed. We drove our attackers off and tried to help him. For a few minutes, he could still speak to us. He didn't know what was wrong with him. He died not knowing he'd got a knife in his back. One of our officers, a very experienced man, told me that a thin blade can slip in almost without pain and may not kill at once."

"I've heard that said, as well." George Hillman leant down to take hold of the girl's cloak and pulled its folds wide. "Look. There's no rent in this. She was stabbed before she put it round her, or else someone caught at it and lifted it aside. The weight of it as it swung against that hilt might have driven it that fraction deeper, making the wound more lethal. It can't have happened very long before she got here, but I'd say she had the blade in her when she arrived."

"However it happened," I said, "this was murder. And it's something to do with a Spanish conference. I know nothing about that, but it sounds important – politically important. Is Sir Robert Cecil at court?"

"They took me to Whitehall, to be questioned by Sir Robert Cecil himself!" wept Mistress Bennett, clutching my arm as Meg and I, murmuring "There, there," helped her into her bedchamber and on to her bed.

"I was never so frightened!" wailed Mistress Bennett. I felt sorry for her. She had been in floods of terrified tears when she was marched out of the house, along with John Malton and the two maidservants and probably hadn't stopped crying since. All were now back, unharmed, but the maidservants had been weeping as well and even Malton looked pale while Mistress Bennett was still hysterical. "That Sir Robert – his eyes are so cold!" She continued to cling to me, "If Malton and I hadn't been together the whole time when that girl came here . . ."

"We could vouch for each other and for the maidservants too, and the maids bore us out." Malton had come in with a hot wine posset. He took it to Mistress Bennett. "Drink that, mistress. It will make you feel better. I was at hand when Mistress Bennett opened the door; we showed the girl to the parlour together and we went out together to meet you. The maids were both in the kitchen with the door open and could see all we did and I know they didn't leave their work. No one in this house harmed the girl and I think the authorities are now satisfied."

"But they questioned me and questioned me!" shrieked Mistress Bennett. "They kept asking what I knew about this Spanish conference! What Spanish conference, I said; I've never heard of it; what are you talking about? I thought I'd be taken to the Tower and put in a dungeon. I thought I'd be going to the block, or worse! The way they *looked* at me . . .!"

"Hush, hush!" said Meg kindly. "Drink your posset."

"All because I'm a Puritan and my daughter Kate's wed to one and he does some preaching against fripperies and idle gossip, but he's a respectable man, is Mr White, and nor, I said, is my Kate the girl that died on my parlour floor. My Kate's at her home in Chelsea Village; you go there and see!"

"Dear Mistress Bennett," I said. "I'm sure no one thinks you had anything to do with it. None of us had. Meg and I and Mr Hillman are to see Sir Robert again ourselves tomorrow, after the inquest. Perhaps he will have news for us. Perhaps we'll know by then just who this girl is."

I had been right to seek an audience with Sir Robert Cecil. One mention of a Spanish conference, and he had seized charge of the enquiry into Eleanor Powell's death.

"There are several angles to follow," he said. He sounded tired, and looked worried. "Who killed this young woman, *is* someone trying to ruin the conference and if so, who – and who in the world is Eleanor Powell anyway? So far, we have no answers. Thank you, by the way, Mistress Stannard, for arranging her funeral. If her relatives ever appear, I'm sure they'll be grateful, too. *If* they appear. She had a wedding ring so Powell was probably her husband's surname but as you know, no one came forward at the inquest to claim her. If we knew who she was and where she came from, the rest might unravel at once. As yet, the whole thing is a mystery."

"She obviously knew who I was," I said.

Sir Robert Cecil and I had met in the past but not known each other well before this violent death brought us together. Now, I thought how like his father, Sir Willam Cecil, he was. I had known Sir William, that most able of Elizabeth's councillors, very well indeed, quarrelled with him badly once or twice, but always admired his intelligence and his complete devotion to the good of Elizabeth and the realm of England. His son Robert was shorter of stature and had a crooked spine which gave him a hunched shoulder but this didn't affect his mind, which was as acute as that of Sir William. On his side, he knew my history and was at ease with me, however much he had bullied my landlady and the servants.

"Sir Robert," I said, "I know very little about the conference; only what was said at the inquest. The purpose is to arrange a peace treaty with Spain, it seems. Does anyone really want to disrupt it? Where will it be held?"

The inquest had finished an hour ago. George, Meg and I were with Sir Robert in Whitehall Palace, in the study which his father had used. The sun was out again, making the river outside sparkle, but our mood was sombre.

"An embassy from Spain," said Sir Robert, "has come to settle the terms of the agreement. The conference will be held in Somerset House, not far from your lodgings, beginning on the 7th of August. Somerset House belongs to the king. So does the idea of the treaty. King James would like a signed peace with Spain to be among the first major achievements of his reign. You would think that everyone would welcome freedom from the fear of another Armada, but, yes, there are those who would wreck the whole enterprise if they could. Ardent Puritans who don't want to talk to Papists, ever, about anything, and ardent Catholics longing for a revival of their religion, with a Spanish army to back it if necessary."

"But *how* could anyone wreck the conference?" said George Hillman with some impatience.

"I wish I knew! If only Mistress Powell had lived a little longer! The dainty little dagger that killed her is as nasty a weapon as ever I saw. I cut my thumb just by touching the edge." He exhibited the mark. "The hilt is unusual but we have enquired among silversmiths, weapon-makers and your neighbours too and no one recognizes it. I marvel," said Sir Robert, "that she lived as long as she did."

"I said from the first that she must have been attacked very shortly before she reached us," George said. "The coroner agreed, did he not?"

"Yes. It can only have happened minutes before she arrived at your lodging. Unless she was actually killed inside it."

"That isn't possible," I said grimly.

"So that leaves the street, the interior of a coach, or a nearby house as the scene of the stabbing," Sir Robert said. "No one admits to seeing or hearing anything noteworthy. To comb the whole of London for missing young married women is somewhat beyond us but no London constable or magistrate has heard of a missing girl called Powell – or Eleanor, either. Girls who aren't called Catherine are mostly Mary or Elizabeth! The choice of names for girl babies isn't wide. No young wife of any name or description has vanished from anywhere near you. Your landlady and your neighbour Thomas Furness both have daughters of the right age, who have married and left the district. We did wonder if one of them had come back under a false name for any reason, but they hadn't. Mistress Bennett's girl, Kate – another who was presumably christened Catherine . . ."

"Called after her mother, I think. Mistress Bennett's name is Catherine," I said. "Almost every family has a Catherine – Kate for short – in it somewhere. My father," I added dryly, "was married to three of them."

"So he was. Well, Mistress Bennett's Kate is married to a Mr White and to make sure she wasn't the murdered wench, I sent someone to see her. She was at her home in Chelsea village. By the bye, I'm sorry we questioned your landlady and your servants so fiercely, Mistress Stannard, but they were all on the premises when the girl died. We *must* examine every angle. As it happens, Mistress Bennett and the Whites are all devout Puritans, and Mr White has been officially warned, twice, against preaching in public and speaking against the bishops. However, we concluded they had nothing to do with this." Unexpectedly, he produced a wicked grin. "You were alone with the girl for a few minutes, Mistress Stannard. I know you used to carry a dagger. I suppose you didn't stab her yourself?"

"Sir Robert!" said Meg, outraged. I contented myself with looking at him. He grinned again.

"No. I grant that you're a most improbable suspect. I wish I could find a probable one. If *only* I knew who this girl *was*!"

"She isn't Furness's daughter either, I take it?" I said.

"His girl is twenty-seven years old and her name is Margaret, for a change! She was married eight or nine years ago to a Mr Westley, a smallholder in Kent. Your landlady knew her before her marriage and the Player Will Shakespeare was a guest at the wedding but neither of them can recall what Margaret looked like so they can't tell us whether she is the dead girl or not. However, Furness – he's a widower – said she wasn't his Margaret and he spoke the truth. I sent someone to Kent to make sure."

"I take it that, like Kate White, she was at home with her husband?" said George.

"When my messenger reached the Westleys' farm, Mistress Margaret was not only at home, she was lying in and the midwife announced the birth of a son while my man was actually in the house. Mistress Westley had had a hard time and was very ill. Furness says he didn't even know she was expecting a child. He seems much attached to her. He was horrified to hear how badly things had gone with her and said he would write to her husband. I gather that she was so ill that she may actually have died but, if so, it wasn't on your parlour floor, Mistress Stannard."

"And Furness himself?" I enquired. "After all, he lives next door to my lodgings. Every angle, you said, Sir Robert. No one has stabbed Margaret, but I suppose Furness could have stabbed Eleanor, whoever she was."

Sir Robert sighed. "Furness's father was in trouble several times for not attending church, and once for sheltering a priest who was on the run, but Furness himself seems to be a dutiful Anglican and a law-abiding family man. His fellow actors agree with that. He says he was out at the time of your return from Greenwich and that his two servants were out too, on various errands. There seems no reason to disbelieve him. I can't arrest anyone simply for living next door to you! In fact," said Sir Robert bitterly, "we have found nothing but blind alleys."

"What more can be done?" Meg asked seriously.

"Every precaution has already been taken that anyone can think of, to protect the conference. The King's Players will stand round the walls of the conference chamber and not just for ceremonial purposes. They'll watch for anything untoward. They haven't been officially informed yet of this extra duty but they will be by tomorrow and I think some of them already suspect. They always seem aware of what's afoot in the world. I think they scent it in the air, like hounds."

His look of worry deepened. "I hope we've thought of everything. The Players won't be armed – we're not allowing weapons into the room at all – but there will be armed guards in the antechamber just outside and at all entrances to Somerset House. The proceedings will probably take most of August and last for some hours each day and refreshments will be served during the sessions. Two of the Players, different ones each day, will fetch the trays from the kitchen. We're not letting any servants into the room. Servants come and go; we can never be sure we know the backgrounds of them all. We know more about the Players and they'll watch each other, too. Somerset House will be searched from cellar to roof beforehand, as well."

Meg said: "I've thought of something that George and I might do to help – if you will, George."

"What is it?" said Mr Hillman, but indulgently. He glanced at Sir Robert. "I grew accustomed, long ago, to having married into a family where all the women have inquisitive natures."

"This Eleanor," said Meg, "knew my mother was coming to London and knew where to find her. Very likely she is connected to the district where we're lodging. Well, Kate and Margaret grew up there. They might well remember other girls like themselves who went away as they did, but may have come back – perhaps visiting. We could go and talk to them. Your enquirers just went to see if they were safely at home. Perhaps . . . well . . ."

"Perhaps they didn't ask the right questions, she means," said Hillman helpfully. "From the sound of it, I doubt if Margaret Westley could have answered questions anyway. But if by good luck she has recovered after all, perhaps she could now."

"Very well." Robert Cecil was decisive. "If you will undertake that, I'll see you are given the right directions for finding these two woman. And Ursula, there is something you can do, if you will. Will you be an extra pair of eyes and oversee the refreshments? Watch the preparation and escort the trays to the conference chamber? With your eyes wide open."

"Of course! I wish I could do more," I said.

"If this isn't enough," said Sir Robert, "I'm sure I don't know what is!"

By the tenth day of the conference, I was tired. I had been on duty in the anteroom to the conference chamber day in and day out, except when escorting those who were fetching refreshment trays. My mirror that morning had shown me a face unwontedly pale, and hazel eyes which were still bright but had new lines around them. Sybil was predicting that soon I would collapse and be brought back to her feet first.

So far, nothing untoward had happened except that everyone –

except the Spaniards, who knew nothing of the crisis – was on edge and jumping at shadows. The Players were the worst, perhaps because they were actors whose lives were, literally, saturated in drama.

Richard Burbage, who at first had gone in for striking elegant poses, had given this up and just looked careworn. Big, craggy Furness, when detailed on the second day to help in fetching the mid-morning refreshments for the eleven dignified gentlemen round the negotiating table, tripped in the kitchen doorway and nearly sent a whole trayload of winejugs sliding to the floor.

Edward Alleyn said he couldn't sleep properly and had nightmares when he did sleep, and if anyone burst into the conference room waving a knife, he would be too tired to do anything about it.

"And you should have seen us when there was a tap on the conference room door," the actor-playwright Will Shakespeare had confided to me. "It turned out to be just a clerk with a fair copy of the first draft agreement but, when he knocked, Sir Robert Cecil dropped his pen and we all looked at the door as though the devil might come through it."

Shakespeare talked to me when he could, for he seemed to find me intriguing. "You puzzle us, you know," he said on that tenth day, as he and Furness, vivid in their scarlet ceremonial livery, emerged from the conference chamber, on their way once more to collect the mid-morning trays. "You seem an unlikely person for this task. If anything did happen, what could you do?"

"I know what you see, Mr Shakespeare," I said, rising from my stool to join them. "Just an ageing dame in dove-coloured damask, with an unfashionable ruff. I can't walk fast, and my arms . . ." I held them up in their big quilted sleeves " . . . are like sticks. I am here to observe, to recognize, if I can, any suspicious pattern before it develops, and give warning. That's all." I smiled. "There was a time when I carried a dagger in case I had to defend myself and once or twice I even used it, but I have no weapons now."

I gestured towards the armed men standing round the anteroom. "If there's a crisis, the guards must deal with it; or yourselves and the principals, if it happens inside the conference room. I see that your rota is repeating itself, by the way. You and Mr Furness have both carried out this errand before."

"But we had different partners. The rota is arranged that way," Shakespeare said as we made our way down the short flight of stairs to the kitchen regions. "What an extraordinary woman you are," he added. "And your family is remarkable, too. Sir Robert has told us that your daughter and her husband have gone to Kent to interview Furness's daughter, and why. They are not yet back?"

"No, not yet."

"I hope they learn something but it seems like aiming at a very distant target."

"We felt we had to try anything we could think of. I am sorry I can't go faster." The stairs had a steep curve and I found them awkward. Shakespeare had matched his pace to mine but Furness was tramping impatiently ahead.

"A minute here or there doesn't matter. But it does seem strange that no one can identify Mistress Powell."

We had no more time to discuss it, however, for now we were entering the steamy, vaulted kitchen of Somerset House, where the dinner which the conference members would eat at midday was in preparation under the eyes of wary and suspicious guards, and trays were being laden with a small mid-morning repast: little pies containing fruit or meat, almond cakes, goblets, and jugs of wine. There was a dry white vintage and a light red, both French, and also a sweet and heavy red wine from Tarragona on the Mediterranean coast of Spain. The Spaniards liked it and had brought their own supplies with them.

Furness was already rumbling an enquiry about how carefully everything had been tasted. He was also complaining that we were behind time. He shot me an irritated glance, blaming my slow footsteps for it.

"Everything is ready," said the chief cook, also irritably. "There are the trays and yes, everything has been tasted and the wine casks freshly broached. Nothing venomous ever went out of *this* kitchen or cellar either, believe me! The very idea is an insult. And," he added crossly, "I've had two assistants dismissed for being Puritans so now I'm shorthanded as well as insulted."

"I understand they were known associates of a man called White, who's done some seditious preaching!" growled Furness, as he gathered up his tray. "Come!" he said to me and Shakespeare, and stalked out of the kitchen ahead of us.

As the days went on, I had grown more watchful, rather than less. This time, as we neared the top of the stairs, something unusual caught my attention. Somewhere ahead, was an unexpected murmur of voices.

Furness, also hearing them, came to a sudden stop and once more, his tray tilted perilously. Shakespeare turned to look at me, rolling his eyes heavenwards in exasperation. Furness steadied himself, checked a sliding wine jug, and said anxiously: "That's a woman talking! But no strangers are supposed to come into the house! Who . . .?"

"I think it's Meg," I said. "She and George must be back from Kent. Go on, Furness!" We followed him up to the short passageway at the top and along it to the anteroom. There indeed we found my daughter and son-in-law awaiting us and they wasted no time in greetings. "We have news," said George, stepping forward into our path. His amiable face was unusually grim. "No further, please!"

"But the gentlemen are waiting for us!" protested Furness. Round the walls, the guards tensed, changing their grip on their pikes.

George didn't move. "Meg, tell them what we've learned."

"We went to Kent to see Margaret Westley, who was born Margaret Furness," said Meg. She looked tired and hot, her dark hair straggling damply from under her hat, skirts and boots dusty. "But there's been a muddle. Margaret is nearly as common a name as Kate. I'm called Margaret, really, and there are many many more."

"What *is* this woman talking about?" demanded Furness angrily.

Meg glanced at him. "Your daughter married the younger of two brothers, who lived together on the same smallholding. The elder brother's wife was called Margaret as well. The enquirer Sir Robert sent found a Margaret Westley there with her husband but she was lying in and very ill. He was never allowed to speak to her and her husband was too distracted to be questioned closely. The enquirer wasn't welcome in a household in such confusion. He accepted that the Margaret Westley who was having the baby, was the former Margaret Furness but he never actually asked her maiden name.

"What is all this?" Furness, impatient as ever, made to walk past George Hillman but a guard lowered a pike in front of him.

"The Margaret Westley who was lying in, is not Mr Furness's daughter but her sister-in-law, the elder brother's wife. She did recover from her confinement and we've talked to her. The younger brother, the husband of Margaret Furness, died last year," said Meg. "And as Mr Furness well knows, two months ago his daughter remarried – an innkeeper she met when he came to Kent to visit relatives. She went with him back to his home in Southwark. We've been there, too. She went off, on the morning of the day she died, to visit her father. She meant to stay a week. When she didn't come home as expected, her husband went to find her and Furness here told him she had left for Southwark at the right time and he didn't know what had happened to her."

"Her husband's name," said George, "is Nicholas Powell, and he called her Eleanor. It was her second name, apparently. When she was a Westley, she took to using it, because it was confusing to have two Margarets in the house."

"*You* are Eleanor Powell's father?" Shakespeare said to Furness. "But you said you didn't recognize the body! Was it you who . . .?"

"No, it wasn't!" bellowed Furness. "But who would have believed me if I'd said so? Yes, she came to visit me. Then she set out for home, and the next I heard, a young woman had been found murdered in this woman's house!" With his head, he indicated me. "I was asked to look at her and yes, it was my girl! But I didn't say so. I told her husband I'd report her missing but I kept quiet. Seems she'd been babbling to Mistress Stannard about some threat or other to this conference. I could see myself in a dungeon if I said she had anything to do with me. I held my tongue and my breath! I don't know who killed her. I only know I didn't but I repeat, who's going to believe me?"

"But she was your daughter!" said Will Shakespeare. "How could you not acknowledge her when you saw her lying dead? And then you lied to her husband!"

"If you were me, and your father had been put in prison for hiding a priest, perhaps you'd understand," said Furness angrily. "I didn't *dare* say Eleanor was my girl. And now, please, can we take these trays in?"

I took a deep breath. If I were wrong about this, I would look very foolish and would probably make an enemy for life, but there's one thing about getting older; enemies for life won't be enemies for all that long. Meg and George had delayed the crucial moment and more than that; they had added to my credibility now that it was here. Only, it *was* here and I could not avoid it.

"Before we go any further," I said. "That jug on your tray there, Mr Furness – that's the one with the sweet wine the Spaniards like, isn't it? Would you mind drinking a goblet of it yourself? We can fetch some more for them."

Thomas Furness turned to me, glowering down at me from his considerable height. I would not, at that moment, have wished to be alone with him in a secluded alleyway. "What the devil for?"

"To prove that it's harmless," I said. "Is it?"

"Of course it's harmless! What are you suggesting? Of all the impertinent . . .!"

The door of the conference chamber opened and Sir Robert appeared. "What is this disturbance? And what has happened to our refreshments?"

"Sir Robert," I said, in formal tones, "will you ask the guards, please, to arrest Mr Thomas Furness. I think he put a dagger into the back of his daughter Margaret as she ran from his presence to warn me that he was planning an outrage against this conference. And though I'm not sure, I think that on the stairs just now, when he stumbled and put a hand over the jug of Spanish wine to steady it, he dropped something into it."

There was an astounded silence. Then I said: "The news my daughter and her husband have just brought was opportune, but I would not have let anyone drink the wine from that jug in any case. When Mr Furness tripped, the very first time he was on refreshment duty, it struck me as contrived. I have watched him carefully, waiting for his next turn at this task. I think the first stumble was a rehearsal. He's an actor, after all. Today, on the stairs, he tripped again and something caught the light under his palm. The stairs curve and I had a sidelong view of him."

"I never heard such nonsense," said Furness coldly. "Of course the wine is innocent. I shall prove it!"

Balancing the tray in one hand, he lifted the jug destined for the Spanish delegates, filled a goblet and passed it beneath his nose. "An excellent vintage, from the bouquet," he remarked. In ironical fashion, he raised the goblet to me and fearlessly tossed the contents down his throat.

My heart grew heavy. *I know what you see*, I had said to Will Shakespeare. *Just an ageing dame in dove-coloured damask, with an unfashionable ruff*. I was past my work. I had made a monstrous mistake. I had made myself look foolish, just as I feared and it hurt more than I expected. I should have stayed at home and minded my stillroom.

Then Furness smiled, and I stepped backwards, shaken anew, with mingled hope and horror. A more unpleasant smile, I had never seen.

"I tried to leave Spain free to come to the aid of the old religion, if the day ever dawns when the true faith needs her," he said, returning the drained goblet to the tray. "It seems I have failed."

"What?" said George.

The rest of us waited, staring. "My father was openly Catholic," Furness said bitterly. "He paid fines. For six terrible months he was imprisoned. He died of a lung congestion he caught in that damp cell."

His voice grew angry. "As for me," he said, "All my life, *all my life*, I have pretended. I hoped when King James, whose mother was a true Catholic, came to reign over us, that changes would come, that one day our faith would once more illumine all England. But what is he doing now? Denying himself, and all of us, a way to call up strength to support us when the moment comes. We *relied* on Spain!"

"A foreign army on English soil? Most of your countrymen would have resisted savagely, even if you didn't," said George Hillman. "Have you thought of the bloodshed? The burned crops and houses, the pain, the deaths, the tears of the bereaved?"

"These things are in God's hands. If they are necessary to restore the faith, then so be it." Suddenly, Furness's face had whitened, revealing a passion so intense that it almost stopped one's breath. "I meant to destroy this conference if I could and I thought my daughter would be proud of me when I told her so. I thought she had always been pretending, too. But she hadn't! She said she would betray me! I said I'd kill her before I'd let her abandon me, or our religion. I showed her the dagger but still she wouldn't heed me. She ran for the door. So I silenced her. It was her life or the hope of our faith. Can't you understand? And with my dagger in her back, still she got away!" It came out through clenched teeth. "My daughter failed me and our faith and her soul is now in hell and so it should be. Arrest me, by all means. I doubt if I shall come to trial. The wine is poisoned, of course."

"We've had a narrow escape," said Sir Robert.

Will Shakespeare, sitting in a corner of Mistress Stannard's parlour, nodded soberly, although some of his mind was elsewhere. It was one of those times – he had experienced them before – when crude reality had intruded on the secret world inside his head and the results were surprising. He was shocked; he took Furness's actions as seriously as any man, but they had stirred his imagination. He wanted to be alone, to think.

Meanwhile, at least, there was no need for over-long faces. It was another sunlit day and beyond the parlour windows, the glint of the Thames was now the glint of mirth.

"Mistress Stannard and the Hillmans did the work," Edward Alleyn said. "The Players were the audience this time. At a terrifying drama."

"Very true. We were all badly shaken." Richard Burbage was also present at this final gathering before Mistress Ursula Stannard and her family left for their homes. "We had no idea what we were harbouring in our midst."

Sybil said: "I shudder to think what might have happened. We might be at war with Spain now! But how did he hope to poison the jug without being noticed? Wouldn't the wine have tasted strange?"

"It was a sweet wine, sweet enough to hide the taste." Sir Robert put a hand into his doublet and brought out a rock crystal phial, a tiny glittery thing, ideal as a perfume bottle for a lady's girdle-pouch. "He had the venom in this. He must have palmed it. Thomas Furness was a big man with huge hands. Delightful, isn't it? He liked pretty objects." Cecil's tone was cynical. "Venetian glass and dainty rock crystal phials and charming little daggers with blades like razors. That dagger was new. We've found the silversmith who made the hilt, now. That's why no one recognized it."

"He had only to trip, bring his hand up and clamp it over the jug as if to steady it, and drop the poison in then," Mistress

Stannard said. "He could have drawn the stopper out and had a finger over the neck."

"But what was in it?" asked Meg.

"Deadly nightshade, the physicians say," said Sir Robert, "He didn't need much. The doctors we called to him said that a single berry of nightshade could kill. Oh yes, we sent for physicians. We wanted him alive to be tried and executed."

His voice was chilling, Shakespeare thought. One could almost pity Furness, if he had lived to face execution.

"Though it may be better as it is," Cecil remarked. "This way, we need never let the Spaniards know what happened. I'm happy enough to leave it there. So is the king."

"But to think," persisted Sybil, "if any of the Spaniards – even the ambassador himself! – had been poisoned! At a peace conference . . .!"

"Oh, it could have been worse than that," said Sir Robert. "Nightshade berries not only kill; they sometimes inspire wild delusions first. It would have been even more appalling if the first symptoms took the form they did with Furness. Suppose the Spanish ambassador had leapt from his seat, torn all his clothes off and then taken to smashing up the furniture, or even attacked the Players or the other gentlemen at the table! Before spewing all over the room."

"Is that what Furness . . .?" asked Burbage, struggling visibly with a mixture of awe, horror and a species of ghastly amusement, while George Hillman actually turned pale.

"Yes. He stripped naked and smashed a small bench against his cell wall before the guards rushed in and then he went for them too. They seized him and then he started to throw up. They said they had never seen nausea like it. The physicians could do nothing for him."

There was silence, while they all contemplated the idea of such a debacle at the conference that was meant to seal the first main achievement of King James' reign. No one felt inclined to speculate aloud on the possible consequences.

At length, Shakespeare said: "And he murdered his daughter?"

"Yes. The daughter he claimed he loved. He did some talking on the way to the Tower. He boasted to her about his plans because he thought she cared for the old religion as he did and would admire him. He was wrong. By then, he had already let out to her that Mistress Stannard was next door. And she had heard of Ursula Stannard."

"He must have cursed himself for that," George Hillman remarked.

"He did. When she tried to run from the room; he snatched at her cloak and must have thrust the dagger into her beneath it. No doubt she felt something but probably didn't realize she was really hurt. She tore herself loose and fled next door. He was furious."

"He must have been quite out of his mind," said Burbage in a hushed voice.

"Drunk on his religion," said Sir Robert heavily. "It happens."

"Her death was my fault, in a way," said Mistress Stannard. "If she'd never heard of me, she might have lived. Poor girl."

"I know. But if it hadn't been for her, and you, it would have been poor England," said Sir Robert seriously.

Shakespeare made his way on foot back to his own lodgings in the City, plodding through the hot streets in which the odours of horse-dung and dust mingled with the appetizing smells, drifting from windows, of suppers being cooked. He dodged the carts and horsemen without noticing them. He was alone at last, and free to think.

Furness's attempted crime had been ugly but the creative stimulation which such encounters with real-life drama so often produced was working strongly now. He had in the last few days met some astonishing people. That woman, Ursula Stannard. Telling him so calmly that she had once carried a dagger in case she needed it to defend herself in the course of her career as an agent – a most unlikely career for a woman. It would be interesting to write about a woman who was handy with a dagger.

How could he fit her into a play? He could see her . . . snatching a dagger, perhaps, from a man too infirm of purpose to use it himself. And what about Furness, murdering his own daughter, the daughter he was said to love! That was horrible. It was the proper business of a father of daughters to care for them and protect them; to stand by them always and never to abandon them. The girl had apparently protected her father. At least, she hadn't said his name to Mistress Stannard, or told anyone that she was his daughter. It was probably a deliberate omission for his sake. The wretch hadn't deserved her.

It reminded him of that old folk tale which the Players – the Queen's Players, they were then – had worked up into a drama just after he first joined them. He had acted in it himself. It was about a king who turned on a once-beloved daughter. He understood it better now. He could improve on that original version.

In the pit of his stomach, he felt the curious thud which was the first symptom of a burgeoning idea. What was the name of the king in that story, now? Ah, yes. *King Lear* . . .

THE DUKE OF YORK

P. F. CHISHOLM

P. F. Chisholm is the alias of historical novelist Patricia Finney (b. 1958). Under both names she has written historical mysteries set in the Elizabethan period. Under her own name she is probably best known for her Becket and Ames secret agent series that began with Firedrake's Eye *(1992) and includes the events behind the Spanish Armada in* Gloriana's Torch *(2003). More recently she has started a new series featuring Lady Grace Cavendish at Elizabeth's court, starting with* Assassin *(2004). She has also written contemporary children's books such as* I, Jack *(2000).*

As Chisholm she has written four novels featuring Sir Robert Carey, starting with A Famine of Horses *(1995). He was a real historical character (1560–1639), the grandson of Anne Boleyn's sister, Mary (and therefore, some argue, also the grandson of Henry VIII – his father had a marked resemblance to the king), and served the Queen loyally, becoming Lord Warden of the Marches. Although he briefly fell out of favour with James I, his loyalty was unquestioned and he was soon reappointed to the royal household, in events that unfold in the following story.*

Elizabeth Lady Carey heard the impatient sound of hooves clattering to a halt in the small courtyard below her chamber in Whitehall, and immediately moved to look out of the window. She knew it was her husband because Sir Robert Carey was the only man at the unmartial court of King James who still rode headlong. You would think he was following a hot trod on the now theoretically abolished Border.

Robert was swinging down from his horse, wearing a face of thunder and Elizabeth sighed. She hadn't expected him to like selling Norham castle, no matter how essential the sale was. But had he in fact got the price agreed for it? It didn't look as if he had.

Before she could call to him, there was a squeal of happiness down below.

"Father, father! Gertrude had four puppies and they're yellow and black and brown and the smallest ate sugar and it was sick and my Lady Aunt said . . ." Little Philly, in an old kirtle too short for her, was sprinting from the small still-room where she had been gorging on sweetmeats under the excuse of learning huswifery from her Aunt. With only a second's pause for a sketchy curtsey, her eight years of healthy growth thumped into her father's midriff and his face instantly cleared to delight. He swung her up, grinning and gave her a smacking kiss on the cheek.

"Now there's a sight to soothe my eyes," he said with mock severity, "My daughter completely plastered in sugar . . ."

Little Philadelphia left the subject of puppies, took her father's hat from his head and put it on her own, curling the long feather around her finger.

"But, sir, I must learn to catch a husband by his stomach," she said reasonably, "as I am not like to be a beauty."

Her father scowled theatrically.

"Where's the ruffian who dares say so?" he demanded. "I'll fight him for you."

"Well, it was Robert," she said, naming her 11-year-old brother while she began to play with the pearl earring in her father's ear. Behind them a groom was seeing to the horse and leading it to the horseboxes in the corner of the courtyard.

"Ah. I see. And you believed him? Don't you know it's the duty of all elder brothers to keep their sisters down?" Her father caught her hand to save his earlobe. "Go and ask your aunt for the tale of all the terrible things I used to do to her and be grateful *I'm* not your older brother."

Philly sniggered as he put her down. "I heard about the senna-pods in your tutor's wine," she said.

"Hmf. Ask Philadelphia who was it stole them from the still-room for me. Now where is your mother?"

Philly rolled her eyes and pointed upwards to where Elizabeth was watching from the window.

As always, even now after twelve years of marriage, Elizabeth felt a shock under her breastbone as his vivid blue eyes met hers and she answered his smile with her own as she curtseyed to him.

"By God, my lady, I am right glad to see you!" he said, very heartfelt as he bowed with a great court flourish in return, retrieving his hat from his daughter's head as he did so. "Off you go, Philly, and try not to eat yourself sick."

Philly ran back to the stillroom, a rip in her petticoat, her straight brown hair falling out from under her white cap and the long nose she had unfortunately got from her mother still smudged with pounded sugar.

Carey's feet were already on the stairs and Elizabeth moved to open the door just as her husband erupted through it and wrapped her in his arms.

A few minutes later, pinning her cap straight again, Elizabeth sat her husband down and called a page to bring water for him to wash the dust of travel off him. She put his swordbelt and buff-coat on the stand herself and after discovering that he hadn't bothered with breakfast because he was in a hurry, sent the lad scurrying off again for bread and beer.

"Now," she said, sitting herself down opposite Carey and wearing her most severe expression, "what has happened? Was it Norham?" She couldn't help grimacing nervously. "Did my lord of Dunbar actually pay what he said he would for it?"

"Of course he did, with Cecil brokering the deal," said her husband, piling new butter on manchet bread and swallowing down mild beer at a remarkable rate. "He's not mad. And I got another £800 off him in cash for the contents of the kitchens and the other insight. Here."

He stood up, unbuttoned his doublet and produced a money-belt which he handed to her. He fished a wad of paper out of his sleeve and gave her that: it was three banker's drafts for £2,000 each in the name of Dunbar, payable to Sir Robert Carey at Gresham's Exchange over the next six months.

Hiding her instant horror that her husband should have galloped the length of a kingdom swarming with sturdy beggars and other riffraff with so much money on him, Elizabeth laughed with relief and kissed his cheek. Carey looked mildly concerned.

"Nobody's sworn out another warrant for debt against me, have they?" he asked, with his mouth full.

"Not yet," she admitted, omitting any details, "And now they won't. I shall go and pay the tailor's bill this afternoon in gold, personally."

"Maybe I should do it . . ."

"Oh, no need," Elizabeth said quickly, terrified her husband would take a fancy to one of Mr Bullard's latest doublets and beggar them again. "I'll take the steward and make sure he's reckoned up the interest correctly. You know how Bullard never makes a mistake in anybody else's favour."

She was watching carefully. Carey's face had darkened, not smiled. "Come, my love," she said, "what's troubling you?"

Carey left the second pennyloaf buttered but uneaten, finished the beer, wiped his hands and face with a napkin, leaned back and sighed.

"You see, after I had finished the business at Norham and gotten the money, something my lord of Dunbar said made me fancy a little trip north."

Elizabeth smiled encouragingly to hide the freezing of her blood: her adored husband had also crossed the still dangerous Borders, presumably twice, while carrying a fortune in gold and banker's drafts.

"Oh," she said brightly, "And how is everybody in the Marches?"

". . . Er . . . much quieter and more law-abiding," said Carey hurriedly. "So I went to visit my lord of Dunfermline."

Elizabeth raised her eyebrows. Alex Seaton, Lord Dunfermline was indeed one of Carey's many friends, but as well as being the Lord Chancellor of Scotland he was also the current Governor of the King's youngest son, the Duke of York.

"And how is his Grace the Prince?"

"Bloody terrible," said Carey, looking straight at her, "I don't know what's going on in his household but he's half the size he should be; he can't walk, he can't talk. I never saw a sorrier-looking little boy. He's supposed to be four years old but he looks two."

Elizabeth shook her head. She knew Dunfermline's lady and thought her a giggling little fool but, more importantly, the woman had never been a mother. There had been rumours that all was not well in the Prince's household and Queen Anne was worried.

"Is he like to die?"

Carey shook his head again. "I could see no trace of fever nor consumption but, by God, Elizabeth, he's as pale as a winding cloth. The Dunfermlines want rid of him in case he does die."

Carey scowled as he said this. Elizabeth knew he was more than just concerned about the second in line to the throne. Unlike most men of his lordly background, he genuinely liked children. He was personally angry about the condition of the Prince because the Prince was a lonely little boy.

"We must make suit to have the keeping of him," he said directly, to her horror and complete lack of surprise. "I know it will take you away from your place with the Queen but we can't just let the poor child fade away and die."

She smiled at him and his faith in her. "But Robin," she said, using her pet name for him, "I'm no miracle-worker if he's genuinely sick . . ."

Carey shook his head impatiently, "With you looking after him, he will recover. Of course he's sick. Christ, Dunfermline's got four physicians treating him!"

It was a serious gamble. Carey had just sold their only asset and not very willingly, despite the way they needed the money. Elizabeth no longer had her jointure. They were courtiers, both of them, making their living at the new Court of King James. Thanks to factional infighting and the numerous enemies he had made amongst the Scots infesting the court, Carey had lost his lucrative place as Gentleman of the Bedchamber to the King. It had been the only reward he had asked for his three-day ride to Edinburgh when the old Queen died. Elizabeth's place as one of Queen Anne's ladies in waiting and Mistress of the Sweet Coffers was worth a great deal to them in gifts and bribes plus the small courtyard of the palace of Whitehall they were using as Grace and

Favour lodgings. If they had the care of the young Prince and the lad did in fact die, they would not be able to attend at court any more. What did Robin propose to do for money then? Go to the New World in search of El Dorado? Probably.

She sighed and put her hand on his velvet-covered sleeve.

"If you're sure we should do it?"

"Of course I am." Carey smiled at her, took her hand and kissed it. "We'll take him to Young Henry's house in Widdrington and I'll teach him to ride."

To achieve anything at Court took time and much manoeuvring. Elizabeth started the process by mentioning her interest in the Prince to one of the Queen's Danish women and then went north with Queen Anne on progress as Mistress of the Sweet Coffers, in charge of the Queen's linens. King James travelled separately on horseback, surrounded by his Scottish courtiers and Robert Kerr, his new favourite, hunting from morning till night. Carey, meanwhile, was given funds, horses and attendants and sent north to meet the Scottish Chancellor and his wife and bring them, plus the Prince's household, south to meet the King.

The households met at Sir George Farmer's house in Eaton, Northamptonshire, the carriages of the Queen and her attendants leaving a thoroughly chewed-up Great North Road behind them. Elizabeth wished she could have ridden in the fresh air, instead of being cooped up in the leather-smelling carriage with the Queen who never seemed to mind the constant swaying.

Queen Anne sewed and chatted and dozed during the long journey. Elizabeth concentrated on not being sick and waited for questions about the younger Prince. They took a while to come: the Queen adored her sturdy eldest son, the 11-year-old future Prince of Wales, and loved her daughter Elizabeth, as did everyone who met her, but seemed embarrassed by her youngest son.

At last, as the carriages rumbled and swayed the last few miles to Eaton, over a disastrously potholed track, while the outriders cantered ahead, the Queen folded the linen she had been stitching.

"Your husband saw my little son, no?" she asked Elizabeth.

"Yes, your highness," murmured Elizabeth, turning from the window to the Queen and hoping she wouldn't feel any more queasy.

"I hear bad things. The doctors they say he is very sick."

"Sir Robert was worried about him, ma'am," said Elizabeth carefully, "He thought the boy very small for his age."

"Ay, but my Lady Dunfermline has such care tae him," said the other lady in the carriage, a stout pleasant-faced Scottish woman who was probably being paid by the Dunfermlines.

"I do not know what is wrong," said the Queen, shaking her head. "He was well enough with his wetnurse."

"Perhaps he needs a change of care," Elizabeth said carefully.

The Queen pursed her lips.

"I wish you to receive him for the moment, my Lady Carey," she said, "You may have what you need to make him comfortable."

Elizabeth caught a small smile of triumph on the Scottish lady's face and felt foreboding. It was the wrong reaction. The woman should have been looking jealous because to be asked to take care of the second in line to the throne was an honour, surely. Unless the Dunfermlines really were trying to unload their responsibilities for the Prince.

"Your grace does me great honour," she began.

The Queen's face was worrying, too; there was a guilty look on it.

At Eaton house there were riders drawn up and musicians playing trumpets to greet the Queen. Elizabeth waited for the carriage door to be opened and the steps arranged, then carefully held the Queen's skirts out of the way so she could step down easily. Once on terra firma at last, after hours in the cursed coach, Elizabeth took a deep gulp of air and smoothed her satin apron. Queen Anne was already going into the house where Sir George and his ugly wife were bowing and curtseying extravagantly.

Elizabeth turned and found Sykes, her deputy, with four husky-looking serving men, ready to assist in the unloading of the Sweet Coffers. After supervising their stowing in the Queen's dressing room, Elizabeth hurried to rejoin the Queen as she sat at meat in the parlour. All of the ladies of the Queen's household were there and rather than disturb them all to sit where precedence said she should, Elizabeth tucked herself in on the end of a bench. She happened to be near some Scottish wives, chatting confidentially in Scotch. As it happened, Elizabeth spoke Scotch quite well, from many years living on the Border, but she never made a point of it and so listened impassively to the gossip while she ate the meat pies, sliced duck and sallet.

"Did ye ken the young Prince is ay on the road here, he's like to be here the morrow," said Lady Home.

"Ah heard he was dyin'," said another lady in a conspiratorial whisper.

"Och no, he's ainly a wee thing, he's well enough," sniffed Lady Kerr. "It's only Lady Dunfermline at the worriting again. Nae doot the Queen will ask a woman she can trust to have the care of the young prince." She sounded smug.

Lady Home sniffed eloquently. "Ah'm verra sure that her highness will ken the importance o' the Prince ganging tae a woman who's been a mother," she said.

Lady Kerr coloured – married to Robert Kerr, the King's current favourite, she had never produced an heir, and rumour said she never would unless it were a virgin birth. Elizabeth resisted the impulse to ask if Lady Home could pick her children out in a crowd, since she rarely saw them.

There was a mob of highborn and highly pretentious women waiting to greet the young Duke of York when the Dunfermlines finally arrived. Elizabeth placed herself firmly at the head of them, despite scowls and elbows. Carey had sent a man ahead to warn her that the Prince's household would arrive first, followed by the Dunfermlines whom he was escorting.

Carriages ground their way to the entrance of the handsome mansion, followed by three wagons of luggage and a few outriders. The carriage decorated with the Duke of York's crest halted, and two nurses climbed from it, reached back to lift someone, followed by a sulky-looking groom who was carrying several bags with a martyred air.

The women surged forwards to get a look at the Prince, who was still in his green damask baby-skirts. The rumours had only hinted at the truth. The little Prince was a pearly white and crying fretfully, his arms and legs dangling like twigs. There was a silence in the constant babble from the ladies and Elizabeth could hear shuffling. Then a combined rustle of curtseys, followed by murmurs, followed by footsteps. She ignored the full retreat behind her and stepped forwards, with no competition.

Close up, he looked no better, with hollow temples and dull eyes like a little old man.

That child is going to die, Elizabeth thought, and could almost hear her adorable but impractical husband growling at her: even if he does die, we must still succour him and God will provide for us.

She would have preferred it if God could be persuaded not to always leave things to the last minute, offered up a prayer that this venture should not be a disaster.

"Your Grace, welcome," she said, curtseying again formally to the little scrap in his heavy damask clothes. There was a strong smell of vomit and a stain down his little doublet.

The Duke of York buried his face in the nurse's neck and whined sadly.

She escorted the nurses to the Prince's suite of rooms, then found her daughter hanging about in one of the window seats along the passage nearby. Philly wanted to see the Prince.

"Princess Elizabeth says his legs are so weak he can't walk," she explained to her mother. "And his tongue is tied so he can't talk and he's like to die soon."

"I hope not," said her mother warningly,

"And she thinks it's a pity but she says her brother says it might be for the best because younger brothers of Kings always cause trouble, look at Monsieur in France, and she wanted me to peep at him and then tell her the truth and . . ."

"That's enough, Philly," said her mother sternly. The Princess had not yet been given her own household but travelled with her mother. "If her grace the Princess Royal asked you to, then . . ."

"Oh, she did," nodded Philly vigorously.

So when she went back she let Philly tag along behind her, carrying a mysterious basket.

They had drawn the heavy velvet curtains although the sun was friendly and bright. The Prince was being held by the junior nurse, sobbing softly and hopelessly, while a surgeon bled him from his twiglike left arm. The room seemed full of men in long brocade robes and skullcaps.

"Does he need bleeding?" Elizabeth asked sharply.

"Good day," said a dark-robed doctor. "And you are?"

"Elizabeth Lady Carey, whom the Queen has asked to receive his grace," said Elizabeth, looking down her nose at him and waiting for him to bow.

"Ah, Dr Hughes at your service, ma'am," said the doctor with a shallow obeisance, "and this is Dr Pike, my associate."

Dr Pike bowed a little. The two other doctors looked over. One nodded gravely, the other actually brought himself to bow properly.

"Those are Dr Cunningham and Dr Stott," added Dr Hughes, with great disdain.

Elizabeth nodded back.

"The bleeding?" she asked.

"Ah yes, my dear madam. Please do not concern yourself. It is only to clear some of the ill-humours that have accumulated during his Grace's travels south and caused him an emetic attack . . ."

"Was he not simply made seasick by the coach's motion?"

Dr Hughes smiled indulgently at her. "No indeed, ma'am, for we are not at sea, are we?"

Elizabeth said nothing and wondered if the learned doctor was being deliberately offensive or extremely stupid. Finally the surgeon stopped the slow drip and wrapped a bandage around the wound. He was keeping his head down but Elizabeth saw that his square hands were careful to be gentle with the fragile arm, which looked as if it might snap if breathed upon. The Prince wasn't an ugly child, in fact his little pointed face had something unworldly about it in its delicacy. He seemed even paler.

"In simple terms, ma'am, the Prince suffers from an excess of phlegm which is the root of the problem with his legs," explained Dr Hughes kindly.

There was a snort from one of the other doctors. "The excess of phlegm is, tae be sure, ainly a presenting symptom . . ."

The senior nurse, whose name was Mrs Gates mixed medicine with mead in the Prince's silver cup and gave it to him on a spoon, followed by some mild ale. The Prince turned his head and whined fretfully at the offer of a rabbit pasty on a silver platter and was set back in his elaborately carved cot where he lay listlessly. The doctors huddled, arguing in vicious Latin mutters.

Elizabeth frowned at the child who seemed so utterly different from her own when they had been boisterous four-year-olds, while Philly peered round her skirts, still clutching her basket.

"I don't know what to do with him, Lady Carey," said Mrs Gates with a worried frown as she gave the cup and napkin to the junior nurse to be cleaned. "We're following all the doctors' prescriptions exactly but he never seems to do any better."

Elizabeth longed to pick the child up and give him a good hug for being so brave about the bleeding, but didn't want to frighten him.

"His poor little stomach's dreadful at the moment," said Mrs Gates. "Nothing seems to settle it, he won't eat and if he does eat he purges soon after."

"Have you tried sugared milk with a little brandy?"

"I've tried sugar and the brandy, of course, but the doctors won't hear of milk, they say milk is too phlegmatic and fit for peasants only and a Prince must have none but the hotter drier foods such as meat."

Elizabeth raised her eyebrows. It seemed to her that mollycoddled children whose diets were supervised by doctors often had the problem with soft bones that had turned Robert Cecil into a hunchback. Her children were not mollycoddled and ate fish when it was a fish day, white meats such as milk and cheese and cold moist foods like sallets and fruits despite the doctors' condemnation of such things as fit only for peasants. Except during famines, peasants normally had sturdy children, she had noticed, and so, thanks be to God, did she. However, for the moment she held her peace. The Latin argument in the corner had switched to English again.

"Clearly further bleeding at regular intervals is indicated in this case . . ." whispered Dr Hughes firmly.

"I would prefer a course of steam baths to attempt a complete clearance of phlegmatic matter . . . " insisted Dr Cunningham.

"Followed by cupellation . . ." added Dr Pike, nodding wisely.

"The physic clearly answers well and should be persevered with," said Dr Stott with a sniff.

"Doctors," said Elizabeth pleasantly, "I have a suggestion to make." They turned towards her, Dr Hughes with another kindly smile. "Perhaps as the Prince is so tired after his journey and being bled, he would benefit from no treatment at all."

Amused and patronizing looks, accompanied by raised eyebrows.

"Mistress," began Dr Hughes.

"Actually, doctor, you should address me as my lady," Elizabeth explained pleasantly. "Lady Carey."

Dr Hughes coughed but rallied. "Lady Carey, it is of course the Queen's expressed wish that her younger son be cured as soon as possible . . ."

Elizabeth advanced towards them, herding them towards the door.

"It is imperative that the treatment be continued until it succeeds, my lady," said Dr Cunningham. "Although I would advise certain changes . . ."

"Imperative?" said Elizabeth.

Glances were exchanged. "Yes, Lady Carey, *imperative*, which means *urgent* and *important*," explained Dr Hughes with kind helpfulness.

Elizabeth took a deep breath. "Nonetheless," she said with a smile that she hoped would not look too much like the furious baring of teeth it actually was, "the Prince is tired and requires his rest. I will see you in the morning."

She was ushering them firmly to the door, mentally cursing Lady Dunfermline for letting the doctors get so completely out of hand, when there was an odd bubbling noise from the cot and a gasp from Mrs Gates. She pushed Dr Pike through into the passage and shut the door herself, before she turned to see what had happened.

The Prince was sitting up next to the carved bars and was putting his fist through the gaps. The bubbling noise was coming from him, and in fact he was giggling. Mrs Gates was looking horrified while the two cradle-rockers who had just come in, tutted to each other. And there stood Philly holding something awkwardly in her arms so the Prince could see it.

Elizabeth wondered for a split second if Philly had a doll in her arms and then if it was a very odd looking baby. Finally she worked it out.

Philly was holding out a small plump puppy, dressed for company with a baby's linen cap tied over one ear. The little Prince was trying to pat its brown head while the puppy squirmed and tried to lick Philly's face.

"Oh, now, you take that dirty beast away," snapped Mrs Gates, "The Prince cannot . . ."

"But the Princess Royal sent him, she said he should have a puppy to cheer him up," insisted Philly.

Elizabeth came up behind her. "Well, Mrs Gates, at least it's made him laugh," she pointed out, as one of the cradle-rockers folded her arms and opined that the dog would certainly bite.

Philly dumped the puppy in the cot with the prince. It

plumped down on its fat bottom, looking surprised, and then rolled over as the Prince patted its fat tum, still gurgling. The puppy started to scrape its paws at the baby's cap it was wearing.

Mrs Gates was scowling. The puppy managed to get the cap off and began to eat it. Philly scolded and tried to take the cap away and ended up in a game of rag with the pup, who growled with soprano ferocity until Mrs Gates swept over and picked it up by its scruff, held it at arm's length with a disgusted expression.

The Prince's tentative giggles turned instantly to a fretful wailing. He held up his skinny arms.

"N-no, no! Wanta *puppy*!" he cried.

The puppy, frightened by the noise, widdled on Mrs Gates who didn't even notice.

"Your Grace!" she whispered, transfixed.

"He spoke," said one cradle rocker to the other.

"He never," said her friend.

"What . . . what did you say, your Grace?" asked Mrs Gates, still holding the puppy absent-mindedly. Philly reached up, took it from her and put it in its basket, trying to tuck the mangled remains of the baby cap in her sleeve.

"He said," she explained to Mrs Gates, "no, no, wanta puppy. It means he likes it," she added complacently.

Mrs Gates was blinking down at her.

"But he never spoke before," she breathed. "Not a word."

It was impossible to keep something like that quiet. Knowing how things went in Courts, Elizabeth left as soon as she decently could, scurried Philly into the chamber they were sharing with Sir Robert's sister, Philadelphia Lady Scrope and three servants. The overcrowding was typical of progresses and Elizabeth was just grateful they had beds to lie in and that Carey's sister was willing to share with her young namesake, so that she and Carey could have the double bed to themselves. Their bodyservants were making do with straw pallets on the floor.

Elizabeth assumed that young Philly must have been climbing trees that morning, judging by the black streaks on her petticoat and kirtle. She stripped off the grubby clothes at speed, wiped her smudged face with rosewater, put her in a smock that was now too short, combed her hair and then piled on a clean petticoat, false front, stays, bodice, kirtle and clean embroidered cap just in time before the page came to fetch them to see the Queen.

Both of them knelt to Queen Anne in the parlour that was acting as her Presence Chamber. The Queen had red-rimmed eyes, which surprised Elizabeth.

"He truly said 'I want a puppy,'?" she asked with great intensity.

"Your highness, he did," said Mrs Gates, also kneeling, "I was so shocked."

The Queen smiled at Philly. "You are Philadelphia Carey, yes?"

Philly stood up, curtseyed, said, "Yes, your highness," and plumped down on her knees again, turning bright pink.

"Why did you bring the puppy to see the Duke of York?"

Philly looked puzzled. "I knew he'd like his grace the Prince, your majesty, he's a very friendly puppy and I'm going to call him Gustavus . . ." Elizabeth had to cough while the Queen's eyes twinkled. "Oh, and I was talking to her grace the Princess Royal and she said she wished the Prince had a puppy and so I took him with me, you see."

"The doctors disapprove very much and the Chief Nurse is concerned that your dog might bite his grace."

Philly blinked and shook her head vigorously, "Oh no, your majesty, he's only got little teeth and he only chews things like caps and I'll watch him very carefully."

The Queen looked puzzled. "When?"

"When you let me bring him back to his grace, because the Prince cried so much I'm sure your majesty will want him to play with Gustavus."

"Ah," said the Queen, "Well, yes, child, I think I will permit you to again bring the puppy . . ."

Philly's face lit up. "I knew you would!" she explained, "I *knew* you wouldn't let Gustavus be sad."

The puppy certainly seemed to cheer the Prince up a little, though he didn't say any more and he seemed to get no better in his stomach and was often ill after he ate. At least he seemed to enjoy Philly's daily visits with Gustavus. The puppy was allowed in the Prince's cot until the day there was a puddle in the corner. The next day, the Prince was set down on a Turkey rug to play and Philly brought a ball as well as the pup. She talked constantly to the Prince, ignoring the fact that he didn't talk back, about the puppy, about what she had been doing, about the court and her father and mother and the horses and dogs in the stables and her Aunt Philadelphia and what she thought about all of it. To Philly, to breathe was to talk and the young Prince seemed astonished by it.

The whole Court moved on to the next stopping place where the Prince's royal father could hunt boar. So far, apart from one Royal visit, the King had not shown much interest in his youngest son, although the Queen visited daily. She thought her son was growing to know her better. And yet the child still lost weight, still seemed very listless and sleepy and still didn't speak or walk.

Then one afternoon Elizabeth found Philly weeping inconsolably in the corner of the chamber.

"What's the matter?" she asked, bending down to her.

Philly turned a woebegone tear-grimed face to her mother. "Mrs Gates told me never to bring Gustavus to the Prince again because he was naughty and broke his lead when no one was there and ate all the cakes and the pies and everything in the bedchamber and then he puked in the rushes and she shouted at me and *look* . . .!"

Philly pointed dramatically. The pup was lying on his side, panting, his eyes half shut and a little pile of bloody puke next to his head. Elizabeth frowned and looked closer. She didn't like what she saw.

"Philly, I want you to go and fetch a page immediately," she said. Her husband was still out hunting with the King and all the rest of the Court. Philly jumped up and trotted downstairs. By the time the young Scot came thundering up the stairs ahead of Philly, Elizabeth had already written a message which she gave him and he clattered off to fetch a horse from the stables.

"Did you send for Father?" Philly asked anxiously.

"Yes, I did."

"Will he know how to save Gustavus?"

"Perhaps," said Elizabeth, not explaining the real reason why she had sent for her husband.

She and Philly did what they could. For distraction she talked of people she had nursed and how a lady must know as much as possible of practical medicine so she could keep her household healthy.

The clattering of hooves and Robert's feet on the stairs at last were very welcome. He came into their chamber looking both puzzled and concerned, especially when he saw the puppy.

"My lady," he said, "Why . . .?"

She had used their codeword for urgency in the message.

"Philadelphia, tell your father what you told me."

Philly did with only slight embroidery about the vomiting. At once Carey's puzzlement cleared away to be replaced by sharp blue focus. He bent over the puppy and his long fingers passed expertly around the little animal, while his face grew grim.

"Everything in the Prince's chamber?" he asked.

"Yes," sniffled Philly, "He didn't mean to be greedy, he can't help it, he's descended from your dog Jack . . ."

Her father held her shoulders and looked very seriously at her. "Philly, you're a wise little maid and quite old now at eight years?"

She nodded, still sniffling.

"Then I will be honest with you, my heart, and you must repay me by being brave. I'm afraid the little pup is dying."

Philly covered her eyes with her hands, "Could he not have a doctor to him?"

"No, the doctors only trouble men. And I fear no dog-leech nor horse-coper could help him, he has taken such a – such a mighty fever in his gut. So all you can do for him is hold him so he knows he is not alone. Can you do that?"

Philly snortled, wiped her nose firmly on her sleeve and took the pup in her lap and cradled him, whispering softly. Her parents moved away and also whispered.

"Is it what I thought?" Elizabeth asked.

"Oh yes," said Carey, passing his hand over his face, "I've seen poisoning before. In the Prince's chamber. Christ."

Elizabeth was appalled and furious. She could not imagine how anyone could bring himself to try and poison a little mite like the Prince, nor any reason why either, since he was only second in line to the throne. Unless . . .

"Sir," she said urgently, "we must warn the other Royal households as well as the Queen."

"We must also keep it very quiet," said Carey, "Not a word to anyone else. It's the only way to catch the bastards."

Elizabeth sent a page to fetch Philly's Aunt Philadelphia, to keep Philly company. As soon as she could she went to attend the Queen while Carey went to talk to Mrs Gates. She explained what had happened privately while the Queen was choosing her clean shift for the next day. Anne of Denmark was no fool and her eyes narrowed.

"Does anyone else know?" she asked.

"Myself, my husband and my daughter."

"I will send new tasters to Princess Elizabeth, and the Prince of Wales. His grace should be here soon. What is Sir Robert doing?"

"Your highness, his service as Warden on the Borders has given him great experience at investigation . . ."

"Yes, certainly, so his Majesty has told me often. I shall give him a privy Warrant."

Meanwhile Carey was blinking at the destruction a determined half-grown lymer pup in search of food could cause. Mrs Gates was standing, arms folded, face red with fury while the Chamberers cleaned and scrubbed away.

"Can you tell me what the pup ate?"

"Hmf. Two caps and his grace's dinner and the sweetmeats upon the sideboard and he knocked over all the physic while he did it and then he ate a pillow as you can see, sir . . ."

Carey could indeed see. The Prince's Bedchamber looked as if it had snowed, there was a sticky smear around the scattered medicine bottles, there were crumbs and scattered plates from the Prince's meal, the sweetmeat bowls from Venice were upended and one was smashed in the rushmats, there was a pile of sick and another pile of dogturd and a wet patch on one of the tapestries, the lower border of which had obviously been chewed.

"That monster is never coming here again."

"Where is the Prince?"

"He is in the garden, sir, despite the lateness of the hour, with Mary, one of his rockers. I only hope he takes no tertian fever."

Carey suspected that he had been shouting, "Wanta puppy!"

"How is his health?"

Mrs Gates sighed. "Not well. He has that little stomach to his meat, he wanes daily and is so pale. Nor his legs are no better, sir, the King is talking of putting him in iron boots which Dr Cunningham recommends."

Carey nodded and wandered about the Chamber, touching the rushmats and sniffing at the vomitus.

"Who are the Prince's attendants?"

Mrs Gates looked puzzled. "Why do you want to know, sir?"

Anticipating hysterics if he mentioned his suspicions, Carey said, "There are rumours of ill-affected Papists in these parts."

"The King is too soft with them," snorted Mrs Gates, "String 'em up, I say, with all their foreign notions."

"Quite so. The Prince's attendants?"

It took a while but finally he had a clear list of those who could come to the Prince's chamber – four chamberers to clean, two cradle-rockers, Mrs Gates the senior nurse and Susannah Kerr the junior nurse, his daughter Philly of course.

"And where is the Prince's food made?"

"It depends," said Mrs Gates, "In Whitehall he has his own kitchen, but on progress we use cookshops or the main kitchens. His food is ever of the best, sir, it's just he won't eat it."

"Who does eat it?"

"Well, we don't let it go to waste, of course, sir, I mean it would be a shame . . ."

"So you share what the Prince doesn't eat?" Mrs Gates nodded, looking nervous. "And what about the sweetmeats?"

"From the Royal Confectioner herself, wonderful suckets and kissing comfits she makes. The Prince eats them sometimes and so do I, though they pain my teeth, since I'm his grace's Taster."

There was clearly nothing wrong with the Senior Nurse. Carey questioned the chamberers as they worked at rolling up the ruined mats. As was often the case at court, they both came of families whose parents and grandparents had served the monarchy of England for decades. Neither could remember any intruders or anything strange happening and the other two chamberers had already gone ahead to the next stopping place for the Progress to ready the Prince's chambers there.

After a short conference with Elizabeth, Carey mounted up thoughtfully and rode the short distance into the village. It was easy to find the cookhouse for despite the lateness of the hour there was a queue of courtiers' servants waiting and the woman at the window looked flushed, floury and exhausted while she did a roaring trade and charged ridiculous prices for her remaining pies.

Very unwilling she was to be interviewed by Carey, but she left the serving hatch to be womaned by her youngest daughter and stepped into her bakehouse where the large oven was being filled full of faggots ready to be fired up again.

"I hear that the Duke of York's Senior Nurse considers your pies so fine she has been giving them to the Prince," said Carey with a smile.

Mistress Kate flushed bright red.

"Is that a fact, sir? My pies going to feed his grace? Well, I never!"

"Did you not know?" Carey asked, watching a promising theory crumble to dust.

"No, sir, not till you told me, though thinking about it, I've seen Mary the cradle rocker here often enough, every day since the court came. She buys a great deal, a dozen pies each time."

"And they are not specially made for the Prince nor marked in any way?"

"No sir. Do you think I should do that, perhaps?"

Carey shook his head and left her musing about asking to have the Duke of York's coat of arms to be painted on her sign. He found the Deputy Clerk of the Confectionery at dinner at the wildly overcrowded inn.

The Deputy Clerk was intelligent enough to be worried by Carey's questions. "Yes sir, all the sweetmeats are packed up in baskets for the Prince's chamber, but not marked specially. I carry them personally, sir, and they are never out of my sight until I hand them to Mrs Gates."

Carey kept to himself his suspicions about how the Deputy Clerk could afford to stay at the inn. The staff of the Confectionery always travelled on progresses to make the subtleties and jellies for the many banquets, and normally did a roaring trade in leftovers.

"There has been no problem with the sweetmeats, sir?" asked the Deputy Clerk.

"Not at all," lied Carey and took his leave. He had seemingly covered the obvious suspects, though he also spoke to the Deputy Butler about the supplies of ale for the Prince's household and found everything there as secure against tampering as possible, as he expected.

There were only two possibilities left and Carey had a shrewd suspicion which one it might be. He went immediately to see the Queen.

Elizabeth had seen her husband arrest Border reivers and thought she had seen every possible reaction – but Mrs Gates's outrage and fury was a surprise to her.

"That you should dare to think I would poison . . . poison his grace, the little child that I have brought up since his birth . . . How dare you, sir!"

"Mistress," said Carey coldly, "I am as shocked as you. However, the puppy was poisoned by something he ate in his grace's chamber and I have been able to find no other person who could have had the possibility of doing it."

Mrs Gates whitened further. "I will stake my solemn oath upon it," she hissed, "Nor me nor none of the chamberers, nor the cradle-rockers, nor Mistress Kerr would so much as dream of it. How can you believe we could do such a thing, sir? How can you?"

Carey nodded impassively. "You would do well to think upon it, Mistress, but for the moment, you must be confined to other quarters."

Normally the Nurses slept in the Prince's suite of rooms but a small storeroom had been found for Mrs Gates and, on the Queen's insistence, a bed put in it. Mrs Gates walked there firmly and with head held high, not deigning to even look at Elizabeth, who felt horribly guilty about the whole thing.

When Carey returned from escorting her, he shook his head and said she had made no confession yet, only insisting that God would justify her. Elizabeth was not at all surprised. She turned to comforting Philly, who had held an heretical funeral for the puppy while her parents were busy. The dog-boy and one of the pages had helped by digging the grave in the centre of a main flowerbed. Philly was so grubby and sad that Elizabeth ordered a hot bath to be drawn in the corner of the chamber and when the child was in a clean smock, gave her milk laced with sugar and brandy and sang her to sleep.

Next day Susannah Kerr took over the day-to-day care of the Prince quite smoothly. Every single scrap of food that had been left in the chamber after the puppy attack, was gathered up and taken to feed some handsome Tamworth pigs in the village who showed no ill-effects. Elizabeth would have banned the doctors if she could, but Carey himself said that it was important that the Prince still have his medical treatments.

And so Elizabeth stood by while the four learned men came swooping grimly into the Prince's chambers. Dr Hughes felt the Prince's twelve pulses, while Dr Cunningham uncovered a bowl of pungently smelling hot water which was intended to cause the Prince to sweat out his excess of phlegm. The Prince was wailing sadly and holding his stomach which was starting to swell. Elizabeth was reminded of some of the terrible sights she had seen during the northern famine of the late nineties. She had to force herself to remain still as the doctors talked in Latin over the child and herself.

"Dr Stott, pray continue," said Dr Hughes after a learned disquisition. Then he turned to Elizabeth, "His grace is to have a new medicine which I believe may answer well, designed to soothe the irritation of the tissues caused by the Nurse's treachery."

Dr Stott advanced, holding a small bottle and poured a dose into the Prince's cup, smiling as he did so.

"Now please do not be alarmed if the Prince needs to sleep after his physic, he shall be far better in the morning . . ."

Elizabeth took the cup from him as he advanced towards the Prince.

"Yes, thank you Dr Stott," she said pleasantly and rapped quickly twice on the wall beside her.

Carey stepped through the door from the passage.

"My apologies, Mrs Kerr," he said smoothly, "However the Queen has ordered that everything that the Prince eats or drinks must first be tasted by the person who brings it. Which includes you, Doctor."

Dr Stott seemed to be standing very still, the pleasant smile fixed on his face.

"Sir?" he asked, seeming confused.

"Only a routine test, doctor. Please be so good as to taste the medicine before you give it to the Prince."

Elizabeth moved towards him, holding out a silver cup. He reached for it, but seemed suddenly clumsy and dropped it on the floor. Dark liquid spilled stickily into the rushes.

"How unfortunate . . ." said the Doctor, smiling again. "Alas, I must now mix some . . ."

"Guards!" said Carey quietly. Two of the Gentlemen of the Guard stepped through the other door and took hold of his arms.

"What is the meaning of this?" demanded Dr Hughes, starting to swell like a turkey-cock.

It was Elizabeth who saw what Dr Stott was planning. She barged forwards as he lunged towards the Prince who was still in Mrs Kerr's arms. Instinct made her pull back as the small scalpel in the doctor's hand flashed past her, and she swung her padded hips into him as hard as she could. He stumbled sideways; Carey moved in the same moment and punched him on the chin.

The doctor fell to the floor, half-stunned, was grabbed and his arms twisted very ungently up his back as the Gentlemen hauled him out. Drs Hughes, Cunningham and Pike simply stared with their mouths open, looking exactly like a row of codfish.

The Prince pulled his face out of Mrs Kerr's neck, pointed imperiously at the doctors and said his second sentence ever. "B-bad!" he shouted, "Go away now!"

Carey was rubbing his knuckles ruefully. "You heard his grace, gentlemen," he said drily. "Off you go." He smiled at Elizabeth.

"B . . . but . . . You have no evidence . . ." gobbled Dr Hughes.

"Fortunately," Elizabeth explained, trying not to let her shakiness come out in her voice, "I kept the original medicine poured by Dr Stott so what he knocked to the ground was simply a wine syrup." She looked at the stuff in the cup. "Although I think Dr Stott's actions have convicted him, we will try and learn what this physic would have done."

The piglet who slurped up Dr Stott's physic died in its sleep shortly afterwards and Mrs Gates was immediately released. Elizabeth had to explain to her how she had been arrested simply to trap the real culprit and after a gift of a handsome new shawl she grudgingly agreed that it had been for the best.

The Careys attended on the Queen in her Presence Chamber, and Sir Robert paced up and down to explain.

"When I was sure it could not be something in his food then there were only two possibilities," he said as the Queen listened intently. "Either one of his nurses or cradle-rockers had been somehow induced to do it or it must have been one of the doctors.

After all, among other crimes, when the puppy raided the Prince's chamber he knocked over the physic bottles and licked up the spill. And yet the Nurse would at least lose her place if the Prince died and all the doctors had sworn the Hippocratic Oath – and yet, when a doctor's patient does die, the doctor is not usually blamed. So I was more suspicious of the doctors. But it was a puzzle to know which one it could be. And so I made the arrest of Mrs Gates to reassure the learned gentlemen that they were not suspected and my wife laid the trap."

"Sir Robert had warned me that the first person to offer the prince anything to eat or drink should be suspected, because they would wish to finish the job whilst Mrs Gates could still be blamed for it," Elizabeth explained. "When Dr Stott offered his physic, I had two silver cups ready, one already filled. I exchanged one for the other and when my husband told him he had to drink it, sure enough, he contrived to knock it to the floor, believing this would prevent his treason being discovered."

She drew a great breath because the memory of the scuffle still made her heart pound. "As for what happened after, I can only think he must have panicked or perhaps have been half mad before . . ."

"Lady Carey, you put yourself between my son and the traitor's knife," said Queen Anne softly, "That I will not forget." She turned to Carey, "As to the doctor's reasons . . .?"

"His colleagues only know that he came from the Prince of Wales's household and seemed a learned man, able to converse in Latin as well as them."

"Could the Papists have suborned him? Or the Puritans? Or some ill-affected men of Scotland?"

Carey spread his hands. "Your Highness, he is being put to the question as we speak, but . . ."

"But?" asked the Queen with her eyebrows raised.

"I doubt that torture ever gets the truth from anyone. I would have preferred to question him over time myself."

"His majesty the King has ordered it," said Anne of Denmark flatly. "He is convinced it must be a connection of the Ruthvens."

Sir Robert bowed politely.

"Lady Carey," said the Queen, "I have decided that you will be in sole charge of the Duke of York's household from now on."

"Thank you, your highness."

"Do you think he will die?"

Elizabeth swallowed hard. "Your Highness, it is in God's hands. But if I have free rein with him, I will do everything in my power to bring him up as healthy and happy as mine own children."

"Do so," said the Queen.

"With your permission, I shall dismiss all the doctors since they did not see that he was being poisoned."

"Certainly," said the Queen firmly.

As the Careys walked down the wide stairs where the Royal households were packing up ready to move again, Elizabeth looked sidelong at her husband.

"What did Dr Stott really say when you questioned him?" she asked.

Carey smiled ruefully. "He informed me that while he was in the household of the Prince of Wales he was told by an angel that when he was King, the Duke of York would cause the destruction of the Crown of England. He claims to be on a mission from God."

"But Prince Charles won't be King," Elizabeth protested.

"No, the next King will be King Henry IX, of course," agreed Carey.

"Did Prince Henry know of this prophecy?" Elizabeth asked, a nasty thought occurring to her.

Carey sighed. "I'm afraid he did."

Historical note: Elizabeth Lady Carey did in fact have the care of young Prince Charles for the rest of his childhood. She battled with King James himself to prevent the young prince having his legs put in iron boots to cure his incipient rickets and having his tongue cut to help him speak. Under her care the Prince became healthy and strong, though still very short, and when he was old enough Sir Robert Carey took over as his Governor.

THE TOWER'S MAN

MICHAEL JECKS

Catholics, who had long been disaffected during the reign of Elizabeth, initially felt some hope when James came to the throne. He was the son of a Catholic sympathizer, Mary Queen of Scots, and they may have felt he would give strength to their cause. Alas, such was not to be. Indeed, James reinforced the penalties of old at the Hampton Court Conference convened to discuss religious grievances in January 1604. When the Catholic concerns were not addressed, Robert Catesby and his fellow conspirators plotted to blow up Parliament and with it, the King. So was hatched the infamous Gunpowder Plot. Despite how much we know about the Plot, there are many discrepancies between the various accounts, some of which were testimonies given under torture. Like so many other key events in history, there is the official account and the rumours.

The possibility that all may not be as it seemed is the starting point for the following story. Michael Jecks (b. 1960) is best known for his long-running series featuring the Keeper of the King's Peace, Sir Baldwin Furnshill, and Bailiff Simon Puttock, set in Devon in the fourteenth century and which began with The Last Templar *(1995).*

There is a particular smell, a sort of musty foulness, that is the stench of terror and despair. It cleaves to those who sit in anticipation of their execution, like those poor devils in the Tower. As I sit here before my fire, I can still detect it upon my clothing, even though it is over an hour since I left that abominable little chamber.

I can recall it to mind with a startling precision. Strange for, as I entered, I felt as one who was blind. There appeared to be no light when the gaoler took his lantern away. Perhaps the fact that my eyes could only gradually acclimatize to the filthy interior imprinted the details upon my mind more acutely because each aspect was brought to my attention individually. I could notice, comprehend and appreciate each detail.

First, of course, there was the noise. The steady *drip, drip, drip* of water into a shallow pool; the chuckling of a guard in some corridor close by; the brief scuffle of a rat; and then the slow step of the gaoler as he continued along the passageway. There was no need for him to remain. Not with this prisoner.

Then, suddenly, there was the odour: the rankness of a body which had remained unwashed for many days, the wounds festering, drool and vomit mingled with excrement. Oh, but there were so many elements of that reek: the nostrils were overwhelmed in a moment, and a relief it was, too.

The last sense was sight. And by the time my eyes could discern objects within the room, my heart was already steeled in preparation.

A thin, sickly light came from the grille set high in the wall. The sun could scarce penetrate, for the wall faced north, and with the rain lancing down outside, the battle was too much. Still, I could tell that the floor was stone-flagged as I walked in. And the light showed me a scraping of ancient rushes. There was neither stool, chair nor bench, let aside a table. On the floor I saw a leathern pail for his water, and a cracked wooden trencher with a bowl filled with a watery pottage made his meal. The very look made my stomach clench.

He sat limply at the farther corner. His back was at the wall, as though he wished to keep in view any man who entered, like the cautious man he was – except he would not now – or could not. His head was pitched forward, one arm over his skull, his hand hidden in the gloom. While his body was hunched, his left leg was up, knee crooked, and his right lay on the ground with a flaccid, useless, immovable look to it. At first I thought he might already have cheated the executioner and died, but no. The torturers knew their job too well. He was alive, but ruined.

It was unlikely he would recognize me – it had been many years since we had last met – but I considered it prudent to stoop and try to disguise my voice to prevent recognition.

"You have confessed," I rasped gruffly.

I heard him grunt with quick fear, and his head lifted, face peering through the gloom towards me. "I've told all I can!" he wavered. He thought his inquisitors had returned.

It was all I could do to remain in there with him. The sight of that broken face, bruised and ruined, was so repellent to me that I wanted nothing more than to beat at it still more. Yet there was a spark of Christian sympathy in my heart, and no matter that I wished to curse him, I had to tell myself that he was – what? – scarcely six years younger than me. A fool, an idealist, and finally a traitor and attempted regicide, but I could feel some compassion for a man who had been so cruelly used.

"You have spoken enough."

"I know nothing more, I swear it!"

His voice was slurred, as though he had taken a strong draught of wine. I knew that if I approached I would see the bruises, the mashed lips and bloody chin. But even as I felt the stirrings of pity, I drew in my mind's eye a picture of the carnage this man had tried to unleash. I saw the noble victims, their blood flowing freely into the Thames, limbs torn from them, splashes of gore on the rubble, and in among them, I saw a little girl, her blue eyes lifeless, clutched by her dead mother.

It was enough to kill any soft-heartedness. "Is there any more you could say? Or *would* say?"

I don't think his ears worked any more. Perhaps it was just that his mind was addled after the pain, but he seemed incapable of listening to me. Maybe that was why he didn't recognize me. "I have confessed. They all trusted me because they knew I was reliable."

"Reliable enough to slaughter many innocents. You had ample time to warn people of their plans."

"It was a year ago that my master asked me to see him."

"And you told no one."

He seemed to hear the contempt in my voice. "I could do nothing. If I had spoken, they would have murdered me! What could I do? I was nothing, but they were all rich and powerful men!"

I couldn't help but sneer at that. "You were born well enough. Not many men are made to be good yeomen in our kingdom; all too few can afford armour of their own. You had a wife, servant, and money, so don't tell me you were a poor pawn in the hands of so many important men!"

"I don't say I was innocent. God knows, I was guilty enough. Yet this was a blow for our Catholic church. No one could stand aside as evil men seek to ruin the true faith."

Aye. There was the rub. A man of any condition could burst from obedience and honour at the thought that his betters were seeking to destroy his religion. There was little else for which a man would willingly lay down his life, but set his priests as naught, and see how even the mildest little mouse would roar and bite.

I was quiet a moment, considering his words, then said, "So all those who profess the Catholic faith should be destroyed."

"In Jesu's name, no!"

"If you could be persuaded to commit murder of so foul a nature, so could any of your co-religionists. And the kingdom cannot tolerate those who may commit treason."

"It was different!"

"What was? *You* were? What sets you apart from others who follow the Pope and the Jesuits?"

"I was devoted to my master. Robert Catesby was a most determined man, and I admired him!"

"You followed him because you admired him? You were happy to commit your immortal soul to damnation for his gratification? To murder with a bomb? To slaughter the king and his government?"

"No. To help him do God's will and protect all the innocent souls in the land. That was why I followed him. He persuaded me."

"A year ago."

"Yes. He thought I had noticed something. I had. Of course I had. It was obvious something was going on. My master had taken a house next door to the House of Lords, and I wondered *why*? He was talking with strangers, and I noticed he was buying a lot of tools. It made no sense, and he noticed I was wondering, so he called me to his house in Puddle Wharf . . ."

"Where you found him and Wintour?"

"Yes. They made me promise to keep their secret. I had to swear an oath and take the sacrament to prove I would keep it."

"And then you helped them to dig their tunnel."

"They were constructing a mine beneath the houses and leading into the cellars under the House. But then we learned that the cellar was to be let, and Percy took it over."

"And you filled it with gunpowder. How much was there?"

"Thirty-six barrels, all found."

"Sweet Jesus!"

That thought made me want to kill him there and then. The thought of such a massive bomb, right under the King as he began to speak . . . it filled me with horror. "Did you have no care for others, for the innocents who would be there?" The picture of the mother and child returned to me.

"Of course I did! But it was like my master said: 'Dangerous diseases demand a desperate remedy.' It was plain enough as soon as the King took the throne that he intended to keep the old *hag's* laws, God rot her!"

He wouldn't have dared speak of her like that in the street! I turned from him at the bile in his tone. She had ruled the kingdom for decades and protected us, her people, to the best of her ability. God Himself had defended her, and us, delivering us from all our foes. Queen Elizabeth was a good, honest, true queen. I would not willingly hear anyone speak ill of her. Yet this poor cretin had been persuaded to take the Catholic faith and as a result hated her. Poor men brought up in the country, seeing little of the real world, were so easily led I could almost pity him.

"You would have our church overturned and return to the butchery of Mary?" I sneered.

"I would have the country brought to the true faith. It is a man's duty to serve God."

"You believe He would prefer the corruption of Rome to our own good . . ."

"You blaspheme! You know nothing of the church and real faith."

"I know enough to know you are talking out of your arse."

"The Holy Father in Rome seeks to mediate between heaven and earth, friend. It is this new faith, Protestantism, which is wrong. Pray for your understanding, and God will enlighten you!"

"It was Catesby who taught you all this?"

"My master was a charismatic man. Bold, energetic, generous, he persuaded many gentlemen to revert to the true faith."

"And has brought them to destruction in their turn."

The fellow peered up at me as though he had heard something in my voice, but then he shook his head. "What can you tell of these matters? You know nothing of them."

"Catesby died in the explosion at Holbeche House?"

As soon as they realized that their plot had been discovered, that was where they had fled, out of London and into Staffordshire. At least Guy Fawkes had the credit for courage. He had remained in London hoping to set off the powder under parliament while others chased his confederates.

He frowned. "No, of course not! Catesby died when he was shot."

"He had been injured, though?"

"In the explosion? Yes. All in that room were hurt. When the posse came to catch us, we were drenched from a long ride, and we'd set powder by the fire to dry. A spark must have caught it, and two pounds went up, wounding everyone in the room."

"Not you?"

"No. I was in a different room."

"And you decided to flee?"

"There was no point remaining. It was clear that when the sheriff and his men arrived, the house must be taken. The plot had failed."

"So you fled. And took a hundred pounds with you."

"Christopher Wright threw it to me from his window."

"Before the sheriff had arrived, then?"

"What?"

"You say that he threw it to you. Plainly that must have been before the sheriff and his men arrived. Otherwise they would have seen you and shot you. As they shot and killed all the others there."

"Yes. I suppose so."

"And all the others did die, or were captured."

"Yes."

He had grown quiet now, and his face was averted. It was plain to him that I knew something, from the way that he avoided my gaze. I suppose with any other felon I would have been able to remain dispassionate, but this man was different. I loathed this bastard as I had no other in all my years.

"Why did he throw money to you?"

He shrugged, a slow raising of his shoulders that nonetheless made his teeth click together and sent a shudder of anguish through his thin frame.

"You said that he wanted much of it to go to his wife?"

"Yes. But I didn't see her."

"So what happened to the money? A hundred pounds is a goodly sum. Especially for a *mere* yeoman like you!" I added sarcastically.

It made no impression upon him. I was convinced that he'd stored the money somewhere. If he had, I only hoped he would somehow get it to Martha, his wife. She would need it when he was executed if she wasn't to be starved soon after. They had several children.

I tried another attack. "The house has been the haunt of Papists for many years."

"It has?"

"You escaped the place in broad daylight, I have heard."

"Yes."

"And you rode off. You were caught on the twelfth, I understand." He made no comment. "There were numerous shots from the house at the sheriff's men."

"They were attacking. I suppose the men inside defended themselves."

"You mean they deliberately resisted arrest."

"They protected themselves as best they might. Every man in this country has the right to defend himself."

"Not from the King's own lawful officials. Not when they are being arrested for treason. Be that as it may . . . there were thirteen or fourteen captured. How many others were there in the plot?"

"Others? That is all there were."

I smiled. "You expect me to believe that you were the only menial there? What, Percy had no one he could trust? The owner of Holbeche House, Littleton, he had no servants there?"

"There was none but those you captured."

"And you escaped from the house on horseback, passing miraculously through all the forces at the disposal of the sheriff? You must be a clever man indeed!"

"I was careful."

"*Careful*! I should think you were! To elude so many men just as they were looking for you . . . perhaps you paid one of them a hundred pounds for your life? That would have been careful."

"I did not!"

"I wonder where that cash has been stored, then." It was nothing to me. There were greater matters. "You were caught in Staffordshire on the twelfth . . . that was four days after Catesby's death and the arrest of the other assassins. Where had you been until then?"

"Living on the land. I spent my time in hedges during the day and rode on at night."

He looked up just then, gazing at the grille set so high up in the wall, and I couldn't help but feel a pang. Memories of fields, fresh air, birdsong, even the grim drizzle that had settled over the country that miserable November seemed so far from that dreadful dungeon. He was harsh indeed who wouldn't feel sadness for a man in his plight. Then I thought again of the explosion he had tried to cause, thought of the men, women and children who could have died, and my heart was hardened against him.

"Who was with you?"

"I was alone."

"You were the only coward?"

He flinched at that, and winced with the sudden pain. "If you say so."

"I do. The others in the house had the courage to stand and die, but you rode off."

There was a faint glimmer of light, and when I peered closely, I saw that he was giving a twisted smile, his remaining yellowed teeth showing. "You think running was cowardly? I wish I'd remained and died and been saved all of . . ." He waved a hand about him. There was a catch in his throat. "You think my end will be easier? I should have remained and taken a bullet like my master."

"Yes. At least then you'd be considered honourable."

"I wonder."

"An *honourable* man would never have bolted, hoping to escape the punishment due to him."

"No."

I knew that he was close, then. I leaned forward. "Unless he had another reason to leave, of course."

There it was again, that quick stillness I remembered so well. He was never so still as when he was guilty and sure that his secret had been discovered.

I continued: "I wonder how the King's men learned of the plot."

"That is plain enough. There was that letter."

That strange letter. Yes. I had seen it and read it, and I have to confess, I thought it a fine piece of nonsense.

It had been sent to Lord Monteagle, and it advised him to keep away from the parliament because it would "recevue a terrible bloue". Lord Monteagle professed himself to be entirely unaware of the meaning – in fact he told me he thought that it might have been a joke in poor taste – but no one would dare to conceal a potentially dangerous letter like that. He took it himself to Robert Cecil, Lord Salisbury, that same night. The King's chief of spies.

"We know that Winter heard about the letter on Sunday twenty-seventh of October," I said. "And he went straight to Catesby and told him that all was up. I understand they thought that Francis Tresham had sent it."

"Perhaps they did."

"Of course, he's dead now."

It was curious. Tresham had been ill just before he was arrested, but all had heard that he had died in gaol two days before Christmas.

"Tresham always struck me as a strong fellow," I commented.

"Perhaps so."

"Somehow he convinced Catesby and Winter that he had done no such thing, though. Surely, if anyone was to warn Lord Monteagle not to attend parliament, it would have been Tresham."

"You believe so?"

"Tresham was Lady Monteagle's brother. Any honourable man must have wished to prevent his sister becoming widowed."

"I know nothing of that."

"I said an 'honourable' man. What would *you* know of that?" I spat, my rage overcoming my caution.

There was a slow change in his posture at that. He turned to face me, and I saw that his leg slid down as though he was suddenly unnerved and sought to rise and escape.

I must control myself. "Being honourable, Tresham wanted to save his brother-in-law. He sent an anonymous letter to the Lord, trusting that his Lorship's good judgement would see to it that he protected himself. And that would probably have been fine, except he didn't read it quietly to himself. My Lord Monteagle was eating his supper, so he had one of his servants read it aloud in his hall, where all could hear. It was instantly clear that the letter was dangerous, and he hurried with it to my Lord Salisbury's house, where he passed it over."

"It was an act of the blindest treachery to tell anyone."

"You would not have done any such thing?"

"No!"

The emphatic nature of his denial made me want to strike him. I could have wept to think that any man could have so lost his soul as to think of eradicating a single man, let alone the massed hordes of parliament. And he saw it as obnoxious that a man could have sought to protect his sister and her husband from widowhood and death. He was indeed a perverted figure. The sort any man should detest.

"I suppose not. You were a retainer of Catesby for most of your life, weren't you? And he rewarded you well for your work."

"I never gave him reason to regret employing me."

"And any man who betrayed your master, you would see as an appalling traitor. Especially one who had been trusted."

It was in his face again: uncertainty. He had been badly beaten. I could see now that his right eye was swollen and blinded, but his left narrowed as he gazed at me. That was little concern – he had always suffered from poor vision in that eye. He was lucky to see his laces to tie them! Still, I remained stooped so that I could remain anonymous.

"Any man would see it as an act of treachery."

I had to catch my breath and force myself to be calm. I would not submit to my passion, there was too much at stake here. "If there had been a means of escape from Holbeche House, that would have made a man think immediately of seeking revenge."

"How could any man escape from there?"

"There were rumoured to have been many men in there when the sheriff and his men arrived. They were shooting from the upstairs windows, from the doorway, from every available position. Even as the sheriff's men wounded and killed the traitors inside, more took their places. And none of their servants were present when the house was taken. That is astonishing, is it not?"

"I know nothing of all this. I had ridden off before that."

"So you say."

"I couldn't have forced my way past all the sheriff's men, not knowing the country."

He seemed to be so confident of his story that he didn't hear my words at first.

"What?"

"I said, what of the tunnel that led from the house?"

He was silent, so I continued, "It would have been an excellent means of escape for all those retainers who were with their masters, but who chose not to stay to the bitter end."

"You're talking rubbish. There's no tunnel," he bluffed.

"No tunnel? I have walked it. It brings you out inside the mill by the river. But you knew that, of course."

"I know nothing of all this."

"Strange. A leather jerkin was found in there, and three men have sworn it was yours."

"There are many leather jerkins," he said with a repeat of that twisted grin.

"So there are. But when you were captured you had an old tunic and cloak, no jerkin. That seems strange. Where did you lose it?"

"I left it behind in London."

"Ah, but you see there was no mention of it in the inventories. I know: I have checked. And it wasn't in the house itself. The sheriff's report was very detailed about everything they found there."

"Perhaps it was stolen, then."

"And perhaps this is a wafer of lies. You escaped along that tunnel with your comrades, and then made your way from there."

"It means nothing. I escaped then; I was caught later."

"Yes. You were caught later. Four days later."

He grunted and turned away again. "This is tedious. Is your

questioning intended to torture my mind as your men have already broken my body?"

"Four days would have been enough time to ride at speed to Rushton."

"What of it?"

"Why, strangely enough, that was where Tresham was. He went to his house to put his papers in order before he was arrested and died."

"He thought he might escape."

"He knew that his part in the plot must become known. Poor man! He wanted to help because he was an idealist, and then he inherited all his family's wealth and realized that life was too precious to expend in foolish ventures."

"He was a coward and a fool! He betrayed all of us. If it weren't for him . . ."

"Yes, if it weren't for him, his sisters would have been widowed. Lady Monteagle and Lady Stourton would have lost their husbands. They might themselves have died. You would have orphaned his nephews and nieces."

"He was all for it!"

"Before he was wealthy, yes. It was only because he was rich that Catesby decided to approach him, wasn't it? Catesby needed money, and was happy to take it from one who'd declared himself for the Pope. It was just that a man desires nothing more than change all his life until he becomes changed himself. When a fellow has money, life is all the sweeter. And a decent man would detest to cause his sister's husband to die, either by his actions, or by his inactions."

"He convinced Winter he was innocent and didn't send it."

"Winter was infallible? *You* don't believe Tresham was innocent any more than I."

"No. Tresham sent that letter, and by so doing he signed our death warrants."

"You signed your own. He had no part in it until the end. You all chose to set your faces against your lawful king and his government. You chose treason and murder."

"We killed no one."

"Did you not? I say *you* did! You murdered at least one man."

"Who?"

"Francis Tresham. You rode to his home, you met him there,

and you gave him poison. You said that he would soon be captured, and that his name would be dishonoured forever. His sisters would be tainted with his guilt, their husbands would be ruined by their association with your conspiracy, and Tresham must surely be an object of contempt. A co-conspirator without the guts to carry through his part in the crime, who lacked even the courage to warn those whom he loved in an honourable manner. He was a figure of ridicule. And you made him see it."

"I didn't poison him."

"No. You gave him the means to kill himself and sat there until he took it, I suppose?"

He put a hand to his face, covering his good eye and turning upwards as though the sun could shine through the thick walls and warm him. "Yes. I went there, and I gave him the poison. I had thought it would work faster . . . but it was better that it took so long. The revenge was delicious."

"You watched him take it?"

"Yes. His servants thought he had a belly-ache from the food he'd taken earlier that day. I was hidden behind the tapestry when he started crying out to them, but he didn't know I was still in there and didn't denounce me. The servants hurried in, took one look, and carried him up to his bedchamber. I just sauntered out to my horse and left him. I'd meant to get to Stafford, but they found me too soon. So here I am."

"Here you are. You killed him in punishment for trying to save lives."

"He betrayed us to Salisbury! *Damn* him! He sold us, *and for what*? Two paltry lives which were not worth one Catesby or Winter! Just to protect his sisters, you say? What of *them*? Two harpies whose sole claim to significance lies in their loins and wombs. For them Tresham was prepared to see my master . . ." he choked a little, and for a moment I feared that he would suffocate, but then he caught himself and rested his skull against the wall, eyes closed.

"What of them?" he repeated. "I apologize, sir, if my coughing alarmed you. It's the instruments they use in here. First there was the beating, then knives, pliers and pincers, then the heated bars and last of all, the rack. Well, when all your limbs have been wrenched from their sockets, you know the meaning of pain. I do. I have suffered – and for why? Because I seek to change my country from this heathen existence and bring her back into the fold of the holy Mother church. I have seen a man killed in that ambition, but if we had succeeded we would have benefitted all the poor souls in the land. You tell me with horror that I should have cared for those two women? I tell you I would have strangled them both with my bare hands, aye, and their whelps too, if it would have assisted in even a tiny part of our scheme to bring this kingdom back to the Church of Rome. It is where we all belong."

"Tresham did not die so quickly, though."

"No. He survived to be arrested. It is good. He suffered greatly."

"Especially here in the tower."

"I heard him," he said cruelly. "It made me smile, even when they pulled the nails from my fingers, I smiled to hear him groaning."

"You are an evil man."

"I am a man of conviction. You could not understand."

"You talk to me of understanding?" I hissed. "I would think that I comprehend vastly more than you. I know you were born well enough, that you came of good yeoman stock, that you were taught to think of generosity of spirit, and that killing was only right when it was to protect yourself from attack. You weren't brought up to be a conspirator!"

"And what do you know of me, King's Officer? Do you understand my mind?"

"No, but as your brother I had hoped you might comprehend mine!"

"I . . . Simon?"

I could hardly bring myself to answer. It hurt so much to see him like that, his expression cracking from anger into pain. Yet I could still see that picture in my mind. The dead, the wounded; gore splashed against the walls . . . I felt sick at the thought of it.

"I am Simon.'

"Sweet Mother of God!"

"I am not here to save you, brother," I warned him sharply. Dear Heaven, how I wanted to think that there would have been a purpose in that! "I am verifying details of your testimony."

"You must, though! Think of Martha and the children, brother! Think of them! You can't let me be hanged."

"Do you really think you could escape from here? No one escapes from the Tower."

"Men have escaped, though," he said.

My scalp moved. It was impossible that he should know – and then I realized his comment was innocent.

"There is no possibility of escape, brother. You have to accept that and take what comfort you can in the knowledge that you will soon be judged. I pray that you will be saved before the end."

"Simon, my soul is safe – but you could save me! Others have lived, why not I? All I need is a fleet horse and clothes. Perhaps a roll of blanket, some food, a little wine, I mean, an outlaw must have sustenance! Then I could ride northwards . . . if I made it to Scotland, I could be safe enough. A ship may take me to Spain, and there I could start afresh. You could come with me, Simon! We could do it together! Escape to a new life. Freedom, and the true faith – who could ask for more?"

"Shut up! You think I would consider running away? Run from what? From your evil conspiracy? Your gunpowder plot? I am safe here. I've proved my honour, and I can live contentedly."

"What does any of it matter? You and I, we're brothers, Simon. That's the thing! Come, save me and we'll . . ."

"Tresham was honourable enough to try to save his family. What did you do, Thomas?"

"Me? What should I have done?"

"Did you never think about who might have been there in the House of Lords when you blew it up? Did you never think about your own brother?"

"Simon, I would have tried to save you, but there was no time. No, I couldn't . . ."

"And you never thought about your niece, I suppose, or your sister-in-law? They were to have been there as well. I had arranged for them to be present in a near chamber to view the majesty of the occasion."

"They were going to be there?"

"I saw the results of Essex's rebellion four years ago. Were you there? No? There was a fight. I believe your master Catesby won some renown for his sword-play. The Earl of Nottingham demanded that he should come out, and Essex said boldly that he'd rather be blown to heaven than surrender. But he gave up in the end. And meantime, while I was there, I saw a young woman caught between the earl's men and Essex's. She was there with her daughter, mere innocents who happened to walk into the wrong road that day. They died, Thomas. They were killed. What happened to their souls, I wondered. Surely God would take them to himself? Would you have wondered that, if you walked past the House of Lords on the sixth of November and saw my wife and daughter lying amid the rubble?"

At last he understood my rage. He saw he could expect no assistance from me. He was, in my eyes, damned. Trying to destroy government, he would have destroyed me and my family. How could he expect me to forgive that?

"I didn't know they'd be there, Simon."

"You knew *I* would. You were prepared to see *me* killed."

"For the faith. Never for anything other than that."

"Me, my wife and child. You would have seen us torn to pieces, brother. So don't harangue me about brotherhood or loyalty. They mean nothing to you."

And his face crumpled. My little brother's face crumpled. The sobs tore at his breast just as the gunpowder would have torn mine, had his conspiracy succeeded.

Sitting here now, by my fire, I can see his wretched features again. Despair ravaged, his hopes built up when he recognized me at last, only to be dashed to jagged, cruel splinters when I revealed my loathing for him.

Except it wasn't true. I still loved him.

There was a knock at my door. A serving girl answered it, and soon thereafter my master was in my rude hall. I rose and offered him my seat, but with his customary generosity he waved me back into it and stood before my fireplace, holding his hands out to the flames. "You saw him?"

"I did, my Lord."

"And he knows?"

"Less than we'd hoped. He thinks he killed Tresham. Thinks he heard him screaming as he died here. The secret is safe."

"A good agent, Tresham. Or I should say Matthew Brunninge. You are sure that there was no hint that your brother knew of his escape?"

"He has no idea that Tresham was your agent, nor that the confederate who rode with him to Tresham's house was another of your men. He has no idea that Tresham has escaped to Spain. I am convinced of it."

"Good. In that case I must return to my house and prepare papers."

I saw him to the door. There was nothing else I could do. And as I stood there watching my Lord Salisbury walking with that long-legged stride of his, I wondered whether Tresham, or Brunninge as he now was, would ever be safe. No agent who could betray one side to another was ever entirely safe. Lord Salisbury was a man of honour, yes, but he was also pragmatic. I only prayed that I remained useful to him.

So I shut the door and smiled thinly at my wife. She was safe, and our child was upstairs sleeping. I drank a quart of wine and stared into the fire for an hour or more before I could bestir myself to go to my bed, and strangely all the while I saw not my wife and child's faces as I had earlier. No. Now I saw only poor Thomas's features, agonized as he was hanged, castrated, and finally drawn.

It was an appalling scene, made all the worse by the knowledge that I would have to witness it for my Lord Salisbury.

Loyalty, under the new king, was more important than horror at seeing a brother butchered.

A DISOBEDIENT DAUGHTER

JEAN DAVIDSON

Perhaps the greatest dramatist of the Jacobean age was John Webster, yet we know virtually nothing about him – perhaps even less than we know about Shakespeare. We know his father married in 1577 so Webster was probably born around 1579/80 and it is possible he was a coachmaker before he became involved in the theatre. The earliest reference to him as a playwright is in 1602 in connection with a now lost play, Caesar's Fall. *Most of his work was in collaboration with others apart from his two great plays,* The White Devil *(1609) and* The Duchess of Malfi *(1613). There is much darkness and violence in these plays, such that you can't help but wonder what might lurk in Webster's own life and origins.*

The following story is set early in Webster's career, around 1606. Jean Davidson is the writing alias of editor and literary agent Dorothy Lumley. She has also written the Victorian romantic thriller A Bitter Legacy *(1993) and the contemporary crime novel* Guilt by Association *(1997).*

John scarcely noticed that it was a bright spring day, albeit a chilly one. As he strode the mile or so down Holborn from the Inns of Temple towards Smithfield, with its stinks from the cattle market and slaughterouses, he felt his black mood settle even more heavily on his shoulders, his enemy of old. His family knew it only too well.

"You're a Changeling, I'm sure of it," his mother used to remark when he was younger, the implication being, why can't you be like Edward? His younger brother was warm and sunny where he, the eldest son, was stormy and dark. They knew to tread warily around him until the storm had passed.

Perhaps it was the thought of a morning helping Edward work on their father's accounts. He loved Edward and enjoyed his company, as he did all his family, but hours poring over Webster's Wagon's books, however healthy they were, filled him with gloom. Likewise the hours of pen scratching as a legal clerk. All he really wanted to do was sit in the ale houses and ordinaries with the actors from the Men from Blackfriars, Manager Henslowe, and his fellow scribblers such as Dekker and Myddleton. It was this that filled Webster Senior with gloom.

But he had an inkling that there was a deeper, more hidden frustration. His writing skills were far below where he wanted them to be, and likewise his standing as a playwright. He could add his name to the others on the title page for the odd couplet, for sparking ideas, but working on his own was a struggle – slow and weary work to squeeze out a few lines. Even more hidden was that he had no belief yet in what he was doing. He hadn't found what he wanted to say.

Turning left under the archway into the yard he nearly collided with Rufus and Queen, his father's oldest dray horses.

"Whoa there, Master John, watch out. I've to be on my way as fast as I can." The horses pulled his father's oldest flatbed wagon and were being driven by the oldest driver, Sam.

Frowning, John stood his ground. "Where can you be off to in such a hurry, Sam?"

"Dead body. Found drownded in the Fleet Ditch. Sergeant wants it moving and we were the nearest but only this old wagon was left in the yard this morning."

"Dead bodies are always being dragged out of that foul sewer. You only have to breathe the contagion filled air over it to fall in. No one usually cares about those bodies – vagrants who've been camping out by St Paul's and other sinks and stews usually. What's different about this one?"

"It's a woman, a woman of title, so I heard."

John's mood began to lighten at this distraction. "Then what's holding you – let's go." He swung himself up beside the old man who picked up the reins and the horses moved out into the narrow street. John heard the rattle of a casement being opened above.

"I thought you were coming to help me, John!"

He looked up and saw his brother leaning out, grinning. His ruff was neat and white, the crown of his hat smooth and rounded, his fair hair tamed and straight. John tugged at his stained and untidy ruff and pushed a hand through his unruly black hair.

"Later, brother, later. This intrigues me. Besides, I trust you to count our father's gold!"

"More fodder for your hack writing friends, you mean. Trust you to be cheered at the thought of viewing some poor bloated corpse." Both young men grinned and waved to each other. Edward withdrew and closed the window, and John settled beside Sam as he forced his way through the throng and jostle of the narrow streets where vendor and hawker rubbed shoulders with high born and cleric alike and they were carried along by the din of a thousand voices, the clang of metalworkers, the trundling of barrows over cobbles. Soon St Paul's tower rose majestic behind them, its environs haunted by whores and beggars, alongside publisher's row and its fluttering pamphlets, and reminding John of the story of Jesus and the moneylenders in the temple.

What a city London was. Not far away King James and his courtiers plotted and connived in the corridors of power at the Palace and in the Houses of Parliament, safe from Guy Fawkes and his co-conspirators only last November. And beyond lay who knew what secrets were carried in the lives of the multitude of this city. From glittering palaces to the steamiest stews, like the contrast between the sweet River Thames with its gardens running down to iris-clad banks, and the stench of Fleet Ditch. Not an original thought, he knew, but none the less true for all that.

And it was not, as Edward thought, that he relished looking at corpses. They did hold a fascination for him, it was true. The great mystery, the final tearing of the soul from the body and the transformation from the physical to the spiritual. But also, he longed for action, to be caught up in the pulse of this great city to be part of its lifeblood – that too lifted him out of himself and his dark thoughts.

A small knot of men and one ancient crone standing close to the gluey mud and liquid that passed for water marked their journey's end. Sam ceased his tuneless whistling and manoeuvred the wagon so that its rear end was to the Fleet.

"At last, you've taken your time." John recognized Sergeant Lightbody from the City of London watch, who managed to be dour and pompous at the same time. He was more pleased to see his second in command, Constable Jeremiah Smith, a young man whom John had met many times during his legal work at Middle Temple.

While Sam soothed the old horses, and the Sergeant commanded his men over the disposition of the body, John greeted Jeremiah, who was looking paler than usual.

"This is a terrible business, John. The messenger came to our gaol just after midday and we have been here for nearly two hours. It took us a long time to bring the body out, she'd become entangled with some branches down there . . ."

"How was the corpse discovered?"

"That old woman there." Jeremiah pointed. The old crone was bent double with rheumatism, and her clothing was tatters and rags, but her eyes were bright with cunning and darted among those present.

"No doubt waiting to see if she'll receive a reward for her labours," John remarked cynically. "D'you think she had anything to do with it?"

Jeremiah shook his head. "Not strong enough. She was scavenging in these foul liquids, as she does every day, to see what might have been dropped here one way or another. She caught sight of some handsome threaded cloth and used her stick to try and pull it out, thinking to boil it clean and then sell it. After a while she caught sight of a hand, then some hair, and she gave a boy a coin to come and fetch us."

"I was right then, she still hopes to get something for her day's work. She wasn't going to leave the corpse unguarded for some other person to take her prize." As if she heard his words, the old woman looked his way and John felt the chill of her cold eyes. "Sam said the body is a woman of noble birth."

"She wore just one piece of jewellery, most exquisite I was told, and her skin and hands are fine and soft."

The body, wrapped in a sheet, was being lifted onto the cart.

The waterlogged clothes made it heavy and awkward to lift and the sheet slipped, exposing her face and upper garments.

"As you can see," Jeremiah went on sadly, as her swelling belly was now obvious, "she was expecting a child."

"I wonder how this accident befell her," John said, stepping closer, thinking of her last moments as death closed in on her. What had been her last thoughts, for her child? For its father?

" 'Twas no accident," Jeremiah said. "That's why there's such a turnout of the watch. We found a cord around her throat, pulled so tight it cuts into the flesh. The Sergeant told me, I could not look myself."

John shuddered, moving closer to the wagon. "A terrible crime." He felt the shrouds of his earlier mood return. The day seemed darker for her violent death. The wind blew more icily, the faces of those around him took on a more sinister aspect. He took an involuntary step forward as they were closing the tailgate and the movement of the cart made her head loll to one side and her face was completely visible to him.

He was later told he cried out. He did remember being consumed by murderous rage. He knew her. "Meg, little Margaret, who has done this to you?"

Arms held him back or he'd have gathered her up and cut the cord from her neck, touched her eyelids with kisses. Choking, he struggled to break free, and then the rage left him. His mind began to whirl with questions. "Pregnant? By whom? When did she marry – we've heard nothing of this. I – don't understand," he gasped. "Who is her husband and where is he?" At the same time he pulled back the sheet further and another part of him registered that her clothes were, for one of her birth, cheaply made and she wore no jewels, and her hair was loose and unkempt making her look like a serving wench. "What has happened here?"

Sergeant Lightbody positioned his solid bulk square in front of John, forcing him away from the wagon so that it could leave. "You knew this woman, Master Webster? Rather too well, it would seem from your outburst. When was the last time you saw her – this morning perhaps?"

"Last year, in the summer, long before the discovery of the Gunpowder Plot. Jeremiah can vouch for that because he –"

Jeremiah was retching into the Fleet, adding to its reek, but he managed to nod. "I did not recog–recognize her before," he said through chattering teeth. "I tried not to look at her."

"She is – or was – the sister of Earl Derwent's nephew, the one who is due to inherit if the Earl dies without issue. Richard is his name, and he studied with us at the Inns. He brought her to view our masques and she was beautiful then, innocent and lively. I partnered her in the dancing. What dreadful turn has her life taken?"

The Sergeant's severe expression did not relax. "A turn for the worse. And now we know her identity we can begin to establish the events that led to this. As soon as you give me directions to this young man's lodgings, we can begin."

John did so, then added, "I heard she had gone into the country to stay with an elderly aunt. September it must have been."

Beside them Jeremiah coughed, his eyes watering. They turned to him. "I do know what course her life took," he said miserably. "Richard revealed it to me but I had to swear not to tell anyone on pain of death because of the shame she had brought his family. Her aunt lived in Buckinghamshire, near Uxbridge, and there a lowly yeoman, who worked in the gardens of a great house there, took her fancy. Margaret turned her back on her home and family and married this common man in secret. Her family have disowned her. That's all Richard told me – he'd drunk a great deal of Rhenish wine."

The rage that had filled John earlier had been born of pity. Now he felt the piercing sting of jealous passion. She had thrown her duty aside and married a common man when he, John, had –

"I'll want to talk to you again," The Sergeant said, disturbed by the gleam he saw in John's eye. "You stay with him, Jeremiah."

John and Jeremiah were left alone by the Fleet – except for the old crone. Now she grasped John's arm with her claw-like hand. "Am I to get nothing?" she whined. "What about me compensation? I've lost a good piece of cloth and all for a good deed. Pah." She spat on the ground.

"Get off me," John pushed her away. "Someone is dead and all you can think of is money . . ."

John remembered little of the next few hours. They stumbled into an inn on Holborn, later met up with some of the King's

Players. Odd fragments remained. A heated argument about the position of the sun and the planets, a satirical review of the newest play at Blackfriars Theatre, drunken speculation on the likelihood of further Popish plots against King James. Anything but think of that once beautiful girl, now a hideous cadaver at the mercy of the Surgeon, worse to think of her as a defiled woman . . . Somewhere along the way he lost Jeremiah and at last came to consciousness again sitting beside the Thames. It was dark now and the river was filled with the bobbing lights of the lanterns on the boats of the watermen as they ferried passengers across to the Globe Theatre, and the lurid pleasures of Southwark. Tears began to course down his cheeks. He realized they were not just for Meg, but for himself and the innocence he had lost today and he hated himself for that weakness.

He'd been sick with love for her for most of the previous year, 1605, ever since he first saw her at their Christmas masques of 1604 celebrating the succession of James from Scotland to the throne of England, thus uniting the two crowns. Her eyes had held such a sparkle of mischief and she had a ready smile. Her hair was decorated with tiny pearls and her neat slippered feet trod delicately through pavane and galliard alike. Who wouldn't fall in love with such perfection?

It was more than that for him though. He had enjoyed talking to her and was never happier than when she was present. His desire had burned in him at night, tossing and turning with physical fever. She was constantly in his thoughts. But he never once entertained the idea of courting her. He knew that, despite his education to the highest level at Merchant Taylor's School, his father's increasing wealth, his own small part in the world of theatre and legal affairs, he would never be considered a fit match for her. She was of noble birth and her duty lay wherever her father directed. But instead, instead –

He clutched his head in his hands and shook it in jealous anguish. She had given herself to someone more lowly than him. She may as well have painted her face and walked the streets. This was not the way of the world. She had destroyed the right order of society and thus threatened its security. The edge of his notebook pressed sharply against his chest. He reached inside his doublet and took it out. The pages were filled with extracts, thoughts, quotations. Sidney, Shakespeare, Jonson – anything he heard or read that struck him of substance, or a happy sequence of words. John Donne's love poems were recorded here, they'd struck such a chord with him. And he'd written sonnets to Margaret, poured out his emotions and private passions in these pages.

Feverishly he scrabbled through the book, ripped out the sonnets he'd written, tore them into pieces and threw them into the sweetly flowing river.

She was dead and with her his entire trust in womankind. He paused, thinking of his own Nell. Yes, he loved her but in a different way. And she was not womankind, she was – Nell, the ordinary, the everyday who shared his confidence and returned it. His feelings for Margaret had been quite different. Intense and overpowering.

He stood up, swaying slightly. He could hear the lap of the water and the cries of the watermen. There was a slight tang of salt on the easterly breeze, he could taste it on his lips. Alcohol still warmed his blood even though he was without his hat and cloak.

He looked down at the dark water. To kill Meg, someone else must have felt such overpowering feelings too. Could Richard, his friend and her brother, have killed her to avenge the family honour? His father even? Or what of this husband in the clandestine marriage she'd undertaken, surely no genuine marriage in the eyes of the world. He pictured a lumpen lout digging turnips in a field and returning home to her where she sat in a hut beside a tiny fire. Perhaps she'd changed her mind and wanted to leave so he had killed her. He'd picked up what lay closest to hand, a length of rope, snuffed the life out of her and then tossed her in the Fleet Ditch.

That was the one image he could not shake. Meg clawing at the cord crying and struggling as her breath was slowly cut off. Or had she met her end with quiet acceptance? And whose image had been the last imprinted on those once sparkling eyes?

As always the thought of the last moments before death when a man's senses and thoughts must be heightened beyond anything he'd ever known, to be almost preternatural, made John's heart beat faster, excited his temperament. Restlessly he began to pace up and down. He had to know what her final moments had been like before her soul had been wrenched from her body. A terror or an ecstasy?

Restlessly he began to pace and a new question gripped him. Why had Margaret come to London from Uxbridge, and had her husband been with her? Perhaps she had run away and was the victim of a thief or cutpurse who had carried his job too far. And Uxbridge – there was something there . . . but no, he could not recall it.

Almost without knowing it he found he was retracing his steps and heading for the area of Westminster and Richard's lodgings. At this early hour of the night there were plenty of revellers abroad and light from torches and windows. But the flickering shadows that were cast seemed to scurry around him and to follow him, like so many rats. The time is indeed out of joint, he thought to himself, as he'd heard said.

John hesitated on Richard's doorstep for a moment. They had grown apart, mainly because John had wanted to distance himself from his hopeless passion for Margaret. Perhaps his old friend would not be pleased to see him, especially in his dishevelled state. But it was only right he should give his respects and besides, he was driven now by the need to know, to uncover what had led Margaret to her untimely death.

An elderly serving man opened the door eventually to his knock.

"Master Richard is keeping vigil," he was informed. "He could not have the body in the house. She is in the crypt of St Simon's on the corner of the street there."

Candlelight guided him down the cold stone steps of the small church. He prepared himself for the sight he would see. Her body lay on a wooden bier in a shroud, hands folded across her chest her face exposed, looking very small but in contrast her pregnancy even more visible, thrusting itself into their consciousness. Richard was alone, kneeling at her side praying. He sprang up when John entered and as he came to embrace him John saw the signs of strain and grief in his expression.

"Thank you for coming," he said. "Father and Mother would not come. Their disgust and anger are still too great. But look at her, John, she was my little sister and, despite everything, I cannot bear to –" He broke off and buried his face in his hands.

John crouched down beside the bier and for the first time

looked at her fully. Her skin was an odd bluish grey and coins had been placed on her closed lids. Her fine red-gold hair had been combed out and spread around her head – something like Ophelia's as she floated down the river, he thought. He resisted the urge to plunge his hands into the hair and touch for one time the object that he had been forbidden when she was alive. The slumbering rage kindled to life again. How could she have been so wilful and turned her back on duty, on everything she'd been raised to uphold? What had corrupted her spirit so? His gaze travelled down to her neck where a gap in her clothing revealed the bruising on her throat. Rage warred with pity and grief in his heart. This time he did touch her. So cold! Like wax. He traced the line of the bruise. There was something odd here–

"What are you doing? Leave her be." Richard's hand clamped on his shoulder.

"I'm sorry," John said. "How could someone have done this?"

"The Surgeon said that no other violence has been done to her. Her death was mercifully quick. Thanks be to God."

"What happened, Richard? The last time I saw her she was dancing and laughing – we all were."

Richard led him to a bench at the side of the room, collapsing wearily on to it.

"I should never have let her go," he said. "I should have been firmer with her, forced her to stay and carry out father's wishes. It was my parents' choice of husband. Lord Neville has estates in Norfolk and Huntingdon. Lordsake, I don't know what she had against him. Wealthy and with a position in the King's household too."

"I've seen Lord Neville. He must be twenty years older than she, but an active man. He funded one of the expeditions to Virginia in the New World." Tall and slim, fashionably dressed, a man expert at politicking and intriguing at court, John recalled.

"Well, she wouldn't have him." Richard sighed. "My father had arranged the match but she insisted she was too young, though she was nearly seventeen already. She persuaded him to allow her a year's grace. He agreed, but only if she went to our aunt in the country."

"Jeremiah told me that her eye fell upon a yeoman there and they secretly married."

"I've never seen father so angry as when the news came that

she'd been so disobedient and had left my aunt's household to go and live with this man. He disowned her on the spot and her name has not been mentioned since – until these last few days."

Both men contemplated the dead body.

"Why had she come to London then?"

Richard shook his head. "This is the worst part of it," he said softly. "She wanted reconciliation and forgiveness for the sake of her unborn child. She wanted that child to be allowed its inheritance. 'Why should it suffer because of me?' she said. Mother and Father refused to receive her. She and that man were lodging near St Paul's, she told me."

"You agreed to meet her."

"I refused at first but then – I saw her two days ago. A lifetime ago."

"What happened to her after that?"

"I don't know. I said I would speak to our parents on her behalf, but the right moment had not arrived. And now it's too late."

John had kept quiet vigil with Richard for a while and then, exhausted, went to his own bed and fell into oblivion for a few hours. At dawn, he was awoken by a hammering on his door.

"Go away," he groaned, turning his face to the wall.

"Master Webster, Sergeant Lightbody demands your presence. You are to come at once."

At those words the events of the previous day came unwelcome into his mind. "Then give me time to wash," he replied, "and I'll come with you."

He was escorted to Sergeant Lightbody's domain near London Bridge.

"You managed to escape from Constable Smith yesterday. Where did you go after that?"

John was about to protest then saw Jeremiah's downcast expression

"We did become separated. Then I joined Richard in his vigil for his sister."

"The sister you want me to believe you have neither seen nor talked to for over six months. Or perhaps, Master Webster, you have been using your power over words to send her love letters, arranged a tryst, then killed her in passionate jealousy," Lightbody sneered.

John managed to swallow his temper. "As you well know, she and her husband came seeking reconciliation with her parents."

"I still want to know how you 'happened' to be on the wagon that fetched her dead body, and how you 'happened' to recognize her. This isn't the first time we've met. Your fists and temper have brought you here before."

And if you'd had your way I'd've been rotting in Newgate or Bridewell Prisons, never to be seen again, John thought. He went on the attack.

"Have you thought about where this husband, William Mantle, is from?"

"From Uxbridge. What of it?"

"I was told he worked at a great house there and the only one I know of is Morecrofts, home to Catesby, co-conspirator of Mr Fawkes. Supposing Mantle was a Catholic sympathizer and has been threatened to stay silent, but Margaret refused? Or perhaps he was forcing her to become a Catholic and she threatened to betray him."

Lightbody snorted. "And suppose men were living on the moon? Put him in with Mantle and see if he's more prepared to talk later."

Jeremiah took John's arm and led him to the room that served as a cell.

"He doesn't really think you've any part in her murder," he whispered. "He's angry because Mantle has a strong alibi which we are trying to check now. If it holds up, then all we can say is it was a passing cutpurse or vagabond."

John was indeed familiar with the room he entered. Rough stone walls, a bench along either side, one small barred window. His heart began to pound at the thought of meeting the man Margaret had betrayed everyone for.

A figure lay curled up on the floor, face to the wall. "Get up," he said thickly, resisting the urge to kick him. "Get up, Mantle, and face me."

The hunched figure stirred after a moment then climbed to its feet, only to sit down instantly on a bench, as if his legs were too weak to hold him. He stared dully at the floor. John saw nothing but a young lad. Fresh-faced, smooth-skinned, handsome in his own way but nothing out of the ordinary. He could only have been a year or two older than Margaret.

"Mantle, I'm sorry for your loss." The words came out unbidden. The lad raised his face briefly and John saw his lips were cracked and swollen. He banged on the door. "Ho, Jeremiah, fetch some small beer and bread."

"I – couldn't eat or drink," William said quietly.

"You must. Would Meg want to see you this way? Of course not. You've got to fight back." Jeremiah arrived and thrust a plate and two flagons at John, then locked the door again. John sat beside William and fed him as if he was a child and held the flagon to his lips, urging him to drink.

"You loved her," he said.

"She – we did not mean any harm," William said. "We wanted to be together but we knew our families would forbid it."

"Who performed the marriage, some hedge priest?"

"Oh no," William looked more animated. "We are no recusants, but non-conformists, another reason we knew we would be forbidden each other. I have a cousin who is ordained and persuaded him."

John drained his own flagon and set it on the floor. Mantle had no connection with Fawkes after all. "I cannot think of any reason she was killed," he said.

William gazed at the floor and answered in a monotone. "She met a misadventure."

"True." John was silent. His emotions were mixed. He wanted to like William, but his jealousy was still a barrier between them. "How did you live?" he made himself ask.

Suddenly the floodgates opened and the lad talked of Margaret, of how they fell in love, how they both shared a passion for horticulture and how they planned a future together creating new gardens. He repeated himself, rambling, until abruptly the door was opened.

"You can go, both of you." Jeremiah brought the welcome news. "The lighterman you were working for down at the docks has been found and confirms your story. He was earning some money by labouring for a few hours," he explained to John.

William did not move. "I have nowhere to go," he said. "You may as well hang me."

John grabbed him under an arm and pulled him up. "You will go to Richard's lodgings and see to your wife's funeral," he said roughly. "You know where he lives. Now go." He gave him a push in the back and the lad stumbled away.

"He says Mistress Margaret Mantle's death was a misadventure – she was attacked, found to have no money, and killed for it. That is Sergeant Lightbody's conclusion," Jeremiah said.

"But I can tell, John, that you are still troubled," Nell murmured from where she nestled against his chest. She turned her head to look up at him and he saw anxiety in her eyes. He knew that with her he could be honest and speak the truth as he saw it.

"Sergeant Lightbody decided that Margaret was the victim of a vagabond who killed her either for sport or to make sure she cannot later identify him. Which, the Sergeant neither knows nor cares. He has found an answer that satisfies her family."

"You don't agree with him." Nell wriggled to sit up beside him, leaning back against the pillows and pulling the sheet up modestly. "You must have reason."

"For one thing, her husband said that she wasn't carrying any coins and they had sold all their last remaining jewellery – save for that one item she still carried which her mother had passed on to her. And it was still on her person."

"A cutpurse wouldn't know that she wasn't carrying any money, would he? Perhaps he was disturbed before he found the jewel she wore. Or perhaps she turned and saw his face. Perhaps he was angry at being baulked of his money and killed her for that."

"I hadn't thought of that, my clever Nell. It could be so if only –"

"If only what? What else did you see?"

"The bruise around her neck. It wasn't a single line. At regular intervals there was a larger blotch."

Nell shuddered. "The poor woman. I know she put herself outside the protection of her family but, all the same – do you mean he used his hands first, before the cord?"

John shook his head. "No. I've heard tell of this before, in my law studies. I am sure it was a knotted rope, the sort that hired assassins use."

"An assassin? I thought the Italians used their daggers."

"This way there is no blood."

"But who would hire someone to kill her? She no longer had

money or position and was soon to have a baby. Her husband – that's who you think, isn't it? To rid himself of this burden he no longer wanted and could not afford to keep."

"My," John turned to her, smiling. "What a cynic you are becoming. Most men will shoulder their responsibilities and I don't think he is any different. He seems a broken man by her loss. He could have killed her in a fit of passion, but not with such cold calculation."

"Then who? Her brother – his vigil could be remorse. Or her father, to remove the stigma from the family name, in case it ever came to light."

"I've considered all those possibilities. At first I thought it was connected to Fawkes and the recusants who could have hired an assassin. But that theory was soon eliminated. And no. I don't think her brother or her father's drive against her was strong enough. This was a drive that was all consuming. Revenge."

"Revenge? Vengeance? For what? What had she done to harm anyone except her father and the family had managed to keep the affair secret up till now. Even you didn't know."

"A truth can remain a secret, yes, but for how long? Remember Pharaoh's wife. Margaret was about to give birth. She wanted her child to be acknowledged, to be part of the family and gain its inheritance. It would need to be christened – midwives and churchmen would be involved, the circle of secrecy would widen, whispers would spread, someone would speak. Perhaps Margaret herself wanted the world to know."

"I still don't see who would kill her for that." Nell was unconvinced.

"I'll tell you who. A man whose life is spent gathering power, whose position in society is all to him. Someone whose pride would not stand for anyone to know that the woman who spurned him was showing herself before the world and his wife. The new baby might soften her parents' hearts, and then everyone would know."

"Who is this cold wretch?"

"The man she rejected, the man her father chose for her to marry. Lord Neville."

Nell gasped in horror and turned to John. "Promise me you won't say anything. You won't speak of your suspicions to another living soul. Promise me, John. He is too powerful and if he can wait in the shadows nursing his revenge for so long and then arrange a killing – I do not want to lose you."

John put his arm around her shoulder and hugged her. "I know," he whispered, kissing her cheek. "But is it right that such a man should sit at the King's feet, to advise him, to pour poison in his ear?"

"I am sure he is not the only one. You must not do it," she said again. "He will have his revenge on you too. He will buy his way out of danger – and anyway, there is probably nothing to link him to the assassin. He might have had that man killed too, or sent him to France. John, promise me."

He released her and leaned forward. "I'd like to but – my conscience troubles me. If we allow such corruption at the heart of government, what else might he be capable of? What, even killing a king?"

They fell silent. Such a thing was inconceivable in this bold new age of King James.

Then Nell said softly. "I have something to tell you. Something that may help resolve your mind."

"What is it? He looked at her and saw again the anxiety in her eyes. So it hadn't been about Meg's death. "What is it?" he asked again.

"John, I'm expecting a baby. Our baby. It's been two months and – I'm sure."

They gazed into each other's eyes for a long moment, then he took her hand.

"We shall get married. And I shall say nothing. Ever."

"Your family – my family –"

"We will face them together and – I do not consider this responsibility a burden, but a joy."

He took her in his arms and consigned Lord Neville to the deepest, darkest regions of his mind.

MURDER UNAUTHORIZED

AMY MYERS

One of the main outcomes of the Hampton Court Conference (already mentioned in relation to the Gunpowder Plot) was the new translation of the Bible into English, which has since come to be known as the King James Version or the Authorised Version. A team of 54 scholars was brought together in six separate companies, each allocated separate sections of the Bible. The work of translation lasted until January 1609 when the work was reviewed and eventually published in 1611. We know the names of only 51 of the 54 translators, so who can gainsay that Septimus Fish, the narrator of the following story, was not one of the other three?

Amy Myers (b. 1938) is probably best known for her stories featuring the Edwardian sleuthing chef Auguste Didier which began with Murder in Pug's Parlour *(1986). More recently* The Wickenham Murders *(2004) launched a series about father-and-daughter researchers Peter and George Marsh who investigate unsolved or unresolved past crimes.*

"See, the witch cometh!"

The raucous cry sat strangely on the lips of the richly dressed old woman at my side. Her eyes gleamed with hatred as she pointed her finger at the fair bride who was now entering the banqueting house of Saxton Hall on the arm of her newly wedded husband. Not a man present but would surely be envying Master Thomas Bell his good fortune in marrying the beautiful Countess of Carlross – if he lived to enjoy it.

"The witch, the witch," the assembled guests around me were murmuring, but none dared speak out in the presence of His Majesty King James I. An authority on witches he might be, but he is also the countess's cousin.

He brought me to the banqueting house, and his banner over me was love. The words consumed me, as I gazed at the bride and her groom. Oh, the Song of Songs, the Canticles of Solomon; they have ruled my every thought for four years now, ever since I had had the honour of being chosen to be one of the fifty-four translators for the new Bible authorized by His Majesty at the great meeting of 1604.

That I, Septimus Fish, a humble vicar of a small Cambridgeshire parish, have been so chosen I owe to my dear friend Archdeacon Clarence Hall. It is because of him that I am here at this wedding today, for he is presently chaplain to the countess.

Did I say wedding?

Perhaps one that foretold a funeral.

For the last two husbands to Lucy Carlross died on their wedding day, and the most recent death, that of the Earl of Lillyfield, I had witnessed with my own eyes. Take care, Master Bell, take care! Death, as that common playwright Master Shakespeare tells us, is a necessary end, and it will come when it will come. And that, for Master Bell, might well be today.

He is a brave man to wed a witch – even one as fair and rich as she.

He that is of a merry heart hath a continual feast, so the proverbs of Solomon tell us, and dear Clarence has indeed such a spirit. At the end of this year of 1608 we translators must submit our scripts to the General Committee of Review, who will check and discuss our work. Clarence is one of its members, and thus many is the evening we have spent over a glass of my dandelion or his rhubarb wine, arguing happily over the perplexities of an ancient Hebrew word or the error in an earlier translation. Fortunately we, as are most of those engaged in this important work, are unmarried.

Indeed such is my dedication to the celibate state that I was chosen as the best suited for the translation of the heady words of the Song of Songs. We fifty-four translators have been divided into six companies: two for the New Testament, three for the Old, and one for the Apocrypha. I am proud to be a member of the First Cambridge Company, entrusted with the task of examining the old texts of 1 Chronicles to The Song of Songs for the new Bible. Its purpose is to expunge all faults from the many texts that have gone before – especially the most recent full version, the Bishops' Bible, which is given to us as our basic text and which is lamentably deficient.

"To no one else could the work be entrusted, Septimus," the leader of our Company discreetly explained, as he told me his wish. "I can rely on you to distil its true theme of the marriage of Christ with his Church. I fear others might be misled by the sensuousness of its poetry into assuming it concerns only King Solomon's more earthly loves. We are all lost sheep, Septimus, but you will find the way."

I humbly accepted his decision, for he knows I am dedicated to my studies (and to my parish of course when time permits). Now my work is almost finished and last evening I proudly read my final decision on Chapter 2 verse five to Clarence. I felt something was weighing on his mind, but I would not be stayed, because I was breathless with excitement. "*Succour me with grape-cakes, comfort me with apples: for I am sick of love.*"

"Succour? And grape-cakes?" quoth Clarence, looking quite aghast. "But what of the rendering of the Geneva Bible, *stay me with flagons*? Why else does that translation precede it with *he brought me into the wine-cellar*?"

"Not wine-cellar, *banqueting house*," I cried in anguish.

It had only been Clarence's little joke, and there was no sign now of anxiety. "Tomorrow," he told me with a merry smile, "it is I who shall bring *you* into the banqueting house. I am bid by the countess to invite you to her nuptials."

"Whom does she marry?" I asked faintly.

Despite my instant delight, I was filled with foreboding. No doubt it was the effect of my dandelion wine, but I recalled so vividly the ashen-faced vomiting Earl of Lillyfield. He had died shortly after the cutting of the sugar paste cake – as, Clarence had told me then, had his predecessor in the role of husband to the countess. Her first husband, Sir John Hengest, had at least died in his bed.

"Master Thomas Bell. He is a most learned gentleman for a

farmer," Clarence answered me with solemn face. "He is well versed in King Solomon's Song of Songs."

"How so?" I asked suspiciously. It seemed I should be well prepared when I met Farmer Bell.

"Why, he is a follower of the Geneva Bible. Every time he hath need of more wine – which is frequently – he calls out with loud voice, 'What ho! Stay me with flagons, varlets!' "

This greatly amused dear Clarence but I am ashamed to say that I wagged my finger in indignation at him. "The word in the Greek text," I almost choked, "is *amoyrs*, referring to the tree, although wrongly translated into Latin as ointments. I follow the Hebrew, a *cake* of grapes, not flagons of wine."

"Flagons!" roared Clarence, helping himself liberally to more dandelion wine. "Upon my soul, what better tribute to the countess and her new husband than to adopt his favourite translation as a wedding gift to them."

Put in those terms, I was forced to consider the lengths to which I would be prepared to go.

"And the banqueting house of Saxton Hall," Clarence now chuckled. "What more fitting place for the translator of the Song of Solomon?"

No one could remain upset with Clarence for long, and together we smiled at this delightful coincidence.

"There will be splendid banquet stuffe there to tempt your palate," Clarence continued.

"Grape-cakes?" I enquired, now scarcely able to refrain from outright mirth myself.

Clarence had no such qualms. "*Flagons*," he declared in delight. "If you do not write Thomas Bell's flagons in your translation, Septimus, I declare the Committee shall alter it to accord with the new Douai Old Testament. I have it on the best authority that they have translated it as *flowers*, which is surely more poetic than grape-cakes?"

I struggled with outrage. The Douai Old Testament, translated by the Roman Catholic English School, is due to appear next year. Clarence was making a terrible threat indeed.

"Flowers?" I cried, near to tears once more. "It cannot be supported."

"Then give the countess and Master Bell his *flagons*, Septimus."

I was torn in two. Did not my integrity as a translator demand it should be grape-cakes?

Clarence roared with laughter at my silence. "Come, let me sweeten the pill, Septimus. With my new duties next year on the Committee, I am forced to yield my post as chaplain, and the countess has agreed you may take my place."

A variety of emotions shot through me at that moment. My advancement would be assured, but would my life? I would forever be under the spell of the witch. I hesitated, because the loss of my grape-cakes would be a heavy price to pay.

I yielded to temptation. "I will accept the invitation, Clarence."

Now I was to be chaplain, however, I must fully understand this charge of witchcraft against the countess. "It is believed," I said slowly, "that if the wedding cake is not cut, then the bride will remain childless –"

"That is so," Clarence said gravely.

"I saw her cut the sugar paste cake with my own eyes when I attended the countess's last nuptials, yet she remains childless through the sudden death of her husband. Does that not prove she is a witch?"

"It does not," Clarence said most firmly. "Her first husband, Sir John Hengest, died of a fit after three years of marriage but I have no doubt it was a fit induced by poison, and not one of her giving. It is my belief her next two husbands died that way too."

"Murder?" I was shocked, but, I confess, keenly interested. "But who would wish to kill three husbands, two on their wedding day?"

"That is easily answered," Clarence replied.

Our rift was over. I could see then what troubled him: that there might be a repetition of these terrible deeds on the morrow.

"Two enemies have good reason," Clarence continued. "The first is her neighbour, the Dowager Lady Hengest, the late Sir John's mother. If Lucy Carlross dies without issue, Sir John's estate reverts to the Dowager. She has no love for Lady Carlross therefore. She had only to poison the piece of the cake handed to each bridegroom at their nuptials to ensure no seed should grow in the countess's womb."

"And the other enemy?" I asked, much concerned.

"The Master of Carlross, the heir apparent to the countess's title and her own lands by birth if she dies without issue. She bears the title Carlross in her own right, as is possible in Scotland. The Master –" Clarence added "– is a most sly gentleman."

Take us the foxes, the little foxes that spoil our vines. I thought once more of my great work. I would keep my eyes open the next day, to see what little foxes might be on the prowl to harm another bridegroom. "Both these devils will be present tomorrow?" I asked.

"They will. And so," he said carefully, his eye on me, "will His Majesty King James. He has asked that he might meet you, being one of his translators."

My heart leapt. King James is generous towards us. We are not paid for our labours, but he has inquired most carefully into our circumstances, and provided money for the poorer among us. I was overwhelmed. I was to meet him face to face. Such good fortune. To meet my king – and after that to serve the bewitching, if not bewitched, Lady Carlross. Clarence need not fear. I shall keep a careful eye on Master Bell for her sake.

Surely Solomon awaiting the Queen of Sheba's arrival could not have rivalled this splendid spectacle. The great banqueting house of Saxton is set on a gentle hill some way from the hall, where today's main wedding breakfast had taken place. The banqueting house was bedecked with velvet and silk hangings, and flags to indicate His Majesty's presence, and he and Queen Anne sat in splendour on a dais with the bride and groom. We guests mingled in the hall, where a sumptuous array of banquet stuffe awaited us in the form of comfits, suckets of orange and citron, rock candies, rasbury cakes and marchpanes, syllabubs and creams of diverse flavours, jellies and white leaches – and many a flagon of Rhenish wine and good claret. Later there would be masques, and I could see masquers here already, princes of Barbary clad in pearl and silver, with long silken stockings, knights of olde in red satin, silver plate and lace, and ladies as shimmering nymphs.

"The masque is of the faerie queen Titania and Oberon her king," Clarence informed me. Again he seemed sad, perhaps aware of all he would be missing now his service as chaplain was reaching its end.

This masque would be too secular for my enjoyment, but I could see it would be a pretty sight. Already musicians were playing on their lutes, and in the centre of the room was a large table with glasses and wine. Its centrepiece however, which drew all eyes, was the wedding sugar paste cake of Edinburgh Castle, a culinary masterpiece.

"In tribute to His Majesty. It was his birthplace," Clarence said importantly.

It was indeed a magnificent sight, and guarded anxiously by its creator, the countess's chef. The castle was a full ten feet in height sparkling in glorious white and coloured sugar paste, and its towers, its battlements, its portcullis of spun sugar and its gatehouse, all delicately moulded.

The countess must have seen our admiring eyes, for she did me the honour of speaking to me in a soft enchanting voice. "What think you of this wondrous castle, Parson Fish?"

Clarence was gaping, and I was somewhat disturbed when I saw how besotted with his mistress. He seemed a different man in her presence, and he was clearly hurt that it was me she addressed. I could understand why she was thought a witch when her eyes looked into mine, and for a moment I almost believed the gossip. After all, there had been a wax image found on the pillow at her first husband's death, and one tucked inside the cake at his two successors' demise. Clarence firmly believed they had been placed there by the Dowager or the Master of Carlross, for he would believe no ill of the lady he served.

I must have murmured something in reply, for the countess laughed. "Our sugar castle holds great secrets. Just wait until it is cut, Parson Fish. You shall see wonders then."

Should I? I wondered if she thought of the last two times she had cut this cake and whether this new groom might suffer the same fate?

As if conscious of my thoughts he waved an arm, shouting at a servant: "Stay me with flagons, varlet."

Despite this discordant note, he looked a harmless enough fellow, albeit dazed by drink and bewildered at the pomp around him. "Long may he enjoy it," I whispered to Clarence.

"He may do so," he replied. "Even the Dowager and Master of Carlross would baulk at yet another murder and in the King's presence. Talking of whom . . ." Clarence gave me a conspiratorial grin.

What a day this was! I was forthwith received by His Majesty, as Clarence, beaming at my side, proudly introduced me as his successor.

King James is not a prepossessing man, but a shrewd and most learned one. He is said to have been able at the age of eight to translate any chapter of the Bible from Latin into French and thence to English. He looked at me most kindly as I fell on one knee before him.

"I bid you welcome, Parson Fish. I hear it is you who translate The Song of Songs."

He could have said nothing dearer to my heart. "I have that honour, your majesty," I stuttered.

"Then tell me, Septimus Fish. Do you believe my fair cousin a witch?" His Majesty wore a brooding look as though the matter much troubled him.

"None who has met her would believe it, sire," I managed to reply, startled at the question.

"Yet it is plain in the Scriptures that Satan can transform himself into an angel of light."

I should tread carefully. His Majesty is not only well known for his learning on the subject of witchcraft, but has written a learned book upon the subject, *Daemonologie*.

"The Second Book of Corinthians, sire," I replied. "But do you not advance the argument in Chapter III of your writings that witches are the Devil's servants, not his masters as are necromancers? They are therefore surely not so blameworthy for their deeds."

"What if it be so, Septimus? By the law of deodand the instrument of death is guilty. It is for God to judge intent."

"A confession would be required," I maintained stoutly. The very idea of the countess being accused of witchcraft was abhorrent and I could see Clarence supported me wholeheartedly. "And witnesses too."

"The countess is my cousin. You would have her thrawn with a rope?" This terrible torture is necessary to root out the evil amongst us, but it was not to be contemplated for the Countess Lucy.

"No, sire," I replied firmly. "I would listen to evidence gathered from others – and be sure they are good men and true."

"I have tried to do so in other cases, Parson. Yet few would speak against Agnes Tompson, save Master Torture himself, and she was most surely a witch. She confessed from her own lips that she would have my death. She took a toad, hung it up by the heels for three days, keeping its venom in an oyster shell until she might obtain a piece of my linen and bewitch me to death. Nor would many speak against Agnes Sampson, who cast black cats into the sea to create a storm for my journey. Worse, she told me what had passed between my queen and myself upon our wedding night. Is that not proof enough?"

Out of the corner of my eye I saw Her Majesty restrain a giggle, and I hastily concentrated on His Majesty. I was aware that His Majesty's cousins could not wed without his permission. Perhaps he would welcome the countess's lack of issue if she were proved a witch. I was all the more determined this should not happen.

"So I bid you, Parson Fish," he continued, "now you are to be chaplain to my cousin, look out for Master Bell. My cousin's choice is not to my taste, but she is a fine persuader."

The little foxes that spoil our vines. I thought of the merry scene around us. Would death intrude once more?

"Your Majesty –" My position before the king was rudely challenged by a splendidly attired gentleman, with a thick Scottish accent. He was a thin man, and sly of face; his eyes flickered everywhere. The watcher in the quiet places, I thought, even before I heard his name.

"The Master of Carlross," Clarence hissed in my ear as we stood to one side.

"A country farmer is no fit bridegroom for a Carlross." We heard the Master drip casual words of poison in the King's ear.

"Thomas Bell looks a fit man to bear fine children," I murmured to Clarence, but the Master of Carlross's fox's ears were sharp.

"Who are you?"

"His Majesty's translator of The Song of Songs."

He sneered. "You are a fortunate man, to work on the poetry of lust and desire."

"Love for the church of God," I replied reprovingly. "As Origen in his commentary declares . . ."

He did not hear me. "It speaks of the body and the desires of men," he said as if to himself. He looked lustfully towards the Countess Lucy, and I thought that he had more than succession to a title after her death in mind. He would marry her himself to enjoy her estates and body now. I thought once more of Thomas Bell. I must watch the Master of Carlross's every move.

It was a full hour before the countess and her groom, now even more stupefied by drink, approached the table. She would plunge the knife into the cake and the first slice be given to her spouse. The King and Queen descended from the dais to stand at the countess's side, with her groom on the other. I had the honour of standing next to Her Majesty. Clarence and I were stood either side of the cook who had created this masterpiece, and opposite the bridal couple, that we might bless the ceremony. If that cake were poisoned . . . No, I would not think that. Even so, I found myself on edge as the other guests crowded round, with the Dowager rudely pushing her way to stand between Clarence and Thomas Bell. The Master of Carlross, taking advantage of her clearing a path to the table, followed in her wake and stood by her side. I would watch them *both* most carefully.

The countess made as pretty a speech as I have ever heard, and there seemed little doubt that she had been deceived into truly loving this fellow Thomas. No thought of danger seemed to occur to her. I saw the Master of Carlross's envious eyes on her groom. I felt the hatred from the Dowager, and I was grateful for Clarence's stalwart presence.

"Dearest husband." The gentle bewitching eyes looked into his, as Lucy Carlross took the knife in her hand to destroy the delicate masterpiece, "I cut this cake that we shall be blest by God with children."

"Never," shrieked the Dowager. "You'll not see him in your bed." The guests gasped, but quickly fell silent, obviously remembering that the Countess Lucy was a witch.

His Majesty turned his wrath upon the Dowager. "Be silent, madam," he roared.

If there were candidates for witch around, it should be the Dowager Hengest, I thought. Every wrinkle of her skinny face proclaimed her hatred of the countess.

"I loved your son, who was my husband," the countess replied to her, trembling, "though he gave me no child."

"A witch cannot conceive."

"No," Lucy declared, turning bravely to Thomas, "but I am no witch. I cut the cake with your son, Madam, seven years ago. We were married three years, and in that time I should therefore have conceived. There is no blame on me." She added gently, "Go, madam, and leave my new husband and myself to our joy."

A harsh cackle from the Dowager. "It will be short, witch."

At a signal from His Majesty, the king's men rushed to stand either side of her to restrain her lest she made a movement towards the countess – or her groom. The Dowager burst into scornful mirth, but it was quickly drowned by the guests' cheers as the countess again took the knife in her hand and plunged it into the sugar paste gatehouse of Edinburgh Castle.

To shrieks of laughter and delight from the guests, it proved not to consist entirely of sugar paste and board. Instead from underneath its cover a multitude of doves flew out from their sugar paste covering, causing great confusion, blundering into ladies' coiffures and gentlemen's hats as they established their newfound freedom. It pains me to say that evidence of the birds' panic was liberally spread over the guests' clothes, including my own. I am told by Clarence there is a court fashion for such conceits in which blackbirds or frogs in pies leap out to amuse the company. I am old-fashioned, and dislike such tricks, but today it served a purpose. Excitement and pleasure, as the guests intermingled and attended to their attire, dispelled all talk of witchcraft.

When order was restored some time later, we resumed our places at the table. The cook had cut the castle of the sugar paste cake into neat slices. Such was the jostling of the guests around us that I could not be sure of how many pairs of hands passed that first important slice to the countess. I saw only that the Dowager and the Master, now free of their guards, were two of those pressing close to Clarence with outstretched hands after he had taken it from the cook, and that it was from His Majesty himself that the countess received it. Bleary-eyed though he was, Thomas Bell suddenly came to life, as she presented the slice of cake to him. He looked at it doubtfully as well he might.

"Stay with me with flagons," he shouted, and his wish was quickly answered, as he picked up the glass before him.

I shuddered again at this misuse of Hebrew, and saw His Majesty's eye upon me. As a scholar he obviously shared my distaste at such a travesty. Then he turned his attention to Clarence, who observed sombrely: "Too many flagons have stayed him already."

I read disgust on my friend's face, but on the Dowager's I saw hatred, and on the Master's envy.

"Dearest Thomas, to thee I pledge my life. May God in His mercy keep us safe and bless us with issue." Lucy seemed not to notice his heavy intake of wine, and Thomas hastily set down his wine and took up his cake, which he obediently ate. That done she followed suit with the piece of cake handed to her. Thomas immediately toasted her again, perhaps emboldened by the fact that no harm had befallen him.

The bridegroom was still alive and the evening was now for merrymaking. No one cried "witch" now, as the company drew back to allow the King and Queen to return to their dais, and the masquers to make ready and the tables be cleared. The Queen looked wistful, for in her youth she had dearly loved to appear herself in such diversions.

"Scantily clad," Clarence had told me in shocked tones.

The festivities would begin with a dance led by the bride and groom. The trumpets played the fanfare, the musicians began to play. I noticed that Thomas seemed ill at ease, holding on to his bride as if for support not to lead her in dance. She seemed not to think it strange, perhaps taking it as an indication of over-indulgence in claret. Then to the general horror of the assembled company, he fell to his knees, vomited, and collapsed, spread on the floor at his bride's feet.

There was a moment of horrified silence, as the countess knelt down beside him. She took one look at him, then blindly held out her arms like a moth fluttering in the candlelight. Perhaps it was not Clarence whom she sought, even though he had hurried to her side, but the aid of a Higher Power.

Thomas Bell was dead. The Dowager had also hobbled to his body, waving a wax image stuck with pins. "'Twas hidden in the cake," she shouted. "The witch, behold the witch!"

Her ladies gathered round the countess to protect her, as the Dowager continued in her triumph, "Your Majesty, even you cannot save the witch now. Let her burn. To the stake with her."

The Master of Carlross was more subtle, but no less eager. "She must have a fair trial, sir. Beat the confession from her. A beating will bring the truth and excise the Devil for the sake of her soul. And," he paused, "for *your* sake, sire."

This point, I could see with sinking heart, was not lost on His

Majesty. With a third husband dead killed in his presence, it was incumbent upon him to act. Our vines have tender grapes, where monarchy is concerned, and little foxes must be stopped.

The Queen was silent; even she did not plead for mercy, though Clarence had told me her liking for the countess was great. So it was I, I realized, who must take the lead if she were not to face certain death. Clarence seemed incapable of speech, so I forced my way forward to His Majesty's presence, with Clarence anxiously beside me. The physician had done his work, although there was little of it, for Thomas was surely dead. Two guards held the countess, and others held back the guests that King James might confer without distraction. *They all held swords being expert in war*. Had I not just settled on those very words for translation?

His Majesty looked at me keenly. "You are her advocate, Parson Fish?"

"More evidence is required, sire."

"Than that clay figure?"

"In this case and in that of the other figures, someone else could have hidden them in the cake and lain one on Sir John's pillow as he died."

Clarence eagerly supported me. "Yes, yes."

His Majesty seized on this. "A Solomon come to judgment is Septimus Fish."

Emboldened, I continued: "There are others who would gain by her death – or by her childlessness. No witchcraft is involved here but foul murder, not just today but for the countess's last three husbands."

Clarence looked startled and somewhat apprehensive that I should speak out so boldly.

"How was this achieved?" His Majesty thundered.

"By poison, your majesty. Poison added to Sir John's food and to the slice of sugar paste cake handed to the grooms."

The fair countess was sobbing, beyond hope, which made me all the more sure of my mission. "Simply in the case of Sir John by one of the many who visited or ministered to him." I continued. "As for the bridal cake, at the nuptials . . ."

I paused, thinking of the scene at the wedding of the Earl of Lillyfield, as well as of Thomas Bell. I could discount the creator of the cake himself, surely, but what of the pairs of hands that passed that piece of cake to the groom? How easy it would have been to add a dose of vital poison if one were fully prepared.

"What poison?" His Majesty questioned me.

"The venom that acts so speedily, even arsenic would not serve so well. The one that masquerades in all our gardens as a flower, well known to the Romans, and one that has speedy reactions as we have just witnessed."

"Hush, Pastor Fish. We know of it. By whose hand was it administered?"

I quickly realized my dilemma, but saw its answer. "That is for a trial to decide. I would arraign the Master of Carlross and the Dowager Hengest forthwith to question them further. Both were between the pastry cook, who cut the cake, and the groom."

A cry of anger came from them both – not unnaturally.

"Both?" King James frowned. "That is not possible. How shall I tell which of them did Satan's work without the torture? And, without knowing which is guilty, torture cannot be applied. An interesting matter of logic, Fish."

I racked my brains for guidance, and the answer came again: "Take them one by one privily, sire. Tell them both that you know their guilt, but that they shall go free if they surrender their rights to the countess's lands and title. He or she who eagerly agrees is guilty, but he or she who protests innocence, protests it with truth."

"A Solomon indeed. It shall be done." King James's face lit up with relief.

The other guests were bidden to retire to Saxton Hall, while the countess remained with the guards to know her fate. Clarence and I prayed together that His Majesty might be successful – although on my part at least it was without much hope that my prayer would be answered.

Alas, when His Majesty reappeared, it was in high ill humour and the Dowager and Master of Carlross walked free. My heart sank.

"Solomon!" His Majesty ordered me to his side. "Both protest their innocence. What say you now?"

"I would ask time to pray further," I said with heavy heart. I could see no way out of this dilemma. God hath indeed strewn my path with thorns. Which of these two and how and why? I prayed long and hard, and so did dear Clarence. When at last God spoke to us, we looked at each other for some time with the love born of those many evenings of conviviality. Eventually Clarence nodded, but his usual merry face showed no signs of mirth now.

"Septimus Fish," His Majesty summoned me once more. "I command you to speak."

I fell to my knees as if pleading even now for what I must say. "*Jealousy is the rage of a man: therefore he will not spare in the day of vengeance*," I began.

"Proverbs Six, verse 34," King James rejoined briskly.

"The first day of vengeance was the death of Sir John Hengest," I continued, "the next that of the Earl of Sully, and the next of the Earl of Lillyfield. And now," I added heavily, "that day is today. The Song of Songs speaks truly, sire. Your cousin is the rose of Sharon, the lily of the valleys. She is all fair. There is no spot in her. How could that jealous man stand by to see her the barren bride of another, then espoused to yet another husband, and another and –" I paused "– to Thomas Bell when that bed was rightfully his? That jealous man would come into his garden, your cousin, sire, and there eat his honeycomb and drink abundantly. Can he be blamed for this? God called him to admire His work in creating the loveliness of Lucy Carlross. This he saw as his work. If there was witchcraft it was in the eyes that God created. They were no work of hers, and no blame of his that he succumbed." I paused again, unable to speak for tears. "O that thou wert as my brother . . ."

"Speak, Septimus," the King commanded me gently.

I sobbed. "I name Archdeacon Hall."

Clarence turned to me, his face ashen, but to my relief I could see no condemnation on that sad countenance so dear to me. He would not repudiate my charge. "Forgive me, Clarence, forgive me," I babbled.

"I do, Septimus. I do. Go in peace and fear not the judgment of our Lord. Nor need the countess, whose beauty and charm are not of her own making, nor her power over men. Sire, she is no witch," Clarence declared. "Those images were placed there by another, the Dowager Hengest, who seized the chance to lay one on her son's pillow, guessing what I had done and why, and reasoning that I might do so again." Clarence embraced me. "I would not have asked to marry the countess, Septimus. Who can wed the sun? I wished only to be her chaplain, without the interference of a jealous husband. Yet she must have suspected me, for she asked me to leave her service. Even then," he embraced me again for the last time, "I could not bear to think of her in the arms of an other, least of all Thomas Bell's. My sister, my spouse, as the Song of Songs so truly calls her."

After Clarence had been led away to leave me in my anguish, His Majesty turned to me, seemingly much troubled. "How did you know it was the Archdeacon, Septimus?" he asked. "Though he passed the piece of cake onwards, I doubt that there was time for him to add poison to it."

"No, sire, there was not, but when the cake was cut, there was confusion as the birds flew out," I said sadly. "He took Thomas Bell's slice from the cook then to poison it."

"Ah yes, the birds. A pretty conceit," the King remarked absently. "And a dangerous one."

"Indeed it proved," I agreed.

"And yet," he continued, "I believe, Parson Fish, the poison was not in that cake, but in the wine. When the birds flew out, advantage was taken of the confusion to add the poison not to the cake but to the glass that stood by Master Bell. The flagons were on the table. It would be an easy matter."

"Sire?" I could not tell where this was leading.

"In my youth, when I translated the Bible, I realized that English is a most dexterous language. One word might have two or yet more meanings. Stay, for example. It means to succour, or it can mean to stop, to prevent. Poor Thomas Bell had a most irritating habit of demanding 'Stay me with flagons' – is that how Clarence interpreted the will of Satan? Prevent me with poison from bedding the countess? Speak, O my translator."

"Alas, I fear so," I stammered, taken aback at his Majesty's acumen.

"You translate the Song of Songs, which is Solomon's," King James said reflectively. "I have no doubt that the Archdeacon is guilty. You spoke eloquently for him. He killed Sir John Hengest, he killed the Earl of Sully and he killed the Earl of Lillyfield that he alone might be my cousin's companion. Cousin Lucy is a witch indeed, but one who is innocent at heart. Losing her must be punishment enough for him. Even so, the Archdeacon would surely face death – were it not for his good deed."

I was shaken. Good deed? "And that was, sire?"

"He let it be thought he killed Thomas Bell. I believe him innocent of that. He stood by me while the doves played their tricks, and poisoned no cake."

My heart jumped. "Then who, sire?"

"You, Septimus Fish. You who spoke so eloquently of Archdeacon's Hall's passion. Which was yours also. You who poisoned the wine doubtless with a preparation from your own garden. You whom I saw place it at Bell's side when the birds flew out. Finish your translation, Fish, and then you and the Archdeacon shall answer to me."

I am sick of love. O witch of Carlross, *thou hast ravished my heart*.

I am guilty. The Devil called me from Bell's own mouth to take my place at my beloved's side. But his words are now my penance, the hardest of all. The Song of Songs must read forever *Stay me with flagons*.

ICE SAILOR

LAIRD LONG

The wave of exploration that had started in the sixteenth century with such notable sailors as Francis Drake, John Hawkins and Humphrey Gilbert, had far from abated by the seventeenth century. One noted, indeed notorious navigator was Henry Hudson (c. 1570–c. 1611), after whom Hudson Bay and the Hudson River are named. Hudson undertook four voyages seeking a passage across the waters of the North Pole to the East. Hudson was by all accounts a mean, even vindictive, man and on the fourth voyage in 1610/11 . . . well, rather than me tell you the outcome, let it unfold in the following story.

Laird Long (b. 1964) is a prolific Canadian writer with stories having appeared in a wide range of print or on-line magazines, including Blue Murder, Handheldcrime, Futures Mysterious, Hardboiled, *and* Albedo One. *His story "Sioux City Express" from* Handheldcrime *was included amongst the top 50 mystery stories of 2002 by Otto Penzler in the anthology* The Best American Mystery Stories – 2003.

When Henry Hudson was told that John Williams had been found in the bush, dead, he finally began to give some thought to just how bad things really were, and how bad they could yet get.

His ship, the *Discovery*, was aground on the southeastern tip of a frozen bay at the mouth of a frozen river, his crew of twenty-two and he seven months out of London – the Strait of Anian, the Northwest Passage to the exotic spices, perfumes, silks, and precious gems of Cathay and Java, still somewhere beyond the horizon. Instead of sailing the warm, open waters of the Western Sea, they were locked in ice at fifty-one degrees north latitude in the New World, winter's full fury fast-approaching. And now the ship's gunner was dead.

Hudson looked up from the map he was sketching of the Groneland coast. "You found him?"

"I did, Master," Henry Greene replied. "Just now. I'd set off early to kill beast or fowl, collect on that reward you'd promised, and not far ashore I found John Williams rigid as an icicle dangling from old man winter's nose."

Hudson set down his quill and sighed. "Rouse my son and the surgeon. You will show us your . . . discovery."

"Yes, Master."

"And, Henry, perhaps you should have the surgeon look at those wounds of yours." Hudson gestured at his friend's dirtily bandaged fingers.

Greene scoffed, tucked his left hand back behind his back. "'Tis nothing, Master. Merely nicked myself on one of those blasted frozen rocks out there, is all." He exited the cabin.

Hudson stood, bundled his fur cloak about his shoulders and stared out the frosted panes of the cabin windows, at the bay. Uneven, unending, ugly yellow-grey ice and the last flecks of what had seemed ceaselessly blowing snow met his cold gaze. This was surely not the land the ship's backers, the Company of Gentlemen (including Henry, Prince of Wales himself), had paid Hudson to find. He turned away in disgust.

The four men met on deck, Hudson, his son, John, the ship's surgeon and barber, Edward Wilson, and Greene. Hudson didn't bother telling the other men why they'd been awakened so early on such a bitter morn, only gestured with a blackened thumb at the gangplank. Greene led the way.

They stumbled across the boulder-jagged beach, across the barren, snow-covered land and into the stunted forest of spindly pine and spruce that grew branches on only their leeward side. Here the snow lay deeper in spots and the going was tough, hard, coarse, half-buried juniper bushes rasping against their clothing as they advanced. The feeble dawn was doing little to relieve the minus thirty degree cold. And this was only the middle of November.

"Here lies John Williams," Greene said at last, stopping and pointing at a slight depression in the snow behind some low-lying brush.

Williams lay on his face, arms at his side, his instantly recognizable bristly red hair encrusted with ice. His hardships, at least, were over.

Hudson banged his arms together, breath steaming out of his bearded mouth in white clouds. "Examine him," he ordered Wilson. Then passed judgment: "The man was a notorious drunk – obviously he became intoxicated and wandered away from the shelter of the ship and fainted, died of exposure to the elements. Who was on watch last night?" he asked John.

Hudson had ensured that a crew member was assigned to one of six, four-hour watches each day. It was his duty to watch over the ship, sound the bell each time that he turned over the half-hour sand glass. It was part of John's duties to make up the watch list. "Mid-watch: Robert Juet. Morning watch: Adrian –"

"I took that watch, actually, Master," Greene intervened. "As I was rising early for hunting anyway, I traded with Mr Motter. And I can say that I noticed nothing unusual during those eight bells – until I ventured out here at first bell of the forenoon watch, of course."

Hudson snorted, turned back towards his ship. He was thinking of his map again, of the course to chart to the northwest when the ice finally broke, of the glory that would surely come to him and England when he reached the Orient by a route shorter and safer from taxes and pirates than any yet known. He was a stubborn man, and steadfast in purpose.

Wilson shuffled forward in the snow, into the depression. He stumbled and toppled over on top of Williams' frozen body.

"You've not been imbibing yourself, have you, surgeon?" Greene jeered.

Wilson glared at Greene. A long, thin teardrop of a man with a wandering left eye, he was as unskilled a surgeon as he was a barber, generally disliked by the men as a result. And the feelings of animosity were mutual, especially where it concerned Greene;

the two had exchanged blows over a goose on the western shore of Iceland, each claiming to have shot the fowl.

Wilson rose unsteadily to his feet and brushed himself off. He touched Williams' neck, clasped Williams' wrist and then dropped it. "He's dead," he stated.

Hudson whirled around. "You bloody sot! We can see he's dead. What of?"

Wilson eyed the corpse and coughed, spat out a sizable chunk of phlegm that froze almost instantly. Like most of the crew, he was sick with cold. "I'd say he froze to death, Master."

Hudson gritted his few remaining teeth. "You and John pick him up and haul him back to the ship. We'll have a service onboard and then bury him in the ground. His belongings will be set before the mast and then auctioned."

John Hudson groaned. He was a slight boy of seventeen, given no special treatment by his father, the Master, whereas Greene possessed the broad shoulders of a river bargeman, and even greater strength, and was given all kinds of special dispensation by his friend and sponsor, the Master. John carefully made his way into the hollow with Wilson and Williams, lifted the frozen man's shoulders while Wilson lifted his legs.

"Oh-oh," John said.

There was a bloody patch of snow where Williams' face had been.

"No use stirring up the men until we have some answers," Hudson intoned, glancing uncertainly at Wilson, Greene, and his son.

They were back in his cabin onboard the ship, the body of John Williams stored in the hold. The gunner's face had been battered to a pulp. Wilson had bandaged the man's head, covering up the wounds before they'd brought him back to the ship. The crew was already nervous about the prospect of wintering further north than any white man had ever wintered in the New World before, and the gunner's bloodied appearance would have only added to that general feeling of unease.

"But obviously someone beat Mr Williams to death," John protested, his ferret-like face twitching with excitement. "Or beat him and left him to die in the cold. You'll have to conduct a full inquiry, father – to catch the culprit."

"I'd know where to look first, if I were Master," Greene commented harshly.

"And where would that be?" Hudson shot back.

Greene's full, red lips blossomed into a cold smile. He used his heavily ringed fingers to wipe that smile away when he met Hudson's angry eyes. "Why, Robert Juet, Master, your former first mate," he said. "We all saw those tiny footprints around Williams' body – the ones left visible after our good surgeon had finished blundering about. No man has smaller feet than that evil dwarf Juet. He said there would be manslaughter, someone's blood would be shed before this voyage was over – back in July, you'll recall, when we were temporarily trapped by the ice. You saw fit to demote him for his treacherous mutterings, Master. Then pardon him," Greene added. "Master Drake would have hung the man from the yardarm for saying such slanderous things, and been done with him."

"You and Mr Juet have been at one another's throats for quite some time," Hudson observed.

Greene shrugged. "He accused me of cracking his credit, spying on him and the rest of the crew – for you, Master."

Hudson waved his hand impatiently. "Enough of that. Could those footprints not have been made by savages, perhaps?"

"No, Father," John quickly answered. "They had a definite heel and toe, like one of our boots. The savages we encountered on our previous voyage to America wore smooth-soled coverings on their feet – moccasins, they called them."

Hudson stroked his beard, his face grim as the outdoors. Gusts of arctic wind buffeted the stout-hulled barke, leeched through the planking and into the men aboard.

At last, Hudson pointed at Greene. "I want you to find out what you can from the crew. You live amongst them and they trust you – but be tactful." He pointed at Wilson. "And I want you to find out anything more you can from an examination of Williams' body."

The two men nodded and departed, leaving Hudson and his son alone in the cold, cramped compartment.

John spoke. "We know Robert Juet is guilty of preaching blood and thunder to the men, father, putting many of them in their sick bed with fear of being trapped in the ice forever. But I trust Henry Greene no more than I trust Juet. They're both villainous men capable of murder."

Hudson looked at his son. "You've sailed on all my voyages in search of a northern passage to the Orient, John. But that does not qualify you to judge men, or handle a ship's crew. Robert Juet has proved himself a first-class navigator over two of those same voyages. And Henry Greene, well . . . his singing and flute and fiddle playing are a tonic to the men's morale – and mine. And both men are needed if we are to survive this winter and sail out of this godforsaken place in the spring."

"Juet is an old man filled with mean tempers," John argued, "while Greene is a roustabout and a gambler, the companion of pimps and trollops in London."

"Hold your tongue, boy!" Hudson thundered. "Mr Greene was a guest in our home not so very long ago. I will hear nothing bad about the man."

"How true," John clucked, before slinking out of the cabin under a withering glare.

Hudson sat down at his desk, ran a gnarled hand over his grey, weather-lined face. What an ill-fated voyage this had been, so far. First, the ship's cat had gone mad when they'd rounded the Orkneys, racing from side to side and staring overboard and yowling like the devil – a sure sign of bad tidings. And then Mount Hekla had erupted as they'd passed it by on the coast of Iceland – a sure sign of foul weather in short time. And the bad weather and bad tidings had indeed come, fog setting in and gale-force east winds driving the icebergs together into a hard pack that could not be penetrated, forcing the ship to anchor for two weeks in Lousy Bay. And only a short time after finally setting sail again, they'd become caught up in ice far from the sight of land, and a mutiny had almost broken out.

Order had just barely been restored by reasoning with the men, congratulating them on journeying farther into the Northwest seas than any Englishmen had before, convincing them to continue the search for the passage that would make them all a part of history. But after successfully navigating the conflicting currents of the Furious Overfall, dodging treacherous ice every league of the way, and finally sailing into a large body of water that promised to be the Western Sea, months of fruitless sailing had proved it to be nothing more than a bay, not an ocean passage at all.

Hudson slammed his fist down on his desk and uttered an oath.

He was fast becoming an old man, and still the riches of the East lay well beyond his bowsprit.

Greene reported back later that afternoon, as the weak sun was being swallowed by the blustery horizon. Hudson was on the quarterdeck, watching his men carry tools and timber from the ship's hold to the leveled clearing in the bush where their winter house would be built. The sailors were stumbling all over each other, hearty seamen used to dancing across rolling decks and scampering up and down singing rigging, not trudging about on frozen, snow-heavy ground with house-building equipment on their shoulders. Hudson shared their discomfort, for on land, a ship's Master was not such a sure and big man, either.

"What have you learned, Henry?" he asked Greene.

"Quite a lot, Master," the man replied, his handsome face alive. "John Williams is remembered as being on-deck and working almost to midnight last night, before retiring below decks." Greene glanced around. "And there he was heard in rather heated conversation with one Mr Juet, in the gunroom."

"What was the nature of their conversation?"

"Well, Master," Greene leaned closer to Hudson in the gathering gloom, "they were discussing . . . mutiny – a topic not unfamiliar to Mr Juet. He was putting forth the proposition that you, Master, had wasted precious summer sailing weather by meandering about in this bay, that you'd lost your bearings, as it were, that we'd never escape this frozen Hell and return to England with you at the helm."

Hudson grunted, wiped his red, running nose. "What was Mr Williams' reply?"

"Aye, Master, that's just it. Williams was having none of it. Juet was trying to get the man onside, no doubt, so he would have ready access to the shot and powder, the muskets and cutlasses in the gunroom – the weapons he and his gang would need to seize control of the ship. But Williams was most adamantly opposed, and threatened to report Juet to the mate. They left it there, so far as my witness tells me. But Juet stood watch the first part of last night, as you know, and he could have easily roused Mr Williams, cooled the man off but permanent so he wouldn't upset his traitorous plans."

"Robert Bylot!" Hudson barked.

The recently-appointed mate came scrambling up onto the quarterdeck. "Yes, Master?"

"You and the bos'n seize Robert Juet and place him in irons."

Bylot looked uncertain, but Hudson's uncompromising face soon sent him scurrying off to fulfill the order.

Greene leaned closer still, whispering familiarly in Hudson's frostbitten ear, "I should like to have Williams' wool coat, Master, if it's at all possible, as I am so very cold in this weather with no proper garment to clothe me. I know it be tradition to auction –"

"It's yours," Hudson gritted.

The surgeon reported back later that evening. Hudson was in his cabin with Greene, helping the man practise writing by having him recopy log entries. Wilson observed the chummy pair, a frown creasing his ragged lips; the passenger's familiarity with the Master, which oftentimes included dining with Hudson to the exclusion of the other ship's officers, had long been a source of bitterment with Wilson.

"Begging your pardon, Master," he said, stifling a burp in Greene's general direction.

"Yes, what is it?"

"My examination of the dead man is complete."

Hudson waited, then rasped, "And what are the results?"

"Well, Williams' facial and head wounds lead me to believe, as a surgeon and barber of some two years' good –"

"Get on with it!" Hudson roared, blowing out the candle on his desk. Greene quickly relit it.

"Well, given the severity of the blows – the broken nose and smashed eye sockets and dislocated jaw – I would say almost certainly that Williams was most probably beaten to death by someone. That is to say, Master, he was likely murdered."

Hudson groaned. "We know he was murdered, you fool! We already have the murderer locked up."

"Oh, well, just confirming the facts, then." Wilson burped again. This time one of his front teeth tumbled out of his blackened gums and rattled down onto the planking. "I, uh, found splinters in the dead man's skin, Master," he said, covering up his mouth, "which would indicate that he was most likely struck with a wooden club of some sort, as opposed to, say, a man's fists, or a metal bludgeon of some sort."

"What do you make of that, Henry?" Hudson asked.

Greene winked. "I'd say this man's got scurvy, Master, and a bad case at that. You best drink some boiled tamarack bud, surgeon, take a taste of your own decoction."

Hudson frowned. "No. I meant –"

"All of the timber was locked tight and dry in the hold till today, Master," Greene said, scratching his chin. "But there's driftwood about, I suppose, if you dig deep enough. And . . ."

"Yes?"

"There's the bos'n's club, Master – three knocks on the head for cursing and all that. Mr Juet could certainly get his hands on that, and know how to use it."

"Yes," Hudson agreed. He dismissed the surgeon. Then he dismissed the whole distasteful subject from his mind. "What say you play your flute for me tonight, Henry?" he asked, clapping his friend on the shoulder.

Greene started. "Uh, perhaps the fiddle, Master?" he suggested.

"Just so."

For most of the night, the north wind whistled through the rigging, hurtled ice pellets rattling against the ship's sides, clawing cold into the vessel and the hearts of her shivering crew. But in the depths of early morning the wind died down and the clouds broke, and the dancing Northern Lights paintbrushed the pitch-black sky in brilliant hues of green and red and blue, dazzling the man on watch and setting the timber wolves to howling.

Hudson awoke at bitter dawn. The clear skies meant a further drop in temperature, but he stood out of bed with the resolve of the deep-water Arctic mariner, the ice-water in his veins bracing him against the brutal weather. Today was an important day, for today construction on the house – the building that would be the crew's home during the long, dark, cold winter ahead – was to begin.

Hudson and the ship's carpenter, Philip Staffe, had quarrelled violently only days before about the house. Staffe had claimed that the order for construction had been left too late, that it was now too cold to build anything. Hudson had dismissed that as nonsense. Then Staffe had insisted that he was a ship's carpenter, not a house carpenter, and would not, therefore, assist in the construction. Hudson had struck Staffe, threatened to hang the man, and there had been ill feeling between the two. Eventually, however, the carpenter had agreed to build the house.

Hudson cleared ice away from the window of his cabin with a dampened hand and looked outside. His eyes widened when he spotted two men armed with muskets striding into the forest on the starboard side of the ship. It was his friend Henry Greene and his enemy Philip Staffe, and Hudson bristled with rage.

Not even bothering to don his cloak, he rushed out of his cabin and up onto the deck, yelled, "Get back here, you two!" But the men were already disappearing into the forest hundreds of yards beyond, and a flock of geese honking loudly overhead served to drown out Hudson's command.

He balled his hands and gritted his teeth. Staffe was desperately needed in the house construction, and here he was gallivanting off for a day's hunting. And Greene! How could his supposed friend, who Hudson was paying out of his own pocket since he was not on the company books, take up with a man Hudson had so recently fought with?

"Bloody traitor!" Hudson roared, shaking his fist. Then roared again, "Bylot!"

The mate was bedded down in the fo'c'sle, but the ship shook with the Master's bellow and all aboard heard it. Bylot rolled out of his hammock and threw on his threadbare coat and stumbled out onto the deck. All was brittle and icy cold, and it took his breath away.

"You want John Williams' coat?" Hudson growled at the bewildered man.

"I –"

"It's yours."

Bylot made for the mainmast, dug the coat out of the pile of clothing there and flung it on his shoulders.

"Morning, father," John said, sidling up to Hudson's elbow. "I see you've changed your mind about who gets the coat."

"I will not provide comfort to those who consort with my enemies," Hudson replied tersely. "Mr Greene has betrayed me."

"As I warned you he would, father."

Before Hudson could say anything, John added, "Why not

search his cabin, as well, while he's away? I hear he's been hoarding food against your orders."

Hudson yelled at the mate, where he was cavorting on the hatch in his new coat. "Bylot! You and John will search Mr Greene's cabin – immediately. Be on the lookout for food or anything else the ungrateful thief shouldn't have."

After a cold, angry breakfast of salt pork and hard biscuit, Hudson made his way down into the ship's hold, William Wilson, great, profane bear of a bos'n accompanying him.

Robert Juet was huddled in a corner. He glanced up as the men approached. "Morning, Master," he grated, a sour smile on his wrinkled monkey-face. Then he sniffed the chill air and added cheekily, "Is that the Spice Islands I be smelling this morning?"

Hudson bristled. The little, old man had always been a cynical, insolent cur, and a demotion and imprisonment were not about to reform his character. "Why did you kill Mr Williams?"

"Did I?"

"Who did, then?"

"Not me."

Hudson rubbed his nose, tugged on his beard. "You stood watch when Williams was most likely killed. Did you see or hear nothing?"

Juet stared down at his chained feet. "Well . . . the truth is . . . I was asleep most of my watch."

"Malingerer!"

Juet glanced up, the wrinkles on his face creasing into a mock-hurt expression. "I was keeping good watch, Master, over the ice and snow – the frozen treasures of the Orient. But I got tired with the eyestrain of looking at all those precious gems and just set my head down in the galley for a moment and –"

"More like you got bloody tired of heating the bloody sand-glass to make 'er run faster," Wilson snarled, pawing his nose.

Juet glared at the giant. "I didn't kill Williams," he said to Hudson.

"Your bootprints were found in the area of Mr Williams' body."

"What bootprints?"

Hudson shook his head, exasperated. "Do you deny discussing mutiny with Mr Williams earlier in the evening?"

"With Williams? Yes."

"Mr Greene says –"

"Aye, Mr Greene," Juet hissed, rattling the chains that bound him.

Bylot and John Hudson found their Master at the helm, staring out at the endless expanse of ice and snow on the bay, his beard made whiter still by the frost.

"Look what we found in Greene's cabin, father," John gasped, running to his side, holding out Greene's heavy, wooden flute. He showed his father the chips and cracks in the boxwood instrument. "It was hidden away in his chest, wrapped in a blanket. It would make a mighty fine weapon, I think." He swung it like a club.

"He would not play it for me last night," Hudson mused.

John blew on the instrument, and the sound was anything but sweet.

"What else did you find?"

"This, Master," Bylot spoke up. He opened the hefty sack he'd been holding and dumped its contents out onto a pile of rope. Salt pork and cod, dried peas and cheese and biscuit poured out, many days' rations.

John said, "Williams was known to have hoarded his rations, too, yet no food was found amongst his belongings."

"Mr Bylot," Hudson gritted, "when Mr Greene returns from his hunting party, have two sturdy men seize him and place him in irons – with Mr Juet."

Henry Greene was furious when he spotted Robert Bylot wearing the warm winter coat he'd been promised. He came aboard the ship just as sunset was setting off the ice crystals in the late-afternoon air, and grappled with the mate. But William Wilson and Arnold Ludlow quickly grabbed him, thrust him kicking and screaming into the hold and locked the hatch above him.

Bylot straightened out his new coat, thrust his hands into its pockets to get them in order. Then he pulled his right hand out, clutching a slip of paper. "Look here, Master!" he shouted.

Hudson took the piece of paper and unfolded it, read: 'I, Henry Greene, of London, do hereby agree that I owe John Williams, of Ipswich, the sum of twenty pounds, that amount being a gambling debt to be repaid in full no more than one year from the date of this note." The note was signed, "Henry Greene", dated "December 1, 1609", almost exactly one year earlier.

"What is it, Master?" Bylot inquired anxiously.

Hudson stroked the frozen tendrils of his beard. "Evidence," he replied thoughtfully.

"I'll bet that we have no further trouble this voyage," John predicted early the next morning.

Father and son were at the house site, watching the crew fumble with tools and nails, their fingers almost too numb to grasp them. "Greene and Juet are villainous men, I've always said so. Juet plotting against you, Greene using you, consorting with your enemies. It's good that they're both locked –"

John's mouth fell open, but no more words issued forth. He was staring at Robert Juet and Henry Greene, as they approached the clearing in the bush, free and unencumbered.

"They seem to have made up their differences after spending some time together," Hudson stated with satisfaction, observing the two men in casual conversation. They saluted and grinned as they walked by. "Good. Their help is needed in building the house."

"The help of murderers and thieves?" John squeaked.

Hudson grunted and shook his head. "You overplayed your hand, son. That note you wrote – about Greene owing Williams twenty pounds – and placed in the pocket of Williams' coat, was your undoing." Hudson gestured disdainfully with his mittened hand. "You see, Greene is illiterate, like most of this rabble."

"But – but I saw him writing the log – in your cabin, father."

Hudson snorted. "He was merely copying what I had written first. I was trying to teach the man the rudiments of reading and writing, helping him as I have so often helped him. But he is a poor student, I'm afraid. And a worse friend."

Hudson looked at his son. "You did a good job of copying his chicken scratch. When did you do it?"

John sighed and hung his head. "I spent yesterday afternoon working on it – put it in the pocket of Williams', er, Bylot's coat just before Greene came back from hunting."

"I suspected so, and now you have confirmed it. The other culprit could have been Edward Wilson, for he knew about the investigation we were conducting, as well, and is literate, and loathes Greene as much as you do."

John looked up. "I was only providing motive. But what about Greene's broken flute, is that not the murder weapon?"

"Remember, one room for the officers and one for the men!" Hudson yelled at his harried carpenter.

Staffe twisted his head around and nodded, then turned back and cursed. The building of two rooms had further angered the already sorely disgruntled crew; they feared there would be two messes, and an unfair distribution of food, as a result.

Hudson looked again at his son. "When I realized someone had deliberately put the note in Williams' coat to further implicate Greene in his death, I began to wonder if there wasn't more trickery at play in the whole affair. So, I confronted Mr Greene with his broken flute and the extra food, and he told me the real story of his finding Williams in the bush.

"He'd remembered the heated words Juet and Williams had exchanged the previous evening, for he'd heard them himself, and he sought to put it to advantage, to implicate his enemy in Williams' death. He retrieved his flute, therefore, not wanting to rouse anyone with a musket shot and having no other weapon at hand, and Juet's boots. Then he battered Williams' face with the musical instrument and made bootprints in the snow to make it appear that the man had died violently and deliberately, at Juet's hand. But Williams was already well-frozen, so he had to cut his own fingers to provide the blood that was necessary at the scene."

"And – and . . . you believe him?"

"It makes sense – he has no reason to lie, for it clears Juet of the crime."

"And himself!"

Hudson winced as a gust of wind sent snow spraying into his face. "He admits stealing Williams' food – like he tried to steal his coat – but there never was any murder, son. Williams was a sick man to begin with, and he got himself drunk on grog and wine and wandered off and fell asleep in the snow and froze to death, as I suspected originally." Hudson slapped his mitts together and spat on the ground, clearing his palate and mind of the whole unsavory affair.

"Both men have promised to be loyal and faithful and well-behaved for the rest of our voyage. And they will be needed to help sail the ship when the ice breaks." The heavy lines on the Master's face lifted momentarily. "When we sail for the Northwest . . ." he paused when he noticed the dirty look from Philip Staffe ". . . for England in the springtime."

John stared down at the snow, thin shoulders hunched in defeat and frustration. "I still say Juet and Greene are villainous men and should be locked up for your own protection."

But Hudson was no longer listening. He was gazing out to the bay, his mind drifting off to the warm, open waters of the Western Sea, where sea salt and exotic spices assailed his nostrils, where riches untold awaited him. He would yet find the Strait of Anian, he was confident, come springtime.

Come springtime, when the ice finally broke and the *Discovery* once again set sail, Robert Juet and Henry Greene led a mutiny that resulted in Henry Hudson, his son, and seven other crew members being thrown into a small boat and set adrift on the bay, never to be heard from again.

SATAN IN THE STAR CHAMBER

PETER TREMAYNE

One of the personal tragedies early in James's reign was the death of his eldest son, Henry, Prince of Wales in November 1612, purportedly of typhoid. He was just eighteen. The following story explores what might really have happened.

Peter Tremayne (b. 1943) is best known for his series featuring the seventh-century Irish solver of crimes Sister Fidelma, whose investigations have now been chronicled in sixteen books starting with Absolution by Murder *(2004). The following story though includes another of Tremayne's series characters, Constable Hardy Drew, who has yet to have a book all his own but who has appeared in several anthologies including my own* Shakespearean Whodunnits *(1997) and* Shakespearean Detectives *(1998). His first three investigations will be found in Tremayne's recent collection* An Ensuing Evil *(2006).*

The noise reminded Master Hardy Drew of the distant report of cannon except that it grew curiously louder and louder. Then he realized that he was awakening from a deep sleep and the noise had resolved itself into a furious knocking at the street door below. It was still black night. He lay for a moment in his warm bed, cursing the fact that his manservant was not at home that night. Exhaling with a sound like a groan, he swung out of bed and padded across the cold wooden floorboards to the lattice window and opened it a fraction.

"Who's there?" he demanded in his best stentorian tone. "Who disturbs the slumber of honest citizens at this hour?"

Peering down, he could see two men, one with a lantern held high, in the cobbled street below. By its flickering light he could see that they were clad in livery, although he could not discern the crests they bore, which would denote in whose service they were employed. Both men were girthed with swords.

"Be you Master Hardy Drew, the Constable of the Bankside Watch?" cried the man with the lantern, lifting it towards the upper window as if to catch sight of him.

"I am," replied Master Drew.

"Then you must accompany us at once, Master Drew. It is a matter of urgency."

Master Drew's brows lowered in annoyance.

"Must accompany you?" he replied, coldly. "Whither? And by whose request?"

"To the Palace of Whitehall, good Constable. By the request of my Lord Ellesmore."

Only a fraction of a second passed before Master Drew bid them wait but a moment to allow him to dress, assuring them that he would be down directly. It would not do to allow the Lord Chancellor of England and Keeper of the Seal to be kept waiting. It was but a short time before he was hurrying behind the two royal guards down the narrow alley that led onto the Bankside, by the dark Thames' waters, where he found two boatmen, also in royal livery, awaiting with a skiff. No word was exchanged as he clambered into the stern of the boat while the others took up positions facing him, their faces stoic and uncommunicative. The boatmen grasped the oars and sent the little vessel speeding across the dank waters of the great river.

From Bankside, on the south bank of the Thames, across to the Palace of Whitehall, on the northern bank, it was a short distance but with the darkness and dangerous tides it took fifteen minutes to traverse the stretch of black water.

No challenge was given as they came to the jetty at the water entrance of the Palace, though clearly they were within sight of many royal sentinels. The two guards were out first, the one still holding the lantern to aid Master Drew to clamber from the boat onto the stone jetty. Then, still without a word, his guides turned and hurried forward through the gates. Guards with halberds stood watch here and there but no one issued any challenge as they hurried through arches into a series of small courtyards before coming to a door which was immediately opened to them. Here the two guards stopped and the man who had opened the door, an elderly man but also in royal livery, beckoned Master Drew to follow. He proceeded to lead him down a maze of darkened corridors before halting before a door on which he tapped respectfully.

He paused a moment and then opened it and coughed hollowly before announcing: "Master Hardy Drew, the Constable of the Bankside Watch, my lord."

Master Drew found himself ushered inside.

There was only one man in the room. He was an elderly man, with a shock of snow-white hair, still handsome and with a sharp pointed beard of which style, Master Drew observed, was favoured by the King himself. The old man was slightly stooped at the shoulders but with bright, blue eyes sparking with humour. He was bending in his chair pulling on a pair of fashionable shoes. The Constable had no difficulty recognizing the 71-year-old Thomas Egerton, Lord Ellesmore, the Lord Chancellor and Keeper of the Seal.

"Sit you down, Constable," the Lord Chancellor said pointing to a chair as he adjusted his footwear. "Excuse me for I am having a little difficulty with these new shoes. I'd fain sign an execution warrant for my cobbler after this. Do you know who I am?"

Master Drew inclined his head and sank nervously onto the edge of the chair.

"I do, my lord."

"How so? I might be anyone. Do you rely on the word of those who brought you hither?"

"No, my lord," replied Master Drew, raising his chin defensively. "Two days ago, at the installation of our new Lord Mayor of London, Sir John Swinnerton, you were in attendance. I was nearby and heard Sir John and divers others greet you tenderly by name. I would not think that they be all mistaken in their greeting."

For a moment it seemed that Lord Ellesmore was about to break into a smile but instead he nodded slowly.

"I have good reports of your sagacity, Constable. Both from my predecessor in this office, my Lord Burghley, and also Sir Thomas Bennett."

Master Drew said nothing and so Lord Ellesmore continued.

"They spoke most highly of your capabilities, Master Drew. They told me that you have an uncanny talent in the solving of riddles. Moreover, they spoke of your discretion. May I trust your discretion, Master Drew?"

The Constable frowned thoughtfully.

"My lord, prudence is important in many of the tasks that I have undertaken and unless they be matters that are inimical to the safety of His Majesty and the Kingdom, or impinge on the liberty of my conscience, then my discretion is something that may be trusted from the lowliest subject to the King himself."

Lord Ellesmore raised an eyebrow and then he smiled wanly.

"You have answered well, Master Drew. You are an honest man and speak forthrightly without fear or favour. Your wisdom and discretion are both needed this night. I am soon to show you something that, if 'twere known outside of these walls, might cause civil war to devastate these now united kingdoms. Do you swear what you see will go no further?"

"My caveat is as I have said, my lord," replied Master Drew, resolutely. "I cannot foreswear to secrecy until I know what this threat may be and whether my secrecy may serve the well-being of His Majesty and the kingdom."

"That word is good enough for me, Master Drew," replied Lord Ellesmore after a moment's hesitation. "Be so good as to follow me and prepare yourself for something I never dreamt I would see the like of."

The Lord Chancellor moved to a side door and led the way down a narrow corridor. Once more, it seemed to Master Drew, that he was being led through a maze of passageways until they paused before a pair of dark oak doors. Lord Ellesmore drew a large iron key from the leather purse that hung at his waist. He inserted it in the lock and turned it. They entered into a large chamber with a high vaulted ceiling. It was the ceiling that immediately caught Master Drew's attention. It was blue and gold and painted with a star pattern. The panelling was of dark oak and there were chairs arranged in a semi-circle around what looked like a raised wooden platform, only one foot higher than the floor but with a single chair placed on it. At one end of the room was another even higher platform, on which were seven ornate chairs, one of which had all the regalia of a royal seat. Above these hung banners and shield crests.

"Do you know where you are?" asked Lord Ellesmore as he closed the door behind them and locked it.

Master Drew shook his head. He had never been in the Palace of Whitehall before.

"This is the Court of the Star Chamber."

The Constable suppressed a shiver that involuntarily began to catch his spine at the name. Back in medieval times the king's royal council used the chamber but in the days of Henry VII it had become a judicial body. During the reigns of the Tudor dynasty, it had even over-ruled all the lower courts. The Star Chamber Court would order torture and imprisonment and now, under King James, its power had grown considerably, being used to suppress opposition to the royal policies, arraigning nobles who were thought too powerful. Its acts were done in secret session with no right of appeal. Here, in this terrible place, punishment was swift and severe to any falling out of favour with the Crown.

"Why am I here?" asked the Constable nervously.

Lord Ellesmore simply pointed to the far end of the room, opposite the royal seats.

It was only then that Master Drew realized this area was in a great state of turmoil. Some chairs were overturned and there seemed a table on which various items had been upset or knocked over, items like candles made of black wax, scrolls of some ancient quality, a golden hilted dagger and curious icons the like of which he had never seen before. One of these was a candleholder, with many arms, of the type that he knew came from the faith of the Jews and there was a strange pentacle star.

Master Hardy Drew took all these things in at a glance before alighting on the dominant object that lay stretched on the door.

It was the body of a young man. His throat had been cut and he had bled profusely. Blood stained everything. His eye caught sight of bloody footprints leading from the body and moving across the chamber but ending abruptly in mid-floor. For a moment or two, they held the Constable's frowning attention. Then he pursed his lips and glanced at the Lord Chancellor.

"It seems that there is great evil afoot here, my lord. These seem to be the devil's accountrements." He gestured towards the objects on the table.

The tall man sighed.

"Know you what day this is, Master Drew?"

The Constable started as he realized it.

"It is now All Hallows Day."

"And this last night was All Hallows E'en."

"God save us," whispered the Constable. "The night when witches and warlocks are abroad to hold their wicked revels."

He glanced again at the partially obscured face of the body of the young man.

"Has he been identified, my lord?"

"You know him not?" queried the Lord Chancellor with meaning in his voice.

Master Drew hesitated. Then a cold feeling began to come over him. He bent down on one knee for a better examination.

"His features are passing familiar. He . . ."

He exhaled sharply, the breath hissing through his partially closed mouth.

He knew the features of Henry Fredrick Stuart, Duke of Rothesay, Lord of the Isles, Duke of Cornwall, Prince of Wales and heir to the thrones of England and Scotland and Ireland.

He came slowly to his feet. There was an oppressive silence. Lord Ellesmore was gazing keenly at him. His expression was serious.

" 'Twere better if names were not uttered," he counselled.

"Who did this thing?" replied the Constable, aghast.

Lord Ellesmore allowed himself a sardonic chuckle.

"This mystery is for you to make a resolution of, Master Constable. Not only who did it but why it was done. Not even His Majesty has been woken to be told as yet but when we do awake him at daylight, as is the custom, it would be better for all of us if we had some answers to give to the questions that he will shower upon us."

Master Drew's lips compressed.

"It lacks only four hours until daylight," he muttered. Then he turned back to the scene. He bent down and picked up a curiously curved dagger with foreign symbols that was lying near the body. It was covered in drying blood. He peered closely at the alien engraving. "It does not need great wisdom to see that some devil's ritual was being made here."

"You have seen the like before?" demanded the Lord Chancellor curiously.

"Not I. But I have a passing familiarity with the work *Daemonologie* that the King himself wrote nearly a score of years past. In my duties as Constable, I have had to make myself familiar of this subject as many lay charges of witchcraft against others. I see many things here that are described within His Majesty's book. These strange hieroglyphs on this dagger, for example."

Lord Ellesmore glanced at him in grudging approval.

"It is true that His Majesty did write that treatise which denounced witchcraft and which many scholars hold in high esteem. Alas, good Constable, His Royal Highness . . ." He paused a moment and corrected himself. "The young man trod paths of impropriety consistent with his station in life. He was corrupted by some of those around him. Many at court, I included, feared for the future. Yet, withal, I find it hard to believe he dabbled in the black arts."

"And yet 'twas witchcraft that seems to be in evidence here," replied the Constable quietly. "Who first discovered His Royal . . . the body?" He corrected himself with a gesture that encompassed the scene.

"The Serjeant at Arms, one Ned Strong. He is a trustworthy man, long in royal service. A man of silent tongue, to be sure. He has served me well and is loyal to me. Knowing that I was residing in the palace this night, pursuing some weighty matters of state, he straightway came to inform me of his discovery, having secured this chamber from idle curiosity."

"And where shall I find this Ned Strong?"

"He is waiting in the guard's chamber in readiness to answer your interrogation. The Serjeant at Arms, as commander of the guard here, is allowed a special chamber for his use."

"Then let us to him this instant and examine his story."

Ned Strong had been in royal service for thirty years and had been privy to many sights that ordinary men could only dream of. He was stalwart, calm of spirit yet with bright brown eyes that seemed piercing and missed nothing. His auburn hair was greying but he was of a muscular, thickset build and, doubtless, he could give a good account of himself with his sword and dirk in spite of the advancing years. He was dressed in the livery of the royal guards, a leather jerkin covering his red and white undershirt with its white ruffs, red breeches, tucked into heavy leather, thigh riding boots, with wide bucket tops above which the boothose showed. He wore a sword and a dirk at his waist. A short cape hung from his shoulders on which was the royal crest.

He stood respectfully as Lord Ellesmore and Master Drew entered his small chamber in which he had been sitting, awaiting them.

With formalities of introduction over, the Constable asked:

"How came you to make your grim discovery, Master Serjeant?"

"It is my duty to proceed through the corridors of this part of the palace at the tolling of each bell, signifying the passing of the night watch."

"Is it your habit to inspect the . . . the Star Chamber?"

The man shook his head quickly.

"The chamber is usually locked and no one is admitted except when the Court of the Star Chamber is in session."

"Yet you have a key?"

"As Serjeant of Arms, I am given keys of all the chambers that are locked. This is done in case of emergency. I have served in this palace for thirty years. I served our good Queen Elizabeth, God grant her peaceful rest. Now I serve King James."

Master Drew frowned slightly. Had he detected a slight change in the man's tone at the mention of the King?

"So you must have served the late Queen for over twenty years?"

The Serjeant at Arms drew himself up proudly."

"I had that honour, good master."

"And on her death, you continued in service."

"I did."

Again was there a slight change in tone. It was a sharper note of disapproval. Master Drew decided to pass over it.

"So what made you open the door on this occasion instead of passing on and continuing your watch?"

"I was approaching down the corridor when I heard a sound as of an object falling. A soft, muffled thud of a sound. I paused and heard the noise of rapid footsteps. Then, no more."

"And so?"

"I took the key and opened the door. The scene that greeted me in the light of the lantern I held was as I have showed his lordship earlier. A body lay on the ground and there were scenes that something diabolical had been enacted there. Once I perceived the body to be that of His Highness the . . ."

Lord Ellesmore coughed warningly.

"Once you perceived the body, you came straightway in search of me," he cut in meaningfully.

The Serjeant at Arms blinked and then nodded quickly.

"That I did and right quickly, sir."

"Locking the door behind you?" queried the Constable.

"Aye, sir."

"You touched nothing? Moved nothing?"

"By the rood, I lay not a hand on anything, good Constable." His voice was indignant.

"It is well to confirm these things, Master Strong," pointed out the Constable in a conciliatory tone. "But there arise some questions. You say that you were alerted by the noise of a soft thud as if something heavy had fallen. Might that be consistent with the fall of a body to the floor?"

The man looked mollified.

"It would, good Constable."

"And you then say that you heard sounds of footsteps?"

"That I did."

"After the thud?"

"Aye, afterwards."

"That presupposes that there was another in this very chamber at the time the body fell."

"That was confirmed, for I also perceived footprints, bloody footprints, which led from the body."

Master Drew nodded slowly.

"These footsteps that you heard, how long did they proceed before you did not hear them again?"

Master Ned Strong shrugged.

"I do not know what you mean."

"A few seconds, sometime? How long a passage of time?"

The Serjeant at Arms was diffident. "I do not know."

"I say this because I saw these prints and they led only five paces from the body, bloody prints, and then disappeared abruptly. Judging from their shape, I would say they were left by a male wearing solid wedge shape shoes with low heels, unlike the high heeled new fashion that is common today with both men and women."

Master Strong was frowning in bewilderment.

"I do not understand, Master Constable. I only know what I heard."

"Very well. Someone was in the chamber with the . . . the victim. You agree to this observation?"

"It seems logical to deduce as much," replied the man.

"And you were standing at the main chamber door during this time. So what other entrances or exits to this chamber are there?"

"Apart from the main doors, I know of only one such entrance or exit and that is at the back of the chamber where prisoners are brought before it or taken below for punishment. The prints, as I recall, led in that direction. A tapestry disguises the door."

"Then you must straightway show me."

They returned to the Star Chamber with the Lord Chancellor, carefully locking the door behind them. The Serjeant at Arms marched clumsily across in his riding boots, passing the body and, carefully avoiding the footprints, went to a tapestry, pulling it aside. A small door of solid oak, with reinforced metal studs and hinges, stood behind it. It was locked.

"You notice that the bloody footprints have come to a halt long before reaching this door?" Master Drew pointed out.

The Lord Chancellor frowned.

"Is that important?"

"Notice how thick the blood is on the prints right until they cease. Why would they cease? There would have been enough blood still on them to make marks, even smudges, not to cease so abruptly. It is as if the person walked to the middle of the chamber and then . . . then disappeared into thin air."

Lord Ellesmore looked worried.

"You imply that there is some devilry here? Some evil phantom at work?"

Master Drew smiled wanly.

"That devilry was at work here is obvious. But, no; I do not ascribe the explanation of this mystery to the supernatural, if that is what you mean."

He turned abruptly.

"Have you the key to this door?"

The Serjeant at Arms nodded and produced a key from his ring.

"This only leads to the dungeons and guardhouse, Master Constable."

"Let us proceed," Master Drew said.

Led by the Serjeant at Arms they went down a small corridor and came to second door that he unlocked. Beyond it was a room in which two surprised guards had been sitting at a table with a flagon of beer between them and dice on the table. They scrambled to their feet astounded at the sight of the Lord Chancellor and the Serjeant.

"How long have you men been here?" demanded Master Drew.

One of the men raised his knuckles to his forehead.

"If please you, sir, we came on watch at midnight."

"On watch?"

"We guard these cells," explained the other, pointing to several doors that led off the room.

"You have been here all this time?"

"We have."

"What prisoners are in the cells?"

"Just three. An Irish noble, Lord O'Donnell, and the lords . . ."

Master Drew waved his hand impatiently.

"Has anyone come this way since you have been here, from midnight, you say?" He jerked a thumb over his shoulder at the corridor behind.

Both men shook their heads.

Master Drew indicated that the Lord Chancellor and Serjeant should return with him to the Star Chamber.

"If the person who made these footprints did not exit by that route," offered Lord Ellesmore once they were back by the body, "then there is only one other entrance."

Master Drew frowned.

"But the Serjeant was at that door."

The Lord Chancellor shook his head.

"I mean there is a special door that leads directly to the royal apartments."

"You did not tell me of this," Master Drew swung round in annoyance to the Serjeant.

The man gestured with raised shoulders and outspread arms. "Even I do not have a key to that door leading to the royal bedchambers," he protested.

"Show me where this door is," instructed Master Drew, irritably.

It was Lord Ellesmore who led the way across the chamber, behind the dais on which the seats reserved for the King and his leading courtiers were placed. He swung back another tapestry behind them and then let out a gasp.

The door stood open and there was a key still in the lock.

Master Drew looked thoughtful. His keen eyes caught a dark stain on the handle and he bent forward, touching it with his fingertip. The blood was not quite dried.

"Was this door checked by you, Master Serjeant?"

The man shook his head quickly.

"I have said, once I observed the body and recognized who it was, I went straightway to Lord Ellesmore. I made no investigation."

"Yet you heard footsteps in the room? Did it not occur to you that the culprit had escaped and if it wasn't through the guardroom and cells then it must have been through this door?"

"To the royal apartments?" demanded the Serjeant in astonishment.

Master Drew did not answer but turned to Lord Ellesmore.

"And when you returned here with the Serjeant, my lord, you did not demand any inspection of this door?"

The Lord Chancellor shook his head uncomfortably.

"I resolved that the matter must be placed in competent hands immediately. That is why I sent for you."

Master Drew let out a sigh.

"Then I suggest we proceed through this door for the stains of blood show us the way."

Master Drew went first with the Serjeant bearing his lantern close behind. Beyond the door was a narrow passage ending in a long flight of stairs that went straight up between stone walls. Now and then the Constable would halt to examine a dark stain which merely confirmed that someone with blood on his or her hands or clothes had passed this way. There was a small landing at the top of the first flight but no doors leading off and then another flight of stairs led up to the dark oak door. Another key was needed and again Master Drew saw that it was still in the lock of the door.

He swung it open slowly.

Beyond was a tapestry that disguised the door from unknowing passers-by in the passageway beyond. This red yew panelled passage was hung with portraits and lit by occasional lanterns. It was opulent in its decorations and furnishings.

Behind him, Lord Ellesmore leant close to Master Drew.

"These are the royal apartments," he whispered.

The red wood made it difficult to discern bloodstains and the Constable was momentarily at a loss as to how to proceed.

It was at that moment a woman came from one of the chambers along the corridor, carrying a china bowl of water and a towel. She was tall, with golden hair and strikingly handsome. She saw them and halted in confusion.

"What are you doing here, my lord?" she demanded of the Lord Chancellor, recovering from her surprise. She obviously recognized him at once.

Lord Ellesmore contrived to give a courtly bow in the confined space of the corridor.

"A grim task brings us hither, my lady. We . . ."

Master Drew stepped forward.

"We wish to know how you obtained the bloodstain on your sleeve, lady, and . . ." He peered closely into the bowl. "Why you carry water so intermixed with blood in that receptacle?"

The woman flushed with indignation

"How now, sir! I know you not." Her chin came up defiantly. "Who are you to dare question me?"

Lord Ellesmore coughed in embarrassment.

"Master Drew, the Constable, is acting under my instruction, lady. Master Drew, this is the Lady Ivowen, lady in waiting to the Queen's Majesty."

There was a silence and then Master Drew said: "We await an answer, lady."

"You are impertinent, sir," snapped the woman.

"As you have heard, I act for my Lord Ellesmore."

Beside him the Lord Chancellor nodded unhappily.

"We would not trouble you, lady, were it not of great import."

Lady Ivowen sniffed.

"If you have to know . . . I cut myself on the arm and was tending to the wound."

"I see." Master Drew smiled. "I am acquainted with such wounds. Perhaps you'll be good enough to show me that I may advise you . . ."

"Really, sir. You are impudent!"

Behind her, a door opened and a tall young man stood there in his shirt, the white sleeves of which were stained with blood. He was tall and had the same features and burnished hair as the woman but without the determined chin. His eyes were red and cheeks tearstained. His lower lip trembled. Master Drew had the impression of an oversized petulant child whose treasured possessions had just been confiscated for misbehaviour.

"It is no good, sister," the young man said in a resigned but tremulous voice. "They have tracked me down and I must face their questions."

The woman turned to him in agitation.

"No, no, Cedric. You are in no condition to . . ."

The Lord Chancellor moved forward, frowning, and his voice suddenly angry and accusing.

"Lord Deenish! We have come from the Star Chamber. Do you admit responsibility . . . ?"

"Of course, he does not!" snapped Lady Ivowen. "He is innocent of any wrong doing. How dare you . . . ?"

"Madam, I dare because I am Chancellor. Your brother's liaison . . ." he chose the word carefully, "with Prince Henry is the scandal of London."

Master Hardy Drew raised a hand for silence. He was thinking rapidly. Certainly, Lord Ellesmore was right. Lord Deenish was the talk of certain quarters of the city as being the favourite companion to the Prince of Wales. And the talk was, as Lord Ellesmore pointed out in unsubtle fashion, that they were more than just companions. Deenish was about twenty-one, three years older than Prince Henry, and rumour had it that he had enticed the young prince into the paths of vice and evil.

"It would be better to repair to Lord Deenish's chamber than discuss this matter in the discomfort of this passage," the Constable said firmly. "Serjeant, do you stand guard here by the door while we retire within."

Everyone seemed mesmerized by his quiet command of the

situation and Lord Deenish backed before them into the room, which was an anteroom to his bedchamber. A fire blazed in the hearth and there were chairs and a table nearby. Master Drew stood back and motioned Deenish's sister, Lady Ivowen to enter, still bearing her bowl of water and towel. These she then replaced on the table. Lord Ellesmore followed and closed the door behind him.

"Now, my lord, my lady, what means this?" the Lord Chancellor demanded, pointing to Deenish's bloodstained clothing. "You cannot deny that you were in the chamber below with His Royal Highness."

As Lady Ivowen began to reply, still with a belligerent expression on her features, Master Drew held up his hand again.

"With your indulgence, my lord," he said to Ellesmore, "I would like to conduct this in my own way. First, Lady Ivowen, you are not wounded and were not washing the blood from any such cut or abrasion on your person. I would like you to tell us the truth. Tell us what you were about before we turn to the matter of what your brother was doing."

There was a silence. Her mouth remained in a thin slit, her jaw pugnacious.

"You know whose body lies in the Star Chamber?" Master Drew pressed on firmly. "This is not merely a matter of murder but it might be construed as an act of High Treason."

Brother and sister exchanged a startled glance.

"We are innocent of any act," Lady Ivowen replied. Her voice less combatant than before. "I was awoken by my brother coming into my chamber in a state of great agitation and with blood upon his hands and clothes . . ."

"Your chamber is where?"

"Next to this."

"Continue. I presume you were asleep?"

"I was. His coming awoke me. It took much persuasion on my part and Malmsey wine to calm his agitation. He said that he had gone looking for Prince Henry and found his body below . . ."

"In the Star Chamber?"

She nodded quickly. Master Drew noticed that she suppressed a shudder.

"What else did he tell you?"

"He was incoherent for much of the time. My brother is . . .

was . . . very close to Henry. They were bosom companions. I brought him here to his own chamber and, believing the blood was from some wound, I took water and towel and washed the blood away. My brother then confessed that the blood was from Prince Henry's death wound. By that time, my brother was calm and told me what exactly he had discovered. He . . ."

Master Drew made a slight cutting motion with his hand.

"As your brother is here with us there is no need for you to tell us this. Your brother may give his account first hand. Now, did you at any time go down into the Star Chamber to verify this story?"

She shook her head.

"Have you attempted to raise the alarm?"

"I have only just calmed my brother and not discussed what we should do," she responded. "I was about to get rid of the bowl of water when you appeared."

Lord Ellesmore grimaced in contempt.

"This looks bad, young Deenish," he said in a brittle tone. "You have affronted God by your conduct here and now you have gone too far, for I have no doubt that it was you who persuaded the young prince to dabble in the black arts. The case against you is obvious."

The young man blinked rapidly.

"I did not do this. You must believe me."

Master Drew contained his annoyance at the Lord Chancellor's intervention.

"We have yet to hear your story, my lord. Let us start with what you might know of the diabolical materials that are laid out in the chamber below."

The young man was pale.

"It was Hal's humour," he muttered.

"Prince Henry's humour?" snapped Master Drew. "You must explain more explicitly."

"You know that His Majesty wrote a work on *Daemonologie*, a work that is highly regarded among the clerics?"

Master Drew gave a sign that he was acquainted with the book.

"Hal – His Highness, that is – was lately out of favour with his father, the King's Majesty, and in filial rebellion against him. I mean," the young man added hastily, "the rebellion that a young man has against his father."

The Constable smiled with humour.

"The challenge of the young bull to the old bull. It happens to all, kings or commoners."

"Hal – that is, His Highness – knowing rightly that his father deemed himself a great expert on witchcraft and that his book has been produced in authority at the various trials of witches and warlocks throughout the realm, thought he would amuse himself by holding a Black Mass in his father's very court – in the Star Chamber. He enlisted my support . . ."

The young man hesitated and licked his lips.

"And did you give it?" demanded Lord Ellesmore harshly.

"I never stirred to help him. I swear so by the holy rood. As much as I loved the prince, I am yet a Christian, and not even to form an amusement or play act would I participate in such a theatre. His Highness was petulant and called me many names, saying that with or without me he was determined to perform the acts ascribed to in his father's books at midnight on the eve of All Hallow's Day in the very spot where his father, the King's Majesty, sat in judgment on all his kingdom."

Master Drew nodded slowly.

"And this came to pass?"

"It is as you have seen. Right until the final moment I refused to accompany His Highness."

"Until the final moment? Did you then change your mind?"

"Not I. Prince Henry left me before midnight and went down by the stairs his father and other members of the royal family use to enter the Star Chamber. He cajoled and pleaded for me to go with him right until the end, using persuasive tones one moment and harsh and jeering taunts another. After he had gone I sat for a long while here in my room. I heard, eventually, the cry of the night watch proclaiming the midnight hour. I waited a while, waited for what seemed eternity, for His Highness to return. When he had not, I summoned my courage and went down the stairs."

He paused and gave a sob and it was some moments before he could control himself.

"You entered the chamber?" pressed Master Drew.

"That I did," affirmed Lord Deenish. "I saw His Highness's body immediately. I went over and tried to lift him . . ."

"Hence the bloodstains on your clothes?" queried Lord Ellesmore.

"He was dead, cold and dead."

"There was no sign of anyone in the chamber?"

"I saw none. As soon as I saw that Hal's throat was cut, a cold fear seized me. I heard someone at the doors and I ran back here to wake my sister."

Master Drew stood quietly for a while.

"That is exactly as my brother told me earlier," Lady Ivowen said, feeling a need to break the silence. "My brother is incapable of any violence, least of all to his . . . his best friend."

"It looks bad, nevertheless," replied Lord Ellesmore. "What say you, Constable?"

Master Drew smiled softly.

"Are those the shoes you have been wearing all evening, my lord?" he asked abruptly, glancing down.

Lord Deenish started in surprise and glanced down at his shoes.

"I suppose so, why?"

But Master Drew had turned to Lady Ivowen.

"And you, my lady?"

Lord Deenish sister was gazing at him as if he had lost his senses.

"I wore these shoes before I retired for the night and put them on after my brother disturbed me."

Master Drew glanced at Lord Ellesmore.

"A word alone with you, my Lord Chancellor. Is there an adjacent chamber to which we may retire?"

"We will use Lord Deenish's bedchamber, with his permission. Remember, the Serjeant is without," he added to Deenish and his sister.

The young man gestured helplessly.

Lord Ellesmore picked up a candle from the table and led the way into the darkened room. Master Drew closed the door behind him.

"I am now sure of the identity of the culprit, my lord," he whispered, placing a figure to his lips to indicate that Ellesmore should respond in a low voice.

"Deenish?" demanded Lord Ellesmore, in satisfaction. "I agree. God help me, but Henry was a weak and indolent young man and his actions were an affront to God and our good Protestant religion. I am afraid it may be said that his death will be of much benefit to the future of our kingdom. Young Prince Charles will be next in line now and being yet a boy we can, perhaps, raise him with a sense of responsibility and protect him from evil influences such as Deenish."

Master Drew did not reply at once. Then he said: "I know that there were many in the kingdom who were unhappy when Her Majesty died and her councillors made the decision to invite James the Sixth of Scotland to ascend the throne of England also."

The Lord Chancellor looked momentarily surprised.

"Seven – no, eight – years have passed since then. We have had to make our peace with His Majesty."

"Nevertheless, there were those who were unhappy."

Lord Ellesmore shrugged.

"Some pointed out that Her Majesty never made a will and that when she died the nation was ill advised to invite a Scot to govern them. It is no secret that I was initially among that number. Many greeted His Majesty as a foreigner, one who speaks in a strange accent and who brought forth all his favourites out of the court of Scotland and placed them over those of England. His Majesty inevitably made enemies; Catesby's plot some years ago nearly deprived him of his life; Melville has been in the Tower these six years, and plots and rebellions occur throughout the kingdom."

Master Drew pursed his lips thoughtfully.

"The Golden Age of England is thought to have passed with Her Majesty," he observed. "Is not her speech to the House of Commons, barely eighteen months before her passing now called her 'Golden Speech'? The one in which she spoke of her love of her people and her people's love of her."

Ellesmore grimaced.

"I know it well. I was there when she made it."

"There are many, such as you, my lord, who loyally served and loved Elizabeth well. Many supported a continuance of the Tudor dynasty by inviting a distant cousin to take to the throne."

Ellesmore's face hardened.

"I know not what you are suggesting, Master Constable. His Majesty of Scotland now has as much Tudor blood in his veins as anyone. Is he not descended from the Princess Margaret, daughter of Henry, the Seventh of his name to sit upon the throne of England?"

"All I am saying is this, plots and rebellions have been many since His Majesty of Scotland came to London. The fact that the heir to the throne of England is . . . *was* an indolent young boy who preferred the company of young men to women was scandalizing many. I believe that this latest indulgence – the performance of a blasphemy in the very chamber where Her Late Majesty, Elizabeth, held court – was, when it was discovered, seen as a final sacrilege and insult to England. The person could not restrain their outrage and slaughtered him."

Lord Ellesmore was staring at the Constable aghast.

"How now, Master Drew, be you serious in this matter?"

"Never more," the Constable assured him,

"And thus are you saying that Lord Deenish must be innocent of it?"

"I am."

"Then do you accuse his sister, Lady Ivowen?"

Master Drew turned to the door.

"Give me a moment more of indulgence," he said.

They re-entered the chamber where Lord Deenish rose uncertainly from the chair where he had been sitting. He had removed his bloodstained shirt and pulled on a woollen doublet. His sister continued to sit moodily staring into the fire.

The Constable went to the door and called in the Serjeant at Arms.

"A favour, good Serjeant," he said, when Master Strong entered. "Be so good as to go and fetch me the shoes that you were wearing when you were doing your guard rounds tonight."

The Serjeant at Arms stared at him in bewilderment for a moment.

The Lord Chancellor was frowning.

"Shoes? You seem to have a preoccupation with shoes, Master Constable."

Master Drew nodded, his eyes not leaving those of the burly Serjeant at Arms.

"I am not so unobservant that I did not realize a night watch in the corridors and halls of a palace does not stalk these echoing chambers in heavy, clumsy riding boots. You have changed your footwear, Master Strong. Shall I tell you how?"

There was a tense silence in the room. The Serjeant was now white faced.

"This night you went on your rounds as usual, clad in your normal footwear. You came to the doors of the Star Chamber and something caught your attention. Perhaps some noise. You quietly unlocked the chamber door and entered and saw . . . well, God alone knows what you thought. Here was the ultimate sacrilege. The young Prince of Wales, heir to the throne, performing some unspeakable satanic rite, in the very chamber where your own beloved Queen Elizabeth once held court among her loyal subjects. You had served her well and loyally, and your religious scruples reinforced your anger. You grabbed the ritual dagger from the young man's hand and killed him."

Master Drew paused. There was no denial, no response, no movement from Master Ned Strong.

"You began to move away from the bloody body, half a dozen paces, before you realized the reality of what you had done. You suddenly grasped the fact that you had blood on the underside of your shoes. They left an accusing trail. So you stepped out of your shoes, there and then, and picked them up. Thus the trail ended. Bearing them in your hands you walked in stocking feet back to the doors, re-locked them, and removed yourself to your guardroom where you put on the other only available footwear – your riding boots.

"Then I think you decided to resume your watch and came back to the door of the Star Chamber when you heard movement within. You opened it but Lord Deenish, who had just discovered the body, had fled back to wake his sister. She was the only person he could confide in. Knowing someone must have made the discovery, you pretended to have discovered the Prince's body for the first time and went off to alert Lord Ellesmore. Am I right?"

Ned Strong glanced to Lord Ellesmore. Some look, a slight nod of acknowledgement passed, and then he cried, "God bless Queen Bess. God bless England!"

The cry startled them all with its abrupt passion.

Then Master Ned Strong was sinking rapidly to the floor. He was dead before he reached it. The dirk was no longer in the sheath at his waist but buried deep under his ribs, through the heart, and his blood was pumping over his clothing.

Master Hardy Drew stood looking down at him in sadness. He had not been prepared for such an act. At his shoulder, Lord Ellesmore was more cynical.

"How shall we describe him, good Constable? A patriot? A religious fanatic? A regicide?"

The Constable shook his head.

"That is not my concern, my lord. But think long and hard about this affair. Should the truth of this be voiced abroad it might do irreparable damage to a realm that is already in turmoil. I am no counsellor, my lord, but things have happened here that the common good dictates should not be revealed to anyone outside these walls."

Lord Ellesmore glanced sharply at him.

"Then I shall return to the question that I asked you earlier – can I count on your discretion?"

Master Hardy Drew returned his gaze earnestly.

"My lord, I have not been here tonight."

It was five days later, on November 6, that London awoke to the announcement from St James' Palace that His Royal Highness Henry Frederick, Prince of Wales, Duke of Rothesay, Lord of the Isles and Duke of Cornwall, heir to the thrones of England, Scotland and Ireland, had died of typhoid fever. He had been removed to his darkened bedchamber early in the morning of November 1 where not even his family were allowed entrance, nor even his chaplain, Reverend Dr Daniel Price, could see him because of the contagion. The announcement provoked a widespread outpouring of public and private grief, English and Scottish poets wrote moving elegies reflecting on human vulnerability, ballads were sung, sermons preached and even madrigalls called "songs of mourning" were performed. The realms of England and Scotland joined together in the grief-stricken release of hopes and expectation for their future king who was now no more. All eyes were turned on the eleven-year-old Duke of Albany, Marquess of Ormonde, Earl of Ross, Baron of Ardmannoch and Duke of York – Charles – the new heir apparent.

Only Master Hardy Drew gave passing thought at the gossip surrounding the swift departure of Lord Deenish and his sister,

Lady Ivowen, who had sailed from Gravesend to make a new life for themselves at Jamestown in Captain John Smith's new colony of Virginia, even before the funeral obsequies of Prince Henry.

It was four years later that Master Drew was attending the funeral of Lord Ellesmore himself.

He was seated next to an elderly and loquacious man.

"A great man, Lord Ellesmore," the man offered. "He was one of Her Late Majesty's most trusted servants and ardent supporters of her dynasty. Did you know him, Master Constable?"

"I knew him briefly some years ago," admitted Master Drew. "And you?"

"I served him as a guard when he was Chancellor. Serjeant Strong was my senior then."

"Serjeant Ned Strong?" Master Drew stirred uncomfortably.

"Aye, did you know him?"

"I have heard the name."

"A fine soldier was Ned Strong. Fiercely loyal to Lord Ellesmore."

Master Drew stirred uneasily.

"Is that so?"

"Indeed it is. You would have recognized him easily had you known him. A strong, muscular man who was proud of the livery he wore. We used to jest with him for when he was on duty, he liked to dress in full uniform, even down to riding boots. Whoever heard of wearing riding boots within doors! But that was his only eccentricity."

The Constable felt suddenly cold.

"It was his custom to wear riding boots indoors?"

The elderly man chuckled.

"He said a uniform was not properly worn without them. But he was a man who would lay down his life for what he believed right. Poor Ned Strong. He disappeared some years ago. The story was that he was probably set upon by footpads one night outside the palace and his body dumped into the Thames. A sad end."

Master Drew nodded slowly. He was suddenly remembering the first time he had seen Lord Ellesmore, seated in his chair and pulling on a new pair of shoes. All that he had accused Strong of doing could equally apply to . . .

It was then the funeral cortège of Lord Ellesmore entered the church.

"A sad end," he echoed. "Ah!" he added, with a little savagery in his tone. "I think I am getting too old to be Constable. I miss the obvious."

GREEN TARTS

DERYN LAKE

Perhaps the most notorious murder trial during James's reign was the Overbury Case. It has fascinated investigators for years and you may find several books on the subject including Cast of Ravens *(1965) by Beatrice White and more recently* Unnatural Murder *(1997) by Anne Somerset. The case is recounted in such detail in the following story that I need say no more.*

Deryn Lake is the author of the John Rawlings and John Fielding murder mysteries set in eighteenth-century Georgian England, starting with Death in the Dark Walk *(1994). Under her own name, Dinah Lampitt, she has produced many historical novels, including the popular Sutton Place trilogy and* The King's Women *(1993) featuring Joan of Arc.*

God grant me grace, but I am getting on in years. I looked in the mirror this very morning and an old man stared back at me. I gazed at him in horror, hardly believing that I had come to this. But sooner or later we all have intimations of mortality. Thus I will do as my conscience dictates and set down a record of those times, so long ago, when a man met his death in the Tower and the part that I played in it all. As far as

I can recall, if memory serves correctly, it all started with a bed.

It arrived in pieces, as was customary, and was carried up to the master bedroom by a team of servants, then handed over to the craftsmen to assemble. Watching them work, its new owner thought it a beautiful thing that grew beneath their hands; richly carved and sumptuously adorned. In fact he could hardly wait for them to finish that he might stretch out on it and measure his length on the silk cover, letting his eyes take in the marquetry panels on the headboard, created by German craftsmen, a number of whom now lived in Southwark. His gaze wandered over the elaborate carvings, one of which was a grinning satyr to represent fertility. It seemed to smile at him in a devilish manner. All in all, he thought to himself, this new bed summed up his status, his standing, his enviable position as the best-loved favourite of that most malleable of monarchs, James I.

Robert Carr, Viscount Rochford, took a step forward and touched the gorgeous draperies, presently being hung beneath the intricately carved oak tester. The workman responsible looked up.

"All right, my lord?"

"Splendid. I think this bed is going to be quite wonderful."

"It will indeed, my lord."

And tonight, thought Robert, I shall show it, totally complete, to my closest friend, Thomas Overbury. He gave a quiet sigh, thinking of the pleasures ahead, and turning, left the room.

As he went downstairs, Robert glanced admiringly at himself in a mirror. He was a handsome man, some twenty-four years of age, with long straight limbs and broad shoulders. He had a head of thick fair hair which he wore tightly frizzed as fashion dictated, meanwhile dressing himself to the inch in fine clothes and jewels, including a sparkling earring worn in his left ear. Unfortunately all this frippery made him appear effeminate, a feature which, no doubt, pleased his royal master enormously. For there could be no doubt that the King worshipped Robert – leaning on his arm, pinching his cheek, kissing him quite openly in full public gaze – a fact which the self-seeking young man positively encouraged, responding with melting looks and suggestive gestures. Yet, despite the love of King James,

Robert had formed another liaison with Thomas Overbury, a bright young Englishman with literary pretensions. In fact the couple were devoted and it was Thomas who was to visit this very night.

In order to pass the time, Robert decided to have a bath, thus causing an army of servants to plod up and down stairs with pails of boiling water. After being towelled dry, he oiled himself then dressed in stockings and doublet, executed in silks and gold and silver thread. On his feet he put on a pair of low-heeled shoes, decorated with an enormous frill of black and yellow. Then, having shaved closely, a feature much admired by the King, he awaited Thomas's arrival. Quarter of an hour later, a thunderous knock announced his presence. Robert immediately assumed a negligent pose, his fingers idly toying with a book, the other hand supporting his chin. He looked up as his friend was announced.

"My dear Overbury," he said.

But once the bowing servant was out of the way, Robert hurried over and embraced the newcomer warmly, kissing him on both cheeks, then on the mouth.

Thomas disentangled himself. "You're pleased to see me, I take it."

"I always am. You know that."

His friend allowed a small smile to light his features, a fact which made him appear more attractive. Older than Carr, he was not so blatantly good looking yet it was a more intelligent face, though spoiled by an expression of arrogance. Now, though, he was anxious to please.

"Have you persuaded the King to like me any better?" he asked eagerly.

Robert pulled down his mouth. "No, I'm afraid not."

"You know why it is, don't you?"

"I think I can hazard a guess."

"Because he's jealous of me. He knows damn well that you love me better than him – and that is something the lecherous old beast cannot stomach."

Robert simpered and for a moment looked utterly feminine. "I think what you say is true. He cannot take his eyes off me, even at court."

Thomas Overbury scowled. "Besotted old fool."

"Shush. Someone might hear you."

"Let them." He turned to Robert. "Now, what is this surprise you have to show me?"

"Come upstairs. Come and see my new toy."

Somewhat mystified, Thomas followed him up the staircase to the master bedroom, Robert firmly closing the door behind him. A few minutes later came the sound of muted laughter as the two men sampled the new bed's delights.

"I am in despair," said Frances, Countess of Essex, bursting into a spectacular torrent of tears. "Oh, my dear, what am I to do?"

The dear in question was a small, comely widow with a pleasing face and hair like golden thread. But at present her expression was one of deep sympathy which did not totally become her.

"Think of it," Frances continued, not waiting for a reply. "Think of being wedded to a lanky brute who at first would not consummate the marriage and now expects me to lie with him, which I do not wish to do. And, sweet Anne, just at this stage I have received a love letter from another man."

Anne's expression changed rapidly to one of acute attention. "Really, my pet? Who?"

"You'll not believe it – the King's favourite! Robert Carr himself."

"Robert Carr? But surely he has other interests."

"So I always thought, but the letter was most ardent."

"What did it say?"

"How much he admires me and how much he would like to converse with me."

Anne shook her head. "I am surprised indeed."

Frances, who was one of the most beautiful women at court, looked very slightly annoyed. "Oh?"

"I'm just surprised that he had the courage to write," Anne answered swiftly.

"I see," answered the Countess, slightly mollified.

"I hold your heart close to mine as I hope you do to me," said Sir Thomas Overbury, dictating.

"Is that grammatically correct?" asked Robert Carr, pausing in his writing.

"Oh, to hell with grammar. It will certainly attract the attention of the silly bitch."

Robert laughed carelessly. "I don't know why I'm bothering with this."

"Oh, yes, you do. It's because you can't resist a challenge and the fact that the lady is in a loveless marriage appeals to you."

"What shall I do if she says yes?"

Overbury gave a careless shrug. "That, my dear, will be entirely up to you."

At that moment both men looked up as there was a noise in the corridor outside. They were in the royal palace at Greenwich, in Carr's apartments, but this did not guarantee them privacy.

"Hide the letter," hissed Overbury and Robert thrust it beneath a book as the door opened without ceremony and they saw, standing in the entrance, his royal majesty James.

He glanced at Thomas unsmilingly. Ever since the affair last year when both he and Carr had been caught laughing at the Queen, any affection the King might have felt for Robert's friend had been totally banished. However, his feelings for Carr remained undiminished.

Now he said, "There you are, my lad. I would ask you to walk with me a little."

Straightening himself from his reverential bow, Carr smiled flirtatiously. "Of course, your Majesty."

Advancing on him, James lolled an arm round his favourite's neck and kissed him on the lips. Carr turned towards him as sweetly as any woman. "If I can do anything to please your Majesty."

The King's rheumy eyes had an inner fire. "We'll walk a little way first, eh, Carr?"

"As your Majesty pleases."

Ignoring Overbury the pair left the room, weak-legged James hanging round Robert's neck as though his very life depended on it. Thomas could not help but notice that the fingers of the King's other hand were fiddling round his codpiece as he shuffled out.

They met privately and for the first time in Carr's apartments in Hampton Court, he full of charm and prattling nonsense, she virtually tongue-tied. Looking at her, intending to use her as a plaything and then discard her, Robert was struck by how very good-looking she was at close quarters. Her hair, reddish-gold in colour, was frizzed out in the latest fashion with an aquamarine and pearl headdress, while her eyes – matching the stone – flashed shy but definite messages in his direction. As for her figure, he could see from her exceedingly low-cut gown that her breasts were truly beautiful. It was rumoured throughout the court that she was a virgin, a fact which stimulated Robert's wicked side with thoughts of deflowering her.

"Well, Lady Frances, how good of you to come."

"I come in response to your letters, Sir."

He had not written one of them; Thomas Overbury was responsible for them all. Thinking of the ribaldry as they had been composed, Robert felt himself flush and turned away.

"Would my Lady like some wine?"

"Yes, please, I would."

Carr poured two glasses and having handed her one, sat down in a chair opposite hers.

"You truly are bewitching," he said, speaking his thoughts aloud.

Frances pulled a face. "Much good it has done me."

"You are not happy?" asked Robert, hoping that this would start off the story of her marriage.

"No, Sir, I am not."

And that indeed released the floodgates. She spoke of her wedding to the Earl of Essex when she had been fifteen and he a few months younger, how her father had at first kept them apart but, following that, when her husband had returned from his trip abroad, he had failed dismally in the bed chamber. So much so that after a year of trying he had given up completely.

"And now?" Carr enquired.

"Now I would hate sexual connection. I dislike the Earl, may God forgive me."

"Why Madam?"

"Because he is not pleasing to look at, he cannot talk to me, and he is only happy in the company of other men." Tears filled the lovely bright eyes. "All in all, he is not a pretty fellow."

There was silence in the room and then Robert put down his glass and held out his hand. After a moment's hesitation, the Countess of Essex slowly put out hers and twined her fingers round his. They said nothing but sat quietly, simply looking at one another.

That evening Overbury, calling on his friend as usual, found him strangely withdrawn.

"Well, Robert, how did it go? Did you woo the hussy?"

"Don't call her that, I beg you."

Thomas was so shaken that he sat down abruptly. "God's life! Do I hear aright? Don't tell me that you have fallen under her spell."

Robert, looking at Thomas Overbury, noticed for the first time that the man had a spot with a head forming on his right cheek.

"Of course not," he said abruptly.

Thomas raised an eyebrow. "If I didn't know you a great deal better I would say that you are extremely interested in the girl. Well, don't do be so I beg of you. The Howards are a poisonous bunch and you know perfectly well that her father loathes you."

"That is hardly her fault."

"Agreed. But I assure you that you will place yourself in great danger if you pursue this."

"Perhaps," Robert answered. He changed the subject. "Now, dear friend, would you care for some wine?"

"I'll have some Alicante."

"A favourite of his Majesty."

"Yes," said Thomas with much meaning. "Let us hope that he does not lose interest in it."

After he had gone, rather abruptly Robert thought – though he had been thankful, for once, to see the back of him – Carr lay on his bed. Over and over in his mind came the vision of the beautiful Countess, so young and so unhappy. A strange feeling came over him, one that he was quite unaccustomed to, and he wondered what could possibly be causing such an unusual sensation. Yet, despite it, he knew that she was indeed dangerous to him. And he also knew for certain that his original plan to use her as a plaything might well have to be abandoned.

Thomas Overbury was in a state of high alarm. There had been a definite change in his friend's attitude, all stemming from the time he had seen that wretched Howard girl on his own. It was a known fact that Thomas detested all the Howards – nobody, himself included, quite knowing why. Possibly, he often thought, he had been born hating them. But the fact remained, he had an obsessive private malice towards the entire family.

He had helped Robert write those silly letters to the Countess of Essex, born Lady Frances Howard, for one reason and one reason alone; to ruin her reputation and thus bring dishonour to her clan. But now it looked as if the entire scheme had blown up in his face. Could it even be possible that Robert Carr, Viscount Rochford, was falling in love with the woman? Alone in his room, Thomas seethed with silent rage.

Yet his position was assured. Robert, frankly, had neither the brains nor the will to wade through interminable papers, and having been raised to the role of Privy Councillor now sent various secret documents to Overbury for him to look over first. Yet this very power was making Thomas unpopular in certain quarters. And one quarter was extremely dangerous. The King himself had conceived a violent dislike of his favourite's best friend, a dislike which he barely bothered to conceal.

"I am deep in love," said the Countess of Essex, sighing.

"I am sure you are, my dear," replied Mrs Turner, wishing she were being paid a guinea for every time she had heard that remark.

"Yet I fear the situation," Frances continued. "If my husband should discover my association he would wreak havoc."

"But he is not a husband in the true sense of the word. Is he?" she added, a trifle uncertainly.

"Most certainly not," Frances replied roundly. "You know I hate the sight of him. And now I love Robert I could not bear to sleep with another man."

"But surely you and Carr have not . . ."

Anne Turner paused delicately and the Countess blushed. "No, not yet. But I fear – what am I saying? – I mean I hope that it won't be too long. That is why, my dear, I want you to take me to your Cunning Man. He has a fearsome reputation in dealing with matrimonial matters."

Mrs Turner nodded her blonde head. "He certainly has. He also has a reputation for taking his clients to bed." She laughed, a little nervously.

"Well, he won't get anywhere with me," Frances answered with asperity. And in that moment Anne saw her determination, her ruthlessness in achieving what she wanted regardless of the cost.

In this way Frances was introduced to Simon Forman, a man who combined the art of medicine with that of magic. An astrologer, a clairvoyant, and most of all a sympathetic listener, she begged him to make Robert Carr love her passionately and at the same time render her husband totally incapable in the bedchamber. She also asked, though this in the greatest secrecy, that the Earl of Essex should die, thus leaving her free to marry again should she so desire.

Then, in the following spring, while still married to the lugubrious Earl, she and Robert met in secret at his house in London. She arrived by coach, heavily veiled, and was immediately shown into the salon. Awaiting her, in a frenzy of love, was the young nobleman, gorgeously attired as was customary but today not caring how he looked, determined, as he was, to get her upstairs to see his wonderful bed.

As soon as the servants had left the room he started to kiss her, wildly and voluptuously, knowing that she would weaken under such a barrage.

"Sweetheart," he said, close to her ear. "Oh, my darling, I want you so badly."

"But . . ." Frances protested half-heartedly.

"But what?"

"I am still married."

"To that miserable fool. To hell with him."

Robert was more aroused than he had ever been before. All his life he had found men more attractive than women but now he was in the throes of a desire so strong that it was barely containable. Turning Frances round he headed purposefully for the door.

"Where are you going?" she asked him

"There's only one place for us to go. To the bedroom."

"Oh, Robert, I'm afraid."

"So am I," he answered truthfully, making her laugh.

But once inside his bedchamber, the door locked safely behind them, she stared in wonderment at his beautiful bed.

"Oh, God's truth," she exclaimed. "I have never seen anything so glorious."

"Do you refer to me or my bed?" he asked, half seriously.

She moved round to face him. "Both," she said.

Afterwards, when they lay entwined, naked as on the day of their birth, she shuddered a little.

"What's the matter? Did I hurt you?"

"A bit. But it was worth every second."

"You belong to me now, Frances Essex."

"Don't call me by that name. I hate it. Call me Howard."

"But the Howards hate me," said Robert ruefully.

"One day they won't."

"It will take a magic spell to make them change their minds."

"Well, who knows, that might even happen."

Overbury was beside himself with anger. He was positive that his friend was deeply besotted with the wretched Howard woman, despite all his warnings of dire peril if Robert continued to associate with her.

"Abandon the bitch now," had become his war cry.

But he misinterpreted the situation. Robert had for the first time in his life fallen deeply in love – physically, mentally, and every other way. He now had one goal and that was to marry Frances as soon as she could obtain a divorce.

Things came to a head between the two men in the following March. Returning to his rooms in Whitehall in the small hours, having spent the evening in the embrace of Frances, Robert was horrified to find Overbury pacing up and down in the Privy Gallery through which he had to pass.

"Are you still here?" he asked angrily.

"Am I here? Where have you been?"

Brushing him aside, Carr went on his way only to have Overbury shout at him, "Will you never leave the company of that base woman?"

"I haven't seen her," muttered Robert.

"It is too manifest," Thomas screamed at him.

Carr wheeled about, his face livid, but Overbury was in full spate. "The King has bestowed great honours and gifts upon you and you overthrow yourself and all your fortunes in the company of that base woman. As you clearly intend to ruinate yourself I think it best if I have nothing further to do with you."

"So be it," growled Robert.

But Thomas was not done yet. "If you would kindly pay me the

£1,500 you owe me then our obligations to one another are at an end. You must stand as you can, and I shall shift for myself. Good night to you." And he stormed off in a towering rage.

"Prick," yelled Robert at his departing back.

"The man is dangerous," said Frances when told of the incident next day.

"No, darling. Difficult perhaps, but not actually menacing."

"He might try and stop my suit for nullity going through."

"On what grounds?"

"On the grounds that you and I committed adultery, a fact which he knows well."

"It would be his word against ours."

"He would dig up other witnesses from somewhere."

Furthermore, thought Robert, Thomas Overbury has been thwarted in his love for me and will never forgive Frances as long as he lives. While Frances, unaware of what her lover was thinking, considered the fact that Thomas might yet reassert his power over Robert and send her packing.

"It would be better for all of us if the man could be spirited away," said Carr quietly.

"I could try and get someone to murder him," Frances remarked brightly.

Robert Carr, Viscount Rochford, merely laughed, thinking that she spoke in jest. But actually the Countess of Essex was in earnest, even going so far as to approach Sir David Wood – a Scotsman with a grudge against Overbury. Unfortunately he refused point blank, saying, "I might be accounted a great fool, Madam, if upon a woman's word I should go to Tyburn."

In the end it was the King himself who provided the solution. He decided that Overbury was to be offered an ambassadorship abroad, thus removing him and his potential for making trouble, yet at the same time treating him very fairly, for to be created ambassador was considered a good promotion.

Strangely, Overbury decided to be defiant. He believed that if he went overseas he would fade into obscurity. His prospects in England were far better, he argued. In view of the King's dislike of him and the fact that Carr had fallen out with him, this was very odd reasoning, to say the least. Yet Thomas would not budge, probably thinking that Carr was behind it all and wanted him out of the way. The possibility of blackmailing

Robert – a difficult thing to do from a distance – had also crossed his mind.

King James was thrown into an almost uncontrollable rage by Thomas Overbury's contemptuous refusal of his offer.

"How dare that arrogant upstart treat me with such derision, Carr? You know I did this for you and I thought it a brave way of saving Overbury's face. And now the poxy pillcock has turned down my offer. I'll have him for this, mark my words."

The spittle was running down from the King's mouth, a sign that he was labouring under some great emotion. Robert, not so keen these days on giving his Majesty whorish looks and flirtatious glances, felt genuinely alarmed. Yet alongside this alarm there rose a ray of hope.

"What do you mean, Sire?"

"I'll call him before the Council and then send him to the Tower. I'll teach him to treat me with disrespect."

Robert was so overcome that he had to sit down suddenly, despite the King being present. So their problem was going to be solved for them. Overbury was to be condemned to imprisonment.

James looked at him from a little eye. "And what do you have to say to that, eh, my Carr?"

"I say good riddance."

"I think it well if you take to your bed for a few days, Robert. And when the news does come to you, plead ignorance."

"I will, Sire, never fear." And Carr kissed the royal hand more fervently that he had done for the last several months.

At long last Frances's marriage was declared null and void. But what a terrible time she had had to endure in order to obtain her objective. The entire Howard clan had been thrown into a panic when the Court of Commissioners had insisted that she be investigated by midwives and ladies of rank to see whether she was "virgo intacta". The fact that she was having an affair with Carr was common knowledge among the family so they had substituted another girl – very young and heavily veiled – to undergo the examination. However the head of the commissioners, Archbishop Abbot, had expressed doubt about the proceedings, but once again the King had intervened. He had issued an order that each commissioner was to vote whether he was for or against the annulment without stating his reasons. Seven to five voted in favour of the Countess's marriage being annulled.

The populace at large were vaguely amused by it all and some wit wrote a ditty which went into common circulation:

This dame was inspected, but fraud interjected,
A maid of more perfection
Whom the midwives did handle, whilst the knight held the candle,
O there was a clear inspection.
Now all foreign writers, cry out on those mitres
That allow this for virginity
And talk of ejection and want of erection,
O there is sound divinity!

Seventeen days after Thomas Overbury was admitted to the Tower, the Governor, Sir William Wade, was dismissed and Sir Gervase Elwes was appointed in his place. Behind this extraordinary turn of events lay the hand of the Earl of Northampton, great-uncle to Frances and himself very attracted to Robert Carr. No sooner had this happened than Richard Weston, a shady character who had once worked for Mrs Anne Turner and who had latterly helped Frances and Robert to meet in secret places, was appointed as Thomas's gaoler.

Shortly after this, Mrs Turner sent for Weston to come to Whitehall to meet the Countess of Essex, as she still then was. She asked him to give Overbury "a water", insisting that Weston did not take it himself. He suspected at once it was poison but on his way to administer it he was stopped by Sir Gervase Elwes. Weston was then approached by a strange man called Franklin in the White Lion on Tower Hill, who enquired about Overbury's health. Weston told him that the man was far from well and had to have enemas regularly. Franklin immediately suggested that a strange apothecary would come and give him a poisoned glister, or enema. Weston promptly reported the matter to Sir Gervase.

Right from the start of his imprisonment, Thomas had been writing to Robert in letters that showed he had no conception of how deeply wounded Carr had been by his references to Frances. Instead he spoke blithely of plans to get him out of the Tower, most of them saying how sick he was, indeed fit to expire. In a welter of self-deception, he begged Carr to say that he – Robert – would die of a broken heart if Thomas were not released. In other letters still he tried to manage Carr's affairs, just as he once had long ago. But his greatest mistake was to refer to Frances as a "catopard"; a derogatory term that he had used about her when Robert merely regarded the girl as a plaything.

Meanwhile a steady stream of tarts and jellies had been arriving at the Tower, purporting to come from Robert. But, shortly, other foodstuffs arrived, from the Countess of Essex. Elwes kept these particular tarts, which were a bright green in shade, in the Tower kitchen and noted that after a day or two they had turned black and foul. While the jellies, left standing, grew fur on them. Then came the day when she sent another batch of emerald green tarts, this time accompanied by a letter. In it she insisted that Sir Gervase should not allow his wife or children to taste the tarts or jelly, and that they were to be given to Thomas Overbury. "Do this at night and all will be well," she concluded.

That evening, lying next to Robert in the great and beautiful bed, she whispered, "Darling, why do you write to Overbury? Surely you must hate him as much as I do."

There was a silence, so profound that she thought her lover must have dropped off to sleep, but eventually he spoke in the darkness.

"No, I don't hate him. I just wish he weren't such an arrogant bullying creature. I truly hoped that being in prison would make him see sense and that he would swear allegiance to your family. But he continues to write in his old vein; ordering me about and . . ."

His voice died away.

"Insulting me?" asked Frances.

Carr propped himself up on one elbow. "I didn't say that."

"No, but you meant it. Oh, sweetheart, I fear that fellow. I fear his influence even from the heart of the Tower."

"What influence, pray?"

"That he will poison you against me. That he will regain his place in your heart."

"Never," answered Robert forcefully. "I swear to you that he shall never do that."

"All the same I wish he were dead and leaving us all in peace."

"Shush. You are not to say such things."

"But I think them."

The final straw in the relationship between the imprisoned Overbury and Robert Carr came in August. Thomas's brother-in-law, Sir John Lidcote wrote to him and told him of a visit he had made to Carr. Having read the letter Overbury, much enfeebled since his commital to the Tower, made a gesture of despair.

"What's the matter with you?" asked Weston, who had just come into the room.

"It's Carr. He's played me false. Listen to this. My brother-in-law told him of my plight in this place and the fellow gave a counterfeit sigh. And then do you know what he did?"

"No."

"He grinned widely in Lidcote's face. Just couldn't help smiling. And to think of my miserable condition and the number of times I have begged him to help free me. Why, I would like to kill the bastard."

"No chance of that," remarked Weston dourly.

"Indeed, indeed," replied Overbury heavily. "But at least I can put pen to paper. That is if I had any."

"I'll get you some," Weston answered, suffering an unusual moment of pity for the shambling wreck that Overbury was fast becoming.

Later he took the letter to be posted without telling Sir Gervase Elwes, little realizing that its contents would finally give Robert Carr a motive for murder, because in it Overbury threatened to expose all the secrets he and Carr had shared over the years, ending with the ominous words, "Thus, if you deal thus wickedly with me, I have provided, whether I die or live, your nature shall never die, nor leave to be the most odious man alive." He also stated that he had made copies of this indictment and sent it out to all his "friends noble".

Knowing that the contents of the letter would send Frances into a frenzy, Robert did not show it to her. But going about the Court as usual he heard nothing to make him believe that Overbury had kept his word and written to various noblemen. On the contrary, everyone was cheerful and nobody mentioned a word about receiving such a libellous document. Carr concluded that Thomas simply had threatened in vain.

But the sands of time were running out for Thomas Overbury; that arrogant bully was now seriously ill. Throughout the month of August, 1613, his condition slowly deteriorated. According to Weston, his gaoler, Thomas had a large sore on his back which he kept covered with a plaster. Apparently the changing of this caused him so much pain that he would shout and swear when Weston did it.

At the end of the month Sir John Lidcote wrote to Robert that it was virtually impossible to contact Overbury and asked if he knew anything about it. Then, almost immediately, Carr was informed that the wretched man's condition was deteriorating fast. He immediately wrote to Dr Mayerne – who was visiting Bath at the time – and told him of the situation. The physician replied that he was sorry but there was nothing he could do at the moment. Might it not be better perhaps if Overbury wrote to him direct describing his symptoms.

But the time for writing letters was almost over. On the morning of the 14th September, Overbury begged Weston for an enema.

"It might ease me a little."

Weston looked noncommittal, his usual expression. "Aye, it might. Shall I ask Paul de Loubell, Dr Mayerne's apothecary, to make you one up?"

"If you wouldn't mind."

Two hours later an apothecary's boy had come into the room where Overbury lay, looking quite ghastly.

"You're wanting an enema, Sir?"

"Oh, God, yes. I'm in a terrible state and I'm hoping it might afford me some relief."

"Should do, Sir. Now let's to your arse."

"What's your name?" asked Weston as the boy administered the glister.

"William, Sir."

"Do you know what you are doing?"

The boy had given him a look from the eyes of a leopard. "Oh, yes, sir. I know what I am doing very well."

That evening, as Weston lay fitfully slumbering, he heard the most terrible cry from Overbury's room. Going to him he saw that the man had thrown himself half out of bed.

"What's up?" he asked laconically.

But he had to bend over Overbury to hear the reply, which came from a mouth with the lips drawn back and upwards in a kind of terrible snarl.

"I am in agony, man. For the love of Christ, help me."

"Where does it hurt you?"

"Everywhere. I have never known pain like it."

"I can change the plaster on your back if you like."

Overbury nodded. "It might help me. Can you do it beneath the bedclothes?"

"I can try."

Fumbling about beneath the sheets Weston did his best to follow Thomas's instructions as to where the ulcer was, but when sticking the plaster down he heard Overbury give vent to a terrible oath as he touched the place where it was situated. He pulled back.

"That's the best I can do."

There was no answer. Weston looked down and saw that Thomas had closed his eyes, but not peacefully. Instead there was an agonized expression on his face.

Throughout that night the gaoler kept close watch, listening to the screams and groans of the sick man. He even moved him to another bed to see if this might ease his sufferings. As dawn broke Overbury spoke to him in a feeble voice.

"Weston, go and buy me some beer, I beg of you. I have such a thirst that I think it will kill me if I don't drink."

The gaoler, paid creature of Mrs Anne Turner, took another look at the prisoner, then did what was necessary. After that he went out of the Tower for fifteen minutes. When he returned he was greeted by death. For the corpse of Thomas Overbury lay alone in the chamber to which he had been brought exactly four months previously. It was finished.

The wedding was one of the most splendid the court could remember. It took place on 26th December, 1613, exactly three months after the death in the Tower. Celebrated in the Chapel Royal at Whitehall – where Frances had married the Earl of Essex, her first husband – the service was conducted by the same man, the Bishop of Bath and Wells. Frances played the part of virgin bride by wearing her hair loose, Robert Carr – who a month before had been raised to the status of Earl of Somerset – was dressed resplendently. It was indeed a sight to behold.

The marriage was followed by extravagant festivities. A specially written masque was performed, then came dancing in which both bride and groom took part. The couple finally got to bed at about three o'clock in the morning, utterly exhausted and too tired for consummation. Acting on a whim, the new Earl had had the great bed dismantled and reassembled in his apartments at Whitehall. So that when Frances finally entered the room she exclaimed aloud in delighted surprise. And later when the groom was brought in surrounded by his male attendants, he found her sitting up in it, smiling at him.

"Oh, sweetheart, you've brought our bed here," she whispered as the last one left the room.

"Yes, goodnight, darling."

And she laughed a little as she saw that he had immediately fallen asleep.

The celebrations went on interminably. At court the entire twelve days of Christmas were taken up with masques and feasting, while poets wrote verses praising the bride's beauty and purity. On New Year's Day a tournament was held in which the teams wore the colours of either bride or bridegroom, while on the 4th January the entire court rode through the streets of London to feast with the Lord Mayor. The bridegroom went on horseback, Frances rode in a brand new coach, richly ornamented, drawn by a team of horses presented to the Earl as an additional wedding present.

It seemed as if nothing could ever go wrong for this glittering couple. Robert had made up his quarrel with Frances's family and still stood high in the King's estimation. He had estates, money, a key position, and, above all, a wife with whom he was deeply in love. Life had never been more worth living. And yet, somewhere, a worm began to turn.

Making his summer progress through the country, the King stayed at Apethorpe in Northamptonshire. And it was there that he first set eyes on George Villiers. It was love at first sight undeniably. James had never seen such a vision. For George's face and hands were effeminate yet handsome, his hair hung in chestnut curls, he was tall and well made. From that moment on the star of Robert Carr, Earl of Somerset, began to go into the descendent.

Robert's many enemies met at Baynard's Castle, four Earls being amongst their number. They determined, almost gleefully, to use Villiers to bring Carr down. They decided to clothe George, giving him spending money. The impecunious young man, owner of one threadbare suit, was now dressed in the very latest fashion. He was young, he was attractive, he was gleaming with self-awareness. At long last the Earl of Somerset had been outshone.

Furiously, Robert did everything to block his rival's rise to power. But to no avail. He had finally met his match.

"But, sweetheart," said Frances, who had been sitting patiently listening to her husband's complaints for a good thirty minutes, "surely you should try and win the King's favour back."

"I do try."

"I beg to differ. You sulk and show him open fury. You will never gain his love again like that."

Much to her surprise, her husband rounded on her. "How dare you? I know the King of old. Leave the way he is handled to me, if you please."

"Certainly," Frances replied, and stalked out of the room.

But walking down the corridor she had a frightening experience. She thought that something moved in the shadows, a dark shapeless thing.

"Overbury!" she exclaimed. And just for a second the thing took form and raised its hand at her before it vanished.

Frances ran to the bedroom and flung herself down on the bed – that wonderful bed that had accompanied her throughout her love affair with Robert Carr. She felt cold and afraid as if something unknown were rising from the grave to come and taunt her. Turning, she looked up at the woodwork but all she could see was the face of a grinning satyr.

By that summer, with George Villiers now knighted and made a Gentleman of the Bedchamber, something else, something far worse, began to worry Robert Carr. A whispering campaign had started about the death of Thomas Overbury. Talk of poison and poisoners was spreading, and all this nearly two years after the event. It occurred to the Earl of Somerset almost at once that his enemies at court had deliberately rekindled the old scandal.

Meanwhile Mrs Anne Turner, Frances's friend and confidante, to say nothing of Frances herself, was growing distinctly worried. It was widely believed that Richard Weston had been working for them and that he had insisted on being paid for his services – namely the demise of the prisoner. Had he anything to do with Overbury's death or was he demanding payment under false pretences? He continued to badger the women who had supplied him with the green tarts until the time when, in order to keep him quiet, they gave him £100 in gold, followed by another four score pounds, also in gold, both sums paid to him by Mrs Turner.

In the spring of 1615 Frances felt certain that she had become pregnant and removed herself to Greys, near Henley. Mrs Turner, who had moved in with the Somersets a short time after their marriage, accompanied her. Walking in the garden, certain that they could not be overheard, they conversed.

"My dear Anne, what are we going to do?"

"I have no idea, my dear Frances. After all, we did send in the green tarts."

"Not to mention the jelly. It was full of poison as you know."

"We must just deny everything and hope that these wretched rumours will stop."

Frances Somerset burst into tears and stamped her foot. "Horrible Thomas Overbury! He will make trouble for us yet, I swear it."

Mrs Turner made no reply but simply pursed her lips and walked steadfastly on.

Robert Carr, Earl of Somerset, had now grown frantic. He had sought from King James a pardon which would absolve him of crimes he had previously committed. But though the King seemed willing enough to sign it, it had come unstuck before the Council when the Lord Chancellor had refused to seal it. The King had become angry and had walked out of the meeting, straight to the Queen, who had, hating Somerset as she did, put the final nail into the coffin and told James not to sign.

Shortly after, His Majesty left on his summer progress. And it was while he was staying at Beaulieu that news reached him of the fact that Sir Gervase Elwes had set down an account of the events leading up to the death of Sir Thomas Overbury. Having thus been informed, it left James no option but to order a full enquiry into the death of the prisoner.

The Lord Chief Justice himself, Sir Edward Coke, who seemed to be everybody's enemy, headed the investigation, driven by his own desire to punish Somerset. He interviewed hundreds of people, everyone from the highest to the lowest – well, almost the lowest – determined to capture the big fish via the little minnows.

In mid-September Richard Weston was arrested and confessed that he had been given a phial of greenish liquid by a Doctor Franklin, a quack that both Frances and Mrs Turner had consulted to aid them with their respective love affairs. That night Franklin was summoned to the Whitehall apartments of the Countess. As he entered the room, Robert Carr, who was present with his wife, gave him a dark look and walked out, leaving him alone with the two women.

"Weston has been taken into custody," said Frances hysterically.

She looked terrible; pale, her hair wild, her body swollen by the child she was carrying.

"How very regrettable," Franklin answered, not knowing quite what else to say.

"Regrettable! It's a tragedy," she answered. "You will be next, Franklin, mark my words, and you must deny everything. If you confess anything you will be hanged. By God, if you confess, you shall be hanged for me, for I will not be hanged."

"No, Madam," said Mrs Turner in a quiet voice, "I will be hanged for you both."

Frances did not reply but left the room. In the silence that followed they could hear her speaking through the wall, and Robert answering her. When she came back again she looked slightly calmer and warned Franklin again about remaining silent when being questioned.

He bowed and left. Two days later both he and Mrs Turner were arrested and questioned.

That night, climbing into their bed, Frances and Robert hugged each other like two children.

"What shall we do?" she asked him in a tiny, frightened voice.

"Deny," he answered. "We must deny everything."

"But Weston will tell them about the green tarts, about the jelly, about the apothecaries . . ."

"Say no more, not even between these walls. All we can do is swear they are liars."

"I'm terrified, Robert."

"We should have thought of that before," he answered bitterly.

Like a rat in a trap, the Earl of Somerset did everything to defend himself; burning letters, writing to Overbury's servant, pleading with the King, objecting to the panel of commissioners investigating the case. But all to no avail. On 17 October an order was made placing him under house arrest in his apartments at Whitehall. Frances – now seven months pregnant – was similarly confined to a room in Greys.

Now, it seemed, that Overbury reached from the grave and claimed his victims. Weston was hanged by the neck until he was dead; Sir Thomas Monson, a shadowy figure who had worked behind the scenes assisting the Countess of Somerset, was arrested pending trial; Sir Gervase Elwes was stripped of office and placed in confinement; Mrs Anne Turner was taken into custody, James Franklin, the quack doctor, likewise. Somerset himself was transferred to the Tower. Because of Frances's pregnancy she was placed under house arrest in the care of Sir William Smithie, a London alderman. She was now completely isolated.

The trial of Mrs Turner proved sensational because various magic dolls were produced, all coming from the time when she and Frances had consulted cunning men about their love affairs. But in the eyes of the public it meant that she was a sorceress, a dabbler in the black arts, and it was hardly surprising when the jury found her guilty. Thomas Overbury had his second victim.

Sir Gervase Elwes was hanged, swiftly, because one of his servants took hold of one foot while the hangman's assistant tugged the other. There was a general feeling that no one thought he deserved the verdict. James Franklin was sent to the gallows and died muttering as the cart was driven away and he was left hanging. Four people had now gone to the grave.

On 9th December Frances gave birth to a baby girl after a normal confinement. The child was christened Anne a few days later. Then, on 4 April, 1616, the Countess and her daughter were parted, for the mother was taken to the Tower pending the court hearing. She lived separately from her husband – who had yet to see his baby – and it was elected that she would be the first to go to trial, to be prosecuted by no less than Sir Francis Bacon. As she entered court every man present drew breath for that day she looked radiantly beautiful. She held up her hand for the reading of the indictment.

"Frances, Countess of Somerset, what sayest thou? Art though guilty of this felony and murder, or not guilty."

Curtseying to the Lord Chancellor, the Countess uttered a single word in a low voice, wondrous fearful. "Guilty," she said.

That, you may feel, was the end of the story. The Earl and Countess of Somerset were both found guilty and condemned to die, she by the rope and he by the axe. But, strange as it may seem, they received royal pardons and eventually walked free from the Tower.

What does that mean? Had Overbury been murdered or had he died of an illness contracted in the Tower? Had all the so-called evidence been doctored by Coke in his determination to condemn Somerset?

And what of me? You see, I was the smallest player. No one asked me what happened, but I knew all the facts.

Poor little Frances. She supplied green tarts and jellies to the prisoner, but they were intercepted by Elwes and never eaten. They were each and all so convinced of the parts they played that they trapped themselves by their own guilt.

So did anyone kill Thomas Overbury, I hear you ask?

Indeed. I killed him, dead as pork.

I, William Reeve, apprentice to Paul de Loubell, the apothecary who made up prescriptions for Dr Mayerne.

On the way to the Tower to give Sir Thomas an enema, I was approached by a shifty fellow – I have no idea who he was – and given a substance which I was asked to substitute for the one I was carrying. He offered me £20, more money than I could earn in years. So I did. I applied the enema right under the eyes of Weston, who had no idea what was really happening.

Then I fled to Paris and stayed there for several years until the whole affair was over, before returning to London and setting myself up as an apothecary. I heard the whole story from my master, Paul de Loubell, just before he died, and I have set it down for you as he told it to me.

Yet even he did not know the truth about my part in the affair. Now you alone know how I outwitted them all, even the greatest in the land. Will you find it in your heart to forgive me?

"O, POISONOUS WEED!"

F. GWYNPLAINE MACINTYRE

The first English colony in the Americas was established at Roanoke, Virginia, in 1585. They were ill prepared and when food ran out the colonists returned to England, thanks to Francis Drake. However he left several men behind but these vanished and were never heard from again. One of the native Americans connected to the colony was Powhatan whose daughter, Matoaka – better known as Pocahontas – became famous when she saved the life of Captain John Smith. However Pocahontas's death in 1617 at the age of only 21 is itself something of a mystery. F. Gwynplaine MacIntyre uses both these puzzles as the basis for the following story.

MacIntyre (b.1948) is the author or co-author of several books, including the science-fiction novels The DNA Disaster *(1991) and* The Woman Between the Worlds *(1994). His non-fiction has been published in* The New York Daily News, Literary Review, Games Magazine *and many British and US publications. In 2003, he was short-listed for the Montblanc/Spectator Award for his arts journalism.*

27 August 1587 (Old Style)
Hatarask Island
Cittie of Ralegh, Virginia

"You die here, if I abandon you," Governor White told the assemblage.

"We perish here, if you remain," vowed Ananias Dare. "The colony is doomed, without sufficience for the coming winter. Only you, of all our number, can persuade England's support for our enterprise. You can convince Thomas Harriot to finance the victualling of a ship to provision our colony. If you remain here, and another of us – lacking your talents of persuasion – should return to England in your stead, our beseechings will go unanswered."

"Here is the compact, sir." Dyonis Harvie stepped forth, and pressed a vellum scroll into White's unwilling hands. "Every man of our colony has signed his name, or made his mark, to show you leave us at our urging. 'Tis no abandonment."

John White hesitated, rejecting the scroll.

"Take it, father," spoke Elenor Dare from the doorway of her hut at the southern limb of the four-pointed palisado. The wife of Ananias was giving suck to her child, birthed only nine days ago and baptized four days later. By God's grace, Virginia Dare – John White's grandchild – was the first Christian born in this new land. But not the last. In the next hut along the palisado, still recovering from childbirth, lay Dyonis Harvie's wife Margery, nursing their new son Dionysus, two days old and not yet christened.

"The tide is high, sir, and the moon is quartering," said Nicholas Johnson. "If you leave now, you have moonlight for the first three se'n-nights of your journey back to England. If you tarry, it goes the worse for us all."

Reluctantly, John White accepted the scroll bearing his fellows' signatures, testifying that his departure was at their request, and in no wise a cowardice. Sadly, he took one more look round the compound, at these goodwives and artisans assembled.

This enterprise should have prospered. John White had selected men and women endowed with a wide range of talents and trades, to ensure this colony's fortune. He himself was a surveyor, painter and tiler. His son-in-law Ananias Dare was a bricklayer. Nicholas Johnson and his brother Henry had been stonemasons in London: now this island Hatarask had proved to possess no stone worth the quarrying, but there was much red clay . . . and the Johnson brothers had swiftly built a kiln, to bake the clay into bricks. Ambrose Viccars and John Spendlove were tanners, James Hynde and the Wyles brothers were blacksmiths, whilst Griffen Jones was a gunsmith and cannoneer. A dozen of the men beside were skilled hunters, and the women were wise in the crafts of farming and crabbing and building fish-weirs. The nine boys of this colony – not counting newborn Dionysys, of course – were willing and true.

To one side of the delegation stood a tall man the colour of burnished bronze, clad in a dressed leather cloak. He was a native of this savage and unchristened land, yet the proud Manteo was both an honest Christian and a nobleman into the bargain. Fourteen days ago, John White had baptized Manteo into the Protestant faith, and dubbed him Lord of Roanoke, in honour of the nearby island where his people the Croatoans dwelt.

Now, solemnly, John White clasped each man's hand in turn. He kissed Elenor, stroked the fine hair of her infant daughter: his first grandchild, but – God willing – not his last.

"Farewell, father," said Elenor Dare.

"Not farewell," said John White. "I will return."

To his son-in-law Ananias Dare – joined in marriage to Elenor on Christmas Day, two years past – Commander White spoke tersely: "You remember the token?"

Ananias nodded. "If our colony is forced by privation to leave this fort, I will carve our destination on the gatepost. Now hasten to England, and speed your return."

Governor White strode across the compound, to the edge of the palisado where Manteo stood with one other red-skinned native, his manservant Towaye. "Lord Manteo," ventured White, "I hope that your kinsmen will help protect our colony if Powhatan threatens."

Manteo had voyaged to England twice over, and dwelt more than eighteen months there, mastering the grammar. "My mother Mishcosk is chieftain of our Croatoans," he said now. "If Powhatan or the warriors of Dasamongupuek move southward upon us, you may rely on my kinsmen's aid."

The two men clasped arms. John White took one last look – no; it must not never be his *last* look – round the desperate palisado.

The flyboat *Peradventure* awaited, but the tide would not linger. He pocketed the vellum, and hurried toward the western gate.

With favourable winds and proper navigation – a backstaff to quarter the latitude, and a good log-line and sandglass to estimate the longitude – White was confident that his flyboat could reach Plymouth in six weeks, and another six for the return to Hatarask. He tried not to contemplate what Walter Ralegh had told him in April, before the colonists' departure: namely, that Philip of Spain was readying for war against England. No matter how eloquently White might plead for his colony's aid, the Queen's admirals desired that all England's ships be kept reserved for battle against the gathering Armada.

And how long would that war last? John White trembled as he saw the two masts of his waiting flyboat. His return to this alien shore might be delayed for several *years* . . .

18 August 1590
Hatarask Island
This date held grim significance, as John White well knew. As he knelt in the thwarts of the *Hopewell*'s tiltboat, scanning the shore for any signs of habitation, he reviewed – a thousandth time – the events of the past three years, and as well the past three days.

As he had feared, Spain's armada had delayed his return to Virginia. At last, freshly victualled and provisioned, White had hired the galleon *Hopewell* and the consort *Moonlight* to convey himself and his equipments to the desperate colony. Three days ago, they had anchored in five fathoms off Roanoke's treacherous coast. Smoke was seen rising from the island, and White had felt the first stirrings of hope that his daughter and granddaughter might yet be alive.

By next morning, the smoke had oddly moved south. A watch-fire? The *Hopewell*'s master gunner fired off chain-shot, yet received no reply from the island. Governor White anguished while the two ships' captains commanded their men to take on fresh water, wasting a full day without relieving the colony. Yesterday, two tiltboats had made for the shore . . . but a sudden northeaster had raised huge swells against the shoals, swamping both vessels. Captain Spicer of the *Moonlight*, with his master's mate Ralph Skinner, and five more men beside were swiftly drowned. Abraham Cocke, commander of the

Hopewell, delayed the rescue mission another day until the northeaster subsided.

Now, finally, blessedly, the shore was near . . . on the eighteenth of August, precisely three years to the very day since the birth of Governor White's granddaughter Virginia Dare. He urgently bent to the oars with Cocke's crewmen, speeding the tiltboat toward's Hatarask's northern shore. Now they were beached, and White seized his wheel-lock pistol as he and Cocke scrabbled upshore to the hill.

The colony's walled enclosure Fort Ralegh was shaped like a four-pointed star. It was a goodly fortress – with bulwarks and a surrounding barrow ditch – having been built five years ago by the soldiers of Ralegh's first colony here: a contingent of menfolk only, under the command of Ralph Lane and Thomas Harriot. John White had taken part in that original endeavour, and he well remembered when Lane's colonists quitted this place in June 1586. But White's only thought as he crested the hill was: what lives and souls would he find here *now?*

The palisado was overgrown with vines and shrubs. With Abraham Cocke at his heels, White circled to the western point of the star: the landward side, and so the only entrance. The gates of the fortress stood open.

"Elenor!" shouted White. "Manteo! Dare! Johnson! Spendlove! *Anyone!* As you love Christ, give answer!"

A raven cawed. The wind stirred the vines.

The Roanoke colony was not merely deserted: it was abandoned. In the storehouse, thick with weeds, White and Cocke found a man's skeleton.

One man only, of one hundred and seventeen colonists?

The huts were empty. The hearths contained no ashes. A half-built kiln stood unmortared.

At the centre of the compound, the weeds grew blood-red. Blood? No; *rust*. With shouts, the arriving sailors of the *Hopewell*'s tiltboat discovered several articles that had lain here long neglected: a dozen iron bars, four fowlers, two pigs of lead, some quantities of sack-shot and locker-shot. All flung about as if by madmen. Or by savages?

In the brown clayed soil beneath his own hut, White had secreted certain items against his return, buried in five wooden chests. Now, entering the weed-grown house, White found a ravaged ditch. In the hole were the remnants of the chests, all a-flindered. In horror, White recognized the portions of his own suit of armour, now rusted. His precious books, his manuscripts, his sketches of this island's fauna . . . all these lay wallowed in algae and old rainwater.

None of the colonists, himself aside, had known that Governor White had buried these things here. Yet someone had found them, and scattered White's most valued possessions, in search of . . . *what?*

And where were his daughter and granddaughter? Or *any* of the colonists?

"You told me," said Cocke, " of an unchristened savage whose dominion is near this place."

Governor White nodded, teeth clenched. 'The native warlord, Powhatan."

At the gates, a sailor of the *Hopewell* gave shout. John White hurried forth, to see what several of the searchers were staring at.

On a tree betwixt the landing and the fort, on the eastern side of the tree's trunk – facing the sea – were carved in knife-cuts the letters CRO. That was all.

Another shout. A sailor pointed. At the entrance to the compound, someone had debarked an oak tree, exposing the pale wood beneath. Five feet above the ground, across the broad flat surface of a large bole, were cut the letters CROATOAN.

No more was found.

3 June 1616
Drake's Leat, Plymouth
"*MURDERER!*"

Their ship from Virginia had harboured, safely enough, at Sutton Pool. From there, Rolfe had secured a Cockside bargeman to convey his group upriver. The journey had gone well enough, thus far. Yet now, as they neared Plymm Bridge . . .

"*Red whore!*" screeched a voice. "*Which of you lot is Powhatan's daughter, then?*"

"Ignore those jackdaws," said John Rolfe to his companions. At his side, his young wife Rebecca – scantly twenty years old – spread her cloak to enfold their infant son Thomas, fourteen months old. Rebecca Rolfe was dressed as an Englishwoman, yet the others – her sister and half-sister, three more women beside, as well as her father's counsellor Tomacomo and four more men – were all clad in the leathers and feathers of their native land, and were an easy target for ungentle English tongues. Tomacomo especially must have made an eerie sight to Christian eyes, for his head was plucked entirely hairless, save for a single region above his left ear, where he had permitted his black hair to grow into a thick chieftain-lock reaching nearly his waist.

"*Murderer!*" the screech came again. Something dropped from Plymm Bridge – or was thrown? – but it fell far astern, as the barge had already passed beneath the bridge's stone arch.

John Rolfe glanced northwest, towards the spire of Saint Budeux's church. "I never expected this," he told his wife. "Though you are baptized a Christian, and you wear an honest Bible-name, there are people here who would charge you with the deaths at Roanoke – deaths *before you were born* – and who call you by the red name you've forsaken."

Rebecca Rolfe nodded grimly, tugging downward the wide brim of her beaverskin hat, to go less recognized. "I wish they would learn: I am no longer Pocahontas."

27 November 1616
Wakefield Tower prison

"The Wizard Earl is at his madness again," came the news at the watch, and all the sentries in the Tower of London were forewarned 'gainst the arrival of strange odours or explosions.

Henry Percy, ninth Earl of Northumberland, age fifty-two, had committed no sin against the Crown. Yet he was cousin to Thomas Percy – a conspirator in the Gunpowder Plot – and had employed the bloody Thomas on his estate at Syon House. For those reasons alone, King James had seen fit to imprison the earl in the Tower of London. Upon the King's orders to confine the earl within the multiple fortresses comprising the Tower of London, the prison's governor had assigned him to a well-aired cell on the ground floor of Martin Tower, adjoining a garden: well-aired, so as to disperse the fumes and sulphurs of his wizardries. By dint of his wealth and influence, the earl was granted also a still-room in Wakefield Tower, containing a furnace as well as a still. This room made shift to be the laboratory for the Wizard Earl's alchemic *experimenta*. Wakefield Tower has the thickest walls of any building in the Tower of

London, and so 'twould be the most standfast against the Wizard Earl's explosions and alarums. So long as he exploded no-one other than himself, his eccentric follies were tolerated.

The earl was bent over a flaming brazier and a simmering bolt's-head flask when the unlatched door of his still-room swung open and Thomas Harriot arrived, clutching a handkerchief across his nose and mouth. The foul phosphorus odour arising from the earl's newest *experimentum* was one reason for the presence of Harriot's handkerchief. As the earl extinguished the brazier and dispersed the fumes, the second reason for the handkerchief became more evident. When Harriot lowered the cloth and revealed his face, Percy observed that his servant's disfigurement had worsened since their last meeting: the ulceration of Harriot's left nostril had spread, and now his upper lip was contorted along that side.

"My friend, 'tis well to see you," said the earl, covering his phials and alembics. "How stands Syon House?"

"Your estates are in good order, my lord," said Harriot. "See you, I've brought the books you requested from your library, and taken back the ones you have finished. I bring books for Ralegh as well, and the saltpetre you require."

"Excellent!" said the earl, eagerly accepting the proffered volumes, and a packet of saltpetre crystals. "And my visitors from America? Have you given them the comforts of my estate?"

"Witness for yourself, my lord." Through the open door came a tall man, thirtyish, with piercing blue eyes. He gently escorted a woman ten years younger, clad in a long black cloak and tall beaver hat. Her cheekbones were high and prominent, her eyes slightly obliqued. "My lord," said Harriot to the earl, "I have the honour of presenting . . ."

"You must be John Rolfe," said Percy to the newcomer, interrupting Harriot. "And this dark-eyed lady is your wife, the famous Pocahontas."

Rolfe bristled slightly at this name, but his wife remained stoic. "I have never understood," she said gently, "why that name, and not my other, is so famed in England." The foreign-born young woman spoke with a slight tendency to lean upon hard consonants, but her English was clear. "Yes, among my blood-folk, 'Pocahontas' was my along-name . . . you say *nickname*? But my father Powhatan named me Matoaka, so that is my birth-name.

And I am baptized into your church, so I pray you call me by my christen-name. I am my husband's wife, Rebecca Rolfe."

As she spoke, the former Pocahontas inclined her head slightly and doffed her hat, revealing two long plaits of raven-black hair, and magnificent earrings of white mussel-shells. Harriot stiffened, and John Rolfe observed his manservant's upper lip curling slightly in contempt . . . or was this due to the spreading ulcer at Harriot's nose?

"I must ask you to speak a bit louder," said Thomas Harriot, while Henry Percy cupped a hand to his right ear. "My lord the earl is slightly deaf, in cost of the explosions which his experiments produce."

Now the meeting that ensued was largely of commerce. John Rolfe had done much to introduce one of America's tobaccos – the Varina broadleaf – to England: an endeavour financed by the earl's patronage. The terms of Lord Percy's imprisonment allowed him nearly everything he could afford excepting his liberty, and so Harriot brought him frequent visitors. Rolfe now gave report of the success of his tobacco crops. Normally, any news of the outer world fascinated the inmate Percy, yet now he waved aside Rolfe's comments and gazed at Rolfe's wife as if enchanted by her alien beauty.

"My dear Pocahontas: forgive the liberty, but that is the name by which I have read of you," the earl began. "Speaking as a man, I am intrigued by your grace and beauty. Speaking as a scientist, I am intrigued by your earrings. They are *white* mussel, I see: a rare species, unknown to England's shores. As my deafness grows steadily, I have come to perceive the human ears as useful chiefly for ornamentation. I have much leisure time here. Would you do me the kindness of lending me those earrings? I would mount them in silver bands, as a tribute to your beauty."

The maiden glanced at her husband, who nodded his assent. Swiftly, Rebecca Rolfe unhooked the graceful shells from her pierced lobes, and gave the earrings to the earl, who bowed as he accepted them.

"Thank you, precious lady," said Henry Percy. "Today marks the beginning of the eleventh year of my imprisonment in this tower, so you have brightened this dark anniversary. I will have my servant Harriot return these earrings to you, freshly silvered."

Harriot bowed, indicating a bundle of books beneath his arm. "Will my lord excuse me? Your friend Ralegh has requested some books as well. While you converse, I will take them to his cell across the way, in Brick Tower . . ."

Twelfth Night, 6 January 1616/7 (Old Style)
Banqueting House, Whitehall Palace
The rituals are clear in their particulars: the antimasque precedes the masque. 'Tis accustomed that the antimasque will boast of grotesque costumes and elaborate dances, whilst the costumes of the masque are traditionally lighter and less cumbersome. So, professional masquers perform the antimasque, whilst the king's favourites perform the masque afterward.

King James's current favourite was his gentleman of the bedchamber, George Villiers, whom the king had only recently – yester-noon, in fact – elevated to the title of the Earl of Buckingham. It was widely known in the court that King James had little passion for heavy dramas or low comedies, oft declaimed by English actors in accents which the Scots-born king was slow in apprehending. The monarch favoured masques which afforded opportunities for lithe young men in elegant hose and tight-fitting bullions to display their graceful limbs as they capered in sprightly dances. Of a certainty, the Earl of Buckingham would figure prominently in tonight's masque, and all would be engined to suit the king's tastes.

The Banqueting House – the tallest building in this modern London – is architected as a doubled cube, precisely twice as wide as it is broad and high. The two long sides, east and west, are tiered with high rows of benches for the spectation of His Majesty's guests. The choicest seats – at the southern end, favouring the best view of the stage on the hall's northern side – were of course on the royal dais, reserved for King James and his retinue. A seat on the king's left was reserved for his Danish queen Anne, but at present she was at the centre of the hall, dancing with the Earl of Montgomery . . . although she was a-hobbled by her gouty foot, and her movements consisted largely of waving her plumed fan. Queen Anne's overdress was of silk, in the sky-blue colour known as *watchett*, which set off her bright auburn hair. The other gentlefolk upon the green baize carpet of the dance-floor took caution to give the queen wide berth for her footings, but in truth there was room for all the company. King James had forbade all ladies at Banqueting House to wear the farthingale – "that impertinent garment", he called it – as such selfish skirts filled the whole floor, and so left less room for dancing. In the east balcony, twelve French musicians played a brisk galliard, whilst their leader Alfonso Ferrabosco kept the time with his viola. Eightscore beeswax candles shed their gleam against the gilded balls and silvered pyramids of the wall-sconces.

To the left of the king sat his son Charles, invested the Prince of Wales this recent November. Aside from the monarch himself, the place of honour was in the alcove of seats at the king's right hand, in the niche which King James in his Scots accent referred to as "the great Neech". As the musicians struck the first notes of the antimasque, it was remarked that two seats in the Neech tarried empty, for guests yet unarrived.

"*A-hall! A-hall!*" announced the footmen. This call notified any guests on the dance floor to return to their seats, and leave the way clear for the performers of the entertainment.

The antimasque had begun. Its title was "Phantasms", and the dancers personated the ghosts of poets murdered for their art. They wore grotesque skull-faced masks, and their costumes were of tight-fitting black stockingette, strategically daubed in white paint to represent the bones of the human anatomy. The make-shift skeletons capered and leapt across the green baize carpet, new-laid for dancing. The counterfeit skeletons' weird movements seemed weirder in the flickering gleam of the braziers that illumined the hall. The leader of the masquers' company, personating Lord Death, recited the antimasque's verses while his bony courtesans beckoned and swerved, wielding pikestaffs and tridents. Although Lord Death was masked, his face concealed in a vizard, his athletic form was sheathed in a costume which encased him so tightly that it served to reveal his identity rather than obscure it. Recognizing Lord Death as the king's favourite, the audience of the masque applauded. Lord Death removed his vizard, revealing the long black hair and beardless face of George Villiers, new-made Earl of Buckingham. He gave a kiss-sign to his applauding admirers, while his long graceful limbs danced a saraband.

From the wings of the stage came a many-legged she-monster,

who now squatted and gave birth to six pups, which proceeded to suckle at her paps whilst they danced in their turn. Truly, an ingenious stagecraft. The scene transformed to the bower of Zephyrus, where Peace sang of myriad pleasures. The next tableau depicted the revels of Aurora, as a chiaroscuro moon descended from above the stage.

Of a sudden, the lights went out, as footmen snuffed the braziers. In the darkness, all the guests along the tiered benches gasped and then applauded . . . for the white paint of the dancers' costumes and masks now showed a *phosphorescence*, causing the ribs and skulls and capering bones of the dancing skeletons to glow in the darkness while the musicians played on.

As the footmen brought tapers to relight the braziers, the oaken double doors at the far end of Banqueting Hall opened, and a trio of latecomers arrived. A servant stepped forth in the dark blue velvet livery of a *huisher* – King James preferred this Scottish term to "usher" – and now John Rolfe and his wife and the heathen Tomacomo were ushered to the great Neech at the king's right hand.

Throughout the hall, there was a murmuring, a huzzbuzz, as the newcomers made their way across the wide hall. Rolfe heard the muttered name "Pocahontas" several times. More darkly, he heard someone whisper "Powhatan" . . . and then a word that might have been "*killers*". He glanced quickly into the crowd of Twelfth Night revellers along the benches, yet he could not be certain of the whisper's source. Beside him, his wife coughed: from nervousness, no doubt.

In the centre of a cleared area at the far end of the hall, King James bade his guests to approach. "We meet again, Rolfe. And is this your wife, the legended Pocahontas?"

Rolfe bowed deeply, averting his gaze. "If it please Your Majesty, my wife is churched and baptized with a Christian name. She is rightly the Lady Rebecca."

"Yet *Pocahontas* is so musical a name," said the king, admiring the garb of the tawny woman. He had expected Rebecca Rolfe to arrive clad in feathers and animal skins, and was faintly disappointed to find her dressed as a fashionable Englishwoman: in crimson bodice, scarlet cloak, and an olive skirt with a dark grey underskirt. A white lace whisk encircled her throat, along with a pearl necklace, and she nervously clutched a high-crowned beaver hat. The most unusual aspects of her costume were the long plaits of her lustrous black hair, and the exquisite diadems at her ears: the jewelled ornaments, whatever they were, gleamed a-silver in the light of the braziers.

The king beckoned to a guest seated behind Prince Charles: a brawny man, above forty years old, who looked quite undistinguished . . . yet who clearly held some importance, as he was permitted to sit in the king's presence. Among the gaudy revellers of Twelfth Night, this man wore a plain black jerkin and sported a short chestnut beard tinged with grey. "We present to you, Rolfe," said the king, languidly, "the author of tonight's entertainments: our court poet, Ben Jonson."

The bearded man bowed to Rolfe's wife, and then shook Rolfe's hand. As he did so, Rolfe noticed a long T-shaped scar at the base of Ben Jonson's left thumb. "I am pleased to meet you, sir," said Ben Jonson, "and pleased the more to meet your wife . . . for I write about foreign continents and alien shores . . . and you, good lady, are the first genuine else-born whom it has ever been my honour to encounter." The daughter of Powhatan simpered at this fulsome praise, turning aside from Jonson while she stifled a cough. Her earrings glittered anew as the candle-light found a fresh angle.

"Your earrings, dear woman," said Jonson. "Might I scrutiny them?" She nodded, seating herself with her head turned sidelong so that Ben Jonson might have the best view of her left-side earlobe while her own gaze favoured His Majesty.

Ben Jonson studied Pocahontas's earrings with keen interest now. Each earring consisted of a matched pair of white mussel shells, girdled by a double hoop of fine silver. "The metal, I observe, is newly worked," said Jonson. "Yet the shells betray their age and tarnish."

Rebecca Rolfe nodded, her earrings bobbing slightly in the candle-gleam. "His grace the Earl of Northumberland hooped them for me, in his prison workshop. My husband and I are his guests at Syon House, and . . ." she broke off suddenly, noticing the sour expression on the king's face.

"Northumberland! *Bah!*" King James gestured derisively, while close to hand the skeletons capered and danced. "His father and mine were both murdered, yet he has taken nothing from the lesson. His kinsman tried to bombard my Parliament!" The king's countenance shifted, gentling his face. "But the music is sweet, hear you? Let us savour the masque."

Rebecca Rolfe most gratefully made curtsey; she had no desire to discuss politics in this place. A matched pair of liveried huishers gave haste to seat her and Tomacomo in two chairs in the Neech, near the king's hand. John Rolfe, intending to sit beside his wife, found no third chair waiting. One of the huishers pointed discreetly upward and afar, to a seat in the balcony near Ferrabosco's violinists. Rolfe grimaced; to be seated amongst French fiddlers and flautists was a clear insult, but he knew that the whims of the king were to be indulged. The foreign-born Lady Rebecca Rolfe and her father's counsellor Tomacomo were alien and exotic, and therefore King James was eager to display them to his court. John Rolfe, for all his dealings in exotic tobacco-leaf, was merely a common-born Englishman . . . and so he was exiled to sit among French pipers. With a bow to the king, as Queen Anne seated herself and placed her gouted foot upon a hassock, Rolfe withdrew to the upstairs alcove.

The antimasque had ended, the masque had begun. A curtain dropped from the fly-lofts, to reveal the cunning stage-design of Inigo Jones: a series of buildings ingeniously fashioned in perspective, so as to make a whole vast city seem presented on the brief stage. In sequence from the rear to the foreground, Inigo Jones's counterfeit edifices consisted of a tower, a scaffolded house, a church, a colonnade, and lastly a triumphal arch.

As the audience gasped and applauded, now began Ben Jonson's masque "The Vision of Delight". Actresses personating the roles of Delight, Love, Harmony – escorted by actors portraying Revel, Sport, Laughter – now bestrode the stage, declaiming verse.

The lights dimmed, and Night emerged in her winged chariot bespangled with phosphorescent stars. Assisted by some unseen apparatus, Night and her attendant the Moon rose into the fly-lofts, to the gasps and applause of all present. The lamps brightened, and a single figure took the stage: an actress in the role of Fantasy, clutching a bag which – she proudly declaimed – held all manner of dreams.

As sweet Fantasy began to list the dream-bag's contents, a courtier approached the king's bench with a tray of quaking-pudding and some spiced comfort-bread for the guests. As

Rebecca Rolfe saw these sweetmeats, she bent towards it and away from the stage, while Fantasy spoke:

> "... *dreams that have wings,*
> *And dreams that have honey, and dreams that have STINGS!*"

A sudden movement at the edge of the stage. One of the creatures in the antimasque – a dancing skeleton – entering a-sudden from the wings, clutching a pikestaff and creeping stealthily towards the king's bench. In his seat behind the Prince of Wales, Ben Jonson stiffened. "Who is that actor? His entrance is not in my script ... and I *wrote* it."

"*Pocahontas!*" rasped a voice beneath the skeleton's mask.

"*Oh!*" A gasp. In the balcony, John Rolfe leapt to his feet. Ben Jonson turned just in time to see the skull-masked skeleton moving away from Rebecca Rolfe. The dancer's pikestaff had jabbed her just above her female privities, where her overskirt and bodice met. John Rolfe shouted, and moved towards the balcony's edge ... but just as hastily, the masked figure melted into the bony throng of the suddenly returning skeleton chorus. Rolfe stared into the whirl of masquers: with their weird costumes and masked faces, it was impossible for him to perceive which of the disguised dancers had jabbed his wife.

He hastened to the Neech, where Ben Jonson had borrowed Queen Anne's ostrich-plume fan, and was fanning Lady Rebecca. As Rolfe arrived, he quickly asked: "Wife, are you injured?"

"Scantly a pricking, it was. Nearly nothing." Rebecca Rolfe smiled weakly, then coughed. She seemed suddenly faint. Her husband glanced along the tiered walls, wondering if a casement might be opened.

At that instant, there came a fanfaronade of trumpets as the scenery on the stage shifted again. There was a clattering of wooden shutters as two courtiers slid aside the backdrop of the Night's chariot ... replacing this with a series of forestscapes, in forced perspective, beseeming the woods of Arcadia.

For a moment, John Rolfe was dazzled by this bold effect. Then his wife moaned, and he looked to her. She seemed definitely ill. Nearby, a courtier muttered: "See there? The red woman Pocahontas. Daughter of the murderous Powhatan."

Rebecca Rolfe swooned. Her husband caught her as she fell, and two huishers rushed to give assistance . . .

21 March 1617
Christopher Inn,
Gravesend, Kent
Pocahontas was dying.

She had sickened on the night of the masque, and ever since Twelfth Night her health had steadily worsened. Now the ague was upon her, and a fit of coughing and shivering.

John Rolfe had made plans to transport his wife and their son back to Virginia, and a fleet had been mustered for the voyage: Samuel Argall in command of the *George*, Ralph Hamor captaining the *Treasurer*, and a pinnace besides. They had sailed downriver from London, intending to reach open sea before the winds lost their favour. But Rebecca Rolfe's ague had ripened and grown, and Rolfe had reluctantly taken his wife ashore here at Gravesend. Now the ships lay anchored in Erith Reach, by the hithe, whilst Rolfe and two sailors had brought his sickened wife to the Christopher – as its name betokened, an inn that welcomed travellers – and made her as eased as possible.

The master of the Christopher Inn – all unwitting of the ill health of Rolfe's wife – had greeted their arrival at the Gravesend hostel with a jest that was popular hereabouts: "*All men come to Grave's End soon enough.*" Then, discovering the Lady Rebecca's distress, he swiftly apologized and withdrew.

A physician was summoned: Josiah Goldstone, who had examined Rebecca Rolfe in London when her ague first announced its presence, following the Twelfth Night masque. He had come swiftly downriver after consulting with his colleague William Harvey, and clutching a new copy of *Pharmacopoeia Londinensis*, typeset in galley-proof but not yet published. Even the faithful Tomacomo had performed some heathen ritual with a bone-rattle and the burning of herbs: a pagan ceremony which Rolfe would have welcomed if it did any good.

Doctor Goldstone assured John Rolfe that his wife's flesh was unbroken, showing no sign of injury from without nor tumour from within. Yet she steadily sickened . . .

John Rolfe had summoned other assistance: the reverend Nicholas Frankwell, rector of Saint George's parish church, just uphill from the Thameside hithe. It was clear to Rolfe that his wife was past the aid of physicians and apothecaries, and that it would be best to ready her for her final journey.

A floor-board creaked. In his grief, Rolfe looked up and saw Josiah Goldstone, fitting his physician's instruments back into their segmented case. The look on Goldstone's countenance told John Rolfe what the nature of the doctor's words would be. Goldstone closed his medical satchel, his fingers nervously clutching his copy of *Pharmacopoeia Londinensis* while it lay open to its frontispiece illustration of the crowned lion and the unicorn.

"I will speak plainly, sir," said Goldstone. "The Lady Rebecca is in her last hours. She is not yet expired, yet her body is strangely cold."

So it was true, then. Pocahontas was dying. True, she had forsaken the false god Okeus of her pagan breed, and been confessed an honest Christian when she took her baptismal name Rebecca. But John Rolfe knew the ways of Englishmen, and the habits of fickle history. He had no doubt that, if his wife Rebecca were remembered at all, she would be known forever by her heathen nickname.

And now Pocahontas was dying . . .

28 March 1617
Blackfriars

Ben Jonson's residence, in the Blackfriars parish of Saint Anne's, was close by Fleet River, the tributary emptying into the Thames. Such closeness – a *closeness* in more than one sense – lent both convenience and inconvenience. A constant stench in Jonson's nostrils reminded him that all the residents of Bowyer Row and Ludgate emptied their chamber-pots and cess-pits into the Fleet. As well, the Fleet River was where the butchers and slaughtermen of the Smithfield stockyards drowned the rancid offal they were unable to sell. By daylight, the surface of the Fleet as far as Holborn was crammed with barges and canal-boats filled with raucous watermen. Fleet Prison, on the river's eastern bank – the side nearer Jonson's house – supplied its own uniquely vomitous perfume, especially at cock-crow when the inmates were permitted to slop out their cells. There was, however, one attribute of the neighbourhood which had aroused Jonson to settle in Blackfriars in the first place.

Fleet Market! From the Fleet Valley to Ludgate Hill, here spanned a little universe of wonders. Each market-day when Johnson visited here, he discovered fresh amazements in the lanes and barrows of Fleet Market. Today, walking east along Fleet Street towards Ludgate, Jonson came to a book-stall in Bear Alley which he had patronized before. The stall-man's name was Wat Collinge. Knowing Jonson's literary tastes from previous custom, he reached beneath his counter and drew forth for Jonson's approval a volume which he dared not display openly: Pietro Aretino's bawdy verse-book *Sixteen Postures*. Jonson had mentioned this volume in his play *The Alchemist*, and now he seized it eagerly: "How much, then?"

"Double crown in gold, sir. Or eleven shillings in silver."

Eleven shillings! Most Londoners would never see as much coin in a year. Jonson had several of the gold double-crown coins in his pocket now: each carried the sign of a Roman X to signify its ten-shilling coinage, but the rising price of gold in King James's economy gave each double crown the worth of eleven silver shillings.

Opening the book of Aretino's verses and glancing through its pages, Jonson observed that one sheet had been neatly sliced out of the book: near to the binding, where its absence would not easily be seen by someone less observant than Jonson. "The Straight Tree is wanting," he told the book-dealer.

Collinge touched his cap respectfully, then pointed to a page near Jonson's thumb. "It's right there, sir." Indeed, Aretino's sonnet describing the sexual gambit of the Straight Tree was on this page, intact.

"Yet the illustration has been cut out," Jonson insisted. From previous acquaintance, he knew that Aretino's woodcut depicted a naked man standing upright while engaged in sexual congress with a woman held upside-down in his arms, wearing only a nun's headdress. Without a complete set of woodcuts illustrating each of Aretino's bawdy sonnets, Jonson had no desire to purchase the book. He returned it to Collinge, then asked: "Have you the volume I requested off your shelves, last market-day?"

The bookman nodded, and brought forth an octavo volume bound in green kidskin. "This is Henry Lyte's edition, sir, translated from the French."

Jonson glanced at its title: *A Niewe Herball, or, Historie of*

Plantes. Thumbing its pages, he swiftly ascertained that the type-blocks were clear and legible, and – most importantly – that the woodcut illustrations of the various herbs were detailed.

"Excellent. We had agreed on fourteen shillings?" Ben Jonson handed the bookman a small gold coin bearing the likeness of King James aboard a ship, brandishing a sword and shield.

Wat Collinge's eyes widened as he saw this coin, so seldom minted. "A spur-ryal!" He dug into his pouch, and gave Jonson two shillings and sixpence in change. Touching his cap's brim again, the merchant asked: "If I may make as so bold, sir: why did you bid me fetch this particular book?"

Ben Jonson placed the volume in his quarter-sack. "I find myself in sudden need of knowledge."

"Of herbs, sir?"

"Of poisons." Jonson slung the sack across his shoulder, and moved on.

The streets were filled with their usual filth, and therefore Jonson – like most residents of this district – had strapped a set of *pattens* beneath his shoes upon leaving his house: these stout iron bands lifted him a few inches above the mire, as well as protecting his shoes from the cobbles.

As Jonson moved eastward past some screeching oyster-women, he practised the custom of "jostling for the wall": each time he approached someone travelling the other way, they both competed for the privilege of passing on the side nearer to the buildings and farther from the kerb. A successful jostle kept Jonson away from the filth in the gutters, and it also gave him some protection from the garbage – usually, a chamber-pot's treasures – that oftentimes plummeted unexpectedly from windows overhead. By good fortune, Fleet Street was less crowded this morning than usual: only three days had passed since Lady Day, when the annual rents came due, and so there were fewer loose coins a-jangle now.

At White Lion Court, Jonson's progress was blocked by a pair of dairymaids: one carrying a milk-stool, the other a pail, and both of them leading a milch-ass while bellowing their wares: "*Milk, oh! Milk, oh!*" A market-woman gave signal to buy; at once, both milkmaids stopped in the midst of the street, and proceeded to milk their she-ass on that very spot.

Passing them at last, Jonson came to a halfpenny-glimpse in

which a Holland sailor permitted the paying onlookers to view a wicker cage containing a live dodo-bird. In a younger time, Jonson might have paid to look upon this weird fowl of an alien land. Yet now, having met the Novo Orbe princess Pocahontas, mere birds held no interest for him.

At the foot of Ludgate Hill was Queen Hithe. Passing among the Ludgathians, halfway up the hill Jonson came to a row of stable-yards and carriage-houses, and three outdoor ovens where perspiring women readied meals for the passengers in the daily coaches. Overhead, a tavern's signboard displayed the gaudy painted image of a red-skinned woman, naked as Eve, surrounded by bright green foliage. Below this sign was the entrance to Jonson's destination: the Belle Sauvage Inn.

He had made previous inquiries, and so he was expected. Straight away, Jonson found himself in the presence of a large red-faced man wearing a most impromptu apron of book-muslin. "Are you the proprietor of this house?" Jonson asked.

"I am, sir. Ingram Charnock's my name." He did not extend his hand, being busy wiping it with the other one. "I was cautioned that you had questions of me. Question away, then. Nothing transpires beneath my roof without I have the knowledge of it."

"Most excellent." Ben Jonson took an instant liking to this man. "But might I speak as well with your inn's porter? Sometimes the porter of a house knows its secrets better than the master."

"I am landlord and chief porter, sir," said Ingram Charnock. "Likewise the publican. And on slow days, I curry the horses."

"It is my understanding," said Jonson, "that your house lately afforded its comforts to Lady Rebecca Rolfe."

"Who, *sir*?"

"Better named as Pocahontas."

"*Ah!*" The taverner shuddered. "Now *there's* a party of customers I'm not likely to forget in a sudden. Came here this half-year ago – last September, she did – with her husband and child, and a ragtag of them red-faced Indians. *Savages* they were, sir!" The innkeeper made a gesture as if beginning to cross himself, then interrupted this as he saw Jonson watching him intently. "Three o' them wore feathers, mind you. And *scalps!*

Filthy beggars; they skin their enemies, and then they wear the skins! Not like your civilized Englishman."

"Indeed not," agreed Ben Jonson. Glancing south and across the stable-yard as he spoke, full down the length of Ludgate Hill, Jonson had a splendid view of Tower Wharf, its gatehouse thickly bristled with pikestaffs displaying the impaled heads of felons and vagrants.

"Tell me," he inquired casually. "While she was here, did the Lady Rebecca . . . did Pocahontas eat of the same food as her husband and your other patrons?"

"She did that, sir. Honest Christian food, as ever it was. Although I marked that she seldom ate meat."

"And did she use the same close-stool as everyone else? Did you remark anything unusual about . . . her fewmets?"

"Lord, sir! What a one for questions you are!" It is difficult to embarrass a Ludgate innkeeper, but clearly Jonson had succeeded. Ingram Charnock reddened. "We've had the cess-pits cleaned just the once since she left. As for anything unusual . . . well, crying your pardon, sir . . . but one person's turds are much the same coinage as another's, if you take my meaning."

"I do," said Jonson, not failing to notice the subtle reference to coins. "Tell me, did Pocahontas seem in any way *ill* while she bided here?"

"She did that, sir." The innkeeper wiped his florid hands with his apron. "Loudly complained as how she couldn't stomach the smells from Fleet Valley."

Jonson felt his senses quickening. "Now this is important, if you please. Did the lady seem genuinely blighted with disease, or merely discomforted?"

The innkeeper seemed afflicted with a sudden loss of memory. Jonson drew forth a new James shilling, and two Queen Bess silver groats. At once, Charnock brightened. "Ah, sir! I'collect now: 'twas merely distress the lady had, not disease. My tavern is no pest-house."

"Did she cough, then? Any show of the ague?"

"No, sir," said Ingram Charnock. Jonson gave him the coins, and the innkeeper smiled. "In early October, the lady Pocahontas and her companions moved out of my inn. Out of London entirely, they said."

"And might you know where they went?"

"To a house name of Syon, I think, sir."

Ben Jonson thanked the man, and bade him a good day . . . then turned, and strode back downhill towards Fleet Valley. The wind's direction had changed: now it was coming from the south, and the stench from the Thames was overpowering.

10 April 1617
Syon House,
Isleworth, Middlesex

The odours of the garden were intoxicating. The moon was full tonight: Thomas Harriot had set up his Dutch telescope on the southern border of the mansion's great lawn, and now – with the aid of a *matita* pencil from Italy – he was sketching the moon's face as it hung inverted in the lens of his apparatus. To the west of his position, he was aware of the strong aromas of the various herbs and plants in the garden he husbanded. He worked in silence, occasionally coughing in the still night air.

Tomorrow, Harriot decided, he would bring a new supply of books to his patron the earl in the Tower of London. For now, he gave his full attention to the lunar mountain range in his eyepiece. Yet as he traced its contours, on the sudden, he heard a rustling sound among the shrubs and stalks of the garden.

"How did you do it, Harriot?" asked the intruder. "What noxious weed performed your murd'rous task?" A cloaked figure stepped forth into the moonlight. He was bearded and diskempt, in his usual accustom, and so Harriot easily recognised him.

"Greetings, Ben Jonson," said Thomas Harriot, setting down his drawing implements.

"You know me. Good. As I know you," said Jonson. "I have spent this past fortnight researching your achievements. Are you the Gogmagog and counsel of this Syon House? The Earl of Northumberland pays you well, does he, to manage his estate?"

"Do you think me a butler?" asked Harriot. "Henry Percy is my patron, and I am his pensioner. His grace the earl has most generously granted me a residence on Syon House's grounds. In return, I perform some modest errands for my patron."

"Including murder?"

"I admit nothing."

"I was present when a masked skeleton – a costumed dancer – jabbed Pocahontas with a staff," said Ben Jonson. "She took ill with an ague soon after, then sickened and died. Yet I have questioned Doctor Goldstone, who attended her. There was no swelling of her privities, no puncture. So, the pikestaff did not wound her. The masked dancer was not the killer. Yet I think he wanted her to die."

"There are many Englishmen," said Harriot, "who wanted Pocahontas dead, in vengeance for her father Powhatan's grim deed at Hatarask: the slaughter of Walter Ralegh's colonists."

Ben Jonson nodded, stroking his left thumb with the fingers of his right hand. "I have read your chapbook of the Virginia surveyance: *A Briefe and True Report*. Harriot, you were a partner in Ralph Lane's first attempt to colonize Virginia. And you helped finance and victual the second attempt: the so-named Lost Colony."

Thomas Harriot made a theatrical bow, acknowledging the honour. "The Lost Colony vanished twenty-seven years ago. You seem strangely concerned with them."

"Not so strangely," said Ben Jonson. "Two of the colonists were my brothers: Nicholas and Henry Johnson. Our stepfather was a bricklayer, and he taught them the trade. I shifted the spelling of my name when I became a playwright."

At this, Thomas Harriot fell strangely silent.

"I'll wager you've attended Will Shakespeare's piece *Hamlet*," said Jonson. "And it inspired you to murder your victim in the same wise as his tragedy's Gonzago: by means of poison *in the ears*."

Thomas Harriot said nothing. In the moonlight, Jonson noticed something peculiar about Harriot's nostrils . . . or the *tonnels* of his face, to use the term which Jonson preferred. Thomas Harriot's left nostril was severly ulcerated, and the ulcer had ripened and spread along that side of his upper lip.

As if resenting Jonson's scrutiny, Harriot now turned suddenly aside. The scientist took up his *matita*, and resumed sketching a lunar mountain range, as if Jonson were elsewhere.

Ben Jonson strode through the hedgerows of Syon House's garden, pausing at each plant in its turn. "The Wizard Earl has been prisoner in Wakefield Tower for eleven years; these plants show only a few years' growth, so he cannot have sown them. What did you choose, Harriot?" Jonson paused in front of a plant with furred leaves and small bright flowers. "You grow henbane here, I see." Jonson moved past this to a tall plant with a high brush of deep purple blossoms, just beginning to blossom in mid-April. "And here is monk's hood, as well." Jonson strode past the bush of monk's hood, careful to thrust it aside with the elbow of his jerkin, so as not to touch it with his bare flesh. Now he noticed a small inconspicuous tuber, its bushy head barely visible amid a circlet of dark green erect pointed leaves. "Here is what you used, I think." Jonson knelt, seized the plant by its head, and tore it from the earth. The night air was pierced by a sound like a whispered scream, as if the plant protested its uprooting. Jonson brandished the tuber: a brown root, nearly two feet long, forking out at its base and then forking again higher up, as the legs and arms might branch out from the body of a homunculus.

Ben Jonson brought forth from his quarter-sack a sheet of paper, bearing a sketch which he had copied from a woodcut in Lyte's *Niewe Herball*. He compared this to the object in his other hand. "Mandrake root," said Jonson, nodding. "Known to the Levantines as Satan's apple . . . for the poisonous fruits of the mandrake carry the scent of apples."

"As well their *taste*," said Thomas Harriot. "Though on this point I must rely upon the experience of others."

"I have questioned the physician who attended Pocahontas, concerning the ill humours that foresaw her death." Ben Jonson turned over his sketch of the mandrake root, and consulted a handwritten list on the sheet's other side. "Josiah Goldstone attested that Pocahontas had a strange coldness in her form and limbs, yet she was feverous in her head. As well paralysis, stomach pain, erratickal pulse and slowed breathing. Each toxin has its countersign, and *those* – I have learnt – are the symptoms of mandrake poisoning."

Harriot seemed unmoved.

Ben Jonson flung the mandrake to the ground. "Harriot! Rogue, you are the courier who conveys books and goods from the outer world to the Wizard Earl's prison in the tower, and you are the selfsame go-between from the prisoned earl to the world beyond. Pocahontas was healthy enough when she dwelt at the Belle Sauvage in London. But her coughing had already begun when I met her at Whitehall Palace, on Twelfth Night. By then, she was living here at Syon House. When the Earl of Northumberland applied silver bands to the seashell earrings of Pocahontas, it was you who brought them back to her. But you applied a pulp of mandrake root between seashell and silver. Over the weeks and months, the poison seeped gradually into her body . . . *through her ears*. Thus you had your revenge for the deaths of the Lost Colony."

Throughout this encounter, Thomas Harriot's face had remained a stoic mask. Now he permitted of a faint smile . . . and the left side of his face was contorted by the ulcer that deformed his nostril and lip. "Here at last you are mistaken, Jonson. Yes, I murdered Pocahontas, but the method you have named is too theatrical."

"How so?"

Harriot stifled a grin that threatened to crack his pocked mouth. "Poison *in the ears!* With such fanciful ideas, man, are your plays as bad as Shakespeare's? Here at Syon House, I have access to the kitchens. While John Rolfe and his wife stayed here as the earl's guests, I took pains to sophisticate the meals prepared for Pocahontas. I fed her mandrake-flavoured sillibubs, with heavy cream to mask the pois'nous spice. Truly, Jonson: the *ears*? The human mouth, I'll warrant, is a far more efficient viaduct to the organs within. As the savage princess was unfamiliar with English food, she did not remark on the flavour of my extra ingredients."

Jonson's mouth tightened. "So you poisoned her, rogue . . . to square the account for her father's slaughter of my brothers and all the Lost Colony."

"Aye, 'twas in revenge." Harriot nodded. "But not upon the Lost Colony's account."

"For whose vengeance, then?"

"Mine own." Harriot pointed to his ulcerous face. "When I journeyed to Virginia in 1585, it was Powhatan and his savages who persuaded me to take up their custom of inhaling the smoke of a plant they cultivated for burning: the tobacco broadleaf." Harriot convulsed. "O, poisonous weed! I am become addicted to its fumes." Now he barely suppressed a cough. "The tobacco has poisoned my lungs, my throat, my very tongue. Yet still I yearn for another pipe-bowl of the stuff. I feel a strange hunger for its seductive poison."

Jonson nodded. "I understand your motive now. Pocahontas

was the intermediary between Powhatan and John Rolfe, who brought tobacco to England."

". . . and so inspired the poisoning of myself and hundreds of other Englishmen," said Harriot. "Have I murdered Pocahontas? Let us say that she and myself have merely *exchanged poisons*." Harriot grimaced. "She deserved to be slain, as surely as her father slew the Lost Colony."

"Only one piece of the conundrum yet eludes me," said Ben Jonson. Now he gestured extravagantly, indicating the garden and the manor beyond. "Your patron the Earl of Northumberland calls this place *Syon* House. Many leagues south of here, in Sicily, the Knights Templar perform their unholy rituals in the Priory of *Sion*. Might there be some link a-tween these?"

Thomas Harriot nodded. "Word has lately reached me that the Templars even now are dismantling their priory, this very month. It soon shall be as dead as Pocahontas."

"Aye, dead by your hand. You have done murder, sir," said Ben Jonson. "D'you think you can play gleeks with human lives? And play jackdaw with souls?"

"Ben Jonson, do your masque-plays have such ripe dialogue?" asked Thomas Harriot, seeming unimpressed. "Quit you these metaphors! You cry me killer, but I am not the only murderer here. As you have detected me, in the like manner I have detected *you*." Harriot raised his pencil, and aimed it at Jonson's left hand. "Mark of Cain! You bear the Tyburn brand."

The playwright Ben Jonson extended his left hand, displaying the T-shaped scar at the base of his thumb. "Yes, the fruit of the hangman's tree," he acknowledged. "It is a matter of publick record, so I freely own of it. Nineteen years ago, whilst fighting a duel at Hogsden Fields, I killed an actor named Gabriel Spenser. Some actors are in need of killing, and he was one of them. I 'scaped the gallows by pleading benefit of clergy, reading a Latin neck-verse, forfeiting all my property, and . . . as you see . . . submitting to the branding-iron."

Thomas Harriot grinned, and his ulcer-pocked face twisted grotesquely. "Very well, then. Now that we have exchanged confessions, what justice do you contemplate for me?"

"None," said Ben Jonson. "As you have murdered the woman who brought tobacco to England, so the tobacco has murdered *you*." As Jonson spoke, Harriot stifled another cough. "That ripe sore on your face steadily prospers, rougue Harriot. I doubt that you will live another five years. In the remainder of your time, try to achieve something to count against the evil you have done."

"I have achieved much already," said Thomas Harriot. "Not all of it murderous."

"True," said Ben Jonson. "I have apprised this in my inquiries. Your patron the earl, when I visited him in the Tower of London, made free to boast of your achievements." Jonson drew forth another sheet of paper now, and consulted the list which he had written: "You were Walter Ralegh's navigator in his voyages, and derived new methods for ascertaining latitude at sea. A shipwright you are, a keeper of accounts, and a land-surveyor. In your journeys to the New World with Ralegh and Francis Drake, you made copious notes of the Virginia savages and their diets and customs, as well the botanies of their native land. You have discovered laws of refraction and opticks, and o'erthrown Aristotle's fallacies in the laws of projectiles. You are the first astronomer in England to make use of the telescope, and you have charted comets and eclipses. 'Twas you who discovered that the very face of the sun is spotted like a pudding." Ben Jonson put away the list, and confronted Harriot again. "Even now, I see that you are scribing the countenance of the moon."

Harriot bowed once more, less theatrically this time. "I would that my own face were only half so cratered as the moon's." He coughed again, and in the moonlight Jonson saw that the cankerous flesh of Harriot's nose was now cracked and bleeding. "As you say, Jonson, I have achieved much. Of a certainty, I am full worth a dozen or more of any Pocahontas."

"*In that you are wrong, man,*" said Ben Jonson. "Despite your voyages to Virginia's new lands, and your inspections of the comets and heavens, there is one place you have never journeyed." Ben Jonson's scarred left hand now touched the left side of his jerkin, at his chest. " 'Tis here. The *heart*. Pocahontas, in her brief life, has touched men's hearts, and caught the fancy of their humours. She lies dead in Gravesend, but in Englishmen's hearts she lives and breathes as the ripening she-child of a virgin land. She symbolizes all that's new and wondrous. Depend on't, rogue: in years and centuries to come, Pocahontas will live, and stand remembered, whilst Thomas Harriot falls dead of canker . . . and all your achievements lie forgotten."

Ben Jonson drew his cloak about himself, and turned away. Once again he strode past the bush of poisonous monk's hood, giving it a wider berth this time. And then he was gone in the moonlight.

Thomas Harriot frowned. The night had suddenly grown cold. He took up his pencil once more, and turned again to his unfinished sketch of the lunar mountains. But in the darkening sky overhead, the position of the moon had shifted . . . and now his vantage was spoilt.

A DEAD MAN'S WISH

JOHN T. AQUINO

One of the unforgiveable acts during James's reign was the execution of Sir Walter Ralegh. Note the spelling of his name. Although we tend to spell it as Raleigh these days, it was never spelled that way during his life time. It was also pronounced "Rawley". Just why Ralegh was executed and the real story behind it is the subject of John Aquino's tale.

Aquino (b. 1949) is a writer, editor and media-law attorney. He is also the editor of the Waste Age and Recycling Times's Recycling Handbook *(1995) and the author of* Truth and Lives on Film: The Legal Problems in Depicting Real Persons and Events in a Fictional Medium *(2005).*

The life-beaten face of Sir Walter Ralegh looked up at Henry Bagnet and said to him softly but firmly, "I've asked you here to find out who killed me."

Bagnet, sometimes investigator for Sir Francis Bacon as well as those of less renown, held his breath. The quick answer to the old knight's assignment was simple enough. "You're to be executed in eight hours on a warrant from the king. So the king has killed you. That'll be £10. Payable now, if you please."

But Bagnet knew that was not what Ralegh meant. Since his return to England and his imprisonment in the Tower in August,

Ralegh had been the talk of London as he proceeded, inch by inch, closer to the block. There were hearings in August and September of a commission of privy councilors, with Bacon and Sir Edward Coke momentarily burying their loathing of one another to please the king by working together. In early October, Coke, having failed to convince anybody of Ralegh's current crimes, had recommended execution based on the old death sentence of 1603. But not feeling comfortable with using the 15-year-old order, the commissioners insisted that hearings be held, and there were three of them, one in private on 22 October, and two others on the 24th and four days later, the afternoon of the day when Ralegh asked for Bagnet's help.

Bagnet had been in the crowd as Ralegh was led on the long final walk from the Tower, through Eastcheap and Cheapside, near the Mermaid's Tavern where the late Master Shakespeare had dined, and passed St Paul's. It was then that Bagnet saw Ralegh's eyes fill with tears, not only as the shadow of the ancient church consumed him, but at the sights and sounds of the shops and homes he had just walked by, the London of his fame and triumphs, now all gone. This feeling of loss was driven further home as the procession of Ralegh and his 60 armed-guard escort passed Durham House, and he craned his neck to see his study or any familiar site of what had been one of his homes until his imprisonment in 1603 when the bishop got it back. But it is likely that the gathering crowd gradually convinced Ralegh that his reputation was stronger than it had been, perhaps stronger than ever, as they cheered a bit, touched him when they could snake their hands through one of the 60 guards, and shouted words of encouragement as he walked down Fleet Street and the Strand to Whitehall and then Westminster where he was to appear before the King's Bench. Enough was enough, they seemed to say, and you have to admire his salt.

The hearing began, and just half an hour later Ralegh was walking to the Abbey Gatehouse where he would stay the night before execution. Sir Henry Montagu, the chief justice, had not unkindly told him that Sir Edward Coke had been right, that Ralegh, having been sentenced to death in 1603, was a "dead man in the law" and had been spared only by the King's whim. That whim having ended, the treason for which he had been sentenced could not be pardoned. Montagu praised Ralegh as a valiant and good Christian before informing him that he would be actually as well as legally dead in the morning.

After the hearing, Bagnet had stayed in town with his wife Jessica. In tribute to a fellow soldier whom he had met but once five years before in investigating Prince Henry's death, Bagnet planned to attend the beheading. They dined at the Mermaid's, and Bagnet reminisced about the recent Ralegh events, describing what she already knew but doing so simply because he enjoyed telling stories on the pretext that since she was from Italy he would need to explain it more carefully. Loving him, Jessica indulged him. He recalled how at a September commissioners' hearing Bacon had pressed the French ambassador to explain what would have happened had Ralegh gone to France when he returned from Guiana in February rather than staying in England for certain arrest. The Frenchman rejected any suggestion that Ralegh would have stayed and worked on behalf of France by answering, "*Il mangera, il boire, il fera bien* – He would have eaten, drunk wine, and had a good time." It was then that Bagnet felt a hand on his shoulder and feared that his words had been overheard and misunderstood. He looked up and saw that the hand belonged to one of the two Weddington brothers who worked for Bacon. Jessica brought her cupped hand to Bagnet's cheek just as he was ushered out, desperately looking back for one last glimpse of her red hair. The small Weddington, who was built like a rook on a chessboard although not as gracefully designed, prodded Bagnet toward Westminster, but rather than to Bacon's chambers or the King's Bench they veered toward the gatehouse, and Bagnet knew he had been summoned by a dead man.

As they approached the entrance around midnight, a cloaked woman was leaving. Bagnet knew without seeing that it was Ralegh's wife, Bess. He stopped, and Weddington sympathetically let him stop. Bagnet bowed his head. Bess Ralegh slowed in her steps, curtsied of a sort, her gloves and handkerchief at her face, and in the slowing down one of her gloves fell to the street. "Wait," Bagnet shouted, and Weddington reached for his blade. The glove was white and light of lace. He held his hand up to show Weddington what he was doing, bent, retrieved the glove, and brought it to her. She turned, accepted it with a timid smile, and then he saw her face. Her eyes were light brown surrounded by some lines caused by the strain of marrying a buccaneer who had been dead-alive for 15 years awaiting execution in the Tower of London. But surely they were not the eyes of a woman over 50 whose skin was white like porcelain newly made. He remembered the words that Ralegh wrote that all of London said were about her,

> *Nature that washed her hands in milk*
> *And had forgot to dry them.*

No wonder Ralegh had risked the ire of the late Queen Elizabeth by wooing and winning her lovely lady-in-waiting.

She accepted her glove, smiled, and walked to her waiting carriage as Weddington seized his arm and dragged him to the room in the gatehouse where Ralegh asked for his help. They were already building the scaffold where Ralegh would stand and kneel in less than eight hours, and the hammering provided an obbligato to Ralegh's proposal.

"Oh, I know," Ralegh said. "I know what you are thinking. As Sir Edward Coke insisted and insisted and as Sir Henry agreed, I have been a dead man for 15 years. If anyone killed me, I killed myself by not reporting rumors of attempts on King James' life, things that I would not have minded had they happened. I am paying for my arrogance and momentary lack of patriotism, and that is fine. I have been expecting any moment for 15 years for the King to simply decide in a bad mood to go ahead and behead me." Ralegh noticed that Bagnet was standing and not a young or lean man. He started to rise to offer the chair to him, but Bagnet placed his hand on Ralegh's shoulder, seeing the old knight's weakness. Ralegh nodded in thanks and continued, "But what I mean when I ask you to find out who killed me, is this, Bagnet. I had it set. I am a resourceful man, always on the scramble. To secure my release, I offered to go back to Guiana to find gold because the King's coffers are bare. He could not refuse my offer. All I had to do was find the gold of El Dorado in the spot where the old Indian told me and Keymis," and here Ralegh misted a bit but continued, "told us it was. Also I was not to fight with the Spaniards, damn them because James and the Spanish ambassador toad Gondomar are still trying to arrange a wedding of state between Prince Charles and the Spanish princess. That Gondomar had it in for me for past adventures against his lying, thriving people. But even he could not touch me if I brought back the gold."

"Everyone knows what happened, Sir Walter. You sailed for Guiana, you became ill, Keymis took a party to find the gold, he did not find it, and in returning to you he fired on the Spanish-held town of San Tomé, during which encounter several Spaniards died along with your son," Bagnet slowed his recital here out of respect, "Walter."

"That is not what happened! I mean, yes, yes my beloved Walter boy is dead, but everything else –"

"Then tell me."

"And I will be quick," Ralegh panted as if his fever were returning or he was on fire mentally in remembering the events, "for you do not have the time for a long discourse. We sailed from Plymouth, were held in Falmouth, and then blown to Cork, where we lost two months. We left Ireland full of supplies and enthusiasm, and yet from that moment on everything went wrong. I became ill, the men disgruntled as if enflamed by wild rumors, and when we landed I had to send Keymis and Walter on without me. But, and here is the wrong part, Walter sent word back that they had found the gold and all was well. And then, when Keymis arrived, he said my son had been mistaken, there was no gold, that a fool one of us had set fire to San Tomé, and that Walter had died leading a charge, which makes no sense because Walter was not in my image that way, if you know what I mean."

"Perhaps," Bagnet said gently, "he portrayed a heroic death for your son to –"

"Comfort me, yes I know. But Walter said that he had found the gold, and when Keymis returned he said one thing and then another, contradicting himself –"

"He had been in a battle and lost you your son –"

"– and I persisted, demanding the truth. He ran to his cabin, locked the door, I heard a shot, and when I broke in the door, Keymis was on the floor, a knife slipped under his bloodied ribs and into his heart."

"The common thinking is that he shot himself with a pocket pistol that broke his ribs but did not penetrate and that then he stabbed himself out of grief and shame."

"Yes, I know," Ralegh panted, in some pain. "Very tidy. Bagnet, you were a soldier I have heard, as am I and as was Keymis. If you were going to shoot yourself with a pocket pistol, would you aim at your ribs or your head?"

Bagnet nodded uneasily and shifted his weight to continue standing. "But if he was distracted –"

"– because he lost me my son, yes, I know. And when we came to England, and it became clear the King would not listen, that he intended to carry out the old sentence, Bess and I had chance after chance to escape," Ralegh said louder, pounding his fist into his hand for emphasis, "and they knew. They knew where we were going, what we were going to do."

Bagnet stood stiffly. "And so you feel you were entrapped –"

"And made to fail – meaning I would be beheaded."

"In spite of your success."

"Keymis found the gold. He must have. Walter said he did." Ralegh, having recounted it all, stretched back in his chair with his arms high and dangling as if relieved of a great weight. "This has troubled me. It will be easier to die if I know. Find out if you can who has killed me. Not that I am loathe to die. I am content. And I am especially pleased that Gondomar has left for Spain and that I will not have to die with that wretched man gloating up at me." He was silent for a moment, thinking of a somewhat sad thing. "I just said goodbye to Bess. She's a beauty and rock, that one. Enduring so much, doing so much. She raised the money for my ship the *Destiny*, and she has fought the king for money and Sherbourne and Durham. She can take care of herself. She told me she has already arranged to dispose of my body. I told her that that was good since she had not always the disposing of it while I was alive. I will miss her until I kiss her in heaven. But she is better off."

"I take it given my escort that Sir Francis –"

"– is aware and does not care. I know it is past midnight, Bagnet, and that your chances of uncovering all of this are few. I would give you more time if I had it. Just try. If you do not return, I will understand." Ralegh nodded as if dismissing him and pulled his chair to the table that was the only other furniture in the room where there was paper and pen waiting for him. "There is so much I would like to write," he said aloud to no one in particular. "A poem for her. A treatise on this gatehouse, which used to be the monastery of St Peter's, a fitting place to absorb the remnants of holy thoughts. But I must settle my affairs. Perhaps I will find time for the poem. Perhaps not."

Weddington brought Bagnet outside and left him. Jessica was waiting and ran to his arms. He was upset that she had been standing alone in the dark of London after midnight, but he admitted to himself she was good to hold again. He explained what Ralegh had asked of him and told her that Weddington had said that Bess had been taken home by Ralegh's cousins the Carews. He urged her to stay with Bess until morning.

After Jessica had left, Bagnet looked around the empty and silent streets and absorbed the pointlessness of his task. There was no way he could refuse a man in Ralegh's position. But from midnight to dawn and the world asleep, how could he succeed? Who would be around for him to talk to?

Bagnet sighed and heaved his chest and eyes up and then saw that candles were burning in the Abbey's buildings' windows. Then it became clear that by happenstance or Providence, he did have a chance after all. This was not just any execution. This was to be the execution of a famous and infamous man. And it was an execution fifteen years in coming and the subject of months of recent conniving by Bacon, Coke, and those who served them. Of course, these people would be up at midnight, if only to savor the expectation of the end of years and years of effort. Knowing Bacon, Bagnet was sure that there was a campaign being developed to scotch the image that Bagnet had felt among the crowd that afternoon of Ralegh being a martyr to the ideals of days gone by. There would plenty of people around for Bagnet to interview.

The only ones Bagnet was sure would not be around were Count Gondomar, whom Ralegh said had been returned to Spain, and the King himself, who, rumour among the crowd had it, had left that morning for a spot of hunting and to work on writing a meditation on the Lord's Prayer.

As Bagnet approached the side entrance, the door was opened as if he had been expected by Weddington, or perhaps his brother, he could not tell them apart. It turned out he was expected, but only to be turned away. The door to Sir Francis's chamber was opened a crack, and he heard him call out in his Lord Chamberlain's voice and authority, "I know why you are here, Henry Bagnet, and I respect it but will not see you. I made a vow after our last unpleasantness to stay clear of you. Besides, I have more important things to do than waste it with a fool dead man's errand." The door was yanked shut from within with a gush, enabling Bagnet to smell something sweet. His first thought was to remember Bacon's penchant for Welsh serving boys and to assume that the aroma was of some tempting treat.

He was taken from his lurid thinking by a noise. Bagnet turned and out of the corner of his eye glimpsed a man retreating behind a curtain. He saw enough of him to say, "Sir Edward Coke." A tall, well-kept noble with beard and ruffles underneath emerged. "You are out of office, are you not? And yet you are here."

The former attorney general bowed. "Your friend Sir Francis has seen to my dismissal. But the king needed me to put your client on the block. I have been given access. Excuse me," he bowed with a flourish and turned to leave.

"Sir Edward, you quarrelled with the King because you believe you are above the law."

"No," he said sharply. "That is your patron Sir Francis talking. I believe the law is above the king."

"As you heard, he is no patron of mine. But having had Sir Francis manipulate your position against you, it would be good to have found an opportunity to regain the King's favour. Sir Walter's failure gave you that opportunity."

The noted attorney smiled broadly. "So, I stand accused without evidence of what – arranging the ruin of Sir Walter's mission to Guiana?"

"What an interesting idea. I do not believe I said that, but it is interesting that you thought it –"

"Come, man. How could one do that?"

Bagnet walked close up to Sir Edward to face him directly. "It is widely said, Sir Edward, that you will do most anything to stay in power. You and Sir Francis have been jockeying for position, he gets you dismissed, you arrange to have your daughter marry the brother of the King's new favourite, the Duke of Buckingham. And when she and your wife object and go to Sir Francis for help, you have your daughter kidnapped, wedded, and bedded against her will. Surely anyone who would do this –"

"That is a family matter, sir. Things family members do to one another are one thing. But I am a loyal servant of the crown. Good night." Sir Edward Coke sweepingly bowed again and left.

"A lawyer's trick," Bagnet whispered to an empty corridor. "Defending his patriotism when I did not dispute it. It is your ambition, sir, that is at issue."

Bagnet returned to the street and saw a man quickly entering a gold-decked carriage. Bagnet shouted after him, "Diego Sarmiento de Acũna, Count Gondomar, I believe."

A man who did indeed bear a slight resemblance to a toad wearing a cloak leaned out of the carriage. "You have the advantage of me, Señor, although you have the good taste to refer to me by my name and not my territory."

"I have been to Gondomar," Bagnet said quietly. "I know what it is."

"As a soldier, no doubt."

"No doubt because you know exactly who I am from your friends at court."

"But how did you know who I am? I am –"

"– supposed to be in Spain, yes. But I felt in my heart of hearts you could not miss this event. And I knew Sir Francis was with someone when he would not open the door. I could also detect the smell of something sweet which I now think were cakes from Gondomar, Ribadavia wine, and Galician ham since I have heard you have them shipped here along with casks of water and bring money and presents to Sir Francis to arrange a marital alliance."

"You have me with the wrong suitor, but you are right about my victual preferences. Wretched country with your terrible water and burned churches. It has been my duty to serve here –"

"– turning Elizabeth's and Ralegh's suspicions about Spain to James' unbounded love."

"For the benefit of both our countries."

"So you say. You opposed Sir Walter's voyage to Guiana and relented only –"

"– only when the King assured me no Spaniards would be harmed."

"And they were. Just as you predicted. Or arranged?"

"I arranged? I?"

Bagnet grabbed onto the side of the coach and hauled himself in, plopping down across from Count Gondomar, pushing aside sausage and bottles of wine and banging his knees against casks in the process. "Ralegh says he found the gold of El Dorado."

"Nonsense."

"You still have troops there. Have you ever thought of looking, just to see? Of course you have! With Keymis dead and Ralegh dead this morning, few would know the secret. And by keeping the gold away from King James the stronger his need for an alliance with Spain and an arranged wedding that you support. Added in is the pleasure of having your enemy Sir Walter Ralegh finally executed."

"That pirate! That butcher!" Count Gondomar hissed. "But it was not a personal matter between him and me, never!"

Bagnet asked quietly, "Then why are you here, Count Gondomar, and not in Spain? Why did you return? You did know that you are here in time for the execution?"

It was four o'clock, three hours before dawn when Count Gondomar's carriage pulled away in haste after Bagnet disembarked. Bagnet was familiar enough with Italian through Jessica to guess what the barrage of Spanish words beginning with "M" that Count Gondomar spat at him meant. The departing carriage rode low with the weight of the sausage and wine. Having been so close to them, Bagnet believed that they were not the sweet scent he had detected in Bacon's apartments after all and so returned to his suspicions about the Welsh serving boys. Bacon was a sneaky, twisted man, as Bagnet well knew, and was more than willing to take lives for his benefit and for what he believed was England's. Still, there was Coke. Both of them were willing to share Gondomar's bed, Coke only figuratively, if it brought them closer to James' favour. What had Count Gondomar said about Bagnet linking him to the wrong suitor? And what of Gondomar himself? Plots and counterplots. Webs of deceit. Oh, this England!

His deductions were stopped with the rushing sound of carriage wheels and a mass of horse and dark vomited from the night and on top of him before he could move.

The inn where Bagnet and Jessica were staying was a short distance from Westminster. When he stumbled into the room, Jessica was there lying on the bed, his arm over her eyes. "Oh, you're back," she said, jumping up. Then she saw his right arm hanging loose and blood dangling from his limp fingertips in drops.

His large form filled the chair as she bandaged his forehead and gently jammed his arm into a sling. "At least it is nice to finally sit down," he said.

"Do not joke with me," she scolded. He saw she now had blood on her face, which he wiped away with his thumb. "For five years now I have patched your battered body up, and each time you vow that you are nearing 60 and too old for taking risks."

"I did not have a great deal of choice, my dear. The carriage ran me down. What is that wonderful smell in your hair?"

"Never mind that."

"Besides I thought you were staying with Bess Ralegh?"

"She sent me home. In fact, she drove with me in her carriage. *È fredda. Come un cetriolo.*" Jessica sometimes used her Italian for colloquial expressions. She found it easier.

"What did you say: 'she is a cool one, like a cucumber'?"

"*Si.*"

"Unusual, given the fact that her husband will be executed soon."

"Well, some women – *come se dice*? – keep it in."

"That is true. And she has to endure a great deal, as he himself said." Bagnet felt that he was sitting on something, reached, and pulled it out.

"Whose glove is this?" Bagnet asked his wife, knowing the answer.

"Oh, it is hers. She must have dropped it in the carriage, and I kicked it when I stepped out. I will send it back in the morning." When he did not respond, she asked, "What is it?"

"I looked into her face seconds after she left her husband for the last time. And her eyes were dry."

"As you say, some women –"

He seemed miles away as he musingly finished her sentence. "Steel themselves. Does that mean they become steel or just act as if they are?"

It was just five when Bagnet arrived at Ralegh's room. A Dr Robert Tounson was there, evoking the Scriptures, and berating Ralegh for not seeming particularly repentant.

"But I am an innocent man," Ralegh was protesting in laughter.

"Men in these days do not die in innocence. By pleading innocent you are taxing the endurance of Divine Mercy." The reverend stopped on Bagnet's appearance. "Sir, go away, I am ministering to a dying man –"

"He is a dead man, and he will need your ministering in earnest soon, but not now," Bagnet said as he pushed Dr Tounson outside.

"What have you found out? Do you know –"

"– who killed you? I think so. But the only way to prove it to you in the minutes we have left is to ask you to go back in time in your mind. You say that after you left Cork everything went wrong."

"That is right. And what happened to your arm?"

Bagnet ignored the question and deliberately stood behind Sir Walter, putting his hand on his shoulder. "Close your eyes."

"What?" The old knight started to turn around.

"No, look ahead and close your eyes. Go back to the dock at Cork as you were leaving. Tell me what you see."

"Well," Ralegh started, with his eyes obligingly shut tight. "I see thin Keymis, who was unusually nervous for some reason, and my son Walter, who was nervous too. I told them there was nothing to worry about, the wind was fair, provisions full –"

"Look around you on the dock," Bagnet persisted. "Do you see anything unusual?"

Ralegh chuckled. "I've left for sea thousands of times, Bagnet. What does one seek on the dock? Shards of burlap, rotten fruit, and –" Ralegh's eyes opened in fright, and he stopped speaking.

"Tell me what you see, Sir Walter."

But the old knight shivered, his mouth open, unable to talk.

It was ten o'clock, and Bess Ralegh was sitting alone in the front room of when Bagnet arrived. It was a small area. The walls were stark white, bowls of pale blue lavender were on white stools, and there was one table where Bess was seated knitting. She turned at the sound of his step but did not see him drop a small bag near the door.

"I remember you. You are –"

"The man in the street this morning. The husband of Jessica Bagnet, who stayed with you for a while and whom you brought home in your carriage, and the man whom your late husband asked to find out who had killed him. I am sure he told you." Bess nodded at the word "late," and Bagnet added, "I am also a witness to his execution and the one entrusted by Sir Francis Bacon to return his remains to you. They are in a wagon outside."

She did not move at the news but stared ahead. "Thank you. May I ask, did he die as he wanted?"

"And more so."

Bess nodded, rose, and started for the door. "I will attend to his body. You have my eternal gratitude, Master Bagnet for all you did or attempted to do. I am sorry that my husband sent you out on a fool's errand and that you wasted this last night –"

Bagnet stepped away from her and placed his free hand on her empty chair, steadying his battered body and hoping to sit there when the occasion allowed him. As he stood, he gingerly slipped his battered arm out of Jessica's sling, as if to have it ready. "Oh, I did not waste my time. I completed my mission and told your husband before he died who had killed him."

"Oh," she said slowly, still near the door. "What did you tell him?"

"Actually, I asked him to tell himself. I asked him to look into his memory for anything unusual on the dock last year at Cork which is when he said everything started to go wrong."

Bess Ralegh moved toward him and asked, flatly. "And what did he see?"

"A white lace glove on the dock. He also remembered the scent of lavender, which women will crush into their gloves to be able to hold them to their faces to provide relief from the noxious smells of a city like London or a dock like Cork. Lavender such as you have here. The Carews tell me it is your favourite."

"I – I do not understand –"

Bagnet eased himself into the chair, knowing he had a ways to go in his explanation. "You seem to have a habit of losing your gloves, especially when you are excited. I smelled the lavender on the glove you lost in your carriage that my wife brought to the inn. I also smelled the lavender in her hair from when she was here with you and in Sir Francis' chambers when you were with him this evening before joining the Carews and when he used the same expression you just employed about your husband's commission for me – 'a fool's errand'. And, of course, I smelled lavender on the glove I returned to you early this morning."

"It is an unfortunate habit, perhaps, losing my gloves, but I do not see –"

"Your anxiety about my investigation caused you to bring my wife to the inn to check on me and to attempt to run me down with your carriage."

"Do not be absurd –"

"It was your carriage rather than Count Gondomar's because his was weighted down with wine and sausage and would not have cleared me, fat and old as I am. But yours was lightly loaded with only you and your coachman, and the undercarriage just grazed my arm."

Bess Ralegh remained calm. "Hardly enough evidence to convince anyone, Master Bagnet. Wine and sausage, really!"

"Oh, it convinced your husband when I told him," Bagnet wheezed, struggling up form the chair. "The memory of your glove proved to him you were in Cork, on the dock, unknown to him, plotting against him. And then everything came together in his mind. How they knew your every move as you and your husband tried to escape the country –"

"Damn you," he heard her hissing behind him. He turned to see her almost on him with nails raised. "Why did you tell him? Why did you spoil his mind about me before he died?"

Bagnet painfully caught her wrists and held them tight. "Because he wanted to know! Because he had to know!" Bagnet let her arms ago and grabbed her by the shoulders to force her to look into his eyes. "Why? Why did you arrange the failure of his mission to Guiana and guarantee his execution? Did you hate him so much?"

Bess Ralegh did not miss a beat. She matched his stare and answered. "Are you mad, man? I loved him more than any woman has loved a man. I still do." She pushed his hands away and moved to her unfinished knitting, which she fingered as if with a wandering mind. "Do you know, the happiest times of my life were the three years he spent in retirement with me after falling out of favour with the Queen because of our marriage. Each moment was a treasure beyond worth. For me, it seems, not for him. He had to – he had to sail, to find adventure, to go to Cadiz, Guiana, and beyond. And when he returned, his boldness brought him to the Tower. It is the fate of the wife of a legend. Which I accepted. Do you know, I would have gladly spent another 15 years, staying with him in the Tower when I could, sleeping next to him in his cell or on the floor when the fever was with him, braving rats and filth. But, no, he came up with this plan to convince James to let him sail again! He must seek out adventure wherever it was. And he did not know."

"Know what?"

"That even when he found the gold James would not have let him live. I have bargained with James. I know how he thinks. He would have killed him anyway, if only to guard the secret of the gold's location. Walter was going to die either way, whether James thought he found the gold or not. If someone had to have the gold, would it not be better if it were we? James had already squandered Elizabeth's treasury. How long would the gold of El Dorado last him? I told this to Keymis and my son in Cork and of my plan."

"Your plan to work with Sir Francis on securing the gold of El Dorado for you and him, of letting it look as if there was no gold, of Keymis firing on the Spanish to doom Sir Walter –"

"Doom him?" she turned, her eyes full of anger. "Canonize him as a hero wronged. Wronged by James. Wronged by the carelessness of his men. Now at least he has died bravely, the victim of a 15-year-old charge that Coke had to dredge up and that the people know is the sign of a weak king killing a better man."

"And what of your son? Why did he have to die?"

Her boldness evaporated in an instant. She brought her back to Bagnet and leaned her head against the wall. "Because he was more like his father than any of us thought. He had agreed to the plan in Cork, but evidently changed his mind and told his father by message the gold was found. Young Walter and Keymis must have argued. Keymis must have panicked."

"And killed your son?"

She appeared to Bagnet as almost a stick figure glued to the white wall as her hollow voice answered, "I knew Keymis was weak. I did not know how weak and stupid."

"And Keymis died –"

"– at the hand of Sir Francis' spy who boarded the *Destiny* in disguise and who had orders to dispatch him if he behaved strangely. Keymis must have fired at him in defence, but the man slipped the knife into Keymis' ribs and made it look like suicide."

"It was that murder poorly disguised as suicide that your husband could not accept and that was your undoing."

She pushed away from the wall, as if switching the topic from her son to Keymis had eased the pain. She turned, and Bagnet was surprised to see her smiling. "And the joke was on Sir Francis, because although Keymis had secured two casks of ore from El Dorado, his killer did not learn the exact location before dispatching Keymis. So what he brought home is what there is. That is what I was telling Sir Francis this evening, for the one-thousandth time. Still, my share of what we brought back is enough for me to support my remaining son Carew and to promote my husband's legend, while with his Sir Francis will have the freedom to plot against the royal marriage he opposes."

Bagnet sighed and then walked to the door, painfully bending to retrieve the black bag he had dropped there. "Sir Walter told me you could take care of yourself. He was right. You are a good woman of business, and until now I did not know there was such a thing, but you are. You argue like a foreclosing banker. Your husband also asked me to give you this." With a lunge, Bagnet looped the string of the bag over her head, and the black sack hung at her chest. "He asked me to tell you that he even knew why you did what you did. He said he had left you without funds, and that he understood. But he also wanted me to hang his head around your neck so that its weight filled your heart forever. And I have a message for you from myself." She sobbed, heaving the bag on her chest up and down. "When you made your arrangement with Sir Francis, you shook hands with the devil. Why do you think he allowed your husband to have me do my investigation? So that someone else knows! I am under orders to put what I found in writing and hand it to him. I have no doubt all reference to his part in this will somehow disappear. You will now have to dance with the devil, Mistress Ralegh. Dance well, and there will be no problem. Dance poorly, and it is you who will be in the Tower for treason, with my papers as evidence. Farewell."

Jessica was waiting in a carriage outside. "It was good of you to bring the body home and comfort her."

"I do not know how much comfort I have brought her."

"Oh," Jessica said, not understanding. "Anyone would feel that way under the circumstances. We do not know what to say."

"But," Bagnet said, settling back in his seat, "at least I satisfied a dead man's wish. Let us go home."

Bess Ralegh did keep the bag with her husband's head with her always, not about her neck, but in a closet, from where she would bring it out to show visitors on no provocation whatsoever, as if as a penance. In spite of the circumstances of her husband's death, she lived in luxury and died in 1647 at the age of 83. Her son Carew became a member of Parliament and was able to purchase the lands of his father that had been lost. Ralegh's reputation grew as the King's declined.

Bess did have to dance with the devil for a short while. Sir Francis died in 1626 but not before using his influence and unexplained wealth to prevent James' plan of a royal marriage between England and Spain. Gondomar died the same year as Bacon, in Spain, in some disgrace. And in 1853, Ralegh's claims of the gold of El Dorado being in Guiana were vindicated when the most productive gold mine in the world was established there.

PERFECT ALIBI

PHILIP BOAST

One individual that we have already encountered in several of the stories is Sir Francis Bacon (1561–1626). A scheming and highly intelligent individual, Bacon was arguably one of the most obnoxious people in Elizabethan and Jacobean England. He was certainly not one to have as your enemy. It was he who was the chief prosecutor of the Earl of Essex on the charge of treason in 1601. Although the shrewd Elizabeth could see through Bacon, James I probably saw much of himself in the man and, for much of James's reign, Bacon's advance was secure. He became solicitor-general in 1607, attorney-general in 1613 (it was he who conducted the prosecution of Somerset in the Overbury trial), Lord Chancellor in 1618 and eventually Viscount St Albans in 1621. But if ever the phrase "pride cometh before a fall" applied to anyone, it applied to Bacon. His enemies succeeded in convincing the House of Lords that Bacon accepted bribes for favours. Bacon offered no defence and was imprisoned but soon released and retired to his estates. There Bacon involved himself in academic and scientific studies – he had always had a fine and enquiring mind. He even wrote a utopian novel, New Atlantis, *in 1624 where he became the first to promote a new society through the study and advancement of science. One can well imagine Bacon in these final years, keen to solve any problems presented to him.*

Philip Boast (b. 1952) has written a number of historical epics, often with a fantasy or religious theme, including Sion *(1999), the story of Jesus and Mary Magdalene, and* Deus *(1997), which deals with the legacy of a crime committed in London in the thirteenth century.*

1624

The girl ran for more than her own life; she ran for two. She ran crying the name "Joabin! Joabin!" but no reply came from the dark.

Her name was Ann, a comely maiden of seventeen or so, with mistletoe in her chestnut hair, her curls now black with wet, invisible in the dark. But moonlight above the rainclouds revealed her terrified white face, and her ankles flashed beneath the hem of her blood-red, rain-blackened dress as she ran.

With a gasp for breath she knelt behind the gorse by Long Ditch, looking back. Still the house lights shone merrily on the hill, small now in the dark; but the lamp swung closer, and she heard footsteps.

Then the rain poured, hiding the sound of them.

She jumped the ditch, slid back, clawed through last season's brambles to the top, ran into Two-Acre Field. Heavy cold mud sucked the pretty red shoes from her feet. She slithered barefoot across the plough-furrows, her sodden dress held her down like an iron weight; gasping she dragged the velvets over her head, threw them away. She ran on, but her pursuer ran faster. Rain turned to sleet but she was past cold. From the field-boundary she glimpsed the lit windows of the village in the dell, and beyond it the scattered glow of St Albans Town, but the lamp swung close behind her now, too close.

Then came a muffled curse as the light was dropped, but was snatched up at once, and again came the mud-splashing footsteps, louder.

She ran into Old Wood. Twigs caught her hair like fingers; she screamed, and behind her the footsteps ran faster, the lamp bobbed between the treetrunks like a terrible glowing eye, and she hid behind an old oak to let it go by. But her heart thundered. And her breath gasped in her throat.

She raised her arm to ward off the blow.
Sleet turned to falling snow.

"Ganymede!" His withered, horny hand slapped my smooth-shaven arse, squeezing my cheek to show he remembered last night. "What, still a-bed, my Lady Gay Ganymede?"

" 'Tis not yet dawn, my lord," I complained. My name, I'll explain, is neither Ganymede nor any shortening, but Toby; and I'm no lady but a manservant and as male as we come, as many a lady and gentleman would swear, if any told truth under oath.

He is, of course, Francis, Viscount St Albans, and almost universally reviled since his fall from power, which as Lord Chancellor was second only to the King's. Everyone, in London at least, knows our Francis Bacon is the greatest lover of men who ever lived, after the King; unlike the King he possesses the greatest mind of any man living, bar none. So he tells me.

Even his enemies admit it.

"Why so early, my lord?"

"No My-lords lie between us while I call you Ganymede." His wrinkled lips tasted of orange and cloves. "I'll wear my green hat with the pearls."

" 'Tis sold, Francis."

"The purple with gold." I shook my head. "Black with silver?"

I fetched it. Great God he looked older since his friends deserted him, his allies betrayed him, the £40,000 fine gutted him. His palace near St Albans sold, only these few Gray's Inn rooms left in London, his magnificent clothes pawned for rent money, which hurt him more than anything. There was a horrible uncertain light in his eyes as he turned to me. "Well?"

"You peacock," I said.

That cheered him and he peeped from the window, all silly hat and scrawny buttocks. "Snow's melting. There's my long-standing arrangement to sleep at Sir John Tyrambel's house tonight at St Albans. His table's plain but good and so's his cellar." This was Francis's way of saying we wouldn't pay to feast and get drunk tonight. Tyrambel, once a near neighbour, was a Crown solicitor, and no doubt thought Francis – who in ascendancy was Solicitor-General and Attorney-General – retained helpful influence. Naturally Francis, who nowadays had shit thrown at him in the street by most of his old colleagues, said nothing to contradict Tyrambel's belief. Francis, I knew, thought Tyrambel had a head of oak; but compared to Francis, most people do.

I found him a black and scarlet doublet which didn't clash much with the hat, and a pair of boots without obvious holes, then scrabbled coins from the coal-scuttle for a carriage. Usually ostlers, like grocers and tailors, are first to hear of a fall and adjust their manners down and prices up accordingly, but this fellow was deaf, and gave over a four-in-hand and driver like the old days. Our arrival would impress even the oaken Tyrambel.

From Gray's Inn to St Albans is hardly over twenty miles, much by the straight Roman road mostly rutted free of January snow, so we'd arrive before dark, after which no travel is possible. Francis spent the day's journey writing in first one book, now the other, some philosophical treatise, or scientific monograph, or play none but him will understand. "Ganymede," he murmured, and I turned from the window pouting, neglected. But instead of speaking of love he said, "I have a theory that the underlying form of Form is numbers."

You see what I mean. Not so interesting as a squeeze on the knee.

"Fascinating," I yawned. Form is one of his words. So is Table. And Idol. These words don't mean what you or I think they do.

"Sufficient numbers acquire Form," he mused. "So I realized last night when I measured the heat of moonbeams."

"The heat of moonbeams!"

"Using a magnifying-glass to focus them on a thermometer."

"Do they? Have heat?"

"Yes. The problem's one of measurement. There's no scale for defining the degrees of heat or cold. I'll devise one," he decided. "The Bacon Scale. There are temperatures colder than the freezing-point of water, but where shall I start? Is there absolute cold? Absolute heat? What's its nature?" He pulled out a wooden rod. "It's all a matter of the measurement of Manifestations. You know what this is?"

"For measuring Manifestations?"

"Yes. A foot-rule." He showed me. "See, the foot scale is divided into twelve equal parts each called an *uncia*, an inch. Obviously everyone's feet are different lengths. However, to establish a universal standard I sent a boy to mark a stick against one hundred feet, and this is the average." He measured my foot. "You have dainty feet, only eight inches long."

"But what does it mean?"

"If all Manifestations of Form can be measured, quantified, standardized, compared, the world is explained."

"My feet explain the world?"

"If only," he sighed, "I could measure your beauty." He added, less happily, "Or your intelligence."

I left him to it. He never stops.

We arrived at Bensalem House before dark, and Francis put on his dignity. It is amazing to watch; his speech slows, authority steals over him like gravity, every gesture is laden with importance. "My good Tyrambel."

Sir John, called to the step by his steward Cambalaine, looked shocked by our arrival. "Such an honour, my lord." His invitation had stood from before Yule (as older people call Christ's-Mass), you'd have thought he'd remember – I whispered it discreetly, so that Francis need not lower himself. "Our best bedroom!" cried Sir John. "Light the fires, Cambalaine! A feast for the table! Wife!" Most satisfactory.

Cambalaine, tall, hollow-eyed, fetchingly muscular, bowed deep.

Francis wore his long black cloak that survived the pawnbroker, and looked around him sharply as we swept into the house.

"Most welcome my lord!" cried Lady Eliza, dark under the eyes, hair unbound, but still handsome. Francis bent over her hand. "Lady Eliza." She almost fainted of nerves. There was a son, Bartholomew, about fifteen, thrice taller since we last saw him, but no more confident, darting his eyes like a kicked dog, as is common with sons of lesser gentry. "And your sister?" Francis enquired. "Ann, I believe?" His memory for names is as phenomenal as his other mental abilities, he'd seen the girl but once or twice since she was swaddled.

"Oh – she – she's –"

"Sick again," Sir John said. "I sent her to spend the winter months at my sister's house on the coast. The sea air is a tonic."

Francis nodded. "The ailment is in her lungs, then."

Sir John said, "Yes–"

"A contagion caught in the village," spat his wife.

"Forgive us." Sir John guided Francis personally to the stairs. "We're worried for her health. Ann, though much-loved, is a trial to us, strong-willed, difficult. Not the first time I've sent the girl to her Aunt Salomana for special care."

Francis's portmanteau, laden mostly with old shoes and motheaten coverlets for weight, was hauled to his room. Naturally I was to sleep on straw in the corner, but the broad bed was plenty for two, and soft. A fire roared but the weather warmed at last, and Francis threw open the window to observe the behaviour of raindrops on glass. "Each drop stands proud, there is a tension on the surface," he called. "Only when smeared do they flatten and run."

"Your head's wet," I called from the bed. "You'll catch a chill."

He turned, the drops standing on his cheeks like beads, for we'd not washed lately. "I have a theory, Ganymede. Science should proceed first by describing how things work, by observation. And only later by understanding why, by experiment."

This is how Francis makes wise men tear their hair, for he thinks thoughts never thought before. Yet they make an odd kind of sense; and do not make him too weary for love.

Supper in the great hall was a poor affair, not the food which was solid and plentiful, or the wine which was excellent, but the company: plainly Sir John and his wife were distracted, and young Bart barely picked his food. Francis helped him with chicken legs leaving nought but bones for me, servants and dogs. A young man, Jack – from a good household behind the hill, Sir John assured Francis – arrived on some small business. "One day you may marry my Ann, eh, Jack," Sir John said cordially, with an eye on Francis. Jack's breeches, once pricey, were a little frayed, she'd be a good catch for him. The gleam in Jack's eye revealed similar hopes.

"But she never looks at me," he complained. "Perhaps you could speak to her, Sir John, on my behalf." Francis glanced at me. The boy seemed very keen to wed a sickly girl, but he was on hard times.

Francis finished with marchpane, syllabub and soft cheese (his teeth being stumped), then in our room threw me the ham-hock and house-cheese he'd concealed in his robes. "'Tis the unhappiest family I ever heard of," he commented, combing his straggly white beard ready for bed. "The girl's sickness has cast a dark oppression on them." And it was at that exact moment we heard a man's shouts outside, and footsteps running, and a knocking on the door. And a frantic knocking it was, with much shouting, and then a moment of silence as the door was opened.

I jumped from bed naked as I was, and leant from the window. There below, by the light cast from the open door, I saw a short man in rugged farming clothes. His eyes were wide, staring, his mouth hanging open like a man who, I swear, has seen Hell. In his hands he held a bloody shovel, still dripping.

"Dead!" he cried, and a scream came from within the house.

I ran downstairs pulling on my breeches, but Francis was first. Lady Eliza had fainted clean away, huddled in her skirts. "Cambalaine!" shouted Sir John, and the steward wrestled the shouting man to the ground.

"Bring him inside," Francis ordered, and the man was dragged in and pushed on a chair. "A gardener, by his clothes?" Francis barely glaned at him. "What's a gardener doing out at this time of night?"

"My gamekeeper," panted Sir John. "'Tis Quinzy."

"Dead sir," Quinzy said, shaking.

"Who's dead?" Sir John demanded loudly.

Francis took his shoulder. "Attend to your wife, Sir John." By now Lady Eliza half-sat against the wall, her hair over her handsome ruined face.

"'Tis her." Her eyes were dull. "'Tis Ann."

"It cannot be, she's with my sister in Weymouth," Sir John said firmly. Then, gently: "My heart, distress not yourself."

Dully: "Run away with that monster. You said so yourself. Stop her."

Quinzy called, "No, master and mistress, not run away, 'tis your own sweet daughter I found lying dead in the woods." His face buckled. "'Tis poor sweet Ann who never hurt a soul!"

Sir John drew his dagger. "You rogue, you killed her!" I grabbed his arm, but there was no force in the blow, I held him. Quinzy sat shaking, Cambalaine's hands pressed firmly on his shoulders.

Francis poured a cup and pushed it at the gamekeeper. "Tell us what happened."

Quinzy drained it in one. "In Old Wood I was. Badgers. Some jobs best done by night. My musket with me."

"And a shovel, you fiend!" cried Sir John, but I kept his dagger hid. "Call the village watchman, lock him away. He'll hang before week's end."

"I can't believe 'tis Quinzy!" wept Lady Eliza, more than half hysterical. "No, no, 'tis the monster."

All this was getting a little much for me. I looked from one grief-stricken face to the other, and then at young Bart who arrived in his nightshirt. "It was Jack," he cried from the stair. "He loved her and she rejected him like before."

"We get ahead of ourselves," Francis said coolly. "The girl convalesces in Weymouth, yet lies dead in Old Wood – if the body, which we haven't seen, really is Ann's. This may be Quinzy's mistake, the body of some vagrant woman mistook when he dropped his lamp." He added, "You did have a lamp, Quinzy?"

"Yes sir, made by myself, of a wooden box with a hole on top, a tallow candle burning inside, and a small window of bottle-bottom glass."

"How did you come by the shovel?"

"I don't use a shovel, sir, unless I got dogs with me, for digging out setts. By night I uses wire traps or musket. That shovel, I fell over it when I dropped the lamp. It was horrible, sir. I saw her poor face, the lamp went out, I tripped backwards, and in the dark my hand found the shovel. Must have picked it up without thought when I ran. Old Wood's thick, like a warren it is, a maze. God knows how I got out in the dark. Only when I reached the house did I see, by the lights –" He covered his mouth.

Francis fetched the shovel, the blade matted with red blood and hair. Sir John covered his wife's eyes. Francis said, "Perfectly fresh. No clotting. No longer ago than dark this afternoon, I'd say." He pulled out a sticky strand of hair. "Chestnut." Even Sir John turned his face away.

"Yes, my lord," Cambalaine said calmly. "Mistress Ann's."

"God preserve us!" cried Lady Eliza. "It's His will." And fainted again.

"I think it best," Francis said, "if, rather than stumble around such a deep woodland in the dark, we endure a sleepless night and await dawn before an excursion."

* * *

"Questions, Toby," Francis whispered my real name because of Cambalaine's presence, "occur to me." Late it was, very late; black beyond the windows.

"Like what day to hang Quinzy on," murmured Cambalaine. We spoke so quiet around the table because Sir John and Lady Eliza paced the room, or sat in chairs, or stared at the dark outside, not sleeping a wink.

"A murderer does not usually run to report his crime whilst brandishing the murder weapon," Francis said. Quinzy, still protesting his innocence, was locked in the pantry for safety.

"Then it was Jack," I murmured. "I know what young men are like. After he left us he met the girl travelling home unannounced from Weymouth with her health fully recovered, pressed his passionate feelings too ardently, she screamed, he went too far silencing her."

"There's a difference between putting a hand over someone's mouth and clubbing them to death with a shovel," Francis pointed out. He asked Cambalaine, "Where are the shovels kept?"

"Outhouse."

"Locked?"

"No, but young gentleman Jack wouldn't even know what a shovel was."

"But you do."

"I served you all evening, my lord."

"Hmm. Any monsters round here?" Francis nodded at Lady Eliza. "She means vagrants, itinerants, tinkers?" Cambalaine shook his head, recalling none. "Any thieving lately, or strangers about?"

"Not recently, sir." He stopped. "Now it occurs to me, about a month or two back, we did lose a shovel."

"This shovel?"

"I don't know sir, a shovel's a shovel to me."

Francis scratched his head. "An extraordinarily premeditated murder for the murderer to steal his weapon months before his crime." He added, "Or her."

We looked at Lady Eliza, then stared at each other, shocked at ourselves. For a mother to kill her daughter is unthinkable. Yet these ancient Greek plays have been discovered in which such behaviour, and worse, seems almost commonplace. I cleared my throat.

"Sir John Tyrambel has a nervous manner," I whispered.

"He dotes on his daughter," Francis said dismissively. "I remember his pride when Ann was born. Once or twice they rode to my house, father and child, she on her own pony. Never was a father prouder." He lowered his voice. "What, is he an actor? I have known actors." Francis has indeed, in more senses than one, and if ever they disturb a certain grave in Stratford-upon-Avon they will find in the bone-dust a brass plaque inscribed *F. Bacon fecit*. F. Bacon made him. Not just the plays but the man too, and his silly name. I digress merely to show that Francis has a deep understanding of acting and actors. "Sir John is acting just as you'd expect of a man who fears he's lost his daughter but cannot face up to it."

"Absolutely," I agreed, which is best with Francis.

"In any event," Francis said, "everyone in the house has an alibi, for we were here. And anyone not here, like Quinzy alone in the dark, or Jack, does not."

Somewhere a clock gonged. The hours until dawn were very long.

The morn was clear and we were out before the sun rose, trudging across wet lawns in the clean grey light of a new day. Yet almost at once we came upon strangeness, and a sense of old sins still doing their work; of course we men in our mercy had left Lady Eliza behind, sleeping at last, but now her scream rent the air and the poor woman came running from the house. "No, I must come! I must see!"

"We don't know there's anything to see," Francis said gently. "Best to wait behind, the vicar is sent for, to pray with him."

But she pointed. "Look."

Indeed strange, for the snow had mostly melted overnight, and the landscape we'd grown used to snow-white was dull and wet. We stood (with a few curious house-boys) by the place Cambalaine, who pushed the empty barrow chained to poor shaking Quinzy, called Long Ditch. The fields stretched out black with mud. Sir John set off to walk around the edge, but Francis pulled a thread from a gorse bush. "Come my lord," I whispered lasciviously, "you'll prick yourself."

He held it up. No thread, a hair. He hummed, "What does this mean?"

"It's a hair," I said. "Heads are covered with them. So are animals."

"A chestnut hair."

"Oh," I said.

"Exactly," he said. "So, what does it mean?"

"Nothing to me."

He said, "I have a theory which I call inductive logic, based on elimination."

"Great God, Francis, these people are suffering! Their hearts cry out for their daughter. Your cold theories say nothing to the complex heat of human emotion."

Francis called them. "She came this way." He showed Sir John the hair. "A matter of observation, of fact. Inductive logic–"

"Perhaps it blew," Sir John said. "It could have been caught there for months, years."

Francis pointed. Across the muddy ploughed field, footprints showed. "From here she ran across the field." He walked out, careless of the clay weighting his boots, following her footsteps. "Someone ran after her." More footprints, not quite on the same line, weaving.

"Her pursuer was drunk!" I said.

"Perhaps," said Francis. He bent, picking a girl's red shoe from the mud. Lady Eliza snatched it at once and clutched the muddy pathetic thing to her bosom, weeping.

"Perhaps drunk," Francis murmured, "or perhaps he hardly saw her because it was dark."

I closed my eyes, appalled. "This happened while we ate and made merry. The poor girl. It hardly bears thinking about."

"Yet we must think about it." Francis looked round carefully but saw nothing. He strode to Old Wood then stopped for Quinzy to be our guide.

Within the wood snow still lay in patches, pocked, grey. "Left," Quinzy said. "Deeper in. Much deeper."

"This is a cursed wood," Sir John said; the trees so close you believed you turned in circles. First one glade, now another.

She lay beneath an oak tree.

"My heart!" Sir John ran on.

Dressed only in soaked petticoats, black with mud below the

knee. He crouched and I thought he stroked something from her hair, crumpled it in his pocket, but I forgot for Lady Eliza pushed hard past me. She lifted her daughter's body in her arms and rocked like a mother giving milk to her baby, weeping.

"Little remains of the face," Francis whispered. "Beaten to death. The shovel."

"I'll hang Quinzy myself," choked Sir John.

Quinzy's lamp lay on the grass among the first blue violets. The outline of the girl's barefoot body was drawn in ice on the ground, melting as we watched. Her arm, raised as if warding off a blow, flopped against her mother's shoulder as her body thawed.

Lady Eliza stroked her daughter's hair, then looked up to her husband, but not in a loving wifely way. Her face changed. "Tell them or I will."

Sir John shuddered, then turned to us. "We know who murdered her. Only let me kill him, let me have justice, and I'll gladly swing for it."

"The monster?" Francis, still kneeling, fixed Lady Eliza's chin so she must look into his eyes. "The contagion from the village?"

"His name's Joabin," she spat. "Give us justice!"

Francis stood. He nodded to Cambalaine. A boy was sent running to the village, but not before Francis had scribbled a note, folded it and on the flap wrote JOABIN, before slipping it in the boy's pocket.

"We've seen enough here," Francis said. "We return to the house."

Cambalaine, helped by two house-boys, lay the poor body in the barrow. Sir John covered it with his cloak. A long slow walk home; the wheel squeaked and stuck often in the mud, so the two boys lifted at the front while Cambalaine pushed at the back. I spoke to Francis in a low voice. "What makes you think Joabin will obey your summons?"

"If he does it tells us much, and if he does not, it tells us much."

"What did your note say?"

"I promised the monster's safety."

"All agree he's guilty."

"Yet," Francis said, "her footprints run away from the house."

"But nobody left the house."

"Running towards the monster's village, not away from it."

"Francis, you make my head hurt!"

He added, "Barefoot, partially undressed. Where's her dress, her other shoe?"

"Do you believe she was . . . violated?"

"I believe," he said, reaching into his pocket and handing me the foot-rule, "that you should make a measurement of every footprint you find in mud and snow." He finished kindly, "Ignoring our own, of course."

"I am Joabin."

I gasped when I saw him, not because I knew who he was, but *what*. His clothes were good but glossy, of deliberately foreign look. His hair, too, marked him apart, long black curls dangling in front of his ears. On the crown of his head, where a monk's tonsure would be, he wore a small black cap. He was indeed a monster. He was a Jew.

And no older than the girl who lay dead downstairs.

Francis, who remained in the front room with the body, had left orders that the monster be shown up here to the library where the light was good. Joabin sat at the long table with his hands resting on the wood, calm, tense, businesslike, the tall gallery windows illuminating his pale intelligent face and large brown eyes. Sir John sat at the far end, staring. Had he a pistol, he'd have used it. Cambalaine and I stood between them.

'You dare show your face in my house, you cur," Sir John swore.

The youth opened his hands. "I've nothing to hide, Sir John." His manner was mature beyond his years, and steady. But so foreign! His nails long and his teeth good.

"Christ-killer!" Sir John shouted. Francis, in the interest of fairness, would have pointed out that our Lord was also a Jew, yet Pilate a Gentile.

Joabin turned to me. "What is this about? Do you need money?"

"We'll wait until my lord arrives."

"Why is Lady Eliza weeping?" Joabin swallowed. "Is there bad news from Weymouth?" Lady Eliza huddled in the padded chair by the stair-top. Francis had pulled her from her daughter's body and sent her up. She couldn't stop weeping. Her noise wore out the nerves of all of us.

"Joabin pretends not to know why!" cried Sir John. "He's clever, the devil."

We heard Francis on the stairs. He stood with his back to the windows so his face was dark, Joabin to the left of his shadow in full daylight, so the sun showed any lie. "You are Joabin?"

"Yes, son of Tirsan."

"You live with your father in the village?"

"We do our business in the town."

"Business?"

"In March my father lends sowing-money to be paid back at harvest. In autumn he lends enough to see people through the winter."

"You work for your father as a moneylender?"

"Yes. And in London, at the 'Change."

"To whom do you lend?"

"Merchants. Aristocrats. Landed gentry."

"Like Sir John?"

"Like Sir John, but not him. He has . . ." Joabin's lips almost formed the word *bribes*, which is how lawyers and judges (and Lord Chancellors) must make a living, but the word he said was, "income. Income from Law as well as fields. He's more fortunate than most of his neighbours."

Francis said coolly, for he was to his neck in debt, "Moneylenders have an unpopular reputation."

"Some do."

"Some are considered monsters."

"I have never been called that. We charge thirty per cent, which is reasonable given our risk."

"Thirty per cent," Francis said, impressed.

"Better to have good debts than bad ones." Joabin raised his voice. "Enough. It's no secret that Sir John regards me as an enemy. Is Ann well? Has she asked for me?"

"Why, Joabin? Why should she?"

"Because I love her, and she loves me." He looked confused. 'Has Sir John not told you?"

"Liar!" shouted Lady Eliza. Sir John went on, "She never loved you, could never love you, Jew, blood-sucker, abomination. God scattered your people to the winds for your sins!"

Francis let a few moments tick by while Lady Eliza wept.

"Joabin," he asked, "where were you last night, after dark?"

"At home with my father, mother, and five brothers."

"That's no alibi," Sir John sneered. "Jews lie to save each other's skins."

Then Francis said a very strange thing. "Joabin, where were you last Christ's-Mass?"

"In London, on business, in a Christian lodging-house by the 'Change, run by Mrs Day. She invited me to the feast with her other lodgers, and I accepted. Along with perhaps a dozen Christians whose names will be in her register, a Moor, and a Puritan, Master Nathaniel Wallington, who stuck his head in to order us to stop our noise."

"That's sufficient," Francis said.

"Then, together with other lenders, I represented my father at Whitehall Palace with Prince Honoré II of Monaco, the Lord Mayor of London, and Prince Charles, Duke of York." We stared. He explained, "His art collection is large and not cheaply bought."

"A perfect alibi," Francis purred. He nodded and I poured a cup of brandy. "Joabin, it hurts me to tell you this. Ann's body was found in the woods last night."

Joabin, pale-faced already, went white as chalk. I pushed the cup into his hands. He drank, choked. "But she can't be dead, not here. Sir John forbade me to see her again and sent her away."

"When was this?"

"Before Christ's-Mass. No." He corrected himself. "It was after. I had returned from London with some difficulty because of the snow. My father had been sent a message that Sir John wished to see me. Because the snow was so deep two of my brothers came with me for safety."

"Lucky for you," Francis said, with a glance at Sir John.

"Sir John made it clear he'd forbidden his daughter's 'false' affection for me and if I ever tried to see or contact her again, ever, he'd see me dead and burn my house."

"I'd do it, and more." Sir John, pouring a brandy, drank it in one.

Francis said, "Did you see her again?"

"Never."

"Or contact her?"

Joabin gave Sir John a wary look. "It would not be the first time they tried to part us. I wrote to Weymouth, to Aunt Salomana's house, under a different name, but one she'd have understood." He tried to make us comprehend. "We are – were – so very, very much in love."

"I know," Francis said. "Ann was pregnant."

In the shocked silence Lady Eliza gave a great scream. She fell forward on the boards. Cambalaine went to her. She covered her face. Sir John watched her, then turned back to us.

"She didn't know," Francis said. "But you did. Ann told you. This was not one murder but two."

Sir John lunged suddenly along the table at Joabin, but I'd kept his dagger, and stuck the point to his throat. He slid back along the wood unblinking, then sat stiff, but anyway I kept it handy under his chin.

"You were here last night yourself, my lord." Sir John's eye acquired a cunning light. "You know I remained here."

"Last night, yes," Francis agreed. "But Joabin has the perfect alibi for when the murder was committed."

Even Cambalaine looked startled. "But she was killed last night! The body's fresh as a daisy, the blood still red with life, wet. There's not a sniff of rot on her."

Francis said, "Joabin, I'm sorry. Your letter to Ann received no reply because she was already dead." He went on gently, "I examined her body carefully. Your child was conceived around harvest-time."

Lady Eliza hissed: "Monster's spawn."

"Be silent, my love." Sir John struggled. I pricked him with the point.

"When we knew God had blessed us," Joabin admitted. "I begged her hand in marriage. She said yes, gladly. She begged her father's permission but dared not tell him of the child. Even so Sir John said no time and again. He damned me. Damned us both, damned even his own daughter's happiness, for we could never be happy apart. What else could we do, but meet in secret?"

"Three months, perhaps four," Francis said. "Ann knew it would show soon. Matters came to a head. She confronted her father at Christ's-Mass, perhaps while the guests were blind with feasting downstairs, up in this very room where it was quiet. Both of them hot with wine – I see Sir John prefers brandy – she told him of the child. She told him that whatever his threats and forbiddings, she was determined to marry Joabin the Jew and bear their child honourably and openly, in wedlock."

"You repeat this unspeakable slur on my daughter at your peril," Sir John said steadily. "I'll sue you for every penny that hasn't been taken from you already, you disgusting old sodomite. You and your prancing catamite, your Ganymede – d'you think people don't *know* about you, you filthy homosexual?"

Francis ignored him. "You saw the time for words was past. Women cannot be argued with once their minds are set; their love turns to scorn. You know you'd lost your daughter. When word came out that she was pregnant by a Christ-killer, your social standing and your career would be finished. You lost your mind. I suppose you lashed out. Ann ran from the house, ran towards the only safety she knew."

"She didn't know I was in London," Joabin whispered. "There was no safety in the village. My father would have handed her back. Jews can't afford argument with Gentiles."

"You know this story of yours is impossible," smiled Sir John at Sir Francis, like a man who wishes his smiling teeth could bite. "It's February, and if matters had proceeded at Christ's-Mass as you say, the body would be rotten by now."

"Nevertheless," Francis said, "having made an hypothesis, I am obliged to test it. *Major est vis instantiae negativae*, the laws of nature cannot be verified, but they can be falsified. So can the laws of human nature, perhaps; a flaw makes the diamond shine, and so it is with the mind. Let us see by experiment. If anything I say is disproved, I must eliminate it from my hypothesis." I kept the dagger pricking Sir John's chin.

" 'Tis best done downstairs," Francis said. "The innocent will be exonerated, the guilty given every chance to disprove their guilt, and I my chance to prove them worthy of the hangman."

The fire unlit; stone cold in the room. The melting body, under a coverlet, laid on the table. The vicar prayed, the watchman scratched his whiskers with his stick. Jack, too, had been sent for, terrified. Bart stared at some painting rather than acknowledge that terrible shape under the coverlet, the drip of icewater from her petticoats. Cambalaine held Joabin and Quinzy, then

Francis shepherded Sir John and Lady Eliza into the room, and bade me stay by the chest as arranged.

"Excellent," Francis said, as though welcoming us to some party-gathering. "Thank you, vicar. I see we're all here. Do sit, Lady Eliza." He swept away the coverlet and we endured poor Ann's frightful distorted stare, the shovel's work.

"The body's fresh after six weeks," I said, as he'd asked me to.

"It is a law of nature," Francis said just a little bit pompously, "a scientific fact that can be repeated by experiment, that below the freezing point of water, corruption of the flesh does not occur." The vicar looked doubtful. Francis claimed, "I have myself proved this by stuffing the carcass of a chicken with snow. The experiment can be repeated any number of times without exception, and applies to all flesh whether chicken or human. *Quod erat demonstrandum*," he beamed.

"But it rained on Christ's-Mass," Joabin said. "At least, in London."

"Turned to snow about nine of the evening," Cambalaine said. "I'd looked out thinking I heard someone, and saw it fell heavy."

"Did you see anyone?"

"No."

"Ann had already run from the house after the argument in the library. The sound you heard was the murderer returning."

"This is fatuous," Sir John said. "Even if your hypothesis were correct, are you saying *I* pursued her? No one saw me. You're a clever fool, my lord. After Ann rushed off pell-mell I sat by the open door of my library, collecting my feelings. Anyone could have seen me there."

"But did not."

He shrugged. "I know not."

"Ann tried to hide in the outhouse, then probably heard your front door slam, and ran when she saw her pursuer had a lamp – several are kept by the door. Enraged by her escape, guessing her destination to be the Jews, the murderer snatched up a shovel."

"I'd never mean to hurt my daughter. I know of no lamp."

Francis turned to me. I opened the chest where he'd bade me conceal various items, and pulled out the lamp.

"This lamp," Francis said. "Splashed with mud. And here, the smear where it was dropped." I showed them. "Replaced among the others as if nothing had happened." He went on, "Ann caught her hair in the gorse by Long Ditch." He held up the pallid forearm, scratched. "Brambles; she jumped the ditch into Two-Acre Field. This morning we followed her footprints and those of her pursuer across the mud, and found her shoe." I held up her red shoe. "Only one. Yet she ran on with *both* feet bare, her toes clearly imprinted. What size, good Toby?"

"Eight and eight-tenths inches," I said. "I measured them."

Francis took the foot-rule and held it to the body's foot. "Eight and eight-tenths inches. Not the same size as the prints left by her pursuer. Ann was weary from the chase, the rain was heavy, she discarded her festive dress to run faster. She ran into Old Wood. There, deep in the wood, she was finally caught and beaten with a frenzy of shovel blows; the shovel dropped by the murderer in horror, or remorse, or satisfaction at a job well done. By then rain turned to snow. The murderer returned to the house, leaving no further prints in the mud to show their return, but only in the overlying snow."

"Now gone," Sir John said. "Your evidence is melted."

"Not all," Francis said equably. "In the deep woodland shadows this morning, some remained. Complete with prints. Not all near the body, indeed none were. Toby, what size were they?"

"Eleven inches and a quarter."

"Allow me, Sir John." Francis held the rule to Sir John's boot. "Eleven and a quarter."

Sir John tried to brazen it out. "Coincidence."

"Hundreds of them," Francis said. "Toby found one half a mile from the body. Because when, calmly, you went early next morning to hide evidence of the crime and bury the body, you couldn't find it. Everything was smooth white snow. Trailing footprints as you were, you couldn't search too obviously or too long lest questions were asked; but you turned up one red shoe in the field."

I held up a red shoe. "From Ann's bedroom, cleaned as though nothing happened. Only one. Doubtless Sir John intended adding the other when melting snow revealed it."

"But the snow didn't melt," Francis said bleakly. "Not all through January, not until now, when *we* found the shoe this morning not he. And the footprints ran from the house preserved in mud. What of her dress?" He pretended thought.

"Red shoes, a difficult match with any colour but red . . . a red dress, I'd say."

"A lovely choice." I lifted a heavy red velvet dress I'd taken from her wardrobe. "Washed." Then I turned the hem inside-out. "Mudstains."

"Oh," Sir John said.

"Oh," Francis agreed, patiently.

"Everything you say is true," confessed Sir John. "I couldn't find her body." He broke down. "I couldn't find where my dear daughter lay."

"A confession!" said the watchman. "Sir John Tyrambel, I arrest you –"

"Father, no!" Bart cried. "My lord, he's a good man, he wouldn't hurt a fly!"

Francis pointed at the body. "Note she wears mistletoe in her hair, a pagan symbol permitted only on Christ's-Mass Day and no other. 'Tis the clinching proof she died on that day." We stared at her bare chestnut locks.

"What mistletoe?" I asked, primed.

Francis plucked a sprig of crumpled mistletoe from Sir John's pocket, chestnut hairs still wound around the stalk. "He took it as he stroked her hair this morning. He's had all this time to think, worry, plot and plan how to cover his tracks, if you'll pardon the expression. He had to hide the mistletoe linking Ann's death with Christ's-Mass, when Joabin had a perfect alibi. He invented ill health for Ann, a convalescence with Aunt Salomana. He planned to shift the murder onto poor Joabin, when the body was found apparently freshly murdered, as last night. A Jew living among Jews, and half the town owing them money, wouldn't get a jury finding him innocent. When the innocent hang, the guilty go free. So, an atrocious crime in every respect, Sir John. A murder not only of your daughter, but of a mother and her unborn child, and an attempt to arrange the judicial murder of that child's innocent Jewish father.

"But," he said, "you did not commit it."

There was a long silence.

"I killed her!" cried Sir John. "I killed her."

Francis held up the foot-rule. "I forgot to mention that the pursuer's tracks across the mud – made before the snow fell – were not eleven inches and a quarter, but nine inches exactly." He handed the rule to me. "Bart, if you please."

I measured Bart's feet. "Ten and two-tenths." I measured Jack's foot, only one-tenth more.

Francis said, "And now Lady Eliza."

I knelt. "I don't think this will be necessary," she said.

"My love, say nothing!" urged Sir John.

I grabbed her foot and held it to the rule. "Nine inches dead," I said.

She stood proudly. "I didn't want to kill her. I wanted to kill his monster." She pointed quivering fingers at Joabin. "His monstrous Jew-child that she carried within her. Yes, I knew." Before I could stop her she leapt, beating Joabin with her fists in a sudden hysteria, beating the air even as I dragged her off, so my mind's eye saw all too clearly the frenzy with which she'd beaten her daughter to death.

"The only monster here is you and your crime, Lady Eliza." Then Francis pointed at Sir John. "And you, for covering up. You'll both swing." He turned to me with a grim smile. "I rest my hypothesis."

Our carriage swayed towards London. "Sir John had a head of oak," Francis nodded, "but Lady Eliza's brain was cold sharp ice." On his lap lay the large, heavy, mysterious paper bag he'd insisted on bringing with him. Naturally I felt rejected.

"Eavesdropping's a sin," he mused, his cheeks flushed, always a sign of strong-felt passion with him. "She should never have listened by the open library door and overheard her daughter's confession. She should never have hated Jews, there was no reason for it. And Sir John should never have loved such a wife enough to hang with her."

"Your passion does you credit," I complimented him, hoping some would come my way. "There's a fine colour in your cheeks."

"Passion, Ganymede? I've more credit than passion." He rubbed his hands. "A hundred pounds at thirty per cent, thanks to Joabin! What a bargain." But still he stared from the window.

"What do you search for?" I asked at last, baffled.

"Ah, there it is!" His knock stopped the driver by a deep gully where snow survived. Rummaging in the bag he withdrew a plucked, drawn chicken. "You remember, dearest Ganymede, my case rested on frozen meat remaining fresh. I deceived Sir

John. I have never in fact tested that hypothesis." He leapt down and commenced busily stuffing the chicken with snow. "A flaw I must remedy. In the service of justice I've been guilty, it seems, of falsification!"

THE RESTLESS DEAD

MARTIN EDWARDS

James I died in 1625 and was succeeded by his eldest surviving son, Charles. Whilst we have now technically moved beyond the Jacobean period we are still firmly in the same world and beliefs.

The following story is based on a real case, that of Arthur and Mary Norcott, which may be found in the Newgate Calendar for 1629. You can find an account of it on the internet at http://www.exclassics.com/newgate/ng11.htm though Martin Edwards has adapted it for his own purposes. It answers the original query that I had that they allowed exhumations this long ago.

Martin Edwards (b. 1955) is a solicitor in Liverpool, and the author of the Harry Devlin series of novels which began with All the Lonely People *(1991). He has also compiled several anthologies including one of historical mysteries,* Past Crimes *(1998).*

What if he is not dead?

George Dakin shivered. By way of compensation for the cold of the night-time graveyard, his imagination was overheating. A twelvemonth of studying dusty legal tomes had not sapped his yearning for romance and mystery; nor had his principal's strictures that the business of the man of law was logic, not lurid speculation. Their nocturnal work was grim and distasteful, but he could not resist a shudder of morbid pleasure. This was his first exhumation.

An east wind howled through the trees. The sea coast was no more than five furlongs distant and George could taste salt in the air. Few places on earth, he would be bound, were as bleak as his native Northumberland in February. But he, like the others gathered around the hole in the ground, was too engrossed to quail at the bite of the wintry gusts. The onlookers huddled closer together as the sexton knocked a clod of earth from his shovel. The soil smelled damp. The candle held by the churchwarden cast a flickering light and George saw the vicar's fleshy jowls wobbling with ill-concealed excitement as he gazed down into the grave. Crouched next to the parson was William Crozier, the coroner and George's principal. Crozier was as lean as the man of God was stout. His nose was quivering; he might have been a bloodhound on a scent.

The candles wavered and George glimpsed a blind cherub guarding a small family vault beneath a gnarled oak. Henry Stokoe's last resting place was marked by a simple stone bearing his name, the dates of his birth and death and the words *requiescat in pacem.* An ordinary grave – until the arrival of the coroner's jury's at dead of night, to witness the disinterring of his corpse.

One of the jurors whispered to his neighbour. "Watch for movement!" A tall man waved his wooden stick. "This is nonsense!" he said to the young fellow at his side.

Yet although he shared John Laidlaw's sturdy scepticism, George knew that many folk believed in the legend that, while flesh remains, a body is still capable of walking. The tell-tale signs of the restless dead are visible on exhumation. The best insurance against becoming such an unhappy creature is to lead a blameless life ending in a good death. Henry Stokoe was a God-fearing man, a staunch churchgoer. Yet his life had been marred by tragedy; his wife had died in childbirth and his own passing had scarcely been peaceful. No, not even the parson, accomplished at making light of any unpleasantness, could describe Henry's as a good death.

Wood splintered. The sexton was panting. George clenched his fists and swallowed hard. He wanted to look, despite knowing that what he would see when the coffin was opened would make his knees shake and his stomach churn.

George glanced towards Henry's sister, standing a yard away from John Laidlaw. Agnes Stokoe was a woman of appealing aspect, but throughout the course of the inquest her distress had been palpable. More than once she had shed a tear. George was glad of the darkness, not wanting to behold her misery. Behind her was the trembling figure of Mary, the dead man's daughter. She was a pretty dark-haired girl, no more than fifteen years of age. Her lovely features reminded George of Agnes, although the round fullness of her cheeks was at odds with her slender frame. She had fainted prior to being called to give her testimony, compelling Crozier to adjourn the proceedings. Thankfully, she was soon revived and gave her evidence in a faltering tone. George's heart went out to her on this bitter night, when her father's body was being snatched from its resting place.

The coffin lid began to crack. George held his breath.

Mary retched loudly and someone in the crowd hissed in agony.

"*No*!"

And then the girl's aunt let out a scream that rent the night asunder.

The jury had previously viewed the body during the course of the inquest. At that point, few questions arose and they were inclined to give up a verdict of *felo de se*. It was a logical conclusion, for according to the depositions of the deceased's sister and daughter, no likely alternative presented itself. Henry's body had been discovered by Agnes when she came to rouse him early one February morning. Widowed a few months before Henry lost his own wife, she had come to live with her brother, to look after the child while he carried on his trade. The work of a baker begins at crack of dawn and Henry was invariably out of bed long before Agnes. When she did not hear him moving around in his room, preparing for the day's endeavours, anxiety seized her and she went to his room to enquire whether he was ailing. What she found, she told the hushed court, she would never forget.

Henry was lying on the bed with his throat cut. A knife from the kitchen was lying on the floor. There was a great deal of blood.

Could it have been murder? Both examinants, the aunt and the daughter, insisted that no intruder could have entered the house without their knowledge. The baker slept in the largest room in the house, which occupied the whole of the top storey. It was reached by a creaking staircase that ran past the tiny chambers where Mary and Agnes slept. The door to the street had been locked. It was inconceivable, they asseverated, that any intruder could have entered the building, ascended two winding flights of stairs, murdered Stokoe, and then retraced his footsteps, without disturbing anyone else in the house. Agnes and Mary were light sleepers – as Henry had been – but neither of them had heard a sound.

Yet why should Henry Stokoe have committed the mortal sin of ending his life before his appointed time? When William Crozier put this question, Agnes ventured that he had been complaining of pains in the stomach and bowels for two days prior to his demise. Their father, Godfrey Stokoe, in his time also a master baker and founder of the family business, had died of a malady of the bowels and endured dreadful agonies before the good Lord in his mercy put an end to his suffering. Agnes testified that Henry had, all his life, feared sickness. He was known as a stern man of considerable resolve, but he dreaded succumbing to the same fate as Godfrey.

George watched as William Crozier fixed his gaze upon Agnes. In the faltering light from the candle, her face was ghost-white. She was weeping uncontrollably, unable even to attend to Mary, who was bent double by her side. From the gathering of onlookers, the tall man limped towards her: John Laidlaw, who scorned the notion of the restless dead. As though he could not help himself, he drew Agnes to him, allowing her to nestle in the crook of his one good arm. Yet within a moment, he stepped back, dropping his arm and muttering a few words to his son, Robert. It was almost as though reason had asserted itself and he had become desperate to rid himself of Agnes. George could comprehend his embarrassment, together with the reason why Crozier was studying the pair with such scientific curiosity.

John Laidlaw farmed a stretch of land within sight of the

fourteen arches of the fine new bridge at Berwick-upon-Tweed, and he and Robert sold produce at the town market, a stone's throw from Henry's bakery. John's wife, long a sickly creature, had died five years ago, but he had not remarried. John was by repute a bluff, likeable fellow, but older folk in the district nonetheless continued to approach him with circumspection. The Laidlaws were a family whose name had long been feared in the Border country. They were Reivers, and amongst the fiercest of those outlaws who had for many years wreaked havoc among peace-loving folk on either side of the boundary between England and Scotland

When King James united the thrones of England and Scotland, he made clear his determination to crush such lawlessness. George had often heard his late father talk of witnessing the proclamation made by the King when he halted at Newcastle on the journey south for his coronation in London. It was to be forbidden to speak of "the Borders". Henceforth, this part of the kingdom, an outpost no longer, would become "the heart of the country" – formally, "the Middle Shires". As for those whose trade was terror, they were to be prosecuted with fire and sword.

Within weeks of the royal proclamation, seven score of the nimblest and most powerful thieves had been slain. Borderers were forbidden to carry weapons; nor could they own a horse valued in excess of fifty shillings. Houses were razed to the ground and families scattered to the four winds. A choice had to be made and John and his father – since deceased – decided to collaborate with the monarch against their former allies in robbery and rapine. The information that they provided led to the deaths of many men, subjected to Jeddart Justice and thereby executed without benefit of a trial. The Laidlaws' reward for showing loyalty to the Crown (or for their treachery, as some saw it) was to be granted ownership of those fertile acres by the river. The clan of Laidlaw duly prospered and twenty years later John, once an unruly and hot-tempered young ruffian, was as respectable as he was affluent.

Yet memories were long in these parts. For George, the Reivers were a dying breed that counted for little, but older folk recalled many instances of their ruthlessness and savagery and it remained common knowledge that, fifty years ago, John's father had led an attack on a farmstead owned by Henry's Uncle Charles. The raid left the old man mortally wounded and all his family's sheep were stolen. No love was lost thereafter between the Stokoes and the Laidlaws.

As for Henry, it was as well-known in the locality that his habitual strictness was wont on occasion to give way to red-faced rage. Within his own household, his temper sometimes manifested itself in violence. His wretched sister was sometimes seen with her eyes blackened and not a soul in Berwick believed her anxious excuses, that a door had struck her in the face, or that she had tumbled down a flight of stairs. Yet she could not leave his house, for her wastrel husband's death had left her with not a farthing to her name and, besides, she would not abandon her beloved niece to her brother's sole care. In truth, she was as much Henry's prisoner as if he kept her under lock and key.

Small wonder that, according to gossip, she had turned to John Laidlaw for comfort and consolation.

Not a word of this supposed scandal was uttered at the inquest, the evidence being confined to the bizarre circumstances attendant upon Henry's death. The conundrum was this: if he did not kill himself, how did he die? It is impossible to cut one's throat by accident. The only alternative to a verdict of suicide was to determine that someone had stabbed Henry to death. Yet if this was a case of murder, it seemed to follow that Agnes was at best a liar and at worst a murderess. From this conclusion, the jurymen had shrunk.

Nonetheless, as William Crozier confided when he and George were alone in chambers, it was plain that a verdict of suicide could not in conscience be sustained. Too many objections were arrayed against it. First, it appeared that Henry had lain in his bed in a composed manner, with the bed-clothes undisturbed. If he had stabbed himself, how could he have portrayed such serenity in death? Second, there was no blood in the bed, saving a tincture on the bolster whereon Henry's head lay. Third, from the bed's head there was a stream of blood on the floor which ran along till it ponded in the bending of the floor in a very great quantity. Further, there was another stream of blood on the floor at the bed's foot, which also ponded, but there was no continuance or communication of blood in either of these two places, from one to another; neither upon the bed. It followed that Henry had bled in two places, severally. Moreover, a doctor deposed that, upon turning up the mat of the bed, there were found clots of congealed blood in the straw of the mat underneath.

A fourth, and highly significant, instance was that the bloody knife was found sticking in the floor a goodly distance from the bed and that the point of the knife, as it stuck, was towards the bed, with the half away from the bed.

Upon mature reflection, the jury – whose verdict Crozier had wisely refrained from drawing up in form – might have been prompted by the combination of these factors alone to desire of him that Henry's body might be taken out of the grave. But their discussions were also coloured by whispers about the relations between Agnes and John Laidlaw. Some said that their acquaintance was innocent enough, and that it arose simply because Robert, a handsome, swaggering boy of seventeen, had set his cap at young Mary. The wagging tongues would not be stilled, however. Henry was not the only man who resented John Laidlaw's good fortune and several of those who knew both families hinted that John was eager to find himself another wife and that his heart was set upon Agnes. Henry, no-one doubted, would have moved heaven and earth to prevent such a match, but once a Reiver, always a Reiver. Had John determined to steal the prize that he coveted so much?

The jury's request to the coroner that he order an exhumation of the deceased's remains was unusual and not to be granted other than in the most exceptional circumstances. Yet William Crozier scarcely hesitated before directing that before he would call a verdict the inquest proceedings would be adjourned and Henry's body disinterred. In truth, George reflected afterwards, Crozier had, by dint of a few discreet observations, led the jurors to follow the path that he regarded as just.

As a consequence, the jurymen, witnesses and all others principally concerned with the case, together with the Laidlaw father and son, invited by the coroner to act as companions for Agnes and Mary, were gathered around the excavated burial place at a time of night when other law-abiding folk were slumbering in their beds.

⋆ ⋆ ⋆

The corpse was of a livid and carrion colour. George flinched at the sight of it. Like any young man, he had a sneaking belief in his own immortality and any reminder of the inevitability of death was unwelcome. Notwithstanding his repugnance, however, he found himself craning his neck as Agnes was summoned to the graveside.

"Step forward, Mrs Milburn," William Crozier said. His voice was low and yet there was no doubting his authority.

The woman took two paces towards the open grave and then fell on to her knees, quietly sobbing a prayer. George could not distinguish the words, and yet he knew that she was pleading to the Lord that He might give up a sign of her innocence.

"Touch the body," William Crozier commanded.

Earlier that day, William Crozier had reminded George of the venerable tradition that, if a person guilty of murder should touch the corpse of his victim, the dead body will respond in such a way as to condemn the malefactor. Stories abounded of corpses that sweated, or blinked, or whose hands moved or dripped blood when their murderers were pressed to brush them with their fingertips. The tales held a gruesome fascination for the young man, and yet he found it them impossible to believe. Moreover, he had never known a man less credulous than William Crozier, a man who insisted upon proof of even the most self-evident proposition before he would credit it. Crozier was more widely read than anyone George had ever met, and his list of accomplishments was as eclectic as it was formidable. He was by nature cautious, and yet unafraid, where circumstances so required, to be daring. Yet George was startled when Crozier announced that he would require those connected with the deceased and his household to touch his body once it was lifted from the ground.

"So – not only Agnes but Mary, too?"

"Certainly."

"Pray, sir, would you not acknowledge that the notion that a suspected murderer should be tested by the ordeal of touching the dead belongs to a bygone age?"

Crozier grunted. "You have the confident assurance of the young. For those of us who have lived longer and seen a little more, matters are not always so straight and simple."

George was alert enough to recognize that he had not received a direct answer. "Surely you cannot believe that the daughter . . ."

"Why not?"

"She is little more than a child!"

"Take another look at her, my boy. She may be young, but she is already a woman."

"A woman with no reason to kill her father," George said hotly. "My understanding is that, although he could be rough with her, she accorded him all the respect that was his due."

"It is not easy to look into the heart or mind of another," Crozier murmured. "Who knows what treacherous thoughts may lurk beneath the most innocent surface, like weed in a woodland pool."

"There would be no logic to it! The crime is apt to bring destitution upon her."

"So you regard young women as creatures of logic?" Crozier permitted himself the glimmer of a smile.

"I have never seen distress in such abundance."

"I do not doubt that the girl is unhappy. Whether that betokens a lack of culpability is a different matter."

George sighed. "I am most reluctant to believe that Agnes killed her brother, far less that her niece is a common murderess."

Crozier clamped him on the shoulder. "You have a good heart, my boy, and that is not wholly out of place in an officer of the court. One must seize every opportunity to utilise one's brain and one's ingenuity, provided they are directed to the service of a just cause. A professional life need not invariably be as dry as parchment. But mark this, a man of law should never sacrifice the ability to think clearly. Even when he is called upon to think about a woman."

"Is it possible that John Laidlaw . . . ?"

"My mind is open to many possibilities."

"Including suicide?" George said quickly.

Crozier grunted, as if to acknowledge the thrust. "We have already established that the indications that Henry Stokoe did not die by his own hand are impossible to controvert. It follows that whoever killed him attempted to convey the impression of *felo-de-se*, but with a crudity that betrayed the subterfuge."

"Very well, then. If he was murdered, who do you think . . . ?"

Crozier lifted his thin hand, requiring silence. "You know me well enough, George, to understand my reluctance to speculate without evidence. Proof is what matters."

"And in the absence of proof?"

Crozier frowned. "This is a case where, I shall admit to you, there is a risk that justice may be frustrated because of the paucity of evidence of guilt. It is right, in my judgment, to take extraordinary steps with regard to the obtaining of such evidence."

"You refer to the exhumation?"

"It is an opportunity to test the tradition of which we have spoken."

Crozier's saturnine features yielded no hint of what thoughts might be coursing through his mind as he gave this equivocal reply. And yet George was sure that those thoughts were more refined than his principal had admitted. William Crozier would have a plan.

The onlookers in the graveyard had broken up into distinct knots. The vicar stood with the sexton, his helpers and the coroner's men; the jurors were clustered together; and the deceased's daughter was close by John Laidlaw and his son. Only George stood apart, watching intently as William Crozier spoke again to the bereaved sister.

"Pray touch the body, Mrs Milburn."

"Have mercy upon me, sir," she pleaded.

"It is a simple matter."

"I cannot touch him!"

"You must."

"Are you a man or a ghoul?" John Laidlaw demanded.

"I am the coroner, charged with determining how Henry Stokoe died," Crozier said, pointing at the corpse. "My word in this matter is law, Mr Laidlaw. You will do well to remember that, my good sir."

The farmer raised his walking stick and, for a moment, George thought that the man was about to approach his principal and knock him down. But if the thought occurred to him, he contrived to suppress it in time. When Agnes Milburn cast a pleading glance at Laidlaw, he gave her the faintest of nods and lowered the stick.

The dead man's sister bent over his dead body and touched the skin of his neck with her forefinger.

George held his breath.

Nothing happened.

Silence reigned in the graveyard as Agnes averted her gaze from the dreadful sight of her brother's remains and stumbled back to her place by Mary's side. John Laidlaw did not reach for her, and George surmised that the man was striving to suppress his emotions, so as not to give the scandalmongers any more fuel to add to their fire.

George cast a glance at his principal. William Crozier's acuity of mind was famed throughout the county; he thought deeply before he spoke, and deliberated at even greater length before he acted. As an adversary, he was formidable. And yet he was not God. He was not infallible.

Did he suspect Agnes of having cut her brother's throat so that she might share her life with John Laidlaw instead? If so, why had Crozier believed that this macabre little play, albeit worthy of a better-lit stage, would reveal the truth of Henry Stokoe's death?

"Step forward, Mary."

Crozier's voice was firm yet unemphatic. If it troubled him that the corpse had not reacted to Agnes' touch, he gave no hint of it.

The girl flinched. She turned to look at the Laidlaws, father and son, and it was as if she found encouragement in their steady gaze, for without more ado she walked towards the corpse and touched it, as her mother had done.

Again, nothing happened.

In anticipating the exhumation, George had considered whether William Crozier might find some reason, and some means, to confront John Laidlaw and accuse him of the crime. Yet he had only to contemplate the possibility that Laidlaw had murdered Henry Stokoe to encounter objections that seemed to him to be insuperable.

In the first instance, the narrow flight of wooden stairs that wound up to Henry's bedchamber was old and unsound. Even a girl as light on her feet as Mary could not help but make a noise as she ascended. Henry would surely have been disturbed had a burly fellow such as Laidlaw climbed up to the top floor. Even if Laidlaw had reached the room without waking his victim, it was impossible to believe that he could have entered and committed the crime without causing a greater disturbance. Henry was not infirm; he would have resisted once wakened. Yet how could an assailant have reached him without breaking into his sleep? Whilst Henry might not have been sufficiently concerned by the arrival in his room of his sister – or, perhaps, his daughter – he would not have remained in repose for a moment on being confronted by John Laidlaw.

As for access from outside the room, there was another difficulty. It was only practicable to ascend to the top floor of the house by climbing from the lower roof of the house next door. In principle, an intruder might have entered unobserved by that route. Stokoe's neighbours were an aged couple who slept on the other side of the house. They might have seen and heard nothing. The window was directly above Henry's bed-head and it would be a simple matter to take him unawares. But the climb would require a monkey's agility and John Laidlaw, for all his strength, was incapable of it. Five years ago, he had crippled his right arm and leg in falling from a horse and since then he had walked with a pronounced limp. For a man of fifty to make such an ascent, armed with a knife, would have been a feat even were he in the prime of health. George could not conceive that Laidlaw would have attempted the endeavour, however fierce his devotion to Agnes. The likelihood would have been another plunge, this time to the street below. John Laidlaw, rather than Henry Stokoe, would have met his Maker.

When George dared to say something to his principal of these conjectures, William Crozier merely gave him a mirthless smile and did not trouble to reply.

"Mr Laidlaw, would you step forward?"

John Laidlaw stiffened. "You wish me to finger the corpse, coroner?"

"My task is to leave no avenue of enquiry unexplored."

"And how, pray, do you suggest that I might have committed such a heinous crime?"

"I suggest nothing, sir."

Laidlaw glared at the coroner and George wondered if he would refuse to obey. However, after a moment's deliberation, he strode forward, dragging his lame leg as he always did. Bending down, he laid his palm full on the deceased's cheek.

There was no response. No blinking, no movement, no blood leaking from the dead man's body.

Laidlaw straightened his back and gave William Crozier a fierce grin of triumph.

The coroner was not, George knew, accustomed to being bested by another. Yet his face gave no clue to what was in his mind. There was no suggestion of embarrassment. Yet the jurymen were becoming restive. George could not see their faces, but their muttered grumblings were easier to discern. They were wondering how long the coroner's whim would require them to linger in the cold and in the presence of a noxious corpse.

The vicar coughed and said, "I wonder, sir, if you are proposing to conclude these proceedings?"

"Shortly," Crozier's tone manifested infinite calm. "We are almost done."

John Laidlaw turned his back on the coroner and started to limp towards the lych gate. His son moved after him.

"Not you, Robert," Crozier said.

The boy stopped and looked back over his shoulder. "What do you want of me?"

Unmoved by his insolence, Crozier said, "That you touch the deceased."

The flickering candlelight caught Robert Laidlaw's face and George saw there an uncharacteristic indecision.

"Will you touch the deceased," Crozier repeated and George thought he detected a barely suppressed triumph in his principal's voice.

The youth seemed to take a breath of the cold air into his lungs, and then strode up to the corpse. He laid his fingers on the dead man's face. As he did so, an eerie voice was heard.

"*Murderer!*"

"John Laidlaw, plainly, could not have climbed into Henry Stokoe's bedchamber and cut his throat," William Crozier said, as the light of dawn crept into his rooms. "It did not seem to be a woman's crime, but at all events I doubted whether either Agnes or Mary were by temperament capable of such a savage murder. Poison would be their weapon."

George shook his head. "I never imagined that Robert . . ."

Yet any doubt he might have entertained concerning the boy's guilt had been extinguished by the foul and terrible confession that spurted from him when the voice – surely not from Henry's corpse? – made its dreadful accusation.

What if he had killed the wretched old man? Everyone hated Henry Stokoe. He was wickedness incarnate, a vile brute who took pleasure in tormenting even the women who cared for him. To rid the world of such a pestilence was no crime. It was an honour. His forefathers were Reivers who hated men like Henry Stokoe. They would have been proud of him.

The onlookers froze upon hearing of the outrage. A dead man had spoken, and a murderer had proclaimed his mortal sin with pride. Only William Crozier seemed unperturbed. When Robert spat on the body and then raced away into the darkness, George had made as if to follow him, but his principal caught his arm.

"Let him run. He will not get far. We have done what we came here to do."

And now, a few hours later, George was wrestling with the enormity of what he had witnessed.

"A corpse does not have a voice," he said at length.

William Crozier nodded. "I admit to a subterfuge, in the interest of a greater justice. It was I who told Robert that he was a murderer."

"*You?*"

"There is a technique for projecting the voice. It dates back many centuries. Have you never heard of belly speakers?"

"Never."

"Scholars have ascertained the origins of this ancient art in the centuries before the birth of our Lord. Wise men held that, by projecting the voice, they might better communicate with the dead. Later, in Europe, there was a widely held belief that the spirits of the deceased went to the stomachs of prophets and continued to exist there. The prophets were thus able to foretell the future by the spirits who spoke from their bellies."

"Absurd!"

"Indeed. There is no place for such views in the philosophy of a man of law. Yet the physical technique is a valuable one. I am a seeker-out of curiosities, as you know, and I have endeavoured to master the skill. It is known, by virtue of a Latin rendering of 'stomach-talk', as ventriloquism. Tonight, for the first time, I had the opportunity to utilise what I have learned in order to serve of justice."

"You decided that the corpse should appear to speak, with a view to wringing an admission of guilt from the boy."

"He is a Reiver's son, wily and resolute. I saw no other way of contriving mattes so that he might so forget himself as to tell the truth."

"But why would Robert wish to kill Henry?"

"Because Henry would never have permitted Robert to marry his daughter."

George stared at the coroner. "What makes you think that Mary would have wished to marry Robert?"

"Unless I am much mistaken, he is the father of her unborn child."

"She is with child?" George gasped.

"So I have surmised. At all events, the theory explains much. Her fainting, her sickness. Even the uncharacteristic roundness of a girl's cheeks is said to be a sign of pregnancy. I have no doubt that it was Robert who cried *no* when Mary retched and then her aunt cried out to distract our attention from the girl's indisposition, encouraging the belief that it was prompted by distress rather than a physical cause."

George put his head in his hands. "And now the father of her child will end his life on the gallows."

"The law requires no less. Henry Stokoe must be avenged."

"What of Mary? Did she know what Robert had done?"

"Strictly between us, I might speculate that she and her aunt know a deal more about what happened than they have chosen to acknowledge thus far. They made much of being light sleepers. Did they really hear nothing on that fateful morning? Of their supposed complicity, however, I have no proof and I do not expect Robert Laidlaw to supply the deficit."

George looked at his principal steadily. "Will you take steps to seek out such proof?"

William Crozier gave a shake of the head so discreet that, in the dimness of the early light, George almost failed to discern it.

"The law must prevail, and it will. But wise men know that the law must also command respect. There is a limit to the sacrifice upon which justice insists."

A TASTE FOR DUCKING

MARILYN TODD

One of James I's early acts had been to extend the Witchcraft regulations introduced during Elizabeth's reign. His Act of 1604 allowed punishment by death for witchcraft without benefit of clergy and it was this law that later witchhunters, most notoriously the Witchfinder General, Matthew Hopkins, used to their advantage. Anyone who was accused of witchcraft, often with the flimsiest of evidence, never seemed to stand a chance, showing the prejudice, superstition and above all gullibility of the age. It was a factor a real criminal could use to their advantage, as Marilyn Todd considers here.

Marilyn Todd (b. 1958) is best known for her series featuring that cunning vixen of ancient Rome, Claudia Seferus, starting with I, Claudia *(1995).*

"Duck the witch!" *Clap hands.* "Duck the witch!"

Dawn was breaking cold and grey, as the procession chanted its way through the little village of Farringham in the South Downs. Hoar frost sparkled on the roof of the church. Wind rattled the tavern's windows. The bare branches of willows reflected like cracks on the frozen duck pond. Betsy didn't notice. The quicker this business was over and done with the better, that was her view.

"Duck the witch!" *Clap hands*. "Duck the witch!"

With her hands tied behind her, she stumbled and slipped down the icy path – past the dairy – past the smithy – down to the miller's place.

"Far enough." Parson Dale held up a hand that had turned blue at the fingers with cold. "Let the Ordeal of Innocence begin."

Most of the faces that had crowded round were a blur, but Betsy did notice the parson's wife leading the clapping while Thomas Collins elbowed his way to the front for a good view. She was sorely tempted to tell him that he, a master carpenter of all people, ought to be ashamed of himself, jeering in public like this. Who was it taught him his numbers, eh? Who showed him how to tie knots in a rope? The best way to harden a conker? When this was over she'd clip his ear, that's for sure, and never mind he was thirty-seven years old!

"Duck the witch!"

The clapping was constant now, fast and eager. Perhaps, she thought, the villagers needed to keep themselves warm.

"Duck the witch, duck the witch!"

At the front of the crowd, the hard lips of Betsy's daughter-in-law were pursed in smugness and malice glittered from her green eyes. Betsy shook her head in bewilderment. All right, Mary wasn't the wife she'd have chosen for her son, but, though they'd never got on, she'd accepted the girl into her family and gave way on everything Mary had asked. Trouble was, and try as she might, nothing could please her, nothing was ever enough. It had reached the point now where she slept in the kitchen and acted as a servant in her own home, yet *still* Mary wasn't satisfied. She wanted Betsy out, that was the problem, and the truth was, she would have gone and willingly so – had she had some place to go.

By her daughter-in-law's side, Betsy's only child fixed his gaze to his boots. Not his fault the lad was weak, she supposed. Took after his granddad on his father's side, did poor Robbie – only soft men were always grist to a shrew's mill. Every time Betsy tried to put her foot down, it was Robbie who caught the sharp edge of her tongue. Robbie who found no comfort in his wife's bed for a week. Betsy couldn't let her son pay the price for his mother's resistance, so she gave way. Shooting him a thin smile of encouragement, she felt a pain in her heart when he didn't once lift his eyes to meet hers.

"Betsy Bellingham, you stand accused of unnatural compacts with Satan." The parson's voice droned through the February bleakness. "Of placing the Devil's familiar at your disposal –"

As though no one else in Farringham kept a cat!

"– and performing whatever vile service Satan demanded of you. Betsy Bellingham, how do you plead?"

"Not guilty, as you well know!"

The priest's black brows joined above the bridge of his nose in a frown. "You deny causing Farmer Preston's bull to turn into a toad?"

Betsy rolled her eyes at the gate that had been left open all night. "I certainly do."

"You deny summoning the dead last Halloween?"

"Of course."

"Of making magic at the crossroads? Conjuring demons? Bringing calamity upon the mash in the brewery?"

"Parson, Nathan Stokes has had a reputation for brewing bad beer for the past six-and-a-half years. What other nonsense do you put forward?"

"How do you plead to the charge that you were seen riding a broomstick over Bramber Down three weeks ago last Wednesday night?"

"With my arthritis?"

The laughter that rippled round the crowd was quickly quelled by the glare of the priest. "Very well, if you persist in denying the charges levelled against you, we will proceed with the test."

Betsy heard a snip and for the first time in three days her wrists were unbound. Numb and leaden, she shook them to bring them back to life, but the action only brought fire to her hands. And it was because of this distraction that the parson had to repeat his request.

"Strip? Naked?" The pain in her fingers was instantly forgotten. "How dare you even ask?" She scowled at the priest. "At my age, as well!"

"You admit to the charges then?" This voice was softer. Like melted lard oozing over a ham.

"I most certainly do not."

"Then I urge you to submit, the quicker we might record your innocence."

Sharp-featured, bearded and with his head cowled, the stranger could have been a monk with all those crosses on chains. He was not. Any time an accusation of witchcraft was bandied, the Witchfinder General sent out an agent. A brodder, whose task was to prove or disprove the allegations.

"And if I don't?"

Where was the ducking stool? Betsy wondered. She'd expected it to have been wheeled down by now and hoped someone would send for it soon. Her limbs were shaking with cold.

"If you don't, we will hang you and bury your body in unconsecrated ground in a grave that will never be marked," the brodder replied softly. "So why not let the Officer of the Ordeal disrobe you that we might be certain there is no mark of the Devil upon you?" He paused. "Dame Bellingham, I assure you this really *is* for your own good."

Behind his shoulder, Mary folded her hands over her chest in grim satisfaction while her mother-in-law shivered with cold and humiliation.

"Let the record read, there is no mark of the Devil upon Betsy Bellingham."

Half the crowd seemed relieved. The other half itched for more entertainment. They were in luck.

"Crouch the candidate, please."

The brodder's voice was politeness itself, while Betsy's teeth chattered too loudly for her to protest.

"Proceed as we discussed, Parson Dale." He might have been overseeing the trussing of a goose. "Right thumb to left toe, nice and tight, now."

"What about the ducking stool?" she finally managed to splutter.

"Ducking stool?" The priest paused from blessing the millpond. "My dear lady, we're ducking witches, not scolds."

"We need to test your innocence," the witchfinder lisped. "For this, we throw you into the waters and if you are, as I truly believe, innocent of these vile allegations, you will sink." A soft hand indicated two stout men standing by, stripped to the waist and ready to dive in and save her. "If, on the other hand, Satan has put lies on your tongue to deceive us, your body will reject the baptismal waters, so have faith in God, my child." He patted her head reassuringly. "Have faith in God."

Betsy did. She always had. And as two pairs of strong arms lifted her over the millpond, His was the only name on her lips.

Of course, she had no way of knowing that the distinctive tying of her bonds was the result of years of painstaking research.

Even when her body plunged beneath the icy waters, Betsy Bellingham firmly believed that her innocence was a foregone conclusion.

Blackestone Manor, with its chimneys and gables, wings and half-timbers, was by far the grandest building for miles. Like Drake and Raleigh, Sir Francis Blackestone had been one of the late queen's most resourceful pirates, and even though his cut represented a mere fraction of the plundering he'd done for the Crown, it had allowed him to purchase what seemed like half the land between Chichester and Brighton and, of course, half the population who lived on it. But despite profits from his farms and forests that more than offset the profligacy of his lavish lifestyle, it was not in cold, dull England that Sir Francis Blackestone made his home. Preferring the warmer climes and even hotter native maidens, he settled in Jamaica to a routine that his only son and heir took great pride in inheriting and which, by all accounts, was set to shorten his life by approximately the same amount as it had his father's.

As a result, Blackstone Manor had remained unoccupied for virtually its entire existence. Occasionally, before his death, Sir Francis would come to England for a month (but no more) to sort out his affairs, gamble away the odd thousand or two and impregnate as many chambermaids as he was able, and, to his credit, his son even made the effort to attend the new King's coronation. But the point is, Jamaica was the place the Blackestones called home. The Manor House was merely the mark of their success.

So when the staff went into a flurry of airing and warming at a time of year when no Blackestone in his right mind would make the crossing, not on those seas, the curiosity in nearby Farringham was relentless. Was young Sir Roger coming home for good? Was he touting at long last for a wife? Would those lazy buggers employed at the Manor finally have to earn their damned wages? Eventually, it was the footman who told the laundress who told the parson's wife who, in fine civic duty, passed it on to everyone else that in fact the house had been lent to a distant cousin of the Blackstones. More pertinently, it appeared that it had been lent to the young wife of that distant cousin, a certain Eleanor Dearborn, who, despite claiming she needed nothing more than a few weeks of rest and recuperation after a heavy winter's cold, was obviously in "a certain condition". Farringham (in the form of the parson's wife) knew this because, dear me, the whole *world* knew that Geoffrey Dearborn had taken a wife thirty years younger than himself in his desperation for an heir to his fortune. Why else would the lovely Eleanor be here on her own, Mrs Dale reasoned? And since Sir Geoffrey enjoyed a reputation for fairness and honesty in these parts, Farringham rejoiced for them both.

"Seven years is a long time to wait for the rock of the cradle," the parson's wife told the newcomer, waiting no time at all herself before popping round with a basket of eggs.

"Indeed it is, Mrs Dale, indeed it is."

My word, the staff had had to move to get those rooms in order, the parson's wife thought. No dust, not a speck, and with that roaring log fire you'd think the chimney had been swept every year.

"You must have been terribly worried," she prompted, once she'd realized that nothing else was forthcoming and that gossip doesn't spread by itself.

"Not at all." The firelight shone on Eleanor's auburn curls as she laid a hand on her visitor's plump forearm. "I put my faith in God," she said, squeezing gently.

"Quite right," Mrs Dale said briskly. "With Him watching over us, the Devil cannot gain a foothold. I must go."

Eleanor glanced at the window. "Won't you stay for tea and crumpets?"

By the time the parson's wife finally made to leave, the sky was purple and heavy with storm clouds, but, bursting with more news than she'd heard in a six-month, she failed to notice the downturn in the weather. Eleanor Dearborn waved her off with a kerchief embroidered with violets.

The stitching, she mused, fingering the petals as she waved, was far from expert. But then she'd only been nine years old when she'd embroidered the thing and how well she remembered sitting in the tiny kitchen behind her father's tailor shop, legs crossed on the floor just like him, while his sister taught her to sew. The laughter, the cuddles, the hilarious unpicking came flooding back, as did the smell of bread baking in the oven, the songs that floated up to the beams and the rays of golden sunlight that streamed through the window while the needle flashed in her amateur hands. Then a thunderclap overhead banished childhood back to memory and, as the rain began to hammer against the window panes, Eleanor watched the parson's wife leaning into the wind, her skirts sodden and her hair dripping wildly beneath her cap as she battled her way down the broad, open driveway. Tossing another log onto the fire, Eleanor Dearborn tucked the kerchief back inside her gown and reflected on how far she'd come from those happy days of embroidering violets.

And sighed.

"That was the house where the witch lived, down there."

In his early forties with rugged features and prematurely grey hair, the stranger cocked one long lean leg after the other over the fallen tree trunk on which Eleanor sat and settled himself beside her.

"Which one?" she asked. "That one?"

"No. The one you were looking at before I arrived."

"I was watching a squirrel."

"Unusual to see one about on a cold day like this," the stranger replied, crossing his arms. "Lucky you."

She said nothing. He made no move to leave.

"Tom Jordan," he said after a while.

"Eleanor Dearborn," and as she turned towards him she could smell pinecones and hay.

"The witch was called Betsy," he said after another long while. "Betsy Bellingham. Wicked woman by all accounts, too. Fornicated with the Devil and his cloven-hoofed spawn." He ticked the points off on his long bony fingers. "Cast evil spells over the village. Kept a familiar that sucked babies out of the womb. Wicked," he added with a cluck of his tongue. "Wicked, wicked woman."

"Is that a fact?"

"Indeed it is fact," Tom Jordan said with a crack of his knuckles. "The old dame confessed to everything, it's all written down. Bewitching horses, bewitching cattle, turning her neighbours' food inedible, and that was just the beginning. If you read her confession, you'll see she cursed James Buckle to bring on rheumatics, gave his wife Janet an ulcer, dosed the carpenter with megrims and gave little Kitty the dairymaid cramps. Oh, and she confessed to night flying over this very hill, too."

"Don't tell me, with the Devil riding pillion on her besom."

Eleanor turned her eyes back to the small thatched stone cottage nestled at the end of the lane, the one with a pheasant made of straw on the roof. She pictured the cottage three months from now, when the garden would be filled with cabbages and peas, parsley and roses, and where chickens would peck and lay eggs.

"That old dame ran quite a coven," he continued easily. "Eliza Crowe, Margaret Drabbe, Jane Parcival, Annie Thomas and her daughter Bess, Katherine Pearson and old Lucy Hewitt. They're all listed in the records, in the brodder's own distinctive hand. Thirteen of them in the end."

She studied the craggy face and dark violet blue eyes.

"I was in Milord's courtroom earlier," he explained cheerfully. "Thirteen trial accounts laid open for all to see."

Not just to be seen, Eleanor thought. To be seen and *feared*. For only the crimes of murder, robbery, arson and rape were tried by the Assizes. Everything else was tried by the local JP. His courtroom carried more traffic than Farringham High Street.

"Still, they say the brodder's work is nearly done," Tom Jordan said.

Over his head, rooks cawed their territories around their nests while the buds of the blackthorn were thickening nicely. In the valley, a pair of hares boxed.

"Apparently, rumours of witchcraft have surfaced in Stoughton and so now, having rooted out all the witches in this part of the world, he'll be wanting to curb their black arts elsewhere." He pointed towards the far hills. "Another two days I give him, no more," he said, nodding thoughtfully, and then smiled. "The King's agent is nothing if not thorough."

The King's agent, she thought. The King's agent . . .

Witchfinder, witchpricker, jobber, brodder, his was a profession which carried a multitude of names yet was charged with but one single task. To confirm or refute allegations of witchcraft. To drive out sin and the Devil.

"*Thou shalt not suffer a witch to live*," the stranger quoted softly, staring up at the cloudless blue sky. "It is written in the Bible. Exodus, Deuteronomy, Leviticus, Samuel, Galatians, Revelations and at least twice in the Acts, I believe. Our King is a deeply religious man."

How true. Translating the Bible into English and taking a Danish wife to strengthen his commitment to the Protestant cause, James had even survived a plot last November to restore Catholicism to the land. A good man, the English cried! A good king! Intellectual and learned, he'd not only taken up Elizabeth's cultural baton, he had positively run with the new flourish in art and literature, whilst continuing to encourage science and the Virginian colonies. To be sure, long live the King!

But there were two sides to every coin. Eleanor wriggled deeper under her furs. Before sitting the English crown on his richly dyed curls, James had researched extensively – some might even say passionately – the subject of witchcraft. Indeed, respected and talented scholar that he was, he was considered an expert on the subject and under him, hundreds (sic, hundreds) of women had been put to death. But of course that was while he was king only of Scotland, which was a long way, a lifetime, away.

Or was it . . .?

The law that he had introduced over here was pretty recent, and what did it say? That it was *a hanging offence for the devilish act of witchcraft and, by the force of the same, killing or laming their neighbours or harming their cattle*? Ah, but the King is a fair man, everyone said so. A just man. He doesn't simply act on somebody's say-so. He sends agents of the crown to investigate these allegations. A brodder, who carries with him a bodkin which he prods into the accused person's flesh – and if the flesh doesn't bleed, only then has he found a true servant of Satan.

And in Farringham's case, Eleanor mused, thirteen true servants who had duly choked to death on the gallows.

"Who are you, Tom Jordan?" she asked quietly. "Why did you seek me out here this morning?"

His grey head turned and his face twisted in a crooked smile. "Seek you out? You have me quite wrong, I fear. I am just passing through." He indicated the cage at the edge of the clearing. "I am the rat-catcher, see?"

"Which is what you were doing in Milord's courthouse? Catching rats?"

"Big 'un, too." His hands spanned a gap large enough for a cat.

"It could be a trick of the light," she said, "but that cage looks remarkably empty to me."

Tom Jordan's chuckle came from deep in his throat. "Dead rats need no cage, Eleanor. It's the live ones you need to keep hold of."

Tipping his cap, he bade her good day and was gone before she could ask why the rat-catcher carried no bells.

Down in the village, ducks dabbled in the melted pond water, primroses lifted their heads to the sun on the roadside and a bearded man with sharply pointed features walked with his cowled head held high. On his chest, several gold crosses dangled on chains. The brodder was proud of each one. Tomorrow morning, when he left this village for Stoughton, he would add another gold cross to his collection.

Another victorious medal in his fight against evil.

"It's Robbie, isn't it? Robbie Bellingham?"

A flabby young man, no more than thirty, whipped off his cap and turned pink. "M-ma'am."

"Do I have smuts on my nose, Robbie? Or do you stare at all the gentry as though they're chops on the butcher's block?"

"No. No, no of course not, begging your pardon, but for a moment there, I thought I recognized you from somewhere." He wiped his hands down the sides of his pants. "No offence, ma'am."

"None taken." Eleanor glanced up at the pheasant made of straw on the roof. Doubted it would last the spring storms. "The thing is, Robbie, since your mother was convicted of witching –"

"I didn't know anything about that," he cut in quickly. "She practised it on the quiet, did Mother."

"Indeed she must have done." She studied the weak chin and blinking pale eyes. "For you not to have noticed any of her abominations in such a small cottage."

The silence was as brief as it was uncomfortable, at least on his part.

"Well, I knew about the cat, of course." He wrung his cap in his hands. "Saved it myself when it was a six-week-old kitten, once Farmer Preston said white cats were deaf and therefore no good as mousers. He'd have drowned it, you know, if I hadn't stepped in."

"That was a very noble gesture, Robbie." Pity he didn't mention it at Betsy's trial. Perhaps it slipped his mind.

"And I saw the candles," he said, "but I didn't think anything of it. I mean to say . . . candles? *Everybody* has candles."

"Except these were different?"

"Not to me, they weren't." Again, he was quick to distance himself. "Looked like any other candle to my eyes, only how was I to know Mother shaped them into human form during the night, melting them so the victim sickened and died?"

"Did someone die, then?"

"No," he said, frowning, "but the Parson got toothache and Thomas Collins started getting the megrims, and like I said at the trial, I didn't think anything odd about Mother's rags, either."

"Rags?" Eleanor queried.

"Aye. She told me it was an old north-country custom, keeping rags to make into a mat. In fact, I can remember as a child her often telling me that she'd been shown how to make rugs with the clippings, only never had the time to make one herself. But the brodder got the truth out of her in the end. She'd been making rag dolls to burn and cause pain, she had. That's how James Buckle got his rheumatics and that's how Farmer Preston's best milking cow came over sick."

"She admitted it?"

"Oh, yes." He seemed almost proud of the fact. "But I'm sure you didn't come all the way down here to talk about me, ma'am."

That's funny, she thought they were talking about Betsy. "No, indeed. As a matter of fact I came because I'd heard that you've been down on your luck since that unfortunate trial and as it happens, I am in need of help at the Manor."

"That's mighty kind of you, ma'am." He turned a different shade of pink. "I won't deny folk don't come near us these days and as a result times are a bit hard, but though I'm a mason by apprentice, I can turn my hand to any job you –"

"Actually, Robbie, it was your wife I was hoping to employ."

"*Mary?*"

"Mrs Dale assures me that she is a dab hand with a needle and in my condition –" she gave a delicate cough "– well, suffice to say a good seamstress would not go amiss."

The cogs of Robbie's brain turned slowly, but turn they eventually did. He remembered now how the rumour mill said Sir Geoffrey's wife had only wanted a few rooms brightened up at Blackestone Manor, at least for the time being. Summer, she insisted, was the time for the bulk of the work. Not March, when she risked a chill from the workmen's comings and goings, and Robbie, who yearned for a baby himself, understood all too well that she wouldn't want to harm a much longed-for child.

And what did it matter, she could see his mind reason, who got the work, as long as food came to the table?

Oh, dear. After ten years of marriage, Robbie still did not know his wife.

Or his mother.

"That's the spot where they buried the witch," a familiar voice rasped in her ear.

"Where?" she asked, squinting.

"The mound you were staring at before I arrived," he said, coming to stand alongside her. "Unconsecrated ground, not blessed by the church and forgotten by everyone else."

"I was watching the rabbits."

"Unusual to see them out at this time of day," Tom Jordan replied, crossing his arms. "Lucky you."

She said nothing. He made no move to leave. He still smelled of pinecones and hay.

"Did you hear about the parson?" he asked after a while. "Took sick during the night with skin rashes and blisters, vomiting and diarrhoea, while this morning he lapsed into stupor interspersed with delirium."

"I had not heard the news, although it sounds a lot like baneberry poisoning to me."

"Exactly the physician's diagnosis. He is of the opinion that his wife, whilst still suffering the effects of the chill she caught from the storm, must have muddled them up with sloe berries, but at least she can rest easily. The malady is not fatal."

True, Eleanor thought, but convalescence is invariably lengthy.

"The other twelve members of Betsy's coven are also spread around in unmarked graves," he said, returning to the subject of the mound with a nod of his head. "Fat lot of good their witching did their families, though. They're nothing short of pariahs in this village, and when rents and prices are rising faster than wages, poverty stares a lot of Farringham in the face. It was kind of you to offer Mary Bellingham work."

Eleanor thought of the speed with which King James was going through the realm's finances while standards continued to plummet.

"Children should not be visited with the sins of their parents. It's hardly Mary's fault that her mother-in-law sold her soul to the Devil."

"Indeed no." His nod was tight lipped. "Though there are some who claim Mary was the first to accuse her."

"That business about turning Farmer Preston's bull into a toad?"

"Rumour has it Mary was seen at the gate that very night."

"Nonsense," Eleanor said. "No respectable seamstress hangs round farm gates at midnight." She tutted loudly. "Next people will be saying she was part of the coven!"

"No, no, the brodder is convinced he has got to the root of the witchery. The number thirteen has a nice ring to it, I suppose. How is Mary's stitching, by the way?"

"Excellent. She is busy embroidering a night gown with violets right now, as it happens, and I have to say her workmanship is faultless."

"Good," Tom Jordan said, and there was an expression in his eyes that she couldn't identify, though it looked for all the world like a twinkle. "I'm sure you two will get along famously." He bowed. "But if you'll excuse me, I have rats to catch."

"Big 'uns?"

He spanned a gap between his two hands large enough for a dog. "Huge."

And with a chuckle that came from low in his throat he was gone.

Sitting alone in his finely appointed quarters, a bearded man with sharply pointed features pushed back the cowl from his head and belched loudly. As the King's agent, the brodder was in a position to command the best accommodation and the finest foods, and, best of all, he never needed to dip his hands in his purse. Not for this flagon of fine, golden malmsey. Not for the succulent capons, nor the dainty sweetmeats, nor the crusty pies bursting with apples. And most *certainly* he did not have to pay for services of that broad-hipped, buxom beauty who did things that his poor wife would faint at. But the hour was late, and tomorrow the brodder was setting off for Stoughton, his work in this village all done. He wished to savour his success with the best company he knew, and he knew no better company than his own.

From the corner of his eye, he thought he saw something black and furry dart across the floor, but when he rubbed his bleary eyes it was gone. He must have been mistaken – rats don't infest such sumptuous accommodation – so he returned to task of counting his crosses.

And licked his lips at the prospect of collecting another in the morning before he left.

Solid gold, they'd be worth a fortune one day.

"Why, Mary, this nightgown is exquisite." Eleanor held it up to the lamp light. "You've done a truly excellent job."

"Thank you, my lady." Her thin lips pinched in pride. "Like I told my husband, good skills will always find an outlet."

A picture formed of a young couple sat either side of the fire, him flabby and pale as he stared into his ale, her hard to the marrow as she carped and gloated in equal measures. Squawking like a magpie as she stitched and sewed, reminding him how she had found work when the man of the house had found none, eroding his confidence with her nagging and bullying, undermining him whenever she could.

"Indeed they do," Eleanor said, linking her arm with Mary's. "Now let us take a walk."

"At this time of night?" Green eyes flashed in distaste. "It's cold out."

"As cold as the grave," she agreed sweetly. "But here. You may borrow a fur. I wouldn't want you catching a chill."

Torn between making excuses or hobnobbing with gentry, the furs swung the balance for Mary. Obviously, you could see her thinking as they strolled through the village, Madam was lonely. And as they climbed Bramber Down with the aid of a lantern, you could see the calculations going on inside her head at how much a live-in companion might pocket.

Above them, the moon rose full and yellow.

"It was good sport, wasn't it?" Eleanor said at last. "I mean a *bull*, for heaven's sake. How the village must have laughed when Farmer Preston found that toad."

"Can I go back now, ma'am?" Mary asked.

"Soon." And even though the smile was warm and reassuring, the hand that clamped her upper arm was like a vice. "Only there's something we need to do first."

Mary looked at the nightgown Eleanor pulled out from under her own furs. "I–I think I'll turn back, miss, if it's all the same with you."

"But it is not all the same to me, Mary." The voice had an edge to it. "You see, by accusing Betsy of turning a prize bull into a toad, you thought you'd found a way to drive your mother-in-law out of the house. Her house, I might add."

"I don't know what you're talking about."

"Because even though you knew she hadn't done it, you also knew that allegations of witchcraft are always taken seriously. But just to be on the safe side, I'm sure you dropped a word in the parson's wife's ear that you'd heard Betsy cursing the brewer's mash, and wasn't it a coincidence that it was around the same time the parson got toothache?"

It only took one drip of malice for the poison to take root. Mrs Dale was a glutton for gossip, and in no time the carpenter's megrims and someone's sick cow had turned into a full-scale blight on the village.

"You're a sensible girl, Mary Bellingham. Have you ever come across rheumatics, or for that matter ulcers, that come on overnight? And I wonder who planted the notion in Kitty the dairymaid's head that her cramps were caused by something other than the onset of her menstruals?"

"You don't know what you're talking about," Mary said defiantly. "Betsy confessed to everything, the parson heard her and the brodder wrote it down."

"What would you expect from an old woman who'd been stripped naked in front of the entire village then trussed up in such a way that sinking's impossible."

Bastards.

Green eyes narrowed. "What do you mean, impossible?"

"Exactly what it sounds like," Eleanor said. "And because of one selfish bitch's bid to turn an old woman out, tragedy rippled right across this village, causing pain, distress and hardship to more people than anyone could imagine."

"It's not my fault." She tossed her head. "I thought ducking the witch meant using the ducking stool. Betsy thought so as well."

"Of course, it's your fault! All of this is your fault!" Eleanor's eyes flashed in fury. "And don't tell me what you thought, because the only thing you thought about was yourself, and dammit, you revelled in Betsy's humiliation. When she was stripped naked, you laughed, and when she was tossed into a freezing cold millpond and floated, you wallowed in satisfaction. Ah, here we are."

She held up the lantern to reveal a freshly turned mound in which a shroud glowed below in the moonlight.

"Betsy's grave."

Mary stared. "You're mad, you are. You ought to be in one of them asylum places."

"Even when the woman who welcomed you into her family was tied in a sack that the brodder strung over the gallows tree, you didn't think about Betsy. You didn't *once* stop to wonder what fear was in her heart when the god she believed in rejected her body on waters that had been blessed by the priest. Shame on you."

"I thought she'd be found innocent," Mary protested.

"If you tell me once more what you thought," Eleanor hissed, "so help me I will leave your body in this grave and no one will be any the wiser."

Imagine the terror of being tied in a sack, knowing it was to swing from the gallows. The knowledge of innocence mixed with holy rejection when the brodder set the sack swinging. Swinging and swinging, back and forth, back and forth, imagine what it must have been like . . .

The rocking motion causes disorientation.

The victim vomits but has no room to move.

She's gagging, but trapped in her own vile stench.

And still the sack keeps on swinging –

"How long did you stand there laughing at her, Mary? How many hours did you watch an old woman struggle for breath and for dignity, until she finally confessed to her sins?"

The brodder had recorded it in delicate detail, insisting the witch give up the name of her accomplice, who in turn, of course, gave up the names of others.

"They call it the witch's cradle and, just like the tying of bonds for ducking the witch, it was designed with great care," she told Mary. "The dice are suitably loaded."

Often the victim suffers hallucinations as well, which was how Lucy Hewitt, eighty-two years old, admitted convening with the coven at the crossroads at midnight, conjuring the dead round the compass of death as they copulated with Satan in turn.

"That's not all."

Anger was rising like a rip tide inside her. She could no more hold it back than turn push back the sun.

"Before hanging, it is the witchfinder's solemn duty to wash away corruption and redeem the soul, and do you know how he does that? Do you, Mary? The brodder ties his victim to the boards naked – oh yes, naked, he's vicious to his core – and then he pinches their nose until they can stand it no more, and when they frantically open their mouth to gasp for air he stuffs a funnel in it and pours scalding water down their throat."

Mary gulped but quickly recovered. "All right, I admit it got out of hand, but I don't see what this has to do with you –"

"No? Well, that's the interesting part, Mary. You see, if you're going to accuse someone of witchcraft, you really ought to know who and what you are dealing with." Eleanor smiled. "Me, Mary. I'm the real thing."

Her face went white and her mouth dropped. "Dear God in heaven!"

"Somehow I doubt that. In the same way that I can't accept cloven-hoofed monsters prancing around waving pitchforks, I find it difficult to believe in a god who idly stands by while decent women suffer the most abominable torture in his name, either."

"So –" For the first time, Mary was worried. "Are you going to make a wax image of me and burn it slowly to twist up my body and make me suffer pain?"

"Worse," Eleanor said, because there was no point in telling the girl that witchcraft had nothing whatsoever to do with the black arts, but revolved around health and wellbeing. "My curse upon you is a conscience. Every day for the rest of your life, Mary Bellingham, you will wake up with a body every bit as sturdy as it is today, and every day you will relive Betsy's torment, your role in it and the tragedy you brought upon not just thirteen innocent women, those who had loved and depended on them."

For as the brodder himself proved, if you plant an idea in a gullible brain, that idea will quickly take hold. And now that Mary had been told she'd be fit and healthy for the rest of her life, as a result, she probably would be. The stronger to relive and repent the wickedness she had done. The damage she had done to them all.

"Now get down into that grave, and wrap the poor woman in a decent shroud," she told Mary.

Aunt Betsy had always had a fondness for violets.

What is witchcraft? Is it the worship of evil for evil's own sake? Is it flying on broomsticks, cooking toads in their blood, whispering spells of cruelty and malice?

In the eyes of King James, witches served the Devil's apprenticeship, causing harm by unnatural means. Through their dark magic and Satanic rites, he saw them conjuring demons and inflicting disease, mixing sorcery that couldn't just bring on death, but was capable of raising the dead. To be fair, his obsession was rooted in personal acquaintance. When the ship on which he was bringing home his Danish wife was caught in a storm, he didn't stop to question how a group of ordinary people could possibly have conjured a tempest, much less what their reasoning might be. He simply attended their trial, believed what he'd heard, then promptly set about protecting himself and his kingdom through the simple expedience of wiping out witchcraft.

Poor James. An intellectual, yet he couldn't see that saintly relics were no different from protective amulets. A scholar, yet he didn't comprehend how the Church was manipulating paganism by propagating tales of demons and witchcraft to deliberately instil fear for its own ends.

Or did he?

If people turned to the Church for support in such dark, turbulent times (and eventually became dependent on it), would the same not be true of the King? That by extending the law to make witchcraft a capital offence – especially without benefit of clergy – might his own influence not grow, too?

But how does one define it? Certainly, Geoffrey Dearborn's wealth and influence could have secured him a wife among the landed gentry, yet it was the full-breasted, auburn-haired daughter of his tailor that he had chosen and adored from that day onward. Bewitched? Possibly, for the feeling was far from mutual; and poor Geoffrey: seven years and still no sign of an heir. But then the rhizomes of water lilies had that effect, even if he didn't know.

A long night of drinking.

A wife who sighs the next morning, tells him he was remarkable.

Oh, no, Geoffrey would never denounce his red-headed love, even if the thought crossed Mary's mind later.

"I'm sorry, but you simply can't keep going round accusing witches, people will think you're a laughing stock," Eleanor tutted, as they wheeled Betsy's corpse down the hill to the undertaker's workshop. "And if my own cousin didn't recognize me, who'll believe you, and trust me, the brodder won't be pointing his bodkin in my direction, I assure you."

The one thing about money is that it can buy you just about anything. Alibis actually rate pretty low on the scale.

"Go back to the stone you crawled under from, Mary." With a soft click, the padlock on the door of the workshop sprang open. "And may you have a long life with the husband who backed you over his mother."

Now both parties get what they deserve.

Prising the lid off a cheap wooden coffin, Eleanor thought back to the tiny kitchen behind the tailor's shop, stitching her violets to hoots of laughter from her aunt, who sang songs and baked bread while her sister-in-law rested from giving birth to the twins, and taking time out between washing and scrubbing to teach the young Eleanor her letters. Covering Betsy's face with her violet kerchief, she hoped that Seth Mabbett, whose coffin this was, didn't mind sharing, but it was important Betsy Bellingham was laid to rest in hallowed ground and the fact that her niece had no faith in God didn't matter.

Betsy had, that was the point.

Blackestone Manor had only just got used to having visitors under its roof before Eleanor was packing her bags, and wasn't it a scandal that the parson's wife had raised poor Sir Geoffrey's hopes by suggesting it was more than convalescence after a cold?

Where *did* she get the idea from, that's what people wanted to know, and now they thought about it, wasn't Mrs Dale *always* exaggerating?

Dear me, she'd even hinted that she'd been deliberately held back at the Manor in time to catch her death from the storm, but why should Sir Geoffrey's wife do a wicked thing like that? It was nothing but a cover for poisoning her husband, if you asked them. Accidental, of course, but all the same. Fewer callers knocked on the parson's wife.

"That was the old man who lived over the road from the witch," a voice said, as Eleanor paused in the lych gate.

"Which one?" she asked. "That one?"

"Not graves. The funeral you were watching before I arrived."

"I was admiring the church steeple."

"Unusual to find the gentry with such a keen interest in gargoyles," Tom Jordan replied, crossing his arms. "Lucky you."

She said nothing. He made no move to leave. The smell of pinecones and hay hung between them.

"Did you hear about the brodder?" he asked after a while. "They found him dead at the table, slumped over his crosses and chains."

Eleanor looked round sharply. "Did they indeed."

"Drank too much, ate too much, it was bound to catch up with him in the end, I suppose."

"More than likely," she said, though it was strange that bane-berries were often used as rat poison, and that the rat-catcher had been setting traps in Milord's courthouse at exactly the same time as the parson was checking the records. Just as he had been eliminating vermin from the brodder's personal quarters –

She looked at his long, craggy face and prematurely white hair, and his words floated back across time.

Another two days I give him, no more.

They had been discussing the witchfinder's imminent departure for Stoughton, to root out the truth of the accusations over there.

The King's agent is nothing, if not thorough.

James might have an obsession with demonology, she reflected, but Parliament wasn't so sure. And since too many allegations were going round for their liking, other agents were also dispatched in the King's name. Men who followed the witchprickers/brodders/call them what you will, to ensure that fair play was done . . .

"It's too early for them to be plentiful yet, but I thought somehow you might like these."

As the funeral procession stopped at the graveside, he pressed a posy of violets into her hand. By the time the mist had cleared from Eleanor's eyes, he was gone, but there was something else with the flowers, she noticed.

A bodkin.

Yes indeed, she thought shivering. The King's agent was nothing if not thorough.

And in the lych gate stood an empty cage.

DEATH KNOWS NO COMPROMISE

DEREK WILSON

I had forgotten until reminded by Derek Wilson that the great Flemish painter, Peter Paul Rubens (1577–1640) was also a noted diplomat, first under Philip III of Spain in 1605 and later under Philip IV. In 1629 he was appointed envoy to Charles I in the latest peace negotiations between England and Spain, during which time he undertook several paintings, including the famous one of Charles I and his wife Henrietta Maria.

Rubens' period in England is the setting for the following story. Derek Wilson (b. 1935) is a noted historian and biographer who has written books about Henry VIII, Charles I, Francis Drake and the Earl of Leicester – the latter also featured in the novels Feast in the Morning *(1975) and* A Time to Lose *(1976). His mystery novels include the Tim Lacy series of art thrillers, starting with* The Triarchs *(1994) plus several historical mysteries, including* The Swarm of Heaven *(2001) involving that great schemer Niccolo Machiavelli.*

"They brought me a body."

The writer paused and laid aside his pen. He pictured his fastidious correspondent, Nicolas-Claude Fabri de Peiresc, in his charming house among the vines and groves of Aix-en-Provence. Rubens smiled. Perhaps he would spare the elegant Frenchman the details of the corpse he had spent much of the day sketching. Even in the cool Westminster cellar where the vagrant had been laid out for his inspection decomposition had set in quickly. Long before the onset of the July evening Rubens had been glad to pack away his sketchbook, carbons and brushes and escape into the fresh air of the waterfront. No, he would not share with his old friend his thoughts about the curious aspects of the dead vagrant's appearance.

The artist cast his eyes over the last lines he had written.

"I have now been here almost a month and the time has passed rapidly and agreeably. Everyone at court treats me with the utmost civility. The day after my arrival the king summoned me to Greenwich Palace (this pleasant residence a little way down river from the capital is where he prefers to spend the months of high summer) and spoke with me *in camera* for more than an hour. Several friends had warned me that I should find his majesty shy and reserved but his manner could not have been more open and friendly. He spoke freely of his feelings about the Spanish and French courts and I have much cause to hope that I shall successfully complete my mission for his Catholic Majesty. He promised me some commissions and asked if there was any way he could assist me in my work. The resources of his court, he said, were at my disposal. I regarded this as princely civility and thought little more of it. It was, therefore, a great surprise when two men in royal livery called at my lodging yesterday. They brought me a body."

Peter Paul Rubens took up his quill again and dipped it in the inkpot.

"I have been working since my arrival on an altarpiece for the Brothers of the Holy Cross in Seville – *Lamentations over the Dead Christ*. I must have mentioned to King Charles certain technical problems I was experiencing in the representation of lifeless form – a live model is never quite right. His majesty obviously remembered my difficulty. He gave orders that when an unclaimed body became available it should be brought to me.

Thus, when the corpse of a vagabond suicide was dragged from the Thames, it was delivered to me. So, you see, my dear Nicolas-Claude, how thoughtful this king is. All his subjects are at my disposal – even dead ones."

Rubens finished the letter with a flourish of personal pleasantries. He rose from the table and walked to the window of his spacious first floor lodgings in Balthazar Gerbier's house. The modest mansion was set on a rise above the Thames no more than a mile from the summer palace and was flanked by clumps of woodland. The painter gazed down an "avenue" through the trees to where the lowering sun made the river into a curving ribbon of burnished brass reaching towards distant London. The details of the view fixed themselves in his mind and Rubens knew that he must paint it. All that was needed was a suitable allegorical subject worthy of this subtly soft English landscape.

As he contemplated the serene Thames his thoughts went back to the body which had been collected in late afternoon and was doubtless, by now, already unceremoniously interred in a pauper's grave. How many poor wretches, he wondered, drowned every year in London's river? Except that his wretch had not drowned and all the evidence suggested that he had not been poor. Rubens was still standing deep in thought when there was a discreet tap at the door and his host entered.

The adjective that came most readily to the mind by someone encountering Balthazar Gerbier for the first time was "wary". The tasteful clothes, well-trimmed moustache and little black tongue of beard spoke of someone who understood fashion and was no stranger to royal courts but his small, dark eyes were seldom at rest and his hands seemed always in search of objects to touch, move or pick up. Now those eyes roved over the sheets of sketch paper laid out on the bed, the empty easel in the corner, the sanded letter, as yet unfolded on the table and the portly, black-clad figure by the window.

"Writing? And the candles unlit? My dear friend. I'll have the girl attend to it directly. But now supper beckons. If you are ready." The words came out in short, jerky sentences as Gerbier moved fussily round the room.

Rubens watched his friend and, not for the first time, wondered about him. He had first met Gerbier in Paris in 1625, four years earlier and had soon realized that the younger man was cultivating him. That did not trouble or surprise him. He was by that time acknowledged as one of Europe's foremost artists, was court painter to Isabella, Governor of the Spanish Netherlands and a member of the diplomatic corps frequently entrusted with delicate negotiations. All manner of men sought his acquaintance and for all manner of reasons.

Gerbier, however, was different. For a start he was a Calvinist, the son of Huguenot parents who had fled from France to the Netherlands. Although he did not wear his religion on his sleeve, it was an encumbrance in the sophisticated courts he aspired to frequent. After various adventures he had come to London and entered the service of the Duke of Buckingham, that capricious and arrogant royal favourite for whom Rubens had nothing but contempt. In the pay of this philistine popinjay Gerbier had toured the royal and noble palaces of Europe buying up paintings, sculptures and antiquities by the wagonload as though they were so many farthing candles. The little dealer had a remarkable gift for sniffing out works of art and impecunious owners who might be obliged to sell. He had survived the assassination of his patron the previous summer, finding other leading courtiers ready to make use of his talents.

Gerbier was a rogue but Rubens could not help liking him. He was a natural connoisseur, with a knowledge matching his enthusiasm. If he hunted like a hawk and accumulated like a jackdaw, it was because he loved beauty and craftsmanship and derived a thrill from acquiring for patrons those works of genius he could never own himself.

Now he was standing by the open curtains of the bed, admiring Rubens's sketches.

"Today's work? The drowned pauper?"

Rubens smiled, as he affected the economical speech of his host. "Today's work. Not drowned. Not a pauper."

Gerbier arched his eyebrows. "But I thought . . ."

"Look at the hands."

Gerbier picked up one of the sheets of tinted paper. He carried it to the window and there admired the simplicity of the brush strokes which had yet miraculously captured the textures of skin and nails. 'Oh, yes, I see. Very elegant."

Rubens nodded. "They have never done rough work. And here–" he strode to the bed and took up another drawing "– see the soles of the feet. Not a callus, not a cut, not a scratch. I'll wager they were accustomed to nestling inside boots or shoes of the finest kid. But this is the most interesting." Rubens gathered up more leaves and handed one to Gerbier. "There, see that mark below the left shoulder blade?"

"Yes. What is it?"

"A clean – a very clean – wound. The sort that might be made by one of those Venetian stilettos. One thrust, expertly made, straight between the ribs into the heart."

Gerbier gasped. "Murder?"

"It would take a remarkably agile suicide to stab himself in the back."

"There must have been much blood."

"Not a trace."

"But even the river would not remove all the stains."

"Very unlikely – if he was thrown in wearing his own clothes. The foul, ill-fitting rags the poor man was wearing bore not so much as a speck of blood."

Gerbier shook his head and sighed. "My friend, what barbarous times we live in."

Rubens nodded agreement. "Barbarous and puzzling."

"Not in London. Cutpurses are everywhere."

"Cutpurses who strike a man down for his money, then go to the trouble of dressing him as a vagabond?"

"Fine clothes are valuable."

"Then why not dispose of the body naked or trussed up in a sack? No, I'm sure the rags were an attempt at disguise. The killers wanted to make their victim look like just another destitute beggar. That way no-one would be interested in him. I wonder who the poor fellow was." Rubens held at arm's length his drawing of the anonymous victim's face.

Gerbier stood at his elbow and scrutinized the clean-shaven features, the square jaw and the wisps of dark hair flattened against the dead man's cheeks and forehead. Rubens felt rather than saw Gerbier stiffen.

"You recognize him?" he asked.

"No. Not at all." Gerbier shook his head. "It's an intriguing puzzle, though. Tell me, what do you intend doing about . . . this?" He pointed at the scattered drawings.

Rubens shrugged. "What can I do? I have to remain on the best possible terms with his majesty. I cannot go to him and say, 'Sire, that body you kindly supplied was the corpse of some poor gentleman, brutally murdered.' "

"You're right, of course." Gerbier seemed very eager to agree. "What's done is done."

Rubens laid the papers on the table. "Yes. Yes." He paused. "Of course, if you hear of anyone missing . . ."

"I'll show them the portrait you've made. Perhaps you could give me a copy?"

"Certainly. Certainly. But I don't suppose . . ."

"No. Very unlikely. Now, come. Supper will be spoiling."

It would be incorrect to say that Gerbier had recognized the dead man or even that the flaccid features in their frame of straggling black hair had triggered some vague memory. What he had experienced when he looked at Rubens' drawing was an almost physical sensation, a tingling of excitement, a frisson. It was a feeling that came to him rarely but which he had learned to trust implicitly. It was the kind of intuitive reaction he had when he came face to face with a painting supposedly by an anonymous hand but which he recognized as the work of a master. Some people referred to this gift as a kind of aesthetic "nose"; highly sensitive to beauty and genius. It was that but in Gerbier's case it was something more. It extended to people as well as *objets d'art*.

Balthazar Gerbier was a man who lived by his wits. He had come from nowhere and had exploited to the full his artistic talent and obsequious personality to gain access to the highest political and social circles. The position of trust (or, at least, grudging respect) he had gained among the cognoscenti of several countries had not been achieved without an awareness of people who might be useful to him. He "knew" when he was in the presence of potential patrons or buyers or sellers. Now, he had that excited inner conviction that the nameless victim of some hired assassin would be important to him.

It was not difficult to conclude that he was dealing with a professional killing. The single, clean blow from behind with a narrow, needle-sharp blade had all the marks of an expert in his craft. He had seen such men during his visit to Venice and Rome eight years before. They were not hired cheaply. So, whose death was worth such a price and who was prepared to pay it? Gerbier scented information that could be valuable.

The enquiries he made over the next few days were discreet in the extreme. Necessarily so. Whoever had done away with the mysterious unfortunate had gone to considerable lengths to conceal their crime. Gerbier had no intention of alarming them and himself ending up as a piece of riverain flotsam. His questioning spread out in an ever-widening circle like ripples from a thrown stone. First, he approached those he felt he could trust. But no friend or close acquaintance at court recognized the face in the drawing. More surprisingly none of the goldsmiths or drapers on Cheapside could identify the man. Seemingly, he had not been a regular purchaser of fashionable clothes or expensive geegaws.

Only when Gerbier risked approaching strangers did his luck change. A week after his discussion with Rubens he took a boat from London Bridge to have himself rowed home from the City. The burly waterman who skilfully plied the oars was both talkative and inquisitive. As the boat pulled clear of the medley of sea-going vessels moored in mid-channel he cast a quizzical eye over his dapper fare.

"Not from these parts, are we, sir?"

"I am English and a friend of his majesty," Gerbier replied somewhat haughtily. At least part of the statement was true for he had deemed it advisable only the previous year to change his nationality. "But, you are right; I am by birth French."

"No offence meant, sir. It's all one to me. I get a lot of frogs in the boat, specially when I work the upper river. You'll be part of the queen's household, no doubt. We've seen no end of frogs in London since the king's marriage."

Gerbier nodded, seeing no need to let this fellow know his business.

"No doubt you'll be glad of the peace just made with your old country." The boatman rambled on. "I had a cousin killed at La Rochelle. Bloody waste and all down to Bloody Buckingham, God rot his soul."[1]

1 The Duke of Buckingham, Charles' favourite, had rushed England into war with France in 1627. Only after the duke's assassination in August 1628 was it possible for peace terms to be discussed. The Treaty of Suza was finally signed in April 1629.

"I'm sorry for your loss. Peace is always preferable to war." The platitudes slipped effortlessly from Gerbier's lips. Then he was struck with a sudden inspiration. "I, too, have lost a cousin – though I hope not dead."

"How so, sir?"

"I received a letter from him some weeks ago, telling me that he was coming to London and asking me to arrange lodgings for him. Well, the fact is, he never arrived."

"Changed his mind, doubtless."

"No, I have since heard that he definitely took ship from Calais soon after the treaty was signed."

"Pirates, then. Sure to be pirates. Scourge of the Channel. Now, my cousin – the one I was telling you about . . ."

"Possibly." Gerbier hastened to interrupt the burly Londoner's reminiscence. "But I've a feeling he did reach London. I wonder whether, by any chance, you have come across him. You watermen are excellent at remembering faces. Look, I have his likeness." Gerbier opened his purse and extracted the drawing. He unfolded it and held it up for scrutiny.

The waterman rested his oars and shielded his eyes against the fiery reflection of the sun on the water.

"Now there's a funny thing," he said, wrinkling his brow in concentration.

"You recognize him?" Gerbier leaned forward.

"I'd swear I know that face but it don't belong to no frog."

"What do you mean?"

"If you'd asked me straight off if I recognized that gentleman I'd have said 'Yes, he was one of my best customers last winter –'."

"Really?" Gerbier tried not to sound too eager.

The boatman bent again to his oars. "Always asked for me, he did. Very generous, too. He didn't like to have anyone else row him."

"That's unusual, isn't it?"

The other man grinned and winked. "Not under certain circumstances."

"I'm not sure I und . . ."

"Look, let's just say I used to pick him up regular at Blackfriars' Stairs of an evening and take him to Chelsea and he always asked me to collect him first thing the following morning. And it wasn't his house we went to and it wasn't his wife who sometimes met him at the staithing. You take my meaning, sir?"

Gerbier allowed himself a man-of-the-world chuckle. "And this went on all last winter?"

"January to March. It's my guess he was a parliament man. The Commons were meeting all that time and I never saw him the session before or after the king sent them all packing. Anyway, sir, that's of no comfort to you. My regular certainly wasn't French."

"A Londoner?"

"No, not that neither. Country gent. That's why I reckoned he was here for the parliament."

"And you don't know his name?" As soon as the question left his lips Gerbier knew that he had pressed too far.

Suspicion clouded the waterman's face. "No more than I know yours, sir. Anyway, he's of no interest to you, him not being, as I say, a froggy."

"No, indeed. It was just that I hoped against hope . . ." Gerbier hurriedly changed the subject.

Rubens, meanwhile, was feverishly busy. As an envoy from Philip IV of Spain it was his responsibility to frequent the English court as much as possible, to gather information and to commend to Charles and his ministers, at every opportunity, the necessity for a peace treaty between the two monarchs. It was exhausting work. The French and Venetian ambassadors did all they could to obstruct him and promises of aid from self-professed allies on the royal council never seemed to result in any advancement of his cause. The painter soon came to realize the reason for this: there was a vacuum at the centre of government. A year had passed since the death of Buckingham but the young king was still immersed in grief and even in shock. His close friend had, as courtiers were always ready to point out, with a contemptuous sneer, controlled every aspect of policy, had, in effect, run the country. The disastrous results of Charles' abdication of responsibility were obvious to everyone but Charles and now that his viceroy was gone he seemed unable to fix on clear decisions or initiatives. Fortunately for Rubens there was one subject on which the King of England was well informed and about which he was passionate. The royal enthusiasm for art provided several opportunities for Rubens to enjoy the privilege of private conversations with Charles.

"You must forgive my coming almost unannounced, Mr Rubens. Since you told me that the *Lamentations* was finished I have been all impatience to see it."

The arrival of a messenger one August morning with the news that the royal barge was already on its way along the river had thrown the Gerbier household into utter confusion. Balthazar was away from home and his young wife, Debora, though pregnant with her fourth child, rushed from room to room shouting at the servants to make everything ready, getting in their way as they tried to do so and, all the time, being accompanied by her maid who was trying to dress her. When the small, twenty-eight-year-old king stepped ashore Debora greeted him at the staithing, attempting an obeisance which her condition made virtually impossible. After a few courteous words Charles addressed himself to Rubens who was standing close by, and demanded to see the painter's latest painting. They turned towards the house, Charles linking his arm in Rubens' and talking excitedly. They climbed immediately to the attic room which had been converted into a studio.

Charles had dismissed his attendants and the two men stood alone amidst the array of completed and partially-completed canvases, paper sketches pinned to the rafters and the scattering of jars and bowls of pigments and oils, brushes and crumpled rags. For a full two minutes Charles stood silently before the picture on the easel which stood immediately beneath a fan light. It was some one and a half metres square and depicted the body of Jesus laid on a stone slab and surrounded by his mother and three disciples all displaying tearful anguish. Rubens stood behind him, anxious to hear the royal verdict.

"A difficult subject, Master Rubens," Charles remarked at last. "So still. No movement."

"Your Majesty has unerringly identified the central problem," Rubens replied and the comment was far from being empty flattery.

"Yes, yes." The King turned, hand gestures emphasizing his excitement. "With an *Entombment* or a *Descent from the Cross*, there is action the artist can freeze depicting straining muscles and tension, the contrast between the active participants in the drama and the limp, lifeless from which yet remains the central point of the composition. You must come and see my Titian *Entombment*. But here," he turned back to the canvas, "here all is stillness. The tension, the emotion is in the faces. How do you do it?" Without waiting for an answer Charles hurried on and Rubens noticed how the king's celebrated stammer disappeared when he was carried along by his enthusiasm. "Caravaggio, you know achieved dramatic effect by the interplay of light and shade. I have his *Death of the Virgin*. But this . . ." He sighed. "What is your secret, Master Rubens?"

"I was much helped, sire, by the body you loaned me. As I made my sketches I fell to thinking, 'Here is an anonymous bundle of flesh, muscle and bone that once was a living, breathing man. Someone, somewhere knows who he was. Is there a wife, children, those who would grieve for him if they could?' Then I imagined such people and how they would look, coming upon their loved one so cruelly slain."

"Ah yes." Charles stepped forward to peer more closely at the painting. "And how masterfully you have captured their varied expressions. Now," he turned abruptly, "I have a very important commission for you. You know that Whitehall Palace is to be completely rebuilt. The architectural centre point will be the Banqueting House Master Inigo Jones built for my father."

"A fine edifice, sire."

"Yes, yes, indeed. But it lacks ceiling and wall decoration to do justice to its excellent proportions. There are several large empty spaces which need to be filled by magnificent paintings. I want you, Master Rubens, to undertake the work. Your subject will be the peace and prosperity of the reign of King James." Charles stepped across to the door. "In two weeks the court returns to Westminster. I will send for you and show you what I have in mind." He held a kerchief to his nose and began to descend the staircase.

Balthazar Gerbier's quest for the identity of the murdered man became more and more determined as the days passed. The little Frenchman was cat-like in his stealthy pursuit of anything he wanted. It was a quality that had served him well in his work as an art agent for wealthy patrons. Many were the masterpieces he had wormed out of reluctant sellers or persuaded owners to part with at bargain prices. It was partly habit that impelled him to seek out information about the adulterous MP and his assignations at Chelsea. He was temperamentally unable to abandon a search once he had begun it. But there was also calculation in his persistent enquiries. Whoever had paid for the despatch of the anonymous Lothario was a man with a guilty secret and men with guilty secrets were always prepared to pay to avoid exposure.

Gerbier now knew the name of the murderer. A river journey to Chelsea had located all the waterfront houses where the illicit meetings could have taken place. A second visit, this time on horseback, had narrowed his search. Casual conversations in the local tavern had provided the information that there was only one wealthy resident who had a younger wife whose behaviour was the subject of servant gossip. His name was Thomas Shearman, a master tanner and leatherworker with premises in Southwark. Gerbier now had to move cautiously. He had no intention of venturing into the rough and malodorous backstreets around Pepper Alley where the tanners' vats polluted the air as their effluent polluted the river. Strangers entered that notorious area of stews and cutpurses very warily and did not pry into the activities of its inhabitants. Gerbier needed to be very sure of his ground before confronting Shearman. That meant that he had to find out more about the man cut down by some minion of the cuckolded merchant.

That would not be easy. If Shearman's victim had been a member of the Commons (something by no means proved) he might have come from anywhere in the realm. Since the king had dissolved parliament (vowing never to recall it, as some said) MPs had all dispersed to their own homes. There were, of course, some who lived in or near the capital but Gerbier was not on close terms with any of them. There was the added difficulty that he was known as a "king's man", a frequenter of the court and, therefore, as someone not very popular among the closed ranks of parliament men who were obsessively critical and suspicious of their betters.

The obvious person to turn to was his latest patron, Lord Weston. Weston had served as a king's man in the Commons for many years before his recent elevation to the peerage. The problem about approaching this trusted royal servant was his violent antipathy towards the "insolent" members of the lower house who were so presumptuous as to try to dictate terms to the king. If Gerbier declared an interest in one of these "lewd fellows" Weston would certainly want to know why. Only after worrying at the difficulty for several days did Gerbier come up with a stratagem he thought might work.

On a morning in early September Gerbier presented himself by appointment at Weston's quarters in Whitehall. The nobleman was celebrating his elevation (and the increase of wealth attendant on his appointment as Chancellor of the Exchequer) by completely rebuilding his family home at Roehampton and had appointed Gerbier as his architect. The little Frenchman now brought a folio of his latest designs to discuss with his lordship. Weston, a stout, high-coloured man in his mid-fifties, welcomed Gerbier affably and had a servant clear a table before a broad window overlooking the Thames. On this Gerbier placed his folio case and untied the cords. The two men bent their heads over the architectural sketches and were soon engrossed in discussion of porticos, pediments and pilasters.

It was on turning a new leaf that a sheaf of smaller papers was revealed. They were figure drawings, some of his own and some by Rubens and the one on top was the dead man's portrait.

"Oh, a thousand pardons, my lord. How careless of me to mix these daubs with Your Lordship's designs." Gerbier hastily set the drawings aside.

But not before Weston had spotted the anonymous image. "What are you doing with a picture of that rogue?" he demanded gruffly.

"What rogue, my lord?" Gerbier affected innocent bewilderment.

"Heythrop! Foul-mouthed, seditious, devil's whelp!"

"I know nothing of that, my lord." Gerbier turned to his next sketch of the south front of Putney Park. "Those are just some drawings that Master Rubens was kind enough to lend me as models for my own work – not that I shall ever approach his genius. Now, Your lordship will want the south windows to be as wide as possible consonant with the overall proportions."

"Heythrop! Heythrop!" An hour later Gerbier made his way back downriver congratulating himself on his own cleverness.

It was now relatively easy to fix the identity of his mystery man. William Heythrop, one of the two MPs for Reading, was a gentleman of the shires who had made his first appearance in parliament in March 1628 but quickly shown himself to be an eloquent and forceful speaker. Accordingly, Gerbier's investigation now took him to the Lamb in Tothill Street, a favourite resort of the Commons' men. For this excursion he made himself appear as nondescript as possible, choosing a low-crowned hat and a light russet cloak. The Lamb was not a recognized meeting place for royal servants and court hangers-on but Gerbier preferred a modicum of disguise in order neither to be recognized nor identified as a member of the fashionable elite.

It was a wet morning with no sign of the sun at its zenith. A dozen or so men were dining – lawyers and shopmen, traders come to do deals, travellers newly arrived and travellers waiting to depart and hoping for a break in the weather. Gerbier chose a table where two elderly men he took to be locals were gossiping over their ale. They talked readily with the stranger and Gerbier soon managed to steer the conversation around to the comings and goings of the parliament men.

"Heythrop? Heythrop?" The smaller of the two men, wrinkled his brow with the effort of memory. "Wasn't that the name of that young firebrand who was in here a few weeks back?"

His companion, an ill-kempt man with a straggle of grey beard, shrugged noncommittally. "That it may be. The landlord will know. George!" He called to the bald, aproned figure who stood in the doorway talking with two departing guests.

The Lamb's proprietor came over and, at Gerbier's invitation, sat down and accepted a beaker of ale from the jug Gerbier had paid for.

"This gentleman's looking for someone called Heythrop, one of the Commons' men."

George raised his eyes ceilingwards. "God save us, not another one! What's Master Heythrop done that all the world wants him?"

It took little encouragement for the innkeeper to explain.

"Yes, I know Master Heythrop. He used to meet here regular with some of his parliament friends. Sat in that corner by the fire, they did, setting the world to rights. Heythrop always had plenty to say for himself – not that I take any interest in politics. Tall fellow. Some might say handsome."

"Yes, that sounds like my man. You say others have been here looking for him."

George drained his drink. Gerbier took the hint and refilled the beaker. "First there was three of them. Rough country types. Tenants of Heythrop's, so they said, come to talk local business with him. I told them that if they came back in the evening they'd likely find their master here. Which they did but I could tell that he wasn't at all pleased to see them. He wanted to talk to 'em private so I let him use my back room. Well, they soon fell to a real jangling. You could hear the shouts and oaths in here, though the door was firm shut. Fair scared my girl they did when she went in to serve 'em. She told me there'd as like be murder done before the night was out.

"Murder?" Gerbier tried with difficulty to conceal his excitement.

"That's right. I was all set to get some help in throwing them out but, praise be, they quieted down and parted with no more than black looks."

"And that was quite recent, was it?" Gerbier asked.

"Oh, no, sir. That must have been, let me see, about the beginning of March. No it was Master Heythrop's brother who came looking for him a few weeks back. Younger man but cut from the same dark cloth, I'd say."

"William Heythrop had disappeared?"

"Run away, according to his brother. The story he told was that there was some unfinished family business to be settled but Master Heythrop, the head of the family, had simply ridden off without warning. That was why the brother – Thomas, I think he said his name was – came to London to search all his known haunts."

"He must have been very worried about his brother."

The innkeeper chuckled. "Worried? Not him. He was furious. Talked about marching Master William home to face his responsibilities. Well, I couldn't help him. Haven't seen Master Heythrop since parliament was dissolved. And now you've turned up, sir, on the same quest. Who is this Heythrop? What's he done?"

Gerbier took his cue from the landlord's story. There were, indeed, he said, important estate matters to be sorted out and, as a financially concerned party, he, Gerbier, needed certain documents to be signed. When he left the Lamb, replete with mutton stew and overripe cheese, the Frenchman realized that this Heythrop case had assumed fresh complications and that they would only be resolved by a journey into the country.

Rubens, meanwhile, was much enjoying his stay in England. He was feted by the king and his leading courtiers, many of whom were eager to show off their artistic treasures. He enthused in a letter to Fabri de Peiresc:

"In this island I find none of the crudeness which one might expect from a place so remote from Italian elegance and when it comes to fine pictures from the hands of the greatest masters, I have never seen such a large number in one place as in the royal palace and in the gallery of Lord Weston."

The high point of Rubens' English sojourn had come on the day that Charles spent several hours alone with the painter in his cabinet at Whitehall. The King had eagerly been buying up the best works of art on the market in order to establish a collection which would be the envy of Europe and he loved nothing more than showing it off to other members of the cognoscenti.

As Rubens moved with his host from canvas to canvas he was, without dissimulation, stunned by the array of Raphaels, Tintorettos, Caravaggios, Titians, Mantegnas and Coreggios. Some were hung on the walls; some stood on easels; others lay casually stacked against each other. It was as though some goddess had poured from her cornucopia of beauty an abandoned profusion of masterpieces.

The conversation ranged over many issues and Rubens found the king both affable and frank. Diplomatic language was laid aside as though out of place in the brotherhood of art. Charles spoke freely of his mistrust of the French, his desire for peace with Spain, his wish to disentangle himself from the political and religious conflicts tearing the continent apart.[2]

The King stopped abruptly before Titian's *Pardo Venus*. "I sometimes think, Master Rubens, that your calling and mine are very similar."

"Sire?"

"The balancing of so many elements." He pointed to the large canvas with its numerous classical figures in a wooded landscape.

2 The Thirty Years War, 1618–46

While Venus slept, Cupid fired his arrows, lovers were absorbed in their own activities, huntsmen and hounds pursued their quarry. "I, too, have many concerns that I must hold in equilibrium."

"Kingship is an art, sire."

"Exactly!" Charles turned to face his guest, eyes gleaming. "Yet, it is more. Like painting, it is a divine calling, a divine gift. To be able to paint as you do, Master Rubens, is something that can only come from God."

Rubens nodded. "I thank Him for it daily."

"Yes, yes, as do I praise Him for my gift. For the ability to rule can also have no other source. When I was but a child my father taught me that kings are gods. Just as you bestow divine beauty on the world, so I am charged to provide divine peace and order for my people."

"It is a great responsibility, sire."

"And one that knows no compromise. Just as you must paint what you see, what you know, what you feel, without limitation, without restriction, so I must be free to follow my divine mission. Do you not concur, Master Rubens?"

"Well, your majesty . . ."

Charles fixed him with an earnest, intense gaze. "You may speak freely, Master Rubens. I have sycophants enough who agree with every word I utter."

"Then, sire, I know nothing of the art of government but I suggest that the artist's life is not quite as simple as you suggest. Every work presents him with many compromises. The skill lies in knowing which to accept and which to reject."

Charles looked displeased and moved on to the next canvas, saying nothing. When he did speak it was without looking at his companion. "Any l-l-limitation must surely destroy the p-p-purity of the work."

Rubens phrased his reply carefully. "A painter is limited first and foremost by his own talent. The vision he has inside his head will never be what appears on the finished canvas. Then there is the constraint imposed by the subject. Should the artist depict every leaf, every cloud formation, every flesh tone precisely as it is or amend it to fit better with the overall design? Beyond this lie the dictates of fashion. Tastes change and the artist must live. He cannot afford to please himself and ignore the rest of the world.

Finally, of course, there is the patron. His instructions must always be considered and followed – if the artist hopes for more commissions. That is why, sire, I say that the artist lives with compromise. He may be master of his craft but he is the servant of his public."

Charles looked thoughtful and, after another silence, changed the subject. As Rubens later reported to Madrid, the king was so courteous and reserved that it was difficult to know what he was thinking.

William Heythrop was lord of a modest estate at Polham, five miles north-east of Reading. This much Gerbier's further researches revealed and thus a blustery autumn day found him riding along the Great West Road. The morning's journey allowed him plenty of time to think. He was building in his mind a detailed picture of his elusive quarry. He envisaged a country gentleman of modest means who had come into his inheritance at a relatively early age but had little interest in settling to his rural responsibilities. His eyes set on the life of the city, he had managed to get himself elected to the Commons. But unlike many provincials come to the capital to seek their fortune, he had made no attempt to ingratiate himself with the court party. On the contrary, he had raised his voice along with Puritan ranters and traitorous malcontents to criticize the king. As if that were not enough excitement, this lecherous bumpkin had seduced the wife of a wealthy citizen. Adulterer, wastrel, negligent landlord, radical and quarrelsome politician – there must have been many people who would have been tempted to rid the world of William Heythrop.

The story was becoming altogether too hydra-headed, too confusing. Long before the church spires of Reading came into view Gerbier had decided that the next twenty-four hours would see the end of his quest. If his visit to Polham did not produce any convincing evidence about Heythrop's murderer he would abandon his enquiries. Yet, even as he made this resolution, there came into his mind the image of Ruben's dead Christ. Gerbier had been greatly moved by the recently completed work. Who would not be stirred to compassion by the grieving faces of a mother and friends, gathered round the body of their dead Saviour. But the corpse so poignantly depicted was, in reality, that of William Heythrop. His family – and Gerbier supposed there must be some who had loved him – were being deprived of their right to mourn. Surely, they deserved the truth?

He came upon Polham Manor early the following morning, having obtained directions in Reading where he stayed overnight. Local gossip placed one fact beyond a peradventure. The town's junior MP *had* disappeared in June, much to the consternation of the burgesses. The house – timber-framed with brick facing – stood on a rise above the young Thames flanked by a fringe of woodland rich with autumn foliage. Cattle grazed the water meadows and the arable fields either side of the lane leading from the village were recently ploughed. To all outward appearances Heythrop lands were well cared for.

Gerbier presented himself as a traveller from London with news of the missing landlord and was immediately admitted. The house, though built to an old pattern with an all-purpose hall on the ground floor, had seen some concessions made to modern notions of comfort and it was to a small upper solar that the visitor was shown. When Heythrop's widow joined him there minutes later Gerbier had a double shock. Margaret Heythrop was beautiful and she was a cripple. She was dark, with smiling brown eyes and lightly-coiffed hair. Her complexion was fresh and quite unlike the painted faces to be seen about the court. Gerbier guessed that she was in her mid-twenties, though her slow and obviously painful progress across the room, leaning heavily on a staff, might have been more in keeping with the movement of a lady twice or thrice her age.

When Gerbier had introduced himself and his hostess had carefully taken her seat in a straight-backed chair, she said, "They tell me you have news of my husband, Master Gerbier."

The Frenchman hesitated, suddenly aware that he had not prepared himself for this moment. "Aye, Madam," he replied. "News which, I fear, can only bring you pain." He produced the drawing, now well-creased. "Do you recognize this as your husband's likeness?"

Margaret gave the picture no more than a glance. "Yes, that is William beyond a doubt. It is an amazing portrait. May I ask who made it and how you came by it?"

As gently as he could Gerbier briefly explained how Rubens had come by the model for his painting. He watched carefully for her reaction.

No change came over her features. She simply nodded slightly and, after some moments of silence murmured, "Poor William. I suppose it was much as we expected."

"You know, then, who might have been responsible for this outrage?"

Before she could reply the door burst open to admit a young man with mud on his boots and wisps of straw in his tumbled fair hair. "Margaret, what's all this?" he snapped, striding across to place himself beside her chair.

Mistress Heythrop made the introductions. "Monsieur Gerbier, this is my brother-in-law, Thomas Heythrop. Tom, Monsieur Gerbier comes from the king's court. He brings the news we've been seeking all these weeks. William is dead. It seems he was murdered." At the word "murdered" Margaret's composure faltered slightly. Her lower lip trembled and she hastily raised a kerchief to it.

Thomas's reaction was quite different. "God be praised!" he almost shouted. Then, frowning, "There's no doubt? This is not some stratagem of Will's to escape his responsibilities once and for all?"

"There is a reliable witness, who will swear to it if necessary."

"Good, good. Doubtless the lawyers will want proof."

After an awkward silence Gerbier said, "I was just asking Mistress Heythrop if she knew who might have been responsible for this crime."

"Whoever it was has spared me the task." Thomas stared unblinking at his visitor. "Do I shock you, Monsieur? Then, perhaps I should tell you a few things about my brother and the torment he inflicted on those closest to him."

Margaret looked up at her brother-in-law and reached out a hand to his. It was not difficult for Gerbier to read from their expressions the feelings these two had for each other. He listened with growing sadness to the tale of domestic misery that Thomas unfolded.

William had inherited Polham from his father five years before and it had soon become clear that his only interest in the estate was to milk it for the money needed to fund his own pleasures. Despite Thomas's protests William had mortgaged several parcels of land so that the estate was soon struggling to meet the repayments. There was nothing to spare for repairs to farm buildings, and tenants' dwellings and what had once been a well-run property was soon in rapid decline. Yet, despite his poor reputation as a landlord, William had managed to have himself elected as an MP for Reading in 1628.

"Bribery and hypocrisy, Monsieur Gerbier. That's how he managed it. Persuaded some of the burgesses that he'd stand up for them against the king's illegal taxes. Those he couldn't convince he paid to vote for him."

"That's not quite fair, Tom. Will was honestly opposed to the king's wars and the forced loan."

Thomas nodded. "True enough, Meg, though you should be the last person finding excuses for him. Anyway, my dear brother went off to parliament last year and became a great speechifier. He was always good at putting on an act. At least with him away we could make a start on pulling the estate back together."

Thomas explained how they had heard very little from the head of the family. Even when parliament was not in session he had spent most of his time London. Then, out of the blue, a letter had arrived from a man called Shearman. In it the writer accused William Heythrop of having seduced his wife and urged his friends and family to take him in hand. If they failed to do so Shearman vowed that he would deal with the matter himself.

Then, late one evening in mid-March William had returned unexpectedly to Polham in a state of great agitation. He arrived on a lathered horse and immediately ordered the servants to bag up the family plate and all the money they could find. Then he went to his wife's room and pocketed her jewellery.

"That was too much, even for sweet Meg." Thomas continued. "She stood up to him and there was a violent quarrel."

"He was in a terrible state," Margaret added. "He said he was going straight away and there was nothing I could do to stop him."

"Meg was clinging to him as he left her room. He struck her repeatedly. Then when she still refused to let go, he picked her up and threw her down the stairs. You can see the result, Monsieur Gerbier." Thomas's face was scarlet with rage as he recalled the events of that terrible evening. "He would have left her there, Monsieur, not caring whether she died or lived. He actually called for his horse and was at the door when I arrived. I'd been in the village and hurried home as soon as one of the servants came to find me. Would to God I had got here sooner. Still, I stopped him," he added grimly.

Thomas had laid out his brother with a single blow. Then he had tied him up and locked him in his room while he and the servants tended Margaret. When the two brothers confronted each other the next day William ranted and swore. He said his life was in danger and he dared not stay.

"Did he say who he was afraid of?"

"No, we assumed it was Shearman. It was some days before we heard about the battle between the king and the Commons. You'll have heard all about that."

Gerbier nodded. Everyone knew about the bad blood between Charles and the lower house of parliament. He had tried to put a stop to its discussions but angry members had held the Speaker in his chair while votes were taken against royal policies. The quarrel had ended up with the dissident MPs scattering and nine of them being thrown into prison.

"We wondered whether the king's men were after William, especially when we heard other reports which suggested that he was a marked man. Well, days passed and nothing happened. I was more concerned about Meg. She was very ill and the doctors talked about removing her right leg. But, praise God, she recovered – or, at least, she lived."

"And William?"

"Stayed home for a couple of weeks. Then, suddenly, one day he was gone. That was in April and we've heard nothing from him since."

"You didn't try looking for him?"

"I'd only have looked for him, Monsieur, if I wanted to find him. But, God's my witness, I devoutly hoped never to see him again. And now I'll never have to. Between us," he squeezed Margaret's hand, "we can return prosperity and peace to Polham."

Gerbier smiled. "And in that I wish you every success – both of you."

Margaret returned his smile. "You're very kind, Monsieur. Thank you for taking so much trouble to bring us this news."

The Heythrops prevailed on Gerbier to stay for dinner and, it being by then too late to reach London by daylight, it was the next morning before he was back on the road.

He ambled his way eastward. Now there was even more to

think about. He was no nearer to discovering Heythrop's killer. Shearman? Some zealous servant of the king? An aggrieved tenant? Or an angry, vengeful brother in love with his sibling's wife? Gerbier wanted very much to believe Thomas's version of events and was inclined to accept that it was substantially true. But why had the young man lied about not going to London in search of William? And if William had simply disappeared as the couple at Polham claimed, how did Thomas know that his brother had returned to the capital? If danger lurked for him there it might have been thought that he would give the city a wide berth. For mile after quiet country mile Gerbier turned over in his mind all the facts he had unearthed. At last he abandoned the effort of trying to reach a conclusion. After all, what did it matter? William Heythrop was dead and his demise was no loss to anyone. The man had been a traitor to all who had a call on his loyalty – king, wife, family and everyone who looked to landowners like the Heythrops as the very substance of English rural society. Gerbier decided to concern himself no more in a business which promised no profit.

He had just come within sight of the castle at Windsor when he heard the sound of galloping horsemen on the road behind him. The highway was wide and traffic was very light but he steered his horse into the side to let the hurrying travellers pass. They did not pass. They reined in as they drew level and one edged in front blocking his path. Quickly, Gerbier reached down for the pistol in his saddle holster. Before his hand closed over the stock something heavy and hard struck the back of his head. He fell across the horse's neck, tried to right himself but ended up slithering sideways. His shoulder struck the flinty ruts with a jarring jolt. Head swimming he looked up at his attackers.

Thee were three of them, all in dark riding cloaks. Gerbier tried to make his eyes focus but the faces staring down at him were little more than a blur.

Someone said, "Frogs should stay in their own pond and keep out of other men's gardens."

Then one of the assailants hit him again and he plunged into a black void.

What followed was a confusion of images and sensations. Sometimes conscious, sometimes unconscious, Gerbier felt juddering motions and sensed the smell of animals. He heard street noises – horses, wagons, people. Yet, terrifyingly, he could see nothing, nor could he call out for aid. But at last the darkness did lift and the pain in his head had subsided to a dull throbbing. When he opened his eyes he saw the familiar sight of his own bed hangings and the anxious faces of his wife and a cluster of children and servants. Somehow, heaven knew how, he had reached home safely.

It was two days before the concussion lifted and Gerbier was able to sit in an armed chair by the window. There were still gaps in his memory but with the aid of servants who had found him on his own doorstep the chain of events became reasonably clear. His attackers had bound and gagged him and stuffed him inside a sack. He had then been brought back on a farm cart to his own house at dead of night. When he had been untrussed a note had been discovered pinned to the collar of his cloak: *He lives. If he meddles further with the Heythrop business he will not be so fortunate.* Since Gerbier had told her nothing about his investigation Debora was both bewildered and frightened. He tried to calm her and assured her – which was the truth – that he had no intention of pursuing his enquiries. Not until Rubens came and sat with him did he unburden himself and try to make sense of his misadventure.

"A pox on the whole Heythrop clan!" he muttered. "They all have deviousness and violence in their blood."

Rubens suppressed a smile. "You are sure that it was they who mishandled you?"

"It must have been. That plausible rogue Thomas Heythrop was afraid that I might not swallow his lie about not following his brother to London, so he sent his men after me to frighten me into silence."

"Hm, possibly." The artist looked dubious.

"What other explanation could there be?"

"Well, it just occurs to me if Thomas Heythrop was a deliberate and skilful murderer he would not have balked at having you despatched and leaving your body at the roadside, apparently the victim of highway robbers.

"That's as may be."

"And then there's the problem of delivery."

Gerbier wrinkled his brow in a frown. "My friend, please don't speak in riddles. My head is still buzzing."

"I mean that if you did not give your address to Thomas Heythrop how could his paid ruffians know where to bring you?"

Gerbier took a sip from a glass of some livid green herbal decoction and winced at the astringent taste. "The same objection must apply to everyone involved in this affair."

"Possibly." Ruben's face was expressionless.

Gerbier stared at him. "Do you know something you are not telling me?"

Rubens stood and moved towards the door. "I know that these English are phlegmatic by nature but unpredictable when roused. I know that it is unwise to become involved in their quarrels. And I know that you, my friend, need to rest and put these troublesome events behind you. I'll come and see you again tomorrow." He left, closing the door quietly behind him.

He climbed to his studio, where a young apprentice was, with intense concentration, working at the foliage sections of a large allegorical landscape. It was the view of the Thames from the painter's chamber window and Rubens was pleased to have found a subject worthy of the peaceful, sylvan scene. It was the king, himself, who had suggested it. He wished to be portrayed as St George freeing his people from the bondage of war abroad and discord at home. In this idyllic scene, men, women and babes in arms rejoiced to be led into a sunlit world of peace and harmony and raised their hands in praise of the saint who had slain the dragon. And what was the dragon, if not the visible metaphor of an evil, unruly parliament, a body of men who had set themselves against the Lord and his anointed? It was a beast that had to be eradicated and the king, the great Christian champion, had destroyed it. The House of Commons was no more and the mood among Charles' ministers and courtiers was one of unreserved glee.

Rubens dropped into an old wainscot chair and watched the young man carefully mixing and applying his pigments but his thoughts were elsewhere. He recalled the king standing before the *Lamentation over the dead Christ* and displaying neither surprise nor emotion at the suggestion that the model for the central figure might have been murdered. The muted suspicion that had murmured in Rubens' inner ear then had now become a shouted certainty. The more he pondered poor Gerbier's rough handling, the clearer it became to him that there was only one man who could be responsible. A man who had the wealth and the power to command desperadoes and assassins. A man dedicated to carrying out the wishes of his royal master, spoken and unspoken. A man well acquainted with Balthazar Gerbier and determined to deflect him from his inconvenient enquiries. Yet a man who would not wish to harm the little Frenchman seriously. For why would Lord Weston want to incapacitate a useful protégé?

Yet the ultimate problem lay not with overzealous, mindlessly ambitious courtiers. It lay with politicians, whether royal demigods or radical demagogues who claimed to speak with the voice of the Almighty. For such fanatics the word "compromise" had no meaning. Rubens sighed. If England's king and parliament could find no way to live together then it might be that they would die together. The fate of William Heythrop, God forbid, could be a portent of things to come.

A HOUSE DIVIDED

JUDITH CUTLER

The English Civil War, which erupted in 1642, was a direct result of both Charles I's and James I's intransigence and their total belief in their Divine right to rule. It divided not only the nation, but individual families, and that forms the basis for the following story set in the midst of battle.

Judith Cutler (b. 1946) is probably best known for her series of novels featuring Sophie Rivers who, like Cutler, was a lecturer at an inner-city college in Birmingham. That series began with Dying Fall (1995). *More recently in* Power on Her Own *(1998), Cutler started a new series featuring Kate Power, a former Metropolitan Detective now working in Birmingham.*

"My son would never run away from battle, Mistress Biddy, let me tell you that." In his anger, Master Bulstrode smote the floor so hard with his stick I feared he would smash through the ceiling below. "And if you persist with such a foul slander, I shall have you whipped at the cart's tail. Do I make myself clear, woman?" he bellowed, for he thought that all were as hard of hearing as he. "Speak up!"

I bobbed my curtsey, though my knees found it harder with each day. But I held to the truth, as I saw it. "I cannot lie, Master.

Not though I were whipped a thousand times. Your son was wounded in the back. I have seen the evidence with my own eyes, as I washed his dear body."

There can be nothing worse, to prepare your nursling, the child you suckled at your breast, for his funeral. The old should die first, not the young. Not that Master Thomas was young any more, I had to remind myself. He was no longer a gold-haired babe whom a painter might have used as a model for the Christ child – in those sacrilegious days of such heathen depictions. He had reached his middle years, thirty-five, when all notions of fighting should have left with the heat of his loins.

But all was topsy-turvy in this year of Our Lord 1648. God's anointed King was now a villain. In our village his name was not mentioned without the speaker spitting into the dust. Master Bulstrode, once famed for his preaching from the pulpit of our parish church, had been one of the first to seize a labourer's pitchfork and smash the stained glass windows of the church he had served for more then half a lifetime.

His eldest brother, Sir Peter, screamed and railed at the sight, clinging like a sailor in a shipwreck to the cross some said was built before the Conquest. In moments he was thrust away, and the heathen symbol was no more.

Would Sir Peter condole with Master Bulstrode? Both had lost their first-born, after all, though they'd fought on opposing sides. I doubted it.

But Master Bulstrode was busy with his stick once again, veins a-bulge in his forehead, as if he were like to have an apoplexy. "I saw the wounds with my own eyes, when they brought him home. A musket ball to the shoulder, his thigh cut almost to the bone by a pike. My son fought bravely."

"I dare swear he did." He had always had more passion than sense, young Master Thomas, whether it was climbing the highest trees or chasing the prettiest wench. "But the blow that killed him was here, sir." I reached to the fleshy part of my shoulder, or thereabouts. "A deep knife wound – very deep, sir. That was what killed him. Begging your pardon, sir." I forced my knees into another curtsey.

It was only because Master Bulstrode was such an important man in the village that they had brought his son home. I had seen the pits they dug for other men, officers and foot soldiers alike, the bodies stripped not just of their armour and weaponry, but of anything else that might have given a little dignity in death. Other women didn't have the privilege of preparing their loved ones for a decent burial in a quiet corner of a country graveyard. Husbands, sweethearts and brothers alike – all were tumbled together like discarded playthings. And I had a home, thanks to the kindness of Master Bulstrode, who had taken me into his household when the bloody flux had carried off my husband: other women, camp followers no better than they ought to be or decent dames trying to provide a few home comforts for their soldier husbands, had nothing. Less than nothing. There were tales from both sides of the violation of women. Not just the slicing of noses to the bone, yes, and cheekbones too, but rape – men supposedly fighting for their God, rutting like animals knowing no better. And trying, God help them, to justify their bestiality.

"And where have you laid him? Until the funeral." Master Bulstrode demanded, in tones more of accusation than grief.

"The dairy's coolest," I said. "I'll watch him over night."

"No praying for his soul! I'll have no papish practices!" The spittle flew in his passion, though I dare swear he'd have given his own hope of salvation to save his son's.

But I nodded. "Of course not, sir; but I wouldn't want him lying there on his own." Not the little lad who was always afraid of the dark. How many times had I rocked him after a nightmare, promising all would be well in the morning? Master Bulstrode had raged each time, saying his son must learn to be a man. But how could any nurse let a poor, motherless child – Mistress Bulstrode had died giving birth to him, a fact the master never let him forget – sob like that without loving him better?

I hobbled downstairs, leaving the master to his bread and small beer. His room was as good as a trap these days. I'd had to slip a coin to Sergeant Briggs and Pikeman Walters, the soldiers who'd brought back Master Tom, to help him downstairs to receive the body: he'd never have been able to make the short journey down to the entrance hall and back without them. Another coin guaranteed their return tomorrow, to carry him in his chair across to the church.

For all that, I dared not disobey him, whatever my own desires.

In the dim light of the dairy, shrouded in a linen sheet, Tom looked so like the child I'd loved. But as I touched his cold face, smoothing back his now coppery hair, I knew he wasn't. When had he grown those deep lines, which even the sleep of death could hardly soften? When had the anger creases become furrows? When his father had forbidden him the puppy he'd set his heart on, and he'd tried to tear it apart rather than let anyone else have it?

Perhaps it was the scar of that on his conscience that transformed him into such a godly youth. Look at those long straight legs of his: made by the Lord to cut a sweet caper, if ever limbs were. But no sooner had Master Thomas – I must no longer call him Tom, he'd frowned – come down from the university, he'd stood apart from the heathenish maypole, staring down any maiden foolish enough to make sheep's eyes at him. He was no stranger to the more tender emotions, however: he would pen verses he took care to lock away when I came to clean his closet. My letters never came easily to me, and I was never book-learned, but those times he forgot to hide his scribblings I could work out "To Mistress A –" or whoever she might be. And such things he wrote – many a blush would they have brought to my cheek, had I been that way inclined, and many a beating had his father found out. His father, or Master A –, of course. But he was my little Tom, and I would have done nothing to harm him.

Now he was as cold as the marble monuments in the church. I folded his hands, so they were seemly in prayer. He lacked the armour and a little dog by his feet, but otherwise he might have been Sir Clifforde, his great-great-great-grandsire, whose tomb alone stood undamaged in the church. A justice Sir Clifforde had been: by all accounts a fair man, but stern and unyielding, he had made many enemies. He died the day he had some old woman bridled as a scold: some said it was she who killed him by her witchcraft, and drove her family from the village. Others said that it was an angry scullion had poisoned his master's food to avenge his beloved mother.

At least my Tom had had a swift, clean death. But who had hated him enough to stab him in the back, a fellow man at arms, fighting for the same just cause? Who must be punished as a murderer? – for even in these troubled times justice might prevail.

Gathering my shawl about me, I went to stand, as I had on so many nights in my life, in the dairy doorway. I could smell the animals – not many left now, most seized by one army or another foraging legally or illegally – and hear the murmur of voices. Women tended to gather round the village well after the heat of the day had passed. If I moved closer I could identify them. Mistress A – might not be there, but Sally, her cook, might be. Like the parsonage, the Manor House had its own water supply, but Sally was never averse to a pleasant gossip. Soon she joined me in the dairy.

"He makes a fine corpse," Sally sighed, only just managing not to cross herself. "Has anyone else –?"

"Not yet. I've not long made him decent. And the Master doesn't want any fuss. But you can't just let the light go out from a life and not say your farewells. Do you think," I began, dropping my voice even lower, so she had to crane forward to hear, "that anyone else might want to come? Anyone at all?"

She jumped back as if I had put her hand in the fire. Then, more thoughtfully, she nodded. "But I cannot think that she will be able to leave the household. The master was wounded in the same skirmish. Not grievously, but enough to want his wife to bathe his brow. And she will – she will do what she must do."

"Is there still no ease between them?"

"With her coming of Royalist stock and him as devout a Parliament's man as your master? And the young master too sickly to know which side he's supposed to be fighting for?" The young master's carroty hair was something we all contrived to ignore. "There's be some wanting to see him laid out like this just to make sure he's dead – saving your presence, Mistress Biddy," she added hurriedly.

"Just let them say that to my face, Mistress Sally, and my poor Tom won't be the only one awaiting burial tomorrow."

"But Mistress Berry's family –"

"I dare them to show their faces here!"

"But Master Thomas was overzealous, perhaps?"

"He's got his forebears' blood within him," I said, by way of apology or explanation – I hardly knew which. "And he was doing no more than his duty," I insisted, lest she sense my weakness.

"Indeed, it is every man's bounden duty – aye, every woman's too – to report witchcraft. But burning is a terrible thing, Mistress Biddy. A terrible thing. And there are many in the village who would say that Mistress Berry was more mad than bad."

"She was a witch," I averred firmly.

She nodded, her fingers twitching to cross herself. "I suppose there's no news of –" she swallowed and dropped her voice even lower "– of his brother?"

I answered question with question. "Is it likely? If he returned, the Master would surely be taken off with a seizure. Master Simon is worse than dead to this household, Mistress Sally. Worse." The brothers had been as like as peas: Master Simon perhaps an inch taller, broader, and with hair a more lustrous chestnut, tumbling on to his shoulders in a manner of which no girl might have been ashamed. Modesty apart, of course.

"But with your master now without issue? And Master Simon the first-born son, for all he's in exile over the seas?"

I shook my head. "When the time comes I shall know what to do."

Scarcely had she slipped into the deepening dusk than there came a scratch at the half-open door: in slid the wraithlike figure of Will, the verger.

"I never thought I'd live to toll the bell for the young master," he whispered. "And it's a long grave young Luke and I have had to dig – and him no more than a lad, scarce able to wield a spade. Yet he'll be off to join the army, soon as his mother's back's turned."

"And who will run the farm then?" Without the crops, without the animals, I could see nothing but starvation for us all.

Will shrugged his shoulders, looking down at the pale face almost glowing in the dim light. "The wages of sin is death," he said. "For us all, Mistress Biddy, for us all." He took my hand, kissing it gently. We'd always had soft spots for each other, but my duty to the young master had always overridden all else.

"Indeed!" agreed another voice.

Sir Peter! My knees struggled to their lowest curtsey.

"Enough, Biddy: we who are old are all equals in the sight of the Grim Reaper." Despite his frailty, he lifted me firmly upright. "As I shall tell my brother in five minutes. I hear you've sent for Master Simon."

"Nay, sir! No I! You hear wrong! Not till Master Bulstrode –"

How could it be, that in the presence of death I could not frame the word?

"But they say he was seen – that was why I assumed my brother was on his death bed!"

I shook my head dismally.

"Are you sure, woman?"

"Certain sure." Without realizing I slipped into the assurance my young master would give when denying his latest exploit.

He nodded, hardly anything visible of him now except the wisps of white hair escaping his hat, and the ivory of his gnarled hand on his stick.

"Sir," I blurted, "might I have a word of you?"

"In private?"

Before I could speak, Will touched his hat and slipped silently away.

His face was full of pity. "Biddy, you do not have to be nervous speaking to me: you are not my servant!"

"And this is not your son. But he is your kindred, sir – and someone has murdered him."

"Woman!" he cried aloud.

I lit the candle, and eased poor Tom so that his uncle might see the fatal wound.

He shook his head, laying his hand on mine. "No man lives such a rackety life as Thomas without making enemies, Biddy. In these grievous times, leave well alone."

But leave it I could not. What were we fighting for, if not God, the fount of all goodness and justice? Someone must pay for this! Kissing my Tom gently on the forehead, I pulled my shawl about me and set forth through the now starlit night towards the camp.

Camp! It was scarcely more than a straggle of improvized tents, with naught but a terrified boy on guard. Young Jacob Ashcroft! Indeed, he nearly shot me in his desire not to let me through what he grandly called the lines, but I reminded him of the tartlets I'd slipped him from my apron pocket during tedious long sermons, and very soon I was before the young man Jacob called reverently the Commander.

"Sergeant Briggs and Pikeman Walters brought him home, you say?" he asked, graciously gesturing me to an ammunition box to sit on. His face was thin and weary, in another age a true model for the image of a saint. "Did they look furtive or guilty?"

I remained on my feet. "Nay, sir, they carried him boldly – tearfully, in truth, but as men proud of their burden, reverent for all Sergeant Briggs had had to sit the whole of one Sabbath on the penitents' stool, him and young Phoebe Dyve, after Master Thomas had seen them doing what I won't soil my lips to speak of."

"So you don't think it was they who, charged with taking an injured man for succour, took the chance to slay him? After all, no man likes to be publicly humiliated."

"True, there was blood on their hands, sir – but they had fought in the skirmish themselves, and how am I to know whose it is? Nay, sir, I want to know who fought alongside him, even behind him! For I know that such a man as Thomas Bulstrode would lead his men from the front."

"And would be in the midst of any action," he agreed, "indeed, taking the flat of his sword to those who tarried, Mistress Biddy."

"And who might those have been?" At last I might be succeeding.

"Many, truth to tell. We are all weary, in God's name."

"Names, sir: I came for names."

He counted off on long, thin fingers: "The sergeant and the pikeman you know already. There were others from hereabouts. The Lord of the Manor."

"Master Ashcroft?" I gasped.

"He, with that halfwit son of his; three young men by name of Berry; several strangers to these parts, all licked into something like shape by young Thomas. None loving him, Mistress Biddy. Except Sir Waller Massey – he and Thomas seemed something like friends."

"I thought he had defected from the Royalist side – can he have become a friend?"

" 'There is more joy in Heaven over one sinner who repenteth', Mistress," he reminded me with the sort of smile I gave young Jacob. I would have rebuked him, had he not rubbed his hands over his tired face. "Oh, and but very lately come amongst us is a tall man, approaching but not in his middle years. Well set-up, knowing his weapons. Besides these gentlemen? The usual assortment of ill-lettered, well-meaning dolts with only their scythes as weapons. Dear God, what a rabble, to resist a well-led Royalist force." He pressed the heels of his hands into his eyes. "Question them if you will, Mistress Biddy. But not now. Leave it till the morning, in the Lord's name."

"Till the funeral?" I was appalled.

"Why not?"

"May I not speak to his friend? To this tall stranger?"

He shook his head firmly. "I'll give those who want it leave of absence for an hour – no more, mind – to attend his obsequies. I shall lead a detachment myself, in fact. And now, good night to you, Mistress." He summoned Jacob to lead me home.

If only I had a tartlet now. If anyone could speak without dissembling, it was Master Jacob. But he was so full of his new responsibility, I doubted if I could remind him how well he used to do my bidding.

"You must see everyone who comes and goes," I murmured, as we picked our way through the thicket protecting the camp.

"Indeed I do, Mistress. But I may not tell who."

"May not? How so, Master Jacob?"

"Because I may not. The gentleman told me."

"A gentleman!" I echoed. "Not a soldier?"

"A gentleman may be a soldier," he muttered. "And a soldier may be a gentleman."

"But this gentleman was not a soldier?" I prompted. "And did you know this gentleman?"

"How could I, Mistress Biddy? He was swathed to the ears. And spoke thus." Jacob laid his arm across his face, as if to muffle his mouth with his cloak.

"But did you know his voice?"

"No, Mistress."

"And what did the gentleman do?" Cool as the night was becoming, my palms sweated.

"Nothing, Mistress. Except to speak to other gentlemen."

"And which other gentlemen might they be? Were they soldier gentlemen?"

"I may not tell, Mistress. They said they'd slit my throat if I looked. But the one gentleman was kind, Mistress, and made them put up their swords so they might not get rusty in the dew, he said, and he laughed. But I know not why. And then he gave me a bright penny, and ruffled my hair and told me to run away."

"So you ran away and did not listen?"

"I ran, but not very far, and did not listen – but I heard, Mistress, because try as I might I could not stop my ears."

"So you heard the gentlemen say things. Now they are not here, now you are safe, you can tell old Biddy, who makes you tartlets and other sweetmeats, what they said."

Was I wrong so to question the child? If I was, think how much worse they were who used children as messengers, even though they knew the enemy recked not for youth or innocence, and tore out their fingernails if they caught them.

"The stranger asked for what he said he'd come for. But the other gentleman – the kind one – said he'd get no more. That he'd done wrong and would not do it again. I would not have dared speak thus to the first man, lest he kill me. For that was what he threatened to do, Mistress – kill the kind man. But at last he thrust him away, and seemed to leave the camp. But then he spoke to another man, and he gave him something in a bag."

"And would you know that man again, Jacob? You may tell old Biddy, you know."

He nodded, hard. But try how I might, I could not lure him into an answer. So I kissed him on the cheek, and promised more sweetmeats if he came to my kitchen, and left him guarding the camp.

Although the night was now old, and the candle I'd set surely long guttered, a pale light still filled the dairy. I saw the shadow of a familiar profile.

He had risen! He had risen indeed! And with the rushing in my ears and the lights blinding my eyes, I knew no more.

Someone was burning feathers under my nose. Choking, eyes awash, I found myself awake once more, a beaker of water pressed to my lips, my back supported by a strong arm.

" 'Tis not Thomas, dear Biddy. 'Tis I, Simon," a familiar voice whispered.

I struggled to my feet. "Then 'tis you who slew him! You, you monster!" I beat at his chest with my fists, but clasping my wrists with one hand he pushed me away.

"Hold your peace, Biddy! Do you want them all about us?" He pressed a finger to my lips. "Nay, nay – enough of your shrewishness. You were never wont to be like this."

"I was never in the presence of a – of a brother-killer before."

He shook his head. "I'm no fratricide, Biddy. Though were I one, I would be one amongst many. This terrible war – to what hideous crimes have men been driven! All in the name of God knows what."

"You, Master Simon – a man of the cloth and you say that?"

"A man of the cloth so saddened by the excesses of his brethren he has left his church behind and sought a better life in the New World. I returned – never mind why I returned. Let us say it was to say farewell to my brother. That is why I came to say farewell to my father. And now, it seems, to my brother." He covered the face with the shroud.

"If you did not kill him, who did?" I asked.

"Biddy, you loved him dearly, but even you must grant that there were many who did not. And men fall dead every day. Why not leave it at that?"

"Would you, in my position?"

"Nor I, in my position!" he admitted with a grim smile.

I recounted the events of the night. "The commander says I may question them all in the graveyard," I concluded. "But, dear Master Simon, I think I may do better than that." As I explained my plan, his eyes rounded in horror. Then I saw him nod, slowly at first but then with enthusiasm.

"But first I must pay my respects to my father. What time does he awake, Biddy?"

"If he gets two hours' sleep together, he'll do well. Many is the night I've watched with him, or read aloud to take his mind off the pain."

"Will you go and tell him I'm here? God forbid I give him the shock I gave you."

"Indeed, it would kill him, Master Simon."

But nothing now could touch my old master. Shock, grief, joy were now all as one: fled, as it were, a shadow. I closed his eyes gently, and – privately, secretly – prayed for his soul.

"Send for Master Will," I whispered to the new master. "We will need two graves."

Will grumbled and grouched his way through the following hours, sending his lad to the next parish for a clergyman to replace Master Bulstrode. The news of the double tragedy seeped through the village with the morning mist, and by the time milking was over and the beasts fed, a regular trickle of mourners made their way to the church.

Sir Peter took his place in the pew he'd long since abandoned: you could hear the gasp of shock from those who knew of the family bitterness. He looked bleakly around him but once before burying his face against his clasped hands. Perhaps he could not bear to see the violence inflicted on the fabric of a building he loved more than his home. At last he looked up, stood as if searching for something – and then limped down the aisle to where I stood at the back of the church.

"You were part of the family, Mistress Biddy, more than just the poor man's wet- nurse. You are the chief mourner." He could not have escorted that foreign queen herself, the one who ruined the king, they say, with a more gentlemanly air.

I was glad of his arm. And glad of the chance to murmur in his ear before the service began. Even I did not know the moment Master Simon would choose to make his declaration.

We had left the church and were gathering round those two unforgiving holes in the sward, sombre and anxious after a sermon less concerned with speaking kindly of the two dead men than with ranting about eternal perdition. The God of Love was nowhere to be found, it seemed. Master Bulstrode was interred first, the clods of earth sounding like a death knell into the quiet corner that held all recent the family graves. It must be soon! My heart thudded painfully as the preacher begged the Lord to deliver us from the bitter pains of eternal death. Even as he signed to Sir Peter and me to gather a fistful of earth, the coffin lid rose and up stood Master Simon, wrapped like his brother in a good linen sheet. He stood still as a statue, his eyes closed.

Slowly, slowly, relentless as death itself, his right arm rose.

The gasps of shock gave way to screams of horror.

There was silence again. Would the dead speak? The body turned, slowly, taking in all who were there. Any moment now we knew it would speak.

But to whom?

When they were young, before the theatre was found to be sinful, there was nothing my lads had enjoyed more than reading a play.

My late master had oft wiped tears of mirth from his eyes, until he realized that he was encouraging them in sin. After that, there were no more plays.

But Master Simon might have been in Shakespeare's own theatre as he stood upright and looked around the circle of terrified mourners. Slowly, slowly he moved his right arm, pointing in turn. Surely someone must be driven by that accusing finger to confess, and soon. Would it be the Berry family, with their natural grudge? The cuckolded Lord of the Manor? Even Master Will, whose courtship of me when I was a comely widow in my middle years had cut sadly short by Tom's scathing words?

As no one moved, I shook with fear. Had our daring, some would say dangerous, plan come to naught?

There was too much of the Bulstrode blood in Master Simon for him to give up, however. Pulling himself from the very grave, he paced in clear fury. Some prayed aloud for all our sakes that he would stop before the stranger, Sir Waller Massey. No one wanted the accused to be anyone from what little that was left of our once close community. But to my horror and that of all of us he headed straight for poor, simple Jacob. From his grave-clothes, he produced a purse. "You have seen this before, young sir?"

The child nodded.

"Whom does it belong to, child?"

Jacob looked wildly about him. "He is not here, sir."

"And is the kind man who told the other men to put up their swords here?"

"Yes, Master – it's you! Master Thomas! Fresh risen, sir!"

I went to comfort the lad, but Master Simon stayed me with a gesture.

"To whom was this purse given, Jacob?"

"To that man there, sir! The Commander!"

"It was when the child spoke of putting up the bright swords, lest the dew rust them, I knew the man refusing further orders must be my brother," Simon reflected, drawing on the wine he'd found buried deep in his father's cellar. "Think of all those nights we read Shakespeare, us lads."

I nodded sadly: there had been such joy then. "'Tis sad to reflect he was a spy, Biddy, but in this dreadful age, no one can say any longer who fights for what is right. But why did you suspect the commander of the killing?"

"He threw so much dust in my eyes, young Master, that I thought he wanted to hide something. The killing of an enemy informant. And why not make it look like a battle wound? Kinder, in fact to his family. It was only the meddling of a foolish old woman that brought it out. Thank God the old Master did not live to know his son's disgrace."

"I think he knew some of it. Why else should he have summoned me? No word of explanation, of course, lest the missive were intercepted and Thomas hanged for the villain he probably was. Do you know, I am proud that at the last he refused the blood money."

"And he was kind to Master Jacob." The lad he dared not admit was his own son. I opened the window a little wider to let the smell of the roses into the parlour, unused for so long it was musty.

"Indeed. And now, Biddy – what will you do?"

I stared. "Stay here and care for you, Master. If it pleases you."

"It pleases me indeed. But not here. Not in this place of strife, Biddy. There is too much hatred. I know others think so too. Your old suitor Will, now: he longs to quit the village, but will not, as long as you are here. I've already offered him a position."

"In the New World?"

"In the New World. Tell me, Biddy – will you come too? I cannot promise you an easy life over there, but already I have a snug farm, good beasts and a fine dairy. Say you will come."

I nodded. "Perhaps I will, Master. It is as you say: nobody can tell what we have fought about all this while."

TWO SIDES

MIKE STOTTER

During the Civil War some more forward-thinking radicals, such as John Liburne (1614–57), had advocated the complete overthrow of the monarchy and the House of Lords and that all politicians in the House of Commons should be elected by the people on an annual basis. He formed a political party called the Levellers. There was a lot of sympathy for the Levellers and Cromwell even went some way towards meeting their demands but it was not enough. Liburne became a relentless agitator and eventually was imprisoned in the Tower. Despite a public outcry Cromwell refused to release him. This turned the Levellers, now led by Edward Sexby, into anarchists, determined to overthrow the government.

Which brings us to Mike Stotter's story set in the midst of all this fear and turbulence. Mike (b. 1957) has worked at various jobs ranging from BBC TV through to Asset Management. His short stories have appeared in such anthologies as The Best of the American West *(Volumes 1 and 2),* Desperadoes, Future Crimes *and* The Fatal Frontier. *He is the editor of* Shots Magazine, *which continues on his website devoted to the genre, <www.shotsmag.co.uk>.*

A weak shaft of winter sunlight reflected on the axe blade as it descended. With a single blow the head was severed from the neck, ending up in the wicker basket placed alongside the vast wooden chopping block. The crowd gathered outside the Banqueting House of London's Palace of Whitehall let out a moan. Richard Brandon, the executioner, expected a roar of celebration not this display of empathy. He did not remove his black leather mask as he moved across the raised dais to collect the severed head. He lifted it aloft, displaying the gory remains for the onlookers, and obeyed the order that he was not to announce: "Behold the head of the traitor!" as was the normal practice. Brandon saw both men and women alike weeping.

Charles, by the Grace of God, King of England, Scotland and Ireland, and France, Defender of the Faith – no more. Charles Stuart, King of England, executed as a traitor. On 30 January 1649, his death brought an end to the monarchy's claim to absolute power by Divine right. Long live Parliament and Cromwell's new Republic.

It is a well known fact that if you stood on London's Fleet Bridge and looked down upon the Fleet River itself for long enough, you would see any manner of things taken by its lazy current into the Thames. It would be a brave soul indeed to endure the powerful stench emanating from the butcher's sweepings of dung, guts and blood of dead cats, of human excrement and the entrails and hides of dogs. The dying days of December 1656 had not deterred Londoners from continuing to use the ditch as an open sewer.

The fog had come in off the Thames at early evening and shrouded Davy's Wharf on the east bank of the Fleet in a dense cloud so thick you could almost grab it with your hands. A small group of people were huddled together despite the intense cold. They spoke in soft tones out of respect for the dead. The fog muffled their voices and hid their forms making them appear as spectres in the night. Some yards away, armed men carried pitch and tar torches that threw a hellish light around the still form on the wharf side.

"The body was found thus?"

The Alderman was startled at the sound of the voice so close in his ear. He turned, his right hand instinctively dropping to the hilt of the dagger on his belt. Many a thief, pick-pocket, night walker and murderer came to this area of the city to either escape the law or ply their trade. The dark alleyways and the huddle of buildings and warehouses provided an excellent refuge. The stranger was quick, and wrapped his fingers around Hemsby's wrist, squeezing with enough pressure to stop him drawing the weapon.

"Put away your weapon, sir. I have come to assist you."

He seemed to have materialized out of the night, bypassing the guards, arriving with an air of authority that even he, Alderman Joseph Hemsby, did not question. The newcomer had the bearing of a man from the military. He was dressed in the sombre tones of the day: a dark woollen cloak fastened about him so only the white falling ruff gave any relief. His tall conical hat was decorated with a simple buckle, whilst the wide brim concealed his upper face. He was freshly shaven and smelt of herbal soap.

"Was the body found here, sir?" The stranger pressed.

"Only after he was dragged from the ditch," Hemsby replied.

The newcomer did not take his eyes from the corpse, saying, "That much is obvious, Alderman Hemsby. I wouldn't expect a dead man to climb out of the ditch and lay out on the quayside for our convenience!" He pointed to a large lump above the man's right eye. "Was that the killing blow?"

The alderman glared angrily. He was similarly dressed but gave into vanity by wearing a lace neck ruffle. Obviously the elder, Hemsby nevertheless gave in to his superiority. He moved closer to the body sprawled out on its back and kicked at the man's foot, showing little respect for the deceased.

"I assume so," he muttered. The stranger knew his name and position but had not introduced himself. "Do you have a name, sir, or credentials as you see fit to trespass my province?" he asked.

"Sir, my name is William Titcomb. I am from Mr Thurloe's office."

Hemsby's stomach lurched and swore under his breath, wondering how news of this death had reached the Lord Protector's spy master so quickly. And why was this corpse of interest to him?

The evening held a promise of snow, and a cold wind whipped around the men, shifting tendrils of fog in its motion. Rats, undeterred by human presence, ventured out of their holes and began to sniff around. Torch light reflected in their black soulless eyes. The fog brought an eerie quietness, only broken by the soft lapping of water against the wooden supports below their feet.

William turned to face Hemsby. "Sir, I fear this is not the place to examine the body. Have it removed to the Guildhall for the coroner's inspection."

"With due respect, sir, what interest is it to the Secretary of State of a poor waterman who more'n likely had his fill of ale, fell and struck his head and ended up face down in the Fleet? It wouldn't be the first time, and surely not the last. Who is he?"

"Is that how you see his death?"

Hemsby shrugged. "I only offer a possible explanation."

William sighed loudly and turned around and strode over to one of the guards taking the torch from him. He commanded Hemsby to hold the torch for him. The light made the shadows dance, making the dead man's pale countenance as grotesque as a church gargoyle. The Chancellor's man squatted down on his haunches over the body, ignoring the foul smell of putrid water, and moved his eyes back and forth over the torso. The neck ruffle was stained black with spilled blood. With great care, William pushed it to one side.

"Bring the light closer, alderman."

Hemsby moved in closer, pushing the torch in front of him.

"By God, sir! There!" William snapped, one hand grabbing Hemsby's cloak, the other pointing at the exposed flesh.

There were two puncture wounds around the area of the windpipe. There could be no doubt – it was murder.

"We have many such warnings sent to us, Mr Stoupe. His enemies, royalists, republicans and Anabaptist clamour against him. And it would be seen as weakness if we acted on every single claim. What signal would that send the world? That the great man was living in fear of his life?"

John Thurloe sat back in his chair, his fingers pressed together to form a temple under his cleft chin. His large eyes were fixed upon the minister of the French Protestant Church in London opposite, whose large bulk was barely contained by the seat provided.

"But Mr Thurloe," Stoupe's high-pitched voice filled the

room. "I have a name from a reliable source. The disclosure would be of the greatest import for His Highness, and yourself."

Thurloe fixed him with a piercing stare. It was unlike him to not think charitably of another person but there was something about the Frenchman that got under his skin. It might have had something to do with the fact that the minister had initially approached Cromwell directly by way of a note. Cromwell being in Council at the time, and thinking that it was a matter of intelligence, had deferred the minister to his Secretary of State. Now the two men sat opposite each other, both resolute in their demeanour to one another.

'Sir, I have acted on similar information relating to attempts on the Protector's life and they were of no consequence. Why should yours be different?"

"I trust my information without reservation."

"Indeed."

"Quite so."

Thurloe leaned forward, his right thumb and forefinger stroking his moustache. His head was thumping with an ache that had troubled him all week. He was finding it increasingly harder to concentrate in the meeting. He was fatigued and his mind had been distracted with family these past couple of weeks. His youngest was dangerously ill, and lay in his sick bed. Physicians had come and gone but to no avail. Thurloe had prayed every day that his son be spared.

"Mr Thurloe, I can provide a name of the chief instigator and where he may be located." Like it or not, the French minister was insistent that an attempt on the Protector's life was at hand.

Thurloe made an open-handed gesture for Stoupe to continue.

"He is a Leveller by the name of Miles Syndercombe, an Irishman who was once a soldier in your New Model Army. In 1649 he mutinied with his regiment but fled when it failed. Six years later he arrived in Scotland and became a member of a cavalry unit and attempted to take control of the army. Alas, this also failed and he fled to Flanders."

"Your friends are well informed, sir," admitted Thurloe.

Stoupe gave a little bow of his head. "Thank you, sir. The message was conveyed to me by well-meaning friends, and I am bound to secrecy of their identity."

Stoupe continued, "Evidence of Syndercombe's activity in

Flanders is documented and it is known that he is in the pay of Colonel Edward Sexby, another of your Levellers hiding abroad, who has supplied both arms and money. I know that the Lord Protector would not wish to see an injustice performed on his person or England. You may rest assured that I have not acted in haste, and came to you at the earliest convenience."

Thurloe suppressed his indignation that the French were giving the impression that their intelligence department was superior to his own office. The agitators known as The Levellers rose to prominence during the Civil War within the ranks of the New Model Army. Their aim was to bring about a less class-driven regime, believing – and here Thurloe could quote Richard Overton, one of their most vocal supporters – "*by natural birth all men are equally and alike borne to like propriety, liberty and freedom*," and that there should be complete religious freedom.

Thurloe said, "Sir, we have not been troubled by the Levellers since its break-up in '49 when the leaders, Thompson, Perkins and Church, were hung after the attempted mutiny at Wellingborough. It is a well-known fact that all Leveller support in the New Model Army was crushed. Pray tell me, what harm can this man do?"

"Syndercombe is back in England. He has rented a house upon King Street. Spain supports Sexby, who in turn, provides monies and arms to those like Syndercombe. There is a plan to restore the Puritan republic as believed by the Levellers. Thus he plots to remove Oliver Cromwell as the head of the republic by violence if necessary."

Thurloe looked at the Frenchman's gaunt face and said nothing.

Stoupe rose to his feet and gathered his hat and cane.

He said, "I fear that you do not take this of import, sir. I come to tell you that an attack on the Lord Protector's life is imminent, plus the name of one of the would-be perpetrators, and yet you sit there and say nothing. You insult me, sir!"

"Hold fast, Mr Stoupe," Thurloe cried out. "Be seated and rest. I shall send for a steward to take a statement from you. Perhaps some wine or ale?"

"In God's name, do not trouble yourself, for I have nothing left to say."

"You are in error, sir. Before you depart I pray that you write a report and send it to Brussels."

The minister was stunned into silence. Had he misjudged Thurloe all along? Was he privy to the information from his spies abroad? Stoupe hesitated for a moment before turning on his heels and leaving the room. Thurloe lay back in his chair and closed his eyes. The small battle of wills was over and the victory was his. Had Stoupe continued to press him on Syndercombe, Cromwell's head of intelligence might well have told him that he already knew of the agitator's presence in London. His address on King Street was a touch of irony that didn't escape his attention.

Neither Thurloe or Cromwell were under any illusion that the Levellers had been quashed. Spies and informers in the exiled king's circle in Spain knew that there were negotiations between the two parties, who swore to see Cromwell destroyed. The Lord Protector and his Secretary of State had gathered about them one hundred and sixty brave men who should always be on duty near his person on a rota – his Life-Guards. They knew that the plotters would take every advantage to murder Cromwell. His death would signal the rise of the Levellers and royalists, and an expedition of hostiles would set sail from Flanders.

The coroner was a wizened small man, bereft of hair and bulbous nosed. His breath reeked of stale ale. As he straightened up from the table his bones cracked in protest. "Poor man, God rest his soul."

"Amen," replied William Titcomb.

"You seem at ease at the presence of death, sir."

"Aye. I've seen it on the battlefield. It is an image that, once seen, cannot be erased from the mind's eye."

Though it had been more than six years since he had seen a dead man William felt a coldness all over his body as he stood close to the deceased. He watched the coroner as he went about his task of examining the body.

The coroner nodded sagely. During the war he had been pressed into service into the Parliamentary army.

"Strange that our paths have not crossed at some other time, Mr Titcomb."

"Quite so, Mr Newman."

The coroner began to strip the body naked, discarding the clothes to one side and initiated his investigation. There was a cool efficiency about him that made Titcomb feel he had performed such a task on many an occasion. Newman spoke to Titcomb on every step of the procedure. Titcomb moved across to the pile of clothes, lifting each item and examining them, then searched through the pockets.

"He was dead before he entered the water," Coroner Newman said. "Any one of those knife wounds to the heart would have been enough to kill the man."

The body was now fully naked on the table, and in the light of the morgue William saw that there were around half a dozen wounds around the heart, two more near the neck and one to the belly.

"Whoever did this was no assassin."

The coroner looked up. "What a curious thing to say. Why would he be assassinated? Do you know the man?"

William nodded. "He was a groom in the stables at Glass House Yard. He and my brother were friends as their parents came from the same village in Wiltshire."

"I can confirm that the man was indeed murdered, but you mentioned assassination – why?"

William felt a sudden chill. He had said too much. "Sorry, I didn't mean that. I am confused with another investigation. He and the other victim lived in the same area. An assassin would strike quickly and cleanly. Why stab a man so many times?"

The coroner overlooked the point. What concern was it of his that this representative of the Secretary of State was lying? He was sure of that. All he needed now was a name to sign off the certificate and he was done. But the question piqued his professional curiosity. He stood by the body and raised a hand, closing his fingers around an invisible knife and brought it down nine times, mimicking how the perpetrator might have carried out the deed.

"In my opinion the attack was carried out in a state of frenzy," the coroner explained. "The position of the wounds suggests that perhaps the first blow was to the belly, followed by two to the neck area. He probably fell onto his back when the other injuries were inflicted upon him."

William removed the man's valuables from his pockets, placing them with a reverence upon a small table. He looked at the paltry possessions: a comb, a handkerchief, one large brass key and four pennies. He shook his head sadly. Then his fingers brushed against a cold item. He used his fingertips to trace around the jagged edges, feeling the raised areas in the centre. He palmed the coin-sized object and slipped it into his vest pocket.

"And the blow to the head?" William asked.

"Oh, post mortem. Suffered when he fell into the water."

"Or pushed?"

"Or pushed indeed, sir."

"Sir, I need your verdict."

"Murder, sir. Murder."

In the morning William Titcomb brought John Thurloe the bad news. He arrived at the Secretary's office shortly after nine, having had one of the most restless night's sleep in a long while. His master appeared to have not fared well either. His shoulder length hair was matted against his forehead, his face ashen and his eyes swollen.

"Are you unwell, sir?" William enquired.

"A sickness that will pass, Mr Titcomb. Pray sit down and tell me the news." He waved at the empty chair opposite his desk.

"I'm afraid it is as we feared, sir. Mr Slade is murdered."

Thurloe seemed to shrink back in on himself and let out a small moan. "We shall pray for his soul, William."

Both men lowered their heads and gave up a prayer in silence.

"Do we know the murderer?" Thurloe asked after a suitable moment of reverence had passed.

"No, sir. But he had this upon his person." William brought out the object he discovered on Slade and placed it upon Thurloe's desk.

Thurloe looked over the item before picking it up. "Do you know what this is, William?"

"A wax seal."

"Not just any seal, my boy. This is the seal of the King of Spain."

"Why would Slade be carrying a Spanish royal seal?"

"He reported that he had intercepted a letter from an Englishman named John Fish to the Spanish Ambassador in Brussels. Fish requested a hundred pounds and a cache of weapons to be smuggled into the City, and left at the wharfside by the Thames. It appears that the parchment did not survive the ordeal in the water but the seal did not perish."

"Slade was expecting this John Fish to be at the rendezvous?"

"Yes."

"Why did he go alone? Why weren't there soldiers despatched to help him?"

"Fish is just one man. There are many plotters."

"So Slade was to follow Fish to discover the agitator's headquarters?"

"No. Slade had actually infiltrated the Levellers. He knew Fish was planning something outrageous but he could not find out what. At any given time there may be thirty or forty people operating but not all the plotters are known to one another. That the King of Spain is openly financing any rebels who help Charles Stuart regain the throne and bring back the monarchy to rule England is a serious threat in itself. I believe Slade was discovered and murdered."

"By Fish?"

Thurloe shook his head. "That is just conjecture at the moment."

"Then we must get proof. Do you know the whereabouts of Fish at the moment?" William was already planning to gather some men and arrest the murderer.

"We know he is in London. I am as anxious as you to get my hands on the man. He is intelligent, make no mistake about that. How he discovered Slade's identity is beyond me. I admit that to you. But we must tread softly; this Fish is a clever and dangerous man."

Miles Syndercombe arranged to meet the others at the house in Hammersmith. It was here that he had planned to shoot Cromwell as he rode in his coach on the way to Hampton Court. An associate had provided him with seven guns which could carry a number of balls, but his designs were thwarted as a clear shot could not be taken for the multitude of spectators. Under the name of Fish, he continued to rent the property. The expense meant nothing; he wasn't paying for it.

John Cecil stood to one side of the upstairs window and looked down upon the street. His eyes searched for any familiar faces or inappropriate activity. He was an overweight man given to sweating profusely, always dabbing at his forehead with a handkerchief. John Toop was the third man in the room and was very edgy. He had already upset a flagon of ale.

"I have to admit to being very nervous," he said. "I don't know if I can go through with this."

"I don't regard myself as a violent man," Syndercombe said, easing his bulk away from the wall. "But you have already received twenty pounds on account."

Toop picked up the broken pieces and carefully placed them on the table. He was a tall, stone-faced man, whose clothes hung loosely about him. He said to Syndercombe, "Whatever you have paid me, I have returned with good information. There is no need for threats, sir."

"If I make a threat, sir, then I intend to carry it out to the full. I merely am pointing out the obvious."

"What is it you want, this time?" Toop asked, admitting defeat.

"If you were offered a troop of horses, how would that sound?" John Cecil said.

Toop turned around. "A troop, sir?"

"Yes," Syndercombe said. "Plus an annual sum of one thousand and fifty pounds. How does that sound?"

He felt that they were playing him like a fish on a hook. The thought of such a high position, plus the money was too great a temptation.

Toop turned back to Cecil and asked, "You can provide that?"

The fat man nodded his head.

"What support is there in the Life-Guards for the Levellers?" Syndercombe pressed.

As a trooper in Cromwell's Life-Guards, Toop was in a position to report on the Protector's movements. Syndercombe had approached him after he overheard his anti-Cromwell rhetoric during a drunken session. It was a simple business deal: in return for twenty pounds, Toop was expected to provide information on Cromwell's future activities. Now they provided a lucrative inducement.

"I would hazard a guess that at least three-quarters are in support of the Levellers."

Syndercombe smiled. "And they would support us, and the Army, if the Protector were to be killed?"

Toop felt a cold, unyielding pressure across his chest. He was not prepared for such a bold statement. And he understood the full implication of the deal. Could he come to terms with the fact that he was a traitor?

"Yes," he said softly.

Syndercombe crossed the room and placed both hands on Toop's shoulders. "It is far better that we are in league with Spain than with France," he said. "But there cannot be peace with Spain until this tyrant is removed. I have prayed to God on this, and he has answered that this is the true and rightful path to take. He is the common enemy of the liberties of this country and the rights of Spain. Once the Protector is dead, the way would be cleared for a new Utopia. You are doing this country a great service, sir."

"A great service indeed Mr Toop," Cecil added, slapping the man lightly on the back. "Now back to the barracks before your presence is missed. You will be contacted in the very near future, sir. God speed."

Toop did not hesitate and left the building without looking back over his shoulder.

Syndercombe sighed heavily.

"Do you think that he can be trusted, Miles?"

"Toop? As far as I can throw him! But he is well connected in the Life-Guard, and the guardsmen trust him. Did you see his greedy little eyes light up at the thought of all that money? As long as we can grease his palms, he will do what we expect of him. But we have a problem. Edward's last remittance of eight hundred pounds has been seized by that damned Thurloe. He is determined to cross over to England and make arrangements, then return to the continent."

"No, sir. He must not come over. It is far too dangerous."

"My thoughts exactly. I sent word to him but I fear that has been foiled."

"How so, Miles?"

Syndercombe began to pace the room. "Not two nights ago," he said. "One of our patriots was found murdered at a designated meeting place."

"Murdered, sir? By whom?"

"I surmise that it was one of Thurloe's dogs."

"Surely not! Even they would not stoop so low as to kill a man without trial. If he were suspected, then they would have arrested him and extract information from him."

"Mayhaps, John. But what a strange coincidence that Joseph Slade had provided us with the fleetest of horses to assist our escape."

Syndercombe stopped his pacing and went across to the window, where he looked down at the road. "We must act again. I have a feeling in my bones that time is running short. No more guns, this time. I plan to burn down the Palace of Whitehall with the despot inside!"

Three days later Thurloe gave instructions to arrest the plotters. It was Toop's change of heart that made it possible. He approached the Chancellor and revealed Syndercombe's plan that he, John Cecil and Syndercombe were to place an explosive device in the palace chapel, and the intention was for a fire to break out about midnight, and in the confusion, the Protector was to be killed. They were captured as they locked the chapel door. Toop had to be there. It all depended on that. The three of them a party to the act. Cecil, the facilitator; Syndercombe the instigator who burned with an intense hatred of Cromwell. And Toop as an associate. He had to make sure that they could get into the Palace chapel, plant the explosive in a basket, then set the candle burning on a timed fuse. Cecil confessed all he knew but Syndercombe remained silent. Toop escaped with his life by turning informer. Thurloe was happy with the outcome.

William Titcomb walked up and around the Fleet area every day and night after the arrests. There was something that didn't sit right in his mind about Slade's death but he couldn't put his finger on it. He called in on warehouses, shops and inns, asking questions about the brave fellow found murdered at Davy's Wharf. At first he found that many people feigned ignorance, whilst others had no interest. Titcomb visited the stables at Glass House Yard and questioned the ostler. He repeated that Slade was an honest man, a hard worker, reliable and of good character. He didn't know of anyone who would harm him. *Yes, but someone did,* Titcomb said to himself.

When he returned home later that evening, it was late, as it was every time for the last month, his wife was sitting up waiting for him.

"Sarah, you shouldn't be up," he said.

"I need to speak to you. The children are asleep. I had to wait for you."

"Why? What's the matter?"

"I was going to ask you that."

"Sarah, that man's death . . ."

"Yes, I know a man died, William. I know that you have worked diligently to find the killer, and how important it is to you. You're out every day and night scouring God knows where. But you're never here for me or the children of late."

"How can you say that, Sarah?"

"Are you looking for the killer?"

"Yes."

"Are you?"

"Of course. What else would it be?"

"I was going to ask you that."

"Sarah?"

"Is there someone else? Are you seeing someone else?"

William's mouth dropped open.

"Is there another woman, William?"

He shook his head. "No. You should have to ask me that?"

"What else am I to think? You have been acting quite strangely about me. It seems that you don't want to touch me any more."

"No, Sarah, you're wrong. Absolutely wrong."

She stood up. "Are you sure?" she asked.

He nodded. "There is no other woman."

"Are you bored with your life with us, William. Is that it?"

"For God's sake, Sarah! No. No. No!"

She looked at him and then turned away. Without looking back she said, "If you are, I'd–I'd kill you."

"My God, Sarah!"

She turned around, tears streaming down her face. "It's true, William. I swear by Almighty God, that I'd take your life rather than have you commit adultery and bring shame on me."

She didn't push him away when he came over to hold her in his arms. He wasn't angry with her and when he pulled away and looked into her face, he was smiling.

"My dear, sweet Sarah," he said and kissed her.

It took him two days to find the house in Smithfield. Twice he had to retrace his steps. He had visited some of the most squalid places he had ever seen, almost certainly risking his life, but at last his cautious questions delivered a name and a place.

A gust of wind came up carrying flakes of snow and the stench of the river. He turned away to wipe his eyes and saw it then. It was a decaying building, dirt besmearing its walls, windows broken and patched over, debris piled knee-high around the doorway. It was the most loathsome place he had ever seen. William was told it was a haunt and hiding place for all sorts of burglars, footpads, fences and other villains. He was certain that no ordinary citizen would step across the threshold.

Inside the squalor continued. Rats ran merrily across the bare wooden floors. The room was small and smoke filled. About eight men and women sat around on chairs or on the floor itself, all in various stages of drunkenness. William counted up to three to himself and entered. He made to walk further into the room when a muscular man stood in front of him barring his way.

"Whad'ya want 'ere?" he leered into Titcomb's face.

Titcomb stood his ground, one hand slipping inside his cloak pocket and resting upon the hilt of a pistol, cocking back the hammer. The muscle man heard it clearly and stepped back out of his way.

"There's a girl here named Mary," William said.

"Lots of girls 'ere, an' you can call 'er anyfing you want!"

Titcomb checked in his rage. "She's around seventeen . . ."

"Likes 'em young, does ya?" Someone said behind him.

He ignored the comment and said, "Listen, I want to speak to Mary Lewington. Just tell me if she's here or not."

From the shadows at the end of the room a voice asked, "What's it to you?"

"Step into the light. Let me see with whom I speak."

An overweight woman shuffled into view. Her arms hung down at her side, hairy like a man's. The sight startled Titcomb but he soon gathered himself together. He said, "Is she here?"

"What's she to you?" the woman asked.

Beyond her, others moved in the shadow.

Titcomb knew he was playing a dangerous game. He withdrew the pistol and held it out. One pistol and one ball. What good was that against so many surrounding him?

Something passed over his face. Just for a fleeting moment but the woman saw it. She said, "Upstairs. First on the left. Don't hurt her, mister."

"I have no intention to do that, mistress."

The door to her room stood at a crazy angle. William knocked, then pushed it open. Mary was kneeling on the floor, hands clasped in prayer. The fireplace was empty and the room was freezing. The wind whistled through the broken window with a keen wildness. She wore a plain shawl across her shoulders, her hair was tucked beneath a cap, but despite the cold her face was soaked with sweat. She looked around when William entered. There were dark circles under her eyes, as though she hadn't slept for some time.

"Come to arrest me, then?" Her voice was just above a whisper. "Took your time, eh?"

William put away the pistol, carefully lowering the hammer. He walked into the room and stood in front of her. "No," he said.

She began to weep. She put her arms around her and began to rock back and forth. "My baby," she said. "My baby, my baby."

He let her cry herself out and compose herself. She rose to her feet and slumped in the chair and talked.

"They said I was a loose woman. His father and the vicar both said that I'd got pregnant to force Joseph to marry me. They even said that the bastard belonged to another man. But it's not true. I loved him and he said he loved me. He wanted to marry me but his father would have none of it. They forced Joseph not to see me anymore."

William did not find it strange at all that Mary spoke perfectly easily to him. Yet he was in the absurd position that Slade's murder had been attributed to Syndercombe. But the man was dead. He had been imprisoned in the Tower but had taken his own life rather than face being hung, drawn and quartered. John Thurloe was content that the murderer had been caught. But William couldn't let it rest there.

"They even told my employer that I carried a bastard child and they dismissed me. What had I now? An unmarried mother, no job, and no home. What employment could I gain with a character reference?"

"Couldn't you have gone to your parents?" William asked.

"And bring shame on them? No."

"And Joseph wouldn't marry you against his father's wishes?"

"He was married three months before our baby was born," she said, simply.

He knew from her face that she was troubled by this. Her life was ruined. William looked about him.

"The baby, Mary. Where is the baby?"

There was no sign of the child. In fact, no sign at all that a child's presence. No cot, no clothes, the room was devoid of anything to do with a baby.

She saw William staring at her. She raised her arm and pointed to the window.

"Oh, God. No, Mary."

"That's what he said. He found me. Told me he'd been looking for me. Said that his marriage was a farce and that he wanted to be with me and the baby. He said he'd come into some good fortune and had money. That he wanted us to be a family. I told him that there was no family. He didn't understand. I told him about the baby."

She hadn't meant to kill him. He'd rushed at her, putting his hand roughly about her. He was crushing her, screaming what had she done with his child. He was hurting her. She hated him. He made her kill their baby. With every thrust of the knife she took her anger out on him.

In this room she had taken the life of both father and son.

On cold winter nights when the wind blew fiercely, it would come back to him. Sometimes just snatched images of the room, or the smell or sound. Other times he remembered everything clearly. When it was quite like this, William Titcomb lay next to his wife, feeling the warmth of her body against his and remembered Mary Lewington.

THE PALATABLE TRUTH

CAROL ANNE DAVIS

After all of the dark and murderous stories we have had it seems timely for a little light relief. Anything I say about the following story is likely to give the game away so I shall say nothing other than that it was in 1657, during Cromwell's Commonwealth, that a Frenchman opened the first ever shop in London for a certain commodity.

Carol Anne Davis (b. 1961) has been dubbed the "Queen of Noir" by Booklist. *Her books deal with the dark and violent underbelly of crime, both in fact and fiction. Her first book,* Shrouded *(1997), was about a necrophiliac, whilst one of her more recent true-crime books is* Children Who Kill *(2004). No wonder she also needs some light relief.*

Everyone was pragmatical of thought when Lady Hardwick of Mellankoly House collapsed and had to be carried insensible to her bed-chamber. Bella the cook thought that partaking of too much olive pie had made Madam slack of digestion, whilst several of the serving girls were convinced that staring at the clowds for halfe an hower that very afternoon was to blame. A hastily summoned physician declared that it was merely a case of the windy vapours, but when Lady Hardwick died that very evening, he decided that the guilt lay with a particularly outrageous spell instead.

Mr Jeffreys the silversmith was given the news when he arrived at the house to give the good lady her latest coffee pot. He had spent the previous days fashioning a particularly neat one embossed with the Hardwick motto which matched the silver chocolate pot she'd recently purchased from him.

"I shall not intrude on your grief, ladies," the silversmith said to Lady Hardwick's three ugly sisters – who had come all the way from Scotland to attend her burial – though, truth to tell, they did not strike him as particularly grief-stricken or particularly ladylike.

"Give us the merchandise," the largest one said crossly and Mr Jeffreys handed over the coffee pot and was duly paid.

Just then the head nurseryman rushed in looking exceeding perplexed: "Someone has had an excess of my fig trees and sat on my lovage," he said crossly.

"Noisome boys to blame, no doubt," the oldest Hardwick murmured, though all present would later swear that she brushed some lovage flowers from her dress and removed a fig seed from between her teeth.

A stranger to the ways of plants and fruits, Mr Jeffreys returned to his workshop and made another kettle, as – the wealthy Lady Hardwick excepting – there still wasn't much call for chocolate pots. After all, chocolate cost thirty shillings per pound, three times the cost of the silver chocolate pot in which it was served. No, the middling classes had to make do with a Turkish coffa dish or a plate of Chinese Tcha, whilst the poor had to be content with their vivid imaginations or a glass of Adam's wine.

He was hard at work on a pewter chamber pot – as there was a recession looming – for a local merchant when he was next summoned to Mellankoly House. "I've moved in here now and would like a grater for the chocolate as cook grinds it exceeding rough," the youngest Hardwick sister said.

Jefferson looked longingly at the chunk of chocolate on the table. "I shall fashion one tonight."

Just then, Cook busied in with sallets, fricase, boyled meats and gilded salmon. The mammoth sister fell on the feast as if twere a wonderous novelty. "You can oh," she said to Jefferson through a mouth filled with fish and fowl. Assuming that he had been dismissed, he made for the door.

"Wha fu afters?" he heard her bark at one of the serving staff. To the silversmith's surprise, she seemed able to interpret the woman's mumblings. Leastways she replied "Quinces, ma'am, and comfits and wafer cakes, roasted pears and wine."

"No florentines?" shouted the lady and Jefferson winced as the slap she gave to the hapless girl resounded throughout the hall.

No one was surprised when Madam was stricken with a dead palsie later that very evening, though – palsies fast going out of fashion – the physician gave the official cause of her demise as being strangled with apoplexies.

By now, the neighbours were taking more than their fair share of interest in Mellankoly House, and one of the braver – and one must assume more educated – of the local wags put a sign saying Inveterate Moral Contagion on the door.

But the local apothecary remained unconvinced that there was any such pox in the air, and encouraged the third sister to move in and stake her claim to the mansion. He told her to avoid Colchester oysters and to purchase a large bottle of surfeit water, something he conveniently happened to have about his person and that was for sale. Cook was equally reassuring and suggested that the lady avoid milk vapours if she wanted to forgo polyps of the heart.

Everyone offered the best advice, and everyone was extraordinarily wrong for within the hour the new homeowner was taken by a rebellious distemper. Never a woman who could refuse a lobster or a chine of beef, some say she swelled overnight to twice her original size.

Even before the funeral could be arranged, the remaining sister had moved in and whipped the chambermaid, flogged the stables lad and slapped the butler. And some said that the very dogs and cats in the neighbourhood ran and hid when she flexed her mighty arms.

The following morning, the mighty-armed one took a nostril's worth of Angelick snuff, guaranteed to ward off the plague (or so said the sellers) but it had the opposite effect and she was soon on her way to meet the angelick hordes.

By now the townsfolk had decided that the very building had a hex on it and they swore that they would raze it to the ground – but first common sense commanded that they spirit away its many treasures. And so every impoverished man, woman, child, dog and cat in the location set off in the direction of Mellankoly House.

Somewhat to their surprise, Jeffreys the silversmith headed the race – and some say he achieved the four minute mile though this was clearly an impossibility. Despite his spindly legs, he rushed ahead and was seen to claim his silver chocolate pot, molinquets and assorted paraphernalia, though only an inquisitive dog saw him bury them in the Mellankoly garden, digging deeper than a young mole with a price on its head can go.

Re-entering the dining room, Mr Jeffreys watched as the blacksmith took the best table and chairs whilst the toymaker helped himself to the kettles and porringers. Meanwhile a flower-seller made off with one of his best-wrought low-looped silver teapots, the one with the handle set at a right angle to the spout. Someone even stole the sack of tea, rumoured by travelling medicine men to be a chimical quintessence, though not one which prevented them dying in droves.

The hungry fell upon the hams and capons whilst the thirsty partook of the sack and elsterrune, each drink strangely making them thirstier still.

For himself, Mr Jeffreys only wanted one thing – several large chunks of the purest chocolate. He stowed the confection in his bag, his pockets and even under his best feathery hat. Back home, he grated some of the sweet perfection and had soon made himself a pot of that most marvellous concoction. He quaffed down the brown nectar then helped himself to a second cup and a third. By now he was happier than he had been on his wedding night, for, in truth, the late Mrs Jeffreys had been fonder of eating cake than of conjugal bliss.

The chocolate was everything he'd remembered and more, from the time when he'd brought Lady Hardwick her first ever chocolate pot. She'd tried it out in his presence and a thin stream had dripped from the moulinet onto the cloth. Without thinking, he'd scooped it up with his finger and licked it off and the caramel-coloured bittersweetness had flowed around his mouth and down his throat, waking his senses like no other essence. "If I might have a cup, madam?" he'd ventured shyly, and she'd flicked at his hand as if it was a pestilence.

"It's not for the likes of you," she'd said, mindless of the fact that he'd made her the best silverware in the whole of Christendom, that he was the hardest working man in the neighbourhood.

Mr Jeffreys had gone sadly back to his widower's accommodation and had brooded on the injustice – on a lifetime of injustice. He gave and gave and gave others took and took. He'd given his life to his craft, and as a result his eyesight was failing and his hands were rheumy. He'd eventually have to give up work and might end up in that most discreditable of endings, a pauper's grave.

The quiet silversmith had thought bitterly of his end but had thought longer and harder about the wondrous new drink of chocolate. And by the time he went to his lonely bed that night, he knew what he must do. After all, if he – a hard working craftsman who never overcharged for his wares – was never to enjoy the exquisite sweetness on his tongue again, why should the lazy rich?

He'd waited until Lady Hardwick gave him her next order for a chocolate set then had coated the inner surface of the pot and every one of the matching silver cups with powdered white mercury. For good measure, he had added some to the sugar bowl when the cook's back was turned. And after the Lady's premature death, when one of her sisters had asked for a grinding machine, he'd coated it with the same deadly poison, dipping the molinquets into an equally lethal dose.

Revenge was literally sweet and Mr Jeffreys was proud that he'd rid society of four cruel harridans and created an end which had never been known before – Death By Chocolate.

THE COMEDY THAT BECAME A TRAGEDY

F. FRANKFORT MOORE

The following is the only reprint story in this anthology and is set just after the Restoration of the monarchy in 1660. And if Charles II is now king, can Nell Gwyn be far behind?

The story first appeared in a series called "Nell Gwyn, Comedian" which ran in Pearson's Magazine *in 1899 and was later collected as* Nell Gwyn *(1900). The author, Francis Frankfort Moore (1855–1931), was a noted Irish journalist who had been writing for many years and who eventually met with success with* The Jessamy Bride *(1897), a historical romance involving the Georgian theatre and society. His series about Nell Gwyn was an attempt to repeat that success and in the process he produced the following pioneer historical murder mystery.*

"My good creature," said Mr Killigrew, the Master of the Revels and the Manager of the King's Playhouse, Drury Lane, "my good creature, 'twere vain to deny the truth of all that you have said so eloquently with your voice and so entrancingly with your eyes – on the subject of William Shakespeare. I have always held that he was a dramatist of the highest rank. His Grace the Duke of Buckingham goes still further, and avers that Shakespeare was the Buckingham of his day."

"His Grace's flattery is overwhelming," said Mrs Hughes, with only the least little curl of her lip.

"Ay; but 'tis in your mind, my good woman, that 'tis the Duke of Buckingham whom he flatters, not William Shakespeare," said Killigrew, who had noted with his customary care the little expression of disdain on the very pretty face before him.

"Nay, Mr Killigrew, I will not deny that I hold William Shakespeare to have been the greatest man that ever lived, while I know that the Duke of Buckingham is – is – the most impudent – there, I have said it, Mr Killigrew," cried the actress.

"Nay, now 'tis you who are flattering overmuch to His Grace," said Killigrew. "In these evil days in which it is our good fortune to live, Mrs Hughes, the impudent fellows are held in the highest esteem. Even I myself, though the manager of the King's Playhouse, have but an indifferent reputation for impudence. Did not I once try to kiss you, Mrs Hughes?"

"I have a short memory in such matters, sir," said the actress with a flush and a laugh.

Just at this point in the conversation the half-open door of the green room was pushed to the wall and there danced in a gorgeously dressed and very beautiful young woman. She was Nell Gwyn.

"What is the subject of your pointless discourse, good people? I have come to find a new dress for our masque at Hampton Court, but I can wait."

"The beautiful Mrs Hughes hath been asking an impossibility," said Killigrew.

"What, hath she been looking for Tom Killigrew to tell her the truth?" cried Nell.

"Nay, Nelly, I have but asked him to let 'Othello' be played, so as to give me a chance of appearing as Desdemona – the part hath never yet been played by a woman, and 'tis plain to me that it could never be faithfully played by one of the boys," said Mrs Hughes eagerly.

"And I say that while the playgoers might stand the strangling of one of the boys –"

"By the lud, Tom, they will stand such a strain upon their tenderness without flinching," cried Nell, interrupting the manager. "I'll swear that I could e'en strangle some of them myself, they play the women's parts so vilely."

"That is my contention," said Killigrew. "The playgoers will tolerate the deadly slaughter of a boy in a night smock, and still smile; but they will speedily hustle off the stage any black negro man who would go about the murder of a young woman who is a young woman, and a very lovely young woman into the bargain."

"And what is this play you are talking about?" asked Nell. "'Tis sure not 'The Indian Prince'?"

"Nay, the play is 'Othello!'" said Mrs Hughes.

"An early work of Mr Dryden's," suggested Nell.

"Good lud, no; 'tis by William Shakespeare," said Mrs Hughes.

"Oh, the grand-uncle of Tom Betterton of the Duke's House?" said Nell.

"The same," replied Mrs Hughes.

"Ah, that accounts for my knowing naught about it," said Nell. "I have often heard of William Shakespeare, but, 'snails, sir, however much one may like Tom Betterton, one cannot be expected to spell through a doleful tragedy simply because it was writ by his grand-uncle. Nay, the heartiest friendship hath its limits."

"William Shakespeare hath some claim to be read, quite apart from his relationship to Mr Betterton," said Mrs Hughes. "And as for his tragedy of 'Othello' – well, I do not believe that Mr Dryden at his best hath ever writ anything more elevating."

"Elevating!" shrieked Nell. "Oh, lud! the notion of me reading aught that is elevating! Look ye, Caroline Hughes, for a play to be elevating is a step beyond a play being dull. Now, Mr Dryden is often dull, but his worst enemies could never accuse him of being elevating. But come, Mr Killigrew, tell us what this play in dispute is about, and I will decide if Mrs Hughes should be permitted to have her own way in regard to it."

"You are an unprejudiced judge, Nell; you will not give a decree in favour of Shakespeare simply because you are a friend of his grandnephew," said Killigrew. "Well, my dear, this play of 'Othello' treats of the love of a Moor for a beautiful lady named Desdemona. He gets her to run away with him, in order that he may have a chance of making a speech in the Court where he is summoned by the lady's father. The poet artfully refrains – doth he not, Mrs Hughes? – from explaining why the father objects to the match, seeing that he had always treated Othello as an equal, and thrown the lovely Desdemona in his way. Well, then, there comes a naughty fellow –"

"Ah! now the play interests me," said Nell. "The naughty fellow always interests me – ay, and everyone else."

"His name is – what is his name? – oh, never mind; he, out of pure love of fun, makes Othello jealous of his wife, and he cuts her throat – no, he smothers her with a down pillow; and when someone rushes in to tell him he did wrong, he runs the villain through the vitals, makes a speech – he never loses an opportunity of making a speech – and then, to save his hearers from dying of the vapours, he stabs himself to the heart. Isn't that the play, Mrs Hughes?"

"But what is the object of it all?" cried Nell.

"Oh, the object is plain enough," said Killigrew. "'Tis to show, first, that one should never become on terms of familiarity with black men; and, secondly, that officers in the army should never become jealous of their wives – they're not worth it."

"And what have you to say to all this, Mrs Hughes?" asked Nell.

"What have I to say?" cried Mrs Hughes. "Ah, Nelly, what can I say if you have not read the play? For me to lift up my voice to plead for Shakespeare would be to degrade him. Put all the wit of all the moderns into one play and that play will contain less wit than the least of his comedies. Put all the tragical passion of all the moderns into one play and that play will be feeble by the side of a scene in 'Othello.'"

"Oh, lud! and pray what else doth it contain?" said Nell. "Is there aught that would sting the Duchess of Cleveland – her that was the Countess of Castlemaine?"

"I have not yet read it with Her Grace before mine eyes, but I dare swear that it abounds in lines which should sting her to the very quick," said the actress.

"If you promise me that there is something in some scene that will sting her, I'll plead with Mr Killigrew on your behalf," said Nell. "But, mark you, her skin is thick: the sting must be sharp and heavy to touch her. An elephant is not even tickled by the sting of a gnat. None of your rapier-thrusts will pierce her skin. Anything short of a battle-axe of satire would produce no impression on her."

"Let me think – let me think," said Mrs Hughes. "I fancy there is some aptness – by the lud, I have it. Did not His Majesty break out in a passion when he accused her of a too great fondness for Harry Jermyn?"

"Well, and if he did?" said Nell.

"Ah, so doth Othello when he accuses Desdemona of a too great fondness for Cassio, who was also an officer in the army – he smothers her on that account. Oh, every scene will stab that creature to the heart," cried the actress enthusiastically.

"Her heart – heart, did you say?" shrieked Nell. "Doth the play say aught about a woman living without a heart?"

"I promise you that it doth, though I cannot recall the exact lines," said Mrs Hughes. "Ah, I promise you that we shall make mincemeat of her; and the King, who is afraid to say to her face what he thinks of her, will hold us in high favour."

"Psha!" cried Killigrew. "You have not convinced me that the playgoers will receive with high favour the strangling of a young woman by a burly black-a-moor – ay, or a brown-a-moor if that pleases you better. And so, Madam Ellen, you may set about the choice of your gown for the new masque at Hampton Court."

Mrs Hughes pouted very prettily, and Madam Ellen said some very hard words regarding his unkindness, and then Mrs Hughes left the green room.

But, for all that, two days afterwards, the actress burst in upon her husband as he sat cooking a fish for dinner, and cried:

"Huzza – huzza, my love; the day is ours – the world is at our feet!"

"Then we shall e'en wipe our feet upon the world and eat a fresh Southwark plaice," said her husband.

"Plaice! plaice me no plaice, sir, until you hear my news. What think you? Mr Killigrew hath resolved that 'Othello' shall be played a fortnight from to-day, and I shall be the first woman to be seen as Desdemona. What think'st thou of that news?"

The husband laid the cooked fish on the table and wiped his forehead with the back of his hand.

"Desdemona – 'Othello' – I can scarce believe the good news," said he. "Dear wife, think that whatever fate may have in store for us, after the tragedy is played we shall have gained immortality – you as the first woman who played the part of Desdemona and I as your husband."

He stretched out his arms to her and she was so excited that she was about to throw herself into these arms until at the last moment she remembered that she was wearing a comparatively new brocade – the gift of Nell Gwyn – which would most likely have to see Desdemona through three acts of the tragedy.

"Ah, you will have to moderate your transports, my James," she said. "Your hands have been dealing with the fish, they would work ruin on my brocade."

"That is the difference between a man and a woman," said he mournfully. "A man is dreaming of immortality while a woman's only dread is that her dress will be smirched. My beloved one, you shall be remembered through all ages as the first actress of Desdemona. People will talk of you hundreds of years hence when the greatness of Shakespeare is recognised as it deserves to be. Just now, alas! – But prithee, what has occurred to cause Killigrew to revoke his original decree regarding 'Othello'?"

"I cannot tell," his wife replied. "I was quite startled when he sent for me on my entering the playhouse, and announced that he had made up his mind to put on 'Othello.'"

"It must be the King's Command; or perhaps Killigrew hath read the play," suggested the man.

"Nay, that is too extravagant a notion," she cried. "What, the manager of a play-house read a play! Dear James, your imagination runs away with you sometimes! Nay, dear, I believe rather that we are in debt to Nell Gwyn for this favour."

"And she is only interested in the play because she fancies something in it may sting her enemy Lady Castlemaine – I beg Her Grace's pardon – the Duchess of Cleveland, I should have said. Alas! poor Will Shakespeare!"

"Good lud! he hath made us even forget our dinner," cried the actress. "And you have cooked the fish as only you can," she continued, looking at the plaice which was cooling on the table.

"Ah, my angel, what is one dinner to such as you who will be supping for evermore among the immortals?" cried her husband.

"What, indeed?" she cried, and then in the exuberance of the moment, she threw her arms around her husband's neck and kissed him heartily on both cheeks.

But all the same she did her best to avert for some time the joys of immortality by making an excellent dinner. Her husband had trained himself to become a capital cook, and thus he and his wife lived on the most affectionate terms. He not only relieved her of her responsibilities in this direction, he, in addition, taught her all she knew about her art, and had even brought her to appreciate in some measure the poetry of Shakespeare. He also went so far as to contribute to the household purse by giving lessons in fencing.

He had had a chequered career. Educated for the priesthood in the reign of Charles I, he had joined the King's army in its conflict with the Parliamentary forces, and had suffered in consequence during the Interregnum. Before Charles II had been many years on the throne, James Hughes married Caroline Swift, and they had starved together very happily until the lady was permitted to join His Majesty's Servants at the King's Playhouse, where she quickly made a name for herself.

On this account, as well as by reason of her continued affection for her husband, she was by no means a favourite with the other members of the company, of whom the men were no better than they should have been, while the majority of the women were certainly a good deal worse.

Mrs Hughes had always shunned, so far as she was able to do so, Burt, the leading actor of Killigrew's company. She had detested him from the first hour she had seen him. He was a vulgar and uneducated man who aped all the airs and graces and vices of a person of quality. He boasted openly of his amours and had more than once been horse-whipped for making too free with a lady's name. He did his best to give circulation to the report that he had in his early years captivated Lady Castlemaine, and he now and again found people who believed that he had actually attained to that distinction.

It was probably with a view of putting the seal upon his reputation as a man of fashion that he had played an infamous part in regard to Henrietta Crisp, who occupied a subordinate place in the King's House. Her husband, Charley Crisp, was a man of good family who had ruined his prospects by marrying her while he was still at Oxford. The two hundred pounds a year, which his father allowed him, would have been sufficient to keep him while he was studying the science of medicine; but before he had been married more than a year he found that he had no time to study anything, save the best way to keep his wife.

She was as foolish as she was pretty, and no one about the theatre was surprised when one day, on her husband's return from a visit to the country, she came down to a rehearsal with Mr Burt.

Charley Crisp was heartbroken at his wife's treatment of him, but he was considerate enough to refrain from publishing his shame by means of a duel with her lover.

"She will return to me – she will return to me," he had often said to Caroline Hughes and her husband.

He spoke the truth. After the lapse of a year, during which it was said that Burt treated her with the greatest brutality, she returned to her husband – to die.

Her knowledge of this incident did not tend to make Mrs Hughes look on Burt with any greater favour than she had previously bestowed upon him. The fellow abated nothing of his odious swaggering, and when some of his boon companions rallied him in regard to her coldness of demeanour toward him, he had smiled significantly, saying:

"Ay, the pretty creature is the best actress in the company."

"Actress! but we were talking of the woman herself, not what she pretends to be," said one of his boon companions.

"Quite so. The woman pretends to be – well, what the woman herself is not," said Burt. "For a pretence of propriety Becky Marshall is clumsy compared to her, the sweet dissembler."

"You mean –"

"I mean, sir, that the man who captivated a Countess – nay, she is a Duchess now – is not likely to be rebuffed by Caroline Hughes."

And he really believed that her constant expression of dislike for him was only meant to draw him on. She had ignored him when they acted together in other plays, but it was impossible for her to maintain the same demeanour in rehearsing "Othello." She was compelled to be with him on the stage for some hours every day, arranging his "business" that led up to the various situations of matchless power. He had thus many opportunities of exercising his fascinations upon her, and it need scarcely be said that he availed himself of all.

At the end of a week his net gains could be easily computed: he had won a single smile from her – no more.

Still this he regarded as distinct evidence that she was repenting of her former scorn of him, and that she meant to encourage him.

On this day her husband, as usual, walked home with her from the playhouse. They had scarcely reached their lodgings when he said:

"My dear wife, I should like very much to hear if you have aught to tell me regarding the play."

"I have nothing to tell you," she replied. "You saw all the rehearsal of the scenes to-day, did not you?"

"I saw – something," said he. "Something that gave me a little shock of surprise."

"What was that?" she inquired.

"You have confided nothing to my ear, and therefore I cannot but think that mine eyes deceived me," he said.

"Tell me what you saw, or fancied you saw," she cried.

"I fancied that I saw that man, that scoundrel, Burt, press your hand and look into your face when the scene between you both was at an end."

There was a pause – an awkward pause – if it had been a few seconds longer it would have been a compromising pause, but she saved those few seconds – before she said:

"You were not deceived, my husband; the wretch had the impudence to hold my hand some time – some moments. That was impudent, but no more than impudent."

"Impudent! And why did you not confess to me that he had done so when I gave you the chance just now?"

"Well, the fact is, my dear, I knew that – 'twas no more than the fellow's impudence, and I did not wish you to be annoyed."

"Heavens above us! you would lead that rascal on to save me from being annoyed!"

"Lead him on – lead Stephen Burt on – I –? Oh, James, I am ashamed of you."

"I shall never give you cause to be ashamed of me, madam, and I would fain hope that you will be equally generous towards me."

He held up his head, and there was a certain subtle suggestion of coldness – of aloofness in that little movement of his. She felt it; and that was why she burst into a laugh – it really did not sound very forced – as she said with a pretty exaggeration of the already exaggerated Iago of Mr Mohun:

"Beware, my lord, of jealousy!"

Then she laughed again, and this time her laugh sounded very forced.

He remained solemn, and in an instant she became so also.

"My dear husband," she said quietly, "have I ever given you cause for uneasiness, even for a moment?"

"You have never acted Desdemona to Burt's Othello," he replied coldly.

"Gracious Heavens! you do not mean to suggest –"

"I mean to suggest nothing, madam. If the opportunity had not arisen, the fascination which that man seems to exercise over all women might have continued harmless so far as you are concerned."

"Fascination! the fellow is detestable to me, I tell you. Oh, I am amazed – hurt – humiliated."

"The amazement and humiliation are not on your side only, madam," said Mr Hughes.

She was tearful as she went into the bedroom to lay aside her cloak. He followed her with his eyes, and when she was gone, he continued looking at the door through which she had passed. Then he gave a long sigh.

" 'Tis a trial – a great trial for her, and much more so for me," he murmured. "But I must be cruel only to be kind; I must force her to put herself in the situation of Desdemona – she must feel what 'tis to be innocent and yet accused – to be the unhappy wife of a jealous husband. Oh, she must carry away the town by her acting of the character. Think of it! think of it! The first true representative of the greatest play ever writ by the hand of man! If she should fall short of what is needed for the true Desdemona, the play may be set back for another half century. God forgive me for my cruelty; but it must be so – it must."

He was walking to and fro in the room before he had finished his mutterings, so that when his wife returned, he seemed to her the embodiment of a man consumed by the demon of jealousy. Then she fancied that she detected a wistful look in his eyes – it seemed to her that he was somewhat ashamed of himself; and, feeling this, her eyes also became wistful and she went to him with outstretched hands. He caught her hands in his own and kissed her warmly – only once, however; then he appeared to recollect his grievance – his imaginary grievance – against her, for he dropped her hands and turned away from her with a sigh.

She had too much pride to force herself upon him. She left the room without a word.

At the rehearsal of the tragedy the next day, Burt greeted her effusively – so effusively as to cause the other members of the company to glance significantly at one another. She would have liked to strike the fellow on the face and then leave the theatre for ever; but she knew that she could not afford to give way to her impulses. She had a full sense of her responsibilities towards the poet whom she had been taught by her husband to love; and she would do nothing that might jeopardise the success of the play.

That was why she suffered Burt without rebuke to press her hand, and look meaningly into her eyes, several times during the rehearsal, and that was why, when she found herself alone with him for a few minutes while waiting for a scene to be set, she only shook her head, and smiled as he murmured in her ear:

"Beloved creature! my success on the night of the performance will be complete because the playgoers will perceive that the words of love which I speak to you come from my heart."

She hurried away from him though he tried to stop her; but when she had got to the other side of the stage, she glanced back at him. She could feel her cheeks flaming when she saw the smile that was upon his face. It was a leer that told her he felt sure of her.

She did not tell her husband of this incident, nor did she say a word to him of the letter which Burt slipped into her hand the next day – a letter full of passionate protestations and implorations. He had loved her for months, he declared in fervid language, but only since they had been brought so close together in the play, had his passion become uncontrollable. Why was she so cold to him, when his heart told him she returned his affection, he asked. Why would she not trust her life to his keeping? Would not their happiness be more than earthly if she would but trust to his honour?

She read this letter when she was alone, and she crushed it in her hand and then with blazing eyes and quivering fingers she tore it into shreds and scattered them to the winds.

When she saw her husband next, he looked at her searchingly – almost insultingly. He seemed to know by instinct that she had come from reading that letter. He was about to speak to her, when Crisp entered to beg of her to come to see his wife – to take leave of her for ever. The doctor had assured him he said, through his sobs, that she could not last another day.

She hastened away with him, thereby evading the explanation with her husband which she felt was inevitable. She did not stay long by the side of the dying woman.

The poor creature was now unconscious except at rare intervals, and Caroline perceived that the doctor's prediction would be realized: she would not live for many hours.

On her way back to her lodgings she came face to face with Burt. The hour was dusk and the lane leading off Holborn was narrow. She would have avoided him if she could, but it was clear to her that he had been lying in wait for her. He admitted as much.

He caught her hand, saying in a passionate whisper:

"My life, my soul, I saw you go forth, and I looked for you to return sooner. You got my letter? Ah, my Caroline, words are too feeble to express what is in my heart. You love me – I can swear that you love me."

He had put an arm about her, and, although she struggled, he was drawing her to him. She cried out, and, making a great effort, freed herself. She stood before him with outstretched hands, breathing quickly from the force of her struggle.

"Wretch – scoundrel – murderer!" she cried. "How durst you talk of loving me? How durst you talk of my loving you – whom I loathe, not love? And now – now – at this moment when I come from the death-bed of one of your victims."

"You are a mad woman!" he cried. "A mad woman! What do you mean?"

"I mean that you are the murderer of poor Henrietta Crisp as surely as if you had steeped your hands in her blood," she said. "And you would murder me just as surely, were I to trust you for one hour. Move back, sir – let me pass."

He did not move. It seemed to her that he was overcome by surprise. Had he never failed before, she wondered.

"Let me pass," she cried again.

"Yes," he said in a low voice. "Yes, I shall let you pass. But – what is't that you have said – murder – I – a murderer? You have said it. You have said that I would murder you were you to trust me." Then he put his face close to hers and she saw the malignant expression that it wore as he whispered:

"You will be compelled to trust me once, and you have spoke your own doom."

"Liar and villain!" she cried. "I will never trust you – never! You know it – you know that I will never cease to loathe you."

He gave a laugh, then a mocking bow, as he stood to one side, and she walked past holding her head high.

Burt watched her until she had disappeared. Then he cursed through his set teeth, and struck the palm of his left hand with his right fist. He had played the villain so often on the stage that the technique of the part came as second nature to him.

"Curse her!" he muttered after the fashion of the stage villain. "Curse her! but she has spoke her doom; I'll take care that her words come true."

He gave another laugh, and a savage oath tripped up its heels, so to speak. Then he walked on, and James Hughes came out of the doorway where he had been hiding, and restored to its sheath the long knife that he held bare in his right hand.

He looked after the other man, thinking:

"*What doth he mean? What doth he mean?*"

All the rest of the night that question remained in his mind:

"*What doth he mean? What doth he mean?*"

It was not until the tragedy of "Othello," which was produced the next afternoon, was approaching its close, that the answer to that question seemed to come to him. He was at the back of the stage, and from this standpoint he had watched the effect of his wife's representation of Desdemona, upon the people in the playhouse. He heard the tumult of applause that greeted the first appearance of a woman in the character of the gentle lady, and he saw that Burt was surpassing all his previous efforts in the part of the Moor. Then suddenly the answer to his question flashed upon him.

He had moved to one side to allow the scene-shifters to put the rude bed for the last scene in its place. The sight of the bed and its pillows suggested the answer. He staggered against the wall, whispering:

"My God – my God!"

In a moment he had regained his self-possession, and had slipped across the stage and hidden himself behind the flowing curtains of Desdemona's bed. The scene-shifters had gone to another part of the stage, and by accommodating himself to the heavy folds of the drapery, he knew that he should be as invisible to any one on the stage as he should be to the audience in the theatre.

A moment after he had concealed himself, his wife came down the stage and took her place on the bed. Then the curtain was raised, and after a breathless moment for the high-strung playgoers, the low voice of Othello was heard repeating the sublime passage:

It is the cause, it is the cause, my soul;
Let me not name it to you, you chaste stars.
It is the cause. Yet I'll not shed her blood
Nor scar that whiter skin of hers than snow
And smooth as monumental alabaster.
Yet she must die.
Put out the light, and then put out the light.
If I quench thee, thou flaming minister.
I can again thy former light restore,
Should I repent me; but once put out thy light,
Thou cunning'st pattern of excelling nature,
I know not where is that Promethean heat
That can thy light relume. When I have plucked the rose
I cannot give it vital growth again
It needs must wither.

What words they were! thought the man who was in hiding. What sublime words!

And then he drew his knife from its sheath as Othello bent for a moment over Desdemona.

Would he kiss her?

If Burt had kissed her, her husband would have put his knife back into its sheath, feeling that the wrong answer to his previous question had been suggested to him.

He saw that Burt avoided kissing her; and then her husband felt with his forefinger the point of the knife.

He heard nothing of the words that followed – the brief dialogue that followed the awaking of Desdemona – it seemed long to him. He waited until the frenzied Othello had raised the pillow in both hands and brought it down – it was no simulated expression of murder that was in his eyes – the actress saw it and shrieked out "Murder!" sending a thrill through the house, and then the pillow fell full upon her face stifling her second cry.

"No, there will be no murder," whispered her husband swaying the curtain, so that when Burt raised his eyes – a look of startled fear had taken the place of the murderous glance – they saw that knife raised over him ready to pierce his throat.

With a cry of dread his hands loosed upon the pillow with which he was crushing the life out of the woman on the bed, not in pretence, but in deadly earnest. He fell upon his knees trembling with fear, and then came the loud knocking of Emelia.

"You have saved yourself, you hound!" said Hughes in his ear. "If you had kept it on her face for another instant you would have been a dead man."

"My love – my husband – it was you who saved me!" sobbed Caroline in the arms of her husband a quarter of an hour later, when the playgoers had shouted themselves hoarse at the close of the drama. "He forced himself upon me – he swore to murder me when I repulsed him."

"I heard him then, but only half-an-hour ago I knew what he meant," said her husband. "Ah, my dear wife, do you fancy I doubted you for a moment? Nay, dear one, I only wished you to realize to the full what 'twas to be the innocent wife of a jealous man."

"I did realize it," she said slowly, after a long pause.

They supped that night with Sir Edmondbury Godfrey, and returned home shortly after nine. Then James Hughes went to a neighbour of his who was a baiter of horses, and borrowed from him a well-knotted postillion's whip. He went to Burt's lodgings. Lights were in the windows. He knocked at the door, and pushed past the woman who admitted him.

"Mr Burt – I must see him," he said. "Which room is he in?"

The woman pointed to a door. He opened it. The room was full of people. They stood around a table on which a dead body was laid. A man moved aside and disclosed to him the face of the corpse – the face of Richard Burt.

"Lord have mercy upon us!" said Hughes. "How did this happen?"

"Run through the vitals on his way from the playhouse," whispered a watchman.

He had not reached his own door before he was met by Crisp.

"She died at five o'clock, and he died before St Giles' clock had chimed six," said he.

Hughes kept his eyes fixed upon him and nodded twice.

"Ah, you think that I am a murderer," cried the man.

"No – no," said Hughes solemnly. "He was the murderer. You are the sword of a just God."

THE DUMB BELL

KATE ELLIS

We are still in the post-Cromwellian struggle to return to some form of normality in this most unusual story. Kate Ellis (b. 1953 – the first New Year's baby in Liverpool that year) is the author of the Wesley Peterson archaeological mysteries that began with The Merchant's House *(1998) and which link past events with present-day crimes.*

My jowls sagged, as did my belly, and my looking-glass mocked me whenever I examined my image. Once I was strong. I fought with the King against Cromwell's army at Marston Moor and then at Naseby before the cause was lost. But that was five and twenty years since and the body turns fat and weak with age.

I was in much need of exercise, for a man with a young and comely wife must do his best to regain the strength of his youth if she is not to seek satisfaction elsewhere. Experience has taught me that women are weak vessels, never to be trusted. And the example set by our new King of late has caused piety and propriety to count for nought.

Mindful of this, I resolved to take up some suitable pastime to exercise my body and reinvigorate my mind. Bell ringing being considered a suitable recreation for a gentleman, I gave orders that a curious contraption – such as I observed at Lord Westham's house at Burton – should be constructed at Mereton Hall. I had great hopes that my new dumb bell – for that is what it is commonly called – would endow me with new vigour. It was many months since I rang a bell at the church of Saint Giles, and then the effort left me weak and short of breath. But if I accustomed my body once more to the exertion, I hoped that I would, in the future, feel able to perform without disgrace.

My manservant, Cooke, supervised the labourers from my estate who constructed my dumb bell. The contrivance was placed in the attic above an unused chamber – left empty and unfurnished since my first wife, Mary, died there – which some of the ignorant servants, in their silly superstition, refuse to enter.

The contraption consists of two upright posts, joined by an iron cross bar, rather resembling the form of a gallows. Around this bar is a wooden cylinder with two iron rods passed through it and at the ends of the rods there are weights of lead. A rope is wound around the cylinder and passed through the floor of the attic to dangle into the room below. One tug causes this rope to be drawn up with considerable force and wound back and forth around the cylinder, thus imitating the action of a church bell as it swings upon its wheel. Such instruments are, increasingly of late, used by gentlemen of fashion who desire to strengthen their bodies and I had high hopes of it.

Once the labourers had completed their task, I was impatient to try out this new plaything. I asked Cooke to accompany me for I have a great affection for the young man who has been in my service only since Candlemas. He is tall and well favoured with fair curls and the bluest of eyes. When I look at him I am reminded a little of myself in the days of my youth when I was strong of arm and spirit and fought valiantly for my King against his enemies in Parliament. The days before my first wife, Mary, betrayed me and was punished for her indiscretions.

I took off my coat and, dressed only in shirt and breeches, I caught hold of the rope attached to my dumb bell. I gave a wary tug and the rope shot upwards with great force, and when it descended I caught it in the middle, still clinging to the tail end with my left hand. I pulled thus for three minutes until my heart began to race and beads of perspiration soaked my brow.

Cooke stood near to the window watching me, and when I was

finished I turned, hoping that I would not see a smile of mockery on his soft lips. But I saw nothing in his expression but pity. And perhaps that is worse.

I wiped my brow before donning my coat and leaving the chamber but I saw Cooke shiver. Perhaps it had been cold in that place but my exertions had made me oblivious to the chill. I have heard the servants say that Mary's spirit walks there. But I shall not believe it. Her soul is in hell, paying for her sins on earth.

And now it seems I must endure a second misfortune, for I have observed my wife, Annabella, talking with a young man near the gate to the kitchen garden. A well-favoured young man of around her own age. I thought Annabella meek and loyal when I took her for my wife. But all women are stained with the sins of Eve.

The name of the man in question is James Vilton and he is staying with Sir William at the Manor House in Paleby, a mile from here. It is well known that he has come from the King's court in London – a fact that impresses the ladies, especially those like Annabella whose lives have been spent in the countryside. His coat and breeches are bright and trimmed with ribbons, as is the mode at court, and he wears a full wig of luxuriant, dark curls, aping the fashion set by His Majesty. It is said that the court of this second Charles is full of vice and is a haven for libertines, for our new King lacks sorely his sainted father's inclination to marital fidelity and, with his return, no trace remains of Master Oliver Cromwell's taste for restraint and piety. It is from this den of lust and depravity that Master Vilton has descended upon our community like a strutting peacock. And it is my wife – my lovely young ewe lamb – who appears to have taken his eye.

I practise at my dumb bell twice each day, morning and night. My wife, Annabella has not enquired about it nor has she asked to see it. She seems much preoccupied and Cooke told me that he saw her walking with her maid, Ursula – a plain, stupid girl with a round, moon face who once served my late wife with dumb devotion – towards the Manor House at Paleby.

I wondered then if I should set Cooke to follow her. He seems keen for the task – his loyalty being to his master like any good manservant – but I do not wish to act hastily. At my request he questioned Ursula discreetly but she told him nothing. Probably the girl is too foolish and unobservant to have noticed anything amiss.

On Sunday myself and my household attended church as usual and I saw that the popinjay Vilton had discarded his wig and beribboned coat to catch hold of a rope and was ringing the second bell with great skill. I resolved to invite him to try my dumb bell, thinking he would believe the invitation to be made in the spirit of friendship and suspect nothing of my true motive.

I know that I must make no move without proof of my wife's perfidy. And yet I begin to feel such jealousy, such suspicion, that I cannot rest. I think of all I have heard of the King's court, of the mire from which the creature, Vilton, has emerged. Of the whores – high born as well as low – and the licentiousness that has infected a people once repressed by the fear of God and Master Cromwell's joyless rule. The seduction of Annabella would be nothing to Vilton and my hatred and anger increases daily.

As my heart aches so do my shoulders from my unaccustomed exercise on the dumb bell. I have asked Cooke to rub my flesh to ease the discomfort. He has most gentle hands, almost like a woman's.

I cannot rest. I have to know if Annabella is unfaithful. The thought eats away at my heart like a worm eats the flesh of the dead. It is common knowledge that Vilton frequents the alehouse in the village and I plan to go there and speak with him. I must know the truth of the matter. And it is certain that Annabella will confess nothing.

I went last night to the Blue Boar but I did not venture inside. Instead I looked into the window, pressing my nose against the windows like some outcast or vagrant to look with longing at the fire lit scene within.

I saw Vilton in the midst of a group of men, some of them his fellow bell ringers – and they seemed to hang on his every word as he regaled them with stories, no doubt of his exploits at King Charles's debauched court. There were occasions when I was a young man when I would enjoy the bodies of girls, whores and virgins alike, with the desperate lust of any man who might die the next day in bloody battle. I used the services of the harlots who followed the King's army around the countryside and I did foolish things which I think of now with regret. And yet I never seduced another man's wife. I was never as sinful as this vile Vilton. Does not the sixth commandment forbid adultery?

I watched him there, laughing with his fellows, a cockerel amongst the dull village birds, without a care for the husband he makes a cuckold, and anger and bitter envy rose within me like an overwhelming flood. When he departed, I followed him a little way behind, like a robber with a pair of pistols primed ready, and I was sorely tempted to strike him there and then in the dark of the lane leading to the Manor.

Yet some nagging voice within me urged caution. I told myself that the man might be innocent of any wrongdoing. Perhaps my first wife Mary's infidelities with my son's tutor have unhinged my judgement. Perhaps I am seeing sin where none exists. I have to be sure.

I have resolved to set Cooke to spy upon my wife. It is the only way I will obtain my proof. Then I shall strike.

Cooke assured me that he has seen nothing untoward between Vilton and my wife. But by his manner, I am certain that he lied. Perhaps he fears that I would be unable to control my fury if what I suspect is true.

After much questioning I wrung the truth from him. He had seen Annabella and Vilton talking together in the arbour. So great was my anger that I went to Mary's chamber and exercised upon my dumb bell a full half hour to quench my pent up fury. I felt much better after my efforts; calmer and in a frame of mind to think and plot rather than to act in haste. I have to be sly – as forbidden lovers are sly. Annabella must suspect nothing.

I fear that Cooke is too soft hearted. I knew he bears me much love but sometimes he looks at me with fear.

Annabella avoids my advances. Another proof of her perfidy. She walks often in the garden with the little dog she keeps by her now, a gift from Vilton. He told her it was a spaniel of the kind favoured by the King and the silly woman believes the fanciful tale. I watched her from the window today, admiring the sheen of her hair and the slenderness of her body, her white neck and bosom on show to all as is the latest fashion, and her hair twined with bunches of ribbons. I think that there is none in the County more beautiful than Annabella. But her beauty is a lure, a baited trap. And when I saw Vilton meet with her by the gate and kiss her hand reverently, a worshipper at Beauty's shrine, I knew that trap had been sprung. I watched as they walked in the knot garden beneath the window of my library, deep in conversation, and I knew from their manner that there was an attraction between them.

I recall how I used to walk there with Mary in the days of our courtship. And before Mary there was another I courted in the same way: that stubborn girl, Kitty, who, being the upright daughter of a puritan father, wrung such promises from me before surrendering her virtue. I look back sometimes with shame, for I went away and I never saw her again.

Perhaps I should have returned to seek Kitty out. But by then my father and Mary's father had made arrangements and I went with the flow of the tide, for her father and mine had been together at the court of King James, the father of our dear martyred King, beheaded and betrayed. What choice did I have if I did not wish to bring disgrace on my family name by entering into an alliance below my station?

But I must not think of the past. It is over. Gazing from the library window at my wife and her paramour has made me maudlin. I have to act, just as I did when Mary proved false. I cannot let idle sentiment cloud my resolve. I shall make plans.

And Cooke will be my trusty lieutenant.

It will be Vilton's desire for amusement that brings him to me. I have sent word to him that he is invited to try out my new dumb bell. As a gentleman of fashion from the king's court, he will surely find the novelty of the contraption irresistible. And the prospect of my wife's presence doubly so.

I have taken Cooke into my confidence and I have his assurance that he will help me, although he seems wary when I speak of violence.

I have a dilemma. Should I make Annabella pay for her wrongdoings as Mary did? Or should I punish her by making her witness her lover's demise and letting her live with the knowledge thereafter? Mary's case was different. Her lover had already left the district when I discovered the truth of her betrayal so she alone had to pay the price.

Maybe I will let Annabella live. She will exist knowing how her husband deals with those who betray him. And from that time on, she will be mine alone. Body and soul. That is an idea I like well.

Cooke was reluctant to aid me in my plan at first. But then his loyalty to me, his master, persuaded him that my execution – for that is how I think of it – of James Vilton is justified. He has stolen from me: stolen my wife's virtue. Every day men are hanged for stealing. And so would Vilton be. He will be strangled by the neck until he is dead.

He is to arrive tonight to dine with me but before we partake of our supper, I shall prepare a decanter of port wine for him. I shall urge him to take a drink to dull his senses and then I shall show to him my dumb bell, inviting him to take some exercise. Then, with Cooke's help, I will strike. I feel no dread at the prospect as I did before I dispatched Mary from this life, holding the bolster on her face as she struggled and fought for breath, testing my resolve with every desperate jerk of her limbs.

For one who has already ended a life, murder is an easy matter.

Cooke came to me in my chamber an hour ago to say he was afraid. I admire him for his tender heart and I told him I would not compel him to take part in the deed. But he assures me that he will do as I ask because of the love he bears me. It may be wrong to persuade another man to imperil his immortal soul and I will forgive him if he absents himself. Perhaps one who looks so like an angel should not become the angel of death.

I wait now for Vilton's arrival, my ears alert for the sound of his horse's hooves in the courtyard. He is a little late – no doubt he is accustomed to the manners of the court – and I grow restless. I have sent Cooke to check the dumb bell is in good order and I have prepared the drink – marking the drugged decanter so I, myself, can drink from the other.

There is little I can do now but pace to and fro across the floor of the great hall, thinking of what is to come. Vilton will, no doubt, consider our hall here, with its tapestries and great oak screen, drab and unfashionable as it has altered little from my father's day. The thought of his contempt keeps my resolve fresh as new picked fruit.

Annabella keeps to her room on my instructions but I have instructed Cooke that she is to be brought to me to witness the deed. How I look forward to watching her face as she sees her lover jerking at the end of the rope like some common felon.

As soon as Vilton arrived he insisted on being taken to the dumb bell chamber at once to see the novel new device. I felt the anger rise within me like bile. Such impudence. Such rudeness. To see to one's own entertainment before greeting one's host is hardly the conduct of a gentleman and my hatred of the man has increased tenfold. How I look forward to the moment when he realizes that my curious instrument of exercise has become the instrument of his death.

I marched towards Mary's chamber with my fists clenched, telling myself that I would soon have my revenge on the scoundrel who would make so free with my house. And my wife.

The door to the chamber was shut but I heard a noise within. The faint, rumbling sound of the dumb bell cylinder spinning round, stopping when the rope reached its full extent, then recommencing. Vilton was already engaged in his act of trespass.

I turned to Cooke and saw the fear and apprehension on his face. His expression reproached me. My young servant has become my conscience. I whispered to him to fetch my wife, instructing him that on no account must she be told my purpose. With a nervous glance he hurried off, leaving me alone there outside the chamber listening to the rumbling and swishing of my contraption as the rope rose and fell in Vilton's treacherous hands.

It was a full five minutes before Cooke returned, walking a little behind Annabella; five minutes that seemed like an hour to a man whose resolve is faltering. But I had killed once without repentance. What is another death to me? But I want it over quickly.

I took Annabella roughly by the hand and Cooke stepped back, as though he wished to have nothing to do with what he knew would follow. I turned and gave him a rueful smile, as though to signal that I understood and he hurried away down the passage. Perhaps it is better that he has no involvement. This matter is between myself and Vilton. And my sly little vixen of a wife. How I shall enjoy her body tonight when she knows who was master.

I pushed the door open, holding Annabella firmly by my side. Vilton turned his cropped head in my direction and smiled, showing a set of even teeth and expressing no surprise at my wife's presence. He had discarded his wig and his yellow, be-ribboned coat which lay on the ground like some common player's motley. He let the rope rise slowly and gently until it stilled itself, allowing Vilton to leave his post. He bowed to me and my wife and I smiled back before asking him how he liked my new plaything. He took a step towards me, clearly suspecting nothing of my intentions.

I confess that I was unprepared for what happened next. As I was about to invite Vilton to take a drink with me before partaking of more exercise so that I could carry out my original plan, Annabella broke free of my grasp and shouted to her lover, "Leave here, quickly. He means you ill. Get out."

Vilton stood frozen for a second with what seemed like disbelief, so confident was he of my ignorance. But he was swift to understand and, before I could act, he had wrested Annabella's hand from my grip and rushed from the room with her, leaving his coat and wig on the ground. The pair were making their escape and, being older and slower than the scoundrel, I lacked the speed and strength to do anything to stop them.

I called to Cooke but, when he did not come, I assumed his tender scruples had caused him to go to some other part of the house, far from the dark deed I planned. I called again but again there was no response. I considered pursuit of my betrayers but realized that it was useless. I could not overpower them and, besides, if my intentions were to come to the attention of Sir William, who is a magistrate and a man of influence in the district, I dare not think of the consequences. If I leave them be then I can deny all, saying they had made up the story to cover their guilt.

It is over. For now. I looked from the window and saw my wife hurrying across the knot garden with her maid, Ursula beside her, her cloak billowing in the breeze, and Vilton some way ahead. In my frustration, I was tempted to fall to my knees and weep with helpless fury. But as I stand here alone I tell myself that I must be subtle and patient. One day I will be revenged but in the meantime I must plan.

* * *

I stood for what seemed like an age, staring at the rope of my dumb bell. My plan had relied on Vilton not suspecting my intentions but now I had lost the advantage of surprise. With a heavy heart I kicked at the coat and wig so hard that they skidded across the boards; then I left that room, shivering at the chill in the afternoon air. I returned to my library where I took a glass or two of port wine from the decanter I had reserved for myself, after which I must have fallen into a fitful sleep in my armchair.

I do not know how long I was asleep but now my head spins as though I have drunk too much strong liquor. I awoke to find Cooke leaning over me, his face all concern.

"You need not trouble your conscience about my wife and her lover," I said to him. My mouth struggled to form the words but I did not know what ailed me. I thought perhaps that I had drunk too much port wine, drowning my conscience and my anger in drink.

"I know, Master," Cooke replied, his voice soft as a whisper. "They've gone. Ursula told me that they were bound for London. Will you pursue her?"

I said nothing. And now I feel wretched. An aging cuckold whose young wife has bettered him with an arrogant young scoundrel. If this comes to light I will be the focus of mockery in every manor house and tavern in the county. I fear that my infamy might spread as far as London. I have heard of plays in the new theatres that blot London like open sores, which mock and ridicule cuckolded husbands of country wives. I put my aching head into my hands but find I cannot weep.

I feel a gentle arm creep around my shoulders. Cooke is helping me up, bearing my weight as if I was a light girl. He must know that I need my bed. Sleep will still the demons that haunt me, if only for a while. I will sleep and wake refreshed. And when I wake, I will consider how to secure the return of my wife. For I shall get her back, whether she wills it or no.

My head spins as Cooke supports me upstairs and I lean on him, glad of his strength. But to my surprise we pass the door of my chamber and I find myself outside Mary's chamber at the end of the passage. I try to ask Cooke why he is taking me there but I find I cannot utter the words. He must have misunderstood and thought I desired some exercise on the dumb bell. But I can hardly stand.

He pushes the door open and helps me inside and as I stagger across the threshold I am half conscious of another presence in that room. Perhaps Mary's restless spirit has indeed returned to that place. The room swims before my eyes, then slowly, gradually, shapes begin to form. The dumb bell rope hangs there, looped at the end like a hangman's noose and four chairs are lined up where the head of Mary's bed once stood. To my surprise my wife Annabella is sitting there next to her lover, Vilton, once more adorned with his player's coat and luxuriant wig, while Ursula, the maidservant is seated at her mistress's side. They have returned. Or perhaps it is my imagination that has brought them to this place. Perhaps I see visions.

Cooke lets go of my arm and I fall, grovelling, to the floor, hurting my knees on the hard oak boards. I raise myself on my elbows and look around, the shapes forming and dissolving into dark clouds as I blink, trying to focus my aching eyes. They are still there. Ursula, Annabella and Vilton, all staring down at me with dark contempt. And now Cooke has joined them, taking the fourth chair.

My mind tells me that I am trapped in some strange dream. A hallucination. I reach out to Cooke for help but he ignores me.

Vilton has stood up and towers over me. Words flow from his mouth and I try to concentrate on what he is saying. I despise him no longer. All my energies are focussed on regaining my senses.

"It is hardly surprising, sir, that you did not know me for I saw you but once and I was then a child."

I try to open my mouth to speak but my lips feel like dead things and will not move.

"It was at your wedding to my Aunt Mary. Do you not remember, sir?"

I tried to shake my head. I feel saliva dribble from my lips. I do not wish Annabella to see me in such a pitiable state.

Vilton continues. "When Sir William met with me at court and told to me the manner of my Aunt Mary's death, I desired to come here and talk with her maidservant. What Ursula told me concerned me greatly and I felt it my duty to warn your new wife of your true nature. She did not believe me at first, of course. But she did believe Ursula who had been too afraid to speak out until I guaranteed her my protection."

Ursula is standing now. My vision is clearing and I can see that the timid creature's hands are shaking with fear. Annabella puts a reassuring hand on her arm.

"I found my mistress dead and the bolster was over her face. You told me to say nothing on pain of death, sir." Ursula's voice shakes. "You killed my mistress. And her innocent of any wrong-doing. She was kind to your son's tutor, that is all. There was nothing between them. She was the sweetest lady who lived."

She begins to cry and I stare at the silly, plain girl with disbelief. She is lying. Still covering up for that evil, adulterous woman. I hear myself groan.

Annabella stands now. "I have not betrayed you, sir. Master Vilton was merely concerned for my safety and . . ."

But Cooke interrupts her. I reach out to him for aid but he looks upon me with hard eyes. "It is you, sir, who are the betrayer."

I try to utter a denial but I still cannot speak. I reach out to Cooke again, hoping that my loyal manservant will help me to my feet for I feel so strange. Perhaps there was something in the port wine I sampled so liberally. Perhaps one of these traitors swapped the decanters, turning my own scheme upon myself.

Cooke ignores my silent pleas and waves a sheet of paper at my face. "I made enquiries at the church of St Bartholomew in Stoke Varley some forty miles from here. My mother was from that parish."

I stare at him. This sudden change in his demeanour makes me afraid.

"There is an entry in the parish register saying that you married Kitty Cookman in 1648. Kitty Cookman lived in poverty and she passed from this life last winter."

He pauses and I feel my body slump to the ground, my arms no longer having the strength to hold me.

"Kitty Cookman was my mother. And you, to my shame, are my father. My mother was the daughter of an honest yeoman farmer, a puritan who fought for Parliament and died for Master Cromwell's cause at Marston Moor. My sweet, gentle mother prized her virtue, so you married her secretly because it was the only way you could get her into your bed. Then when you had had your amusement, you abandoned her to bear and raise me alone. I, sir, am your eldest son and your true heir born in lawful wedlock." He hesitates, staring into my eyes and I am suddenly afraid. "And upon your death I shall inherit all this estate."

He looks around and smiles; a triumphant, confident smile such as I have never seen upon his lips before. At that moment he resembles me as I once was. My son.

"And in a short while," Cooke continues, his face close to mine. "I shall claim my inheritance. And a new wife to go with it."

I see him take Annabella's hand tenderly and kiss it. I feel the roughness of the hemp on my flesh as he slips the looped rope of the dumb bell around my neck.

My head is clearing and at last I manage to speak. "You would not murder me?"

He smiles and shakes his head. "Murder? This is not murder, Father. This is trial by jury. This is justice."

Cooke has given a signal, a chopping action with his right hand. The four are standing up, their faces solemn.

Vilton is speaking, pronouncing the sentence, as I try to form the word "no" with my numbed tongue. I struggle against strong hands and I hear myself let out a terrified grunt of fear, like a beast in the slaughterhouse. Then I see Mary smiling at me from the shadows.

And with the words "The Lord have mercy on your soul", Vilton pulls upon the rope and I am flung upwards with a jerk into the darkness.

THE CURIOUS CONTENTS OF A COFFIN

SUSANNA GREGORY

When I started this anthology I didn't expect to get even one story involving an exhumation, let alone two. However that is all that this story and Martin Edwards's have in common. The following continues the theme of individuals trying to get their lives back together after the turmoil of the Civil War and the Cromwellian period.

Susanna Gregory (b. 1958) is a biologist who spends most winters sunning herself in the Antarctic. Otherwise she is the author of several historical mystery series, most notably the Matthew Bartholomew books, set in fourteenth-century Cambridge, which began with A Plague on Both Your Houses *(1996) and the Crusader series featuring Sir Geoffrey Mappestone which began with* Murder in the Holy City *(1998), written under the alias Simon Beaufort.*

LONDON, 1663

Thomas Chaloner, spy for the Lord Chancellor, hated assignments like the one he had been given that morning. He did not mind the physical labour of excavating a tomb in the hour before dawn – although he would have been happier had it not been raining so hard. And he enjoyed the challenge of disguising himself as a gravedigger – donning the filthy clothes of the trade and staining his teeth brown, so that even his own mother would not have recognized him. He did not even mind manhandling corpses. But what Chaloner didn't like was causing distress to the dead woman's son and daughter, who had objected strenuously to their mother's final resting place being disturbed. Nor did he like the possibility that he might be ordered to steal what was in the coffin with her.

"How much longer?" demanded John Pargiter, wealthy goldsmith and husband of the deceased. He was a tall man, with a long nose and a reputation for dishonesty – the Goldsmith's Company had fined him several times for coin-clipping and shoddy workmanship. "My arm aches from holding this lamp and I'm soaking wet."

"This foul weather is a sign of God's displeasure," declared Pargiter's son Francis, hugging his sobbing sister closer to him. "This is an evil deed, and you will pay for it on Judgment Day."

"Please, father," begged the weeping Eleanor. "Stop this. Let our mother rest in peace."

Chaloner waited to see if Pargiter would agree. He was nearing the casket, and knew he would have to be careful not to step through it. The man who usually dug graves for St Martin's Ludgate – currently insensible after the copious quantities of ale with which Chaloner had plied him the previous night in the hope of learning a few useful tips – had confided that there was an art to dealing with rotting coffins, but had then declined to elaborate. Chaloner would have to rely on his own ingenuity to perform the grisly task, and only hoped he would convince Pargiter that he knew what he was doing. The goldsmith had brought two burly henchmen with him, and Chaloner suspected they might turn nasty if he failed to impress.

He exchanged a hopeful glance with the parish priest, Robert Bretton, a short fellow with a mane of long, shiny black curls. Bretton was chaplain to King Charles, as well as Rector of St Martin's, and it was because of him that this particular assignment had been foisted on Chaloner. When he had learned what Pargiter intended to do, Bretton had approached the King in a fury of righteous indignation – the poor woman had been in the ground for more than three years, and it was shameful to disturb her rest. With a shudder of distaste, the King had passed the matter to his Lord Chancellor to sort out.

But the Lord Chancellor said there was nothing he could do to stop the exhumation, because Pargiter had the necessary writs. What he *had* been able to do, however, was lend Bretton one of his men, assuring the agitated chaplain that Thomas Chaloner would not only ensure the exhumation was carried out decently, but could be trusted not to gossip. When Bretton had demurred, the Lord Chancellor had pointed out that he would have an ally at the graveside should he need one, and the family would be suitably grateful to him for "hiring" a man who knew how to be discreet. And, the Lord Chancellor had added slyly, he wanted his spy present anyway, because he was curious to know what Pargiter thought he might find among his wife's rotting bones.

Bretton peered at the goldsmith in the gloom, to see whether he was having second thoughts. He sighed unhappily when he saw he was not, and nodded down at Chaloner, telling him to continue. The spy began to dig again, pretending not to listen to the furious altercation that was taking place above his head. The family had kept their voices low at first, unwilling to let a stranger hear what they were saying – even one vouched for by Rector Bretton. But as time had crept by and Chaloner's spade came ever closer to the coffin, they had grown less cautious, and the foul weather and their increasing agitation encouraged them to forget themselves. In addition, Chaloner had excellent hearing – a valuable asset for a spy – and a decade of eavesdropping in foreign courts meant he was rather good at hearing discussions not intended for his ears.

"This is very wrong," said Pargiter's cousin and business-partner, an overweight man named Thomas Warren, who was the last of the graveside party. His plump face was pale and unhappy, and the hair in his handsome wig had been reduced to a mess of rattails in the rain. "Had I known you'd cached our gold in Margaret's grave, I'd *never* have asked for it back. I don't want her defiled."

"You're deep in debt," said Pargiter with a sneer. "You lost a fortune in Barbados sugar, and your creditors snap at your heels. Would you rather go to prison? Besides, Margaret won't be defiled. Once the coffin is reached, I shall jump down and remove the gold myself. I was her husband, so she won't object to me touching her."

Francis snorted his disdain. "She would. She hated you – and with good cause." He added something else in a low, venomous hiss that Chaloner could not quite catch. The spy supposed someone – probably his sister – had warned him to keep his voice down.

"Why are *you* so eager to retrieve the hoard, Father?" asked Eleanor softly, so Chaloner had to strain to hear her. "*You* don't need your share of this gold: you're already rich – certainly wealthy enough to lend Warren what he needs."

"Yes," said Warren, sounding relieved. "That's the best solution. Fill in the hole and I'll have papers –"

"I've lent him too much already," interrupted Pargiter roughly. "No, don't you flap your hand at me to be quiet, Warren! I shall talk as loudly as I please. And, to answer my daughter's question, our cache has been playing on my mind of late. Gold can't earn interest if it's buried, and I want it where it can do me some good."

"Tainted money," said Rector Bretton in disgust. Chaloner had noticed his increasing distress as the exhumation had proceeded, and now he sounded close to tears. "It won't bring you happiness, and I strongly advise you to leave it where it is."

"You did a dreadful thing, burying gold with our mother," said Eleanor in a broken, grief-filled voice that made Chaloner wince at his role in the distasteful business. The gravedigger's disguise had been Bretton's idea, and Chaloner heartily wished the rector had thought of something else.

Francis murmured something Chaloner did not hear, and Pargiter responded with a sharp bark of laughter that had Francis spluttering in impotent rage. The spy glanced up and saw Eleanor rest a calming hand on her furious brother's arm.

"Francis is right, cousin," said Warren in a low voice. "I cannot imagine what you were thinking when you performed an act of such heartless desecration."

"I was desperate," replied Pargiter with an unrepentant shrug. "You and I supported Cromwell, but when the monarchy was restored, Royalists surged into London and started confiscating Roundhead goods. Margaret's death from fever provided me with a perfect opportunity to hide our gold where no one would ever think to look."

"That's certainly true," said Bretton unhappily. "But only a monster would have devised such a plan – and only a devil would consider retrieving the hoard."

"Our mother was right to despise you," said Francis. Chaloner saw Eleanor was hard-pressed to restrain him as he glowered at their father. "And so are we."

Pargiter did not care what his son, daughter, rector and cousin thought, and when Warren took a threatening step towards him the two henchmen blocked his path. But the goldsmith did not so much as glance at his kinsman: his attention was focussed on the grave. Chaloner's spade had made a hollow sound, as metal had connected with wood.

"At last," said Pargiter. "Now, climb out and let me take over."

"You don't want me to open the coffin first?" asked Chaloner.

Pargiter shook his head. "I told you: I don't want anyone to see her. I'm not the heartless fiend everyone imagines and, by retrieving the money myself, I shall spare her the indignity of being gawked at. Then we can cover her up again, and be done with this business. Take my hand."

Scaling the rain-slicked sides was not easy, and Chaloner was muddy from digging. He was not halfway out before his fingers shot out of Pargiter's grasp, and he fell backwards, landing feet-first on the ancient casket. There was a crackle of shattering wood, and the top third of the lid disintegrated. Eleanor cried out in horror, and Bretton began to pray in an unsteady voice.

"Clumsy oaf!" yelled Pargiter, while Chaloner danced around in a desperate attempt to regain his balance without doing any more damage. "You've exposed her for all to see!"

Warren looked as though he might cry. "This has gone far enough, cousin. I don't want the gold any more – I'll find another way to pay my debts."

"I'm not leaving without my money," declared Pargiter, climbing inside the hole himself. He soon discovered it was not easy, and slithered down in a way that broke more of the coffin. One of his men handed him a lamp. "Everyone stay back. I'll finish quicker without an audience."

Sobbing, Eleanor appealed to Chaloner. "Please stop him. You must see this isn't right."

"If you have any compassion, you'll do as my sister asks," added Francis in a heart-broken voice. "I'll pay you – twice what my father offered."

"And I'll pray for you for as long as I live," said Bretton. He sounded distraught. "Poor Margaret doesn't deserve this."

Supposing a real gravedigger would at least consider their offers, Chaloner moved forward. He stopped when he saw the body for the first time. Margaret Pargiter had been buried in a lacy shroud and a veil that covered her hair. Her face was much as he would have expected after three years, but it was the glitter of gold that caught his attention. Coins covered her chest and shoulders – too many to count. Pargiter was busily collecting them. The goldsmith glanced up and saw his order had been ignored: everyone, even his two henchmen, was gazing open-mouthed at the spectacle.

"The bag must have broken," he said in an oddly furtive way that made Chaloner sure he was lying. "I put it under her head."

But Chaloner had spotted something beside the hoard, and he edged around Pargiter to be sure of it. "Gold isn't the only thing to have shared her tomb – there's another body beneath her."

Pandemonium erupted after Chaloner's announcement. Warren accused him of being a liar, although his furious diatribe faltered when Chaloner pointed out the grinning skull under Margaret's shoulder. Francis and Eleanor clamoured for the strange body to be removed and their mother reburied alone. Pargiter wanted his gold out and the two bodies left as they were. But Bretton had the authority of the Church behind him, and once he declared his bishop would want both bodies excavated while an investigation took place, the argument was over.

Knowing the frail coffin would disintegrate if he tried to lift it, Chaloner raised the two bodies separately, using planks of wood, although his task would have been easier if Pargiter had not been in the grave with him, grabbing coins. When he had finished, and the corpses lay in the grass next to the tomb, Chaloner reached for his spade.

"Don't bother to fill it in," ordered Pargiter. "Margaret will be back in it soon. Here's a shilling for your trouble – you're dismissed."

But Chaloner had no idea how much gold Pargiter had retrieved, and the Lord Chancellor would be annoyed if he was not told a precise sum. He thrashed around for an excuse that would allow him to lurk long enough to see the money counted. "For another shilling, I'll find out who was the second corpse," he offered rashly.

Pargiter gazed contemptuously at him. "And how would a gravedigger know how to do that?"

"Fossor used to work for Archbishop Juxon," announced Bretton, before Chaloner could fabricate a story of his own. "And he solved all manner of crimes on His Grace's behalf. Don't let his shabby appearance deceive you. Fossor possesses a very sharp mind."

Warren peered at the spy in the darkness. "You've fallen low, then, if you were in the employ of an archbishop, but now you dig graves for a living."

"He does more than that," said Bretton, before Chaloner could prevent him from inventing anything else. "He hires himself out to many of my clerical colleagues, because we all know him as a man of intelligence and discretion. Why do you think I dispensed with my usual gravedigger and hired him instead? Whatever happened here *must* be investigated and the results reported to the proper authorities – and I would rather Fossor did it than some half-drunk parish constable."

Chaloner wished he would shut up, not liking the increasingly elaborate web of lies or the fictitious name. But Bretton gave him an encouraging nod, and Chaloner supposed he was hoping to curry favour with the Lord Chancellor by supporting his spy's proposal. However, all Chaloner wanted was an excuse to see the money counted, after which he would dispense with his disguise and disappear from the Pargiter family's lives for ever. He had no intention of mounting an investigation – Bretton would have to resort to his 'half-drunk parish constable" for that.

"I will discover the truth," he said, hoping he did not sound as unenthusiastic as he felt. "I shall uncover the corpse's identity, and you can make an official report to your bishop."

"Well, I don't want to know who it is," said Pargiter firmly. "It is common knowledge that Margaret made a cuckold of me, and one of her lovers must have contrived to be buried with her. And this *is* a man – he's quite tall and look, the fellow was buried wearing spurs."

"Our mother had no lovers!" declared Francis hotly, shooting Chaloner an uncomfortable glance. "How dare you defame her good name in front of strangers!"

Eleanor tried to pull him away, to talk to him privately, but he resisted. "You know she did, Francis. It was her way of defying the husband she didn't love. And I cannot find it in my heart to condemn her for it. And nor should anyone – including strangers who did not know her and so have no right to judge." She gazed coolly at Chaloner, who pretended to be absorbed with the skeletons.

"Nor me," said Warren. His chubby face was wan in the faint gleam of approaching dawn. "Do you mind if we just count this gold and go home? I feel sick."

"We can't," said Bretton angrily. "Something evil happened in poor Margaret's grave, and my bishop will want to know what. We are duty-bound to discover both this man's identity *and* how he came to die."

Eleanor sighed. "Rector Bretton is right. Once he reports the matter to his bishop, it will have to be investigated. He will think we have something to hide if we object."

"How do we know you can be trusted?" demanded Warren of Chaloner. "We have never met you before today."

"*I* trust him," said Bretton, before Chaloner could point out that anyone could be trusted if enough gold changed hands. "And you have known *me* for a long time. That should be enough for you."

Eleanor nodded slowly, staring hard at the spy. "Very well. If there must be an enquiry, then I suppose I would rather this Fossor did it than that horrible Constable Unwin."

"So would I," said Francis, glaring at his father. "Unwin hates us because *someone* made a fool of him over a consignment of clipped coins, and we don't want *him* poking into our affairs. He'll invent something to harm us, and who can blame him?" He turned to Chaloner. "If Bretton says you're all right, then I suppose you'll do. I'll pay you your shilling, if you find out the corpse's name."

"No," countered Warren shakily. "You might not like what he learns. Margaret was a sociable lady, and you should let matters lie while her reputation is still intact."

"It was *not* a lover," snarled Francis, rapidly losing what small control he had. "And I want to know why my mother has spent the last three years with a stranger. Do your work, Fossor."

"Let sleeping dogs lie," argued Pargiter irritably. "Folk will have forgotten her infidelities by now, and I don't want to be labelled a cuckold again, thank you very much."

"You were unfaithful yourself," said Bretton sharply. "And if Fossor needs to ask you questions to solve this wicked business, you *will* answer them. It is your Christian duty."

"You can't order *me* around!" cried Pargiter. "I'm a City goldsmith –"

"Then we shall summon Constable Unwin instead," said Bretton coldly. He nodded his satisfaction when there were resentful glares from Pargiter and his cousin, but no further objections. "Good. Fossor, you may begin."

Chaloner knelt next to the bodies. First, he inspected Margaret, recalling how her grave-clothes had been carefully arranged to hide the corpse beneath – someone had been to considerable trouble. Then he turned his attention to the second body. There was nothing left of his face, and the only thing of use was a charm on a chain around his neck.

"Does anyone recognize this?" he asked, removing it. The pendant was made of jet, and was in the shape of a bird. There were shaken heads all around, although a brief glimmer of alarm flashed in Warren's eyes.

Chaloner began the distasteful business of peeling away the decaying clothes, hoping to discover how the stranger had died. Revolted, Bretton invited the others to his house, where they agreed to wait until "Fossor" had finished. From the worn teeth, Chaloner concluded the stranger had been an older man, and his silver spurs suggested he had been wealthy. The only injury was a triangular puncture-wound, clearly visible in the bones of the chest and what little skin still clung to them.

The spy gazed at the bodies and reviewed what he had been told. Margaret had died of a fever three years before, and Pargiter had taken advantage of her burial to keep some of his and Cousin Warren's money from acquisitive Royalists. The grave had been opened because Warren was in debt, although the man had become increasingly unnerved as the exhumation had proceeded. Had Warren's unease derived from his fear that an old crime was about to be exposed? And what about his hesitation when

Chaloner had asked about the charm? Finally, it had been Warren who had objected to an enquiry that promised to reveal the dead man's name.

Next, Chaloner turned his thoughts to Pargiter, who did not need more money, but could no longer bear the thought of it lying uselessly underground. From the very start, the goldsmith had made it clear that only *he* was to collect the coins from the coffin, and he had issued all manner of threats to ensure he was obeyed – until Chaloner's fall had inadvertently spoiled his plan. Had he been so determined no one should see the contents of the coffin because he knew what else was in it? He had tried to persuade the others to ignore the grisly discovery, and had joined with Warren in objecting to an investigation. Was it because he had no desire to be ridiculed as a cuckold again, as he had claimed, or did he have a more sinister motive for wanting the matter quietly forgotten?

Then there were Francis and Eleanor, who had loved their mother – or at least, had not wanted her grave disturbed. Were they devoted children, who had taken her side against a hated father? Or had they made use of her death to conceal crimes of their own? But then, surely they would not have asked Chaloner to investigate the stranger? They would have taken the opportunity supplied by their father to have the matter shoved quickly underground again. Or were they afraid that might have looked suspicious?

Finally, there was Bretton, who had also objected to the exhumation. As the family rector, he would have had access to Margaret's coffin three years before. Had he encouraged Chaloner's investigation because to do otherwise would have looked odd – especially in front of the Lord Chancellor's spy? He had always referred to the dead woman as "Margaret", rather than "Mrs Pargiter". The more Chaloner thought about it, the more convinced he became that the rector might have offered her more than spiritual comfort. Did that mean Bretton had dispatched a rival for her affections?

"Anyone could have killed him," said one of Pargiter's henchman, who had lingered to watch. "Although I suspect *you* think it was Pargiter, because this man was probably one of her paramours."

Chaloner shrugged. "No one likes his wife sleeping with

another man, and Pargiter *is* violent – he has been threatening me all night. But I imagine Margaret would have been too ill to entertain lovers immediately before her death."

"She *did* die of fever – I saw her shivering and sweating myself. But I've been thinking. About the time she passed away, there was a fellow who lurked around a lot, talking to Warren. He disappeared after, and I never saw him again."

"Do you know his name, or what he was doing?"

The henchman shook his head. "All I know is that he was tall with a big nose and a stoop."

Chaloner was thoughtful. "There are two peculiar things about Margaret's burial. First, the presence of an additional corpse. And second, the coins were not in a bag, as Pargiter said they would be, but were scattered across her body."

"Worms," said the henchman. "They do odd things underground."

"Not that odd," said Chaloner.

Chaloner did not want to spend too much time with the bodies, in case he missed the counting of the money. He trotted across the sodden churchyard to the Rectory, a grand house boasting ornamental drainpipes of lead – few owners bothered, leaving rainwater to cascade from the roof – and was admitted to a warm, comfortable room with a blazing fire. Piles of gold pieces sat on the table.

"I found these caught in the stranger's clothes," he said, producing two coins he had pocketed earlier, in a sleight of hand no one had noticed. "Are you missing any more?"

Pargiter snatched them from him. "Good. That makes three hundred pounds exactly. It's all there." He had spoken spontaneously and then regretted it in Chaloner's presence. Chaloner wondered how much Pargiter would have left once the find had been reported to the Lord Chancellor – the Court had expensive tastes.

"Tell me about the day Margaret was buried," he said, supposing he had better make a show of investigating the stranger's death, even though he had no intention of furnishing them with answers. His work was done, and he was more than ready to change out of his filthy, wet clothes and move on to the Lord Chancellor's next assignment.

"She died in May, three years ago," replied Bretton with genuine sorrow. "But the churchyard was flooded, and she had to stay in the charnel house for two days until the water had gone down."

"So *anyone* could have shoved that fellow in her coffin," elaborated Warren. "You'll never prove his identity *or* discover what really happened – and if you try, you'll be wasting your time."

Chaloner regarded him thoughtfully. Was it wishful thinking that made him so sure?

"It is a lover," said Pargiter harshly. "Almost certainly."

"No – some felon must have hidden the victim of a robbery," argued Warren, swallowing hard. "And now I must pay my creditors." He took a step towards the door, but stopped uneasily when Francis approached Chaloner and gazed earnestly at him.

"My mother's honour is at stake here, and I want you to prove this was *not* a beau. Perhaps the fellow *was* murdered by felons, as Warren suggests. Go to the local taverns and ask known thieves whether he was one of their victims."

"That will see him killed," said Pargiter scornfully. "Let the matter lie, Fossor. I'll give you *two* shillings, if it's a love of money that makes you persist with this nonsense."

"Margaret's coffin would have been heavy with a second person inside it," said Chaloner, declining to be bribed. "Who were the pallbearers?"

Pargiter sighed irritably when he saw Chaloner was not going to do as he was told. "I was one. My children objected, since Margaret and I were estranged when she died, but I overrode them. The box *was* weighty, now you mention it."

"I was another," said Francis softly. "But I've never carried a casket before, so can't say whether it was abnormally heavy or not."

"We ordered a leaded one," explained Eleanor. Tears began to flow, and Francis put his arm around her. "We wanted her to have the best."

But the one Chaloner had uncovered had been plain wood. Had the killer removed the metal lining, so the extra weight of a second body would go undetected? It seemed likely.

"I understand a tall, stooped man visited you at Mr Pargiter's house around the time of Margaret's death," he said to Warren. "Who was he?"

Warren scowled. "I don't recall. But you're talking about things that happened three years ago, so what do you expect?"

"The visitor was a paramour, I expect," said Pargiter carelessly. "And he was there to see Margaret, not Warren. She often used such devices in an attempt to deceive me."

"That's unfair," said Eleanor, grabbing Francis's sleeve to prevent him from responding with violence. "She was desperately ill and in no position to entertain anyone. Visit the taverns, Fossor, and talk to robbers. We should at least give this stranger a grave with his own name on it."

Chaloner promised to do his best, and took his leave, knowing there were two reasons why no robber was responsible. First, he would have stolen the gold and the silver spurs at the same time. And second, he would not have gone to the trouble of arranging the two bodies with Margaret on top. The more he thought about it, the more Chaloner became certain that the murder was connected to Margaret's family, and that someone she knew had committed the crime.

It was still raining when Chaloner headed for his home on Fetter Lane. He scrubbed the mud from his face and hands, and shoved his filthy garments in a chest that held the clothes he used for his various disguises. Then he sloshed his way to the palace at White Hall, where he was told the Lord Chancellor was with the Swedish ambassador and would not be able to see him that day. Loath to leave a written message in a place that seethed with intrigue, he decided to return the following morning, and deliver his information in person.

With nothing else to do, he walked to Cripplegate, where his friend Will Leybourn owned an untidy bookshop with cluttered shelves. Leybourn ushered him into his steamy kitchen. He wrinkled his nose in disgust when he heard what Chaloner had been doing, but became thoughtful when he learned one of the bodies had been Margaret Pargiter. As a shopkeeper, Leybourn knew a lot of people and listened to a lot of gossip.

"Margaret's affairs were common knowledge – and so were her husband's."

"Was one of her lovers Rector Bretton?"

Leybourn nodded. "He visited her regularly, long before she became ill of the fever that killed her, although Pargiter didn't know the meetings were far from pastoral. I heard she was faithful to Bretton, though, because he was special to her. So, your stranger may have been a *previous* paramour, but he certainly wouldn't have been a *current* one."

Chaloner rubbed his chin. "Well, that explains why Bretton went to such lengths to prevent her from being excavated. No wonder he was upset – it must have been a grim business for him."

"But you say *he* was the one who urged you to investigate? That should mean you could eliminate him from your list of suspects. He wouldn't demanded an enquiry if he had secrets to hide."

"Not so, Will. If he'd agreed to shove both corpses back in the ground with no questions asked, it would have looked suspicious to say the least. He's a priest, supposed to uphold the law, so could hardly turn a blind eye to something so manifestly sinister – especially in front of the Lord Chancellor's spy."

"I suppose not," said Leybourn. "What a pity. I like Bretton – although he does preach the most blustering and wordy of sermons. Never go to St Martin's Ludgate on a Sunday, unless you have a good couple of hours to spare."

Chaloner showed him the charm. "I don't suppose you know anyone who might recognize this? It was around the stranger's neck. It's a black bird, perhaps a crow."

Leybourn's jaw dropped. "No, my friend, that's a raven. And Raven is the name of the man who wore it – Henry Raven. He was in your line of work – a tall, crook-backed fellow with a beaky nose."

"A spy?" asked Chaloner. "Working for whom?"

"For the government, of course. He often came to chat to me, pick my brains – just as you do. But then he stopped, and I assumed something like this had happened. You don't need me to tell you it's dangerous work. Poor Raven!"

"Could he have been one of Margaret's past lovers?"

"Never. He wasn't interested in women – or men, for that matter. Rather, he was consumed by a passionate interest in Barbadan sugar, of all odd things."

Chaloner watched the flames in the hearth, his thoughts whirling. If Raven was a government spy, then perhaps it was not the first time the Lord Chancellor had sent an agent to investigate Pargiter and Warren – and he recalled that Warren's lost fortune had been in the sugar trade. Chaloner supposed he would have to watch *he* did not suffer a fate similar to Raven's.

The notion that it was a colleague in someone else's coffin was enough to drive Chaloner back into his gravedigger costume. The nature of their work meant spies had few friends, and it was tacitly agreed that they could rely on each other to investigate any untimely ends. First, Chaloner went to see Pargiter at his mansion on Thames Street. The coat of arms over the door was picked out with gold, and there were fine woollen rugs on the floor of the hall. Chaloner, wearing clothes that still stank of death, was not permitted inside.

"I told you: I've no idea who the stranger was," snapped Pargiter, standing in a position that kept him dry and Chaloner under the dripping eaves. It was a way of ensuring an unwanted conversation remained short.

"His name was Henry Raven," said Chaloner, watching for any sign of recognition. He saw none. "And he may have been involved in government business."

Pargiter's eyes narrowed. "How have you learned this so quickly?"

"Archbishop Juxon introduced me to a lot of people."

Pargiter stared at him, and Chaloner wished Bretton had not saddled him with quite such a prominent master. "Well, my answer remains the same. I didn't know him."

"When you hid your gold in Margaret's coffin, *where* did you put it, precisely?"

Pargiter looked angry. "Under her head, where it wouldn't be seen by anyone paying their last respects. Look, I know hiding it with her was an odd thing to do, but I was desperate and I didn't think she would object. God knows, she spent enough of my money when she was alive."

Next, Chaloner went to visit Eleanor at an address in Cheapside. She lived with Francis and his wife in a house with a roof that leaked. When he was shown into the main room, buckets littered the floor to catch the drips, and he was told to watch where he put his feet. It was a stark contrast to Pargiter's luxurious mansion, and he commented on it.

"We would never demean ourselves by accepting our father's

charity," said Francis, watching his wife rock a fretful baby. "He might be rich, but his money is dirty."

"There are better things in life than gold," agreed Eleanor, smiling at Chaloner while she played with another brat next to the fire. Chaloner heard Francis's wife snort in disgust.

"We're happier here – with our leaking roof and smoking chimney – than we would be living with *him*," said Francis, glaring at her.

"But the children have no toys," snapped his wife. "They use your carpentry tools instead – a chisel is a soldier and a hammer is a dragon. And the reason these items are available for games is because *you* can't find work. Pride is all very well, but yours is affecting the welfare of your sons."

"You can always leave us and find something better, Alice," said Eleanor coolly. She turned back to Chaloner. "Our father is a selfish man, and Francis and I are better off here. It was his wicked behaviour that led our mother to seek solace in the arms of other men. He made her miserable."

"So did her lovers," said Alice tartly. "Except perhaps Bretton."

"You make it sound as though there were dozens of them," snapped Francis, turning on her. "There were not. But if that stranger was one of them, then he received his just deserts."

Chaloner raised his eyebrows. "You sound as though you're glad he died."

Francis gave an impatient sigh. "I didn't know him, but if he defiled my mother, then, yes, I am."

Eleanor came to stand next to him, resting her hand on his arm to calm him, as she had done earlier that day. "It was a long time ago, and she's at rest now. What else do you want to know, Fossor? Bretton ordered us to cooperate, and we have nothing to hide."

"Where did your mother die? Here or in your father's house?"

"The latter," replied Eleanor. "We all lived there, until she died."

"The stranger's name was Henry Raven," said Chaloner. "Someone recognized his neck-charm."

Eleanor was startled by the speed of his discovery. "Then you've succeeded, and we owe you a shilling. Do you know any more about this Raven?"

"He wasn't your mother's lover. I have it on good authority that he wasn't interested in women."

Francis gaped at him. "Are you sure?"

Chaloner nodded. "Why? Do you believe every man was a willing candidate for her affections?"

Francis was furious, and Eleanor stepped forward to prevent him from grabbing the spy by the throat. "Of course not. But you've exceeded our expectations – learning who he was *and* finding a 'good authority' who says he wasn't one of our mother's follies. You've cleared her name."

"You haven't said why he was in Margaret's coffin, though," Alice pointed out.

"We didn't ask him to do that," said Eleanor, searching in a pot for a shilling. "We only wanted to know the stranger's identity, so he can be buried in his own grave."

Francis grunted agreement. "We should let matters rest now. I don't want an ex-agent of Archbishop Juxon poking around in my family's affairs. Juxon is a creature of the Court, and –"

Suddenly, there was a piercing howl from the child by the hearth. Eleanor bent quickly to pick him up, soothing a cut finger with kisses and croons.

A petty expression crossed Alice's face. "I've warned him before about playing with that particular chisel – it's sharp – but he's just like everyone else around here. No one ever listens."

Warren's house was shabby, although it had once been fine, indicating that its owner had recently fallen on hard times. He answered his door himself, and explained sheepishly that he had no servants.

"I invested in Barbadan sugar, but there were several bad harvests in succession. Still, if I can weather this year, I may yet survive. The crops can't fail for ever."

"Did Henry Raven tell you that?" asked Chaloner. "He had an interest in sugar from Barbados."

Warren regarded him sharply. "Who?"

"The man in Margaret's coffin – as you know perfectly well. The others didn't recognise his neck-charm, but you did. I saw it in your face."

Warren closed his eyes. "Yes, that bauble belonged to Raven, although God alone knows how he got into Margaret's casket. It was nothing to do with me."

"You argued – probably about sugar investments. Did the disagreement end in violence?"

"No! There *was* no argument! He was very knowledgeable about Barbados, so I took him to Cousin Pargiter's house – not here, because I didn't want him to see the full extent of my losses – and asked his advice. He said mine was a bad venture, and recommended I withdraw while I could. I wish to God I'd listened! But I didn't kill him and I didn't put him in the coffin."

"How did you get into Pargiter's house? Does he not keep it locked?"

Warren looked furtive. "I have a key. Margaret gave it to me, a few years ago."

A short while later, Chaloner went to see the last of his witnesses. Rector Bretton was more welcoming than the others, and offered him wine and a seat by the fire. He was clearly under the impression that the liaison forced on them by the Lord Chancellor meant he was exempt from suspicion, and was surprised when Chaloner started to ask questions.

"You can refuse to answer," said Chaloner. "But the Lord Chancellor will want to know why. Everyone else has cooperated, although not always with good grace – people don't like Archbishop Juxon very much, and you should have chosen me a more popular master."

"He is a saint," said Bretton in surprise. "Who doesn't like him?"

"Margaret," prompted Chaloner, deciding he had better change the subject before he landed himself in trouble. Francis was right: Juxon *was* a creature of the Court. "Tell me about her."

Bretton stared unhappily into the flames. "All right. Yes, I was Margaret's lover. I think I was more important to her than the others, but perhaps I flatter myself. I was with her when she died."

"When was she put in her coffin?"

"The morning after her death. Francis had ordered a lead-lined box, and we put her in it together. We left it open for another day, then Pargiter and I sealed it before taking it to the charnel house. I know the others said someone could have put the stranger in at that point, but it isn't true. I stood vigil until her funeral – although I never told *them* that – and I'd have noticed anything untoward."

"The stranger was named Henry Raven," said Chaloner.

Bretton stared at him. "The tall man with the stoop? He came to see Warren around the time of Margaret's last illness, although I have no idea why. During one visit, he told us he disliked close contact with women, because he was afraid of catching the plague. He was an odd man."

"Who was the last person to visit Margaret, before the casket was closed?"

"Pargiter. He asked for a moment alone, and when I returned, he'd placed the lid across her and we nailed it down together. But this happened in Margaret's bedchamber, and unless Raven's body was hidden under the bed . . ."

Chaloner stood. "Will you summon the others? I think I know what happened now."

It was an uneasy company that gathered in Bretton's home. Warren and Pargiter claimed they were too busy for nonsense they never wanted started in the first place, and Eleanor and Francis said the investigation should have finished when Chaloner learned Raven's name. Only Bretton said nothing. The spy began his analysis.

"At first, I assumed Warren was the culprit. He recognized Raven's charm, and it was obvious they'd known each other. They discussed sugar investments, and the debate might have ended in violence. But it was Warren who asked for Margaret's grave to be opened, and he isn't so desperate for funds that he'd risk hanging for murder to claim them."

"But he was deeply unhappy about the exhumation," Bretton pointed out. "His reaction wasn't that of an innocent man."

"That's because he was one of Margaret's past lovers, too," explained Chaloner. "He said she gave him a key to the Pargiter house a few years ago – she would not have done that without good reason. And he still harbours an affection for her. He was torn between a selfish need for money and leaving her undisturbed."

Warren hung his head. "It's true – I did love Margaret. But I didn't kill Raven. Why would I? He gave me some good advice."

"Who *is* the culprit, then?" demanded Eleanor. She turned to the rector, who was regarding Warren with open-mouthed horror at the confession. "Bretton? Perhaps he was afraid Raven would take his place in my mother's heart – that he didn't come to discuss sugar with Warren, but to court *her*."

"Bretton didn't kill Raven, either," said Chaloner, cutting across the rector's spluttering denial. "He knew – from Raven himself – that the man spurned any kind of physical contact, because he was afraid of catching the plague. Thus there was no need for jealousy, and Bretton was more concerned with tending Margaret on her deathbed than in dispatching imaginary rivals."

"Well, *I* didn't do it," said Pargiter, when the others regarded him accusingly. "I didn't even know him. You say he was in my house, but I never saw him there."

"Warren invited him when you were away, hoping Raven would think the mansion was his," said Chaloner. "But Raven was killed in your house – and he was certainly stuffed in the coffin there."

"How can you know that?" demanded Pargiter in disbelief.

"Because Bretton was in constant attendance once Margaret's casket was in the charnel house. Therefore, Raven was hidden *before* you and Bretton closed the lid. At the same time, the killer removed the lead lining, to disguise the additional weight. I suppose he concealed it under the bed, or spirited it out of the house when everyone was asleep – we may never know. But although you lied about the coins, it proves you didn't kill Raven."

"I don't see how –" began Francis, while Pargiter gaped in astonishment.

"Pargiter claimed he put his bag of gold under Margaret's head," explained Chaloner. "But if that were true, he would have noticed Raven, who was already there – and he certainly would have said something. Instead of placing the coins *beneath* her, he tossed them *over* her in an act of defiance."

"I didn't –" began the goldsmith indignantly.

"You resented the amount of money Margaret spent; you said so yourself," Chaloner continued. "You hurled the gold at her, no doubt adding a taunt about her not being able to fritter it away now."

Pargiter regarded him with dislike. "I didn't anticipate that we'd have to reclaim it in the pouring rain *or* that there'd be another corpse to consider while we did so."

"And that leaves you two," said Bretton, looking at Francis and Eleanor. "Did you kill Raven and defile your mother's grave?"

Chaloner addressed Francis. "You disliked your mother's liaisons, and you loathed the men who took advantage of her. But you loved her, and you're the only one who stalwartly defends her reputation – everyone else acknowledges her indiscrtions."

"Indiscretions is putting it mildly," muttered Pargiter. "She was flagrant."

Chaloner's attention was still fixed on Francis. "You said you'd never met Raven, and that's probably true. But you were so hostile to your mother's men that you were more than willing to dispose of the corpse of one of them – especially when it was to help someone else you love."

Francis licked dry lips. "This is pure fabrication. You have no proof."

"You're a man of fierce passions, who either loves or hates – there's no middle way for you. When someone told you Raven was one of your mother's beaux, you were only too happy to get rid of his body. At first, I thought you were the killer – you objected to the opening of the coffin, and you didn't agree to my investigation until Eleanor said it was a good idea. But you're a follower, not a leader, and you hid the body because you were obeying instructions."

Eleanor gazed at him, then started to laugh. "I hope you're not implying that *I* killed Raven!"

Chaloner nodded. "I *know* you did. You see, you jumped to the wrong conclusion about Raven – you *assumed* he'd come to tarnish your mother's reputation because he visited when your father was out. But poor Raven had come to discuss sugar with Warren. You killed him because *you* misjudged Margaret. By this time, she was in love with Bretton, and had forsaken all the others."

Francis rounded on Eleanor. "You said he was –" He faltered when she glowered at him.

"Eleanor told you the man she had killed was another of your mother's conquests," surmised Chaloner. "And you believed her

– which is why you were startled when I mentioned that Raven wasn't interested in women. You realized then that Eleanor had stabbed an innocent man."

"But it was Francis and I who offered to pay you if you discovered Raven's identity," said Eleanor with a bemused smile. "Why would we do that, if we were the ones who'd killed him?"

"For two reasons. First, you were confident that you'd left no clues – especially ones that could be unearthed by a mere digger of graves. And second, you knew everyone would think you were innocent *because* you'd financed the investigation."

"And how did I kill Raven, exactly?" demanded Eleanor with a sneer. "A small woman against a tall, powerful man?"

"If you never met him, how do you know he was tall?" pounced Chaloner. Eleanor did not reply. "You killed him with one of Francis's carpentry tools, which he leaves lying around for his children to play with. Raven's wound was oddly shaped, and will almost certainly match the chisel – and the chisel is sharp, because his son cut himself on it today."

Rector Bretton regarded Eleanor with cold, unfriendly eyes. "Don't you remember the Latin I taught you? *Fossor* means a digger, or a man who delves. And that's what this Fossor has done – delved until he found the truth."

"I loved my mother," said Eleanor quietly. "And she was dying. I didn't want the gossips saying that she'd entertained lovers in her last hours on Earth – and Raven came to our house when Father was out, so who can blame me for thinking what I did?"

"You admit it?" cried Bretton in horror.

"No," said Pargiter sharply. "She doesn't. Fossor has no real evidence, only supposition. But if she confesses to the crime, she'll hang. Conversely, if she keeps her mouth shut, no one can prove anything. We may have had our arguments in the past, but I'll not see my daughter on a gibbet."

He went to stand next to her, gazing defiantly at Chaloner. Francis hurried to her other side, and Warren was quick to join them.

"You won't repeat what you've heard today, Bretton," said Pargiter softly. "You won't want Margaret's name dragged through the courts – nor her beloved daughter swinging on a rope. And who'll take Fossor's word over a family of wealthy goldsmiths and the King's chaplain?"

Bretton hung his head, and Chaloner knew Raven's murder would never be avenged. Pargiter was right: without a confession, there was not a jury in the country that would convict Eleanor.

The rain had abated by the following morning, and the sun glimmered faintly through thin clouds. Eleanor and her father stood side by side at the empty chasm that had been Margaret's tomb.

"Fossor came very close to discovering the real reason why I killed Raven," she said softly. "That Raven only visited Cousin Warren because he wanted to spy on our family; that his real objective was to confiscate our gold and give it to the government. Do you think Fossor will try to do the same – for whichever churchman he is working for now?"

"If he does, I'll call on your services again," replied Pargiter. "Only this time, don't ask Francis to help. He's too stupid for games of deceit, and almost gave you away."

Eleanor smiled. "But Warren played his role well. He was very convincing as the desperate debtor, and is more than satisfied with what you paid him."

Pargiter was less complacent. "What about Bretton? Do you think he was convinced by what Fossor deduced?"

Eleanor shrugged. "He seemed to be. And why not? He loved Mother very deeply, and Fossor's erroneous conclusions made it look as though I was desperate to protect her reputation as she lay dying. As far as Bretton is concerned, I'm a dutiful daughter, prepared to kill a man and hide his body to save his Margaret from ridicule and gossip."

"Well, now the spectre of a murdered government spy is truly dead and buried, you can come to live with me again," said Pargiter, placing an arm around her shoulders. "I've missed you these last three years. Francis can live in self-imposed poverty – he'll never love me as you do – but there's no longer any reason for you to endure leaking roofs and smoking chimneys."

Both jumped when someone emerged from the shelter of the churchyard yews.

"I heard you," said Bretton in a strangled voice. "You didn't murder Raven to protect Margaret's name, but to defraud the government. That's treason!"

"Rubbish," said Pargiter scornfully. "It's business. And if

anyone ever claims otherwise, we shall blame the whole affair on Margaret – say she *demanded* to be buried with the gold as a way to stop the Royalists from getting at it."

"I've been such a fool," Bretton went on brokenly. "Three years ago you paid for my roof to be mended – not out of kindness, but to pretend to your Goldsmith's company that you were a reformed man after they fined you for coin-clipping. The repairs included fine new lead drainpipes – *lead* drainpipes. You used the lining from Margaret's coffin, didn't you?"

"It seemed a pity to waste it – lead is expensive," replied Pargiter with a careless shrug. "And we could hardly sell it as it was! People have admired those drainpipes, so don't pretend you haven't enjoyed showing them off . . ."

The rector suddenly shoved Pargiter towards the grave. With a sharp cry, the goldsmith toppled inside the hole, where his head hit the remains of the coffin. He lay still. Eleanor tried to run, but Bretton grabbed her and hurled her after her father. She spat dirt from her mouth and tried to stand. Bretton struck her with a spade, and she dropped to all fours, dazed.

"I don't want Margaret associated with any more scandal – or her liaisons discussed in a way that make her sound like a whore," said Bretton brokenly. "I still love her, and I shall protect what remains of her good name. If you're dead, you can't harm her, can you?"

He gripped the shovel and began to fill in the hole.

NOTE

Robert Bretton was chaplain to Charles II and rector of St Martin's Ludgate. John Pargiter was a goldsmith, whom the diarist Samuel Pepys considered a "cheating rogue". Pargiter was fined several times by the Goldsmith's Company for persistently shoddy workmanship and coin clipping, and his name was removed from the list of aldermen in 1668, presumably because of his fondness for dubious practices. A merchant called Francis Pargiter also lived in London in the 1660s, although it is not known whether he and John were kin. Thomas Warren was a merchant who traded overseas.

Shortly after the Restoration of the monarchy in 1660, there were many tales of exiled Royalists returning home to retrieve hoards they had secreted years before – some found them undisturbed, others did not. One man was alleged to have chosen his wife's coffin as his hiding place, and was reputedly delighted when he excavated her and found his money just as he had left it.

THE DUTCHMAN AND THE MADAGASCAR PIRATES

MAAN MEYERS

It was the ill-fated Henry Hudson who helped open up the area around the Hudson River to European colonization in the early seventeenth century. The Dutch established a trading post on the southern tip of the island of Manhattan in 1613 which, by 1624, had grown into the settlement of New Amsterdam. The English captured it in 1664 and soon after it was renamed New York in honour of the king's brother, James, Duke of York, the future James II. New York is thus a Jacobean city and duly belongs in this collection.

The husband-and-wife team of Maan (Martin and Annette) Meyers (both b. 1934) have been writing a fascinating series of books set at different times in New York's history and which started with The Dutchman *(1992), featuring Pieter Tonneman, the first Schout (or Sheriff) of New York. He returns in the following story, set a few years later in 1675.*

MONDAY

The man was slim, though broad of shoulder. Ribbons and beads adorned his shoulder-length black hair. He wore a green velvet jacket with elaborate embroidery, black breeches, and tall boots. Tucked into one boot was a long knife that had served him well in the past. His red silk neck cloth was extravagantly fringed.

Against his thigh rested a sword in a jewelled scabbard. In spite of his sun-browned skin, he had about him a foppish air. With his thin mustache he could have passed for a gypsy or even a Spaniard, but was neither. His birth name was Fernando de Souza. The men who served under him called him *El Jefe*. Or simply Nando.

Since Nando had already run out his game in the taverns along the Hudson River docks, where the rewards were niggardly, he was looking to a more worthy neighborhood in which to throw his final dice.

Every tavern in the port of New-York was packed with the usual crowds: Locals with no real reason to celebrate anything but beer or cheap gin, and sailors, few virtuous.

To Nando, locals or sailors, it mattered not at all.

On Manhattan Island thirsty sailors with their jangling purses were gulls for the taking. The curfew was kept by few taverns, but most of the revelry continued in dim light behind shuttered doors and windows, despite the intense heat. Nando made his way easily through the darkness.

The voice of one of the Rattle Watch drifted on the dead air from somewhere in the city as he made his rounds. "Half eleven and all is well. By the grace of God."

Nando was not new to Queen Street, or the Strand as old timers liked to call it, having observed its buzz without yet joining in. His boots crackled on the oyster shells that paved the street, as he viewed the towering masts of the flotilla of merchants in the near darkness, moored up and down the East River where only hours before the crews had unloaded alien goods on Manhattan's docks.

He considered the best place to set up business. On the beach? Or inside where men are drinking. Nando smiled. Where men were drinking, of course. Candles sputtered as he entered the murk of *The Queen's Stallion*.

A humpback was playing an English tune on a small fiddle. Nando rubbed the man's hump for luck and dropped a copper in his cup. He'd chosen well. The tavern's company of drunken men were all competing to overrule each other in a cacophony of tongues they had learned or mislearned plying their trade in the port of New-York, or on the high seas.

It was Nando's experience that two schemes were always better than one. He sauntered to the bar, a thick but well worn plank upon two barrels.

"What?" The stinking barman had a bald pate with a low rim of stringy white hair hanging over his ears. His nose was bulbous. He wore a black patch over his right eye.

"You the boss?"

A laugh sprayed spittle from the man's rancid mouth. "Ha! That's for certain. Hired help would drink the damned place dry in one night." He wiped his mottled brow with the back of his hand and ran his working eye over the stranger, who looked the gypsy but spoke English like a goddamn British Lord. "What's your poison? Gin or beer?"

"No, the question is what's *your* poison?"

"Beer's all right, but gin is quicker."

"Two gins it is." Nando scattered several coins on the bar. One was gold.

The boss of *The Queen's Stallion* poured and withdrew only one of the coins. Not the gold piece.

Nando approved. Greed was good but not obvious greed. Subtlety made life more pleasant. He pushed one drink back and lifted the other. "To riches."

"I'll drink to that." The man tossed off his gin.

Nando did the same.

"I am Vega. They call me One-Eye." One-Eye's nose gave a mighty twitch. He was of the belief that everyone had an axe to grind, but whether he offered the grindstone was another story. He had learned this years earlier as the proprietor of *The Red Rooster*, hardly more than a hut under a stand of pines at the third bend on the road to New Haarlem, but still a thriving tavern. While One-Eye worked *The Queen's Stallion* at the tip of Manhattan, *The Red Rooster* was tended by his younger brother, Two-Eye.

"What's your game?" One-Eye asked.

"Lottery. I am called Nando."

"Keep it straight, Nando, or you'll end up in the river with your throat cut. I get half."

"I was thinking more along the lines of one-tenth."

"Get the hell out of my tavern," One-Eye said pleasantly.

"One-fifth."

"Step away from the bar."

"One-quarter."

"Go stand at the door."

"Your loss." Nando set down his drink.

Vega laid a meaty hand on Nando's wrist. "If you are as hard as you are shrewd we'll make some coin." The tavern owner vaulted the bar and cleared a table of two snoring sots, tossing them out on the Strand.

Nando sat and set up his opening gambit. From his purse he drew three walnut half-shells and a dried chickpea. He barely acknowledged One-Eye who set the large gin before him. Placing the chickpea on the table, Nando covered it with a half-shell and began moving the three shells around with his slender, multi-ringed fingers.

Sure as fish swim in the sea he hooked one of his own. A large, sweating man with short yellow hair, too fat for a sailor, more likely a dockworker. The man took off his hat and fanned his dripping face.

The heat didn't seem to bother Nando at all.

"What are you doing?" the yellow-haired man asked.

"An experiment," Nando replied. "I'm seeking to discover which is quicker. The hand or the eye. Watch." He showed the pea going under one half-shell, then moved all three shells about the table quickly. "Where's the pea?"

"That's easy." The yellow-haired man reached out his hand.

"Not so fast, Zinn," another large blond man said. "The gypsy's after your coin."

"He won't get it with this child's game," Zinn said. "You can't fool a cobbler. I know how to use my eyes. I know where the pea is."

Nando smiled. "For how much?"

"Tuppence."

"Choose."

Zinn chose the middle shell. And much to his and his friend's delight his selection was correct.

Nando paid and invited the two to try again. Wonder of wonders, they won again. And again. When others joined the game, they took Nando's money, too. Not all the time, but often enough to think the gypsy a righteous chap.

One-Eye didn't care. All the players were drinking. And paying.

Nando was pleased, too. He beckoned the musician to fiddle for them. This time he put two coppers in the hunchback's cup when he rubbed his hump.

As he knew would happen, the denizens of the tavern were eager to keep wagering. Only when he had all the fish on the line, firmly in place, did Nando mention the lottery.

TUESDAY

The day began like any ordinary late July day in the year of Our Lord, 1675, in His Majesty King James's thriving city of New-York. Four days of intense heat with little to no breeze had slowed the pace of activity. Shopkeepers along the Broad Way sat outside their doors fanning themselves. Women brought buckets of cool water to their men from the many fresh water creeks. As flies and bees circled lazily, children and four-footers dozed. No dearth of customers in the taverns, however.

Even the sea birds were hiding, though every so often a double crested cormorant would swoop down out of nowhere and pounce on something in the water. One such sat on a piling fluttering feathers with satisfaction as it disposed of a wriggling eel.

Two women, one plain and straw-haired with a keen eye and keener wit, and the other, an olive skinned beauty, dark of hair and eye and fiercely intelligent, had boldly tucked up their skirts and thrown off their caps. They stood, legs strong against the pull of the rushing current, in the exquisite chill of the East River, which was not really a river but a tidal estuary.

Berry stained and dusty with flour, they washed their hands and arms, sprayed faces, hair, and throats, easing the heat. Under their watchful gaze, two sturdy boys, the older a golden-haired child of five, the other, three years, dark like his mother, but with eyes blue as his father's, played in the water beside them, not at all hindered by the strong ropes anchoring each to the stout oak near the shore line.

Several yards away a heron stood on one leg pondering the scene. And all the while the hypnotic currents so near the surface rushed the river ever forward into the bay at the foot of the island.

Keeping their eyes on the boys, the women climbed onto the wooden pier called Coenties Slip and let the sun do its work on hair and clothing.

While Racqel shook out her hair, Antje pulled in a fish from a hanging line, gutted it, and dropped it in a pail.

Many ships lay idle in the bay, for there was little wind to fill sails, and now and then the voices of sailors – those who had watch duty and hadn't wandered ashore to the taverns – could be heard calling out to one another. Despite the calm there were smaller vessels on the river their sails flat, nevertheless propelled by the swift current.

"I could sleep the day away," Racqel said, swatting at a black fly. She ran her fingers through her thick dark hair and plaited the damp strands before tucking the plait under the white ruffled cap.

Antje Ten Eyck, never at a loss for words, would have agreed with her friend Racqel Tonneman, and she would have had more to say had she not been distracted, first by a sudden gust and surging swells that sent waves over the pier, drenching both women, and by the two-masted ship under an arresting halo of sea hawks that was bearing down on Coenties Pier.

"Racqel!"

"Daniel, Benjamin!" Racqel, snatched up the fish knife that lay on the dock and dropped into the river. Antje was right behind her. Fighting the new currents they reeled the boys in by their tethers, cut away their harnesses.

They heard the ship ram against the dock they'd so recently vacated as they made for Coenties Alley and the Ten Eyck house. Almost at the same moment, the sun quickly faded under a dark cloud. Thunder rumbled north of the city.

Antje, fearless, came forward, cupped hands to mouth and shouted, "Ahoy, you aboard ship."

Her answer came with what sounded like the crack of a shot. An explosion of a sort. Carried over the water, the sound could be heard by most of the citizens of New-York. The hawks screeched, dispersing, when the brigantine glanced off the dock and rested as if it had meant to moor there all along.

The heron stirred, but waited. Antje didn't wait. She raced up the alley to her house and joined Racqel and the boys, who were protesting having to leave the cool water. After giving each a cookie, the women stood in the alley watching the excitement outside while what seemed to be the whole city came running in response to the shot. Within moments the shore line was crowded with people.

A loud clap of thunder, then a streak of lightning scattered the curious. Thunder, like the mad bowler in the hills, rolled over the city, then a downpour so heavy, one could barely see. When the short storm was over and the sun returned, people saw the vessel in question lying still in the water nestled against Coenties Pier.

Pieter Tonneman, riding home on the dry, dusty road after a day inspecting some of the buildings going up on land he'd purchased outside the Wall, was thinking what to do about the makeshift shacks that squatters and Indians had put up around and about outside the city. With New-York expanding as it was beyond the Wall, and three thousand souls settled here now and more coming every day, land was becoming a premium. The shacks would have to go.

His gentle dun mare Venus snorted and Tonneman, the man whom the English still called the Dutchman, peered through the dust cloud ahead. He reined to a halt and waited for the dust to settle. A cart lay on its side in the middle of the road, having lost a wheel, while a fine looking gelding, white muzzle, black otherwise, grazed in the dry grass.

Sitting on a boulder surrounded by bundles of goods obviously expelled when the cart lost its wheel, were two little dark haired girls, waiting patiently as their father struggled with the cartwheel. The man was clumsy at his task.

"Hallo, do you need some assistance?"

"That would be a fair statement."

Sweet Jesus, a woman. A woman in man's clothing, sweating like a brute, a man's hat clamped down on dark hair hanging loose over her shoulders. "You're a woman."

"You might say that." She'd responded in French to Tonneman's English.

Tonneman dismounted. "*Permittez moi,*" he said in his limited French.

"I thank you," she said, speaking English now but with a Frog accent.

He made short work of rolling the wheel back onto its spoke, securing it and setting the cart upright. Catching the reins of the grazing horse, he put the animal in charge of the cart once more.

The Dutchman removed his hat, drew his nose cloth from his pocket and mopped the dust and sweat from his face and neck, running the cloth over his cropped sand-colored hair.

"Mistress, where is your man?" He beckoned to the girls, who appeared the age of his two young ones, then lifted them into the cart. The bundles followed.

"My man . . ." she smiled as she said the words ". . . is a sea captain. Captain Isaya Spinoza. I am Lily Spinoza. My husband sent me to find a place for us while he brings his ship, *The Portagee Spirit* and its cargo into the harbour."

Tonneman offered the woman his hand, but she ignored it. As she climbed up on the driver's seat of the cart, the sky darkened. "Come along to City Hall, straight down the Broad Way to Queen Street –"

Across the city from the direction of the East River came a sharp explosive sound, like a gunshot. Tonneman prodded Venus forward. "City Hall," he called to the strange woman. Lightning streaked, followed close on by a huge clap of thunder like the wrath of God. More lightning, torrents of rain, and suddenly as it had begun, it was over.

Tonneman whipped off his hat, shook it out, and followed the surging throng as it pressed toward the East River dock near Coenties Slip. People milled around on the pier gesturing and mumbling. The law, Sheriff Gibb and his deputy Nessel-Vogel, were nowhere to be seen.

The object of everyone's attention was a two-masted vessel, square-rigged foremast with fore- and aft-rigged mainmast, that angled against the pier. Years back Tonneman's last ship had been a brigantine such as this.

Dismounting, Tonneman pushed through the crowd and saw that two Lookermans rascals were jumping around on the pier attempting to grasp a rope ladder that dangled from the vessel too distant for facile access. In fact, it was obvious that boarding the vessel would have to be done from the river itself.

"Belay that, you minnow ninnies," Tonneman called in mocking tones. "Avast, unless you want some great evil pirate to chop off your head and eat it for breakfast." He shaded his eyes from the bright sunlight. "Sweet Jesus," he muttered. The name of the ship was *The Portagee Spirit*.

The boys laughed, but constrained themselves. They knew the former sheriff was a man of good humour, but standing eighteen hands and weighing fifteen stone, some thirty pounds more than when he was Schout of New Amsterdam, Tonneman was a formidable figure.

"There could be pirate gold on board," twelve-year-old Cornelis Lookermans declared with authority.

"It's not your gold, is it?"

And from Jacobus Lookermans, all of eleven and already a man of the world: "What if there's a maiden in distress?"

Tonneman scratched his chin. "Now that's an interesting thought." Moving well onto the pier, he inspected the vessel. He caught the thick hawser line, giving it a sharp tug. It held.

"Ahoy! Anyone on board?"

No answer. "Stand back," Tonneman told the boys. The sea hawks circling over the ship did not please him.

The crowd of on-lookers, not content being at a distance, pushed closer, calling to Tonneman, everyone talking at once, everyone offering an opinion.

"Come no farther," Tonneman shouted.

"Make way, make way!" Jan Keyser, the tanner and notorious scavenger, elbowed his way through, followed by two of his sons. "What have we here, Tonneman?"

"A ship without a captain, or crew, it would appear."

"I claim scavenger rights," the tanner said. "Come, boys, we're going aboard."

"Stand back, Keyser. I happen to know the ship has a captain who might not take to anyone claiming his property."

"We'll see about that," Keyser said. But he stood back.

The ghost ship's groan signified that the currents were harassing, rocking, urging it adrift once more. A faint eastern breeze brought a foul smell from the vessel.

"You two, give me a hand." Tonneman made room for the boys on the rope. "Heave," he bellowed. The ghostly ship bumped the dock. He tied the line to a cleat, pulling the rope taut round and round, making it fast. Arse to the river, holding fast with both hands, he wrapped his legs round the rope and inched upward, hoisting himself onto the ship's deck.

"Halloo, anyone on board?" No response. The stench of death hung over the ship.

The hairs on the back of Tonneman's neck tingled. A line hung over the side. Taking note of its position he pulled the line up. It had been cut. The former lawman rubbed the back of his neck. It might have held a barge or small boat in tow. A seaman up to no good could have cut the line when he took leave.

Tonneman tied the bow rope off with several hitches and tossed the stern line to Lodowyk Pos standing on the dock. His former deputy grinned up at him and secured that line, too. Pos was now Captain Pos, Special Deputy to the First Councillor of the City of New-York.

"About time you got here," Tonneman called down to the short, muscular man with the fine gray beard.

"As Special Deputy to the First Councillor, it is my duty to look into all uncommon events that occur in our city."

Tonneman guffawed at Pos's posturing. He cast an eye about the ship, slowly taking in her condition. The square-rigged foremast was trim if not tidy, but the aft mainsail and its square upper sails were in need of repair. Still, all the masts stood well. He'd hardly begun his exploration, when the ship gave an almost human groan as the currents worked to dislodge it from its mooring. The air was putrid. Tonneman called again. "Anyone aboard?"

Only more creaking and moaning. Then a mighty splash and shout from the pier. Tonneman turned in time to see Pos's dripping head appear from over the side as he climbed the rope ladder. Tonneman gave him a hand and, like a four-footer, Pos shook the river water from his clothing.

"Seen anyone? Pos asked, emptying one boot after the other.

"Not a living soul."

"The stink tells me that," Pos said.

Tonneman moved aft, then up stairs strewn with shards of glass to the wheel deck. Finally! He reached for the knife on his belt, his only weapon. "Stand to," he shouted at the man hunched over the wheel. Rats scattered from the body.

Pos, who had come up behind him, spat, "Horse piss!"

The dead man, clad only in faded blue breeches, soiled with

blood, was lashed tight to the wheel. No life, only the ferocious scent of the dead.

Pos cut away the bindings and they both stood back. What remained of the man after the rats and the hawks had feasted sank to the deck, staring up at them with hollows where his eyes had been. One eye was eaten to the bone. The other was heavily blackened with dried blood. The handle of a blade could be seen buried deep in his chest. Not a musket ball. No blood on the chest. Tonneman studied the corpse. No blood anywhere but the eye. No shattered bone, not a wound one would suffer from a pistol. But what then was the source of the shot or explosive noise?

It was as if they'd been summoned to the site.

Were it not for the glint caught by the sun high overhead, Tonneman might have missed it. Gold. In the dead man's fist. Exactly what Keyser would have wanted for himself.

Tonneman crouched and opened the flaccid hand. Not a gold piece but something familiar. A small casing in which a tiny parchment scroll was inscribed on one side with Biblical passages from Deuteronomy, and the Hebrew word for God, *Shaddai*, inscribed on the other. A *mezuzah*. He had one similar, if not as ornate, attached to his doorpost.

He sat back on his heels. "Sweet Jesus."

"Like the one alongside your door," Pos said.

Tonneman chewed his lip and muttered, "Amen."

Standing, he called down to one of the Lookermans boys. "Cornelis! Run to Asser Levy's slaughter house and tell him he's needed. And Jacobus, go find Sheriff Gibb."

Pos chortled. "You'd think he'd be the first here." He picked up a shard of glass and sniffed it. "Rum, I'd say. What a waste." He sighed mightily and disappeared below deck.

Pos was quite correct. Tonneman could smell it now. Remains of a bottle, perhaps. He'd seen it happen. A bottle of spirits left in the hot sun could explode with the force of a gunshot. He followed Pos below deck.

Here there was no stink of rotting flesh, but rotting food, scraps of clothing and the dark stains of blood and shards of glass. The cargo holds were empty of whatever cargo the ship had carried.

The smell of rum was strong, but not a barrel to be seen anywhere. All signs pointed to pirates, who not infrequently boarded cargo ships looking for rum from the islands of the Caribbean.

"What do you make of it?" Tonneman asked.

"Pirates. Either they killed the crew or the crew joined them."

"I met a woman with two children on the road into town. Their cart had lost a wheel. Her man is a sea captain bringing his cargo to the city."

They climbed back onto the top deck.

"Let me guess," Pos said. "The name of his ship is *The Portagee Spirit*."

"And that well may be what's left of her man we found tied to the wheel."

"Hallo, the ship."

Asser Levy was as tall and broad as Tonneman. His coal-black eyes were deep set in a face darkened permanently from his youth in the Brazilian sun.

"You are welcome to come aboard." Tonneman lowered the ladder.

Though older than Tonneman, Levy was strong and agile, still working with his sons in his slaughter house just beyond the Water Gate. He dealt with the climb up the rope ladder with little difficulty.

"Mister Tonneman. I believe you asked for me." The leader of the Jewish community in New-York, Levy had thick features and a white beard. He was normally a genial man unless his people or his religion were attacked. He remained near the rope ladder, his nostrils twitching, uneasy.

"Thank you for coming."

Levi sniffed the air. "There are dead aboard this ship. I cannot be here."

"You are correct. I'm sorry."

The old man held tight to the ladder, anxious to leave this impure place. "Please tell me quickly how I can help you. Do you believe the dead are Jews?"

"One man is dead. I don't know if he's one of your people, but I found this in his hand." Tonneman showed Levy the gold *mezuzah*.

Levy did not touch the *mezuzah*. Bobbing his head, he mumbled a prayer.

Tonneman waited.

"A gold *mezuzah*. I have not seen one like this in many years."

"You have seen one before?"

"Yes. In Recife before we came here. There were those who –" He stopped, frowning. "There is a way to discern if the dead man is a Jew. And if he is, I will send my people to prepare his burial. Who is he? How did he die? Where did this ship come from and where is the crew?"

"We don't know. He might have been the captain of the ship or simply one of the crew. Murdered by a dagger in his chest. No sign of crew or cargo."

"Piracy," Levy said.

"Our feeling, too," Pos said.

"A strange barge came aground near my slaughterhouse this morning. Its tow line had been severed."

"Ah." Tonneman held up the cut line. "The barge might well have been tied to this ship."

"They could have come ashore last night. I will ask my people if anyone saw them."

"Couldn't be missed with their barrels of rum," Pos said.

"I met a woman this morning," Tonneman said. "She was travelling into the city with her two children. Her husband, captain of *The Portagee Spirit*, was bringing his cargo into New-York port. The name is Spinoza."

Levy sighed.

"You know the name?"

"It is a name that echoes in the history of my people."

"I will see if the dead man is a Jew."

"You know what to . . ."

"Forgive me, Mister Levy. I have three sons and if I'm not mistaken, their mother is one of your people, which makes them Jews. We follow tradition."

Levy did not respond. Since her marriage to Tonneman, a Christian, Racqel had not been accepted by the Jewish community, which was why she had prayed for his conversion, and why he had finally agreed to do so after the Jewish New Year. Levy knew this. Truth be told, Tonneman, who feared little, was in no hurry to take the necessary steps.

An angry yell rent the air. "Damn you, Tonneman, don't touch another thing on that ship. Get off, now. You forget who is sheriff here."

The outraged voice belonged to Sheriff Thomas Gibb. Standing nearly seven feet, Gibb was gaunt of body and face. His temper was choleric.

And in his stormy wake, in sharp contrast to Gibb, the calm and collected Deputy Eric Nessel-Vogel, who stood just a few inches over five feet and was so muscular he didn't appear to have a neck. The muscles simply went from his shoulders to his head. Nothing and no one distressed Eric Nessel-Vogel.

Gibb shouted, "I'll have you leave this ship, Tonneman."

"As you wish, sheriff, but first I must carry out a duty."

Pos followed his friend to the wheel house, clapping him on the back. "Do you know why Gibb is always in a temper?"

"Pray tell."

"Because he doesn't drink beer."

"I don't drink beer. Or anything these days. Why aren't I always in a temper?"

"Ah, that's because you have Racqel."

Tonneman laughed out loud.

"Tonneman!"

From Gibb's shout Tonneman could tell that the sheriff was taking further offence. The Dutchman was not happy with the task he'd assigned himself. But he performed it as he did every chore over the course of his life. One thing at a time. He pulled the dead man's pants aside.

"Poor sod," Pos said.

Tonneman nodded. The dead man was a Jew all right. But being one of the Chosen hadn't helped him any more than it had those who had been caught in the horrors of the Inquisition.

They returned to Asser Levy. The butcher was already on the rope ladder.

"He's a Jew."

Levy grimaced. "I'll see to it."

"I want to have a look at that barge," Tonneman said, placing the *mezuzah* in his purse. It may well have belonged to the dead captain, in which case it was now his widow's.

"Do so."

"And Mister Levy, if our dead man is the captain and a Jew, then Mistress Spinoza and her children are your people as well. I told her to come to City Hall."

"I will send someone to look for her." The old man climbed down to the pier and approached the sheriff and spoke softly.

"When and only when I've investigated," Gibb shouted. He grabbed at the rope ladder and missed, coming dangerously close to smashing himself between ship and pier, all the while cursing Tonneman and all who thwarted him.

Nessel-Vogel used the distraction to speak to Asser Levy. "If the dead man is one of your people, you may see to him after the sheriff inspects the scene."

"You'll have a look at that grounded barge?" Tonneman asked Pos.

"Of course. We can discuss it on the way to Whitehall. There's the matter of First Councillor De Sille. I was sent to fetch you."

"I will see him tomorrow. I take it you don't know what it's about."

"You take it right."

Pos was more than happy to accept Antje Ten Eyck's offer of a tankard of beer while Tonneman went down to the river and doused his head with cool river water.

Before he drank his buttermilk, Tonneman laid the gold *mezuzah* on the table and gave Racqel and Antje Ten Eyck a quick account of what had been discovered on the ghost ship.

"The *mezuzah* was in his hand," Tonneman said. "It was either his or it belonged to the man who killed him."

"I would not like to think that," Racqel said. But she knew it was possible. There were those of her people who could be as murderous as some gentiles.

"He may well have been the captain of the ship, murdered by pirates, the cargo carried off, the crew either tossed overboard or joined with the pirates." Tonneman returned the *mezuzah* to his purse and told the women about Lily Spinoza. "We'll see if Mistress Spinoza recognizes it."

"Poor woman," Antje said.

"Poor orphaned babes." Racqel gathered her boys to her.

WEDNESDAY

The arresting, white-shingled building, once Pieter Stuyvesant's Great House, now known as Whitehall, stood at the foot of Queen Street. As Pos knew well, Tonneman was never happy when he talked to his old boss, Nicasius de Sille. Impatient to get this meeting past, Tonneman raised the lion's-head door knocker and sounded it several times.

A tall young African slave with high cheek bones and a serious aspect, opened the door. His clothing, yellow satin breeches, ruffled white blouse, and blue waistcoat, resembled that of a European courtier. His deep brown skin gleamed in the sunlight.

"Good day, Mister Tonneman, First Deputy Pos. The First Councillor is expecting you." He escorted the men past dark wood furniture on Turkey carpets, their images reflected in mirrors with frames carved in gold leaf.

Before First Councillor Nicasius De Sille became so high and mighty, he and Tonneman had been shipmates together on the brigantine *The Princess of India*. Over the years Nick's demeanour and appearance had altered with his station. He'd come far with the English.

Nick had grown a flamboyant English moustache and was bulkier of form. He doused himself with great amounts of lavender scent, wore a stylish wig, and said "rather" and "bloody" and "damned" all the time as if he weren't Dutch but an Englishman born.

The First Councillor's office was elegant, with silver candelabra, satin and velvet on chairs, an ebony cabinet, and a French carpet. A majestic chandelier hung from the ceiling, its candles lit. The room was suffocating.

De Sille filled his pipe with tobacco from an ivory box, held a candle on a silver stick to flame the burly leaf. "Tea, gentlemen?"

Tonneman kept a smile on his face. "There's a murdered man on an empty ship at Coenties Slip. Let's get on with it, Nick. What can I do for you?"

"Bloody hell, don't you think I know that? I was expecting a shipment of fine Cuban rum. Now some damned pirates have stolen it from me. One hundred and ten barrels. I want you to get it back."

"Isn't that a problem our brave British navy could accomplish faster and better than I?"

"Yes. If the bloody thieves are still at sea. My spies tell me they are in the area peddling my precious cargo to the bloody taverns up and down the Hudson. If we don't act quickly, there will be nothing left of my rum."

"Bloody sad," Tonneman said, ignoring Pos's cough.

"Rather. What? Very amusing. Find my rum."

"And?"

Nick heaved a great burst of air. "I will pay you five percent of the profit I earn on the shipment."

Tonneman considered five percent fair. He doubled it. "Make that ten percent . . ."

"Done."

". . . of the total price you get."

The First Councillor's eyes narrowed. "Done."

"May the sun shine on all your . . . bloody . . . enterprises."

On the Strand once more, Tonneman saw Pos conversing with De Sille's slave. The slave gave Pos an oblong package. When Pos joined him, Tonneman said, "Help me find the rum and I'll share the fee with you."

" 'Done,' as the First Councillor would say. But I'd like a bonus. One bottle of rum for my own personal use."

"Done. What have you there?"

Pos removed a small telescope from the leather case. "I thought it might be helpful."

"Good thinking for a bloody English deputy."

Pos grinned. "Where do you suggest we look?"

"We start with that barge that ran aground near Asser Levy's slaughter house."

As Tonneman and Pos approached the Water Gate and Asser Levy's property near the Wall, a woman's pitiful cry pierced the thick and humid air.

"A widow's wail," Pos said.

Tonneman dismounted in front of Levy's house and tied Venus's reins loosely to the post, among other horses including the gelding and the cart whose wheel he'd replaced the day before. Levy came out on his stoop.

"Have a look at the barge while I talk to Levy," Tonneman told Pos.

"The dead man is Captain Isaya Spinoza," Levy said. "He has been cleansed and shrouded. We are awaiting only the pine coffin. He will be buried before sundown."

"The widow and her children?"

"The Nathans have taken them in. She is, of course, desolate." He seemed about to say something else, then paused, shrugged.

"Mister Levy?"

"Most peculiar, Mister Tonneman."

"You mean her apparel."

"Yes. Of course, a woman travelling alone some distance must be wary. We live in perilous times. Most of their possessions were on the calamitous ship."

"Perhaps she will speak to me. I would like to express my sympathy and return to her the gold *mezuzah*, which undoubtedly belonged to her husband."

Levy looked doubtful, but before he could respond, a group of women in black garments came from the outbuilding behind his house. Lily Spinoza, her face ravaged with sorrow, was among them.

To Levy Tonneman said, "I must tell you that Councillor De Sille has given me the task of finding out what happened on the ship. It seems that the cargo was meant for his warehouse. I could use the eyes and ears of your community."

"Of course." Levy beckoned to Lily Spinoza. "Mistress Spinoza. Mister Tonneman would like to express his sympathy for your loss."

The other women waited, bristling, like a small band of crows. Pieter Tonneman was a gentile who had married one of their own. Racquel had set a bad example.

"You are kind, sir," Lily Spinoza said, weeping profusely. "Kind to help me on the road and kind now." More sobbing. "My poor orphaned children."

"I believe I have something that belonged to your husband." Tonneman took the gold *mezuzah* from his purse.

Lily Spinoza gasped through her tears. She fell to her knees in front of Tonneman, clutching the *mezuzah* to her breast, ignoring the shocked cries from the other women. "You have brought me peace, sir. It belonged to his father and before that, his grandfather. My husband never parted with it. I thank you with all my heart and soul."

Casting a disapproving look at Tonneman, Asser Levy helped Lily Spinoza to her feet.

"Mistress Spinoza," Tonneman said. "What port did your husband sail from?"

"Madagascar."

"A long journey."

"They were to take on provisions in Cuba."

"Your husband's crew. Did he know them well?"

"Oh, sir, do you think –" She began to sob again. "They were not his usual complement. His own men had come off a long voyage and dispersed after they were paid. Then a contract came of a sudden with a bonus if the cargo was delivered quickly, so my husband, blessed be his name, had to hire a new crew."

At the Water Gate, the sentry dozed in the sultry heat, leaning precariously on the side of the guard shed.

"The Indians are coming, Kendall," Tonneman called. To his right were the river and the long pier to Levy's slaughter house.

Kendall blinked, staggered, then toppled over as Tonneman rode past. "That wasn't very nice," the soldier shouted.

"A fine guard you are," Tonneman said. "We could all perish."

Pos fixed the glass to his eye, looking north toward the tanneries. A wonderful instrument, yet nothing of interest appeared. He looked across the river. Again, nothing. But wait. A flash of colour on the rocky Breukelen shore that didn't seem pure, as Racqel Tonneman liked to say. Yes, indeed, a truly wonderful instrument. Breukelen. Of course. The cargo would be sold most easily to taverns on Long Island. They were unloading barrels from a barge much larger than the one he was standing on. Pos chuckled. He could taste the rum already.

No time to wait for Tonneman. After strenuous poling northward along the shoreline, Pos hid the barge in a spot thick with brush near the Dircksen farm. He scrambled up the grey stone slabs and shouted for the ferryman.

Not getting a response, Pos made for the barnyard along with dozens of fat pigs and piglets coming from all directions. Johann Dircksen, strewing ears of corn, was soon surrounded by his hungry pigs and piglets. Johann, like his father and grandfather before him, ran the ferry to Breukelen.

"I'm busy," Dircksen said. "I have a farm to run. You'll have to wait."

"There's no waiting. I'm appropriating your ferry boat," Pos told him.

"You say?"

"An order from First Councillor de Sille. I must get to Breukelen right away."

"And I must be paid."

"You'll be paid. Submit a bill to Whitehall." Pos was on his way down to the river when Dircksen called out to him.

"What?"

"When I win the lottery, I'll have no need for ferrying."

Thunder rumbled in the distance as Tonneman tied Venus near Levy's slaughter-house. When she nickered her objection to the scent of blood, he rubbed her nose and fed her a carrot from his ration bag, then walked down the rocky path to the inlet where Levy had told him the barge had run aground.

"Halloo, Pos?" Tonneman expected to see Pos dawdling about the barge, but both Pos and the barge were nowhere to be seen.

"Sweet Jesus!" Tonneman roared, loud enough for Josiah, one of Levy's sons, to come running along the extended pier that led to the slaughter-house. "Forgive me."

Josiah could barely suppress his smile at the Dutchman's discomfort.

"Have you seen what happened to the barge that went aground here?" "

At the young man's head shake, Tonneman continued. "First Deputy Ludowyk Pos? He should be here with the barge."

"No," the youth said. "The barge was here this morning. I saw nothing of First Deputy Pos."

Perhaps Pos found rum on the barge. Just like him to have a nip or two and think it a wonderful prank to play.

Tonneman was mounting Venus when Nessel-Vogel came along in haste. "Sheriff Gibb is on his way and he's fit to chew tenpenny nails."

"Over what?"

"He was told about a barge aground near here."

"Levy said as much."

"The Sheriff is certain the barge has something to do with the ghost ship. He won't be happy to see you here."

Tonneman turned his snicker into a cough. "I'll be on my way then, Nessel-Vogel. We wouldn't want to upset Sheriff Gibb, would we?"

Crumpled pewter clouds were darkening the sky. More rain

was Tonneman's guess. Venus slowed her pace. Tonneman reached down, stroked the four-footer's withers and whispered into her ear. He nudged her into a trot as he took the long way home along the Wall to the Broad Way and down to Queen Street so as to avoid the angry sheriff.

His boy Moses, sturdy, his mother's dark hair, but Tonneman's keen blue eyes, was sitting on their stoop waiting for him when Tonneman rode up.

The boy leaped to his feet and carefully placed "The Book Of Proverbs" that Asser Levy had given him for his tenth birthday into a velvet bag. Printed in Spain, the Biblical proverbs were presented in Hebrew on one side and Spanish on the other.

Moses rubbed Venus's nose. "Mutti said for you to come in right away." Venus, hungry, nipped Moses' shoulder.

Tonneman dismounted, patted Venus's flank and turned the reins over to his son. "Give her a good rub down before you feed her."

The air was baking hot, stifling. A torrid breeze drifting in from the river just made matters worse.

"Did you hear about the lottery?" Moses asked.

"What lottery?"

"Everyone's talking about it. Are we going to buy a chance?"

Racqel stood at the door holding a bowl of fresh water and toweling cloth. Tonneman removed his hat, lowered himself to the stoop, and washed the dust from his face and hands. She sat beside him, using the toweling to wipe at hidden dirt behind his ears. He quite forgot about the murdered sea captain, Pos and the barge being missing. He put his arm around her.

"Not here in the open," she said, though she didn't pull away.

"Why not?"

"Our neighbours."

"From what Moses tells me, everyone is more interested in the lottery than in us." He kissed her cheek and then her neck.

"Husband," she said sternly. "I have something of importance to tell you."

"Oh, very well," he said, giving her a final kiss on the chin.

"I saw the dead man when he was taken from the ship. He was not murdered. His brain exploded."

"Then he *was* murdered."

"His brain was not attacked from the outside. It was assaulted from the inside. It is my belief that his blood was pumping rapidly. It had no place to go, so it exploded in his brain."

"How do you know this?"

"I don't. I deduced it. From the few facts I had at hand. Mainly from the one eye that was destroyed and filled with blood. Apoplexy."

"Which is?"

"A rupture of a blood vessel. No blade or pistol killed him. Apoplexy ruptured one or more blood vessels and the apoplectic hemorrhaging killed him. If he was fortunate he swooned before the eye burst and then he died."

"But what of the knife in his chest?"

"I saw no blood around the wound. The knife was introduced after his death."

Tonneman nodded. This made no sense. Unless . . . unless someone wanted them to think the dead man had been murdered. Why? To create a diversion. While we were concerned about murderous pirates, what real event was taking place right under our eyes?

Day currents flowed south on the East River. The stream caught Pos quickly. His motion was sure and effortless as his oars propelled him forward with the current. He used it in dips and pulls to get across to Breukelen.

Pos feathered his port oar and dug deep into the water with the other. He passed the barge, now empty. They were so busy carrying barrels up the cliff, they obviously hadn't seen him rowing across, which was good. He counted six. No, seven. Two were Africans. He didn't want to take on the lot of them, but if he captured their leader the rest would run. He hoped. This required careful thought.

He came ashore well below where the pirates worked, dragged the ferry boat up behind a boulder and knelt, watching the scene. A sudden gust of wind blew his hat from his head. But there was no wind. He reached for his hat, which lay on the rocky beach and planted it back on his head. Again the wind blew it off. This time when he reached for it, he was surrounded by laughter. He leaped to his feet. He was also surrounded by men. All with swords drawn.

⋆ ⋆ ⋆

"You've won part one." Pennies flowed to the wagerers as they were assured by Nando that winning early meant they had a better chance of winning late, and they were convinced to increase their investment.

"No matter the calendar, no matter the day of the week, I call this Fat Tuesday, Mardi Gras," Nando said. "Let me see your ticket. Aha! You're a winner."

More pennies flowed. "Now is the time to increase your wager. You are fated to win even more. Happy Fat Tuesday. Happy Mardi Gras."

The city was like the famous Bedlam madhouse in London, or maybe, as Tonneman thought, more like the tulip auction fever in the Old Country, which resulted in a panic. His father had lost everything and Tonneman had to leave university in Leiden and go to sea. Now he saw grown men and boys running up and down the streets and lanes and alleys of New-York stumbling over roaming pigs, nearly run down by carts, selling lottery tickets and half lottery tickets, and one-tenth lottery tickets, while others shouted, "I won, I won." Staid married women sat on their stoops counting their puny winnings, wagering more.

Nando had cleverly set up Before-the-Big-Lottery lotteries, separate from the main contest. They paid very little, perhaps a penny for a thruppence wager. But they paid off often and noisily as Nando and a brightly clad boy, to the accompaniment of drums and cymbals and horns, demanded to see gamblers' tickets.

Tonneman stood on the Strand watching the furious proceedings, which centered around *The Queen's Stallion*. He shook his head in disgust. Where in God's name was Pos? He should have returned by now.

"Tonneman!" Johann Dircksen came on horseback from the direction of Whitehall. His cheeks were puffed up and red and he was bristling with anger.

"What is it?"

"Your man Pos went off with my ferry and never came back."

"How so?"

"Said he couldn't wait while I fed my pigs. Had to get to Breukelen on the First Councillor's business. De Sille says you're in charge. I want my ferry. I hold you responsible."

"Come now, Johann. You know Pos is not one to go off like that. Something's happened to him."

It was late afternoon when Tonneman lowered the sails of De Sille's yawl and beached it on the barren Breukelen shore amid sparse, dry grass, boulders, half eaten fish carcasses and empty oyster shells. Breukelen was a desolate place, though with so many new arrivals, people were taking land here and building farms. But, no port, no thriving business. He saw no future in Breukelen.

What had brought Pos here? And what was so important he could not wait for Tonneman?

A faint hot breeze followed him as he walked along the rock-strewn beach. The sun was edging toward the western horizon when he came upon Pos' hat. Concerned, Tonneman picked it up, looked it over, relieved to see no sign of blood. He shaded his eyes and scoured the cliffs, then called, "Halloo, Pos!"

At once there came a muffled response, but from where? It wasn't until he walked farther up the beach that he saw the upside-down prow of Dircksen's ferry boat nosing from behind a huge boulder.

And it was bucking like a goat.

He flipped the boat over and was struck by the explosive smell of rum. "Sweet Jesus!" Pos was trussed up like a Christmas goose, a red silk neck cloth in his mouth. He reeked of rum. Tonneman pulled the cloth from his mouth.

"Horse piss! Get me out of this. Those treacherous bastards soaked me in rum with no way to drink."

THURSDAY

"I'll have their heads," De Sille squealed like a stuck pig. "And yours for not moving fast enough."

Tonneman had just told Nick, "I guarantee that there'll be a barrel of rum in every tavern on Long Island, not to mention a bottle here and there where the tavern keeper couldn't afford the toll for a barrel."

Pos added, "They're going overland because they surely would have been spied at sea."

"Bah. I'll send soldiers across the bay to warn the tavern keepers."

"It would be too late," Tonneman said. "I took it upon myself last night to make a deal with Keyser. One barrel to him if he and his sons can find the booty and capture the pirates."

"That comes out of your commission, Tonneman," De Sille said.

"From nothing comes nothing," Tonneman said.

"Those damned pirates stole the telescope and De Sille is insisting I pay for it," Pos complained as they walked down the crowded Strand. The sun, already a hot ball of fire, had yet to burn off the steamy morning mist. "If Keyser captures them he'll try to keep the telescope as scavenge, that thieving bastard."

"I let him know that De Sille expects it back."

"You are a good man, Tonneman." Pos paused outside *The Queen's Stallion*, where a boisterous line of men and women were gathered around the gypsy Nando vying to buy lottery tickets. Children ran about screaming and barking four-footers chased them. "I think I'll add to my collection," Pos said.

"Collection? Don't tell me you're buying into this fever?"

"I picture my big winning, guinea upon guinea, a trunk full of them. I might consider taking a wife."

"You are all mad. It's the bloody tulip fever all over again. And you marry? May I live to see the day."

He left Pos to the lottery and inspected the idle vessels in the bay. A new ship had arrived in spite of apathetic winds. Its crew was busy at work on board. He looked closer. Well, well, well. No new ship at all, but *The Portagee Spirit*, and she was being revived by a new crew.

Who had bought *The Portagee Spirit* so quickly? De Sille, perhaps? He had the most money. But Nick had said nothing about it.

Tonneman was curious. At least the Widow Spinoza would have some money for her woe. He came down to the shore, where boys with baskets were digging for oysters to sell door to door. Shading his eyes, he saw a small boat put off *The Portagee Spirit* heading for shore.

He would soon get the answer to his question.

As they came close Tonneman was astonished to see Lily

Spinoza herself sitting in the boat, rowed by a brawny man with olive skin and a bright yellow cloth round his forehead.

"May I be of service, Mistress Spinoza?" Tonneman offered the woman his hand.

Lily Spinoza, in dark trousers and a sea captain's coat, swung herself from the small boat. "You are most kind, sir," she told Tonneman. "I am capable."

"So I see. How are your children faring?"

"Well. Babes have no sense of loss," she said. "Your wife offered to take care of them while I was seeing to my ship." Lily Spinoza removed her hat and fanned herself. Her black hair hung in ringlets past her shoulders.

She was an odd one, he thought. "Your ship?"

"Yes."

"You are preparing it for sale, then?"

"Oh, no. I'm hiring on a crew and I will sail home."

"Then you will sell it."

"Not at all. I plan to carry on my husband's business."

Tonneman saddled Venus and rode to the Water Gate. There was no sign of Pos.

"Have you seen First Deputy Pos?" he asked the dozing sentry.

Kendall blinked, twitched, squinted up at Tonneman, then pointed his thumb to Asser Levy's Tavern, just this side of the Water Gate. Pos' horse, head in the trough, was tied to the rail outside.

"No surprise," Tonneman muttered. He dismounted and stood in the door of the tavern. Pos was drinking beer, regaling all of his adventure with the pirates in Breukelen.

"Deputy!"

"Ach and my saviour has arrived." Pos drained his tankard. "Duty calls. I regret I must leave you, gentlemen."

Tonneman growled.

"You might be of better humour if you imbibed a tankard or two."

"I leave that to you, old friend," Tonneman said.

Beyond the Wall the noise of the city receded. Queen Street was the southernmost and lowest point of Manhattan Island. From there the rise was steady all the way to the northern, densely wooded hills.

Not too far beyond the Wall was a section of marshlands, low and wet, dense with grasses, rushes, tall, reedy cattails, home to mosquitoes, frogs, and water snakes. It was followed by a thick wood on the sharp rise of a hill, falling off gradually to accommodate Shellpoint, a deep, clear freshwater lake, one of the many basins that collected the run-off from the hills and brooks and provided drinking water for the city. On the far side of Shellpoint free Africans had built a village on land given to them.

Just past Shellpoint, the stink of the tannery hit them, all the more foul smelling in the heat. The tanneries had been banished beyond the Wall by Pieter Stuyvesant because of that very stink.

"Couldn't do this without beer," Pos said, gasping. "What do you wager the greedy toad has been successful?"

"What would *you* do for a barrel of rum?"

"What wouldn't I do."

Keyser's tannery, a prospering business, was on a knoll, and always a beehive of activity, what with his two sons, and their six apprentices all busy carrying buckets of water from here to there, scraping decomposing flesh from hides, tending fires which went day and night, boiling bones, making caustic dyes, soaps and candles.

The three buildings were open to the front because most of the work was done outside in cauldrons and pots with carts rolling back and forth. The noise was usually deafening. Not today. Though the fires burned, there appeared to be no living creature about except for the cats that prowled the site amid thick hordes of black flies and mosquitoes, feeding on large chunks of rotten meat that teemed with maggots.

"What do you think?" Pos asked. He was peering up the hill to where Keyser and his family lived: One house for Keyser, his wife, who kept milk cows, and younger son Willem, the other for his older son Adolphus, his wife, and children. A large barn was set well back of the houses.

Tonneman said, "I think we should see why all the cows are milling round outside the barn."

At the top of the hill they tied their horses to the hitching post in front of the house. Groans, curses and many voices came from out back of the barn. They nodded at each other and squeezed through the shifting cows to see why the beasts had been displaced.

Barrels. The barn was filled with barrels.

"Fifty-five, by my count," Pos said.

They slipped quietly from the barn and edged around back. Keyser stood over a massive ditch leaning on a shovel urging speed as his sons and his apprentices rolled barrel after barrel into the ditch.

The sound of Tonneman's sword leaving its scabbard didn't register with Keyser standing over the ditch. Two women, Adolphus' pregnant wife, and Freyda Keyser, and three children watched. Freyda Keyser turned at the sound of the sword. All industry stopped with her scream.

"Thirty-two barrels of beautiful rum," Pos said. "Buried in the earth for the toad's profit."

"Eighty-seven out of a hundred and ten. Not too bad," Tonneman said. "Nick should be grateful."

"He won't be," Pos said. "He has to pay you ten percent. And you have to buy off one barrel for Keyser. And then there's your old friend Pos."

FRIDAY, SATURDAY, SUNDAY

The sale of lottery tickets continued with steadily increasing frenzy before the Jewish Sabbath began at sundown on Friday. Tonneman, returning from his meeting with De Sille, could hardly make his way through the crowd in front of *The Queen's Stallion*.

On Sunday, the Christian Sabbath, the taverns were closed by law. Gambling was not permitted either and the sale of lottery tickets was deemed gambling by the First Councillor and the various chapels and churches. Still, human nature being what it was, there was no law preventing people from buying lottery tickets on the sly.

In addition to the boy, Nando had acquired two aides, Africans, tall, well built, their skin oddly scarred, their heads wrapped in colourful cloth. They stood over his trunks, guarding the coins of every description.

"Slaves?" One Eye said, not liking the look of them. Especially as the trunks and the Africans were positioned behind his tavern.

"Free Africans," Nando said, emptying another bag of coins into one of the trunks. "Sailors, they say, waiting for a ship."

"How much do you think we've collected?" Greed fairly oozed from One-Eye's pores.

Nando gave him a broad wink. "Enough for thirty taverns, partner."

Sunday night arrived with no respite from the intense heat and with the knowledge that the name of the winner of the lottery was to be drawn on Monday at high noon. The city was fraught with anxiety and avarice. Sleep was uneven. Taverns were filled with revellers. The heavens, laden with rapidly moving clouds, crackled. Occasionally a strange light flashed across the northern sky, but there was only a sliver of moon. Darkness fell heavily on the restless city.

MONDAY

One hour after the Night Watch called midnight, a sharp wind came up from the southwest, bringing great crashes of thunder, followed by torrents of rain that fell in such quantity the city was threatened with flood.

In the Tonneman house, a child screamed. Racqel woke from a deep sleep. Tonneman groaned. Two-year-old Daniel slept on a pallet next to their bed.

"Mutti." He gripped his mother's arm with icy fingers and climbed over her, then settled in between them.

"Daniel, are you having a bad dream?"

"The pirates are coming to get me and take me away with them."

"You're safe with us," Tonneman said, hugging his youngest, blotting Daniel's tears with the bedclothes. "No pirates here."

"But Silvie said they're coming for me tonight."

"And who may this Silvie be?" Tonneman said.

Racqel, bemused, said, "Lily Spinoza's younger child."

"A child's fantasy." Tonneman was quiet for a moment. "And who did she mean by they, Daniel?"

"Her papa and mutti, of course."

"Her papa is –" He stopped because Racqel had her finger on his lips.

"Papa, why don't you have a moustache like Silvie's papa?" Daniel yawned. He snuggled up to his mother.

"Sleep now, Daniel," Racqel said.

Even in the dark Tonneman could see her eyes fastened on his. "The dead man did not have a mustache," Tonneman whispered. "You say he died of natural cause." He eased from their bed so as not to disturb the sleeping child. "There's a stink in the air. The stink of conspiracy."

Rain played music on the oyster shells. Soon it lessened. Not the wind. With such a wind sails would fill and a ship could fairly fly . . . Tonneman looked out in the bay at the swaying vessels, their sails billowing. In spite of the storm, dawn was showing the faintest glimmers in the east.

The Portagee Spirit was gone.

Gone as well, as One Eye would find when he awoke on this day of supposed riches, were the trunks of coins, the two African guards, and the master of the lottery, Nando himself.

It was said that *The Portagee Spirit* was sighted off the coast of Virginia several days later, her sails full, heading south toward the Caribbean, at her helm a captain in a green velvet jacket with elaborate embroidery, and at his side, a woman, her long, dark hair flying in the wind.

TOM OF TEN THOUSAND

EDWARD MARSTON

The following is based on a real case, the murder of Thomas Thynne in 1682. Thynne (1648–82) had succeeded to the estates of Longleat in 1670 and was known as "Tom of Ten Thousand" because of his vast wealth. Thynne had been a friend of the Duke of York, but they quarrelled and Thynne allied himself with the opposition party, the Whigs, under the growing power of Charles II's illegitimate son, the Duke of Monmouth.

Edward Marston (b. 1940) is just one alias of the prolific author and playwright Keith Miles. He is perhaps best known for his Domesday series, set in the years after the Norman conquest, which started with The Wolves of Savernake *(1993). Of more relevance to the following story is the Restoration series featuring Christopher Redmayne, which began with* The King's Evil *(1999).*

FEBRUARY 12, 1682

The crime occurred in broad daylight. When the coach reached the main street, it slowed down and rumbled around the corner, its iron-rimmed wheels slipping on the frosted cobbles. Before it could pick up speed again, it was ambushed.

Coming out of nowhere, three men rode alongside the coach so that they could discharge their weapons at its occupant. Two of the attackers had pistols but it was the blunderbuss held by the third that proved fatal. It went off with a deafening bang and split the victim's stomach wide open. Blood gushed out over his velvet breeches and dripped on to the floor. Confident that the man had been killed, the villains kicked their horses into a gallop and disappeared at once from the scene.

Christopher Redmayne saw it all from a distance. He had just entered the other end of the street when the murder took place. He heard the sounds of shooting clearly and the horrified screams from passers-by. He watched the coachman pull the horses to a sudden halt and caught a glimpse of the attackers, escaping in the confusion. Christopher did not hesitate. Riding at a canter, he made straight for the coach around which a small crowd was now gathering. There was an uneasy feeling in the pit of his stomach. An aspiring young architect, he was on his way to meet a wealthy potential client at a tavern in that street. The closer he got to the coach, the more convinced he became that it belonged to the very man with whom he had arranged to dine that day.

Having leapt down from his seat, the coachman opened the door to find his employer doubled up on the floor. He was still alive but he was fading with each second. Christopher's horse skidded to a halt and the architect dismounted at speed. He looked over the coachman's shoulder.

"Is that Mr Thynne?" he asked.

"Yes, sir," replied the other.

"Is he injured?"

Without waiting for an answer, Christopher eased the man aside so that he could see for himself. Thomas Thynne was beyond help. Face contorted in agony, he made a futile attempt to speak then his eyes rolled and collapsed in a heap. The coachman gasped. Christopher leaned in close to examine the body. When he was certain that Thynne was dead, he offered up a silent prayer before taking control of the situation. Having sent a bystander to fetch an officer, he turned to the coachman, a stout man of middle years, deeply shocked at the murder of his employer.

"Do you know who those men were?" asked Christopher.

"No, sir."

"Have you seen any of them before?"

"Never."

"Were they lying in wait for you?"

"Yes, sir," said the coachman, wiping away a tear with the back of his hand. "As soon as we turned the corner, they were there."

"Can you think of any reason why they should do this?"

"None, sir."

"Did Mr Thynne have any enemies?"

"No, sir. He was the kindest man in the world."

Prompted by loyalty, and annoyed by people staring at the corpse with ghoulish interest, the coachman took off his coat and used to it to cover Thomas Thynne's face. Then he waved his arms to force the onlookers back.

Christopher asked for any witnesses and half a dozen came forward to tell the same gabbled tale. None of them, however, had been able to identify the men. It was only when a constable came running to take charge of the incident that Christopher spotted a short, thin, ragged individual, lurking in a doorway on the other side of the street. He beckoned the architect across to him.

"I might know who one of them is, sir," said the man, slyly.

"You *might* know?"

"If my memory was jogged, sir."

Christopher understood. "Who was the fellow?" he said, reaching into his purse for a coin. "Give me his name."

"I could give you his address as well," promised the other, eyeing the purse meaningfully. Christopher took out a second coin and pressed both into the man's grubby palm. "Thank you, sir." He snapped his hand shut. "The person you want is Ned Bagwell. He stays at the Feathers, not two hundred yards from here."

Christopher knew the inn by reputation. After thanking the man, he mounted his horse and urged it forward. He was soon trotting briskly in the direction of the Feathers, situated in one of the less salubrious areas of Westminster. London was a dangerous city and Christopher was always armed when he went abroad. In addition to his sword, he wore a dagger and was adept with both. He was not deterred by the fact that there had been three men in the ambush. They had not only robbed a respectable gentleman of his life. They had deprived the architect of a handsome commission to build a house for Thomas Thynne. It served to harden Christopher's resolve to find the killers.

When he got to the Feathers, he tethered his horse and went into the taproom. Filled with smoke from the fire in the grate, it was a dark, dingy, unappealing place. Customers looked up in surprise. The inn was not used to welcoming someone as wholesome and well dressed as the young architect. Christopher went across to the man behind the counter.

"Does one Ned Bagwell lodge here?" he asked.

"Aye," came the surly reply. "What do you want with Ned?"

"I need to speak to him."

"And supposing he doesn't want to speak to you?"

"Then my sword will give him some encouragement," warned Christopher, meeting the landlord's hostile stare. "Is he here now?"

"Aye – Ned is always here."

"I fancy that he went out a little earlier."

"Then you must think again."

"He had two friends with him. Are they here as well?"

The man folded his arms. "Ned's not stirred from here all day."

"I've only your word for that," said Christopher, whipping out his dagger and holding it to the man's throat, "and I wouldn't trust you for a second. Take me to him."

"No need," said the other, unperturbed. "I'll call him for you." He cupped his hands to his mouth. "Ned! Ned Bagwell, you've a visitor!"

A string of ripe obscenities issued from the next room then Christopher heard the thump of crutches on the wooden floor. When he appeared in the doorway, Ned Bagwell was a one-legged old man who let loose another stream of abuse. Christopher had been tricked. The man to whom he had given the money was already spending it in another tavern.

"Tom Thynne shot down in the street by ruffians!" cried Henry Redmayne in dismay. "It's a devilish crime."

"I mean to solve it," vowed his brother.

"I was at Court when the news came. His Majesty was greatly upset. Tom Thynne was a leading member of the Duke of Monmouth's party. It was his money that has been helping the King's bastard to win support around the country. There's your motive, Christopher," he went on, wagging a finger. "Some scurvy Roman Catholic has set these men on to kill poor Tom."

"I make no assumptions, Henry."

"But it's as plain as the nose on your face."

"Not to me," said Christopher.

They were in the parlour of Henry's house in Bedford Street. It was he who had recommended Christopher to Thomas Thynne. The contrast between the two brothers was startling. Christopher was tall, slim and well favoured while Henry's features showed clear signs of dissipation. As one led a decent, healthy, conscientious life, the other pursued vice in every corner of the city. Though he did not approve of Henry's passion for drink, gambling and lechery, Christopher was grateful for the many introductions his brother had given him to people in search of a talented architect. Henry Redmayne knew everyone of consequence in London society.

"Tell me about Mr Thynne," said Christopher. "All that I know is that he was very rich and recently married."

"Yes," replied Henry. "We called him Tom of Ten Thousand. How I envied him! Think what I could do with an annual income of that size."

"You'd drink yourself to death in a fortnight."

"That was not what Tom Thynne did. He was a sober gentleman but not without an eye for the ladies. The beautiful widow, Lady Ogle, was half his age yet he wooed and won her. There was only one problem."

"Was there?"

"Yes, Christopher. She let him wed her but not bed her. Repenting of the marriage, she fled aboard to Holland and is rumoured to be staying with Lady Temple. One of the ways her husband hoped to lure his wife back was to have a new house built for her. That's why I whispered your name into Tom's ear."

"We were supposed to dine at the Golden Fleece today so that we could discuss the project. Mr Thynne was murdered on his way there."

"The blackguards must be punished."

"They will be," said Christopher, gritting his teeth, "but I may need your help to catch them."

"What can I possibly do?"

"Find out who else knew about the arrangements for dinner. Those men were waiting for him, Henry. Someone told them when and where he would be at a certain time."

"So?"

"The most likely person is employed in Mr Thynne's household. You were a guest there in the past. See what you can learn at the house. The body was taken there. You'll be able to pay your respects."

"But I'm expected at the card table within the hour."

Christopher was decisive. "Solving a murder is more important than gambling away money that you can ill afford," he argued. "Get over there at once."

"I take no orders from you."

"Then take them from His Majesty. You told me how alarmed he was by the turn of events. This news will inflame those who hate the Court and its political friends. What better way to curry the King's favour than by helping to track down the culprits? He would be eternally grateful to you. Now ride across to Mr Thynne's house."

"Very well," said Henry, peevishly. He adjusted his periwig in the mirror then preened himself. "What will you be doing in the meantime?"

"Seeing what Jonathan has managed to find out."

"Jonathan?"

"Jonathan Bale."

"That gloomy constable? A sour-faced rogue, if ever there was one. He has far too many Puritan principles to be allowed in respectable company." Henry snorted. "A hue and cry will have been granted. Westminster will be crawling with officers. Why bother to involve Bale?"

"Because he is so tenacious."

"Too damned tenacious!"

"He once helped to save your life, Henry."

"Yes," wailed the other, "then he read me a lecture on the need to abandon my evil ways. The brazen audacity of the man!"

"Jonathan Bale is a godsend," insisted Christopher. "He's not without his faults, I grant you, but he has a gift for finding out things that other men would never even sniff."

⋆ ⋆ ⋆

"When was this, Reuben?" asked Jonathan Bale.

"Soon after I heard the shots being fired."

"And you *saw* the men?"

"I did," confirmed Reuben Hopkiss. "The three galloped straight past me and all but knocked over our chair."

"Did you recognize them?"

"I recognized one of them, Mr Bale. We carried him from his lodging here in Westminster only yesterday."

"And where did you take him?"

"To the Black Bull."

Hopkiss was a brawny man in his fifties with the strength and stamina needed to carry heavy passengers in a sedan chair. He knew Jonathan Bale of old but was surprised to see him so far from his own parish of Baynard's Castle. Bale seemed to read his mind.

"A certain gentleman has taken an interest in this case," he explained, "and he sent me a note. I was asked to search for anyone who could put a name to the face of any of the killers."

"Lieutenant Stern – that's what he was called."

"Lieutenant?"

"A naval man."

"And a foreigner to boot, then?"

"A Swede."

"That will make him easier to find. Describe the fellow, Reuben."

"Gladly."

As the chairman gave a description of the man, Jonathan Bale memorized every detail. The constable was a big, solid, serious man in his late thirties with an ugly face that was puckered in concentration. He and Christopher Redmayne had been thrown together in an unlikely friendship, and they had solved a number of crimes together. When the request from Christopher came, Bale had responded at once. Other constables had combed the scene of the crime for witnesses. Bale was the only one to wander off into the side streets. His encounter with Reuben Hopkiss had been productive. He now had a clear description of one of the attackers. He also knew where the man lodged and in which tavern he preferred to drink.

Jonathan Bale walked swiftly off to the Black Bull, hoping to catch the Swede – if not his two confederates – at the place. He was out of luck. Stern was not there and neither were any friends of his. Bale therefore retraced his steps and made for the man's lodging. Once again, he was thwarted. The landlord told him that Stern had left early that morning and not been seen since. That worried the constable. He feared that the Swede might have quit London altogether after the crime.

The booming of a bell reminded him that he had been asked to meet Christopher Redmayne at two o'clock. Hastening to Tuthill Street, he found his friend waiting impatiently at the corner. After an exchange of greetings, Bale told him what had been gleaned so far. Christopher was impressed with his diligence.

"I've just come from my brother," he said, nothing the look of disapproval in Bale's eye at the mention of his sibling. "Henry spoke to the steward at Mr Thynne's house. It appears that his master used to dine at the Golden Fleece at least four times a week. Those who lurked in ambush must have known that he would come that way sooner or later."

"Can you tell me *why* Mr Thynne was killed?" asked Bale.

"Henry believes that it may be linked to his support of the Duke of Monmouth's cause."

Bale frowned. "Yet another of the King's many bastard sons."

"The duke is claiming to be the legitimate heir to His Majesty, insisting that he has written proof that the King was legally married to his mother, Lucy Walter, at the time of his birth." Bale said nothing. Having fought against the Royalists at the Battle of Worcester, he remained an unrepentant Roundhead. "It provoked the Exclusion crisis," Christopher went on. "Monmouth is resolved to exclude the King's brother, James, Duke of York, from the succession because he is an ardent Roman Catholic."

"Then you believe this murder to be a Catholic conspiracy?"

"Henry does, certainly."

"What of you, Mr Redmayne?"

"I think that we should look to the lady."

"What lady?"

"Mr Thynne's wife," said Christopher. "No sooner did she marry him than she took to her heels and fled to Holland. Now, why should any wife do such a thing?"

Bale shook his head. "It's beyond my comprehension."

"I can't imagine your wife behaving so recklessly."

"Sarah would never let me down – nor I, her."

"Yours is a real marriage. Mr Thynne's, alas, was a sham. I think that it behoves us to find out why."

"How can we do that?"

"We begin with the Swedish gentleman, Lieutenant Stern."

"But we have no idea where he is, Mr Redmayne."

"Oh, I think I can hazard a guess," said Christopher. "Let's go to the Black Bull. He may not be there but I'll wager that someone will know where to find him. A few coins will soon loosen a tongue. If he is a hired killer, he'll have collected his payment by now."

"That was my reasoning," said Bale. "I thought that he would be spending his blood money with his accomplices."

"Perhaps he sought choicer company."

"What do you mean?"

Christopher smiled grimly. "Look to the lady," he repeated, "though this particular one may not merit that title."

Her name was Jenny Teale and she picked up most of her trade at the Black Bull. The majority of her clients were eager sailors who took their pleasure quickly in a dark alley before moving on. Lieutenant Stern was different. He bought her favours for a whole night. In this instance, he had come to her at midday and adjourned to her lodging. They had spent frantic hours in bed before falling asleep in a drunken stupor. Jenny Teale lay naked across his body. When someone pounded on her door, she did not even hear the noise at first. It was only when Christopher Redmayne's shoulder was put to the timber that she was hauled unceremoniously out of her slumber.

There was a loud crash, the lock burst apart and the door was flung wide open. Christopher stood framed in the doorway. Jumping off the bed, Jenny Teale confronted him.

"You'll have to wait your turn, young sir," she said, angrily.

"I'm here for Lieutenant Stern," declared Christopher, averting his gaze from her naked body. His eye fell on the rapier lying beside the bed and he snatched it up at once, using it to prod the sleeping foreigner. "Wake up!" he demanded. "You're coming with me."

The Swede let out a yelp of pain then swore volubly in his own language. Sitting up in bed, he saw Christopher standing over him and tried to retrieve his sword from the floor.

"I have your weapon, lieutenant," said Christopher, "and I daresay that I'll find your pistol in here somewhere as well. I'm arresting you for your part in the murder of Thomas Thynne."

"Ze devil you are!" roared Stern.

"Get dressed and come with me."

"No!"

Grabbing a pillow, Stern leapt out of bed and used it to beat back Christopher. The Swede then hurled the pillow in his face and, clad only in his shirt, opened the window and dropped to the ground below. Christopher had no need to pursue him. He had taken the precaution of stationing Jonathan Bale in the garden. When he glanced through the window, he saw that the constable had easily overpowered the suspect. Christopher gathered up the rest of the man's clothing together with the pistol that had been used in the shooting. He turned to leave but found that Jenny Teale was blocking his way.

Naked and unashamed, she gave him a bewitching smile.

"Do you have to leave so soon?" she asked.

"I fear so."

She spread her arms. "Don't you like what you see?"

"The only person I'm interested in is the man we just apprehended. He's a vicious killer," Christopher told her. "Try to choose your clients with more care in future."

Moving her politely aside, he went out of the room.

Henry Redmayne had repaired to a coffee-house near Temple Bar. He was deep in conversation with his friends when he saw his brother enter the room. Excusing himself from the table, he took Christopher aside.

"Really, sir!" he complained. "Must you always come between me and my pleasures?"

"Count yourself lucky that you are not Lieutenant Stern."

"Who?"

"One of the men who attacked Thomas Thynne," said Christopher. "I caught him in bed with his whore. He is now in safe custody. You might pass on that intelligence to His Majesty, and you can assure him that this crime did not arise from political intrigue."

"It must have done."

"No, Henry."

"The Duke of Monmouth has grown bold. The King exiled him yet he insists on returning to this country to press his absurd claims to the throne. Tom Thynne endorsed those claims to the hilt. He paid for his folly with his life."

"I think not."

Henry was petulant. "That's only because you are so ignorant about affairs of state. I move among the great and the good, and know how corrupt their greatness and goodness really is. What prompts them in the main," he said, airily, "is envy, malice and perverse ambition. There are hundreds of people who seek to pull Monmouth down. What better way to do it than by having his chief paymaster assassinated?"

"Lieutenant Stern has never heard of the Duke of Monmouth."

"Has he confessed who suborned him?"

"No," said Christopher. "He admits that he was one of the three men who shot at Mr Thynne but it's all he will tell us. That's why I must turn to you again."

"But I'm enjoying a coffee with my friends."

"Thomas Thynne was a friend of yours once."

"Yes," said Henry, blithely, "and I mourn his death."

"By carousing in here?"

"I gave you help. You can't ask any more of me than that."

"I can," returned Christopher. "Your aid is crucial. You can provide information that is way beyond the reach of Jonathan and myself. We must learn more about Mr Thynne's wife."

"Elizabeth, the former Lady Ogle? A pretty little thing."

"Why did she betray her marriage vows and flee the country? Had her husband been unkind to her? Was any violence involved?"

"Tom Thynne would not harm a fly."

"Then what made his wife desert him?"

"Covetousness," said Henry, knowledgeably. "The fault that mars all women. She left one man because another one must have offered her more than he could. Tom of Ten Thousand was outbid by someone with even more money and, most probably, with a title to dangle before her."

"We need his name."

Henry tried to move away. "I need my cup of coffee."

"No," said Christopher, restraining him. "It will have to wait,

Henry. You are part of a murder hunt. Something is missing and only you can track it down."

"Am I to be allowed no leisure?"

"Not until this case is solved. We have one villain behind bars but two others remain at liberty. Additional people may yet be involved but the person who interests me most is the wife."

"Any man with red blood in his veins would be interested in *her*," said Henry with a lewd grin." A most bed-worthy lady in every sense. Tom Thynne was by no means her only suitor."

"She must have preferred someone else."

"I told you – she covets wealth and position."

"Then give us the name of the man who offered it to her."

The second arrest was made early that evening. Bribed by Christopher Redmayne, the landlord of the Black Bull had not merely supplied the name and whereabouts of Lieutenant's Stern's favourite prostitute. He had told them that the Swede's closet friend was a Polish sailor called Borosky. Jonathan Bale went in search of him but not in the guise of a constable. He first returned to his house on Addle Hill to change into the clothing he had worn in his former life as a shipwright. Bale then worked his way through the various taverns frequented by sailors.

He was at ease in their company. Bale talked their language and shared their interest in a seafaring life. He met more than one man who had sailed with Stern and Borosky, but it was not until he called at the Blue Anchor, the fifth tavern on his list, that he actually came face to face with the Pole. Borosky was a sturdy man of middle height with a flat face and high cheekbones. He had clearly been drinking heavily and was off guard. Bale had no difficulty getting into conversation with him.

"Where do you sail next, my friend?" he asked.

"To the Baltic," replied Borosky.

"Under which captain?"

"Captain Vrats of the *Adventure*."

"I helped to build a ship of that name once," confided Bale. "She was a frigate of thirty-two guns with a crew of a hundred and twenty. But your *Adventure* is just a merchant ship, I daresay. What do you carry?"

Borosky talked freely about the vessel and mentioned that it would be sailing in a few days. Bale acted promptly. He enticed his new acquaintance out of the Blue Anchor with the promise of a meal at another tavern. As soon as they stepped into the fresh air, however, Bale arrested him. There was a brief scuffle but Borosky was too drunk to offer much resistance. He was marched off to join Lieutenant Stern in a dank cell.

Buoyed up by his success, Bale went immediately to Christopher Redmayne's house in Fetter Lane to tell him what had transpired. The architect was delighted to hear of the second arrest and, like Bale, guessed the name of the third suspect.

"Captain Vrats of the *Adventure*," he said.

"The Polander talked of him with affection."

"Did he say that the captain instigated the crime?"

"No," admitted Bale, shaking his head, "he swore that the man had nothing to do with it. He told me over and over again that Captain Vrats was innocent."

"What conclusion did you reach?"

"He was hiding something."

"I think we should pay Captain Vrats a visit."

"But he's aboard his ship in the Thames."

"So? You know how to row a boat, don't you?"

"Of course, Mr Redmayne."

"Then let's go out to the *Adventure*," said Christopher, reaching for his sword. "My instinct tells me that we're getting closer to solving this crime. We are entitled to congratulate ourselves – all three of us."

Bale was mystified. "All *three*?"

"Do not forget my brother."

"What has he done to help us?"

"Henry discovered that Mr Thynne was a regular visitor to the Golden Fleece in Westminster. All that the villains had to do was to lie in wait nearby, knowing that he would eventually turn up there."

"Reuben Hopkiss was far more use to us than that," contended Bale. "He guided us towards Lieutenant Stern. With respect to your brother, sir, he has not pointed us towards any of the suspects."

"But he has," said Christopher, holding up a letter.

"What's that?"

"A message from Henry. It arrived minutes before you did."

"What does the letter contain?"

"The one thing that I wanted above all else."

"And what was that, Mr Redmayne?"

"A name."

The *Adventure* was anchored in the middle of the river, its masts pointing up into the clear night sky like giant fingers. Two watchmen had been left aboard but they were too busy playing dice by the light of a lantern to see the boat that was being rowed out to them. A call from below alerted them to the fact that their ship had visitors.

"Ahoy, there!" yelled a voice.

"Who's below?" asked one of the men, leaning over the bulwark to peer at the boat. "Give me your name."

"Christopher Redmayne."

"What's your business?"

"I wish to see Captain Vrats," said Christopher. "I have news for him about a member of your crew – Lieutenant Stern."

"Has something happened to him?"

"He's been badly injured and cannot be moved. But he's calling for your captain. We promised him that we'd convey the message."

The watchman pondered. "You'd best come aboard," he said at length. "The captain is in his cabin."

Jonathan Bale secured the rowing boat then, in spite of his bulk, shinned up the rope ladder with consummate ease. Christopher found the ascent much more difficult and he was grateful that the ship was so stable. He clambered over the bulwark and stood on the deck. One of the watchmen held up a lantern so that he could study them carefully. Satisfied that they presented no danger, he led them to the captain's cabin and introduced them. The watchman returned to his post.

Two lanterns burned in the cabin, illumining a room that was small, cluttered and filled with curling tobacco smoke. Captain Vrats took one more puff on his pipe before setting it aside. He appraised the visitors shrewdly.

"What's this about Lieutenant Stern?" he asked.

"He was stabbed in a fight at the Black Bull," replied Christopher. "It seems that he was drinking with a young woman named Jenny Teale when another man tried to take her away from him. There was a brawl and the lieutenant came off worst."

"You don't look like the sort of man who'd deign to enter the Black Bull," said Vrats, suspiciously, looking at Christopher's fine apparel. "It's not for the likes of you, Mr Redmayne."

"Too true, captain," Bale put in, "but I drink there from time to time. And I saw the fight with my own eyes. I helped to carry the wounded man to Mr Redmayne's house nearby and he sent for a surgeon. There was not much that could be done, sir."

"Stern is dying?"

"He'll not live through the night."

"And he's calling for me?"

"He has something important to tell you," said Christopher. "He begged me to fetch you so I asked Mr Bale to row me out to your ship."

"I see."

Captain Vrats sat down behind a table that was littered with documents and maps. He watched them through narrowed lids. He was a handsome man with dark hair and a neatly trimmed beard. His command of English was good though he spoke with a strong German accent. He pretended to search for something on the table.

"Lieutenant Stern and I are old shipmates," he observed.

"That's what he told us," said Christopher.

"And he's no stranger to tavern brawls."

"He fought well," claimed Bale. "Then a knife was pulled on him. He was stabbed in the stomach. He's lost a lot of blood."

"You'll lose some of your own if you tell me any more lies," said Vrats, seizing a pistol from beneath a pile of papers. "I don't believe that Stern is injured at all. This story is just a device to get me ashore."

"Is there any reason why you shouldn't come with us?"

"I'm holding it in my hand."

Captain Vrats stood up and pointed the pistol at each of them in turn. Their ruse had failed. Bale bided his time, hoping for the opportunity to disable the man. Christopher took over.

"That weapon is a confession of guilt," he decided.

"I confess nothing."

"You ambushed Thomas Thynne with the aid of two others."

"I spent the whole day aboard," asserted Vrats, "and I have members of my crew who will vouch for me."

"Then they'll be committing perjury," said Christopher. "You are right about one thing. Lieutenant Stern was not injured in a brawl. He and Borosky have been arrested. They will hang for their crime and you will take your place on the gallows beside them."

Captain Vrats laughed. "Nobody will catch me."

"You can only kill one of us with that pistol," noted Bale. "Whoever survives will arrest you on the spot."

"What chance would one man have against three? As soon as they hear the sound of gunfire, the watchmen will come running."

"Then we must be ready for them," said Christopher.

He had been edging slowly towards the table and now made his move. Diving suddenly at the captain, he grabbed the barrel of the pistol and turned it upwards. The gun went off with a loud report. Bale reacted quickly. As Christopher grappled with the captain, Bale stepped forward to fell Vrats with a powerful punch to the ear. He then indicated that Christopher should stand behind the door. After blowing out both lanterns, Bale took up his position on the other side of the door. It was a matter of seconds before the two watchmen came hurrying down the steps to see what had happened. Bale knocked the first one senseless and Christopher held his dagger at the other's throat.

"Find some rope," ordered Christopher.

"No shortage of that aboard a ship," said Bale.

The constable left the cabin but came back with some rope almost immediately. He trussed up both of the watchmen then hauled Vrats off the floor. The captain was still dazed. Christopher lit one of the lanterns before holding it a few inches from the captain's face.

"Tell me where we can find him," he demanded.

"Who?" asked Vrats, clearly in pain.

"The man who set you on to kill Thomas Thynne."

"Nobody set me on."

"His name is Count Konigsmark."

Captain Vrats was astounded. "How ever did you find that out?"

"My brother, Henry, kindly provided the name," said Christopher, cheerfully. "He has a gift for smelling out scandal."

Gravesend was rimed with frost. The passengers who waited at the harbour that morning shivered in the cold. A rowing boat arrived to take them out to the ship. Before they could climb aboard, however, they heard the clatter of hooves and half a dozen horsemen came galloping out of the gloom towards them. Reining in his mount, Christopher Redmayne leapt from the saddle and surveyed the passengers. He was disappointed. The man he sought did not appear to be among them.

"Count Konigsmark?" he asked.

Nobody answered. Some of the passengers shrugged, others shook their heads. Christopher's gaze shifted to the man on the fringe of the group. Tall and lean, he had long, fair hair that spilled out beneath his hat to reach his waist. He was shabbily dressed but, when Christopher took a closer look at him, he saw how impeccably well-groomed he was. The man had poise and striking good looks. There was an aristocratic disdain in his eye. Christopher gave a signal and two of the riders dismounted to stand either side of the passenger.

"You must come with us, Count Konigsmark," said Christopher.

"But my name is Lindegren," argued the other, reaching into his pocket. "You may see my passport, if you wish. I am sailing back to Stockholm."

"No, you are fleeing the country to avoid arrest. The passport is a forgery. This, however," Christopher went on, producing a letter to wave in front of him, "is not. Do you recognize your own hand?"

"I told you. I am Oscar Lindegren."

"Then we will arrest you in that name, though we know full well that you are Count Konigsmark. Your countrymen will be shocked to learn that one of the leading figures in their kingdom is party to a brutal murder." He snapped his fingers. "Take him."

The two officers grabbed hold of the man. He was outraged.

"Is this the way you treat innocent people in England?" he protested. "You have made a terrible mistake."

"It was you who made the mistake," said Christopher, indicating the letter. "You should not have sent word to Captain Vrats that you were leaving Gravesend on a Swedish ship this morning. We found this in his cabin when we arrested him. I've ridden through the night to catch up with you, Count Konigsmark."

"I committed no crime."

"You paid others to do it for you and that is just as bad. And if you are as innocent as you pretend, why are you sneaking away in disguise with a false passport?"

Konigsmark was trapped. He was hopelessly outnumbered and was, in any case, unarmed. There was no point in further denial.

"Tell these men to unhand me," he said, peremptorily, "I demand the right to be treated with respect."

"You did not treat Thomas Thynne with respect."

"Mr Thynne was a fool."

"Yet it was he whom Lady Ogle married and not you." Christopher saw the flash of anger in the other man's eyes. "I know that you courted her as well for a time. Was that why you had Mr Thynne ambushed in Westminster? Were you racked with envy?"

"I would never envy such a man. He was beneath contempt."

"From what I hear, he did not have too high a regard for you either." Konigsmark scowled. "Is that what provoked your ire? Were you upset by slighting remarks that Mr Thynne made about you?"

"He should have remembered who I am," growled the other.

"Save your breath for the trial," advised Christopher, slipping the letter back into his pocket. "Captain Vrats is languishing in prison with two other villains. You will soon join them."

The officers tried to move him away. Konigsmark held his ground.

"I am a member of the Swedish aristocracy," he said with dignity, "and I insist on the privileges due to my rank."

"Of course," said Christopher with a deferential smile. "I'll make absolutely sure that you are hanged first."

In fact, Count Konigsmark did not hang at all. Captain Vrats, Lieutenant Stern and Borosky were found guilty of murder and were hanged in the street where the crime occurred. At the Old Bailey trial, Konigsmark was charged with being an accessory but he was acquitted. Captain Vrats went to his death with remarkable equanimity. His body was then embalmed by a new method devised by William Russell, an undertaker. When he was shipped back to Germany fifteen days after execution, the body of Captain Vrats was in an exceptional state of preservation.

THE PHILADELPHIA SLAUGHTERMAN

IAN MORSON

Just as with New York, the site that became Philadelphia was originally a Dutch trading post established in 1623. However the real birth of Philadelphia was in 1681 when Charles II granted a charter to William Penn. The town's name means "city of brotherly love", but unfortunately by the start of the twenty-first century Philadelphia topped the list in the number of violent crimes amongst American cities. Ian Morson follows that back to how it might have all begun. Morson (b. 1947) is the author of the William Falconer series set in thirteenth-century Oxford which began with Falconer's Crusade *(1994).*

1

After the death of Peter Rokesby – the fourth brutal murder in a week in Philadelphia in the sixth year of the city – the Middle Colonies of the Americas were in turmoil. Pennsylvania's famed enlightened tolerance had flown out of the window, banished by each honest citizen's fear and suspicion of virtually everyone else in the city of Philadelphia. Questions were being asked about any Papists who lived nearby. Or odd fellows like

Dutchmen. Or them redskin savages downriver. Or that black slave that lived in the old Hendricksen shack down by the docks, pretending to be civilized. He was surely reckoned capable of the most primitive of savagery. And truly, the murders had been uncivilized and savage according to all reports.

For himself, John Adams kept his own counsel, and the shack door closed. What else could a black-skinned, former indentured servant from the Bermudas do? Most people thought he was an African slave who had escaped the plantations in the West India colonies. And, as such, he had been made welcome in the Quaker province of Pennsylvania. Quakers were, after all, firmly anti-slavery. The truth of the matter was that Adams had been born in England, albeit of an African slave father, and had been a free man until sentenced to be hanged for a petty theft he had not actually committed. With his sentence humanely commuted, he was shipped as a convict to the Bermudas, where he laboured in the sugar plantations along with other black men who did not understand he was an Englishman, and whose strange tongues he did not know. When his chance came to escape on a ship named *Stockton*, he had taken it. The ship had eventually docked on the east coast of the American colonies, at a shore called Coaquanock. Deciding it was best to hide in full sight, John had settled in Philadelphia, the growing new capital of Pennsylvania, nestled between the Schuylkill and Delaware Rivers. The frontier-minded English Quakers had approved of his willingness to work, welcoming him into their industrious and self-sufficient community.

Or so he had thought. Now, with four men dead, anyone who was different was falling under suspicion – and John Adams was patently different, even though he dressed in the same simple knee-breeches and rough shirt as his neighbours, and favoured the tall-crowned and wide-brimmed black felt hat everyone wore to keep the sun off their faces. But the problem was his face was already dark, betraying the colouring of his father, and not his fair-skinned English mother. Though his neighbours' faces turned dark in the sun, they would never match the hue of John Adams's features. It was those features that faced James Bunce when he went to see Adams at his shack.

Bunce, the keeper of William Penn's Great Law in Philadelphia, knocked loudly at the open door. At first, John welcomed him in his usual friendly manner. The day was humid, and Adams had hurried home to cool off, before finishing the stacking of Bowater's produce ready for shipping. Giving Bunce no more than a glance, he pulled off his shirt and splashed cold water over his face.

"Come in, James Bunce. The door is open, and you are always welcome. You know that."

He scrubbed wearily at his face with a work-callused hand, feeling the stubble that had sprouted on his chin since the morning. Doubtless, when he had last drawn the knife-blade over his chin, he would have had no greater cares than ensuring the transport to the docks of Simon Bowater's hemp and flax. True, he must have been as uneasy as anyone about the deaths that had occurred recently. But he wouldn't have feared for himself. Until now, when he was to learn of Rokesby's death, and the suspicions that were falling on him.

Bunce stood in the doorway, unsure how to proceed. The ensuing silence made John cease his ablutions, and pay more attention to his visitor. Bunce had never been so uncomfortable before, and now felt positively shifty. He couldn't bear to look John in the eye, and stood in the doorway, turning the brim of his tall hat nervously in his big fists. As his feet shifted on the elderly timber of the porch, it creaked uneasily. When Bunce spoke at last, it was with a crack in his voice.

"John, I must ask you where you were this morning."

John Adams suddenly sensed the strange awkwardness that had come between them – a barrier that had never existed before. What he did not immediately fathom was the cause for it to be thrown up.

"Why must you ask that of me, James Bunce?"

Of course, in one sense, he knew the answer. Bunce was his friend, but he also acted locally for the Government of Pennsylvania as law-keeper. He was clearly at Adams's door in that capacity. What Adams didn't know was why him, and why now? Bunce gave a low groan.

"Don't make this any more difficult than it is, John. There has been another murder, and I must execute my duties as best I can. Besides, I am answerable to a higher authority."

"I thought the only higher authority here was the Lord our God." As soon as he said the words, Adams realized how bitter, how sanctimonious they sounded, and wished he could retract them. But they were said, and he could only hope that they would not irreparably damage his friendship with Bunce. Adams had too few real friends in the community to be pushing one of them away. For the moment, the words chilled the air between the two men, and Bunce chose to respond with coldness and formality.

"You well know to whom I am referring."

Adams did know. Friend Edward Wilson wielded a heavy hand of authority over Quaker Philadelphia. And his attitude sometimes set him at odds with the mood of careless generosity and shrewd self-help that characterized his fellow settlers in the Province. But his piety was never in doubt, nor his scrupulous attention to the application of the Great Law established by the Founder, William Penn. John Adams, however, found him a sour-faced, and pettifogging individual. Perforce in such a self-sufficient community, they had met on several occasions, neither man taking to the other. So it should have come as no surprise that John Adams should be offered up by Wilson as a suspect in a case of murder. But still Bunce was a little ashamed he had not immediately defended him to Edward Wilson, refusing even to consider him. Maybe their friendship wouldn't survive this. "Another murder, you said. Who is the victim this time?"

"Peter Rokesby, the butcher, who trades down First Street."

Adams was saddened by this news. Rokesby had been a good man, and maybe of all the Quakers in the city had been the most outspoken against slavery. Pennsylvania could ill spare such a man.

"How did he die?"

Without quite knowing why, Bunce suddenly clammed up, staring hard at his one-time friend. He was an outsider, and a black man, after all.

"Just say to me, John, where you were since last night."

"So it's from last night, now, that I must account for myself. Not just this morning."

The lawman lowered his gaze, but stood his ground. This was unpleasant, but it had to be done. The brim of his hat suffered under the increasingly sweaty ministrations of his palms. Adams sighed, and pulled his shirt back over his head, scrubbing the coarse cotton against his wet torso to dry himself.

"As you know full well, James Bunce, I have no one to share

my house and bed. Last night or any night. So you must take my word that when I had finished storing Simon Bowater's crops yesterday, I returned home. I cooked some corn-meal up and ate alone, read from the Bible by the last nubbin-end of my only candle, and retired to my bed when it failed not long after sunset. The passage I was reading, by the way, was from the First Letter of John – the Recall to Fundamentals. The call to love one another, as love is from God."

It was Bunce's turn to sigh now. This time with impatience. His friend was testing him, knowing full well that he was conversant with the passage in question. He was stung to retort in kind.

"Aye. And in the same letter, John asks who is the liar. Who but he that denies that Jesus is Christ."

Adams grinned briefly, having at least succeeded in riling Bunce, but then carried on with the detailing of his recent activities.

"This morning, after a particularly good night's sleep, I arose at dawn. I confess that I awoke with a murderous feeling."

Bunce raised a bushy eyebrow, spying a trap and not willing to be drawn again. Adams continued.

"Yes. As I do every morning at dawn, I desired the demise of Friend Wilson's cockerel, and an end to its tuneless crowing."

In spite of himself, Bunce smiled. He too would have liked to stuff the bird in a pot and broil it for several hours. The gravity of the situation, however, stifled any amusement, and he waved a hand indicating Adams should carry on.

"After rising, shaving, and offering a small prayer to God, I ate the rest of the cold corn-meal bread from yesterday, and repaired to Friend Bowater's sheds once more. Where I spent the day until now."

"Did anyone see you on any of these occasions?"

Adams felt a little sick in his stomach suddenly. It had come home to him that this was no longer a game, and that he was in very real danger. If his words were not deemed good enough, then he could be a suspect in this murder. And the three that had preceded it.

2

Adams racked his brains to recall if he had seen or spoken with anyone yesterday or that morning. If James Bunce – a friend – truly suspected him, then Adams was in trouble. The last time he had said anything to his employer – Simon Bowater – was early yesterday, when the elderly man had stumped his way to the quayside, leaning heavily on his stick. Bowater had been one of Penn's original settlers seven years earlier, and had been a widower past his prime then. But still a man determined to make a life for himself and his son in the New World. However, the work of breaking the land and making a home had not been kind to him. And he had all but given up, when a bitter argument had separated him from his only son, Oliver, who had disappeared into the wilderness on some mad fancy. But he had taken a grip on himself, and had turned merchant for others' crops.

Soon after his own arrival, John Adams had become his right-hand man at Philadelphia's bustling docks. Bowater still liked to see what his business was doing, though, and made it his habit to find his employee between breakfast and noon-time each day. And each day he brought him a joke learned from his collection of chap-books. Adams always laughed politely at the old jokes. Partly because Bowater had taught the adult Adams, along with his own young son and a native, how to read using the books. But chiefly because the old man was lonely and needed companionship. He quickly told Bunce all this.

"And you saw him today too?"

Bunce's question threw Adams into confusion. He suddenly realized he hadn't seen his employer today. He had worked hard at recording and storing the incoming produce in Bowater's warehouse, and had not noted his employer's absence. What is more, Bowater had seemed distracted yesterday, not offering a joke, but merely scrutinizing Adams's hand-written records, and hurrying away. Maybe he had been taken ill.

"No, now you mention it, I did not see him this day. I hope he is not unwell."

Bunce grunted, not to be deterred from his task.

"No, it is probably the return of his son that has distracted him from his labours."

"His son has returned?"

"Yes, did you not know? Ellen, my wife, saw Simon yesterday, and he mentioned it. And talking of yesterday, you spoke to no one else then?"

"I believe I passed the time of day with Peter Booth. And I waved at Ellen, as she passed the end of Market Street. On her way to you with some ale and a pie, I would guess."

James Bunce's wife, Ellen, was a cheerful, if plain woman who always had a pleasant word for anyone she encountered. It was she who had been the first to welcome the travel-weary Adams into their community. She fussed overmuch over her husband's lack of regular eating habits. Bunce reddened at the introduction of his own wife into the list of witnesses. Especially the reference to her propensity for bringing him provender, when he was on serious business. He set that witness aside to check on later, and pressed on.

"And this morning? Can anyone vouch for your whereabouts this morning?"

Adams wanted to ask when Rokesby had been killed, so that he might have been able to set Bunce's mind at rest. But he thought he couldn't ask the question without appearing to be a guilty man seeking a false alibi. The trouble was, his shack was down by the docks, and beyond the edge of the city's environs, which effectively hid it from view. When he had moved into it, he had seen this as an advantage. Privacy was a welcome relief after the communal sheds of the slave plantations on the West India islands. Now, it clearly presented him with a problem. From getting up and making his way to Bowater's warehouse, that itself stood down by the water's edge, he would hardly have been observed. Save only for a brief sighting on the riverbank of a man he only knew by the name of Cartaret. He was a stand-offish man, and aristocratic too – an unusual combination in Pennsylvania – and he lived somewhere upstream of the town. He certainly would never have deigned to pass the time of day with a black ex-convict, so Adams knew little about him. Still he told Bunce about him, adding however that he didn't suppose the man had seen him.

"Oh, Sir Thomas, you mean. No, I don't imagine he would have noticed you."

The implied insult in Bunce's reply shocked Adams, and indeed Bunce himself was embarrassed by it. He blushed, and stumbled on.

"Anyone else?"

There had been the Dutchman, Jan de Ruiter, whom Adams had seen hurrying along the dockside that bounded the eastern edge of the expanding Philadelphia. He had not concerned himself with what de Ruiter was doing at the time. It had been none of his business. But in the new circumstances, what he recalled of the Dutchman's manner and behaviour suddenly struck him as odd. Unlike Carteret, De Ruiter was on friendly enough terms with him, and would have recognized him even though he had been some distance away. His black visage was hardly commonplace in Philadelphia. But the Dutchman had ignored his raised hand, and disappeared into the maze of shacks and warehouses that made up the district called Southwark. Like its English namesake, it was a ramshackle area, home for wood-yards, boat-builders, and mast-makers. The Dutchman, who normally traded upstream with the natives, had little reason to do business there. Had he a guilty secret to hide? Or had he been on a completely innocent mission that had preoccupied him? Adams hated to implicate another man without reason, but told all that he had witnessed. Bunce nodded as he filed it away in his slow-working but compendious brain. Then, when he asked if there had been anyone else, Adams had a strange feeling there had been. But it was only a fleeting memory of a shadow that might have been nothing more than that – the shadow of a tree waving in the wind. How could he implicate the breeze? So he shrugged his shoulders.

"I don't know for sure. This is Philadelphia, James Bunce. Even if the local gossips think they know your every thought and action, it is easy to disappear in the crowd.'

Bunce acknowledged that the virgin capital of Pennsylvania was now as populous as some towns in the Old World. It would be hard to pass a day, even an hour, without brushing shoulders with the mix of humanity that had settled in Penn's province. The city teemed with over two thousand souls, and sometimes it was easy to forget the normal courtesies. Bunce was a Bristolian by birth, and knew how anonymous a big, bustling city could be.

Of course, everyone here was an individual with his own peculiar ways. Philadelphia was a community made up of independent souls, who had been deemed too good or too bad not to be troublesome to the aristocratic and religious powers who held away in England after the Restoration. Dissidents mixed with debtors, and the oppressed with criminals and other failures from old England. But overall, they were individuals, but whose common ideas on reason, and liberty of conscience drew them together as a coherent whole. And this made solitary people like Adams all the more conspicuous in the circumstances that now appertained. Bunce clearly found himself in a dilemma, not wishing to believe the worst of his erstwhile friend. Uncertain how to proceed, he chose finally to answer Adams's earlier question.

'You asked how Rokesby died. He was hanged upside-down by his legs like a side of beef, and split near in twain with one of his own cleavers."

3

The first death in Philadelphia had not initially seemed suspicious. Joshua Burewald had been out hunting north of the city. And it was only when he failed to return at dusk, that his son called on their neighbours, the Chapmans, to come to his aid and locate his father. Burewald was found dead in a ditch, apparently thrown from his horse. The horse lay nearby with a broken foreleg, also dead. He was brought home in the dark on a hurdle, and the close-knit Quaker community began its mourning. At daybreak, though, his son questioned whether the ugly wound on his head could have been caused by a fall. Doctor Söder was fetched from the nearby Swedish Moravian settlement across the river in New Jersey, and he confirmed that the shape of the depression in Burewald's skull must have been caused by a hammer. Edward Wilson and the other elders of the Quaker community rocked from the shock of realizing they had their first murder on their hands. The truth was kept from the other residents, while James Bunce, at the instigation of his elders, inquired most closely of those who might have resented Burewald's acquisition of land, and his prosperity.

Bunce had not even completed his inquiries before the second murder was discovered. Again, the circumstances might have suggested an accident. Silas Peters had a substantial stone house in the north of the city, which allowed him to travel daily by mule to his farmstead near Shackaminsing Creek. He was always a careless, if enthusiastic farmer, and his rural neighbour was not surprised to discover his body crushed into the good earth he had been tilling. It seemed as though he had lost control of his oxen, and the plough they had been pulling had been dragged over his prostrate figure. The body was brought to his city residence, and once again Philadelphia was in shock over another death so close on the heels of the previous one. The community again set about healing its wounds. But in the mean time, Wilson again quietly called on Doctor Söder's services. He was rewarded with the horrifying news that Peters too had been deliberately done to death. Bunce was as puzzled as before, though he did begin to inquire into the lives the two victims had led in England before their relocation to the Middle Colonies of America. Scarcely another day had gone, though, before the fragile peace of Philadelphia was riven by a third death. And it was impossible to put this one down to mischance.

The baker, Perkin Bird, was found by his wife stuffed unceremoniously into his oven. The fire was lit, and the oven hot. Mary Bird's early morning shrieks alerted Edward Wilson, who happened to live next door, to the likelihood of a disastrous situation. Though he rushed out into the street, he was too late to prevent his neighbours from emerging from their houses too. Several men entered the bakery, and quickly emerged pale-faced, followed by the nauseous stench of the baker's self-immolation. One man vomited a mess of breakfast bread and ale over Wilson's best buckle shoes. The secret was out, despite James Bunce's best efforts, and soon everyone knew that a savage murderer was loose in Philadelphia. Someone spoke of wholesale slaughter, and a name was born.

The Philadelphia Slaughterman.

4

John Adams realized his hard-won peace was shattered, and he sat down on the porch, staring over the reeds that edged the shallow river bank. Bunce had hunkered down on the porch steps, also scanning the river as he thought. Adams looked at the back of his friend's head, wondering if James Bunce was thinking of arresting his one-time friend. Even as he rose from his chair, he knew what he had to do. He had to find a name for the murderer that would satisfy Friends Wilson and Bunce. Preferably not his own. Hearing Adams move, Bunce rose too and turned, quick and effortless for such a tall man. Adams had the impression Bunce was afraid now to have his back to his old friend, and that made him sad. Their eyes met, and they stared at each other in something of a silent duel. It was Bunce who spoke first.

"Well, if I am to question all the men in the vicinity of the murder, I might as well begin with finding out what de Ruiter was doing when he turned his back on you this morning."

The morning of Rokesby's death, thought Adams.

"And I will come too. I can help."

Despite Bunce's protestations, Adams would not back down, and both men resolved to get on with their task immediately. The afternoon stretched before them, and Adams's duties at Bowater's warehouse could wait. Besides, he wanted to know what was afoot, and reckoned he knew where de Ruiter was.

"We should try down by the river."

Bunce grunted, and crammed his hat on his head. Adams stopped only to carve off a hunk of bread, and fill a flask of water, thrusting both into a small gunny-sack. Though he hoped de Ruiter would still be in Southwark, if he wasn't, the Dutchman's house was some way upriver at Pegg's Run. So Adams was uncertain how long their search for him would take. As Bunce stepped through the shack door, Adams turned back quickly, and picked up the knife he had used to cut the bread. A little self-consciously, he jammed it in the belt round his waist, slung the sack over his shoulder, and followed Bunce into the grey river mist.

Mindful of his experience of the Great Fire of London, William Penn had laid out Philadelphia on a grid pattern with grand avenues and public parks. But even the noblest of intentions had to give way somewhere to the practicalities of nature. Pennsylvania relied on trade with the Old Country, and trade required ships. Ships meant boat-builders, and sailors, so just like London and Bristol before it, Philadelphia had spawned an undesirable underside along the shoreline. This denizen of boat-builders, mast-makers, and sailors waiting for a berth and fair weather, lay to the east of the neat and regular city. It clung to the sinuous curves of the Delaware River, whose creeks in places cut into the straight lines of Philadelphia's streets like vicious scars on an otherwise perfect skin. Dock Creek was one of those scars, housing a stinking brewery and the Blue Anchor tavern. Honest citizens were rarely seen in its vicinity. It was there that John Adams expected to find Jan de Ruiter.

As the men skirted past the noise and bustle of the shipwrights' yards, Adams kept his head down, and his wide-brimmed hat firmly pulled low. The less he was seen the better, especially if the word was out that he was under a cloud of suspicion over the Slaughterman's murders. The mingled smoke of singeing wood and bubbling tar drifted across their tracks as they hurried up the creek to the door of the tavern. Inside, the fug of old tobacco smoke hanging beneath the low beamed ceiling couldn't hide the fact that the Blue Anchor was unusually quiet. A few sailors were slumped in one corner, but they were already dead to the world, their drinking session having culminated in stupefaction. Maybe they were celebrating their imminent departure from this now dangerous city. But apart from them, there were few other drinkers. The Slaughterman's deeds were obviously bad for trade. Their quarry therefore was not difficult to spot. Jan de Ruiter was sitting at the rough trestle at one end of the room, behind which stood three barrels of home-brewed ale. The short, squinty-eyed man with whom he was conversing threw a glance at Bunce as he entered with the black man close behind, and then quickly departed by way of the rear door. Adams wondered if his undeserved reputation had preceded him. De Ruiter leered at them, and waved them over.

"James Bunce. John Adams. Come here, and have a drink with me.'

By the sound of his voice, and the smell of his breath, Bunce guessed that the Dutchman had been in the Blue Anchor since Adams had seen him that morning. His eyes were clouded with drink, and Bunce hoped this would help his investigation. Maybe the Dutchman was in a state in which he might inadvertently reveal whatever he had been up to that morning. He took up de Ruiter's offer of a tankard of ale, and when it arrived, swallowed deeply of the watery, bitter brew. Adams, who had hung back at first, suddenly leaned into the Dutchman's face.

"You ignored me this morning, Jan de Ruiter. Are we not friends any more?"

Jan peered closely at Adams, screwing his eyes up as if trying to focus on who the man was.

"This morning? I don't recall seeing you."

Despite Bunce's warning hiss, Adams wasn't to be put off that easily. De Ruiter had definitely stopped and stared before turning away, and disappearing down towards Dock Creek and the shipyards.

"That's strange, because I saw you."

"Where did you think you saw me, Adams? I was not in the town. This morning I came downriver by flat barge from my house."

Now Adams knew the man was lying. He had seen him in First Street for sure, and the Dutchman had been coming from the direction of Market Street, where Rokesby's butchery stood. De Ruiter leaned drunkenly forwards, pushing his whiskery face into Adams's, and grinning. He tapped the side of his bulbous nose, turning the tables on his examiner.

"Hunting for a defence, are we? A witness?" He turned to Bunce, who had stood aside, angry that his friend had spoiled his planned interrogation. "I hear a little rumour that James Bunce, here, has already looked no further than Hendricksen's shack for Rokesby's murderer."

A cold shiver ran down Adams's back. Was the rumour already spreading so fast, that de Ruiter had heard even without leaving the tavern? The Dutchman must have sensed Adams's fear, and he drove his advantage home. He squeezed Adams's arm, and whispered into his ear with a beery exhalation.

"Pity. I was betting on you being innocent." Once again, he addressed Bunce, a sly look in his eyes. "Myself, I would have gambled on it being some damned Papist. Isn't it barely ten years since their plotting with your very own monarch was revealed?"

Bunce knew to what the Dutchman was referring, even though he had been no more than a child himself at the time. But then, everyone had heard the rumours from the highest to the lowest in the land. The wild claims from Titus Oates of Papist conspiracies at the heart of power had struck a chord in England. And, despite few facts supporting Oates coming to light, many Catholics had lost their lives in the panic that ensued. Many others had fled the country. Bunce felt sick at the thought of Popish conspiracies in the colonies, and pulled the Dutchman's hand off his arm. Had the taint of the Old World crossed the ocean already, and was it staining the New? Were all the old prejudices still to be found in men's hearts, after all? De Ruiter seemed to think so, for he yelled out his accusations so that anyone could hear.

'It's a Popish plot, mark my words. These murders are revenge for what happened in your country to the Catholics. Go ask that Carteret fellow."

Adams turned away in disgust from the drunken de Ruiter, striding out of the tavern. As he passed them, he saw that the sailors had been roused from their stupor, and were examining him with suspicious, if bleary, eyes. He wondered if everyone would look at him in the same way now. Bunce hurried after him with the Dutchman's final vituperations ringing in his ears.

"Yes, a Papist conspiracy. It doesn't make sense otherwise."

As Bunce crossed the threshold, he nearly tripped over a hunched-up figure by the door. The man, wrapped in a deer skin, seemed oblivious to Bunce's foot crashing into his backside, only mumbling some incomprehensible words. Bunce realized it was the Delaware redskin called Teinane, who drifted round the periphery of Philadelphia like a lost soul. Most of his tribe had retreated further off into the wilderness, but Teinane seemed incapable of leaving, incapable of seeing the unreasonableness of his behaviour. Young Oliver Bowater, before his disappearance, had apparently tried to reason with Teinane. But it had only resulted in a scuffle that Bunce had been forced to break up. But mostly, the Quaker community tolerated him. Bunce now did the same, stepping over his prostrate form, and striding down the darkening lane towards the river and John Adams. He could barely contain his anger, as he grabbed Adams's arm, and swung him round to face him.

"Don't do that again. You must leave the interrogations to me. Now de Ruiter is informed of my suspicions, and will be on his guard when I speak to him next."

The import of his last words was unspoken, but clear to Adams. Next time de Ruiter was questioned, Bunce would be on his own. Crestfallen, he nodded his head, not wishing to be further barred from the investigation. He had good reason to be more than eager to get to the truth. Once before, in England, he had been convicted of a crime he had not committed. The same was not going to happen to him in the New World. Adams guessed that this man Carteret might be their next port of call. As Bunce had called him Sir Thomas, and sounded almost deferential, Adams most definitely wanted to be present when they tested out this paragon of virtue.

5

The sun began to set as the two men hurried down the Old York Road, the main thoroughfare running north across the province. Adams soon dropped behind James Bunce, failing to match the tall man's long, loping stride. When Bunce turned off the dirt road though, and plunged into the woods, Adams hurried to close up with his companion. Some of the Quakers may have imagined a black man would be at home in the wild, but John Adams was a denizen of the city – a Londoner born and bred. And it was at times like this that he missed the dirty, stinking streets of his childhood, the closeness of overhanging tenements, and the proximity of fellow humans. Ironically, he would not have lost his way in the mazy alleys and courtyards of that greatest of cities on Earth. But now, after nearly an hour amongst the trees of the wilderness north of town, he was thrashing his way blindly through prickly undergrowth that grabbed at his shirt, and dragged at his stockings. He would have been lost without Bunce, and thought them both completely alone. Until he saw a shadow in the trees some twenty yards away that moved, and resolved into a human shape.

His hand went to the knife at his belt, for he got the impression the figure was stark naked. Was it one of the few Delaware native savages who roamed the wilderness still? Thoughts of the savage Teinane, and four dead settlers flashed through his mind. He called out to Bunce, but even as the tall man stopped to look over his shoulder, the shadow dissolved into nothing.

"What is it, John?"

"I thought I saw . . . It's nothing. Nothing at all. Just my imagination."

Yet even as he spoke, Adams felt a cold shiver run up his back. He was not normally afraid without a reason, but the fleeting presence seemed an omen of doom. He hurried over to Bunce, and for a few minutes more, the two men walked closer together. Then Bunce stopped, and sniffed the air.

"We are nearly there. You can smell the odour of the tan yards at Pegg's Run. It is not much further to Cohocksink Creek, where Carteret's house stands."

Adams smelled the air. It was true – the rancid stench of the tannery was getting overpowering the closer they got. And as they passed the yard, an evil-looking miasma rose from the tanning pits. Each oblong opening resembled nothing less than a yawning grave. Adams's fevered imagination conjured up the body of Peter Rokesby, his torso virtually sundered, rising from one of them. Followed by a battered Joshua Burewald and Silas Peters, their brains dripping out of their skulls, and finally a lobsterish, half-cooked Perkin Bird. But as he wiped his face, he saw it was just vapours and steam that drifted over him. The sharp, acrid odour of the fluids ate at the back of Adams's throat, and before he could stop himself he hacked, and spat on the ground. He shouldered his gunny sack of provisions, and hurried on to catch up to Bunce. After another quarter hour of walking, they saw the yellow glow of a light in the window of a house.

The lamplight looked inviting, but as they approached, a gust of harsh laughter from inside told them instinctively to keep to the shadows. They skirted round the cleared perimeter of the imposing stone building, and moved ever closer to the riverbank, where Adams could see a flat barge moored. In the dark, he missed his footing and slid partway down the muddy bank. Involuntarily, he cried out, just as Bunce grabbed at his arm. Moments later, the door of Carteret's house was flung open, and the slim Englishman stepped on to the porch, holding up a lantern to the darkness. Bunce could see the yellowish glow reflected in Carteret's staring eyes, and thought it gave him the look of the Devil Himself. He ducked his head, and slid down the bank of the river to join Adams in hiding. Both men crouched ankle-deep in soft cloying mud. The look in the nobleman's eyes had the stare of someone fearful of discovery. It convinced Bunce that Carteret was up to no good. Moreover, he had co-conspirators in the house, who even now called out to him in faltering English.

"It's ghosts. Them redskin savages do say as how they live in the upper air for years before they settle in heaven."

"Shut up. I'm listening."

Carteret's retort was sharp, and peremptory.

Both men held their breath, wondering if Carteret would come down to the riverbank. If he did, they were sure to be discovered. Then, just as they heard Carteret stepping down off his creaky porch, one of the men inside called out something in a heavily accented tongue that made the others laugh. Adams didn't understand it, but knew it was a Frenchman who had spoken. He had laboured in Shadwell docks in the Old Country, and encountered sailors of many nationalities, including Frenchies. The tongue was distinctive. So, Carteret was entertaining some of England's oldest rivals on this new continent. Though the French travelled down the St Lawrence River far to the north, trading in furs, and their contact with the English settlers was rare, still the Old World enmity persisted.

All this made the gathering most interesting to Bunce. Especially as the Frenchies' inclinations were to be Catholic and Royalist, like their host, Sir Thomas Carteret. The two countries were still maritime rivals, but King Charles had supported Roman Catholic France in its struggle with the Dutch Protestant Republic. Neither man's knowledge of the French language was good enough to know what comment had been made to the Englishman. They did understand Carteret's reply, though.

"Very well. Have your joke, if you must. But I'd like to see which of you would dare face even one Englishman in the dark, if he rose up from the dead."

The words disturbed Bunce. Was Carteret referring to the dead men in Philadelphia? Did he know more than he was saying? Maybe he and the men inside his house, with good reason to hate Dissenters and Englishmen, were implicated. He risked a peep over the edge of the riverbank, only to witness Carteret cast a final devilish look into the dark before closing his door again. Adams felt sure they had been seen, but dared not move for fear of being discovered. It seemed like an age, with the muddy waters of the river chilling both men's legs, before three men emerged from the front door, and stood shaking Carteret's hand. They loped down to the river bank just upstream from where Bunce and Adams lay trembling in the cold and damp, but missing them completely. They climbed on board the flat barge, and poled it out into the stream and the darkness. When the plash of their departure had faded, Carteret's voice broke the ensuring silence.

"You, down on the riverbank, show yourself. If I have to come and get you myself, I will undoubtedly kill you."

There was nothing for it, but for Bunce and Adams to rise up from their watery hiding place, and reveal themselves. Bunce went first, then as Adams clambered up the bank behind him, Carteret hissed in anger.

"It's that damned black slave from the docks."

Adams thought wryly that James Bunce was wrong, after all. Carteret did know of his existence, if not of his true ancestry. He forbore from setting the nobleman right as to the nature of his status. It might be difficult asserting he was a free man who had been wrongly accused and convicted of theft, and ultimately an equal of the nobleman. He reckoned Carteret would not be interested in his life story anyway. Besides, it was Sir Thomas's own story that they were here to delve into. Bunce hurried to take control, before Adams was riled again, pulling off his hat deferentially.

"Forgive me, Sir Thomas, for disturbing your . . . er . . . gathering."

Carteret did not speak, merely waving Bunce up on to the porch, but leaving Adams in his place. On the lower level and not to be invited inside. His superior attitude reminded Adams of his former life in the Old Country, and he was a little lost for words. As apparently was James Bunce, and it took Carteret to rouse him.

"Come on, man. Speak up. What is it you want?"

Bunce's shoes squelched as he approached Carteret.

"Sir Thomas, John Adams, here, saw you close to the river in Philadelphia this morning. I do not wish to pry into your . . . private business." The French connection could wait, he thought. But not for too long. "I am only concerned to discover if you know anything of the death nearby of Peter Rokesby."

Carteret frowned, and peered inquisitively at him.

"Who sent you? What do they know?" Before Bunce could answer, Carteret waved his hands in the air, dismissing any explanation. "Don't bother to come out with any lies. Damned Puritans. What care I if they are being slaughtered in their droves. A good thing, I say. They cost me my inheritance. As a Cavalier in the Civil War, my father was fined so heavily he had to sell his estates. He was of a noble line, yet was branded a malignant for supporting his King and Country. Now I am reduced to this."

Carteret swept his hand around the spacious stone house that stood behind him, as though disdaining its proportions. To Adams, it seemed like a palace, and the man's existence idyllic.

"A malignant." Carteret spat out the word with disgust. "A son should walk in the footsteps of his father. But I have nothing. And now I must stand here with . . . common men and black convicts . . . and bear their badgering. The world has gone mad. Well, I don't owe you an explanation. If anyone thinks I am guilty of murder, have them come and challenge me themselves, not send their lackey and his slave."

With that, he turned on his elegant heels, entered the house he averred to despise, and slammed the door behind him. Leaving Bunce to wonder again about the taint of the past in another country re-emerging in the colonies like a disease carried on infected ships. Adams, on the other hand, was preoccupied with what Carteret had said about fathers and sons.

6

Back at the Hendricksen shack, Adams lit a candle thoughtfully provided by Bunce from one of his commodious pockets. Then he fussed around distractedly, eventually finding a jug of small beer, and pouring out two tankards. Bunce could only ruminate on the clues he had gleaned so far, all of which seemed precious few.

"The killer could be de Ruiter, or Carteret, but as yet I cannot discern a true pattern to the murders. And in truth, it could be any number of others. We have Cavaliers, Papists, Dutchmen, and Frenchies on the list of suspects." He sighed. "I might have compiled such a list over the dinner table, without stumbling around in the dark all night."

Though his thoughts were elsewhere, Adams racked his brain for other ideas, finally recalling the other recurring feature of his night's excursion. The lingering shadow that dogged the corners of his vision.

"There is also . . ."

"Yes. The redskin savage, Teinane. I thought of him too."

Adams frowned at Bunce's intervention. He had not meant to mention Teinane by name, but the savage certainly fitted the image he had created in his mind. But there was something else gnawing at the corners of his memory, something that had been stirred by things said by both de Ruiter and Carteret. But before he could drag it out into the light, Bunce interrupted.

"I feel we have been approaching the business from the wrong end, hunting down men who you saw that morning. If the killer is as clever as we suspect, then he would ensure no one sees him at all. No, I think we should look instead at the lives of those the Slaughterman has killed to see if there is a common thread. Perhaps one going back to the Old Country."

Adams smiled grimly.

"I see you are as fearful as I was that some stain from the past we had hoped to have left behind haunts us still in the Colonies."

"Yes. For example, what of our Cavalier, Sir Thomas Carteret? He as much said to us that he was glad to see Puritans murdered. His father lost his estates after the Civil War, so he has good reason to kill those he might blame. And he is in league with French trappers."

"I don't see it." Adams shook his head. "With the deaths of Perkin Bird and Peter Rokesby, maybe. They were good Puritans, and stood by Cromwell in the war. But you told me yourself Burewald was of Cavalier stock, and Silas Peters's father was a Catholic. As for the Dutchman, de Ruiter, he has even less reason to kill Dissenters, for it was they who ensured that King Charles failed to have England side with France in wiping Holland from the map. Rivals we may be, but enemies never."

Bunce had to agree.

"I happen to know why he was hanging around the docks, by the way."

"Why?"

"Because he and that skinny reprobate we saw him with are dealing in contraband. Only I can't prove it, yet. No, John, I too have racked my brain, and cannot see a common thread in the victims' past lives that would account for their being selected. Yet the alternative is inconceivable. It would be madness, pure and simple, if these deaths were random acts."

Bunce's words once more stirred the beast lurking in the shadows of Adam's brain. And he was prompted to speak what was on his mind. But then, as Bunce rose from the table, Adams saw revealed for the first time his little collection of chap-books, some stained by spilled beer.

"Damnation. Bowater will not be pleased that I have allowed his books to be so damaged."

Bunce's eyes narrowed.

"These are Friend Bowater's books, not yours?"

Adams looked somewhat uneasy, but acknowledged they were. He finally admitted that he had not learned to read and write. Bowater had taught him along with his own son, using the chap-books as guides. In fact Teinane had been there too, but sat mainly on the sidelines smiling secretively to himself. Adams still used them to improve his reading. Bunce fumbled in the pocket of his breeches, pulling out some grubby pieces of pieces of paper with ragged edges.

"Then, do you recognize these at all?"

Adams took them and look at them one at a time. They were all crude wood block illustrations of the sort common to cheap chap-books. But somehow these were different, showing scenes that were strange and unnatural. Having perused them, it slowly dawned on Adams what they related to.

"Let me guess. You found these at each of the murders. Look, here is a huntsman chasing fish in the air. It's called 'The Mad Squire and his Fatal Hunting.' That's Joshua Burewald. This one . . ." he indicated the picture of an ox whipping a man who was pulling a plough ". . . is entitled 'The Ox Turned Farmer.' That's Silas Peters. And here is 'The Reward of Roguery, or the Roasted Cook'. Perkin Bird. And the last one . . ." he turned over the picture of a man hanging up-side-down by his legs about to be cut up by an ox. ". . . 'The Ox Turned Butcher.' Peter Rokesby."

James Bunce nodded.

"You are exactly right. I found one of them under the body of each victim. So it must have been placed there deliberately. What do you think they mean, John?"

The room suddenly felt hot, almost stifling, to John Adams. Everything he had heard that night from de Ruiter and Carteret, and even from Bunce's lips, now fell into place. What if reason had flown out the window, and madness taken its place just as the men had bemoaned? Then all their logical pursuit of motive and cause was in vain. The torn-out pages from a chap-book had given Adams the final piece of the puzzle.

"Why have you not shown me these before, James Bunce? They are the very key to the mystery."

Bunce frowned, not understanding what John Adams meant. "How so?"

"Because the chap-book they come from was important to Simon Bowater. I remember how downcast he was over the whole matter of the Civil War turning the world topsy-turvy. He saw the book as some sort of warning text . . ." Adams paused as a shocking thought crossed his mind. "Did you tell me earlier that Oliver had come back?"

"Bowater's son? Yes."

"And do you recall how before he left, he argued with Teinane?"

"Of course. Simon said his son had struggled to convert the savage, then left to continue his mission in the wilderness."

Adams felt cold shivers run down his spine, as he saw what this whole horrible sequence of events was all about. He grabbed Bunce's arm, and squeezed it hard.

"We must find Teinane. You go to his usual haunts, and I will go to Bowater's house. There is grave danger here."

7

The night had been long, and dawn was breaking as John Adams left his broken-down shack on the edge of Philadelphia docks. He marched determinedly across Dock Creek and down Market Street. Hardly anyone was stirring as the vapours that clung around the riverbank dispersed to reveal the substantial brick houses that lined the long straight road running down towards where Simon Bowater lived. His house stood at the intersection of two straight avenues that defined part of the grid that was Penn's Philadelphia. Never would anyone die in a great fire here such as had consumed London twenty years earlier. The houses stood in serried ranks, clean and orderly. But Adams now knew that behind the façades lurked an evil far worse than cleansing fire. An evil unique to this new continent, and Adams knew in his heart what he was to confront.

He paused a moment before Simon Bowater's house, looking up at the building. The windows stared blankly back, as though denying knowledge of his unspoken accusation. Then fleetingly, he thought he saw a pale shape at one of the upper windows. Resolutely, he climbed the short flight of steps, and hammered on the front door. His knocks reverberated inside the house, but noone came to open up. He turned the handle, and pushed. The door was unbarred, and he stepped inside, closing it carefully behind him. He didn't want the taint that was inside to escape. He called out the name of his employer.

"Simon. Simon Bowater. Friend Bowater."

There was no reply, except for the pale echo of his own voice. The house seemed dead, unoccupied. But twining around its tired dampness, he could detect another, ranker smell. He sniffed the air, sure he knew the smell, but he could not place the odour at first. He walked towards the back of the house, then heard a rustling from the room to the right of the hallway, and he stepped that way instead. For a second he hesitated before the door that faced him, afraid of what he was unleashing. As he pushed the door cautiously open, the stench hit him. What was only a lingering scent before, was overpowering in its ripeness. He gasped, and held his hand over his nose and mouth. The smell was of death, but there were two layers to it. The stink of human death, horrible in itself, was overlaid with the stench of rotting fish. It was a moment before Adams could figure out what lay before his eyes.

In the centre of the room was a hip bath full of water. In it lay the indisputable body of Simon Bowater. Though he could not have died more than twenty-four hours ago, his bare feet and legs were thick and purplish in death, as they hung over the lip of the bath. One arm was flung out sideways as if grasping for the heavy ebony cane that lay on the floor at the side of the bath. The cane was Bowater's constant companion, and his gnarled hand was instantly recognizable. He couldn't have otherwise identified his erstwhile employer because the bath was full of rotting fish. Bowater's face and body was under water, and covered with the silvery flanks of a heap of Delaware shad.

He looked around the room for the sign he knew would be there. Eventually he saw it – a torn piece of paper in the mouth of one of the dead fish. He extracted it, recognizing the picture immediately. It depicted a man drowning in water with a fishing line hooked into his mouth. On the bank of the river holding the rod was a large fish standing upright on its tail fin.

"'The Water Wonder, or Fishes Lord of Creation'," murmured Adams, recalling the scene from the chap-book. There was a high-pitched squeal of laughter from the hallway, and the door behind him slammed shut. It sounded like the laugh of a child, but it was not happy laughter. Adams ran to the door, but in his confusion could not open it. At first he thought someone was on the other side, holding the handle. But a child surely did not have such strength. And when finally he did wrench the door open, there was no one to be seen. He heard a sound from above, and looked up the stairs. What he saw made him gasp. It was the naked flank of a savage, his black hair long and greasy, flowing down his back. The figure disappeared, and Adams bounded up the steps two at a time. In any other circumstance, he might have imagined this was merely play. But, with a dead body lying downstairs, the mood was far from playful. The call to Hide-and-Seek masked a deadly intent. Adams wondered if there was a mocking picture waiting to be tossed on his own body. At the top of the stairs he gasped for breath, staring along the empty passageway, wondering if he was chasing a phantom. The only sign of movement were the dust motes that swirled in the shaft of morning light angling through a half-closed door. The disturbed air marked the passage of a corporeal being. He called out into the silence.

"Are you there?"

In reply he heard the wavering sound of a childish chant.

> *"If revolutions strange appear*
> *Within the compass of the sphere;*
> *If men and things succession know,*
> *And no dependence reigns below . . ."*

There was a momentary silence, then the childish voice came again, teasing, tormenting.

"What follows next, John Adams? Come on; you know as well as I."

Adams edged towards the half-opened door through which the sunlight poured. Of course he knew the lines. He had been taught them by Simon Bowater from the chap-book whose torn-out pictures now adorned a series of murders. He also knew now who he was chasing, and it was no child. Adams racked his brain, and began to recite the lines that followed, as he slowly stalked his quarry.

> *"Since 'tis allow'd the world we dwell in,*
> *Is always round the sun a'sailing;*
> *Experience to our knowledge brings*
> *That times may change as well as things.*
> *And art . . . And art . . ."*

What followed next, damn it? Adams could not recall the words. But his tormentor could, and the little child's voice came again.

> *"And art than nature wiser grown,*
> *Turns every object upside down."*

Reminded, Adams joined in, finishing the doggerel off.

> *"No wonder then the world is found*
> *By change of place Turn'd Upside Down."*

When Bunce had showed him the pictures found at the scene of each death, Adams had instantly recognized the wood-block prints as coming from a chap-book Simon Bowater had often read to him. The title was "The World Turned Upside Down", and the dozen scenes depicted were largely humorous in their content: "The Old Soldier Turned Nurse", "The Lovers Catched by the Bird". But some were gruesome images: "The Ox Turned Butcher" and "The Roasted Cook". These were the ones that had driven a troubled soul to bring the images to life in a series of senseless killings that had rocked the complacency of Penn's settlement to the core. Adams recalled Bunce's words to him only a short time earlier.

"It would be madness, pure and simple, if these deaths were random acts."

Both de Ruiter and Carteret had also railed at unreason, and the world gone mad. So it was only when Adams had stopped imagining there was some reason to the sequence of deaths – a reason that hung on Old World enmities – that he had seen the true cause. The reason for the murders was no reason at all. The cause was bound up in the very liberties of the Middle Colonies themselves – freedom to think the unthinkable. And then do it. It was truly a world turned upside down. And now in that world he could hear weeping.

"You can come out now, friend. I understand. I can help you."

Even as Adams spoke the words, he knew he couldn't. Penn's new laws may reflect Quaker idealism, but two crimes were still punishable by death. One was treason, and the other was murder. The fugitive knew this too, and though he may feign a child's voice, he was a fully grown man. Seven years earlier, it had been three young men – two English and one native – who had sat together imbibing new ideas, free of the past and its encumbrances. One of them had perverted those ideals.

Adams could see his adversary's large shadow etched against the sunlight. So he was ready, when Oliver Bowater emerged from the room. Even so, the sight of a stark naked, wild-haired Oliver with tears running down his face almost distracted him. And the arc of the lump hammer came close to bursting Adams's head open. He ducked at the last minute, and felt the wind of the hammer's passage over his head. He grabbed Bowater's weapon arm, and struggled to disarm him. Face to face with Oliver Bowater once again after seven years, he was shocked by the demonic look that haunted the man's features. He recalled a soft-faced young man with an earnest look in his eyes, who had left for the frontier with naïve dreams in his head. This person was no longer that Oliver Bowater, but a man truly possessed. How his father had hidden him away for the week he must have been back in Philadelphia wreaking his havoc, Adams could not guess. Why Simon should have done it, knowing what was happening in Philadelphia, was more understandable. Often, a father loves his son too well. Oliver now looked like a demon, and his strength was that of a demon too. As they fought, Adams felt he was losing the battle. Bowater pushed his face into Adams's, his eyes almost popping out of his head, and grinned.

"Remember the book, John Adams? Father taught us how it was a true picture of the world. Well, I have set about making the world match the pictures. You are next, John. Remember the Duel of the Palfries?"

Adams conjured up the picture from the chap-book: two men carrying horses on their backs, the horses with lances under their forelimbs. He had an image of himself found dead by James Bunce, crushed under the weight of a dead horse. Slowly, his vision began to fade, and his hope along with it. Then suddenly, as if Adams had wished it, Bowater groaned, went limp and crashed to the floor. Adams looked up through hazy eyes, and was aware of James Bunce supporting him with one hand. In the other, he held the club with which he had floored the Philadelphia Slaughterman, and saved his life. He could also see Teinane hovering in the background, smiling his enigmatic smile.

"Thank you, James Bunce."

Bunce blushed.

"You have no reason to thank me, John. When you sent me on that wild goose chase after Teinane, I was sure you meant to come and kill Simon Bowater. I still harboured the thought that you were the man who stalked the Philadelphia streets."

"Me?"

"Yes. I couldn't put from my mind that you were the only person linking the murdered men. Did you not see that Burewald, Peters, Bird and Rokesby all used Bowater's warehouse to store or purchase goods?"

Adams stared at Bunce in astonishment, then burst out laughing. Indeed the fact had not even occurred to him. Unfortunately for the four men, it may indeed have been their association with Simon Bowater that had homed Oliver in on them. Adams had not seen the link, because he knew he was innocent of the murders, even if his friend hadn't. Bunce looked suitably shamefaced.

"Can you ever forgive me for thinking evil of you?"

Adams clasped his friend's hand, and reassured him of his forgiveness. He looked down at the face of Oliver Bowater, which somehow in death had regained its former innocence.

"We both of us feared that the evils of the Old World had followed us here like rats on a ship. It distracted us from the reality. For here we have a far worse evil – a whole new evil – lying in wait to infect pliant and susceptible souls like Oliver Bowater. May God allow it to perish with the death of the Philadelphia Slaughterman."

TO WALK ON THORNY PATHS

PAUL FINCH

We reach the end of our journey through Jacobean crime with a suitably sinister story that could claim to be the first country-house murder. It is set in a snowbound house on Exmoor in the days immediately following the flight of James II from England to France, bringing to an end the Jacobean Age. James II, as stubborn and high-handed as his father and grandfather, had determined to revert to the Catholic faith, despite all that had happened over the previous century or so. Catholic supporters still regard him and his son – who became the Old Pretender (and the father of Bonnie Prince Charlie) – as the rightful kings of England and the true heirs to the throne.

Paul Finch (b. 1964) is a former police officer who has written for TV, including episodes of The Bill. *His first collection,* After Shocks, *won the British Fantasy Award for 2001. He is also the author of* The Extremist and Other Tales of Conflict (2004), Cape Wrath (2002) *and a volume of Viking horror,* Darker Ages *(2004).*

All through the December of 1688, it snowed heavily in the English West Country. A bitter northerly wind blew down from the Welsh mountains, rivers and streams froze, and many of the more isolated roads became impassable. None of this, however, prevented the local populace from coming outdoors to celebrate the stately advance of Prince William of Orange, as he and his fifteen thousand Protestant mercenaries proceeded eastwards from his landing-place at Brixham, in Devon; then, later, from Exeter as he embarked on the final leg of his journey to London.

The reign of the Catholic King James II was over. After four years of intrigue, chicanery, "popish plotting", and aggressive absolutism at the very heart of government, the least popular monarch since Bloody Mary had finally abandoned the throne of England. When the news broke on Christmas Eve that James had fled to France, Whig and Tory gentlemen alike left their country residences to join the merry throngs in the snow-bound villages. This, it appeared, would be a very happy Christmas indeed.

"Not a good night for you, O'Calligan, I dare say," Lord Chillerton said, dabbing his mouth with a napkin.

Captain O'Calligan shrugged. "I'm merely a soldier, my lord. These great political events pass me by."

"Well, that's a novel way to rationalize it," Lord Lightbourne retorted. He was seated directly across the table from O'Calligan, and had been glowering at him from the moment the meal had begun. "If I were you, I'd consider myself lucky that Lady Foxworth is in such forgiving mood."

"No, no, no, I won't have that," Lady Foxworth interrupted in her delightful, sing-song tones. "Captain O'Calligan was always a most gentlemanly gaoler."

"A gaoler, my dear," said Lady Lightbourne, "is a gaoler."

Lady Foxworth waved the business aside as though it was all best forgotten. "And Silvercombe was a most comfortable dungeon."

There were nods and smiles at this. The assembled guests had no desire to spoil their hostess's gay mood. If she was inclined to pardon those who had wronged her, then who were they to disagree? At present, she was as happy as a schoolgirl, as beautiful as a butterfly. An inner-light seemed to shine from her, which, after the uncertain years of James's reign, they could all now comfortably bask in.

Only Jack O'Calligan had difficulty appreciating it. Thanks to the Arctic conditions outside, it was only a small gathering of Exmoor's minor nobility at the Silvercombe Hall feast-table that night, but the tall, good-looking Irishman was uncomfortable all the same. Of Lady Foxworth's guests, Lord Lightbourne and his wife, Loretta, long-time Whigs, were openly against him, while Lord Chillerton, though a Catholic and a Tory, was past ninety now, and his wife, Lady Barbara, much older, so there was little support to be had there. Even Judge Prendergast, who'd presided alongside Lord-Chief Justice Jeffreys at the Bristol Assizes, was keeping a low if corpulent profile at the far end of the table; he hoped to retain his office on the West Country circuit, and was thus being as obsequious as possible to the incoming administration. In any case, even had O'Calligan been seated among close companions, his position here would have been invidious: up until the last week or so, as a captain in the King's Horse Guards, he had been charged with keeping Lady Hannah Foxworth under strict house-arrest. (Three years earlier, her younger brother, Rupert, had taken part in Monmouth's ill-fated rebellion and had then dashed treasonously overseas to find service with the Dutch navy, which had not reflected well on her in King James's eyes.) Granted, Silvercombe Hall, her ancestral home, had made a luxurious prison, but she hadn't been permitted to leave it under any circumstances, except for those frequent occasions when she'd been summoned to Court to answer trumped-up charges of seditious libel. All things considered, her time had been exceptionally difficult, and O'Calligan was the one who'd enforced it. As such, he had no appetite. The repast that evening was delightful – roasted goose stuffed with cherries, a saddle of pork garnished with apples, and all manner of pies, tarts and puddings – while several excellent clarets had been produced from Lady Foxworth's famously well-stocked cellar, but it was more than the Irish soldier could do even to sip at his brimming goblet.

"Conciliation will be the order of events in the New Year, Captain O'Calligan," his prisoner-turned-hostess said, leaning towards him. "You needn't worry so."

He glanced sidelong at her. Even at forty-four years old, and two years his senior, she was extraordinarily handsome. Gemstones sparkled on her bosom, but were dull compared to the sapphire lustre of her eyes. Her golden hair, which she wore high and layered in thick curls, shone in the firelight. Her perfume was intoxicating.

"If you'll excuse me, my lady," he said, pushing his chair back. "I'll take some air."

She smiled and nodded, and watched him as he withdrew from the dining-room.

"By God, I'd have my pack on his heels by now if I was you, Hannah," Lord Lightbourne remarked.

She tittered. "Oh Randolph, you do change with the tides."

He looked hurt. "I beg your pardon?"

"Come now," she said. "You weren't so committed a rebel when the Duke of Monmouth and his army arrived at Lyme Regis. And especially not after the Assizes, when they were all being marched to the gallows."

At the end of the table, Judge Prendergast gazed awkwardly down at his plate.

Lord Lightbourne was no less discomforted. "In my opinion it was an ill-considered enterprise . . . with all respect to your family's involvement."

"That respect is duly noted," Lady Foxworth replied, and she smiled teasingly, which caused Lord Lightbourne to fumble with his cutlery, and his wife – who, compared to their hostess, was owlish and plain-looking – to scowl through her powdered blusher.

Silvercombe Hall was a great rambling structure.

It had originally been constructed during Henry VIII's reign, from local stone, and at the time cast a grim, functional shadow across the bleak wilderness of northern Exmoor. Now however, thanks to the Foxworth family's profitable sea-faring exploits, it boasted parkland and lush, manicured gardens, while its interiors had been paneled throughout in richest oak and hung with portraits and hunting-trophies, and at this time of year, of course, were decked with evergreens.

As he walked down the entrance hall, Captain O'Calligan felt conspicuous in the presence of such grandeur. He hadn't deemed it appropriate to dress for dinner, and still wore his riding-boots and red regimental coat, knee-length and trimmed with gold at the collar and cuffs, but old and weather-stained. His pistol and sabre hung at his hip, but were purely symbolic now that he had no office to enforce with them. Outside the hall, brushing snow from the porch, he found Cedric, Lady Foxworth's oldest retainer, and the senior member of the three household servants she'd been allowed to keep during her period of confinement. Cedric had seen countless years: he was a tall but crooked fellow, with a thin, mournful face and long white hair. Compared to the stockings, wigs and dandified ruffles of his betters, he still preferred the Puritan garb of yore: the dark trousers and doublet, the starched white collar spread broadly over the top. Despite this, possibly because of their lowly birth and uncertain status in an ever-changing world, the Catholic Irishman and the Protestant Englishmen had become – if not friends – polite acquaintances.

"You're a long way from home, Captain O'Calligan," the servant said after a moment. "Especially on Christmas Eve."

"Duty calls, Cedric."

Cedric eyed him curiously. "Unless I'm mistaken, your duty fled with your lord and master?"

O'Calligan nodded and gazed across the snowy wastes. An icy wind whipped up flurries of feather-sized flakes. "Until I receive official notification that my post is terminated, I'll stand my ground for King James."

"You're a strange kind of Irishman, and that's a fact."

O'Calligan acknowledged this, though, as far as he was concerned, he'd had good cause to serve the English crown so loyally. "You remember me telling you about when I was a child in Drogheda?"

"Aye. That I do."

"I saw every member of my family slain, Cedric." The soldier's eyes misted as he recalled the grisly event. "It was Cromwell's Ironsides, who did it. I was three years old at the time. That's the only reason I was spared . . . but I remember it like it was yesterday." He paused to swallow his emotions. "I learned early that Catholic England's fight was Catholic Ireland's fight too. I've seen nothing since to change me of that opinion."

Cedric continued to brush. "Let's just hope that fight's finally over, eh?"

O'Calligan agreed. The religious wars had drained too many men of their humanity, but despite his dismay at the recent turn of *political* events, at least this latest revolution had been bloodless. That had to be a good sign, he thought.

It was in the darkest, coldest hour of the night when hellish screams woke the household. The wind blew shrilly all around the ancient building, whistling through its chinks and rafters, but there was no mistaking what could only be cries of unimaginable horror.

Several minutes passed before O'Calligan and Cedric, both of whom arrived on the upper floor of the east wing at the same time, carrying flaming candelabra, were able to locate the source of the sound, which appeared to be the guest-room allocated to Lord Chillerton and his wife. By this time the screams had ceased, and an eerie silence followed. The two men tried to force entry, but the door was locked from the other side. They knocked and shouted for several minutes, but received no answer. By now, Lord Lightbourne, Lady Foxworth and Judge Prendergast had also appeared, huddled in their caps and bed-robes but white-faced in the early-morning chill. Cedric, on the orders of his mistress, went for a hammer and chisel, and they finally broke the door down.

Inside, the once elegant room was more like an abattoir.

Even from the low fire in the grate and a guttering candle on the mantel, it could be seen that blood daubed everything: the bed-hangings, the curtains on the window, the Persian rug. Lord and Lady Chillerton lay like broken mannequins in a heap of bedclothes, their faces frozen rictuses of agony. In each case, a deep and fatal wound had been gouged across the throat.

Lady Foxworth promptly fainted into Cedric's arms. The other would-be rescuers stood there with stunned disbelief. Numerous items were out of place: a night-stand had been thrown over, its garments scattered; a chamber-pot was broken, its odious contents seeping into the floorboards. Despite that latter, rather foul detail, another stench was in the air – something pungent and carrion-like – though the intruders were too appalled by what they were seeing to even comment upon it. In truth, moments of utter confusion and Bedlam followed. No-one could make sense of the situation.

"Here's a curious start to your loyalist fight-back!" Lord

Lightbourne suddenly shouted, rounding on O'Calligan. "Cutting the throats of your own *toraidhe* companions!"

The Irishman stared at him uncomprehendingly. It was Lady Foxworth, who'd now recovered somewhat, though her pallor was still sickly white, who retorted: "Lord Lightbourne!" Her voice quavered with emotion. "I'd appreciate it if you'd refrain from making wild accusations."

"And I'd appreciate it if you'd put this Irish devil-dog under lock and key!" Again, Lightbourne rounded on the soldier. "Tell me, O'Calligan, isn't it true that as a young trooper, you pursued the brigand Colonel Blood through the Wicklow Mountains, then later through the marshes of the Low Countries? That you also hunted robber bands in Scotland who'd disguised themselves as Covenant rebels?"

The soldier said nothing. But it was true; they all knew it.

"Isn't it also true that you've developed something of a talent for clandestine warfare?"

"My experiences served me well," O'Calligan finally said.

"So I see!" Lightbourne bellowed. "Throat-cutting must come second nature to you."

"Randolph, this is your prejudice speaking," Lady Foxworth chided him.

"Is it, Hannah? Then why, pray, is O'Calligan the only one among us dressed?"

And that was true. Everyone, with the exception of Cedric, who was back on duty in an hour anyway, wore nightgowns and slippers. O'Calligan, however, though he'd loosened his oil-black hair so that it hung past his shoulders, had only stripped to his shirt and breeches. He even wore his boots.

In actual fact, the soldier had spent the night seated by his fire, smoking pipe after pipe as he brooded on his future in a Williamite Britain, but, unused to being questioned, he now remained stubbornly tight-lipped.

"This is absurd, Lightbourne," Judge Prendergast put in. "Why should O'Calligan murder the Chillertons? They were Catholics and Jacobites, like him."

"Maybe he viewed them as collaborators," Lightbourne said. "Maybe he'll view *you* the same way." Lightbourne was a tall, sturdy individual, only in early middle-age but beetle-browed and angry-faced, and he gazed at the Irishman with fanatical dislike.

Judge Prendergast's viewpoint, however, was more measured. "Whoever's responsible, he'll be punished," he stated flatly, "but might I suggest we find the miscreant first, rather than the nearest convenient scapegoat."

"And might I suggest we start hunting for him now," O'Calligan added. He turned to his hostess: "Madam, I no longer have authority here, but it might be a useful thing if we searched these premises. It's possible some vagrant has broken in, seeking shelter."

Lady Foxworth's delicate cheek paled at the mere thought, but she nodded quickly. "Yes, we should search. Of course."

"Might I also suggest," O'Calligan said, "that we remove the bodies to one of your outbuildings. How soon we'll be able to summon help in this weather I don't know, but if we keep them indoors too long, they'll start to putrefy. Outside, the cold will preserve them until an enquiry can be made."

Again, Lady Foxworth nodded: "Cedric, assist Captain O'Calligan."

O'Calligan and the servant wrapped the bodies in sheets, and carried them downstairs. As they did, Cedric voiced a quiet opinion of his own: "If you'll notice, captain, their throats haven't been cut. More ripped, I'd say."

When they reached one of the stables, having ploughed through snow that was now knee-deep and still being driven on a sword-edged wind, O'Calligan saw the same thing for himself. By the light of a lantern, he examined the victims' throats, and noted that, though the outer flesh and the esophagus tissue beneath had been sliced from one side to the other, the wounds were ragged edged and zig-zagging.

"A hooked blade, maybe?" he said, baffled. "And not especially sharp. Good Lord. Whoever did this, Cedric, is a savage. A *real* savage."

For the next hour, the men, now coated and booted, and armed to the teeth, searched every nook of the great manor-house, while the women sat nervously before a rekindled hearth.

It was no small task. As well as its central section and extensive wings, Silvercombe Hall also boasted a number of outhouses. No trace was found of an interloper, however. More to the point, no locks had been forced or windows broken. The search-party even ventured out into the landscaped gardens, though this was fruitless for different reasons: the blizzard howled, and the snow drifted to such depths that sculptures, arbors and topiary alike were all buried. Eventually they returned indoors, having agreed to meet again in the morning and discuss the affair over breakfast, though throughout this conversation Lord Lightbourne's eagle-eye was fixed on Jack O'Calligan.

For his own part, O'Calligan had no intention of retiring just yet, and when various bedrooms had been closed and locks thrown, he summoned Cedric back to the murder-scene. It was now ice-cold in there and pitch-black, the fire having died, the candle having been removed. Cedric produced a fresh one and lit it, and they stood there for several moments, their breath swirling vaporously around them.

"The luggage is untouched," O'Calligan eventually said, nodding to an open cupboard, in the foot of which two heavy portmanteaux could be seen. "Whoever did this was not trying to rob them."

Cedric nodded, then added: "There's another mystery. How did the villain get in? I checked the window before. It's fast. Not even tampered with."

O'Calligan crossed the room to check for himself, but found that the window was indeed securely locked. Beyond its warped panes, he saw a shelf of unbroken snow. No-one had entered by this route. "The only conclusion is that the killer was already in here when they arrived," he finally said.

"Then how did he get out?" Cedric asked. "The door was locked from the inside."

They glanced around the room, the walls of which, with the exception of a stone breastwork over the hearth, consisted of solid oaken panels. O'Calligan even glanced up the chimney, but saw a narrow brick shaft not remotely large enough for a human to pass through. He stood back, even more confused. "Cedric, you know the people gathered here very well. Better than I ever could. Did any one of them have reason to hate Lord and Lady Chillerton?"

"None at all. The Chillertons were regarded as goodly neighbours. I mean, they had political differences with Lady Hannah, but isn't that the way of things all over?"

"Who else is here aside from the guests?"

"Our cook, Agnes, who's an elderly sort, and two chambermaids, Martha and Charlotte, and they're bits of girls. Neither could hurt a fly."

O'Calligan gazed at the blood staining the floor and the bed-linen in the corner. "How wealthy were the Chillertons? Did anyone stand to gain from their deaths?"

Cedric now regarded the soldier curiously. "Am I to understand, captain, that you're taking some kind of investigator role here?"

O'Calligan shrugged. "You've seen how the land lies. At this moment, I'm a very suitable suspect."

"With respect, anyone who knows you knows that that's nonsense. You're a proper gentleman."

"That's not the way the Prince of Orange's magistrates might see it." O'Calligan scanned the room for the least clue. "My future hangs by a thread as it is. For all Lady Foxworth's good will, this incident might turn that thread into a rope."

Cedric considered this, then said: "Well, in answer to your question, there's no-one here like to benefit from Lord and Lady Chillerton's deaths. They have a son at Court – a clerk in the Exchequer, I believe. He stands to inherit everything, but he's not here. Probably wouldn't have had long to wait for his inheritance anyway."

"And what's *that*?" the soldier wondered. He indicated a bell suspended from a cord in a high corner. "There's one in my room too."

"That's from the old days," Cedric explained. "The Foxworths were always sea-folk. They were awarded Silvercombe Hall for services against the Spanish Armada. The family the house was confiscated from was Catholic. They used to hold Masses here, and shelter priests and nuns and such. A bell like that was put in each room. They could be rung from a secret place, to alert guests should the priest-hunters come by."

O'Calligan glanced round at him. "Does that mean there are priests' holes as well?"

"There were, but they're all gone now. The whole inside of the house was refurbished by Lady Hannah's father, thirty years ago."

Despite this, they spent another ten minutes making rounds of the room, tapping on each wall, but there wasn't so much as a hollow *thump* to greet their knuckles.

Not surprisingly, the Christmas Day hunt was abandoned. Even without the atrocious murders, it would have been impossible to send the hounds out. The gardens and moors were still deep under snow, while flakes continued to fall, no longer tossed by a gale, but thickly and heavily in an unrelenting cascade. This also prevented anyone from leaving the hall and heading the sixteen miles to Minehead, where they might summon help.

Shortly before luncheon was served, Lord Lightbourne took it upon himself to question the domestic staff, which he did unduly harshly as far as O'Calligan was concerned. Lightbourne, the Irishman decided, was probably the sort of master who would willingly take a horsewhip to his servants. He sat the cook and her two maids in window-seats in the drawing-room, then questioned their every move on the previous night in a tone so severe that it would have done Matthew Hopkins proud. Needless to say, he reduced them to tears, but he didn't stop there, insisting on regaling them with the ghoulish details of the murders, determined, in his own words, to "break their stubborn impudence".

Lightbourne, however, wasn't the only person O'Calligan formed opinions about that morning. There was a mournful mood: people were understandably subdued, but were, all of them, shocked rather than grief-stricken. Lady Foxworth's relationship with the Chillertons, the Irishman had learned (from himself questioning the maids that morning, albeit in a gentler manner), had not always been as amicable as old Cedric believed. There'd been disputes over land in the past, and once apparently, Lord Chillerton had invested heavily in a sea-voyage to the Foxworth family's trading-post on the coast of Madras; the ship sank in a storm, however, and the Foxworths had refused to recompense him, which had caused a very public row. Judge Prendergast had also had issues with the Chillertons: one time he'd refused to make good on a gambling debt to them, using his period of empowerment following Monmouth's rebellion to bully his elderly neighbours into cancelling it outright. The only person present O'Calligan had no real information about in this respect was Lady Lightbourne, though he discovered a little bit about her in a brief conversation with his hostess.

According to Lady Foxworth, Loretta Lightbourne, formerly Loretta Wilberforce, was a rector's daughter from Devon, who had only married her beau at the age of twenty-nine, a period in life when she might normally have been regarded as an old maid. Lady Foxworth knew nothing of the Lightbournes' courtship and romance, except that Loretta had taken confidently to her life as wife of a country squire. She was a stern-looking woman with a stiff posture and pinched features, but she compensated for her lack of physical attractiveness with a strict and assertive attitude. She apparently ran her husband's household efficiently, and had successfully reined in his one-time gallivanting antics. Not that she seemed to be firmly in control at this moment. As O'Calligan and Lady Foxworth surreptitiously watched her, Lady Lightbourne sent Cedric for a fourth glass of French brandy.

"It must be the stress of circumstances," Lady Foxworth said, still pale in the cheek herself. "I'd always thought her given to temperance."

"Her abrasiveness is clearly a front," O'Calligan observed.

"She has a temper, though. Her husband lives in fear of it, for one."

The Irishman glanced towards the hearth, where Lord Lightbourne stood over the flames, one hand on the mantel; following his normal instinct to be cock of the walk, he was wearing a bright blue coat that morning, trimmed down its buttonholes with gold thread, and with a lengthy, red velvet doublet underneath. His cravat was a froth of intricate lace, his shoulder-length, chestnut wig of the finest quality.

"You'll now be wondering if Randolph and I have ever . . . consorted?" Lady Foxworth added.

O'Calligan pondered this. Hannah Foxworth's scandalous behaviour and frequent affairs were a difficult matter to discount when it came to potential motives for crime. "The question had crossed my mind," he admitted.

She sat back in her chair, and fanned herself. Due to the snow, the house was closed up and, with every fire roaring, becoming uncomfortably hot. "I'm not sure I should answer so impertinent an enquiry from the man once charged with imprisoning me. But the situation has sufficient seriousness to perhaps put privacy aside. The answer is 'no', we haven't. But even if we had, why should that spell death for Lord and Lady Chillerton?"

O'Calligan mused. "Maybe they knew about it? They were blackmailing you? Or *him*. More likely *him*."

"Why more likely him?" she wondered.

"Well, with all respect, my lady, he'd have more to lose, his spouse still being alive."

Lady Foxworth smiled tiredly. "The point is taken. Not that it resolves the main problem. Namely that the murders were committed inside a locked room. You've checked for secret entrances?"

"I have. As has Cedric."

"Well, if Cedric found nothing, there *is* nothing. He's been at Silvercombe since I was knee-high. He's almost part of the furniture here." The woman smiled wistfully. "My mother died when I was still a child and my brother, Rupert, a baby. As a result Rupert was sent to live with relatives in East Anglia, and, with my father being away at sea all the time, it fell to Cedric to raise me. Which of course you already know, having been my keeper for so long."

O'Calligan nodded.

"He's looked after me ever since," she added. "A loyaler servant, one couldn't find."

Again the Irishman considered what he knew about the Foxworth family. Much of it was a tragic tale, especially for Lady Hannah herself. As well as losing her mother at a very early age, her father died when she was sixteen, and her husband expired from influenza when she was seventeen, during only the second year of their marriage. Four years later, in fact on the eve of her twenty-first birthday, she received news that her elder brother had drowned in Hudson Bay when his ship struck an ice-floe. More recently, during Monmouth's abortive uprising, two of her close cousins were killed at Sedgemoor and another two hanged afterwards. Of course, as was often the way with these old baronial families, guile and fortitude had turned disaster into triumph; catastrophe had only made them stronger. On her husband's death, Lady Foxworth had returned to her family home and readopted her maiden name. On her elder brother's death, she'd taken over the running of all family businesses, and had made them even more profitable than before. Though a staunch Protestant and parliamentarian, she'd continued the family tradition of currying favour with the anti-Cromwellian court of Charles II by bestowing on it an endless succession of exotic gifts brought back from the East Indies: silks, spices, fabulous beasts as pets or as specimens for the royal zoological gardens. Even during her three years of house-arrest, Lady Foxworth had run her affairs admirably. The family's mercantile empire had blossomed. They now owned considerable shares in the East India Company, a business that was booming on a world-wide scale. Now that King James himself had gone, nothing, it seemed, could prevent their rising to unprecedented prominence.

Except, perhaps, for this hideous and inexplicable double-murder.

O'Calligan wondered briefly if the outrage might actually have been directed at the Foxworth family rather than their ill-fated guests; an attempt to indelibly besmirch their name maybe. If this had been the case, however, Lady Foxworth wasn't considering the possibility. In fact, she now seemed determined to put the terrible event aside until it could be dealt with by the authorities.

"Let's not dwell on unpleasantness," she said, suddenly standing and clapping her hands for attention. "It is Christmas and we owe it to Our Lord to celebrate his birthday. All gather round, if you please. I have an assortment of presents for you."

The guests assembled uncertainly, not quite sure whether this was seemly under the circumstances. Lady Foxworth would not be deterred. On her instruction, Cedric and Charlotte brought in several gaily wrapped packages, and one by one they were distributed. To his astonishment, Captain O'Calligan received one as well.

"You may open them now," Lady Foxworth decreed. "I understand that it's perhaps against tradition so early in the season, but by sad circumstances we now may have to part sooner than normal this year, and I can't neglect my duty to my guests."

For Judge Prendergast, there was a tub of excellent Brazilian tobacco, of which he approved heartily; for Lord Lightbourne, a fine silken chemise. Ordinarily, Lady Lightbourne would have scowled at so personal a gift to her husband from another woman, especially when that other woman then brazenly commented: "I hope it fits, Randolph, I had to guess your proportions," but the mistress of Lightbourne Manor was by this stage too drunk to notice. She was too drunk, in fact, to even offer thanks for her own present, a scented pomander, which their hostess took care to tie to her wrist with a ribbon.

O'Calligan was the last one to unwrap his gift, and was amazed to receive a handsome fighting-knife, with a stout, curved blade, and a hilt fashioned from ebony and inlaid with gems. "It was taken from a Moorish pirate," Lady Foxworth explained. "What better item, I thought, for a man whose life is . . . how did Lord Randolph put it, *clandestine* warfare?"

O'Calligan shook his head. "I'm honoured, ma'am. But also, I'm shamed. I have nothing to give you in return."

"I'm your hostess, captain. It is not required that you give me anything. I'd also provided for Lord and Lady Chillerton," she sighed. "Sadly, those goods must now be passed on to their estate . . . along with their bodies."

At which point, with astonishing suddenness, Lady Lightbourne began to weep hysterically. For a moment everyone was transfixed with shock. The next thing, however, the normally staid countrywoman was down on her knees, beating her breast, tearing at her carefully coiffed locks.

"Those poor people!" she wailed. "Slain in their beds! Who could do such a thing? What vile monster roams these passages?"

Clearly, the false good cheer of that morning had put Lady Lightbourne under intolerable strain. She was a rector's daughter, O'Calligan remembered; she'd known wealth and breeding, had been raised exclusively in a world where domestic chores and prim conversation were the highlights of the day, and suddenly *this* . . . two close neighbours butchered, their blood left drenching the bedroom walls. Little wonder she'd taken so readily to drink that morning.

There was a bustle of activity in response. Lady Foxworth and her maid, Charlotte, hurried to assist the casualty to an armchair. No amount of consoling, however, no number of whiffs from a jar of restorative would bring the distraught woman round. Eventually, after several minutes of pandemonium, she was taken up to her bedroom, where she consented to lie down. Lady Foxworth took charge of the procedure, with Charlotte and Cedric's assistance.

The moment the little group had left the room, there was a

deafening silence. Lord Lightbourne himself seemed too startled by his wife's unexpected breakdown to pass comment. Judge Prendergast, who, of them all was perhaps most used to hearing screams of despair – as condemned folk were led raving from his court – sat by the fire, re-stuffed his pipe and began to smoke. A moment or two passed, then O'Calligan went out into the hall. On the grand stairway, he met Cedric coming down. Lady Foxworth and her maid were close behind.

"She's resting now, sir," the servant said. "She's taken a sleeping-draught. I'm sure it'll do her good."

"Poor thing," Lady Foxworth added. "Such a sensitive soul beneath all those corsets and starched petticoats."

O'Calligan nodded, though once their hostess had swept back into the drawing-room, and the maid, Charlotte, had scurried off to the kitchens, he drew Cedric aside. "Lady Lightbourne's room is now locked?" he asked quietly.

Cedric nodded. "She herself has the only key."

"And you checked it was empty before leaving her in there? Under the bed, in the closet?"

Again Cedric nodded. "She is absolutely alone."

O'Calligan patted the servant on the shoulder. "Then she at least should be safe."

But she wasn't.

It was shortly after luncheon, and what remained of the party were playing cards and smoking their pipes, while outside another of those early, ominously dark December evenings was creeping over the snow-laden moor, when the *clanging* of a bell suddenly sounded from the upper apartments.

The guests gazed at each other, puzzled. Then, O'Calligan leapt to his feet. "That's an alarm call!" he shouted.

O'Calligan dashed from the room, followed closely by Lightbourne himself and then, more ponderously, Judge Prendergast. Cedric was in the passage outside, carrying a tray of sweetmeats. They almost bowled him aside in their efforts to get upstairs, at the top of which stood the door to the Lightbournes' guest-chamber. As before, that door was locked. They hammered it to no avail – it was solid oak – and, once again, Cedric was summoned with tools. When at last they'd opened the room, a similar gruesome sight confronted them. Lady Lightbourne lay beside her bed amid disordered sheets, eyes closed but a ghoulish grimace on her face. Her throat had been torn from ear to ear, and a wide puddle of blood was congealing on the carpet.

Lord Lightbourne howled and roared when he saw this, and had to be forcibly restrained by O'Calligan and the judge. This time, he switched his accusations from the Irishman to Cedric. "It was him . . . him, the dog!" he bellowed. "He was the only one not present when we heard her ringing for help!"

"It couldn't have been him," the judge insisted. "He was outside the drawing-room, just about to serve us!"

But logic had fled the bereaved man. He wrenched himself free and threw himself down onto his wife's corpse, sobbing bitterly. As he did, there was a gasp of shock from the doorway. O'Calligan turned and found Lady Foxworth there. Quickly, he led her out into the passage.

"How . . . is this possible?" she stammered, her face pale as ice. "That room was definitely locked. I heard Lady Lightbourne do it, herself."

"You're sure none of your domestics have a key?"

"I'm sure, but come and speak to them anyway."

O'Calligan did, going straight down to the kitchens in company with his hostess. There, however, as he'd expected, he found the two maids, Charlotte, and her sister, Martha, huddled together, teary-eyed with fear. Likewise, there was no possibility that the cook, Agnes, was responsible: she was aged and obese, and shuffled about slowly on elephantine feet. After briefly interviewing the woman, O'Calligan – frustrated and dissatisfied – went back up to the room where the crime had occurred. Cedric was standing outside with a lighted candle. He warned the Irishman about going in, saying that Lightbourne had lost his mind. O'Calligan replied that he had no choice.

Inside, the new-made widower, now with sword drawn, was seated on the bed beside the body of his wife, which he'd clearly placed there himself. He'd pulled off his wig, and had gone white in the face.

Aware that he was being watched coldly, O'Calligan went first to the bell in the corner. It was similar to his own in that it hung just below the ceiling. If the poor woman had indeed reached up and rung it, it would have been quite a stretch for her, especially considering that she was at that moment under attack. Next, he contemplated the walls themselves, which, aside from a timber skirting-board, were of bare stone blocks and hung with tapestries. He checked behind the tapestries, but found nothing unusual. After this, it was the window: outside it he saw another unbroken strip of snow on the ledge. Clearly, no-one had entered or departed this way, though the top panel, he now noticed, was open, admitting an icy breeze.

O'Calligan turned to Lightbourne. "Forgive me for asking, my lord, but did you or your wife open this casement?"

There was a chilling silence, before Lightbourne replied: "My wife did. Last night. She always found a stuffy room intolerable."

O'Calligan now noted that the hearth was cold. "Is that why you had no fire?"

For a moment Lightbourne couldn't reply. His eyes were bloodshot, his lips taut and grey and visibly trembling, and for the first time it struck the Irishman that there was more to this arrogant, posturing peacock than he'd first though. Lord Randolph Lightbourne was one of that very rare breed: a rakish squire, a gambling man and a drinker, but, all the same, a fellow who genuinely cared for his wife. "We . . . we made our own warmth together," he finally mumbled, starting to weep again, softly.

There was another moment, then O'Calligan added: "You shouldn't remain in here. Why torture yourself?"

At which the country gent suddenly seem to wake up to the reality of the situation. He snatched at the hilt of his sword. "I'll take no advice from you . . . you bog-dwelling Irish ruffian! Leave me alone!"

"This villain seeks to murder us all," O'Calligan said calmly. "We should stay together."

"Did you not hear me, sirrah? Get out of here!"

O'Calligan did as he was bidden. There seemed little point in exacerbating an already difficult situation. In the drawing-room, he found Lady Foxworth assisting Cedric as he removed the remnants of their afternoon repast, and Judge Prendergast, standing beside the window, stuffing his pipe with more Brazilian tobacco.

"This is a confounded mystery," the judge said, as the soldier approached him.

"I don't understand it," O'Calligan confessed. "We were all of us together when we heard the alarm."

"All of us except the manservant chap."

O'Calligan shook his head. "Cedric was only in the passage. You said that, yourself . . . how could he have attacked Lady Lightbourne, dragged her away from the bell, finished her off, locked the room, then come all the way downstairs and gathered a tray of sweetmeats in time to meet us outside that door? It's not feasible."

"Little about this business is."

"There has to be someone else on these premises," the Irishman said.

Prendergast blew out a stream of fragrant smoke. "We've looked. There's no trace."

"If only we could get to Minehead."

"One of us may need to try."

But O'Calligan was less sure about that. Outside, night had now fallen on the snow-deep tundra. Flakes swirled on a newly risen wind, which would cut anyone stranded in it to the very bones. Even in the unlikely event that one of them decided he and his horse were strong enough to risk such a venture, the chances were that he'd be lucky to find his way off the moor, let alone to the coast and the nearest town.

Despite this, however, someone *did* test the elements that night, and managed, just before the stroke of twelve, to arrive grunting and puffing at the doors of Silvercombe Hall.

With the exception of Lord Lightbourne, who hadn't yet come down from his bed-chamber, the remainder of the household were together in the drawing-room, dozing under quilts, when they heard the banging at the front door.

There was initial astonishment, then O'Calligan, Cedric and Judge Prendergast went to answer it, all three armed. Only after demanding identification through the door, did they admit the callers: two men, both in cloaks and tricornes, thickly caked in snow. Lady Foxworth arrived in the hall as the newcomers stripped off their outer garments. Her handsome face broke into a relieved smile when she saw that one of them – a youthful fellow, with long fair curls and wearing the buff uniform of the Dutch Royal Navy – was her younger brother, Rupert. The second chap also wore Dutch naval garb, though he was larger, burlier, and had a brown, scarred face.

"I expected you over a week ago," she said, clasping arms around her sibling.

"We only left Windsor a couple of days back," he laughed. "We'd have come sooner, but there was a bit of skirmishing with James's Irish militia before an armistice could be reached. I wasn't sure we'd even get here today. This blizzard is the worst I've seen. Edouard here didn't know we got such snow in England. Oh, by the way, may I introduce First Lieutenant Edouard Van Brooner, my most capable officer?"

The Dutchman bowed. "Madame."

"You're most welcome, Edouard."

"It's my pleasure to attend you." His English, though accented, was fluent.

"Well, this is a quiet house for Christmas Day," the younger Foxworth said. "Late though the hour is, for which I heartily apologize." He turned to his compatriot. "I told you I'd come home again, didn't I, Edouard? By damn, no bunch of papists were keeping me from the family nest."

"Rupert," his sister said, now more solemnly. "Come into the drawing-room. There's something I should tell you."

Five minutes later, the entire tragedy had been explained to the new arrivals, who greeted the news at first with slow bewilderment, then finally with outrage and anger.

"We must search the premises!" Rupert shouted at the top of his voice.

"We've already searched," his sister replied, seated by the fire. "Several times. There's no-one here but ourselves."

"What about *him*?" Lieutenant Van Brooner asked, with a glowering nod towards O'Calligan. "Isn't it likely that *he's* responsible?"

"How so?" Lady Foxworth enquired.

Her brother was also now staring at the Irishman. "Well, for one thing, he's James's man," he said. "In fact, we came here specifically to free you from *his* clutches. His world has ended. He's nothing but a powerless, penniless immigrant. He has plenty reason to strike out."

"That's scarcely proof, gentlemen," Judge Prendergast put in,

"By the same token, can he prove he *didn't* do it?" Lieutenant Van Brooner wondered.

"Can you prove *you* didn't?" O'Calligan replied. "You say you've ridden all the way from Windsor. A hundred miles or more, in this weather. Personally I find that doubtful."

"What exactly are you suggesting?" Rupert demanded.

O'Calligan remained calm. "Surmising rather than suggesting, but it's not beyond the realms of credibility that two felons might secrete themselves somewhere nearby to carry out hit-and-run raids on the house. And perhaps tonight the cold simply became too much for them."

Before either Rupert or Van Brooner could reply, however, there came a series of shrieks from the outer passage. A moment later, the maid Martha had stumbled in and collapsed. For a second there was complete confusion, then the girl jabbered out that she'd been upstairs, making up a new pair of rooms, as ordered by her mistress, when she'd heard the sounds "of chokes" from Lord Lightbourne's room. "Fearful chokes, ma-am. The sound o'murder, and no mistake!"

The scene was now a familiar one, though in this case there were several differences.

To begin with, Lightbourne had put up a fight. Slash-marks on the drapery around his bed revealed that he'd struck out with his sword. In addition, his throat, though again rent from ear to ear, was not the only wound on him. His shirt had been torn open, and there were gashes on his chest and shoulder, and, higher up, on one of his cheeks.

"This is demonic!" Rupert bellowed.

"This, gentlemen, is the horror that has afflicted us all through the Yuletide feast," Judge Prendergast remarked soberly.

"Does anyone know who's responsible?" Lieutenant Van Brooner asked.

O'Calligan glanced round at him. "Do you think we'd be standing here like cherries waiting to be plucked, if we did?"

The big Dutchman scowled at him. "You may have been downstairs with us at the time, but I still haven't discounted *you* from this business."

"Nor I you," O'Calligan replied.

There was a tense moment, then Van Brooner's scowl became a

cruel sneer. "I killed some of your countrymen at Reading. What do you think about that?"

"If I was you, Dutchie, I'd watch my bloody lip," came the Irishman's taut reply.

"Enough of this!" Rupert interrupted. "We must search the upper floor. All of us!" And he raced from the room, pushing his lieutenant in front of him.

Judge Prendergast followed, and Cedric was about to leave too when O'Calligan stopped him: "Is there something different in here?" the Irishman wondered.

Cedric glanced around, blank-faced. "I don't see it."

"The fire is lit. It wasn't earlier."

The servant shrugged. "Lord Lightbourne must've got cold. There's coal, a tinder-box. He could easily have lit it himself."

"Yes," O'Calligan said, "but the window is still open. If he'd got cold, wouldn't he have closed the window as well?"

"I don't follow."

The Irishman shook his head. "There must be a reason why he lit that fire."

Cedric crossed the room, took a poker and thrust it around amid the glowing coals. Aside from a few scraps of kindling, the only other thing in there was an edging of paper, gold-trimmed. Cedric scraped it out onto the floor. It was all that remained of a burnt sheet of notepaper; the gold-trim revealed that it was household notepaper, of the sought used by Lady Foxworth in her regular correspondence.

"This doesn't really tell us anything," Cedric observed.

"No," O'Calligan agreed. "It could be perfectly innocent."

He turned to Lady Lightbourne's body, now a grisly sight; sickly-white and visibly stiffening. The blood, a black congealed blanket of it, lay down her entire front. "There's something different about her ladyship too," he said. "I thought so earlier, but couldn't place it. Is something missing, Cedric?"

Cedric looked the body over. The rings still glittered on the dead woman's fingers; the string of pearls hung intact across her ravaged throat. Before they could speak on it further, however, Judge Prendergast reappeared at the bedroom door. "O'Calligan," he said urgently. "Master Rupert and his shipmate are dead-set against you as it is. You must help us search, or they'll be doubly suspicious."

The Irishman nodded, and left the room, leaving Cedric to dignify this latest corpse.

Feeling more confident with the two naval men present, the search-party this time split up into smaller groups and scoured every inch of the property, even the attics and the crawlspaces under the roof. Lady Foxworth was too distraught to partake, however, and repaired to her own quarters, supplied by her brother with a fully charged pistol.

It was now past one o'clock, and that "graveyard" hour of the night when one feels most marooned from the rest of human society. Outside, the wintry wind moaned around the ancient walls; there were creaks and bangs, windows rattled loosely in their frames. It was in the west wing, however, on a stretch of corridor attached only to empty rooms, that O'Calligan heard something distinctly different. He was alone at the time, and so paused and listened. For a moment he fancied he was hearing voices behind the wainscoting: muffled voices, engaged in some heated debate. He approached the wall in question and put his ear to the woodwork, finding it aged and worm-eaten.

"My God," a man was mumbling. "How could you do this to us? And when everything was looking so fine?"

A woman then replied: "I needed to secure what at the time looked a perilous future."

"Good God, woman!" The man's voice rose. "And the Irishman? I suppose you took him to your bed as well. Or was that just his master?"

O'Calligan would have listened to more, but the voices now faded, as though the persons having the dispute had moved away. He considered for a moment. Without any doubt, it had been Lady Foxworth and her brother Rupert, and though, from that brief snatch of conversation, it was difficult to ascertain what they'd been talking about, the fact that they were in collusion about something – a collusion that had now turned acrimonious – put a different complexion on events. More mysterious still, where had they actually been just then? As far as the Irishman knew, the west wing of the house was not used; he'd already searched it several times, and had found nothing. This suggested there were regions of this building still known only to the Foxworth family, even in the light of recent events.

Bewildered, but strangely content – as though he was finally making some ground – O'Calligan rejoined the others a few minutes later, and said nothing of his discovery. He wasn't exactly sure who he could trust here anyway, and it was his intention to return to that disused stretch of passage when everyone was asleep, and force his way through the wainscoting.

The men held a further moot in the drawing-room, where it was decided that, as Lady Foxworth had now withdrawn to her own chamber, they might as well each do the same. Rupert – who seemed a little flustered, O'Calligan thought – insisted that anyone facing an intruder fire a shot immediately: even if they missed their intended target, they would certainly alert the rest of the house. There was general agreement at this. A series of final checks were made: the cook and her two maids had barricaded themselves into the scullery, while Cedric had his own small room off the kitchen, which he could easily defend. After this, they said their goodnights.

O'Calligan returned to his own quarters and allowed an hour to pass. Then, taking his pistol and sabre, he made his way stealthily back into the west wing. The house was now in darkness, of course, so he took a candle as well, which he fixed on a shelf opposite the place where he'd eavesdropped. It was still difficult to locate the exact point, however. The entirety of that wall felt flimsy to his touch. And then . . . he stiffened.

He'd sensed a presence come up behind him.

He turned slowly, and found the hulking form of the Dutchman, Van Brooner, blocking the passageway. Van Brooner was fully dressed, though he'd loosened his long brown hair, which hung in unruly hanks to either side of his truculent face. "Your constant mischief," he said, "is making the household, what remains of it, nervous."

"You too, I assume," O'Calligan replied, "judging by the way your knees are knocking."

The Dutchman smiled grimly, then, without warning, launched a big fist at the Irishman. O'Calligan had been expecting it. He stepped nimbly aside and launched a fist of his own, catching Van Brooner squarely in the gut. The breath wheezed out of the Dutchman, then an uppercut took him beneath the chin. He staggered backwards, but remained conscious. With a snarl, he went for the hilt of his sword, but no sooner had he grasped it than O'Calligan had kicked him in the shin, then slashed down flat-handed, chopping him on the bridge of his nose. Three more swift but telling punches followed, which fractured at least one of Van Brooner's ribs, causing him to squawk in agony. The duo clamped together and began to wrestle, but O'Calligan was still getting the better of it. Another brutal gut-thump doubled his opponent over, and, as a *coup de grâce*, he looped an arm around the Dutchman's head, then barrelled him across the corridor, slamming the crown of his skull into the wall opposite . . . the hollow, rotten portion as it happened.

Instantly, the wainscoting was broken through.

O'Calligan dropped the insensible Dutchman, grabbed his candle and poked it into the hole. On the other side, there wasn't a room, as he'd been expecting, but a junction between two low passages. They were at floor level and no more than three feet high. O'Calligan crouched and gazed into them. Though he could see little more than horizontal brick shafts leading off into darkness, he had no doubt that these were the priests' holes with which Silvercombe Hall was reputedly riddled. While their exterior entrances might have been obliterated by the refurbishments of thirty years ago, the inner structure of the house was likely still networked with them. Such cavities doubtless conducted sound well, and this meant the conversation he'd overheard might have come from some distant region of the house. Even so, he had no option but to investigate. He tore away the remnants of the wainscoting, and then crawled forwards, opting to take the left passage first.

The going was tough, and unsavoury. The tunnel system might once have been intended for concealing frightened clerics, but now it smelled as if it had been used by animals. It was matted with rancid straw, and, here and there, great dollops of droppings. In addition, the roof was low, necessitating that he keep his head bowed, which was not easy considering that he also had to hold the candle in front of him. Maintaining a light, however, paid dividends. After he'd been crawling for several minutes, he reached a point on his left where a wooden panel was fixed to a hinge. When he pushed it, it swung open into a darkened room. He thrust his candle through, and looked, and was not surprised to see familiar blood-patterns on a rug, and arterial spray on the oaken walls. To his immediate right, Lord and Lady Lightbourne lay in quiet repose on their silent, gore-stained bed.

This, then, was how the assailant had twice entered their locked room: a secret hatch concealed in the skirting-boards. Not that O'Calligan, for one, would have been able to get through it. His shoulders alone were too wide.

Feeling vindicated, but increasingly nervous, he proceeded along the tunnel, now passing other junctions. A moment later, it began to tilt steeply downwards, until he was certain he'd reached the ground-floor level, at which point it opened into a cubby-hole of a room that he hadn't seen before despite his now frequent searches of the house. Several things struck him about this room. Firstly, it was tight, compact . . . so much so that it surely couldn't serve any real purpose other than for storage. Secondly, it was slope-roofed, a curious design-feature by any standards. Thirdly, a series of pull-ropes hung into it through holes bored in its slanted ceiling. O'Calligan, who was at last able to stand and stretch his joints, gazed up at them. Slowly, a frightful picture of what might be happening here was forming in his mind. He turned: there were two doors, facing each other from opposite corners of the room, but both were locked when he tried them. The low passage, however, by which he'd entered, continued on the other side. He took a minute to work the cramp from his limbs, then crouched and proceeded.

There were more twists, more turns, more ups and downs.

And then there was light. Just ahead.

He scrabbled forwards, and found access to another previously unseen chamber, though the purpose of this one was more evident. He was now gazing down through a wire grille into an ornate bath-room. A huge, cast-iron tub sat on a Romanesque-tiled floorway. Beside it, a pump and faucet were fashioned from glinting brass. Velvet drapes clad every wall, while flaming candelabra created a scented, rose-red luminescence.

My lady's bath-house, O'Calligan thought to himself. This, no doubt, was where the conversation he'd overheard had taken place. He could easily imagine someone as brazen as Lady Foxworth sitting naked in her tub while engaged in a heated debate with her brother. It was perhaps understandable that no guest had been allowed into this particular section of the hall: the hostess's private apartments would ordinarily be her personal domain, but while searching for the murderer, they'd requested they be allowed to inspect *every* portion of the building. Lady Foxworth had not been honest with them.

He pressed on, turning a corner and crawling downhill again, before finding, on his right, another hinged panel. He paused, asking himself which room this secret entrance gave access to, and wondering if it was locked. Before he had the chance to check, however, the panel was opened. Bright light fell into O'Calligan's eyes. He had to shield them, but that didn't prevent his being squirted with a fine spray of some pungent, almost noxious perfume. He gasped, coughed, wafted in vain at the substance. The next thing, though, the panel was slammed closed again and he heard a bolt being thrown.

For a second he was confused, disoriented. He'd dropped his candle, and it had gone out. As he struggled in the blackness, he cracked his head against the low brick ceiling, which momentarily stunned him. He wasn't sure how long had passed, probably less than a minute, before he then heard something else: a grinding of what sounded like iron wheels, and the groaning of a pulley-system. Another noise followed, like a *grating* of stone. For some reason, Captain O'Calligan imagined a heavy piece of cage-work being slowly lifted. A chill went through him. What exactly was at the heart of this house? What did this twisting labyrinth of passages finally connect with?

A second later – when he heard the fast-approaching *skitter* of claws, and the soft brushing of lank, wet fur against brickwork – he realized that he didn't want to find out. Not in this situation, enclosed in a space where he could wield neither gun nor blade, and drenched with some foul ichor, the sole purpose of which was surely to mark him as prey. He scrambled around and began to lumber frantically back in the opposite direction. Whatever he'd heard, however, was coming swiftly. Claws that were surely the size of eagle's talons, if not bigger, were fairly *clattering* along the straw-covered brickwork.

The Irishman then rounded a bend, and again saw the grille to Lady Foxworth's bathroom. He lunged wildly forwards tearing the knees from his breeches, scraping the flesh beneath. The thing, whatever it was, was maybe fifteen yards behind when he actually reached the grille. Without hesitation he folded his knees to his chest and kicked at it with the soles of his boots. Two such blows, and the grille went through. O'Calligan hurled himself after it, falling full length into the bathroom, landing on the tiled floor beside the tub. He leapt up and staggered away. There would be a door behind one of the curtains, but maybe there was no time for that. He grabbed automatically at the hilt of his sabre, but there was still something else he was looking for . . . and then he spied it! As in all the rooms here, a bell was present, hanging from the bathroom's ceiling, perhaps nine feet up.

Then there came a low, sibilant *hiss*.

O'Calligan froze, before staring back at the high aperture in the wall.

Two burning eyes regarded him from its darkness. They were like buttons, only larger, gleaming with candle-light. The Irishman didn't wait to see more. He drew his sword and, without looking, swept it up and struck the bell, which rang three sonorous tones in response. Still, the eyes regarded him. But, a moment later, as he'd fervently hoped, they withdrew slowly into the blackness.

A second passed, then O'Calligan dropped to one knee and leaned on his sabre. His breath came in heaving gasps. His torso was so slick with sweat that his torn and filthied shirt clung to it like a second skin. Not that he could afford to take too long to recover. The time had come to tell the others what he knew.

"This had better be worthwhile, O'Calligan," Judge Prendergast grumbled. He crouched before the drawing-room hearth in his house-coat and bed-cap, and jammed a poker into the dying coals. "As if things aren't difficult enough, now you're getting us up at three o'clock in the blasted morning."

The other man present, Rupert, was stripped down to his shirtsleeves, wore his sword and pistol at his waist, and regarded the Irishman with deep suspicion.

"Gad!" the judge suddenly added. His wrinkled his porcine nostrils. "O'Calligan, you smell like . . . well, I don't know what you smell like!"

The Irishman nodded. "It was almost the death of me."

"Why, did someone attack you?" Rupert asked.

"I'll explain everything in a moment."

A second later, Cedric came in. He looked bleary-eyed with

sleep, but he closed the door behind him. "Sorry, my lords," he began, "but I was . . . oh, did you wish me to bring her ladyship? Only, I've just been up there. She mentioned something earlier about taking a sleeping-draught. I wanted to ensure she hadn't done, with the murderer still loose."

"It's all right, Cedric," O'Calligan said. "She'll be quite safe."

"Well, O'Calligan?" the judge said. "Hurry it up, man. We need some sleep at least."

O'Calligan turned to face them. "I'm afraid there'll be no more sleep tonight. Not for any of us, and, once we've finished here, not for Lady Foxworth." He paused, then added: "Because, much as it pains me to report this . . . *she* is the instigator of these events."

Rupert's eyes widened. "You Irish rogue! That's a devil of an accusation!"

"I'd shout less and think more if I were you, Captain Foxworth . . . I very much doubt that *you'd* have been leaving this building alive if your sister had had her way."

"It could be you misspeak yourself, O'Calligan!" the judge put in, equally astonished. "I think you'd better explain."

"I will, but first a question of the young captain here." He turned again to Rupert. "How long, my lord, has your sister been King James's mistress?"

There was a moment of stunned silence, before Rupert began to splutter in outrage: "What do you . . . how dare you . . ."

"I overheard you and she discussing it not two hours ago," O'Calligan added.

"You spied on us, you blaggard!"

"Until officially removed from my post, it's my duty to spy. Another duty I had, as her ladyship's official gaoler, was to accompany her on her many trips to Whitehall. Usually she was summoned there to answer some minor charge of libel. I now realize what the real purpose was, however." He shook his head, as though the truth had been under his nose for ages and he hadn't noticed it. "She would spend many lengthy sessions being . . . *interviewed* by His Majesty."

Rupert had turned red in the face, but he was no longer refuting the charge, which Judge Prendergast noticed. "Is this true, Rupert?" the justicier asked.

"I can't deny it," the young man finally admitted, though it clearly agonized him. "But I didn't know myself until this evening, when she told me."

"Good Lord," Prendergast said. "I knew she was profligate with her favours, but King James?"

"The fact that he was king is irrelevant," O'Calligan put in. "He wasn't the first king in Lady Foxworth's bed. His brother Charles had been there before."

"His brother Charles had been in every gentlewoman's bed."

"That's the point," the Irishman continued. "In Charles's case there was no scandal. It happened with mundane repetitiveness. With King James, however, the matter is more delicate. James's daughter Mary is now married to the Prince of Orange, and is a woman notoriously protective of her mother, Queen Anne. It seems highly likely – and no doubt *you* share this opinion too, Captain Foxworth – that once Mary has herself become queen, which must now be imminent, her father's mistresses, of which your sister is only one, will be reckoned with."

There was another moment of silence as the reality of the situation sank in.

"Contrary to popular belief," O'Calligan added, "and I freely admit that I shared in this belief, Lady Foxworth does *not* await the arrival of the new administration with any enthusiasm. If anything, it's likely to be the ruin of her. The very least she can expect is a loss of influence at Court, but probably a dismissal from all royal favour and patronage as well, and maybe a thorough investigation of her affairs . . ."

"All this is true!" Rupert interrupted with sudden desperation. "It was a terrible miscalculation by my sister, and as such she now intends to hide her shame by living abroad. But does that make her a murderess?"

"On its own, no," O'Calligan said. "Is it beyond the realms of possibility, though, that she thought she'd rid herself of a few enemies first. Enemies who, once she was overseas would be beyond her reach."

Rupert shook his head. "This is madness."

"Is it?" O'Calligan wondered. "Lord Chillerton caused an uproar by publicly demanding monies from your family because of an unfortunate shipping disaster. Lord Lightbourne sought your sister as his lover and, though he never enjoyed that pleasure, his vicious-tongued wife spread scathing gossip about her. Judge Prendergast, here, sat on the panel that sent relatives of hers to the gallows. *I* was her prison-keeper, for Heaven's sake. We all of us had wronged her. Even *you* were likely to die . . . because, if you lived, she couldn't lay claim to the entire Foxworth fortune, which she needed to finance her new life abroad."

Again, Rupert shook his head. "Pure supposition."

"I agree. But there's more . . . if you'll come with me."

And now O'Calligan led them upstairs to the chill bedroom where the Lightbournes lay. He took a candle, and approached the section of skirting-board where the trapdoor was concealed. With one kick, he'd broken it open. Beyond it, he showed them the black passages that wound worm-like through the innards of the house.

"There are hidden access-ways, just like this," he added, "in virtually every room in Silvercombe Hall. Either concealed in the wainscoting, the kick-boards or, possibly in the case of the Chillertons, inside the chimney-breast. They are all exceptionally small and skilfully constructed, which makes them very difficult to detect from the outside."

"But who made them, and how?" Rupert asked, suddenly looking more puzzled than distressed.

"It wouldn't be difficult," O'Calligan said. "The tunnels were already there, and your father's refurbishment, which allegedly covered them, was only paper-thin."

"What's their purpose?" Judge Prendergast wondered.

"I'll show you," the Irishman said. "Come."

He took them back downstairs into the main hall, then along a passage that veered beneath the grand staircase. A low door was set there. It was locked, but O'Calligan bade Cedric bring tools again, and a moment later the door was down. Beyond it they found the cubby-hole room that the Irishman had entered via the priest's hole.

"So?" Judge Prendergast grunted. "It's an under-stair wardrobe. Most homes have one."

"But this one's been adapted for a different use," O'Calligan replied. He indicated the row of hanging ropes. "These are bell-pulls, my lord. Each one is connected to a different room. Once they were used to alert Catholic fugitives hiding out at Silvercombe. Now they're used to alert a very different sort of person. In fact, to call him off."

His expression had become grave: "The bell we heard when Lady Lightbourne was attacked, was not rung by her as an alarm. Whoever rung it – and they probably did it from in *here* – did it to recall her assassin."

Judge Prendergast still seemed bewildered. "Then why didn't we hear the same when the Chillertons were slain?"

O'Calligan had already considered this. "The Chillertons' room was the only one on the east wing, whereas the Lightbournes were housed at the very top of the stairs, in a central location."

"And when Lord Lightbourne, himself, was attacked?"

"There was considerable noise in the drawing-room at that moment," the Irishman said. "The maid was frantic, there was wild shouting. It may also be that, once an assault's complete, the beast returns to its lair by instinct. The bell might only be used in the event of an emergency."

"*Beast?*" Judge Prendergast stuttered. "*Lair?* What the devil are you talking about?"

The Irishman now crossed the wardrobe to the second locked door. "With luck, this little-used portal will answer all your questions." And he used the same tools as before to remove the door from its hinges. Beyond it, steep steps descended into a dank and dripping shaft.

"What's this place?" Rupert murmured as they went down, in a voice so wondering that clearly, even though he'd visited Silvercombe many times in his life, he'd never been to this part of the house before.

"The proverbial hidden room, I'm afraid," O'Calligan replied. "It might once have been connected to the cellars or undercroft, but it isn't any more."

Ten feet down, they entered a dirty, dungeon-like area, its low roof supported by heavy brick pillars. A single torch in a wall-bracket cast only a weak, glimmering light, but it was sufficient to show a long work-table, and on top of it a variety of curious objects.

"In here, I suspect, the vile work was both planned and executed," the Irishman added, approaching the table. "The killer is in many ways a mindless brute. It needed a lure to bring it to its victims. *This* is that lure." And he picked up a small mixing-bowl, filled with brownish, oily fluid.

"What is it?" Rupert asked.

O'Calligan shook his head. "Who knows? Some concoction used as part of the creature's training." Next, he showed them a green bottle, with a rubber valve attached. "It was sprayed onto me from this perfume-dispenser, or a similar one." He squeezed the rubber, and moisture puffed into the air. Its odour was quite distinctive.

"It's the same smell," Rupert confirmed.

"The same, I imagine, that you'd notice if you burned one of these," O'Calligan said, sidling along to a pile of tallow candles. "Certain candles in this house have been impregnated with the same agent. I believe one such was given to Lord and Lady Chillerton."

"By Jove!" the judge blurted out. "There *was* a curious smell in that room."

"It probably made itself known when the candle had burned half-way down," O'Calligan said. "A clever device. And, just to make sure it wasn't detected, that candle was later removed. If you remember, Cedric, it wasn't there when we went back to the room?"

Cedric nodded, almost despondently. "That's right, sir, it wasn't."

"Lady Lightbourne's pomander had also been taken," the Irishman added. "You recall I said there was something missing after she'd died? At the time we looked for jewellery, but actually it was the pomander, which Lady Foxworth herself tied to Lady Lightbourne's wrist as a Christmas gift. You see these ingredients?" And he presented a dish containing dried, sliced oranges, bundles of herbs and what looked like a scattering of cinnamon and nutmeg. "That pomander was made up down here. Almost certainly, it too was laced with the fatal material, so that at some point the smell was given off. We didn't notice it when we arrived up there because the window was open. The cold air had wafted it away."

"But if the smell had gone and the pomander been taken, how was Lady Lightbourne's husband killed?" Rupert asked.

O'Calligan moved to the final item on the work-table. It was a block of household notepaper, gold-trimmed. "We found fragments of paper just like this in his fire." He glanced up at them. "An element of conjecture is perhaps required at this point.

Suppose an unsigned letter was slipped under the bedroom door. Who knows what it contained . . . maybe a promise to reveal the identity of Lady Lightbourne's murderer before the night was out. Whatever it said, suppose it intrigued Lord Lightbourne enough for him to keep it secret. Suppose it also instructed him to burn it once he'd read it."

"You mean the letter itself was imbued with the substance?" the judge said. He sniffed at the notepaper. "Good God, it *is*."

"The moment it burned, the smell became strongly noticeable," O'Calligan said. "Again, it became a deadly lure."

"It's ingenious," the judge replied.

"And quite fiendish." O'Calligan moved to a corner, where, alongside another line of bell-ropes, some bulky object was hidden beneath a dingy sailcloth. "Because the real horror, gentlemen, lies under this."

When he whipped the sailcloth back, even O'Calligan wasn't entirely sure what he would find. He'd already heard the thing, but he hadn't seen it. And for a second he was unnerved at the prospect. He hadn't expected, however, to find an empty cage.

It was a filthy cage, admittedly, packed with straw and sawdust, and all manner of foul detritus, but it was empty all the same. Slowly, however, as they gazed at it, their eyes took in other things. The cage was large, for example; much larger than the average rabbit-hutch. Also, it had what looked like a gate in its rear-section, and, thanks to a rope-and-pulley system, that gate currently hung open, though it only gave access to a wire-grille passage, which vanished through a cavity in the wall, almost certainly joining with the labyrinth of priests' tunnels.

It seemed to take an age before the realization struck home.

"It's on the prowl again," O'Calligan said slowly.

And just as he said this, a shrill scream came echoing down through the vaults of the house, amplified by the network of passages. The men gazed at each other, chilled.

"Hannah," Rupert breathed. "Good God, Hannah!" And he dashed to the stairs.

They raced up through the building, drawing their weapons as they did, and at last reached the door to Lady Foxworth's apartments. Inevitably it was locked. This time they didn't wait for tools, but went at it with the hilts of their swords and grips of their pistols, and at last they broke it down and burst through.

The opulent living-chamber within was bare of life, but on the far side of it, another door stood open on the bedroom. They dashed through it as a group . . . and were greeted by a scene of nightmarish terror.

The handsome mistress of the house lay twisted across her divan. Her flowing white chemise had been torn open at the front, exposing her breasts but also her milk-white throat, now ripped asunder and spouting blood. On the far side of the chamber, meanwhile, crouched in a corner as though trying to hide amid the drapes and cushions, the miscreant was still present.

"Behold, gentlemen," O'Calligan cried, "the assassin of Silvercombe Hall."

They gazed, hair prickling, upon a ghastly, misshapen creature. It was a rodent; of that there was no doubt. In fact, by its hooked front-teeth, grey matted fur and blood-dabbled whiskers, it was a rat, a buck-rat. But the size of it! Though huddled in a ball, it was over three feet long from nose to tail. Its crimson eyes were pin-points of evil, its claws horribly twisted, as though they'd many times been broken and re-formed. As it gazed back at them, it gave a hideous, hoarse squeal, a deep, guttural thing that seemed to rumble in its blood-filled guts.

"Good God!" Judge Prendergast exclaimed. "Good God in Heaven!"

They were, all of them, still paralysed with shock when it suddenly sprang on the offensive. This time, though, it was outnumbered. Before it had even crossed the room, either to attack or simply to bolt back through the aperture in the adjoining bath-chamber, they'd discharged their firearms. A succession of explosive *roars* boomed through the house; the room was suddenly swimming in gunpowder-smoke.

And the rat-thing lay dead.

Killed instantly. Torn apart by a great storm of shot.

Slowly, still astounded, Judge Prendergast stumbled forwards. "What in the name of Heaven . . . is this some demon from the pit?"

"Not at all," O'Calligan said. "It is – or was – as real as you or I. One of those many famous exotic pets brought back from the Indies. Or a descendant of one. Either way, it was beaten, mistreated, brutalized to the point where it would kill on command."

"And still you blame my sister?" came Rupert Foxworth's disbelieving voice, suddenly thick with grief. He turned to face them from the divan, his eyes swollen with tears. "You have the nerve to blame Hannah, though she also lies dead by this monstrosity's teeth?"

For a moment, O'Calligan was confounded. Fleetingly, in the shock of the moment, the factor of Lady Foxworth's death had eluded him. But if she wasn't the one, who . . .?

With a loud *click*, a firing-pin was drawn back.

As one, the men turned. To find Cedric in the doorway, a massive blunderbuss in his hands, which he trained on them unwaveringly. "No foolish moves, my lords," he said gloomily.

There was a moment of stupefaction, then O'Calligan gave a long, low sigh of understanding. "Of course. The loyal, lifelong servant. Who loved Lady Foxworth from when she was knee-high, and raised her almost as his own."

"*Him*?" said Rupert incredulously, pointing at the saturnine underling.

"Who else?" O'Calligan replied. "Who else would be party to the inner secrets of this house? To your sister's private affairs?"

"I advised her against it," Cedric said mournfully. "All her life, I advised her. To walk the thorny paths of political intrigue is foolish, I said. Enjoy the comforts of home, be content as lady of the manor. But no . . . the older she grew, the more her ambition to glorify the Foxworth name soared. Especially when King James came to the throne, and all doors seemed to close on her. She became more determined than ever. She was still comely, she said. She knew she could gain from it . . ."

"You killed my sister, you wretch!" Rupert shrieked.

Cedric remained calm, however, if deeply sad. "Once news came that James would flee, the careful work of seducing him was for nothing. In fact, as has been astutely recognized, it backfired badly. My lady thought she'd head to France. Maybe rejoin with His Catholic Majesty there. But with Master Rupert back home again, she'd have had to leave everything . . . Silvercombe Hall, the family plate. In short, she'd have gone there a pauper. And would King James want her then, when he himself was so shriven of wealth?" The retainer shook his aged head. "It's bad enough even for women who succeed in wielding their charms as political weapons. Look at the vilification heaped on Countess Castlemaine after the death of Charles. But if they *don't* succeed . . . they become guttersnipes, drab-tails. Well, I loved her too much to let that happen."

"You loved her, yet you planned a fate for her like this?" Judge Prendergast said, indicating the ravaged body.

Cedric shook his head: "It wouldn't have been like this, but you gentlemen forced my hand. I thought to weave a web of deceit, to eliminate a number of prominent folk . . . and in a baffling, bewildering way that no man would fathom. All along of course, the *real* target would be Master Rupert, the agent of our misfortunes."

Rupert looked aghast. "What's that?"

"You heard me, my lord," Cedric said, his tone turning sour. "You and your cronies, not seeing the way the wind was blowing when King James came to the throne. Making war on him like it was a game in the nursery. And when it's all over, rushing off to exile, leaving your sister to pick up the pieces. Little wonder she did the things she did. She *needed* to, just to survive."

"But, but . . ." Rupert seemed lost for words.

Cedric continued: "But you were to die here because you *had* to, not because you deserved it. As I say, I sought to hide your murder amongst a number of others. And once you were dead, Silvercombe Hall and all its trimmings would belong *exclusively* to my lady. She could then sell it off, and live abroad in safety and comfort. Unfortunately, because of this fellow here, O'Calligan, the plan failed."

Cedric now turned to face the Irishman. "You've always performed your office well, captain. You treated my lady with respect and courtesy but, the further you progressed in your investigations, the more apparent it became that she, herself, might take the blame for my scheming. As you said, she had reasons – unlikely reasons, but reasons nevertheless – to kill all of her guests. Your discoveries tonight were the final straw." He shook his head sorrowfully. "It was an easer decision to end it for her than it should have been. Her life as she knew it was finished anyway. Better to make her a victim rather than a perpetrator, I thought. Better to spare her the shame of the block and eternal infamy."

"Are you a madman?" Rupert breathed. "You condemned my

sister to death rather than face a trial that might very well have acquitted her! And a torturous death at that!"

"She was unconscious," the servant replied. "She'd have felt nothing."

"We heard her scream . . ."

"A fleeting thing, while she was deep in sleep." Cedric seemed utterly convinced of this, or perhaps he wasn't allowing himself to consider otherwise. "When I attended to her earlier, I didn't actually come up here to check that she hadn't taken a sleeping-draught, but to make sure that she *had*. And then I doused her bed-curtains in the carrion-effluent that I used to train the Sumatran rat. Compared to the others, it would be painless for her."

"They'll put you on the gibbet alive for this," Judge Prendergast said.

"Maybe, but *you* won't decide that, my lord. Now gentlemen, if you'll all stand together."

Of the three men, O'Calligan and the judge were beside each other, but Rupert was a good three feet away, close to his sister's bedside divan. O'Calligan saw at once what the plan was. "Don't!" he shouted. "Nobody move. He only has a single blast in that blunderbuss. If we stay apart, he can't kill us all."

"One step ahead of me again, Captain O'Calligan," Cedric said. "As you wish."

And with a sudden move, he grabbed the nearest candelabra and flung it at the bed-curtain, which went up in a roaring sheet of flame. More by instinct than decision, Rupert leaped away from it . . . and found himself next to the judge and the Irishman.

O'Calligan shouted, but it was too late. Cedric already had the blunderbuss at his shoulder. His finger was on the trigger, and then . . . he was grabbed from behind.

It was Van Brooner.

The Dutchman was still dazed, however, his face battered and bloody, and Cedric, though old, was wiry and strong; he slammed an elbow back, catching Van Brooner in the broken rib, severely winding him, dropping him to the floor. Then he raised the blunderbuss again, but in that split-second of distraction there was a blur of twirling steel, and, with an ugly *thunk*, something embedded itself in the servant's throat.

The eyes bulged in his dour face, and the firearm slipped from his fingers.

For a second he tottered there, looking down in disbelief at the ornate hilt of the Moorish dagger quivering under his chin. Then his knees buckled and he toppled forwards.

There was a moment of heavy breathing, before O'Calligan and Rupert turned and tore down the burning hangings, hurriedly stamping them out. Judge Prendergast, meanwhile, continued to stare at Cedric's body and the weapon that had slain him. "A life of clandestine warfare," he finally remarked. "Indeed it *has* served you well, my Irish friend."

The following morning, the cloud-cover had cleared, and a winter's sun shone coldly from a blue but glacial sky. The wastes of Exmoor lay silent under a glistening mantel of pristine snow. O'Calligan and Judge Prendergast stood out on the porch, coated and booted and awaiting the help that Rupert, having ridden for Minehead at first light, would hopefully soon bring.

"I should have realized straight away, once we found the bell-pulls in the under-stair wardrobe," O'Calligan said with self-reproach. "We dismissed Cedric as a suspect because we saw him outside the drawing-room shortly after hearing Lady Lightbourne's bell. Once I knew the bell-pulls were much closer to hand, I should have reconsidered him."

"One thing that puzzles me about him," the judge replied, "is that it's only been known for three months or so that the Prince of Orange intended to invade. How could someone like Cedric have planned everything so meticulously in so short a time? How did he train the animal, for example, or build its bolt-holes?"

O'Calligan considered; the same thing had been troubling him. "Canny men like Cedric see events coming from way off," he eventually concluded. "One wouldn't have had to be a genius to realize that King James wasn't going to last on the English throne. Likewise, one wouldn't have needed a calculating mind to understand what that would mean. Even so," and his brow furrowed, "it makes me wonder if Lady Foxworth was more involved than Cedric has admitted."

"Oh come now, O'Calligan," the judge snorted, but the Irishman shook his head.

"Cedric said it himself. She walked the thorny paths, indulged in Machiavellian games. Maybe this plan to kill her brother was hers after all, a failsafe just in case James was overthrown . . . and the loyal servant only opted to include *her* in the roll-call of death once I'd escaped the creature and it became apparent the game was up?"

The judge pondered this. "Unfortunately, we'll never know for sure," he finally said.

"No," O'Calligan agreed. "In that respect, villainous old Cedric was quite successful."